FEAR AGENT

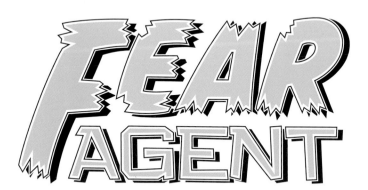

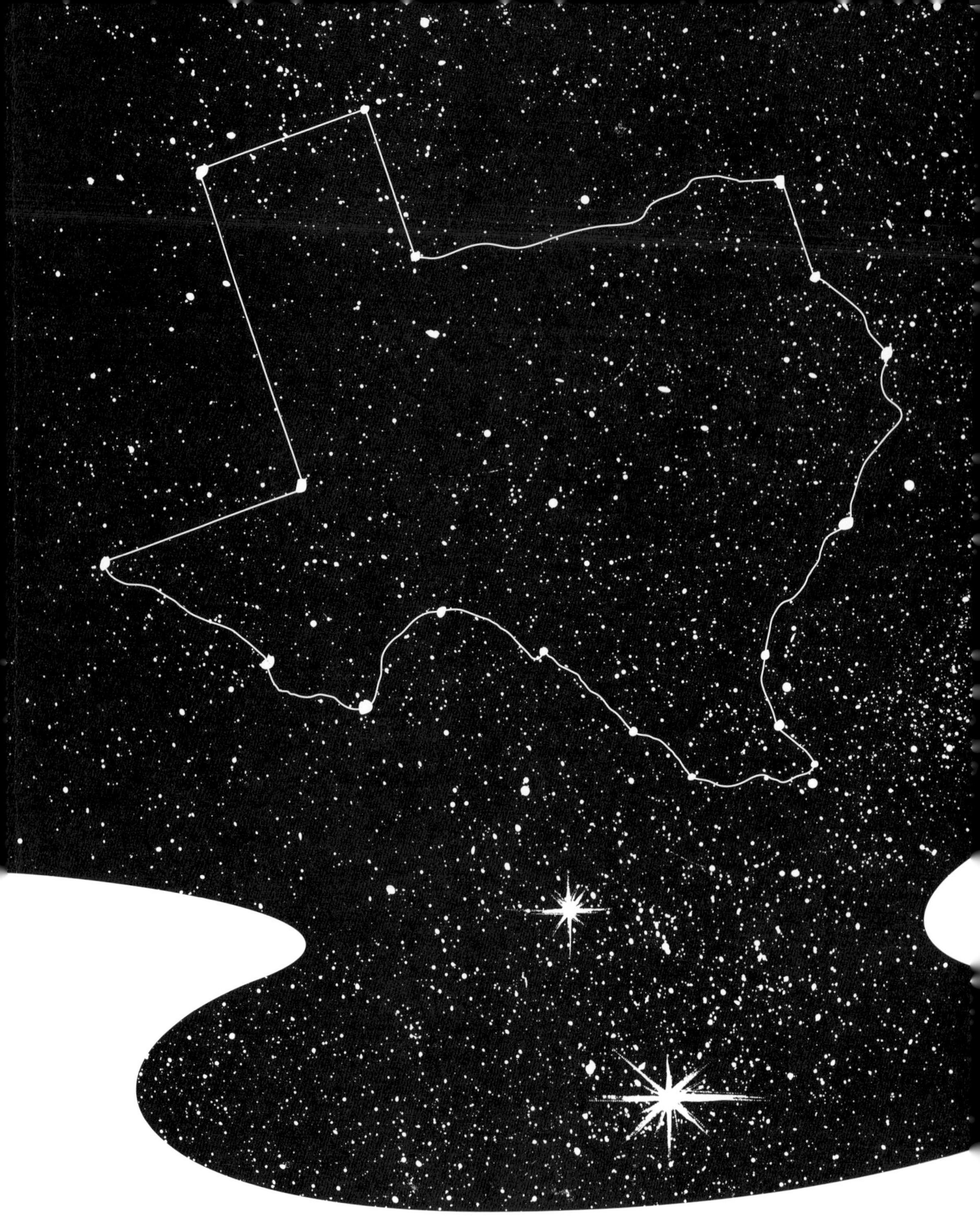

FINAL EDITION
Volume ③

STORY
Rick Remender

I AGAINST I

PENCILS & INKS, CH. 1-2
PENCILS, CH. 3-6
Tony Moore

INKS, CH. 3-6
JOHN LUCAS

LAYOUTS, CH. 6
MIKE HAWTHORNE

OUT OF STEP

PENCILS
Mike Hawthorne
AND
Tony Moore

INKS
JOHN LUCAS

COLORS
LEE LOUGHRIDGE

LETTERS
RUS WOOTON

COVER BY
TONY MOORE

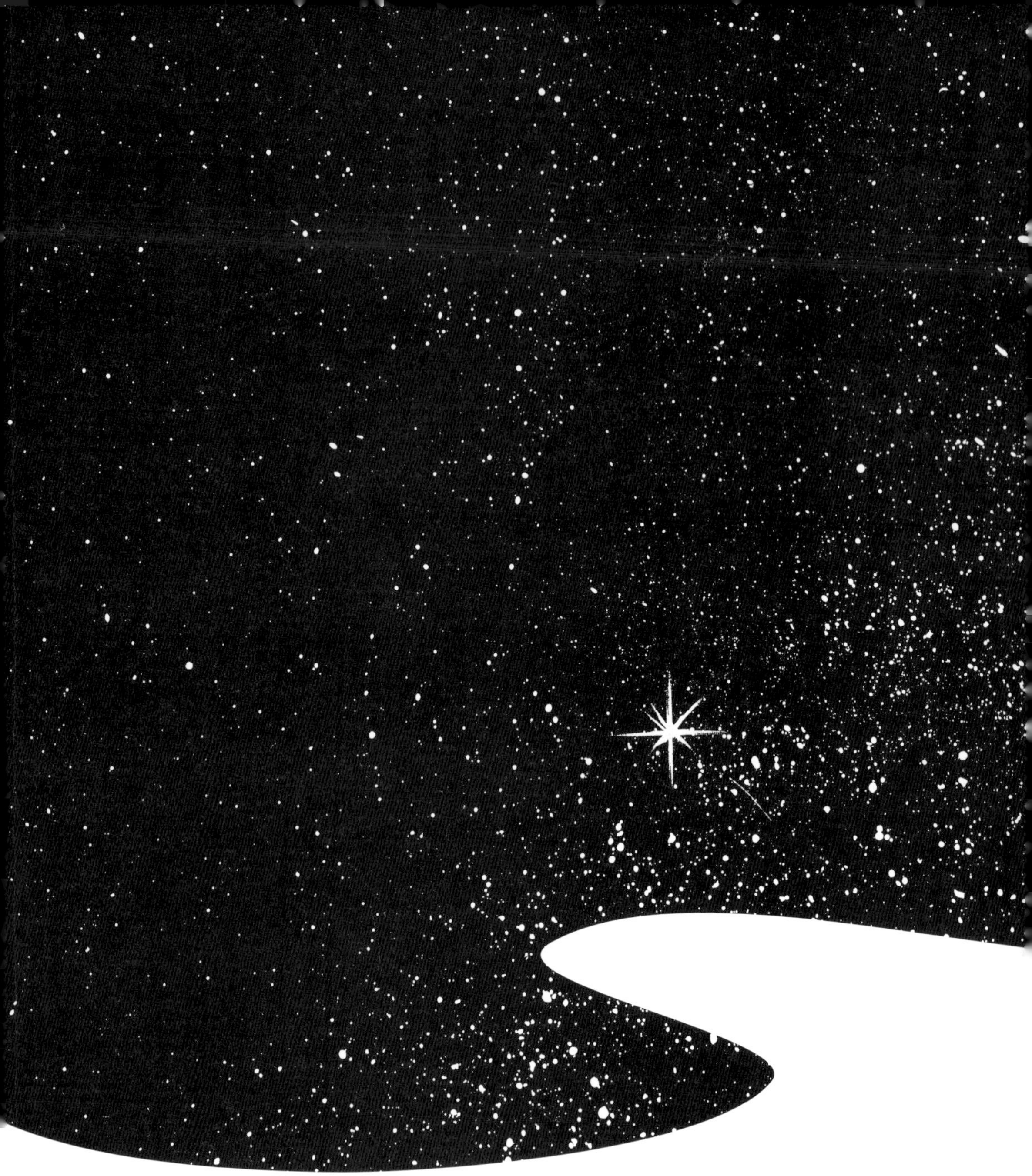

FEAR AGENT CREATED BY **RICK REMENDER**,
TONY MOORE AND **JEROME OPEÑA**

FEAR AGENT LOGO BY **RICK REMENDER**

COLLECTION DESIGN BY **JEFF POWELL**

IMAGE COMICS, INC.

Robert Kirkman: Chief Operating Officer

Erik Larsen: Chief Financial Officer

Todd McFarlane: President

Marc Silvestri: Chief Executive Officer

Jim Valentino: Vice President

Eric Stephenson: Publisher / Chief Creative Officer

Corey Hart: Director of Sales

Jeff Boison: Director of Publishing Planning & Book Trade Sales

Chris Ross: Director of Digital Sales

Jeff Stang: Director of Specialty Sales

Kat Salazar: Director of PR & Marketing

Drew Gill: Art Director

Heather Doornink: Production Director

Nicole Lapalme: Controller

IMAGECOMICS.COM

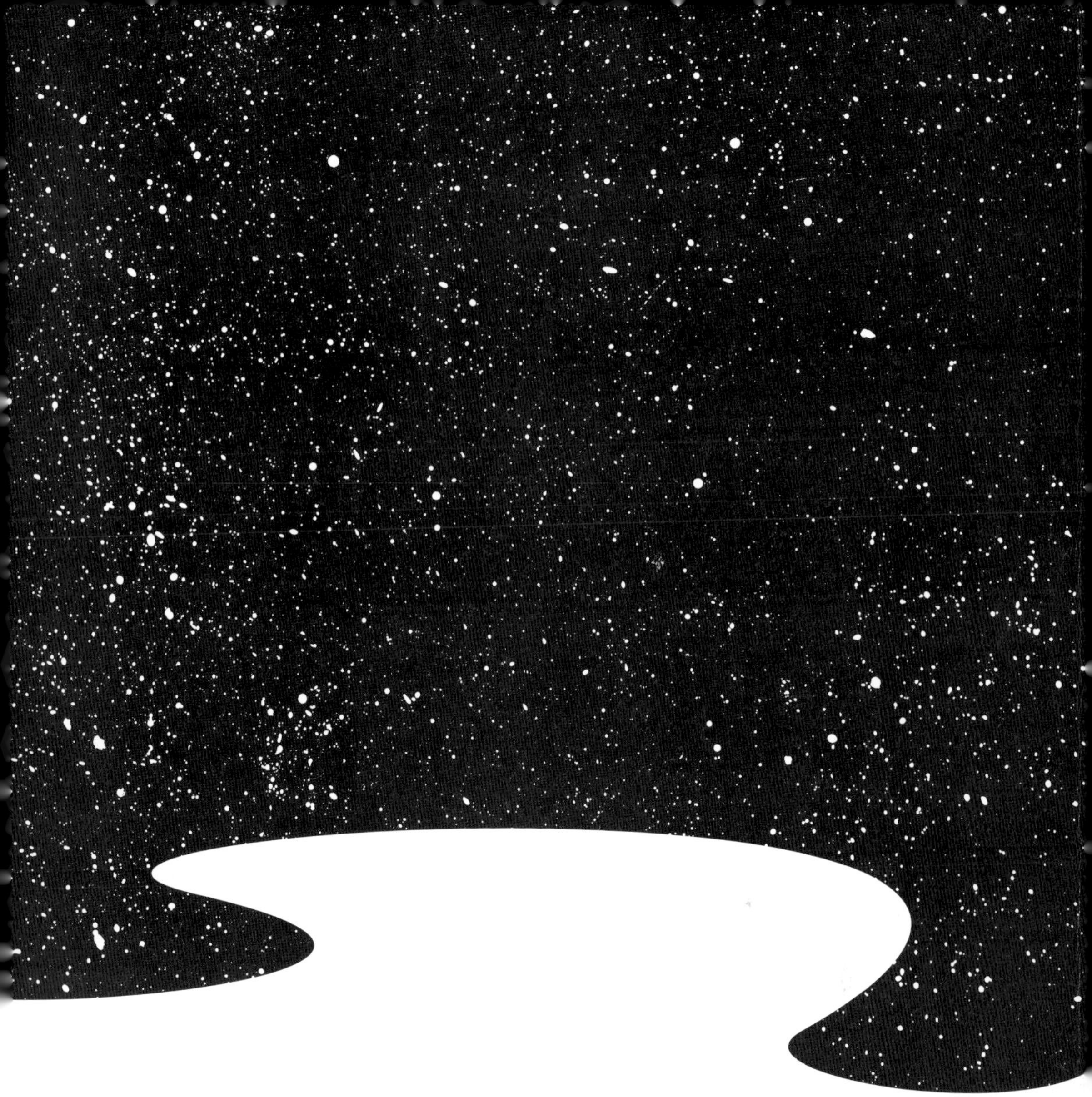

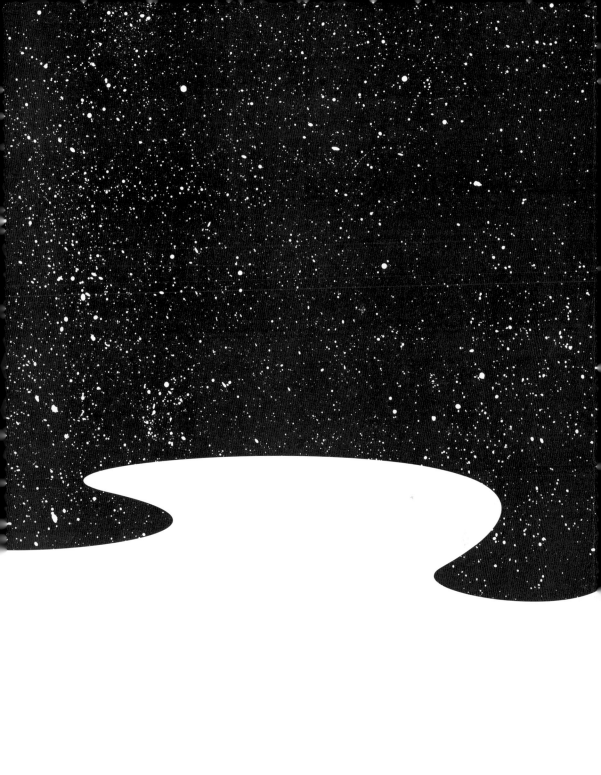

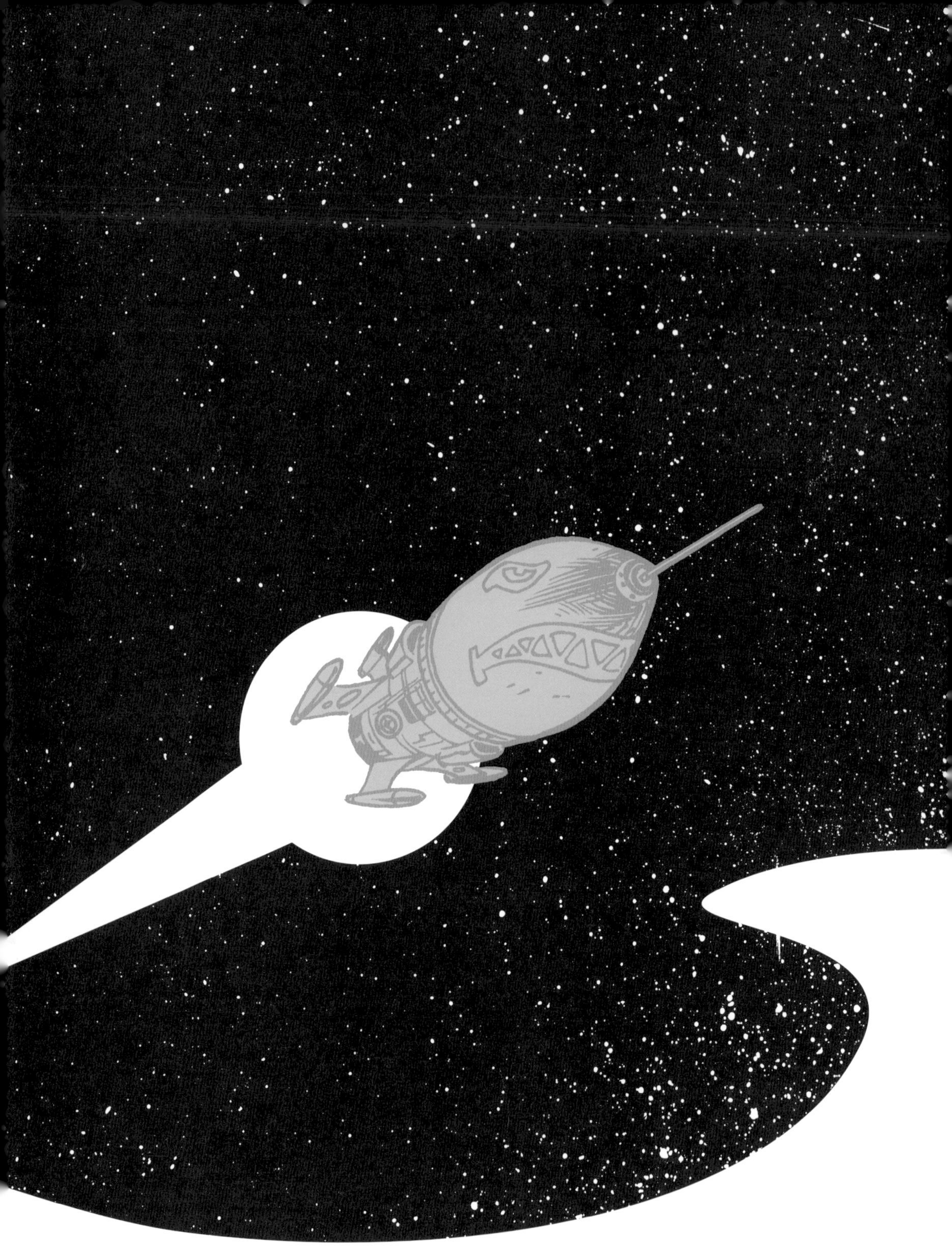

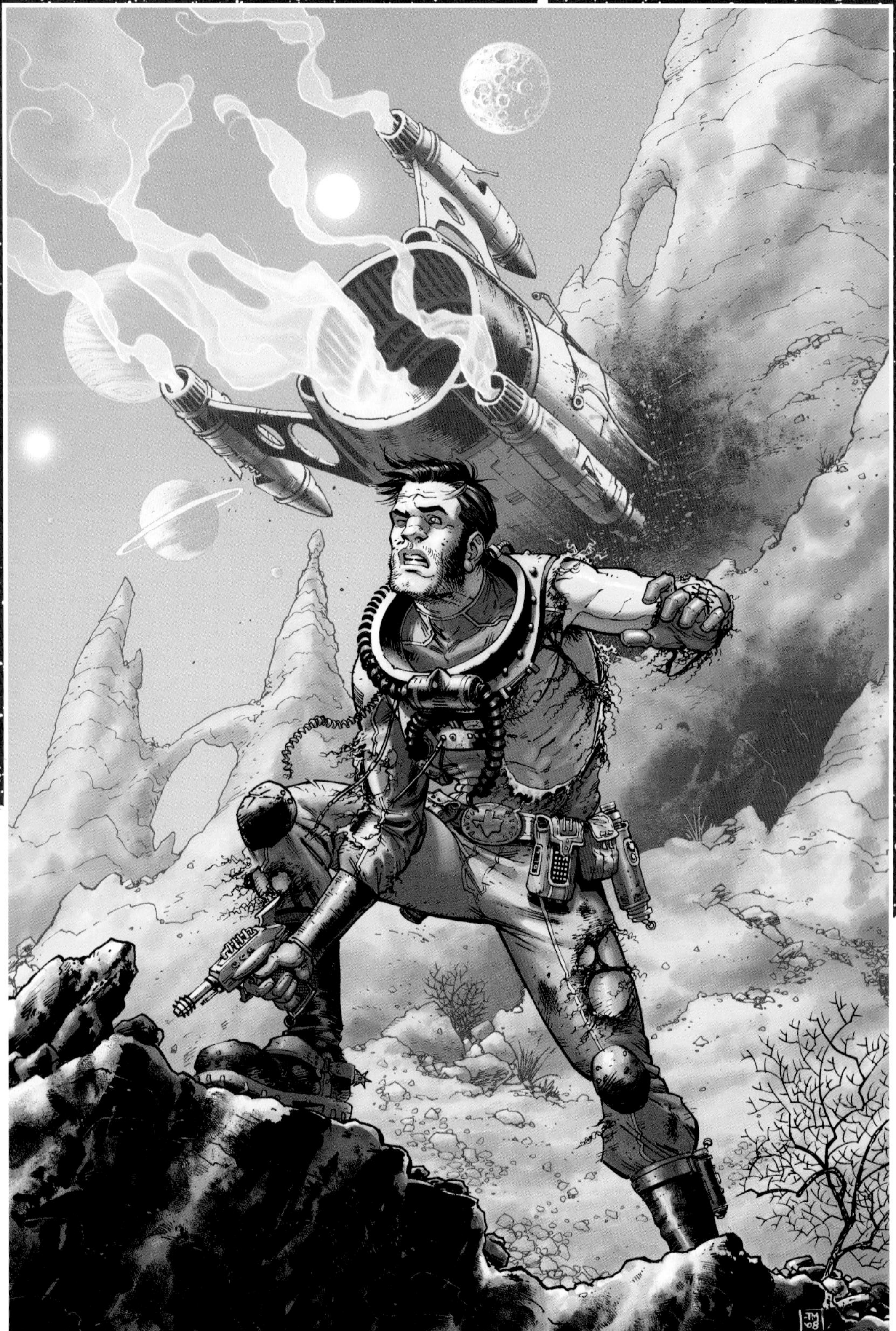

FEAR AGENT #22
ART BY **TONY MOORE**

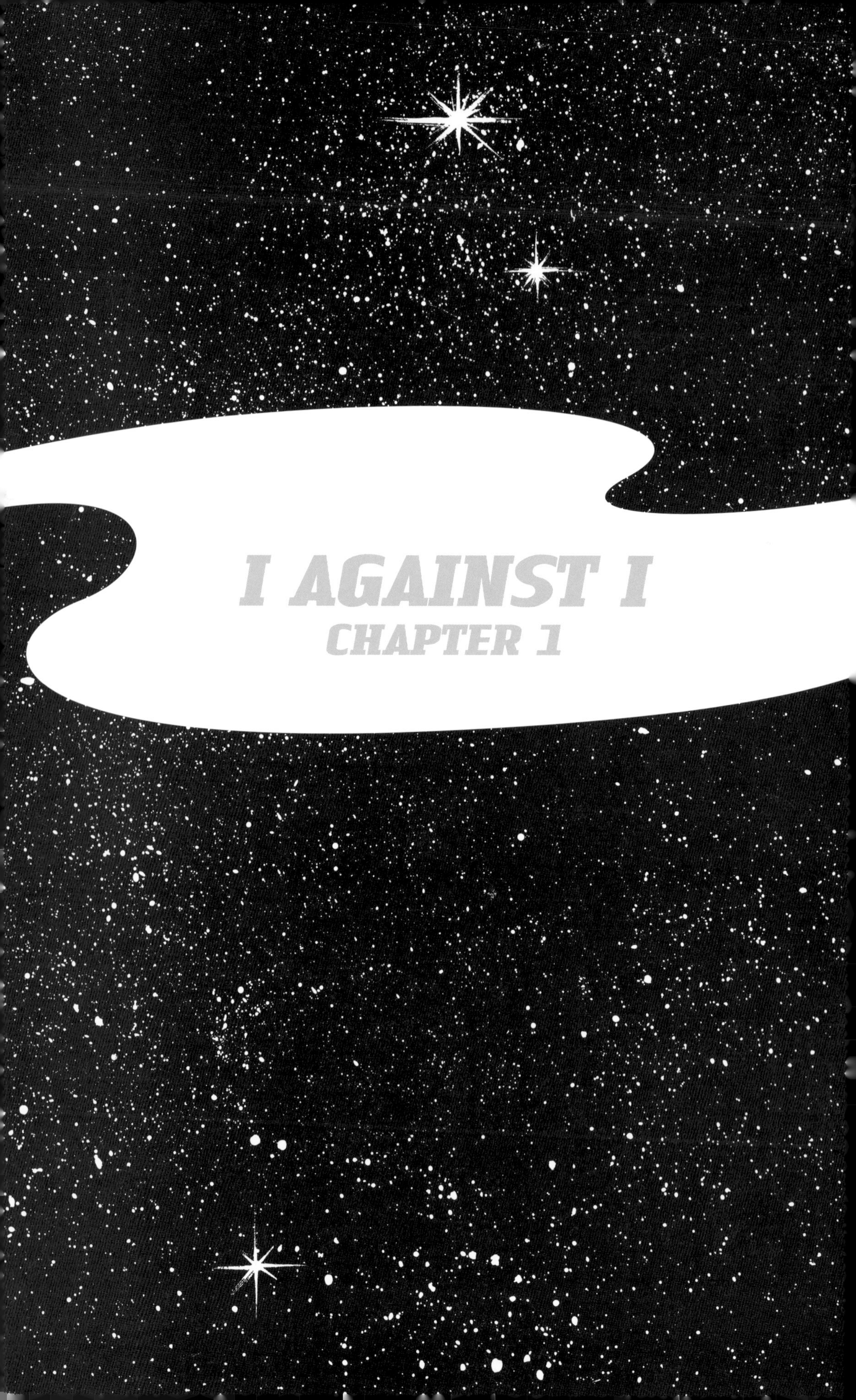
I AGAINST I
CHAPTER 1

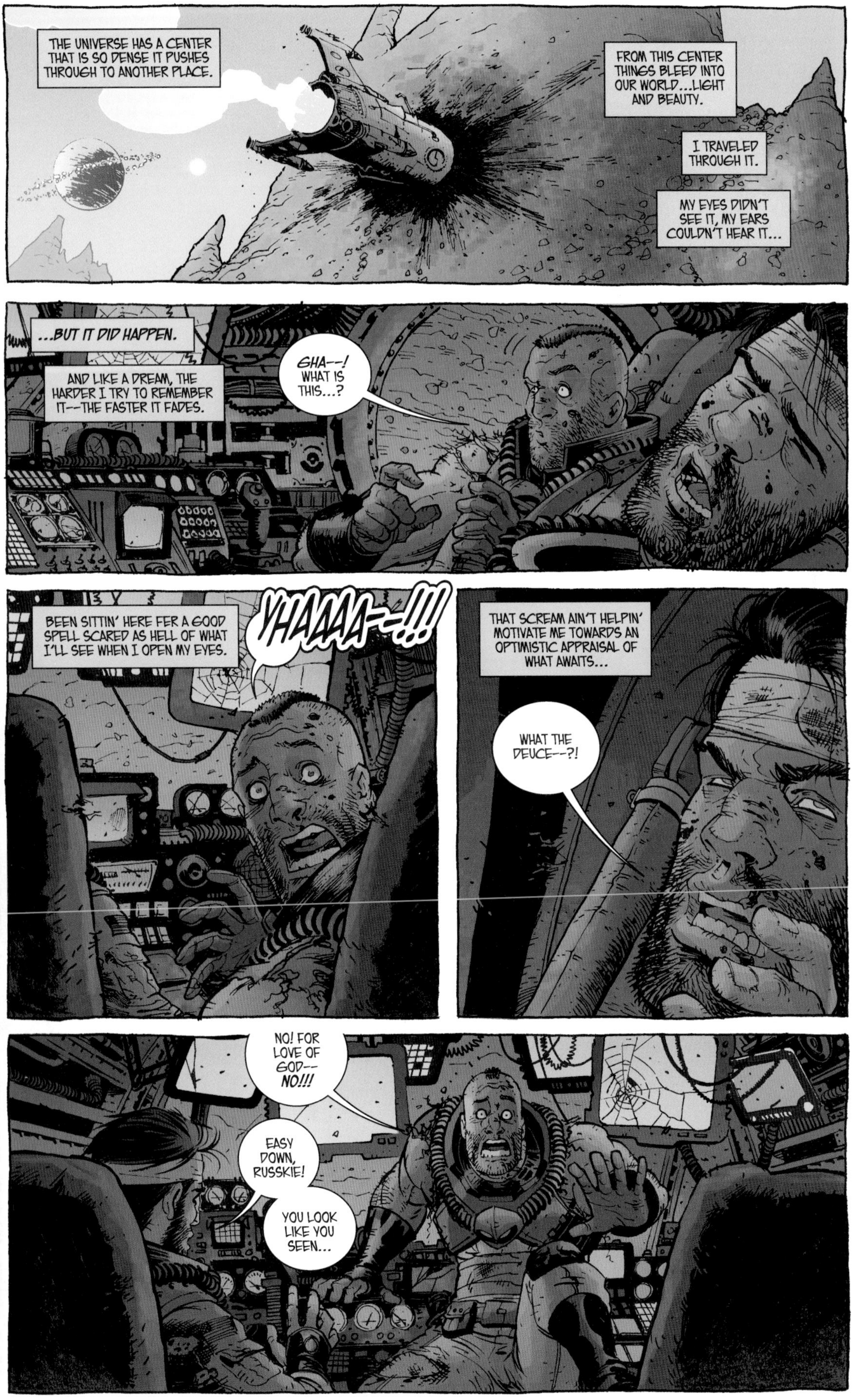
THE UNIVERSE HAS A CENTER THAT IS SO DENSE IT PUSHES THROUGH TO ANOTHER PLACE.
FROM THIS CENTER THINGS BLEED INTO OUR WORLD...LIGHT AND BEAUTY.
I TRAVELED THROUGH IT.
MY EYES DIDN'T SEE IT, MY EARS COULDN'T HEAR IT...
...BUT IT DID HAPPEN.
AND LIKE A DREAM, THE HARDER I TRY TO REMEMBER IT--THE FASTER IT FADES.
GHA--! WHAT IS THIS...?
BEEN SITTIN' HERE FER A GOOD SPELL SCARED AS HELL OF WHAT I'LL SEE WHEN I OPEN MY EYES.
YHAAAA--!!!
THAT SCREAM AIN'T HELPIN' MOTIVATE ME TOWARDS AN OPTIMISTIC APPRAISAL OF WHAT AWAITS...
WHAT THE DEUCE--?!
NO! FOR LOVE OF GOD-- NO!!!
EASY DOWN, RUSSKIE!
YOU LOOK LIKE YOU SEEN...

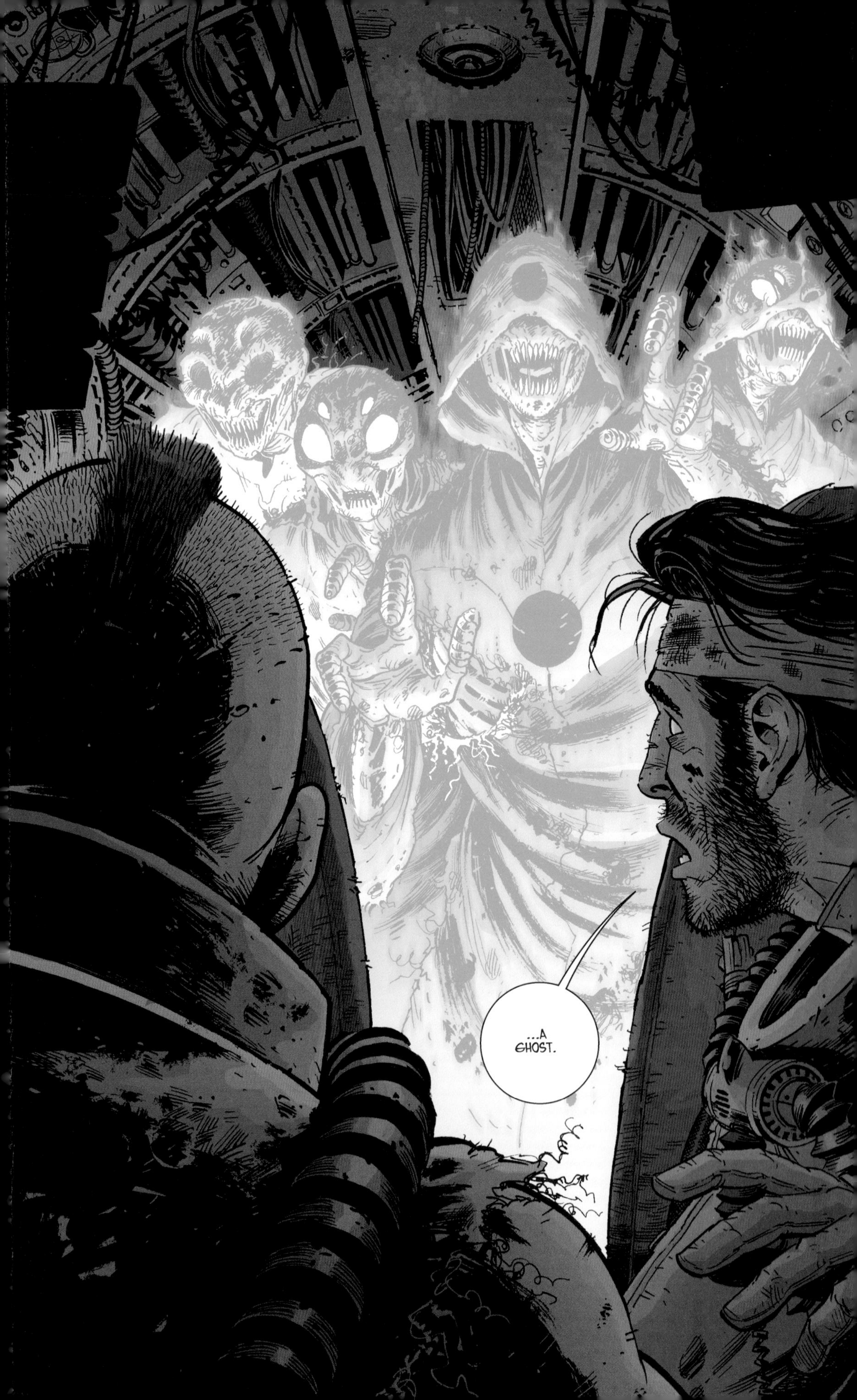
...A GHOST.

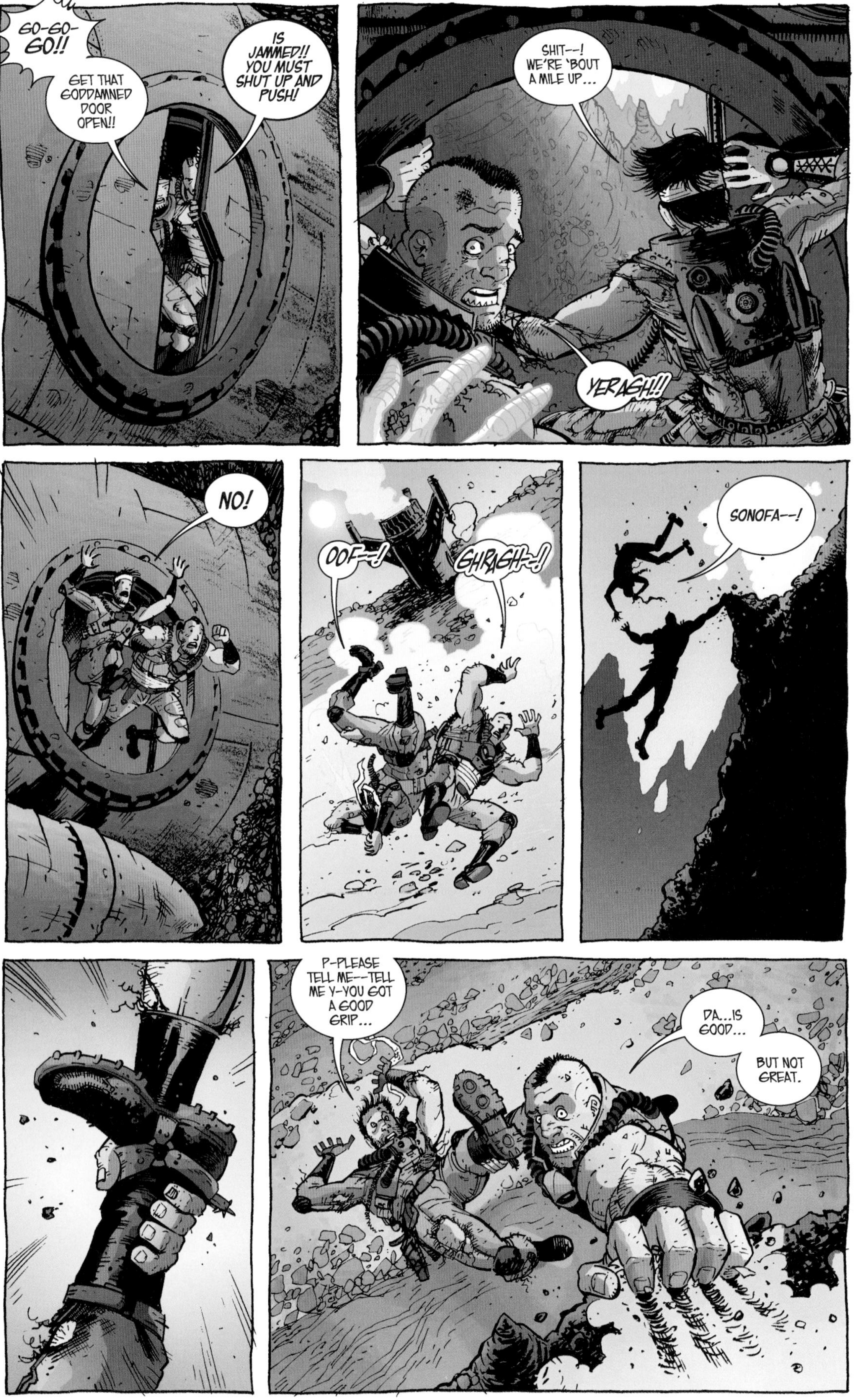
GO-GO-GO!!
GET THAT GODDAMNED DOOR OPEN!!
IS JAMMED!! YOU MUST SHUT UP AND PUSH!
SHIT--! WE'RE 'BOUT A MILE UP...
YERAGH!!
NO!
OOF--!
GHRAGH--!
SONOFA--!
P-PLEASE TELL ME--TELL ME Y-YOU GOT A GOOD GRIP...
DA...IS GOOD...
BUT NOT GREAT.

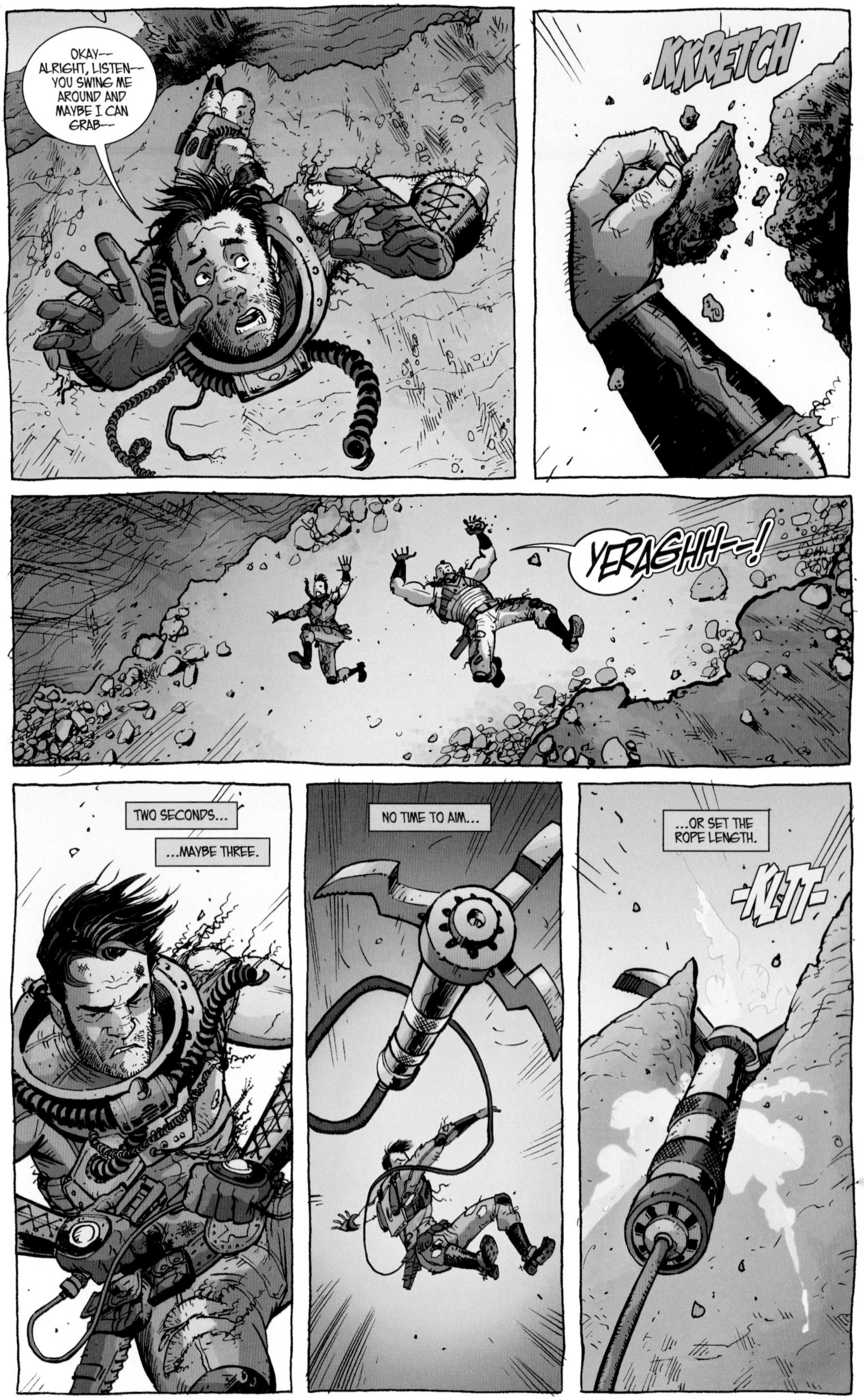
OKAY--
ALRIGHT, LISTEN--
YOU SWING ME
AROUND AND
MAYBE I CAN
GRAB--
KKRETCH
YERAGHH--!
TWO SECONDS...
...MAYBE THREE.
NO TIME TO AIM...
...OR SET THE
ROPE LENGTH.
-KLIT-

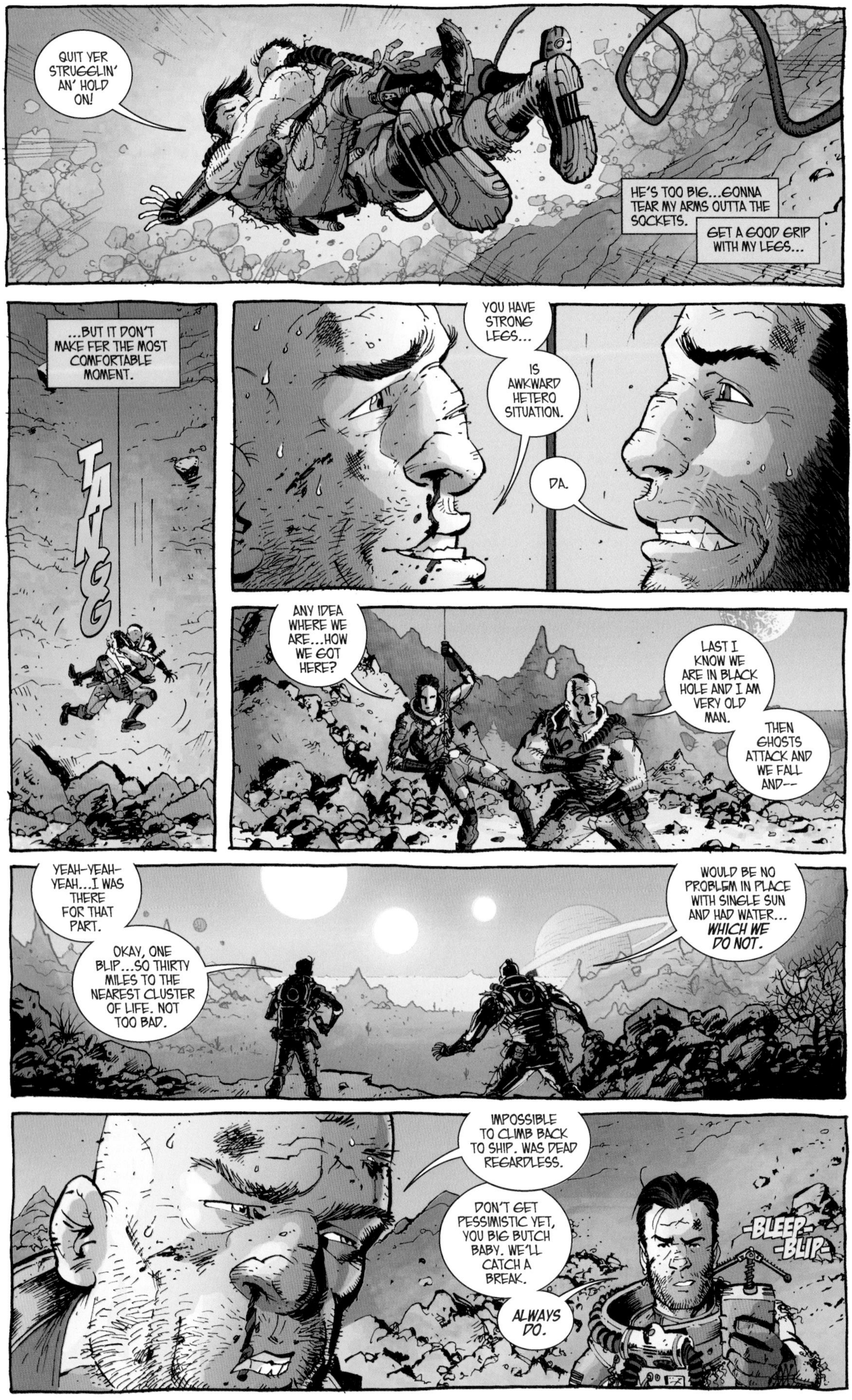
QUIT YER STRUGGLIN' AN' HOLD ON!
HE'S TOO BIG...GONNA TEAR MY ARMS OUTTA THE SOCKETS.
GET A GOOD GRIP WITH MY LEGS...
...BUT IT DON'T MAKE FER THE MOST COMFORTABLE MOMENT.
TANGG
YOU HAVE STRONG LEGS...
IS AWKWARD HETERO SITUATION.
DA.
ANY IDEA WHERE WE ARE...HOW WE GOT HERE?
LAST I KNOW WE ARE IN BLACK HOLE AND I AM VERY OLD MAN.
THEN GHOSTS ATTACK AND WE FALL AND--
YEAH-YEAH-YEAH...I WAS THERE FOR THAT PART.
OKAY, ONE BLIP...SO THIRTY MILES TO THE NEAREST CLUSTER OF LIFE. NOT TOO BAD.
WOULD BE NO PROBLEM IN PLACE WITH SINGLE SUN AND HAD WATER... WHICH WE DO NOT.
IMPOSSIBLE TO CLIMB BACK TO SHIP. WAS DEAD REGARDLESS.
DON'T GET PESSIMISTIC YET, YOU BIG BUTCH BABY. WE'LL CATCH A BREAK.
ALWAYS DO.
-BLEEP-
-BLIP-

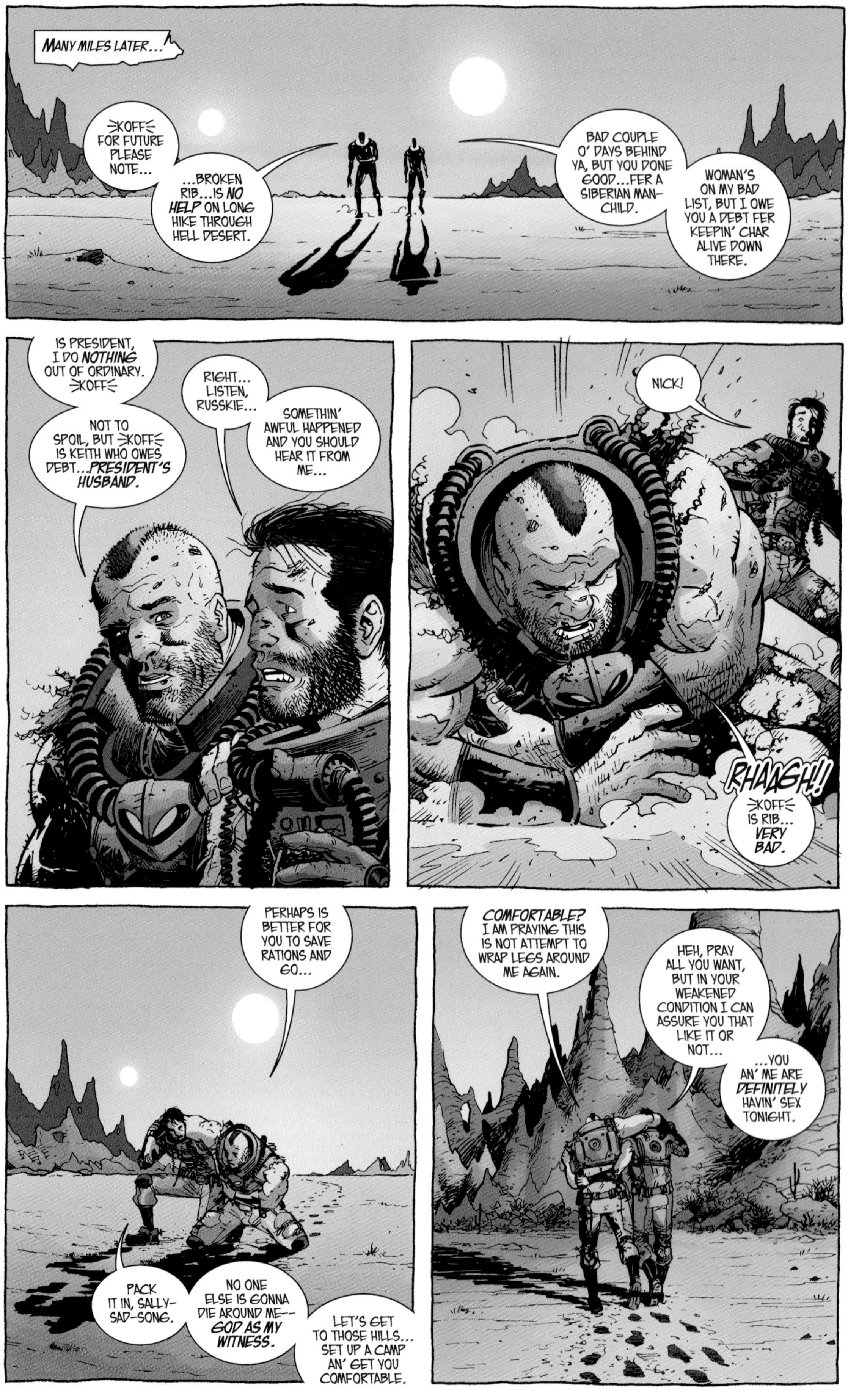

MANY MILES LATER...
KOFF FOR FUTURE PLEASE NOTE...
...BROKEN RIB...IS NO HELP ON LONG HIKE THROUGH HELL DESERT.
BAD COUPLE O' DAYS BEHIND YA, BUT YOU DONE GOOD...FER A SIBERIAN MAN-CHILD.
WOMAN'S ON MY BAD LIST, BUT I OWE YOU A DEBT FER KEEPIN' CHAR ALIVE DOWN THERE.
IS PRESIDENT, I DO NOTHING OUT OF ORDINARY. KOFF
NOT TO SPOIL, BUT KOFF IS KEITH WHO OWES DEBT...PRESIDENT'S HUSBAND.
RIGHT... LISTEN, RUSSKIE...
SOMETHIN' AWFUL HAPPENED AND YOU SHOULD HEAR IT FROM ME...
NICK!
RHAAGH!!
KOFF IS RIB... VERY BAD.
PERHAPS IS BETTER FOR YOU TO SAVE RATIONS AND GO...
PACK IT IN, SALLY-SAD-SONG.
NO ONE ELSE IS GONNA DIE AROUND ME--GOD AS MY WITNESS.
LET'S GET TO THOSE HILLS... SET UP A CAMP AN' GET YOU COMFORTABLE.
COMFORTABLE? I AM PRAYING THIS IS NOT ATTEMPT TO WRAP LEGS AROUND ME AGAIN.
HEH, PRAY ALL YOU WANT, BUT IN YOUR WEAKENED CONDITION I CAN ASSURE YOU THAT LIKE IT OR NOT...
...YOU AN' ME ARE DEFINITELY HAVIN' SEX TONIGHT.

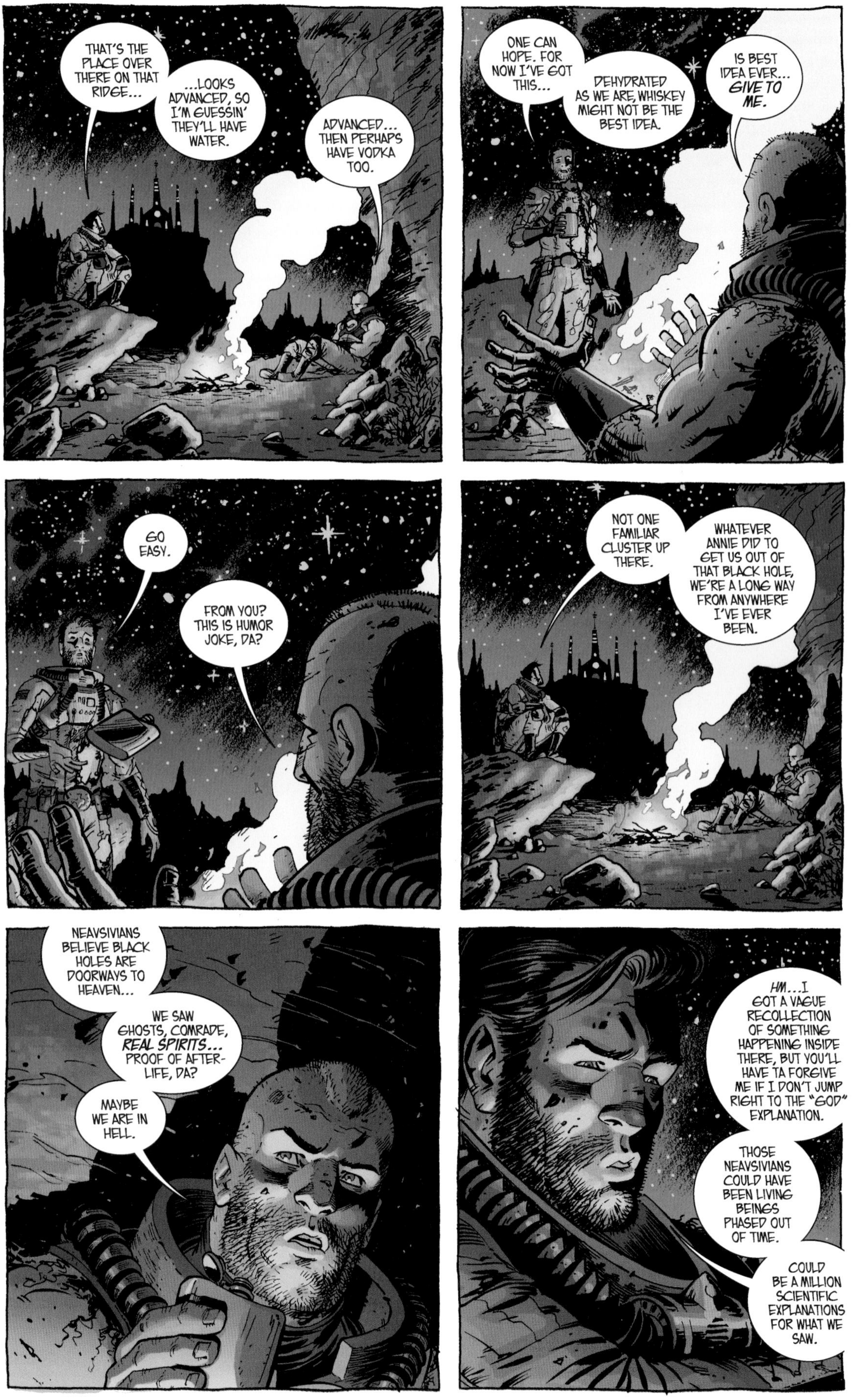
THAT'S THE PLACE OVER THERE ON THAT RIDGE...
...LOOKS ADVANCED, SO I'M GUESSIN' THEY'LL HAVE WATER.
ADVANCED... THEN PERHAPS HAVE VODKA TOO.
ONE CAN HOPE. FOR NOW I'VE GOT THIS...
DEHYDRATED AS WE ARE, WHISKEY MIGHT NOT BE THE BEST IDEA.
IS BEST IDEA EVER... *GIVE TO ME.*
GO EASY.
FROM YOU? THIS IS HUMOR JOKE, DA?
NOT ONE FAMILIAR CLUSTER UP THERE.
WHATEVER ANNIE DID TO GET US OUT OF THAT BLACK HOLE, WE'RE A LONG WAY FROM ANYWHERE I'VE EVER BEEN.
NEAVSIVIANS BELIEVE BLACK HOLES ARE DOORWAYS TO HEAVEN...
WE SAW GHOSTS, COMRADE, *REAL SPIRITS...* PROOF OF AFTER-LIFE, DA?
MAYBE WE ARE IN HELL.
HM...I GOT A VAGUE RECOLLECTION OF SOMETHING HAPPENING INSIDE THERE, BUT YOU'LL HAVE TA FORGIVE ME IF I DON'T JUMP RIGHT TO THE "GOD" EXPLANATION.
THOSE NEAVSIVIANS COULD HAVE BEEN LIVING BEINGS PHASED OUT OF TIME.
COULD BE A MILLION SCIENTIFIC EXPLANATIONS FOR WHAT WE SAW.

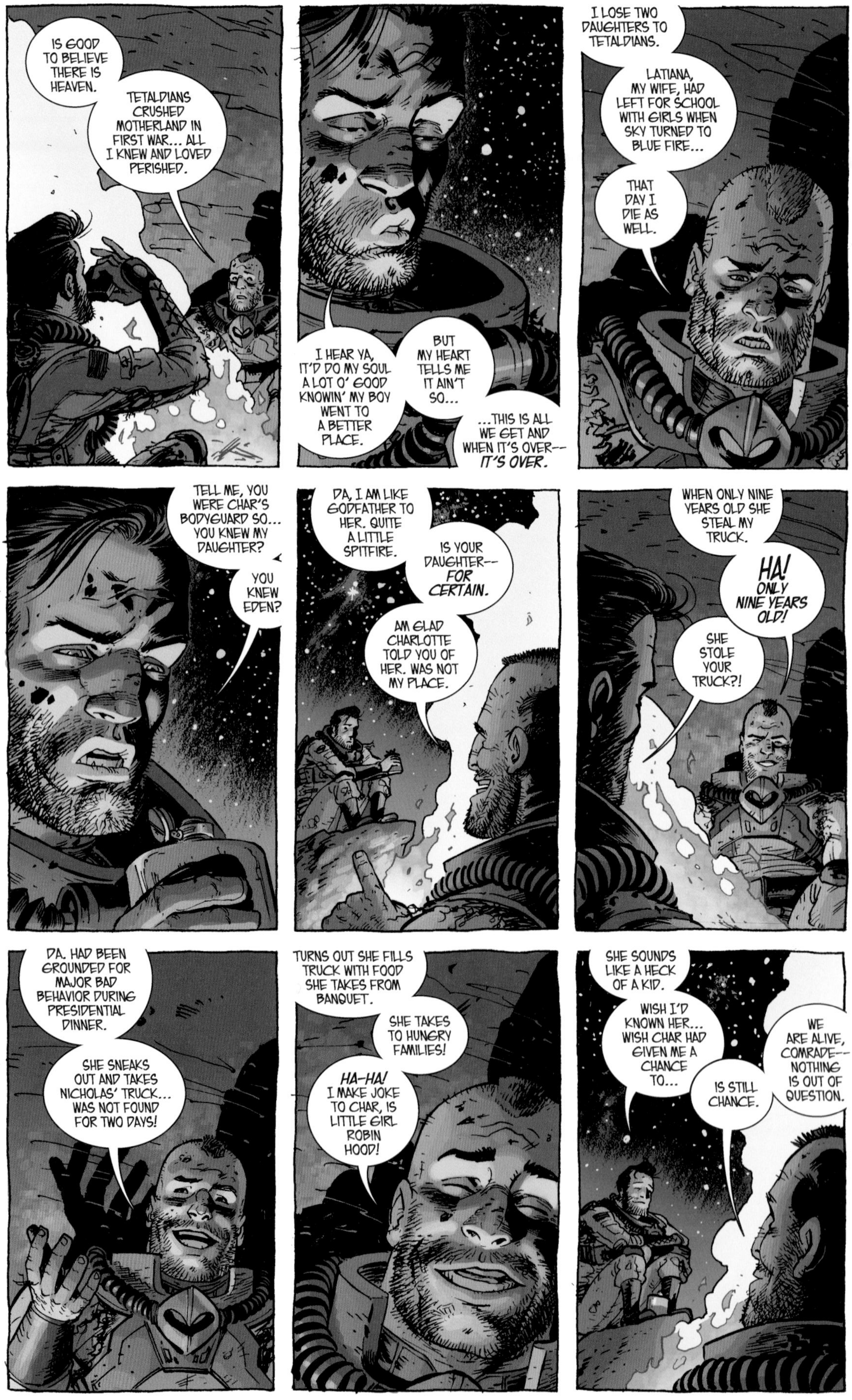
IS GOOD TO BELIEVE THERE IS HEAVEN.
TETALDIANS CRUSHED MOTHERLAND IN FIRST WAR... ALL I KNEW AND LOVED PERISHED.
I HEAR YA, IT'D DO MY SOUL A LOT O' GOOD KNOWIN' MY BOY WENT TO A BETTER PLACE.
BUT MY HEART TELLS ME IT AIN'T SO...
...THIS IS ALL WE GET AND WHEN IT'S OVER-- IT'S OVER.
I LOSE TWO DAUGHTERS TO TETALDIANS.
LATIANA, MY WIFE, HAD LEFT FOR SCHOOL WITH GIRLS WHEN SKY TURNED TO BLUE FIRE...
THAT DAY I DIE AS WELL.
TELL ME, YOU WERE CHAR'S BODYGUARD SO... YOU KNEW MY DAUGHTER?
YOU KNEW EDEN?
DA, I AM LIKE GODFATHER TO HER. QUITE A LITTLE SPITFIRE.
IS YOUR DAUGHTER-- FOR CERTAIN.
AM GLAD CHARLOTTE TOLD YOU OF HER. WAS NOT MY PLACE.
WHEN ONLY NINE YEARS OLD SHE STEAL MY TRUCK.
HA! ONLY NINE YEARS OLD!
SHE STOLE YOUR TRUCK?!
DA. HAD BEEN GROUNDED FOR MAJOR BAD BEHAVIOR DURING PRESIDENTIAL DINNER.
SHE SNEAKS OUT AND TAKES NICHOLAS' TRUCK... WAS NOT FOUND FOR TWO DAYS!
TURNS OUT SHE FILLS TRUCK WITH FOOD SHE TAKES FROM BANQUET.
SHE TAKES TO HUNGRY FAMILIES!
HA-HA! I MAKE JOKE TO CHAR, IS LITTLE GIRL ROBIN HOOD!
SHE SOUNDS LIKE A HECK OF A KID.
WISH I'D KNOWN HER... WISH CHAR HAD GIVEN ME A CHANCE TO...
IS STILL CHANCE.
WE ARE ALIVE, COMRADE-- NOTHING IS OUT OF QUESTION.

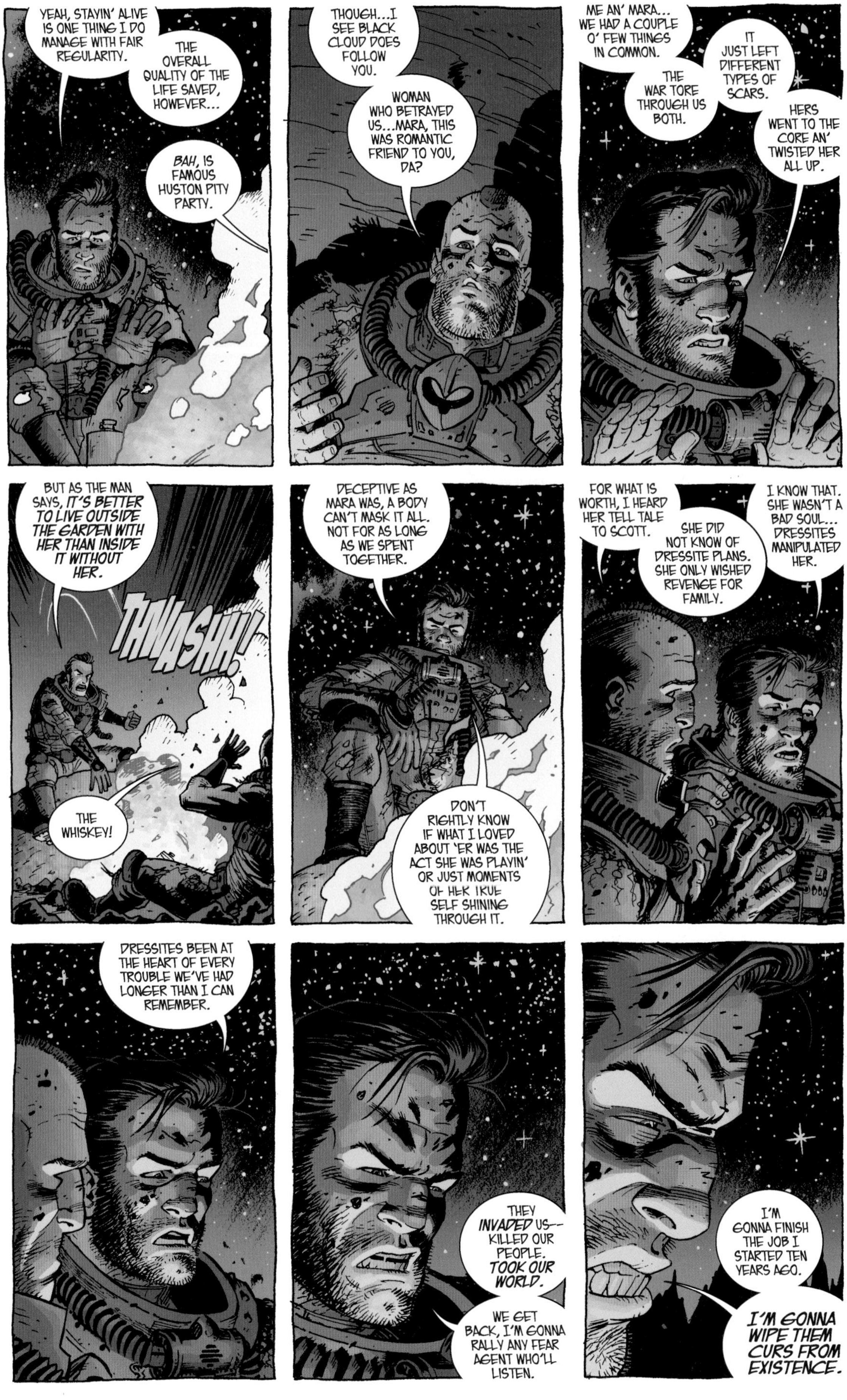
YEAH, STAYIN' ALIVE IS ONE THING I DO MANAGE WITH FAIR REGULARITY.
THE OVERALL QUALITY OF THE LIFE SAVED, HOWEVER...
BAH, IS FAMOUS HUSTON PITY PARTY.
THOUGH...I SEE BLACK CLOUD DOES FOLLOW YOU.
WOMAN WHO BETRAYED US...MARA, THIS WAS ROMANTIC FRIEND TO YOU, DA?
ME AN' MARA... WE HAD A COUPLE O' FEW THINGS IN COMMON.
THE WAR TORE THROUGH US BOTH.
IT JUST LEFT DIFFERENT TYPES OF SCARS.
HERS WENT TO THE CORE AN' TWISTED HER ALL UP.
BUT AS THE MAN SAYS, IT'S BETTER TO LIVE OUTSIDE THE GARDEN WITH HER THAN INSIDE IT WITHOUT HER.
THWASHH!
THE WHISKEY!
DECEPTIVE AS MARA WAS, A BODY CAN'T MASK IT ALL. NOT FOR AS LONG AS WE SPENT TOGETHER.
DON'T RIGHTLY KNOW IF WHAT I LOVED ABOUT 'ER WAS THE ACT SHE WAS PLAYIN' OR JUST MOMENTS OF HER TRUE SELF SHINING THROUGH IT.
FOR WHAT IS WORTH, I HEARD HER TELL TALE TO SCOTT.
SHE DID NOT KNOW OF DRESSITE PLANS. SHE ONLY WISHED REVENGE FOR FAMILY.
I KNOW THAT. SHE WASN'T A BAD SOUL... DRESSITES MANIPULATED HER.
DRESSITES BEEN AT THE HEART OF EVERY TROUBLE WE'VE HAD LONGER THAN I CAN REMEMBER.
THEY INVADED US-- KILLED OUR PEOPLE. TOOK OUR WORLD.
WE GET BACK, I'M GONNA RALLY ANY FEAR AGENT WHO'LL LISTEN.
I'M GONNA FINISH THE JOB I STARTED TEN YEARS AGO.
I'M GONNA WIPE THEM CURS FROM EXISTENCE.

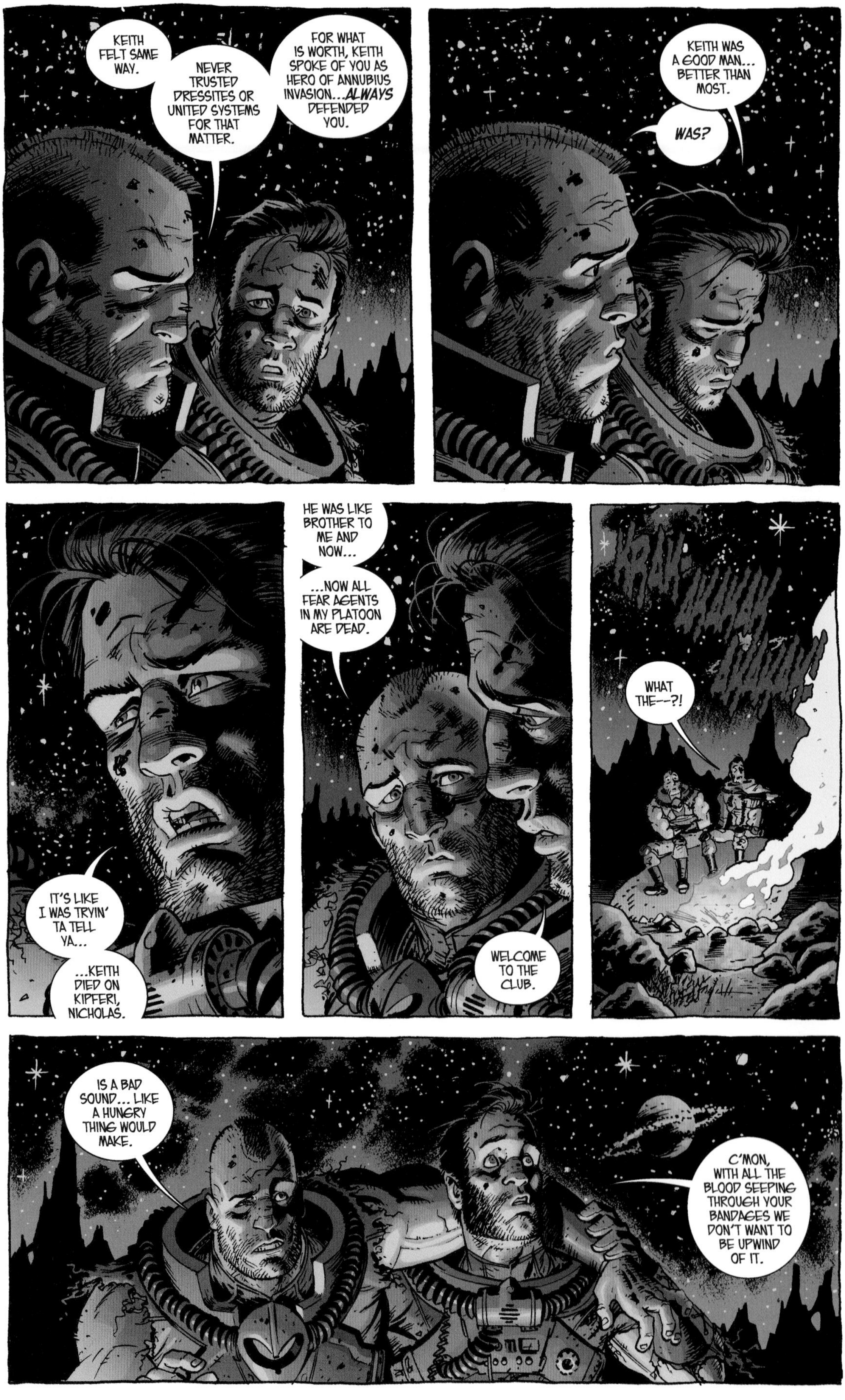
KEITH FELT SAME WAY.
NEVER TRUSTED DRESSITES OR UNITED SYSTEMS FOR THAT MATTER.
FOR WHAT IS WORTH, KEITH SPOKE OF YOU AS HERO OF ANNUBIUS INVASION...ALWAYS DEFENDED YOU.
KEITH WAS A GOOD MAN... BETTER THAN MOST.
WAS?
IT'S LIKE I WAS TRYIN' TA TELL YA...
...KEITH DIED ON KIPFERI, NICHOLAS.
HE WAS LIKE BROTHER TO ME AND NOW...
...NOW ALL FEAR AGENTS IN MY PLATOON ARE DEAD.
WELCOME TO THE CLUB.
WHAT THE--?!
IS A BAD SOUND... LIKE A HUNGRY THING WOULD MAKE.
C'MON, WITH ALL THE BLOOD SEEPING THROUGH YOUR BANDAGES WE DON'T WANT TO BE UPWIND OF IT.

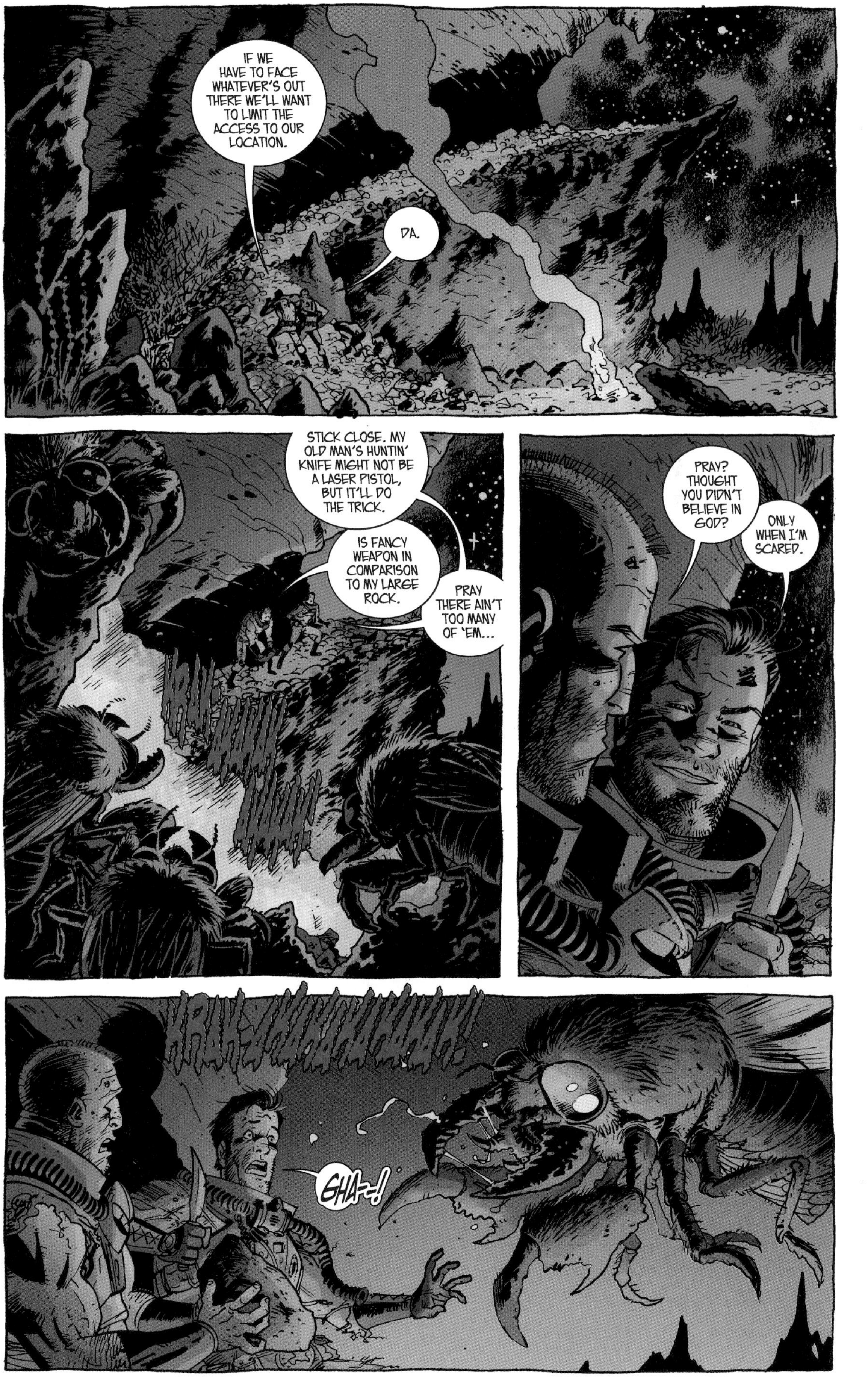
IF WE HAVE TO FACE WHATEVER'S OUT THERE WE'LL WANT TO LIMIT THE ACCESS TO OUR LOCATION.
DA.
STICK CLOSE. MY OLD MAN'S HUNTIN' KNIFE MIGHT NOT BE A LASER PISTOL, BUT IT'LL DO THE TRICK.
IS FANCY WEAPON IN COMPARISON TO MY LARGE ROCK.
PRAY THERE AIN'T TOO MANY OF 'EM...
PRAY? THOUGHT YOU DIDN'T BELIEVE IN GOD?
ONLY WHEN I'M SCARED.
GHA--!

SKRAKK--

GLUKK

PERHAPS YOUR HAPHAZARD APPROACH TO PRAYING DOES NOTHING.

YEAH... WELL, IF THERE IS A GOD, IN ABOUT *TWO MINUTES* I'LL BE ABLE TO MAKE MY APOLOGY IN PERSON...

KRAK KLIKIKIKIKIKIKIK!

IS OPTIMISTIC APPRAISAL.

KRAK KLIKIKIKIKIKIKIKIK!

GHA--!

SCHUNKK

LEG GOES COLD-- POISON--

HARDER I FIGHT NOW--

--FASTER MY HEART BEATS--

--FASTER THE VENOM TRAVELS--

CHNGK

KLIKIKIKIKIKIKIK

GLA-TTWOKK

GODDAMNIT-- THEIR PINCHERS ARE LOADED WITH VENOM!

GRAAA-- YES, I KNOW.

UNFF!

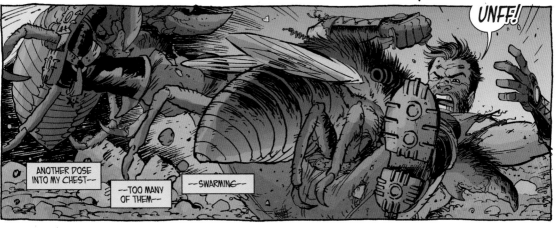

ANOTHER DOSE INTO MY CHEST--

--TOO MANY OF THEM--

--SWARMING--

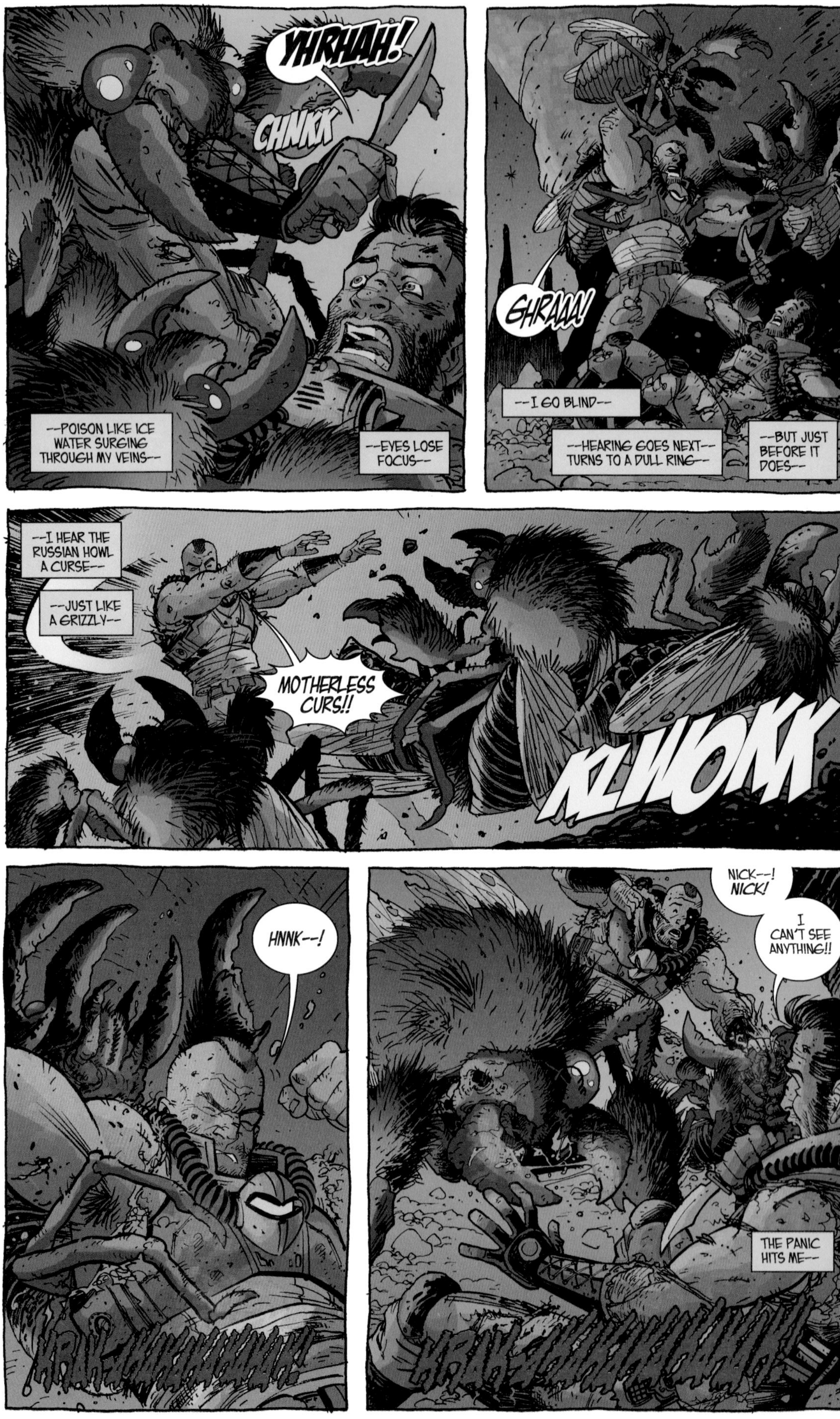

YHRHAH!
CHNKK
--POISON LIKE ICE WATER SURGING THROUGH MY VEINS--
--EYES LOSE FOCUS--
GHRAAA!
--I GO BLIND--
--HEARING GOES NEXT--
TURNS TO A DULL RING--
--BUT JUST BEFORE IT DOES--
--I HEAR THE RUSSIAN HOWL A CURSE--
--JUST LIKE A GRIZZLY--
MOTHERLESS CURS!!
KLWONK
HNNK--!
NICK--! NICK!
I CAN'T SEE ANYTHING!!
THE PANIC HITS ME--

SOMETHING OPENS UP MY STOMACH—

SHNTT

—HOLD THE KNIFE FOR ALL I'M WORTH—

KRAKK—!

—STAB AT THE BASTARD—

SCHUNKK

GAA—!

SCHOPP

—ANOTHER BITE— I CATCH A FULL DOSE—

—I KNOW IT RIGHT AWAY—

GRHH!!

—BLIND—

—WAITING FOR THE FINAL STROKE—

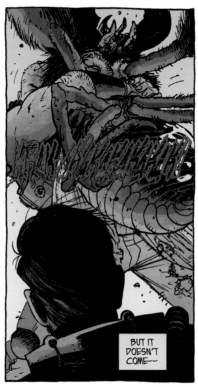

BUT IT DOESN'T COME—

RRRHHOOAAAHHH!!

—AN' BEYOND THE HUM IN MY EARS I MAKE OUT A SOUND—

CRRMBBLE...

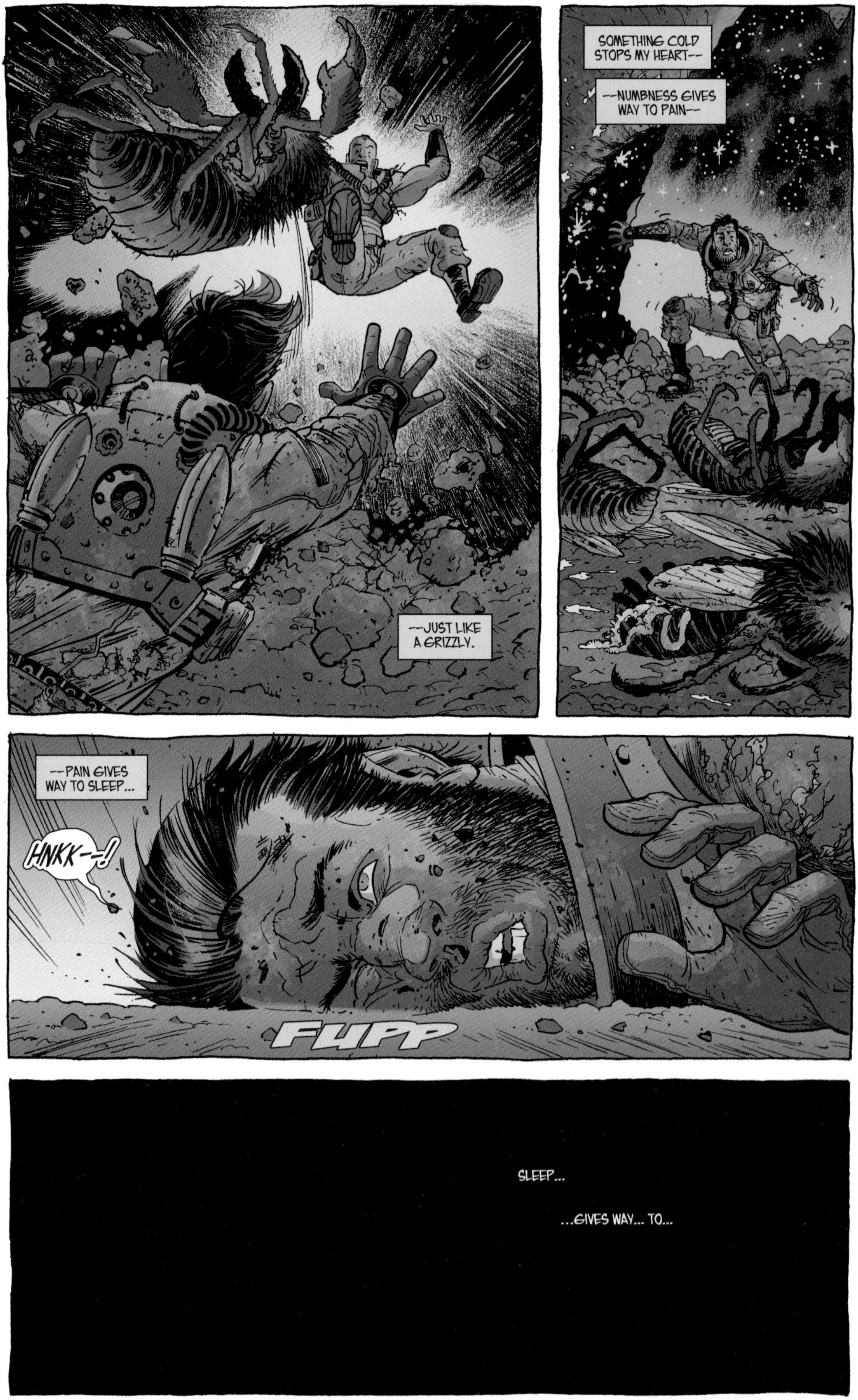
--JUST LIKE A GRIZZLY.
SOMETHING COLD STOPS MY HEART--
--NUMBNESS GIVES WAY TO PAIN--
--PAIN GIVES WAY TO SLEEP...
HNKK--!
FUPP
SLEEP...
...GIVES WAY... TO...

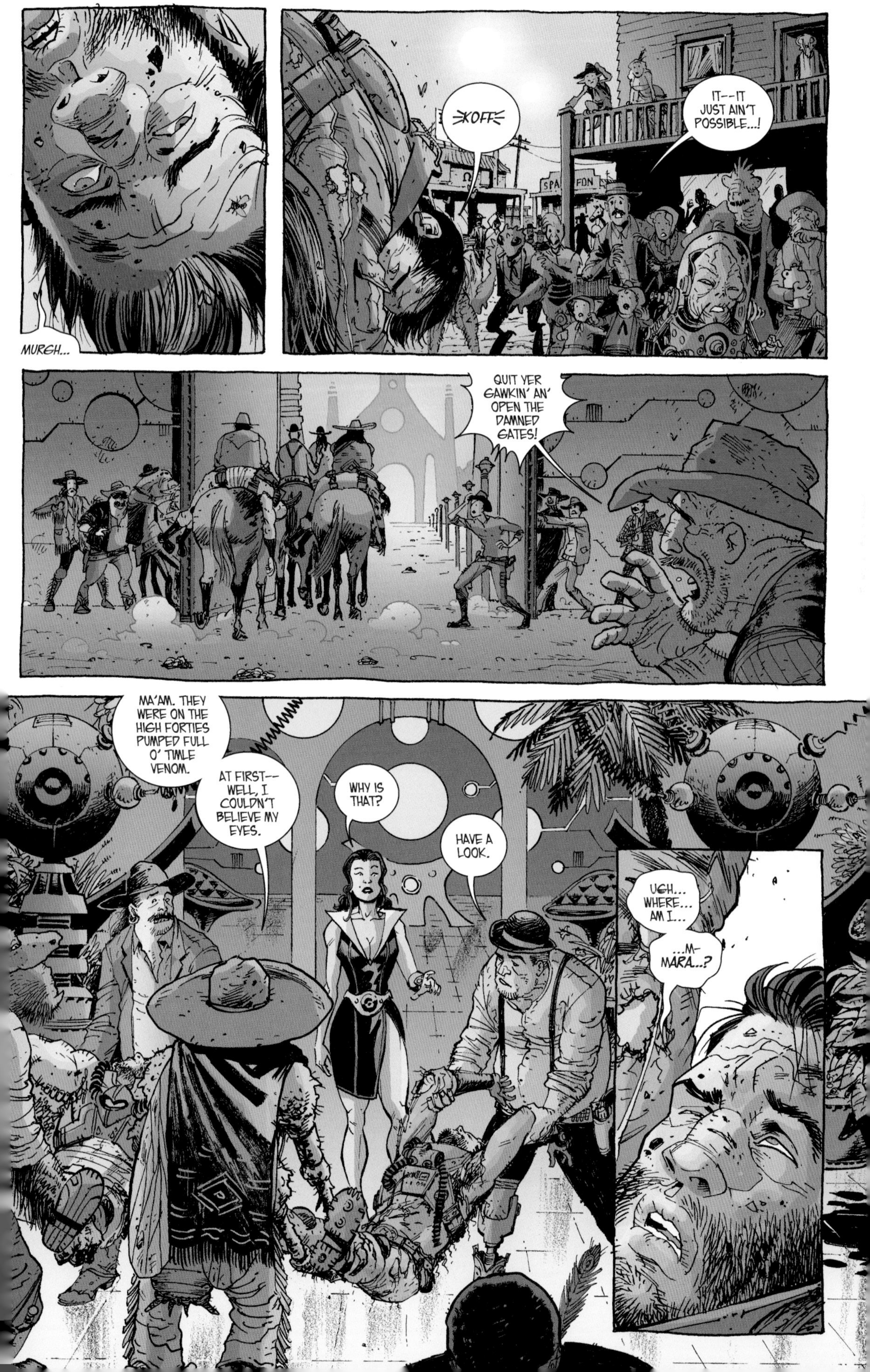
MURGH...
KOFF
IT--IT JUST AIN'T POSSIBLE...!
QUIT YER GAWKIN' AN' OPEN THE DAMNED GATES!
MA'AM. THEY WERE ON THE HIGH FORTIES PUMPED FULL O' TIMLE VENOM.
AT FIRST--WELL, I COULDN'T BELIEVE MY EYES.
WHY IS THAT?
HAVE A LOOK.
UGH... WHERE... AM I...
...M-MARA...?

DAYS LATER...

WELL, LOOK WHO'S UP.

HNN... WHAT THE--?!

WHAT'RE YOU DOIN'?

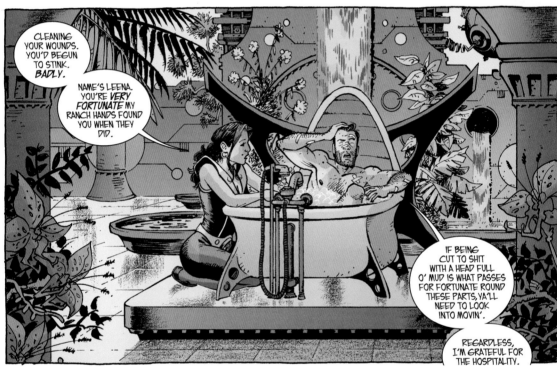

CLEANING YOUR WOUNDS. YOU'D BEGUN TO STINK. *BADLY.*

NAME'S LEENA. YOU'RE *VERY FORTUNATE* MY RANCH HANDS FOUND YOU WHEN THEY DID.

IF BEING CUT TO SHIT WITH A HEAD FULL O' MUD IS WHAT PASSES FOR FORTUNATE ROUND THESE PARTS, YA'LL NEED TO LOOK INTO MOVIN'.

REGARDLESS, I'M GRATEFUL FOR THE HOSPITALITY.

HEY! WHO PUT THIS GODDAMNED PATCH ON ME?

YOU WERE IN PAIN.

OUR DIAGNOSTICS SHOWED US THAT YOU'D USED IT BEFORE AND WE ASSUMED IT WOULD BE PLEASURABLE FOR YOU.

YEAH... WELL... IT AIN'T HALF BAD...

GARBAGE IS ONE SON-OF-A-BITCH HABIT TA KICK, THOUGH.

WHERE'S THE RUSSIAN??

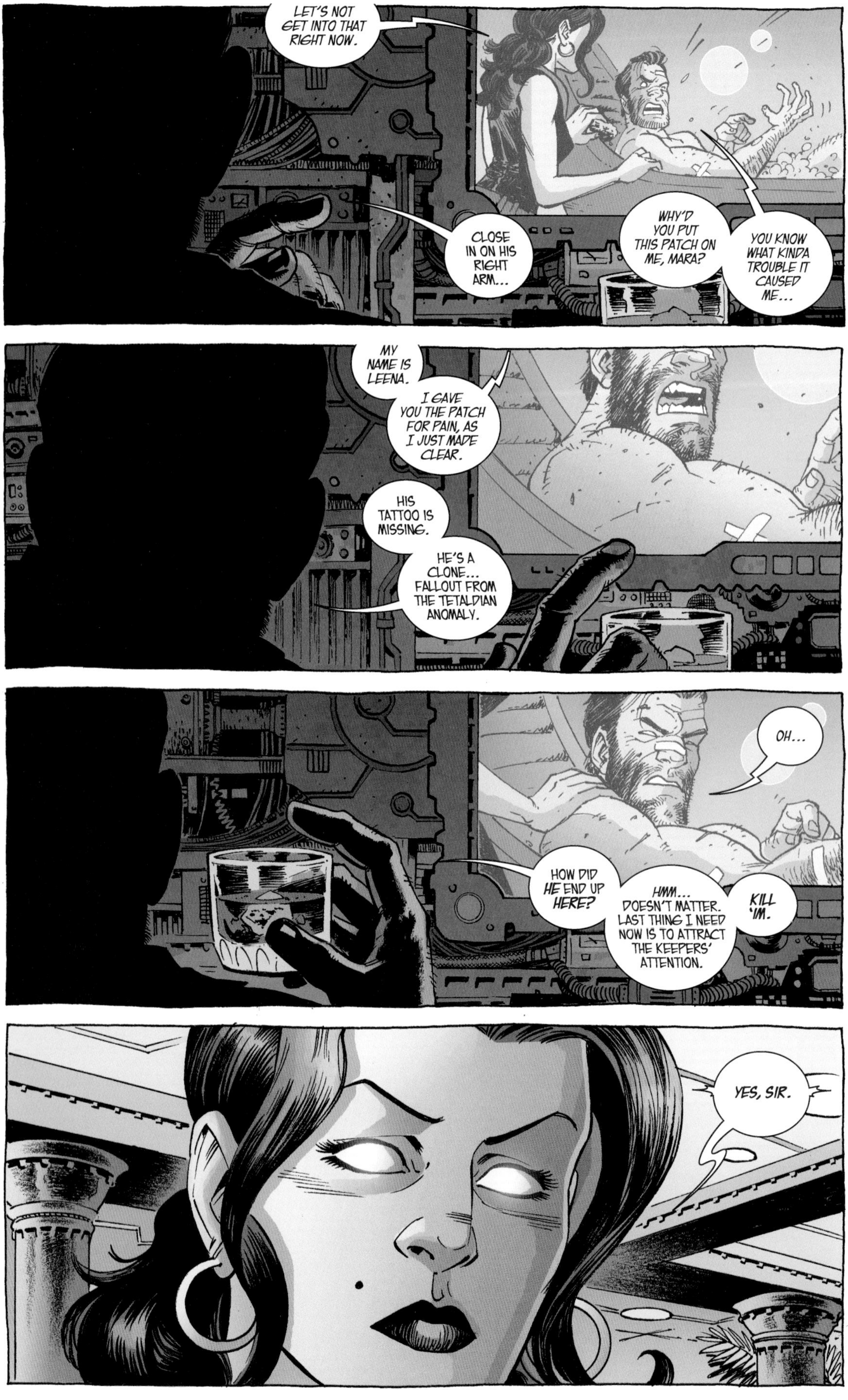
LET'S NOT GET INTO THAT RIGHT NOW.
CLOSE IN ON HIS RIGHT ARM...
WHY'D YOU PUT THIS PATCH ON ME, MARA?
YOU KNOW WHAT KINDA TROUBLE IT CAUSED ME...
MY NAME IS LEENA.
I GAVE YOU THE PATCH FOR PAIN, AS I JUST MADE CLEAR.
HIS TATTOO IS MISSING.
HE'S A CLONE... FALLOUT FROM THE TETALDIAN ANOMALY.
OH...
HOW DID HE END UP HERE?
HMM... DOESN'T MATTER. LAST THING I NEED NOW IS TO ATTRACT THE KEEPERS' ATTENTION.
KILL 'IM.
YES, SIR.

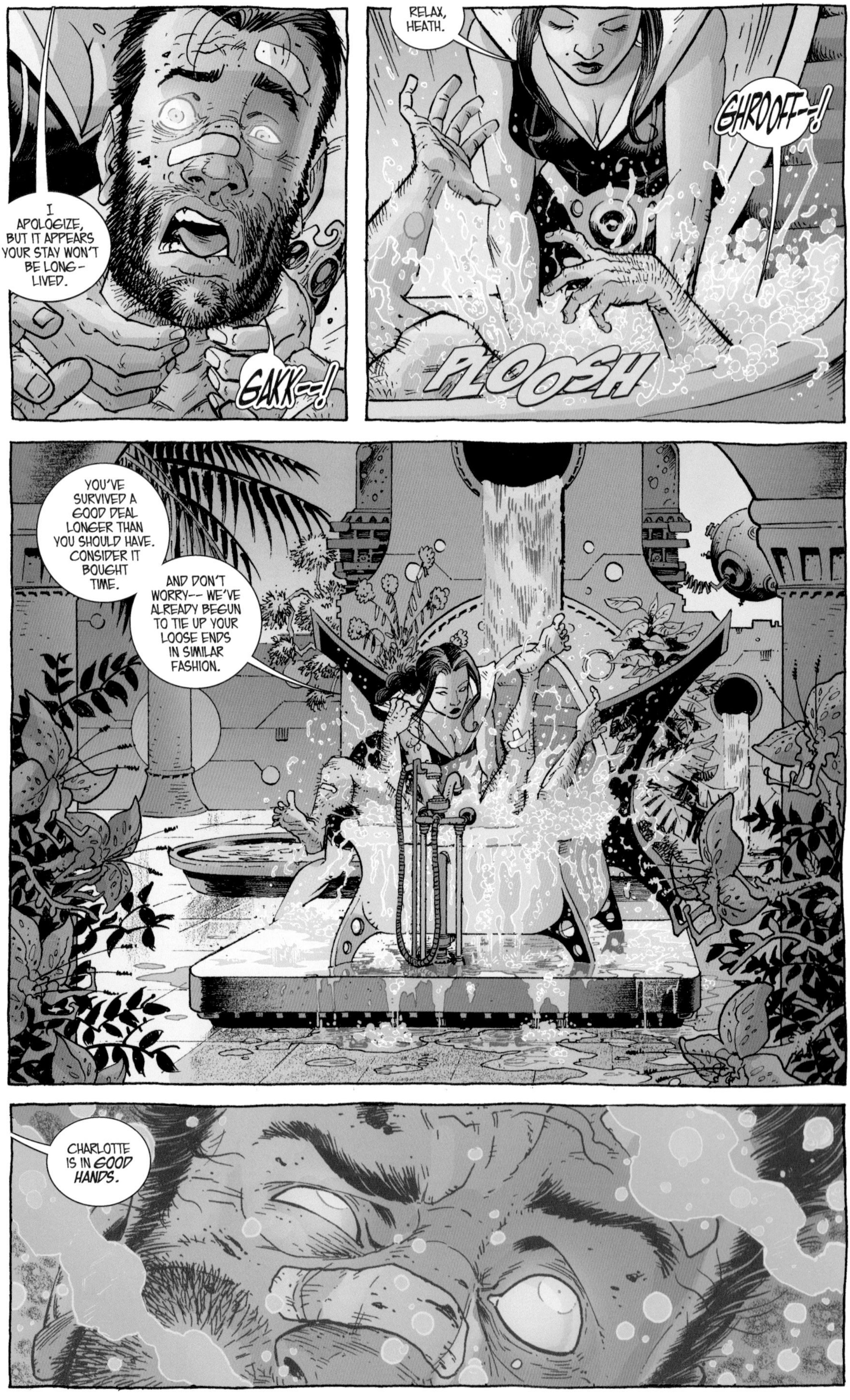
I APOLOGIZE, BUT IT APPEARS YOUR STAY WON'T BE LONG-LIVED.
GAKK--!
RELAX, HEATH.
GHROOFF--!
PLOOSH
YOU'VE SURVIVED A GOOD DEAL LONGER THAN YOU SHOULD HAVE. CONSIDER IT BOUGHT TIME.
AND DON'T WORRY-- WE'VE ALREADY BEGUN TO TIE UP YOUR LOOSE ENDS IN SIMILAR FASHION.
CHARLOTTE IS IN *GOOD HANDS.*

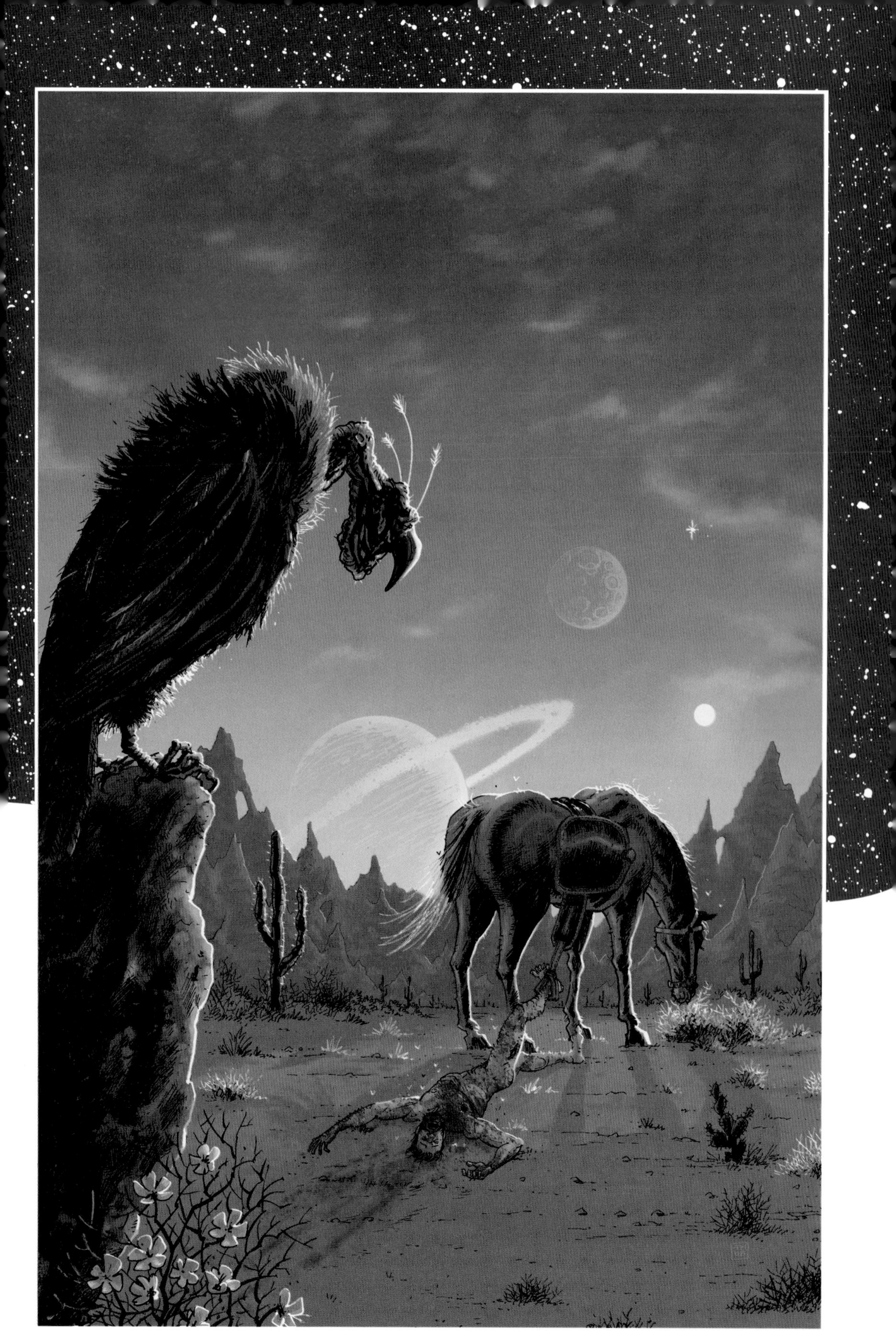

FEAR AGENT #23
ART BY **TONY MOORE**

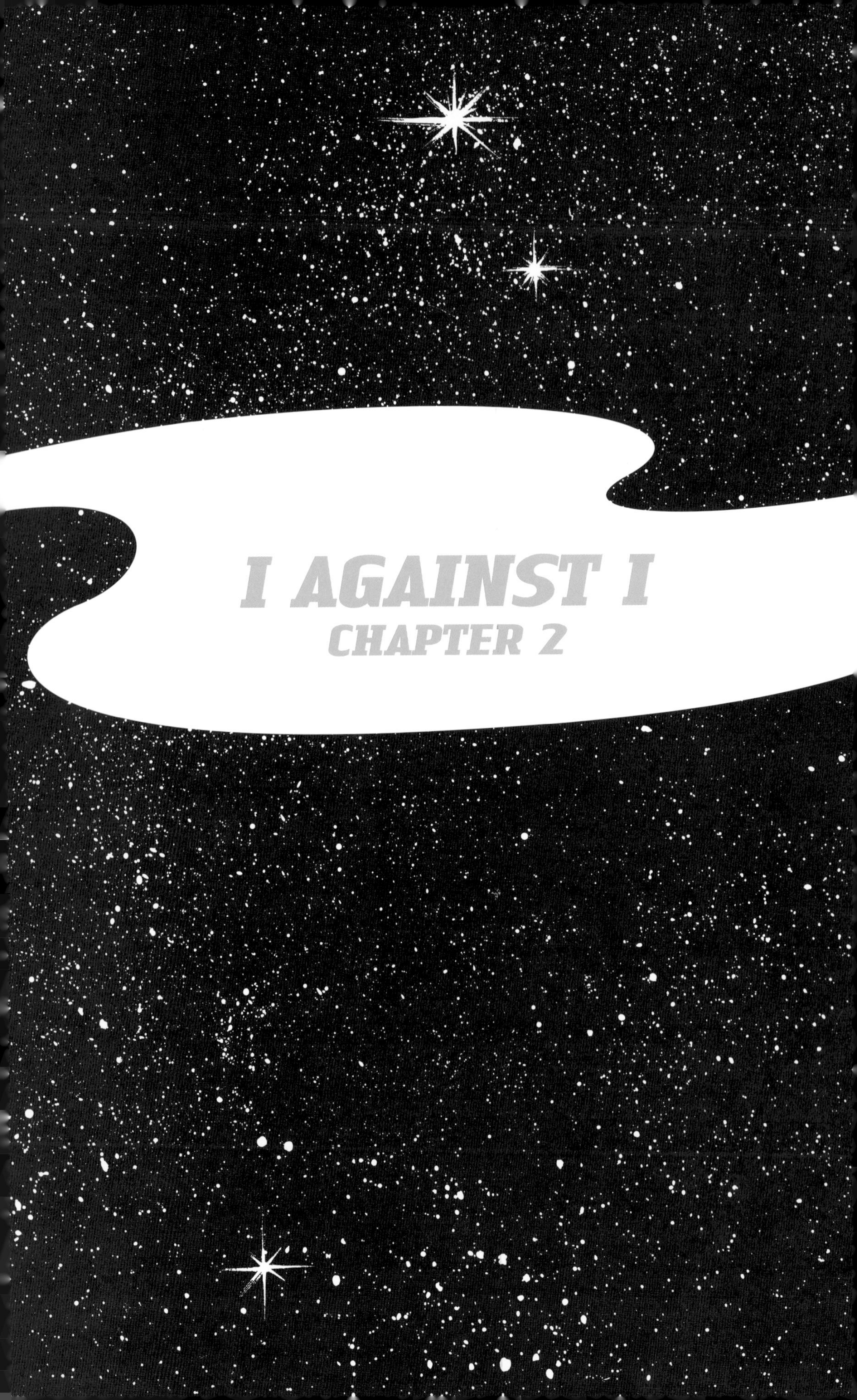
I AGAINST I
CHAPTER 2

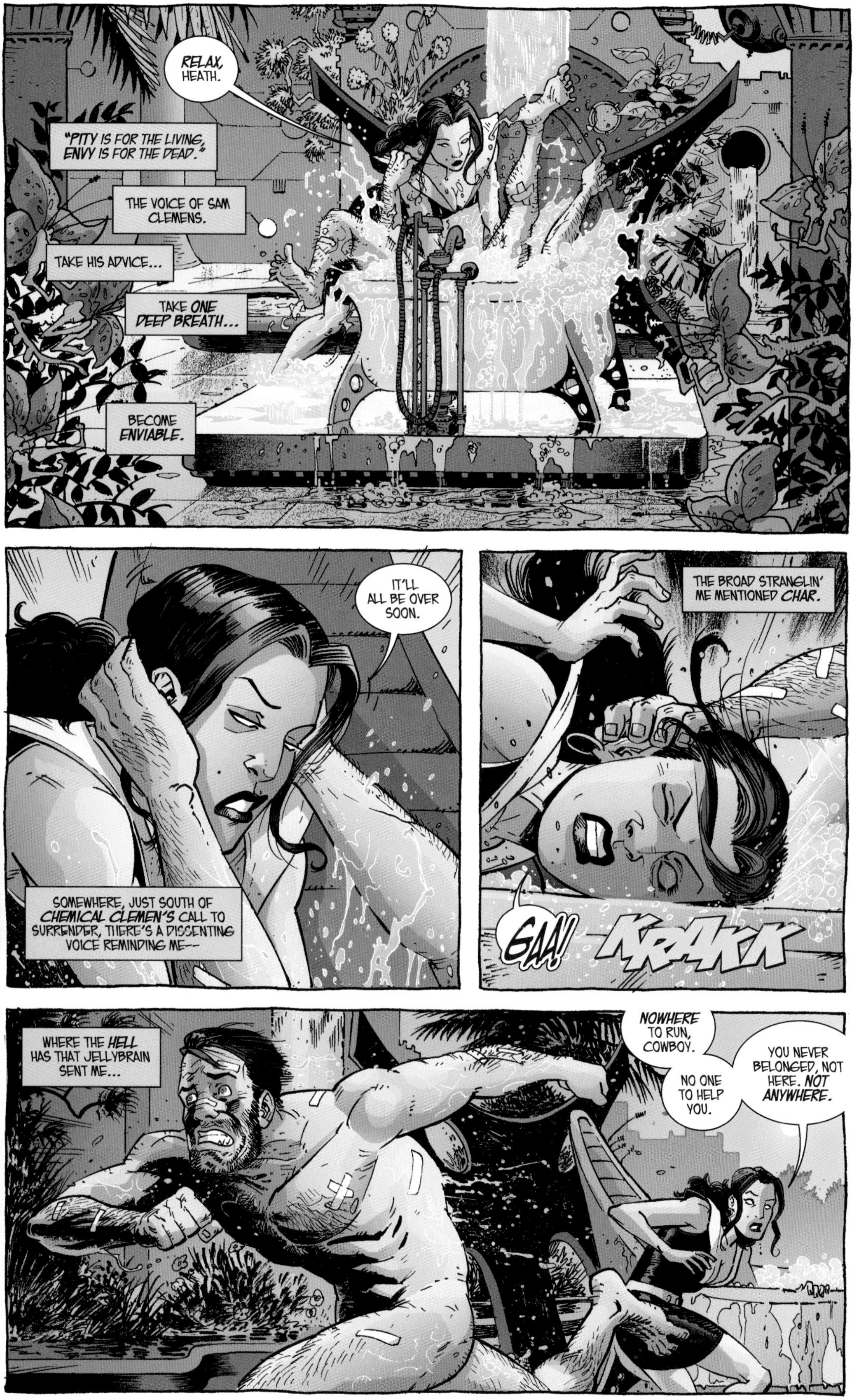
RELAX, HEATH.
"PITY IS FOR THE LIVING, ENVY IS FOR THE DEAD."
THE VOICE OF SAM CLEMENS.
TAKE HIS ADVICE...
TAKE ONE DEEP BREATH...
BECOME ENVIABLE.
IT'LL ALL BE OVER SOON.
SOMEWHERE, JUST SOUTH OF CHEMICAL CLEMEN'S CALL TO SURRENDER, THERE'S A DISSENTING VOICE REMINDING ME--
THE BROAD STRANGLIN' ME MENTIONED CHAR.
GAA!
KRAKK
WHERE THE HELL HAS THAT JELLYBRAIN SENT ME...
NOWHERE TO RUN, COWBOY.
NO ONE TO HELP YOU.
YOU NEVER BELONGED, NOT HERE. NOT ANYWHERE.

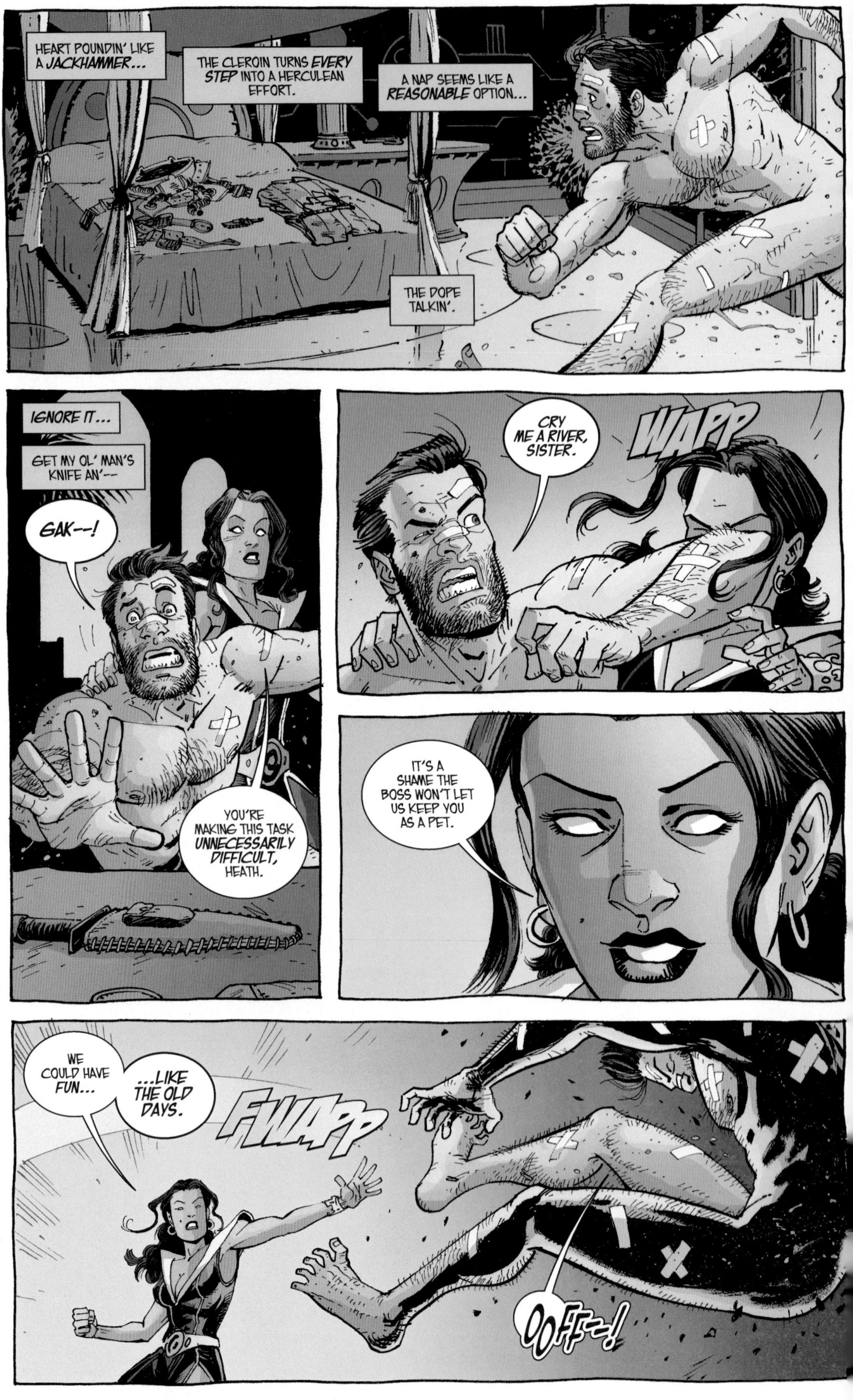
HEART POUNDIN' LIKE A JACKHAMMER...
THE CLEROIN TURNS EVERY STEP INTO A HERCULEAN EFFORT.
A NAP SEEMS LIKE A REASONABLE OPTION...
THE DOPE TALKIN'.
IGNORE IT...
GET MY OL' MAN'S KNIFE AN'--
GAK--!
YOU'RE MAKING THIS TASK UNNECESSARILY DIFFICULT, HEATH.
CRY ME A RIVER, SISTER.
WAPP
IT'S A SHAME THE BOSS WON'T LET US KEEP YOU AS A PET.
WE COULD HAVE FUN...
...LIKE THE OLD DAYS.
FWAPP
OOFF--!

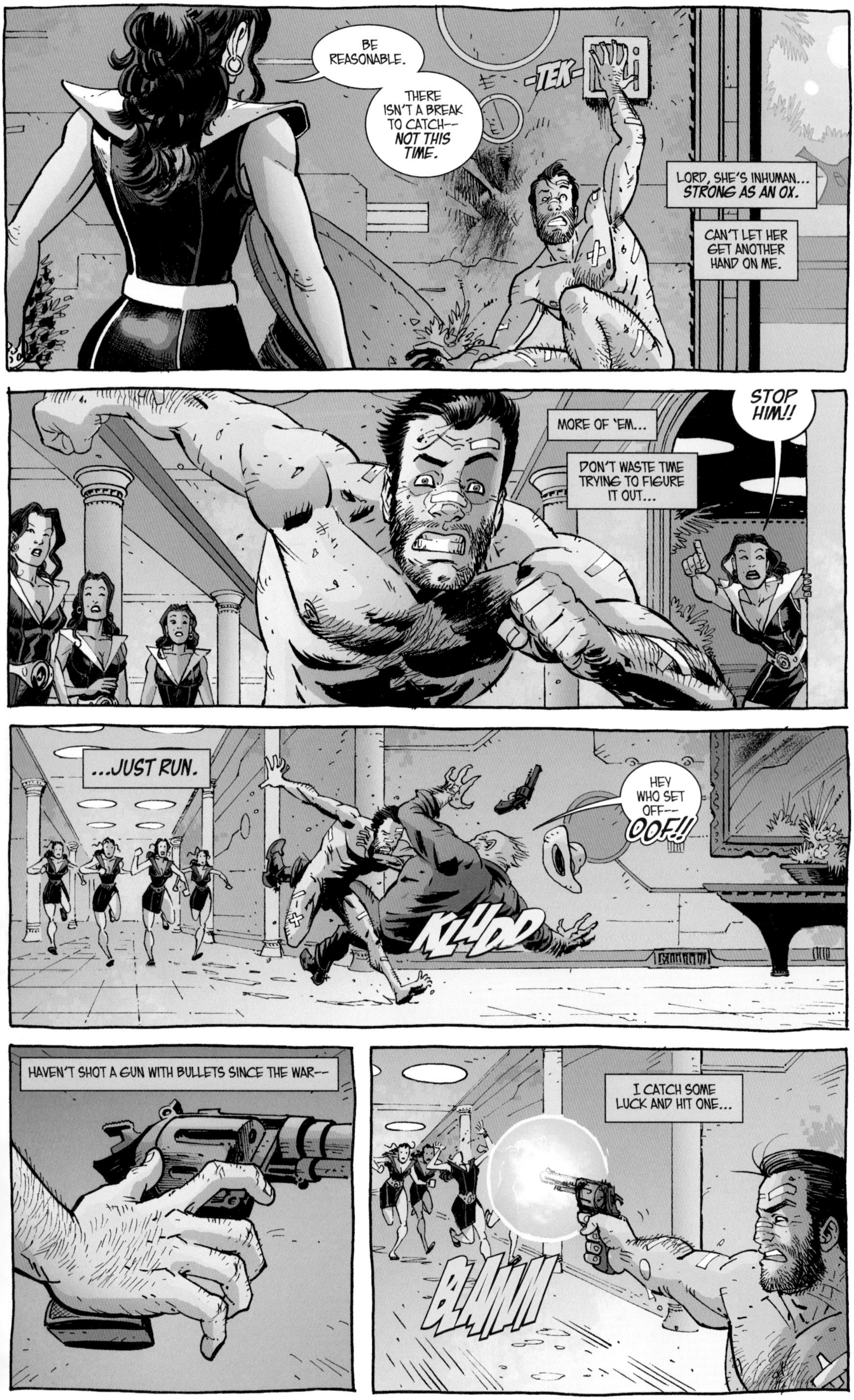
BE REASONABLE.
THERE ISN'T A BREAK TO CATCH-- NOT THIS TIME.
-TEK-
LORD, SHE'S INHUMAN... STRONG AS AN OX.
CAN'T LET HER GET ANOTHER HAND ON ME.
MORE OF 'EM...
DON'T WASTE TIME TRYING TO FIGURE IT OUT...
STOP HIM!!
...JUST RUN.
HEY WHO SET OFF-- OOF!!
KLUDD
HAVEN'T SHOT A GUN WITH BULLETS SINCE THE WAR--
I CATCH SOME LUCK AND HIT ONE...
BLAMM

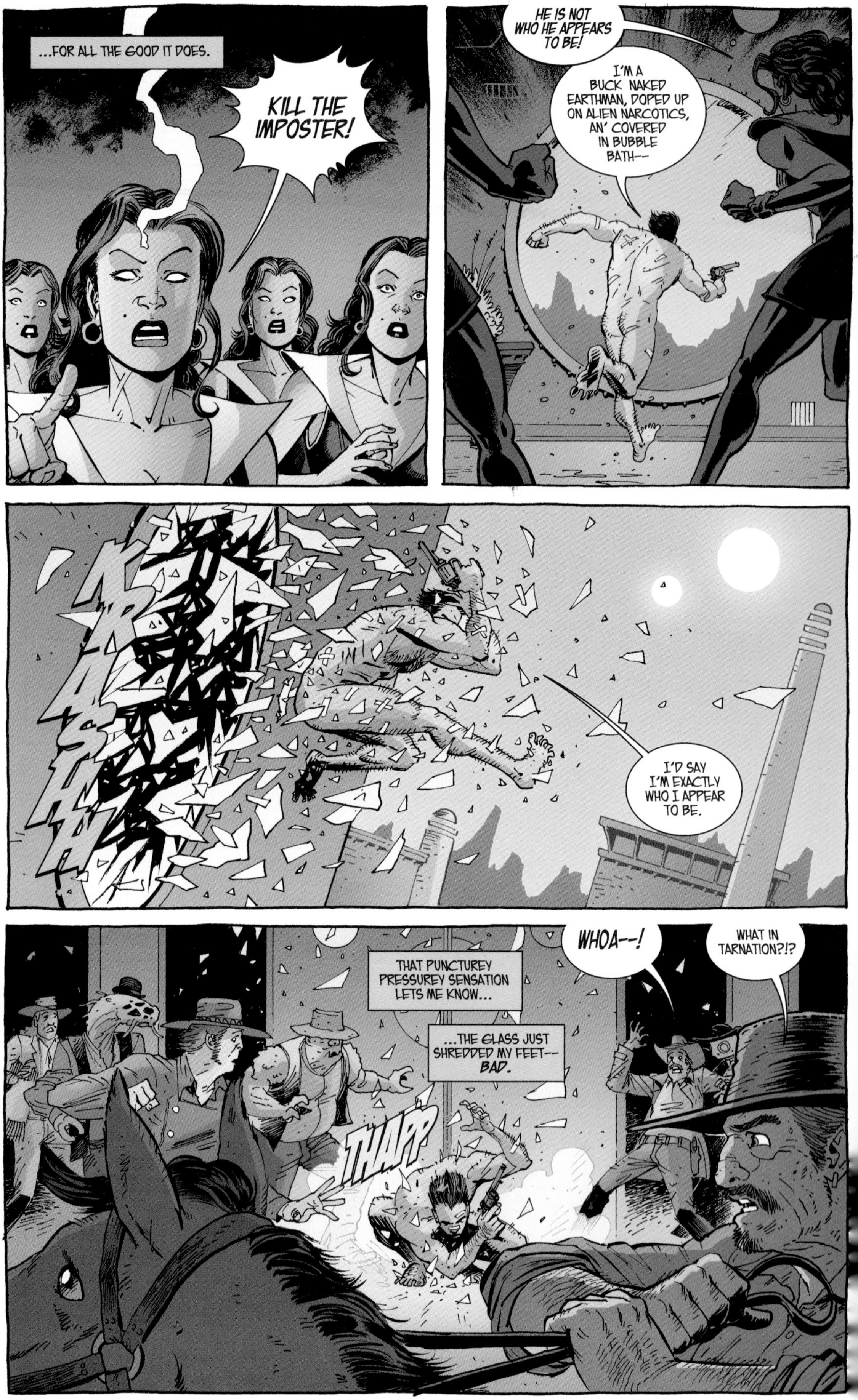

...FOR ALL THE GOOD IT DOES.
KILL THE IMPOSTER!
HE IS NOT WHO HE APPEARS TO BE!
I'M A BUCK NAKED EARTHMAN, DOPED UP ON ALIEN NARCOTICS, AN' COVERED IN BUBBLE BATH--
KRASSHH
I'D SAY I'M EXACTLY WHO I APPEAR TO BE.
THAT PUNCTUREY PRESSUREY SENSATION LETS ME KNOW...
...THE GLASS JUST SHREDDED MY FEET-- BAD.
WHOA--!
WHAT IN TARNATION?!?
THAPP

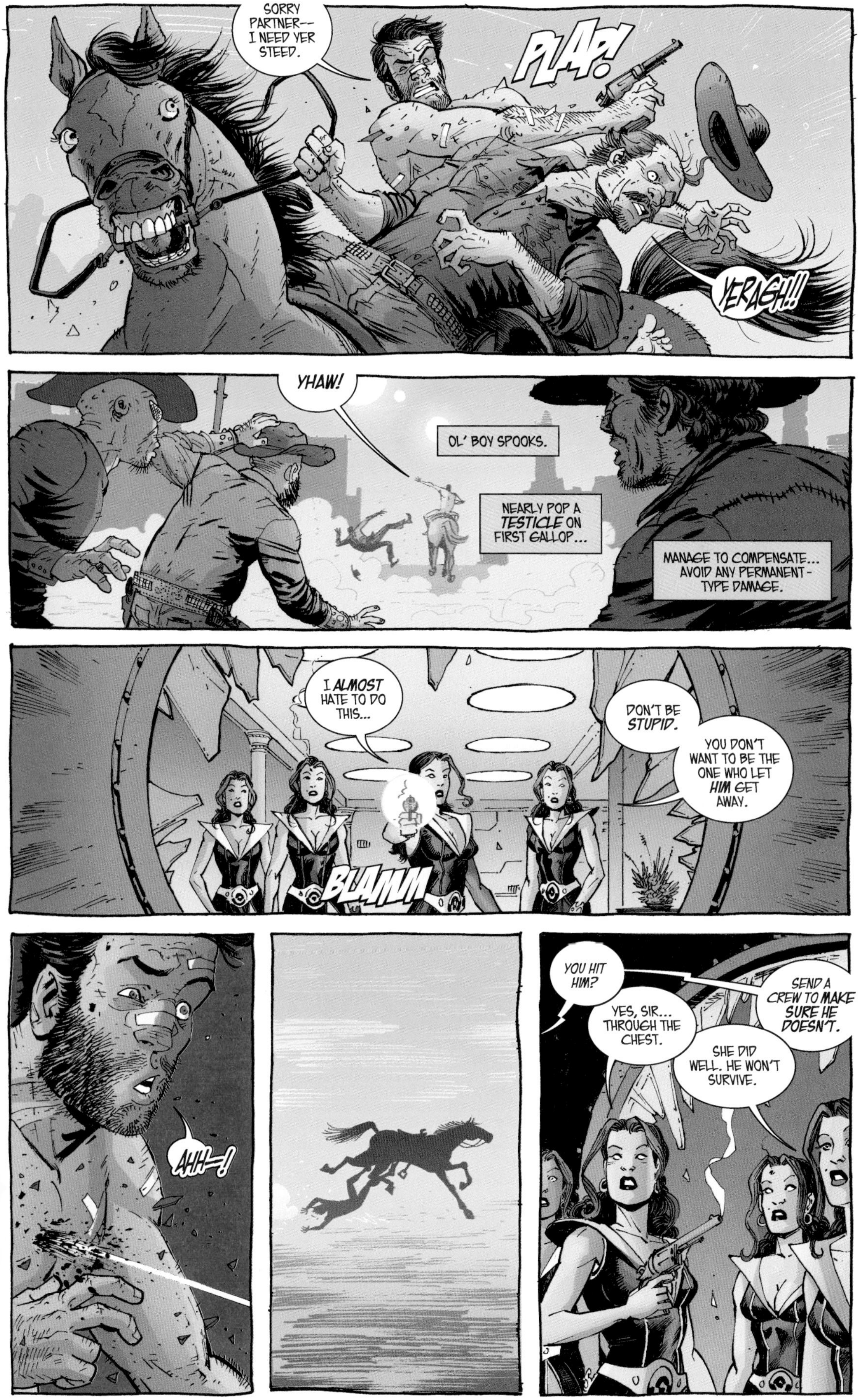
SORRY PARTNER-- I NEED YER STEED.
PLAP!
YERAGH!!
YHAW!
OL' BOY SPOOKS.
NEARLY POP A TESTICLE ON FIRST GALLOP...
MANAGE TO COMPENSATE... AVOID ANY PERMANENT-TYPE DAMAGE.
I ALMOST HATE TO DO THIS...
DON'T BE STUPID.
YOU DON'T WANT TO BE THE ONE WHO LET HIM GET AWAY.
BLAMM
AHH--!
YOU HIT HIM?
YES, SIR... THROUGH THE CHEST.
SEND A CREW TO MAKE SURE HE DOESN'T.
SHE DID WELL. HE WON'T SURVIVE.

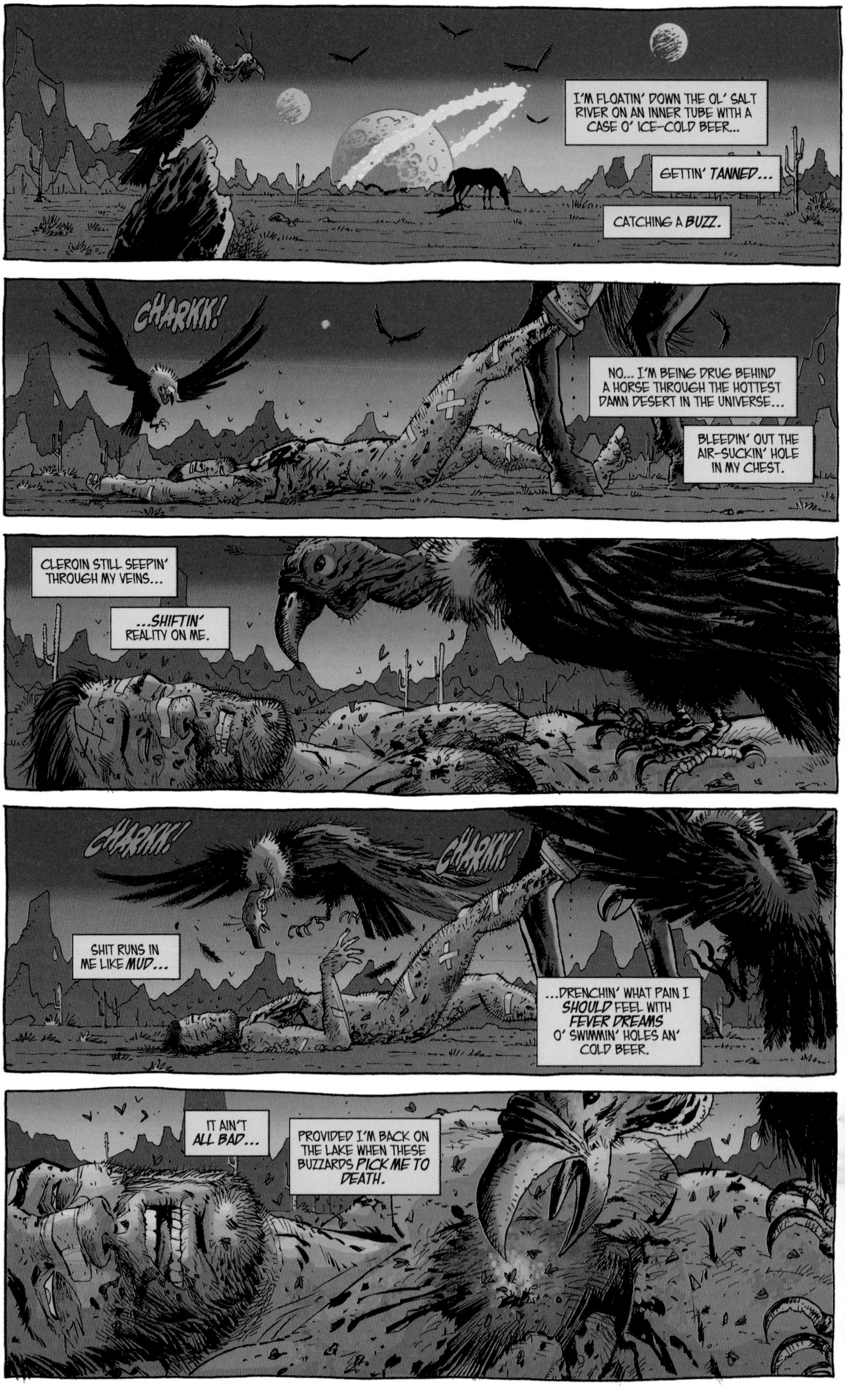
I'M FLOATIN' DOWN THE OL' SALT RIVER ON AN INNER TUBE WITH A CASE O' ICE-COLD BEER...
GETTIN' TANNED...
CATCHING A BUZZ.
CHARKK!
NO... I'M BEING DRUG BEHIND A HORSE THROUGH THE HOTTEST DAMN DESERT IN THE UNIVERSE...
BLEEDIN' OUT THE AIR-SUCKIN' HOLE IN MY CHEST.
CLEROIN STILL SEEPIN' THROUGH MY VEINS...
...SHIFTIN' REALITY ON ME.
CHARKK!
CHARKK!
SHIT RUNS IN ME LIKE MUD...
...DRENCHIN' WHAT PAIN I SHOULD FEEL WITH FEVER DREAMS O' SWIMMIN' HOLES AN' COLD BEER.
IT AIN'T ALL BAD...
PROVIDED I'M BACK ON THE LAKE WHEN THESE BUZZARDS PICK ME TO DEATH.

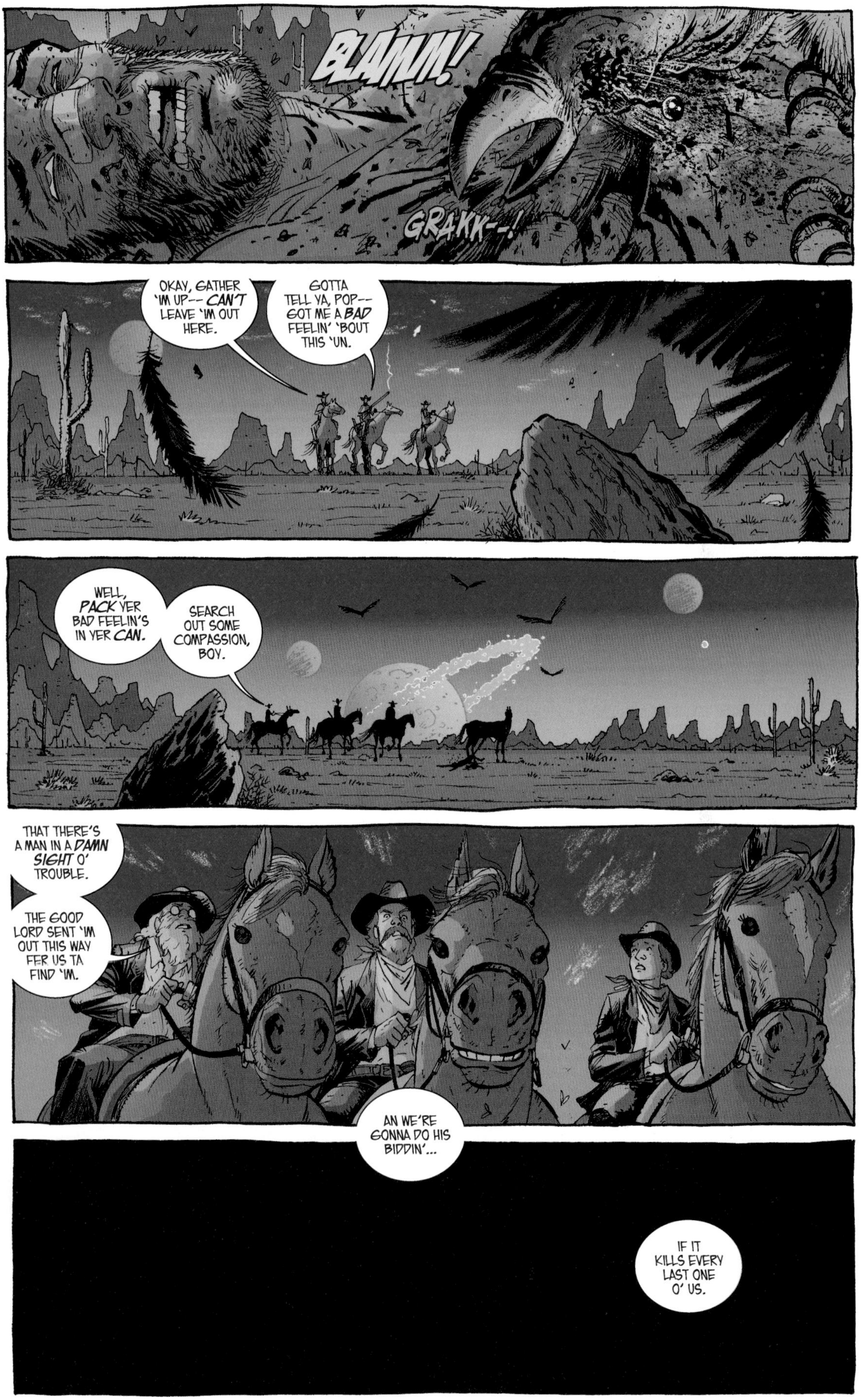
BLAMM!
GRAKK--!
OKAY, GATHER 'IM UP-- CAN'T LEAVE 'IM OUT HERE.
GOTTA TELL YA, POP-- GOT ME A BAD FEELIN' 'BOUT THIS 'UN.
WELL, PACK YER BAD FEELIN'S IN YER CAN.
SEARCH OUT SOME COMPASSION, BOY.
THAT THERE'S A MAN IN A DAMN SIGHT O' TROUBLE.
THE GOOD LORD SENT 'IM OUT THIS WAY FER US TA FIND 'IM.
AN WE'RE GONNA DO HIS BIDDIN'...
IF IT KILLS EVERY LAST ONE O' US.

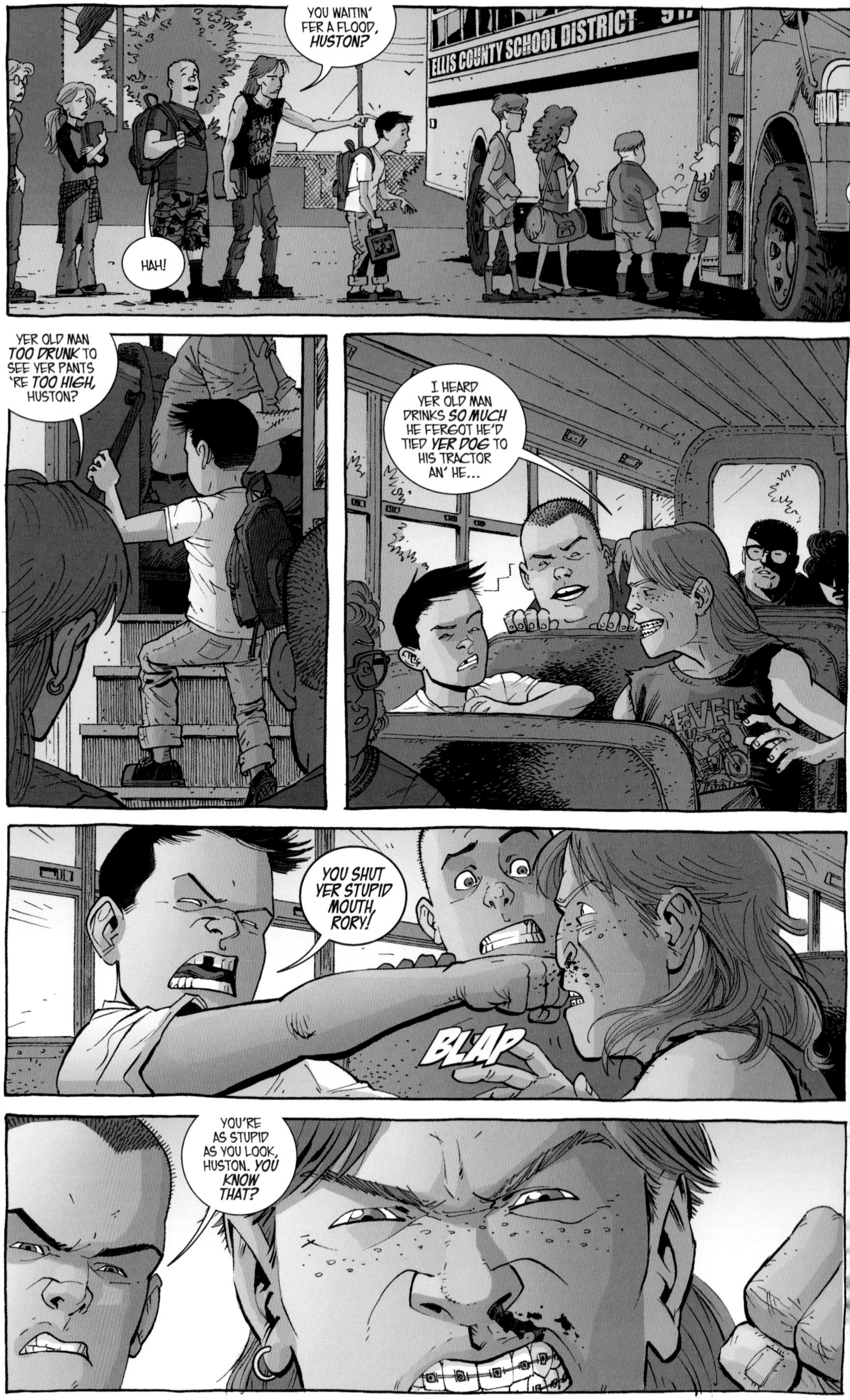
ELLIS COUNTY SCHOOL DISTRICT
YOU WAITIN' FER A FLOOD, HUSTON?
HAH!
YER OLD MAN TOO DRUNK TO SEE YER PANTS 'RE TOO HIGH, HUSTON?
I HEARD YER OLD MAN DRINKS SO MUCH HE FERGOT HE'D TIED YER DOG TO HIS TRACTOR AN' HE...
YOU SHUT YER STUPID MOUTH, RORY!
BLAP
YOU'RE AS STUPID AS YOU LOOK, HUSTON. YOU KNOW THAT?

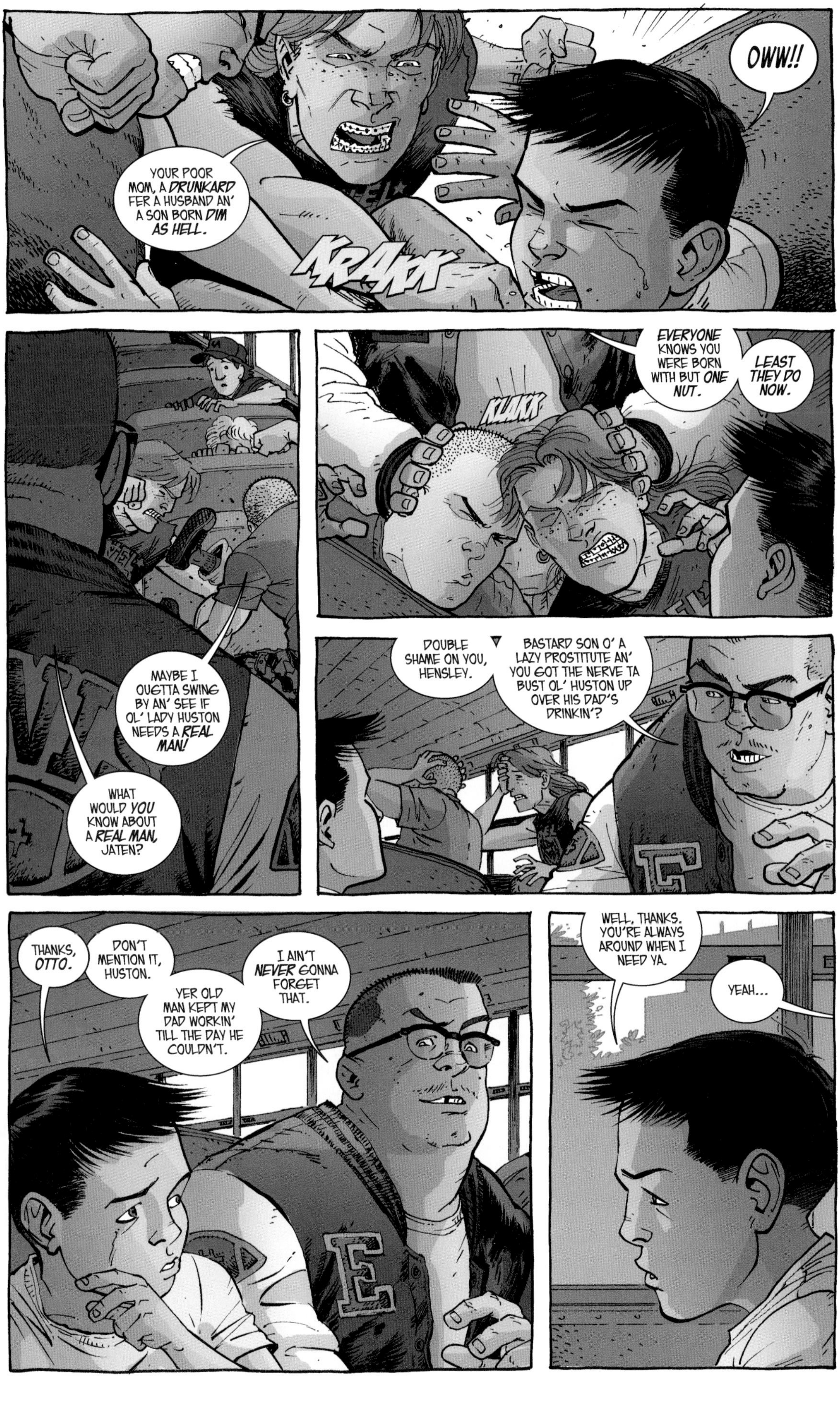
OWW!!
YOUR POOR MOM, A DRUNKARD FER A HUSBAND AN' A SON BORN DIM AS HELL.
KRAKK
MAYBE I OUGTTA SWING BY AN' SEE IF OL' LADY HUSTON NEEDS A REAL MAN!
WHAT WOULD YOU KNOW ABOUT A REAL MAN, JATEN?
EVERYONE KNOWS YOU WERE BORN WITH BUT ONE NUT.
LEAST THEY DO NOW.
KLAKK
DOUBLE SHAME ON YOU, HENSLEY.
BASTARD SON O' A LAZY PROSTITUTE AN' YOU GOT THE NERVE TA BUST OL' HUSTON UP OVER HIS DAD'S DRINKIN'?
THANKS, OTTO.
DON'T MENTION IT, HUSTON.
YER OLD MAN KEPT MY DAD WORKIN' TILL THE DAY HE COULDN'T.
I AIN'T NEVER GONNA FORGET THAT.
WELL, THANKS. YOU'RE ALWAYS AROUND WHEN I NEED YA.
YEAH...

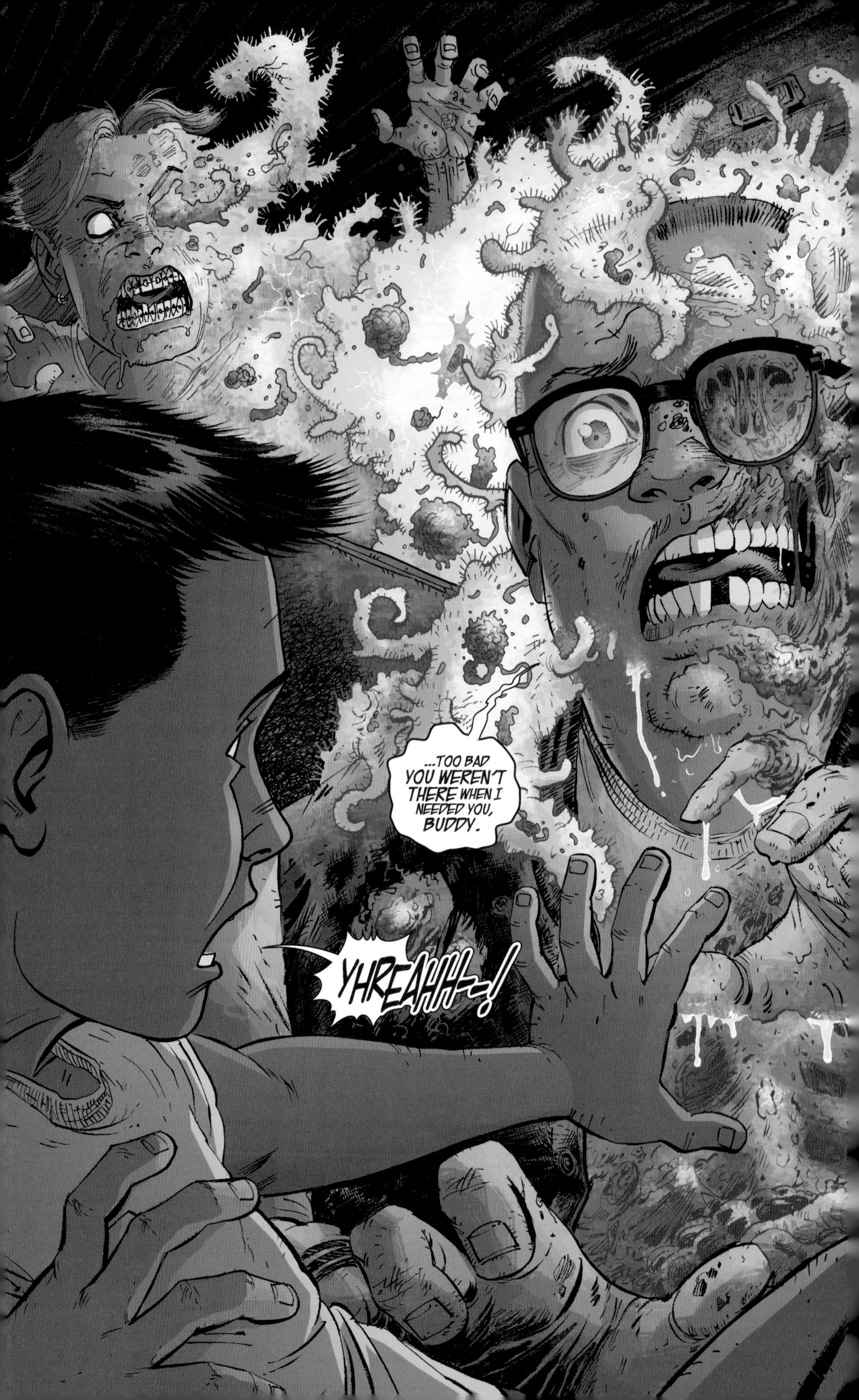
...TOO BAD YOU WEREN'T THERE WHEN I NEEDED YOU, BUDDY.
YHREAHHH--!

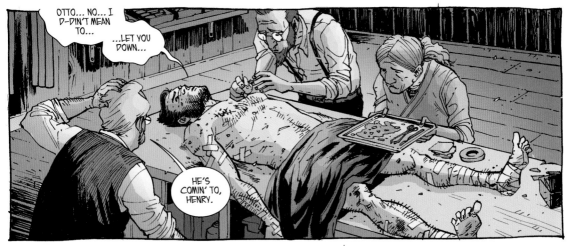

OTTO... NO... I D–DIN'T MEAN TO... ...LET YOU DOWN...

HE'S COMIN' TO, HENRY.

OKAY NOW... EASY DOWN, SON.

CHAR, HE'S BURNIN' UP. YOU GOT THAT TOWEL?

W–WHERE... WHERE THE HELL AM I––?!

YOU'RE IN HEAVEN.

IN MERVIN JOHNSON'S GENERAL STORE TO BE MORE SPECIFIC.

THANK YOU, CHARLOTTE.

CH– CHARLOTTE?

W–WE'RE I–IN HEAVEN?

W–WHAT THE HELL'S GOIN' ON?

HEAVEN, SIR––THE NICEST TOWN IN ALL OF WESTX.

AND I'M NOT SURE WHO YOU THINK I AM, BUT IT'S JUST A DELUSION FROM THE DRUGS.

BOY SEEMS TO KNOW YA, CHAR.

YOU AIN'T NEVER SEEN 'IM BEFORE?

HEAVEN NO, SIR.

I NEVER WOULD CONSORT WITH A DRUG-ADDICTED, REPROBATE GUN-SLINGER ON ANY ACCOUNT.

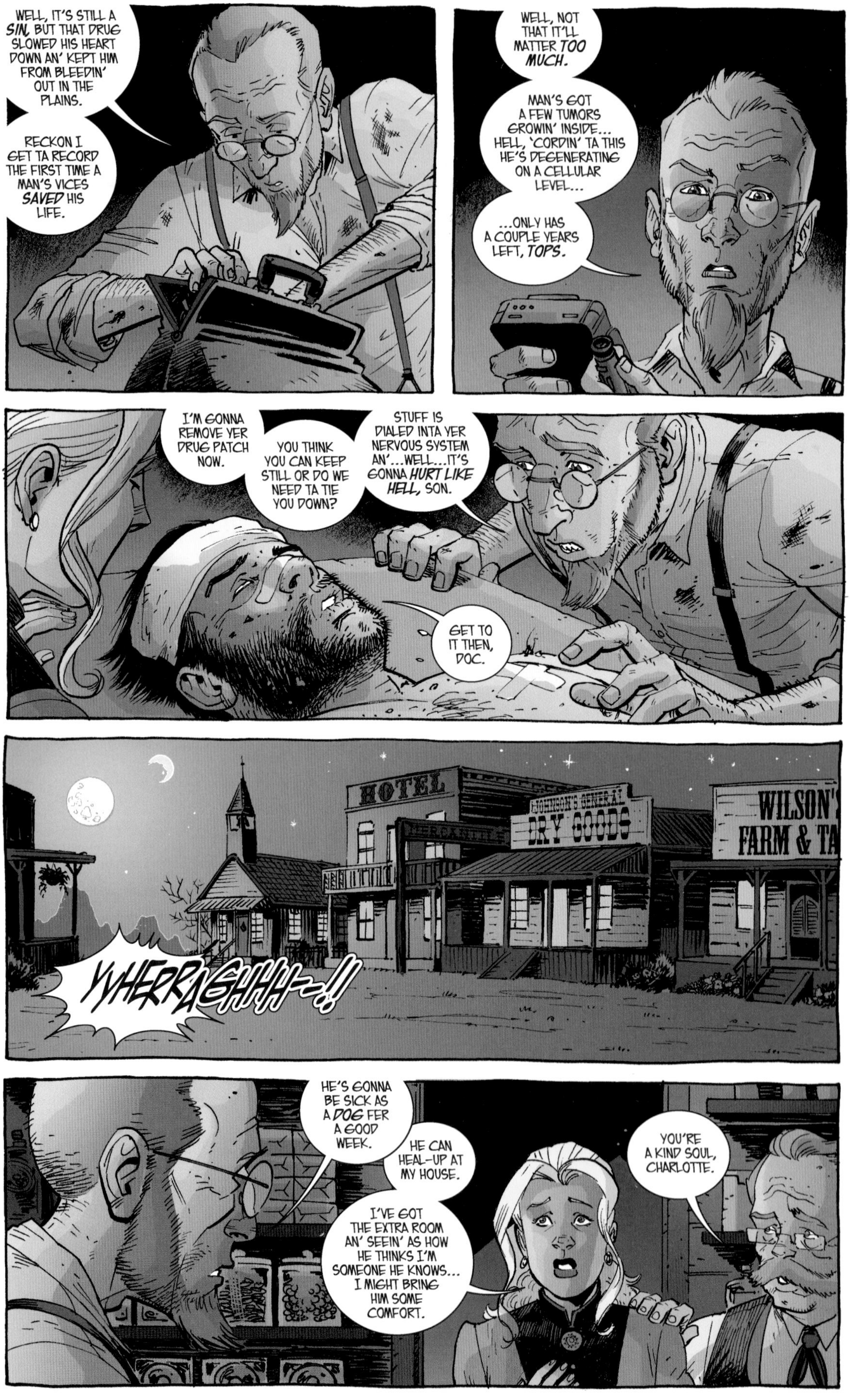

WELL, IT'S STILL A SIN, BUT THAT DRUG SLOWED HIS HEART DOWN AN' KEPT HIM FROM BLEEDIN' OUT IN THE PLAINS.
RECKON I GET TA RECORD THE FIRST TIME A MAN'S VICES SAVED HIS LIFE.
WELL, NOT THAT IT'LL MATTER TOO MUCH.
MAN'S GOT A FEW TUMORS GROWIN' INSIDE... HELL, 'CORDIN' TA THIS HE'S DEGENERATING ON A CELLULAR LEVEL...
...ONLY HAS A COUPLE YEARS LEFT, TOPS.
I'M GONNA REMOVE YER DRUG PATCH NOW.
YOU THINK YOU CAN KEEP STILL OR DO WE NEED TA TIE YOU DOWN?
STUFF IS DIALED INTA YER NERVOUS SYSTEM AN'...WELL...IT'S GONNA HURT LIKE HELL, SON.
GET TO IT THEN, DOC.
HOTEL
JOHNSON'S GENERAL
DRY GOODS
MERCANTILE
WILSON'S
FARM & TA
YYHERRAGHHH--!!
HE'S GONNA BE SICK AS A DOG FER A GOOD WEEK.
HE CAN HEAL-UP AT MY HOUSE.
I'VE GOT THE EXTRA ROOM AN' SEEIN' AS HOW HE THINKS I'M SOMEONE HE KNOWS... I MIGHT BRING HIM SOME COMFORT.
YOU'RE A KIND SOUL, CHARLOTTE.

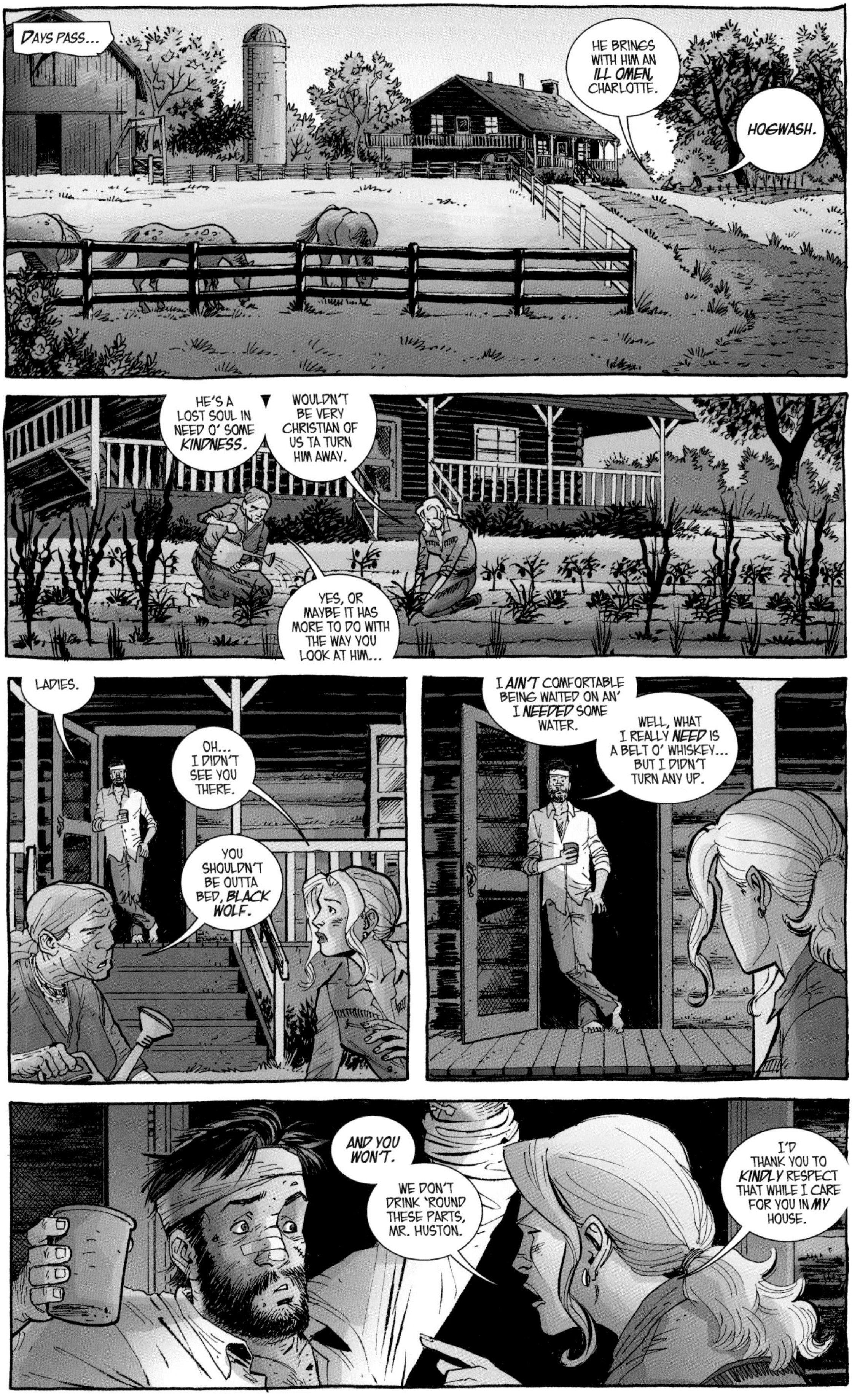
DAYS PASS...
HE BRINGS WITH HIM AN ILL OMEN, CHARLOTTE.
HOGWASH.
HE'S A LOST SOUL IN NEED O' SOME KINDNESS.
WOULDN'T BE VERY CHRISTIAN OF US TA TURN HIM AWAY.
YES, OR MAYBE IT HAS MORE TO DO WITH THE WAY YOU LOOK AT HIM...
LADIES.
OH... I DIDN'T SEE YOU THERE.
YOU SHOULDN'T BE OUTTA BED, BLACK WOLF.
I AIN'T COMFORTABLE BEING WAITED ON AN' I NEEDED SOME WATER.
WELL, WHAT I REALLY NEED IS A BELT O' WHISKEY... BUT I DIDN'T TURN ANY UP.
AND YOU WON'T.
WE DON'T DRINK 'ROUND THESE PARTS, MR. HUSTON.
I'D THANK YOU TO KINDLY RESPECT THAT WHILE I CARE FOR YOU IN MY HOUSE.

I NEED TO GO TO TOWN BEFORE IT GETS DARK. YOU NEED ANYTHING?

I AIN'T PICKY. I'D EVEN SETTLE FER SOME *GIN.*

I TAKE THAT AS A *NO.*

ALL RIGHT THEN-- IT'S JUST THE TWO OF US NOW, CHAR.

CUT THE CRAP AN' TELL ME *WHAT THE HELL IS GOIN'* ON HERE.

LIKE I TOLD YOU, YOU'VE GOT ME MIXED UP WITH SOMEONE ELSE.

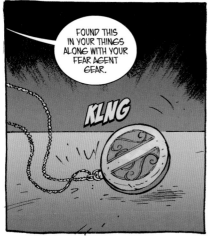

FOUND THIS IN YOUR THINGS ALONG WITH YOUR *FEAR AGENT* GEAR.

KLNG

YEAH, OKAY, OBVIOUSLY IT'S ME, HEATHROW.

SO YOU KNOW NOW-- *BUT THEY CAN'T.*

I DON'T KNOW EXACTLY WHAT IS GOING ON, BUT SOMETHING IN THOSE HILLS HAS THESE FOLKS *SPOOKED* AN' I DON'T WANNA BE RODE OUT ON'A RAIL.

HOW THE HELL'D YOU END UP HERE? *WHERE ARE WE?*

TWO YEARS AGO, RIGHT AFTER YOU LEFT--*AFTER OUR FIGHT*-- I FOUND A SMALL BOX.

HAD A NOTE THAT SAID IT WAS FROM YOU. SAID TO PRESS THE BUTTON FOR A RECORDIN'.

SO I PRESSED IT AN' NEXT THING I KNEW I WAS HERE, IN THIS TOWN.

TWO YEARS?

AFTER I LEFT YOU I WENT BACK TO NEAVSIVIA, PICKED UP NICHOLAS...

COULDN'T O' BEEN THREE DAYS BACK...

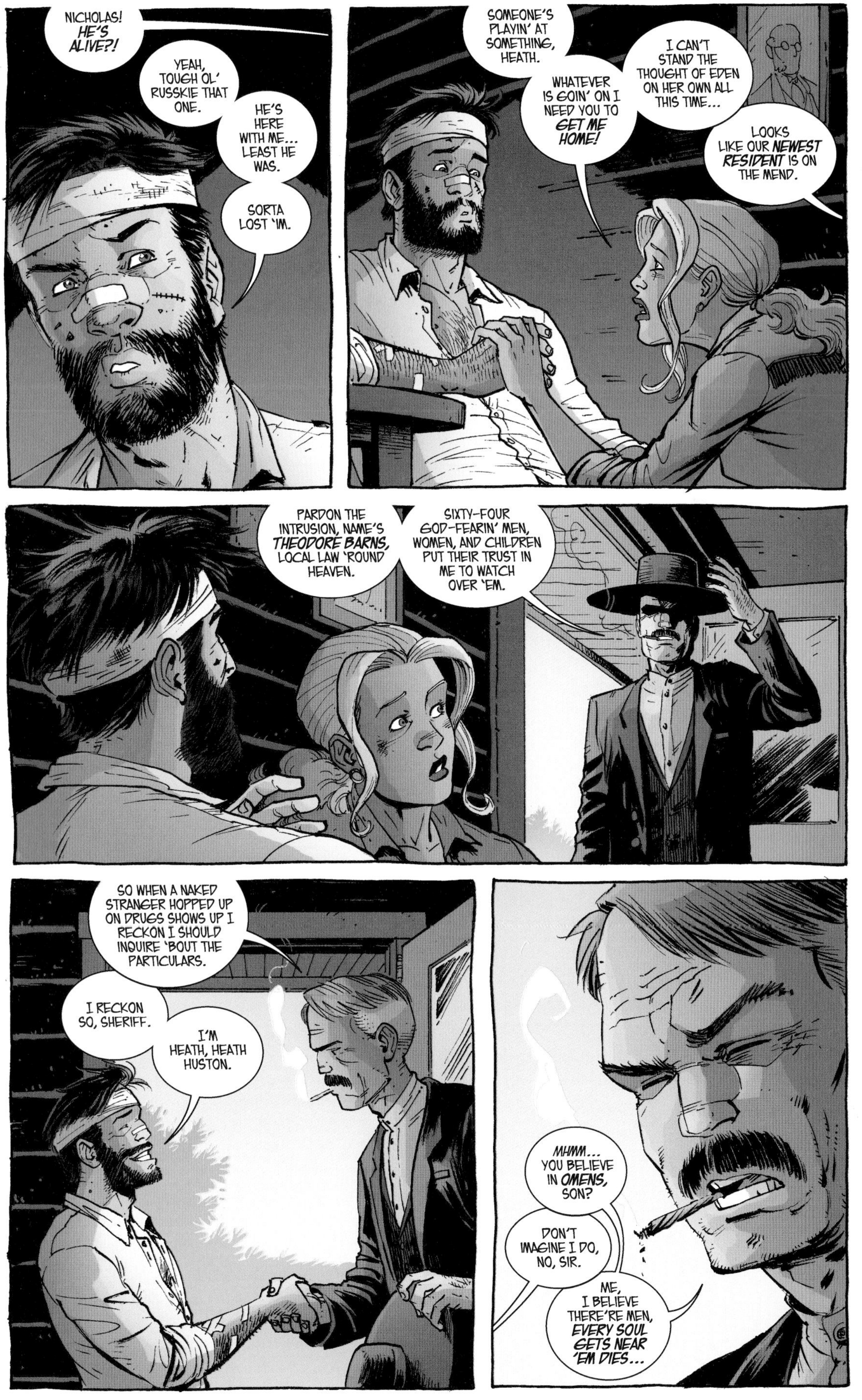
NICHOLAS! HE'S ALIVE?!
YEAH, TOUGH OL' RUSSKIE THAT ONE.
HE'S HERE WITH ME... LEAST HE WAS.
SORTA LOST 'IM.
SOMEONE'S PLAYIN' AT SOMETHING, HEATH.
WHATEVER IS GOIN' ON I NEED YOU TO GET ME HOME!
I CAN'T STAND THE THOUGHT OF EDEN ON HER OWN ALL THIS TIME...
LOOKS LIKE OUR NEWEST RESIDENT IS ON THE MEND.
PARDON THE INTRUSION, NAME'S THEODORE BARNS, LOCAL LAW 'ROUND HEAVEN.
SIXTY-FOUR GOD-FEARIN' MEN, WOMEN, AND CHILDREN PUT THEIR TRUST IN ME TO WATCH OVER 'EM.
SO WHEN A NAKED STRANGER HOPPED UP ON DRUGS SHOWS UP I RECKON I SHOULD INQUIRE 'BOUT THE PARTICULARS.
I RECKON SO, SHERIFF.
I'M HEATH, HEATH HUSTON.
MHMM... YOU BELIEVE IN OMENS, SON?
DON'T IMAGINE I DO, NO, SIR.
ME, I BELIEVE THERE'RE MEN, EVERY SOUL GETS NEAR 'EM DIES...

YOU GOT THAT LOOK ABOUT YOU, SON.

THE LOOK OF A CURSED MAN.

HELL OF A THING TA TELL A BODY AFTER FIRST HOWDY, SHERIFF.

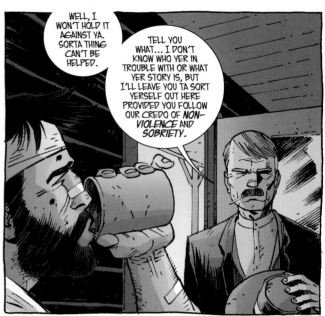

WELL, I WON'T HOLD IT AGAINST YA. SORTA THING CAN'T BE HELPED.

TELL YOU WHAT... I DON'T KNOW WHO YER IN TROUBLE WITH OR WHAT YER STORY IS, BUT I'LL LEAVE YOU TA SORT YERSELF OUT HERE PROVIDED YOU FOLLOW OUR CREDO OF *NON-VIOLENCE* AND *SOBRIETY.*

I'LL BE BY WHEN YOU'RE FEELIN' BETTER TA HEAR YER STORY.

CHURCH SERVICE IS ON SUNDAY. I'D LIKE TO SEE YOU THERE AS WELL...

IN A *CLEAN SUIT* IF YOU DON'T MIND, MA'AM.

WE'LL BE THERE, THEODORE.

APPRECIATE THE *HOSPITALITY,* SHERIFF.

ESPECIALLY SEEING HOW I'M *CURSED* AN' ALL...

DON'T MENTION IT. THAT'S HOW WE DO HERE.

JUST DON'T MAKE ME LIVE TA REGRET IT.

BY THE WAY...

...WELCOME TA HEAVEN, HEATH HUSTON.

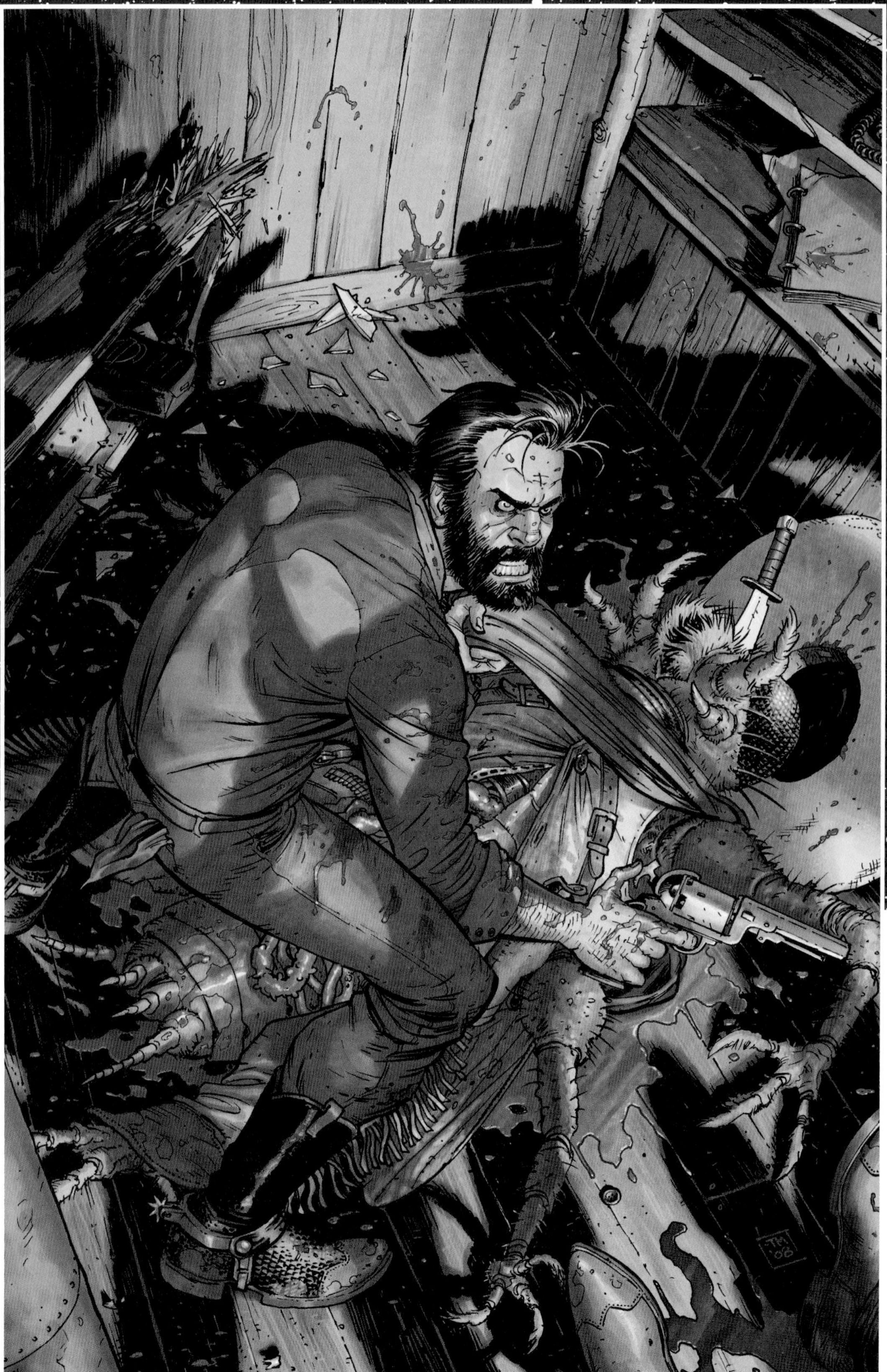

FEAR AGENT #24
ART BY **TONY MOORE**

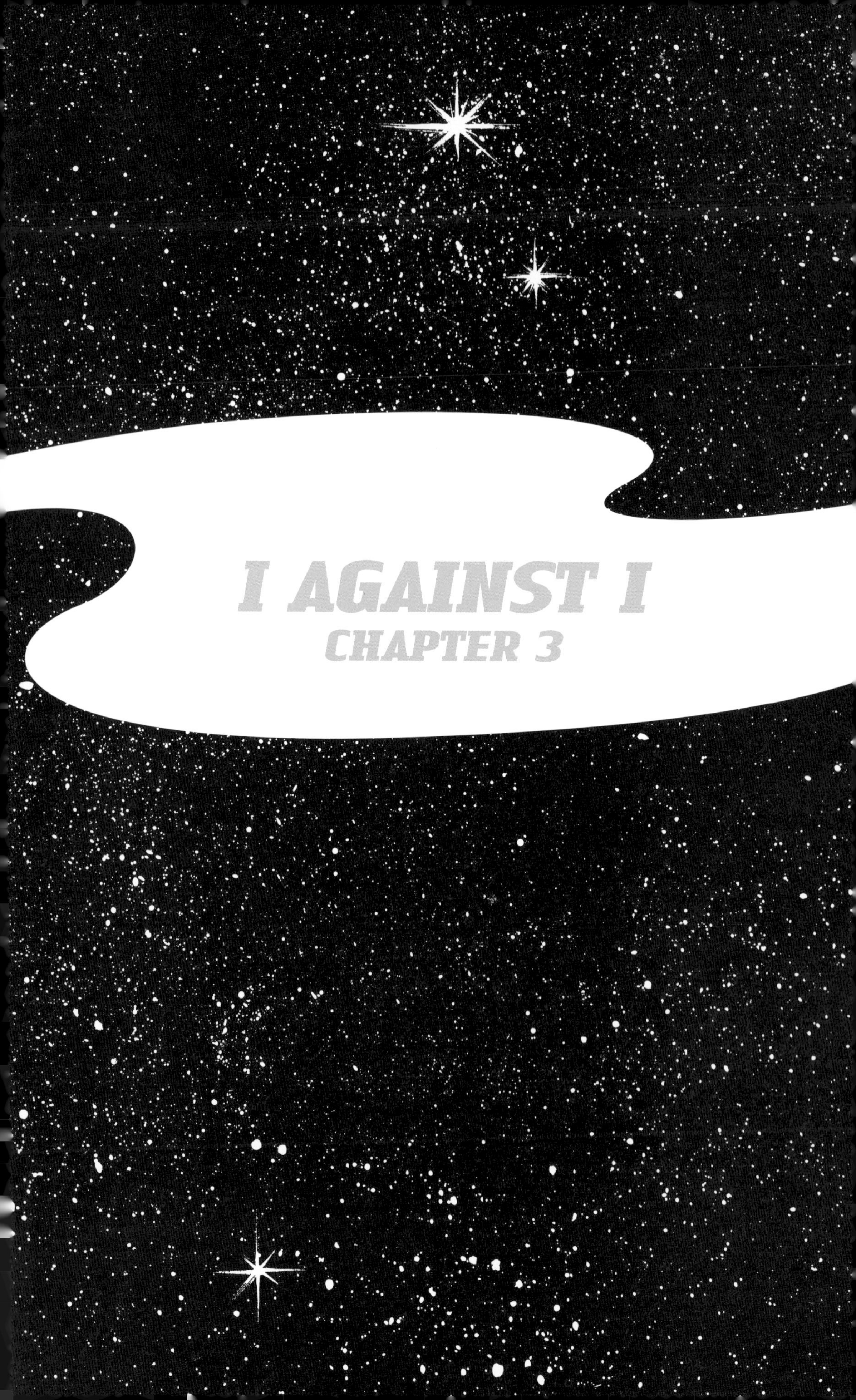
I AGAINST I
CHAPTER 3

LOT O' STUPID FOLKS IN THIS WORLD, SON.

LOT O' UGLY MINDED IDIOTS MIRED IN BLOODLUST.

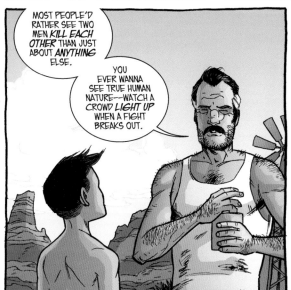

MOST PEOPLE'D RATHER SEE TWO MEN *KILL EACH OTHER* THAN JUST ABOUT *ANYTHING* ELSE.

YOU EVER WANNA SEE TRUE HUMAN NATURE--WATCH A CROWD *LIGHT UP* WHEN A FIGHT BREAKS OUT.

IF YA *NEVER* REMEMBER *ANOTHER* THING YER OLD MAN TAUGHT YA-- *REMEMBER THIS...*

PEOPLE *DON'T WANT* TO SEE OTHER PEOPLE *HAPPY.*

HELL, MOST FOLKS WON'T EVEN LET JOY INTO THEIR *OWN LIVES* MUCH LESS SOMEONE ELSE'S.

DON'T YA *EVER* COUNT ON SOMEONE PUTTIN' YOUR INTERESTS BEFORE THEIR *OWN...*

NOT YER OLD MAN.

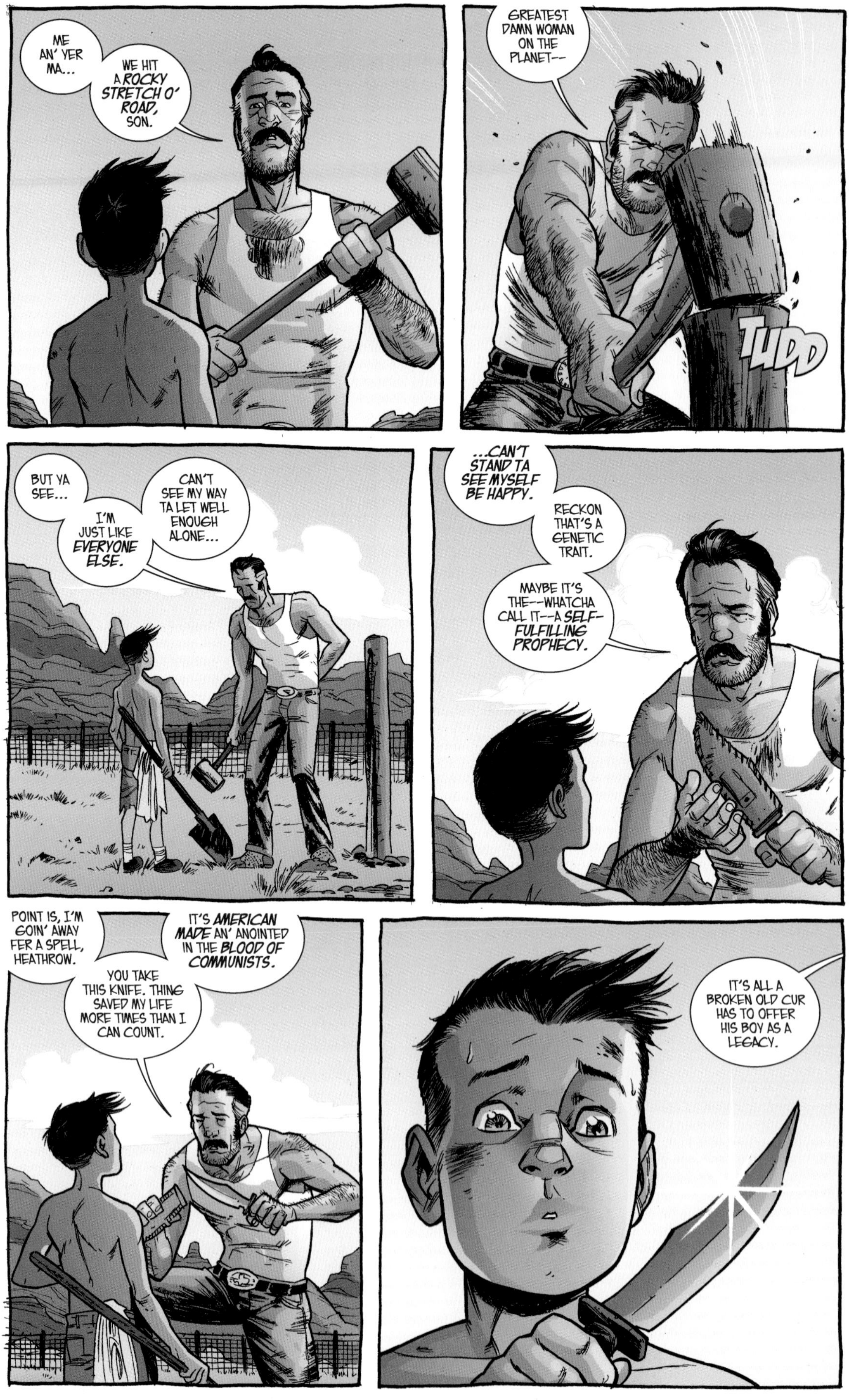

ME AN' YER MA...
WE HIT A ROCKY STRETCH O' ROAD, SON.
GREATEST DAMN WOMAN ON THE PLANET--
TUDD
BUT YA SEE...
I'M JUST LIKE EVERYONE ELSE.
CAN'T SEE MY WAY TA LET WELL ENOUGH ALONE...
...CAN'T STAND TA SEE MYSELF BE HAPPY.
RECKON THAT'S A GENETIC TRAIT.
MAYBE IT'S THE--WHATCHA CALL IT--A SELF-FULFILLING PROPHECY.
POINT IS, I'M GOIN' AWAY FER A SPELL, HEATHROW.
YOU TAKE THIS KNIFE. THING SAVED MY LIFE MORE TIMES THAN I CAN COUNT.
IT'S AMERICAN MADE AN' ANOINTED IN THE BLOOD OF COMMUNISTS.
IT'S ALL A BROKEN OLD CUR HAS TO OFFER HIS BOY AS A LEGACY.

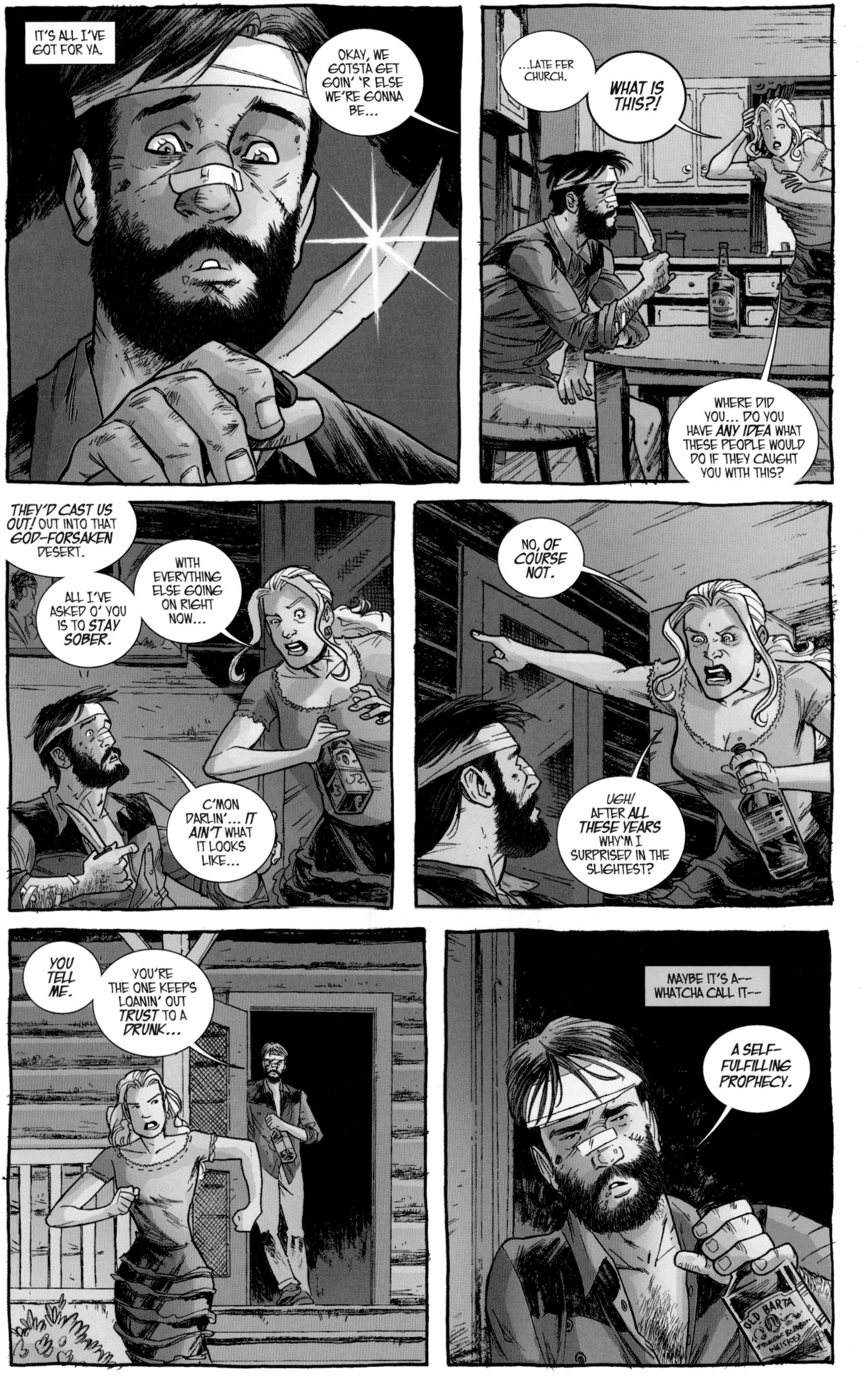
IT'S ALL I'VE GOT FOR YA.
OKAY, WE GOTSTA GET GOIN' 'R ELSE WE'RE GONNA BE...
...LATE FER CHURCH.
WHAT IS THIS?!
WHERE DID YOU... DO YOU HAVE ANY IDEA WHAT THESE PEOPLE WOULD DO IF THEY CAUGHT YOU WITH THIS?
THEY'D CAST US OUT! OUT INTO THAT GOD-FORSAKEN DESERT.
WITH EVERYTHING ELSE GOING ON RIGHT NOW...
ALL I'VE ASKED O' YOU IS TO STAY SOBER.
C'MON DARLIN'... IT AIN'T WHAT IT LOOKS LIKE...
NO, OF COURSE NOT.
UGH! AFTER ALL THESE YEARS WHY'M I SURPRISED IN THE SLIGHTEST?
YOU TELL ME.
YOU'RE THE ONE KEEPS LOANIN' OUT TRUST TO A DRUNK...
MAYBE IT'S A-- WHATCHA CALL IT--
A SELF-FULFILLING PROPHECY.

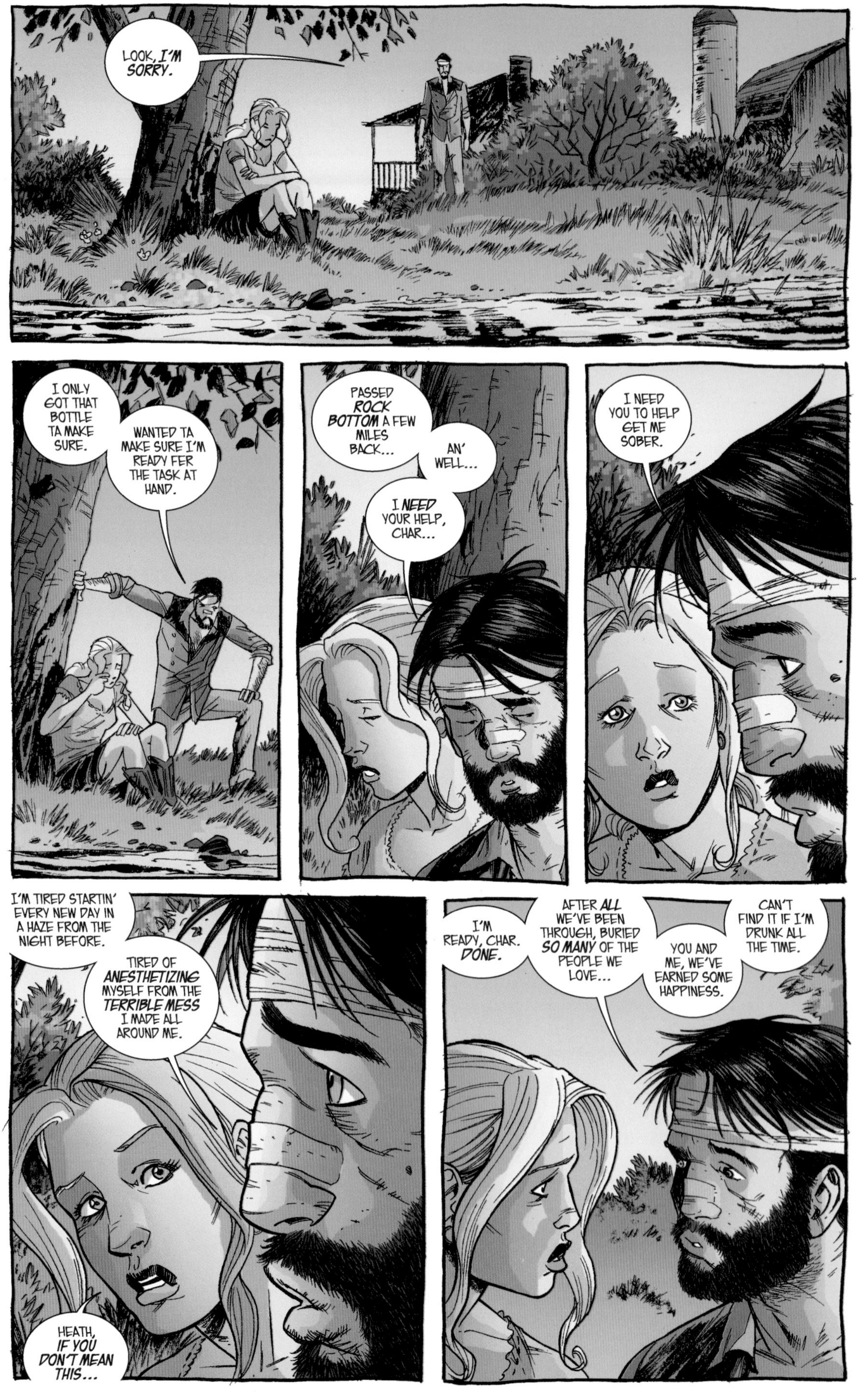
LOOK, I'M SORRY.
I ONLY GOT THAT BOTTLE TA MAKE SURE.
WANTED TA MAKE SURE I'M READY FER THE TASK AT HAND.
PASSED ROCK BOTTOM A FEW MILES BACK...
AN' WELL...
I NEED YOUR HELP, CHAR...
I NEED YOU TO HELP GET ME SOBER.
I'M TIRED STARTIN' EVERY NEW DAY IN A HAZE FROM THE NIGHT BEFORE.
TIRED OF ANESTHETIZING MYSELF FROM THE TERRIBLE MESS I MADE ALL AROUND ME.
HEATH, IF YOU DON'T MEAN THIS...
I'M READY, CHAR. DONE.
AFTER ALL WE'VE BEEN THROUGH, BURIED SO MANY OF THE PEOPLE WE LOVE...
YOU AND ME, WE'VE EARNED SOME HAPPINESS.
CAN'T FIND IT IF I'M DRUNK ALL THE TIME.

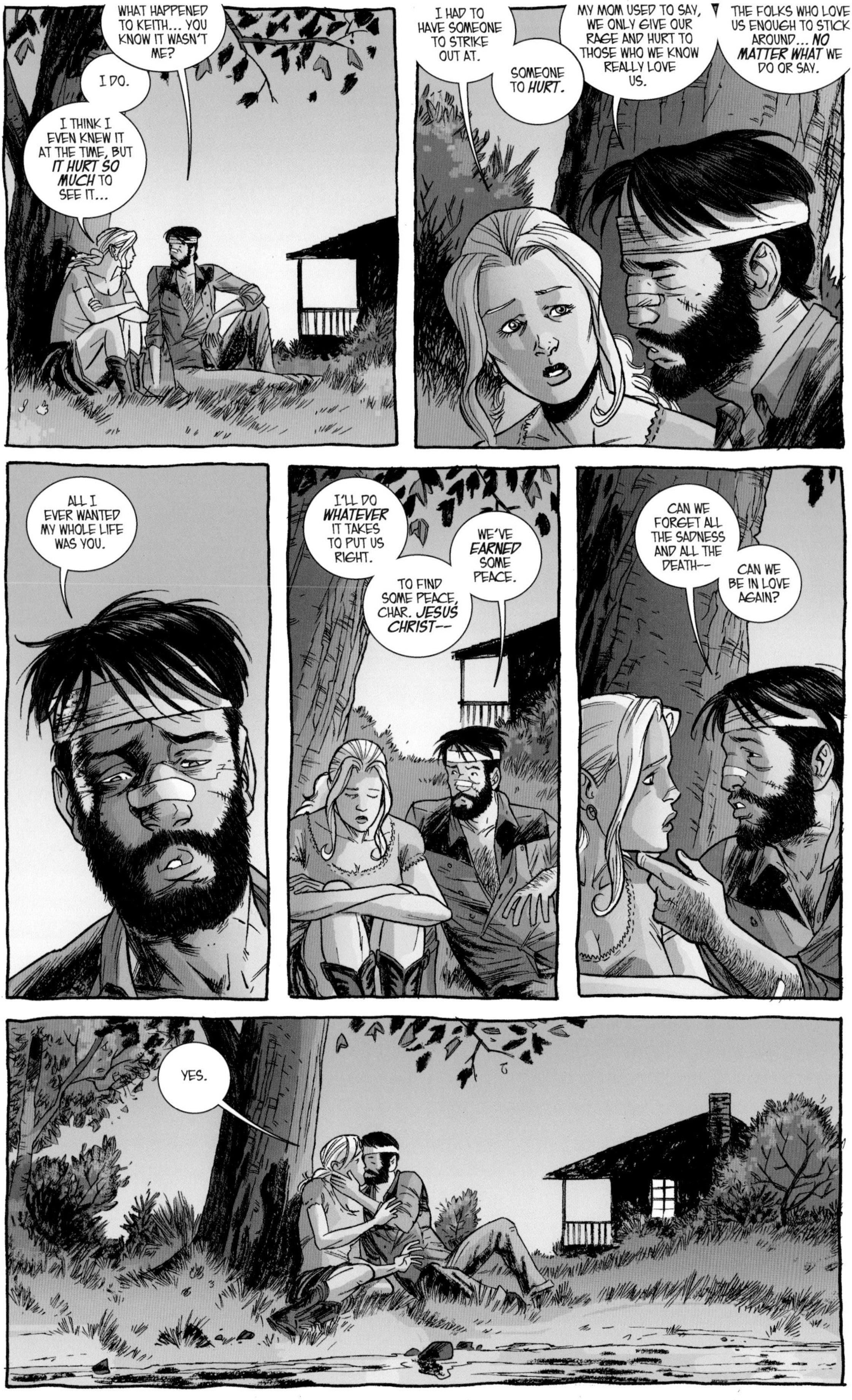
WHAT HAPPENED TO KEITH... YOU KNOW IT WASN'T ME?
I DO.
I THINK I EVEN KNEW IT AT THE TIME, BUT IT HURT SO MUCH TO SEE IT...
I HAD TO HAVE SOMEONE TO STRIKE OUT AT.
SOMEONE TO HURT.
MY MOM USED TO SAY, WE ONLY GIVE OUR RAGE AND HURT TO THOSE WHO WE KNOW REALLY LOVE US.
THE FOLKS WHO LOVE US ENOUGH TO STICK AROUND... NO MATTER WHAT WE DO OR SAY.
ALL I EVER WANTED MY WHOLE LIFE WAS YOU.
I'LL DO WHATEVER IT TAKES TO PUT US RIGHT.
TO FIND SOME PEACE, CHAR. JESUS CHRIST--
WE'VE EARNED SOME PEACE.
CAN WE FORGET ALL THE SADNESS AND ALL THE DEATH--
CAN WE BE IN LOVE AGAIN?
YES.

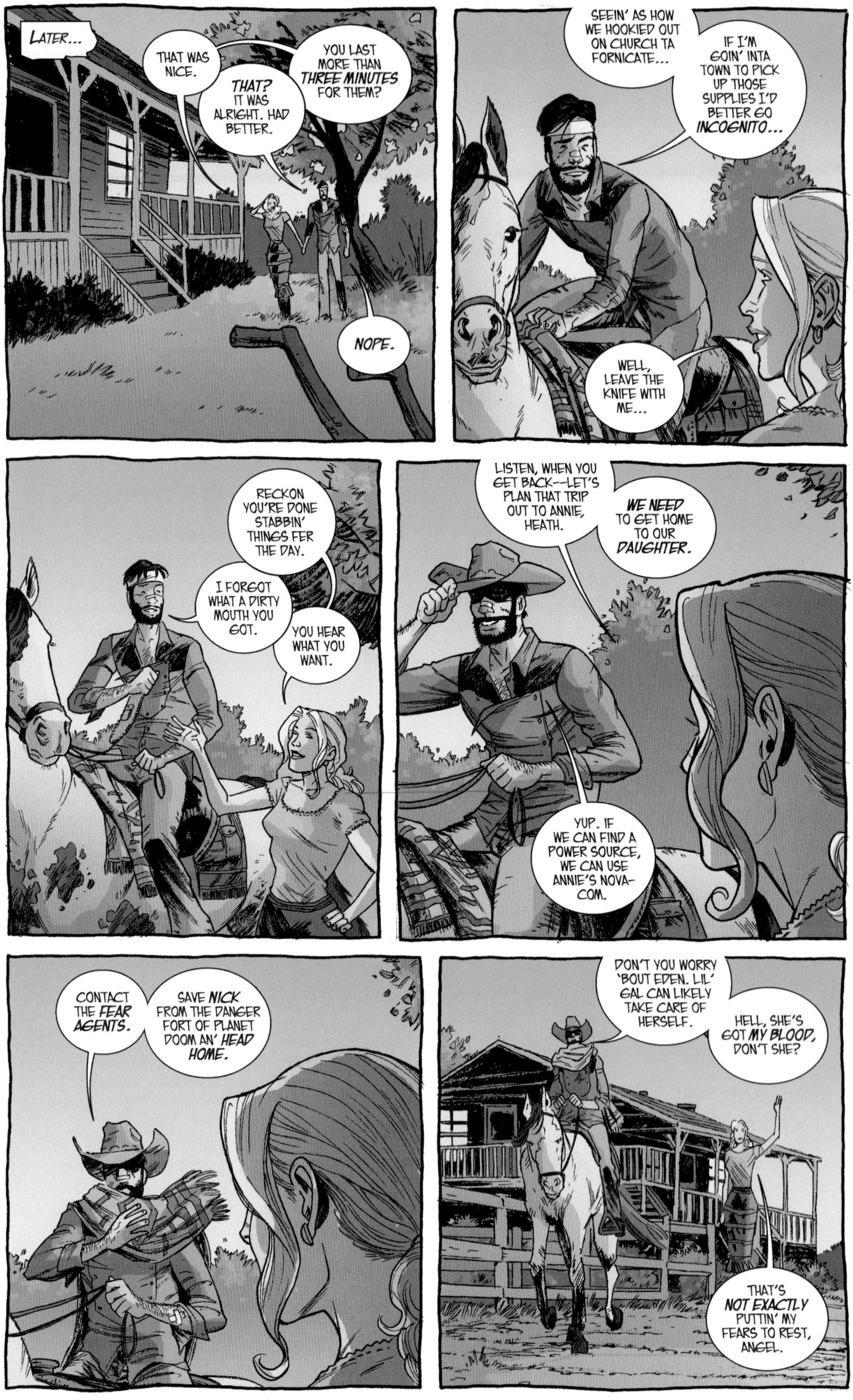
LATER...
THAT WAS NICE.
THAT? IT WAS ALRIGHT. HAD BETTER.
YOU LAST MORE THAN THREE MINUTES FOR THEM?
NOPE.
SEEIN' AS HOW WE HOOKIED OUT ON CHURCH TA FORNICATE...
IF I'M GOIN' INTA TOWN TO PICK UP THOSE SUPPLIES I'D BETTER GO INCOGNITO...
WELL, LEAVE THE KNIFE WITH ME...
RECKON YOU'RE DONE STABBIN' THINGS FER THE DAY.
I FORGOT WHAT A DIRTY MOUTH YOU GOT.
YOU HEAR WHAT YOU WANT.
LISTEN, WHEN YOU GET BACK--LET'S PLAN THAT TRIP OUT TO ANNIE, HEATH.
WE NEED TO GET HOME TO OUR DAUGHTER.
YUP. IF WE CAN FIND A POWER SOURCE, WE CAN USE ANNIE'S NOVA-COM.
CONTACT THE FEAR AGENTS.
SAVE NICK FROM THE DANGER FORT OF PLANET DOOM AN' HEAD HOME.
DON'T YOU WORRY 'BOUT EDEN. LIL' GAL CAN LIKELY TAKE CARE OF HERSELF.
HELL, SHE'S GOT MY BLOOD, DON'T SHE?
THAT'S NOT EXACTLY PUTTIN' MY FEARS TO REST, ANGEL.

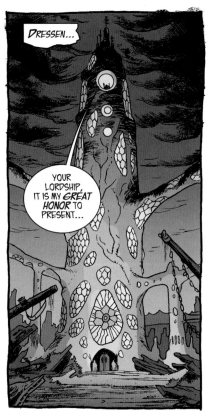

DRESSEN...

YOUR LORDSHIP, IT IS MY *GREAT HONOR* TO PRESENT...

...THE DAUGHTER OF HEATH HUSTON.

YES, YES.

WELCOME TO DRESSEN.

ONCE A FLOURISHING METROPOLIS AT THE HEART OF A VIBRANT GALAXY...

...UNTIL YOUR FATHER *DECIMATED* IT!

MURDERED MY ENTIRE SPECIES!!

KRINK

YEAH, I KNOW. Y'ALL WERE MESSIN' ABOUT WHERE YOU DIDN'T BELONG.

DEAR GIRL. BOTH OF YOUR PARENTS ARE DEAD.

YOU LIVE ONLY BY MY *GOOD GRACE*.

PERHAPS YOU SHOULD *RECONSIDER* YOUR TONE.

MY PA IS GONNA *BUST YOU UP*.

YOU OUGHTTA *TAKE ME BACK HOME* AN' SAVE YOURSELF THE TROUBLE.

YES, FINE... IT DOESN'T MATTER.

I DON'T NEED YOU TO UNDERSTAND.

I ONLY NEED YOUR *BLOOD*.

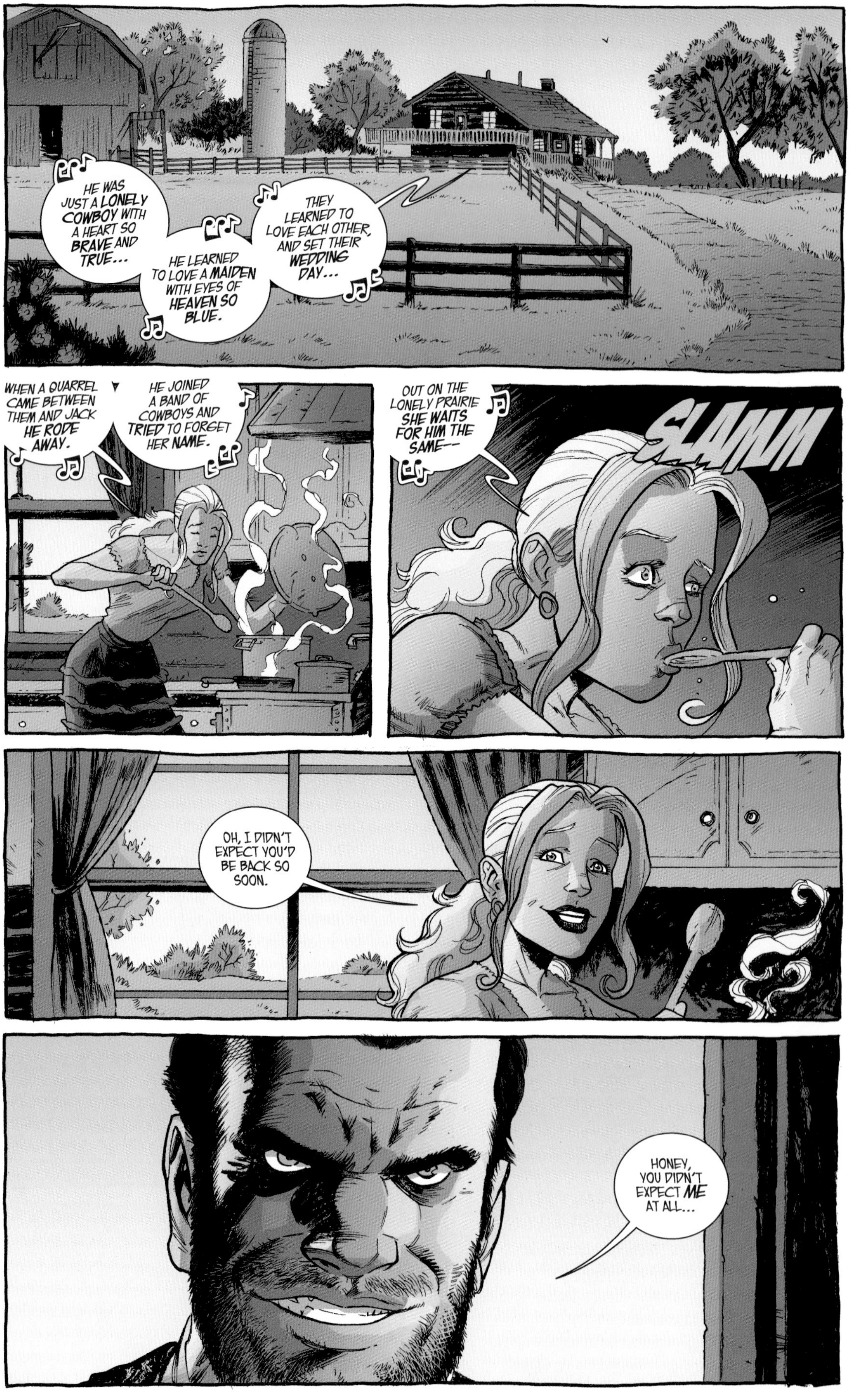
HE WAS JUST A LONELY COWBOY WITH A HEART SO BRAVE AND TRUE...
HE LEARNED TO LOVE A MAIDEN WITH EYES OF HEAVEN SO BLUE.
THEY LEARNED TO LOVE EACH OTHER, AND SET THEIR WEDDING DAY...
WHEN A QUARREL CAME BETWEEN THEM AND JACK HE RODE AWAY.
HE JOINED A BAND OF COWBOYS AND TRIED TO FORGET HER NAME.
OUT ON THE LONELY PRAIRIE SHE WAITS FOR HIM THE SAME--
SLAMM
OH, I DIDN'T EXPECT YOU'D BE BACK SO SOON.
HONEY, YOU DIDN'T EXPECT ME AT ALL...

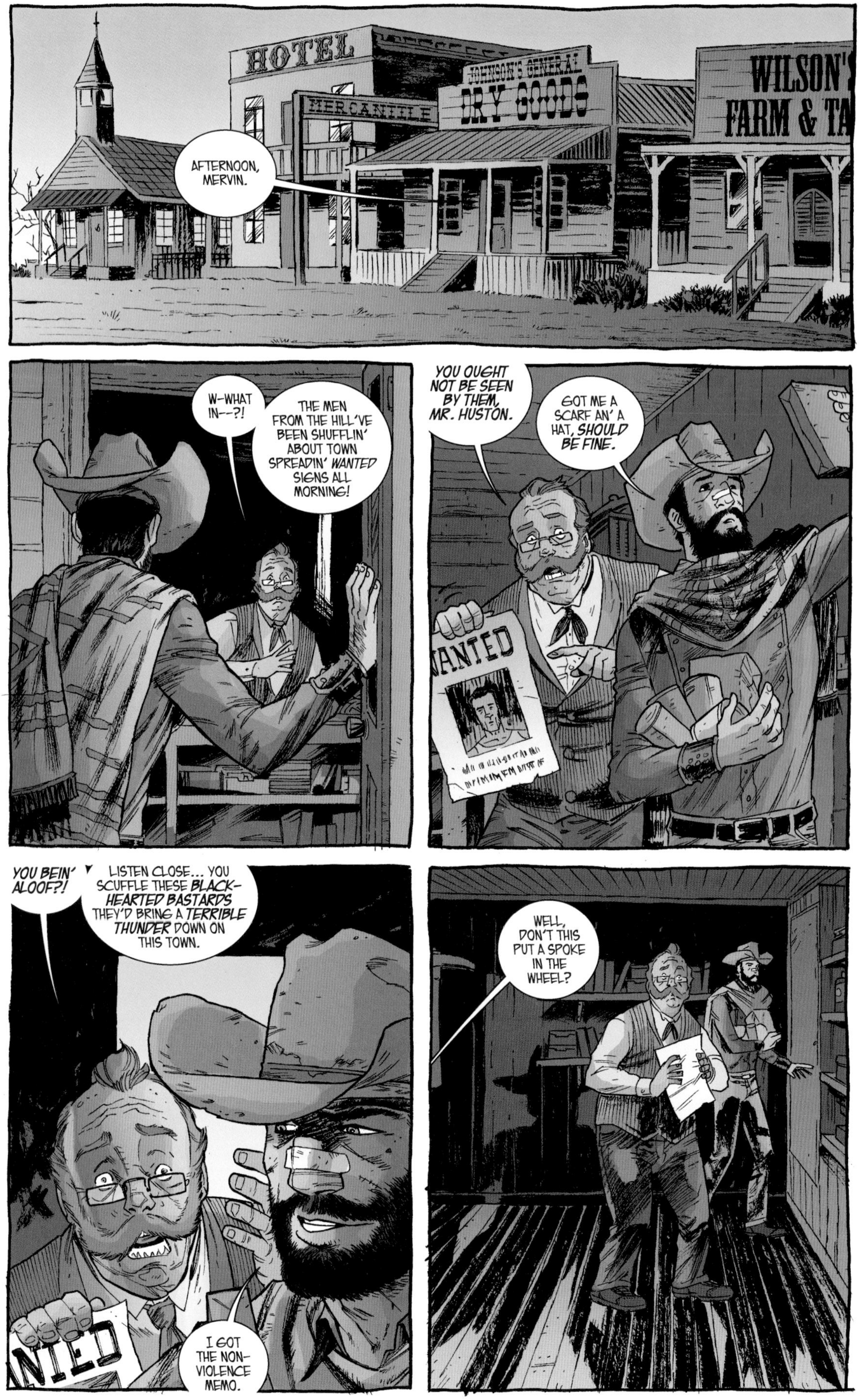
HOTEL
MERCANTILE
JOHNSON'S GENERAL
DRY GOODS
WILSON'S
FARM & TA
AFTERNOON, MERVIN.
W-WHAT IN--?!
THE MEN FROM THE HILL'VE BEEN SHUFFLIN' ABOUT TOWN SPREADIN' WANTED SIGNS ALL MORNING!
YOU OUGHT NOT BE SEEN BY THEM, MR. HUSTON.
GOT ME A SCARF AN' A HAT, SHOULD BE FINE.
WANTED
YOU BEIN' ALOOF?!
LISTEN CLOSE... YOU SCUFFLE THESE BLACK-HEARTED BASTARDS THEY'D BRING A TERRIBLE THUNDER DOWN ON THIS TOWN.
I GOT THE NON-VIOLENCE MEMO.
WELL, DON'T THIS PUT A SPOKE IN THE WHEEL?

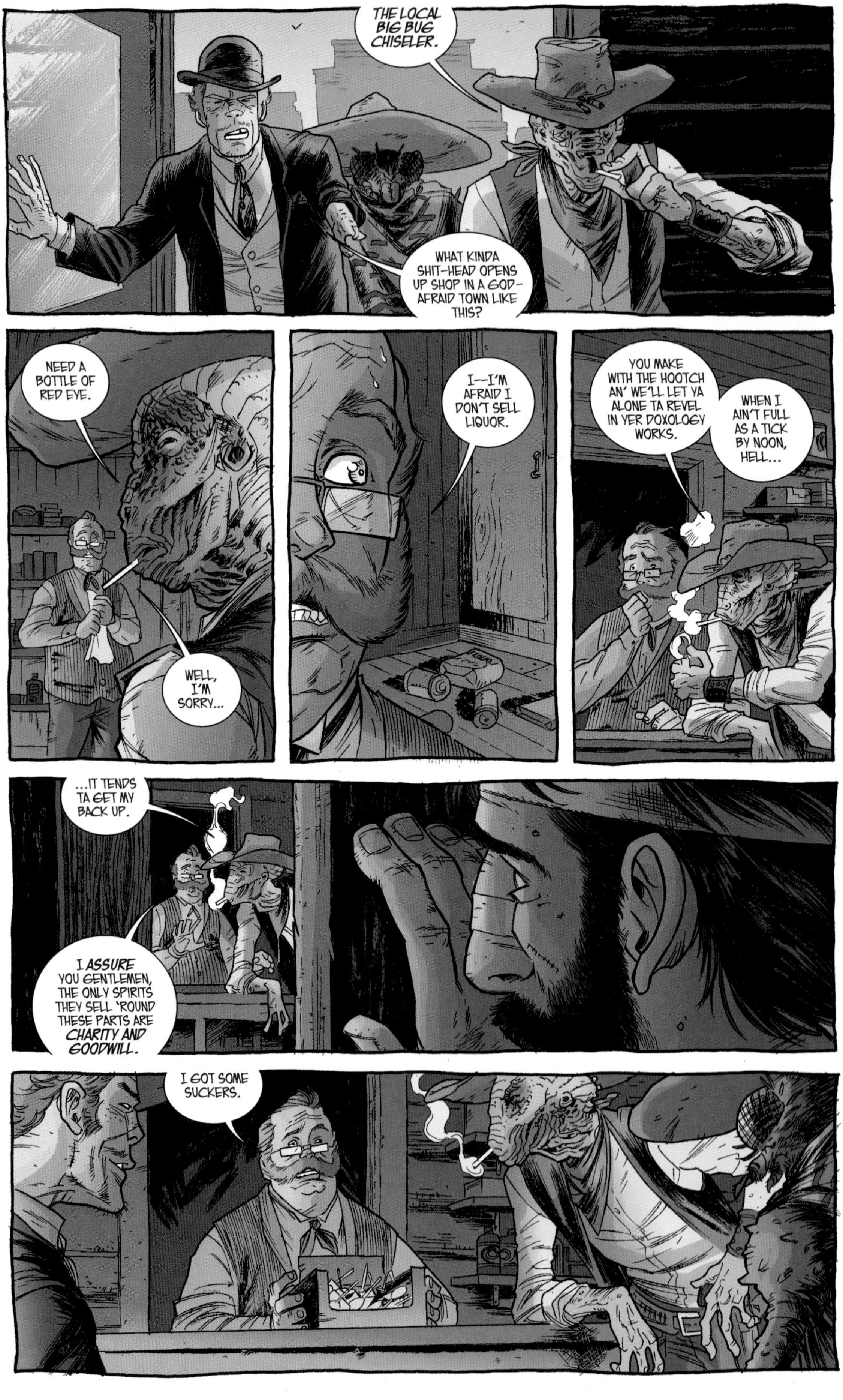
THE LOCAL BIG BUG CHISELER.
WHAT KINDA SHIT-HEAD OPENS UP SHOP IN A GOD-AFRAID TOWN LIKE THIS?
NEED A BOTTLE OF RED EYE.
WELL, I'M SORRY...
I--I'M AFRAID I DON'T SELL LIQUOR.
YOU MAKE WITH THE HOOTCH AN' WE'LL LET YA ALONE TA REVEL IN YER DOXOLOGY WORKS.
WHEN I AIN'T FULL AS A TICK BY NOON, HELL...
...IT TENDS TA GET MY BACK UP.
I ASSURE YOU GENTLEMEN, THE ONLY SPIRITS THEY SELL 'ROUND THESE PARTS ARE CHARITY AND GOODWILL.
I GOT SOME SUCKERS.

ALREADY GOT A SUCKER--
GIVE 'ER A LICK!
CHWKK
GAA!
YOU KEEP FLAPPIN' THEM GUMS YOU MIGHT GET SOME GOODWILL TO WASH THIS CHARITY DOWN.
HAR-HAR! Y'ALL SEE THEM TEETH!
DAMNED IF ONE O' 'EM DIDN'T HIT THE CEILIN'!
ALRIGHT, BOYS. Y'ALL POSTED YER BILLS.
WIND UP THIS BUSINESS AN' HEAD ON HOME-- I WANT YOU OUT OF MY TOWN.
YOUR TOWN??

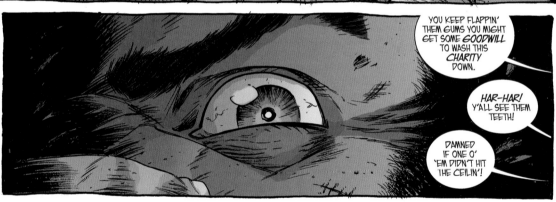

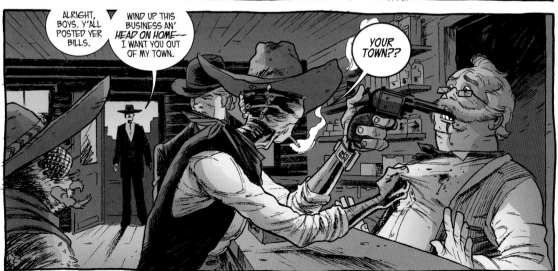

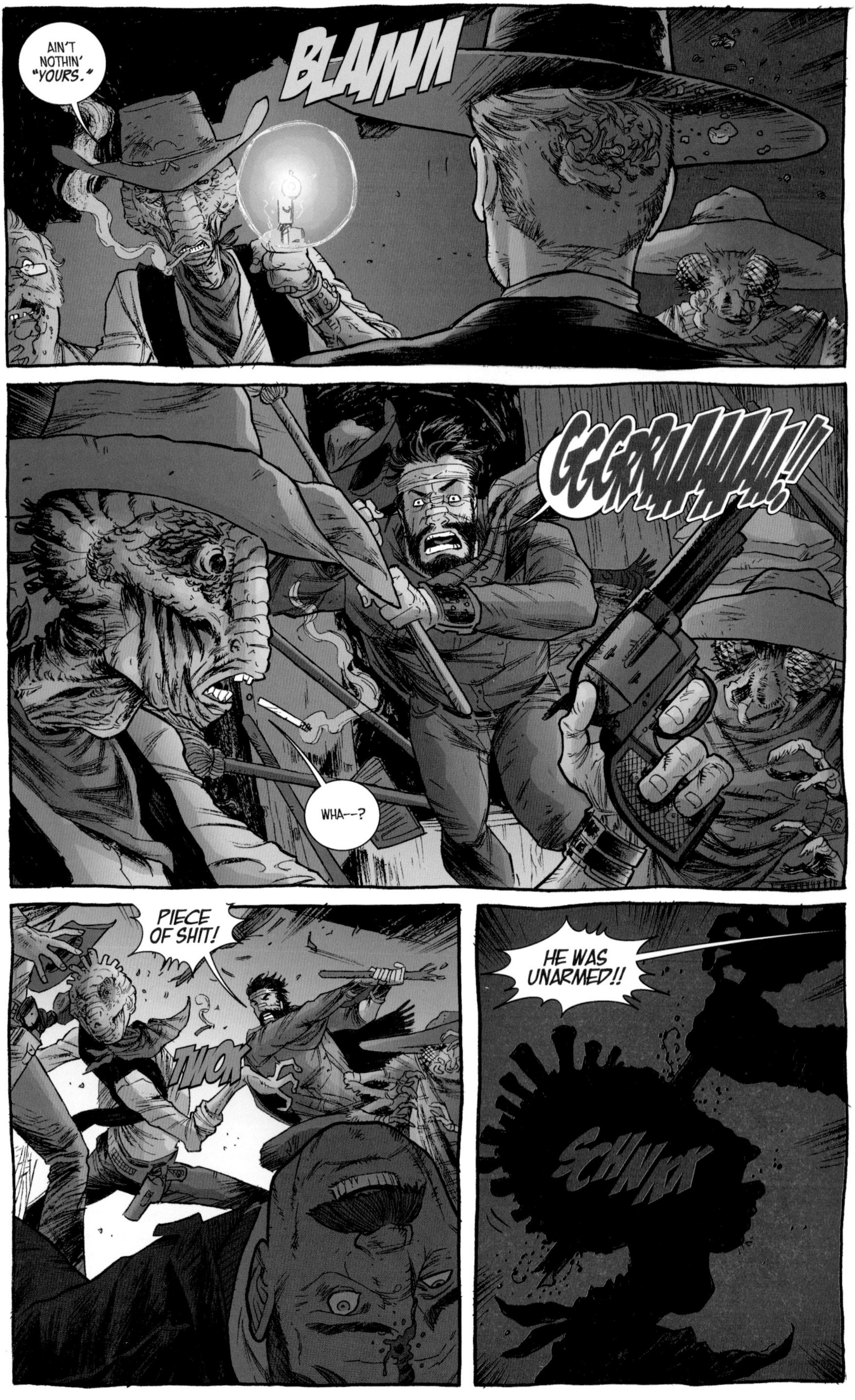
AIN'T NOTHIN' "YOURS."
BLAMM
GGGRAAAAAA!!
WHA--?
PIECE OF SHIT!
THOK
HE WAS UNARMED!!
SCHNKK

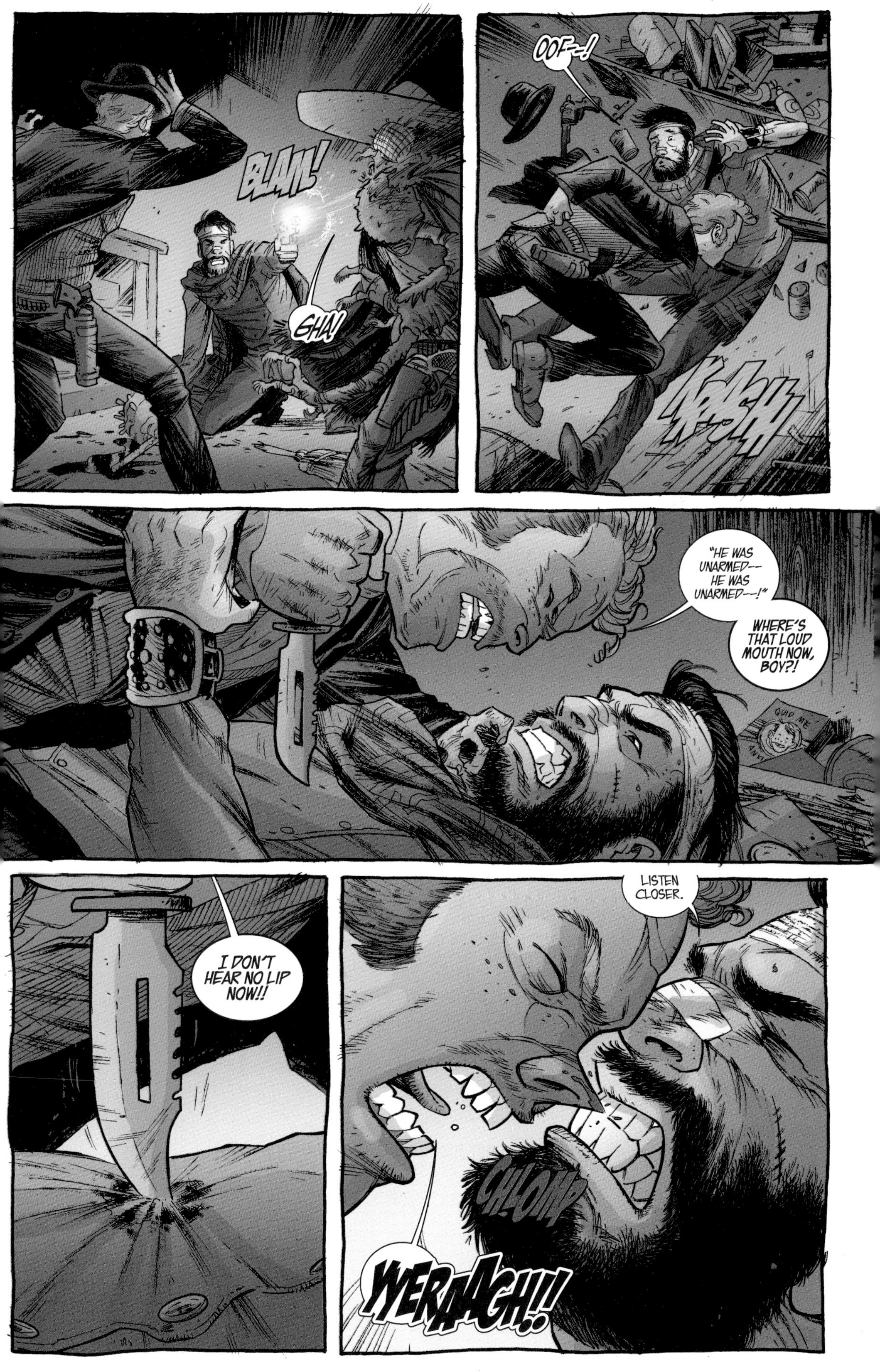
BLAM!
GHA!
OOF--!
KRSCH
"HE WAS UNARMED-- HE WAS UNARMED--!"
WHERE'S THAT LOUD MOUTH NOW, BOY?!
I DON'T HEAR NO LIP NOW!!
LISTEN CLOSER.
CHLOMP
YYERAAAGH!!

MY ROSE!!

HE RIT OFF MY ROSE!!

RO, STUPID-- GHA!!

KLABLAMM

KLABLAMM
KLABLAMM

SCHWOKK

KLABLAMM

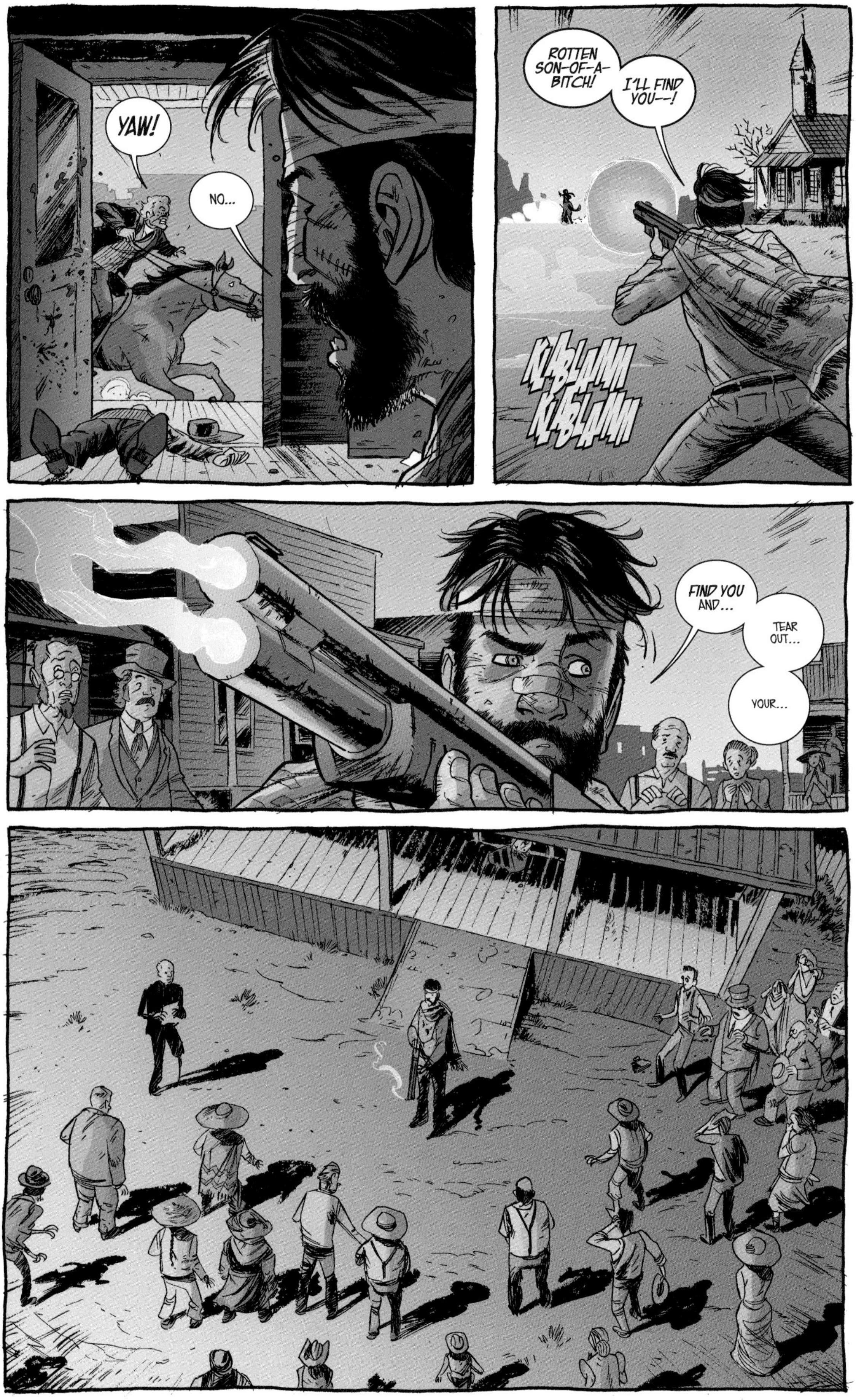
YAW!
NO...
ROTTEN SON-OF-A-BITCH!
I'LL FIND YOU--!
KLABLAMM
KLABLAMM
FIND YOU AND...
TEAR OUT...
YOUR...

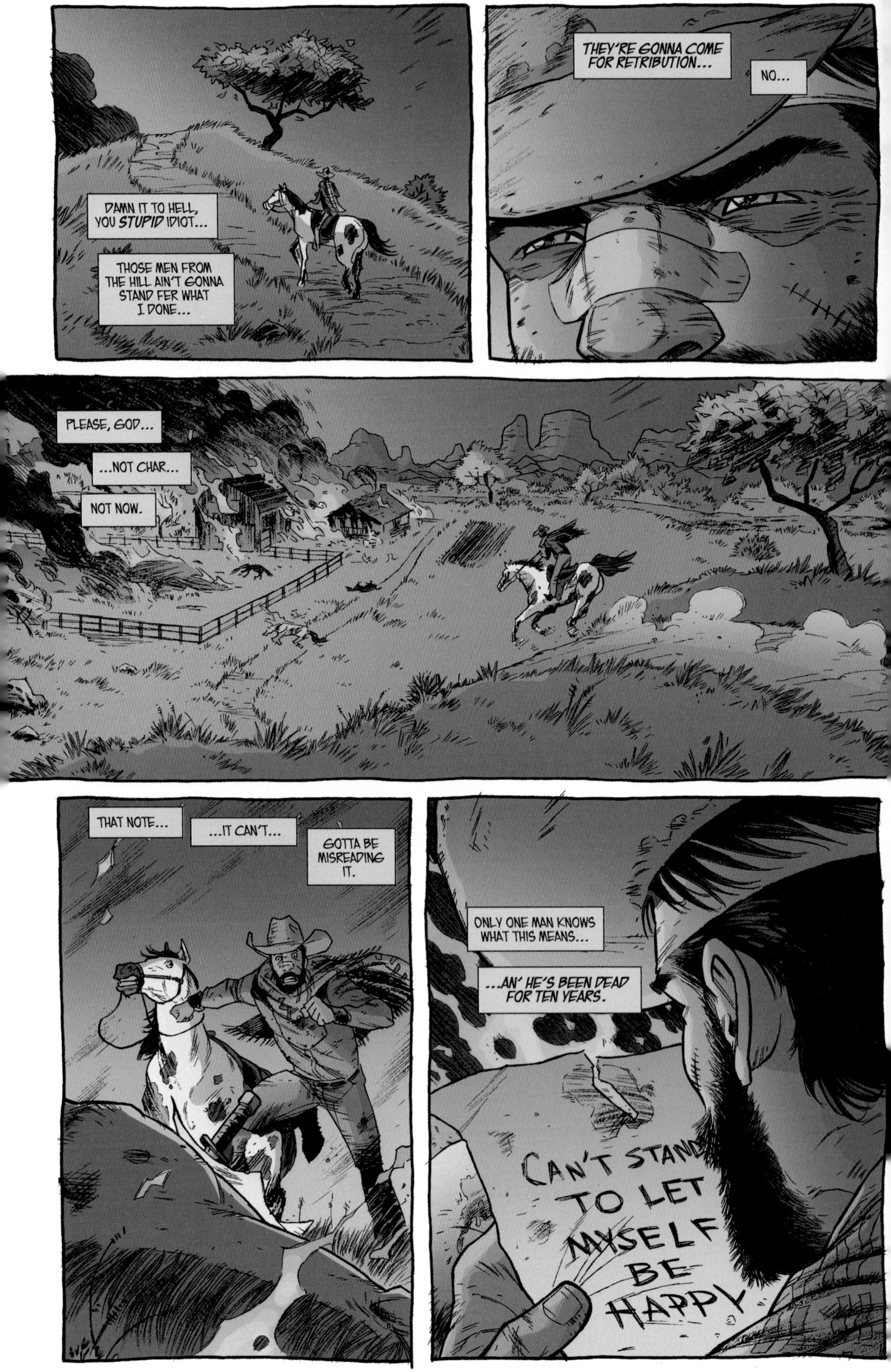
DAMN IT TO HELL, YOU STUPID IDIOT...
THOSE MEN FROM THE HILL AIN'T GONNA STAND FER WHAT I DONE...
THEY'RE GONNA COME FOR RETRIBUTION...
NO...
PLEASE, GOD...
...NOT CHAR...
NOT NOW.
THAT NOTE...
...IT CAN'T...
GOTTA BE MISREADING IT.
ONLY ONE MAN KNOWS WHAT THIS MEANS...
...AN' HE'S BEEN DEAD FOR TEN YEARS.
CAN'T STAND TO LET MYSELF BE HAPPY

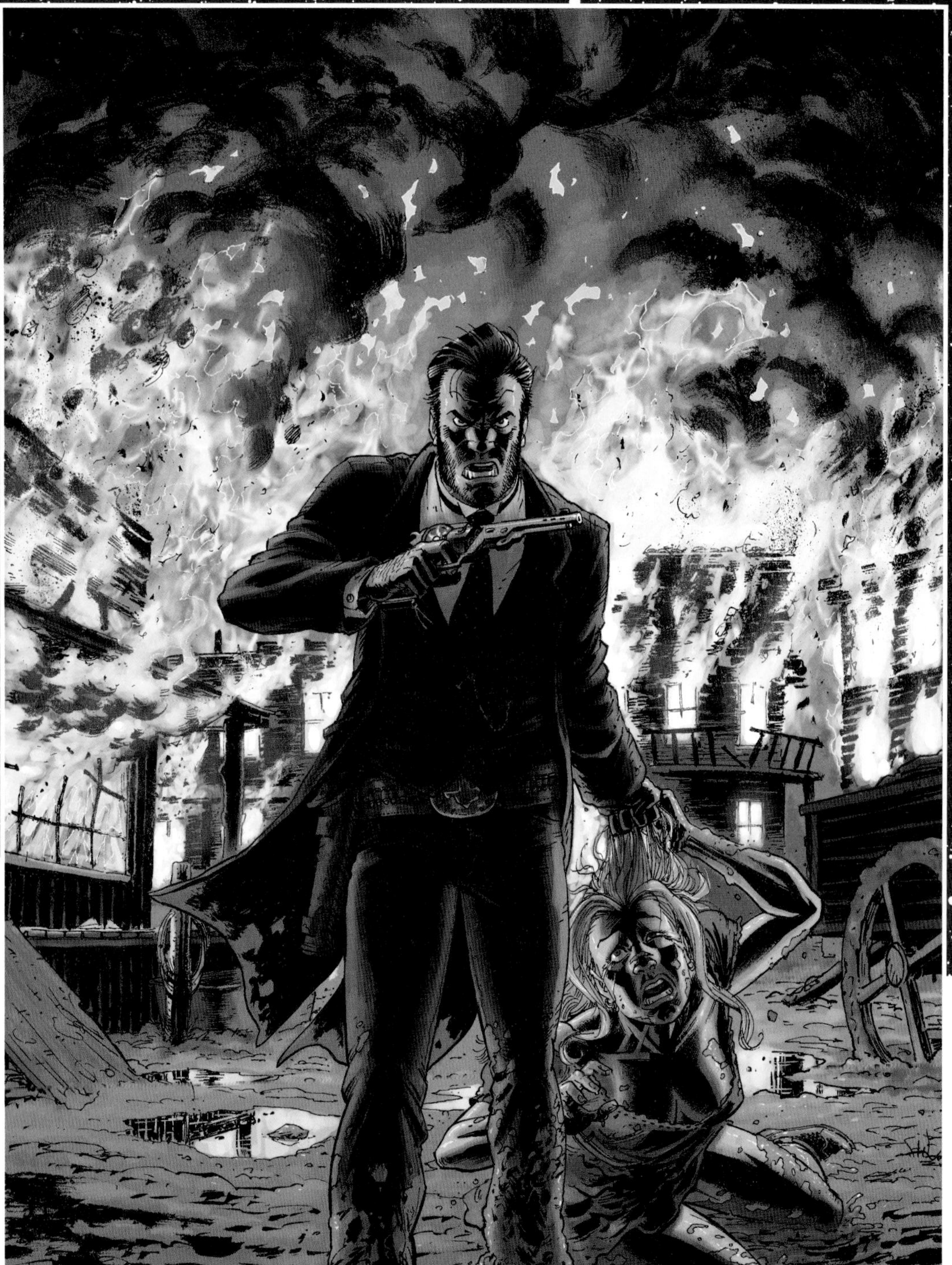

FEAR AGENT #25
ART BY **TONY MOORE**

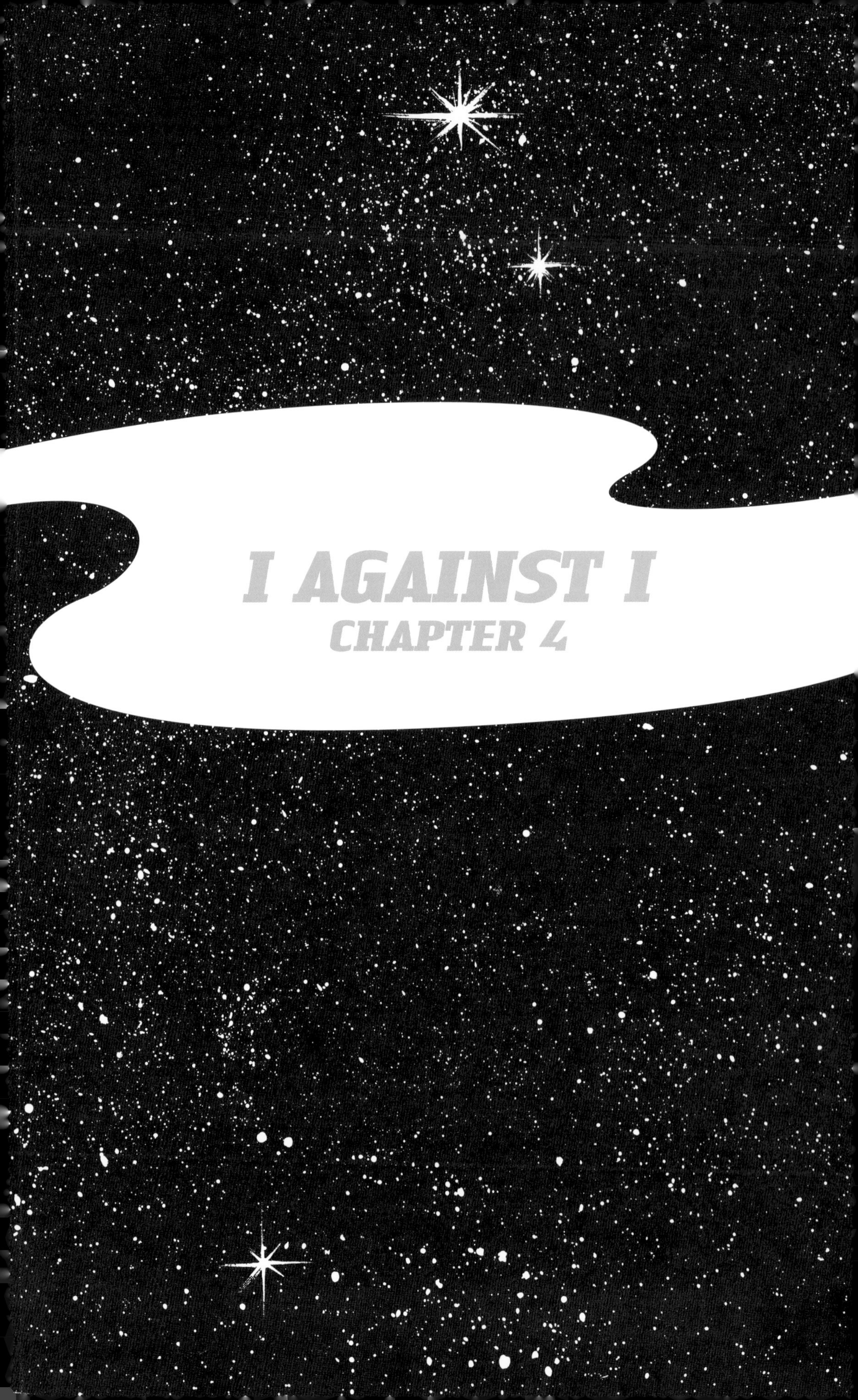
I AGAINST I
CHAPTER 4

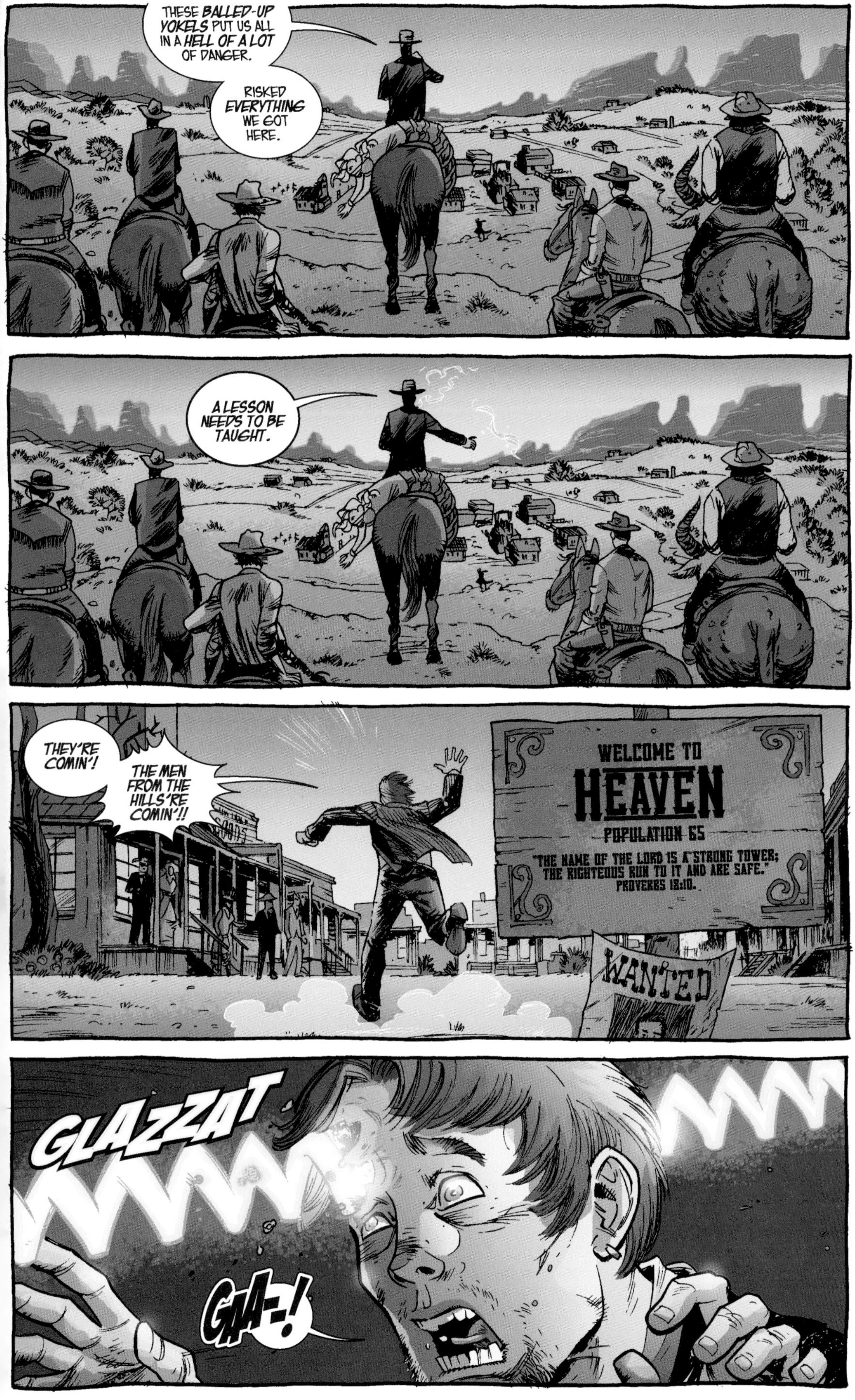
THESE BALLED-UP YOKELS PUT US ALL IN A HELL OF A LOT OF DANGER.
RISKED EVERYTHING WE GOT HERE.
A LESSON NEEDS TO BE TAUGHT.
THEY'RE COMIN'!
THE MEN FROM THE HILLS'RE COMIN'!!
WELCOME TO
HEAVEN
POPULATION 65
"THE NAME OF THE LORD IS A STRONG TOWER; THE RIGHTEOUS RUN TO IT AND ARE SAFE."
PROVERBS 18:10.
WANTED
GLAZZAT
GAA-!

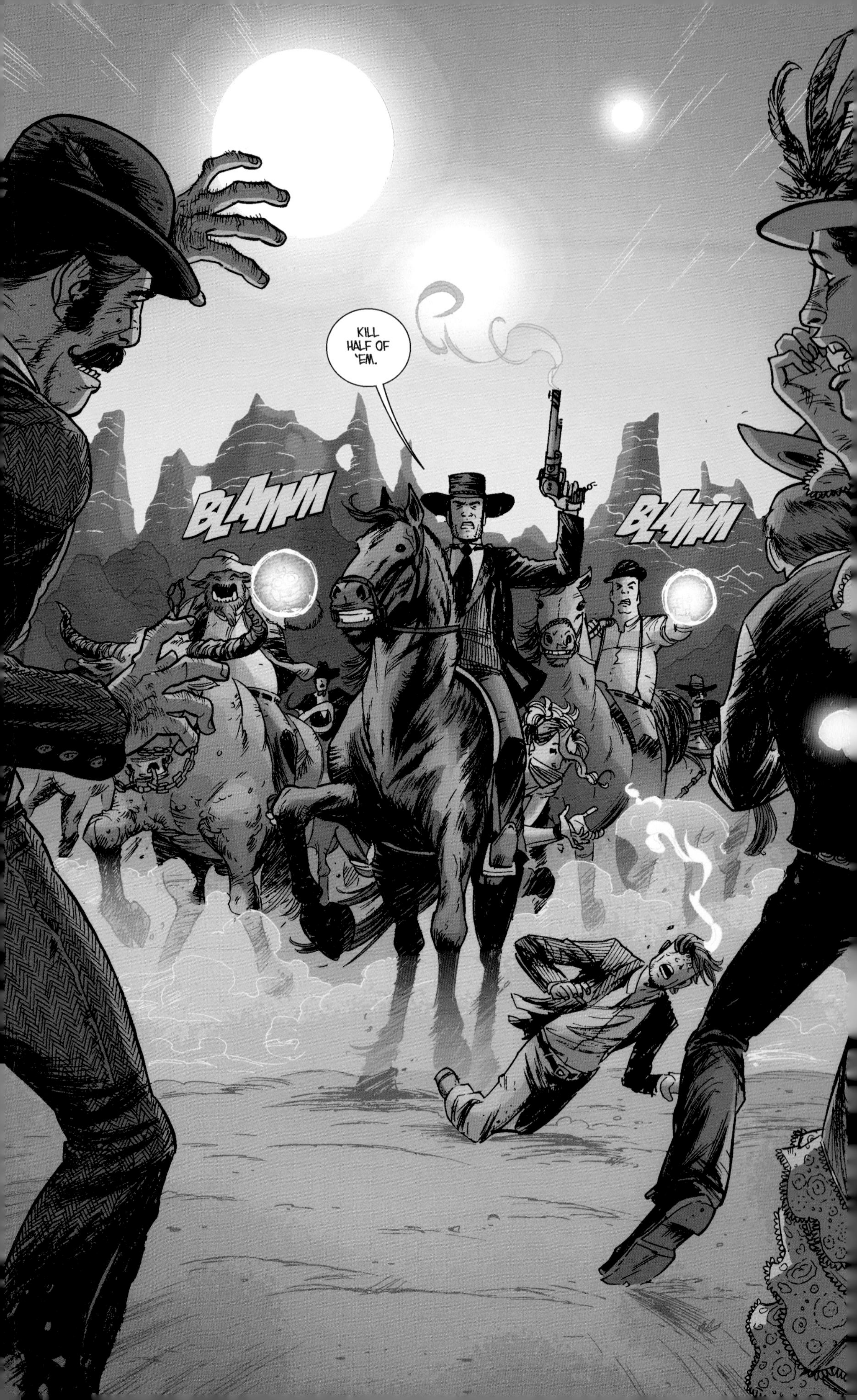
BLAMM
KILL HALF OF 'EM.
BLAMM

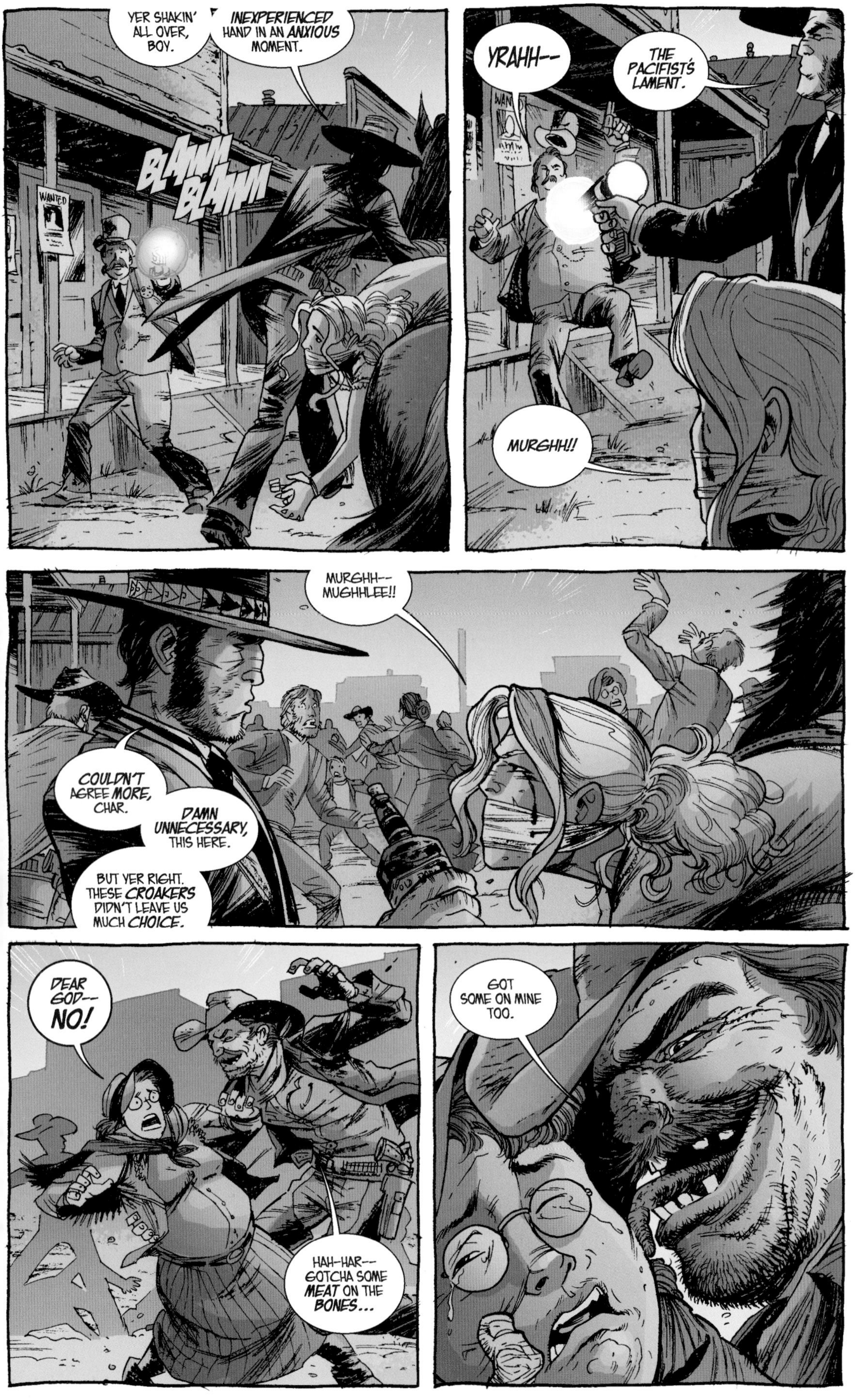
YER SHAKIN' ALL OVER, BOY.
INEXPERIENCED HAND IN AN ANXIOUS MOMENT.
BLAMM BLAMM
WANTED
YRAHH--
THE PACIFIST'S LAMENT.
MURGHH!!
MURGHH-- MUGHHLEE!!
COULDN'T AGREE MORE, CHAR.
DAMN UNNECESSARY, THIS HERE.
BUT YER RIGHT. THESE CROAKERS DIDN'T LEAVE US MUCH CHOICE.
DEAR GOD-- NO!
HAH-HAR-- GOTCHA SOME MEAT ON THE BONES...
GOT SOME ON MINE TOO.

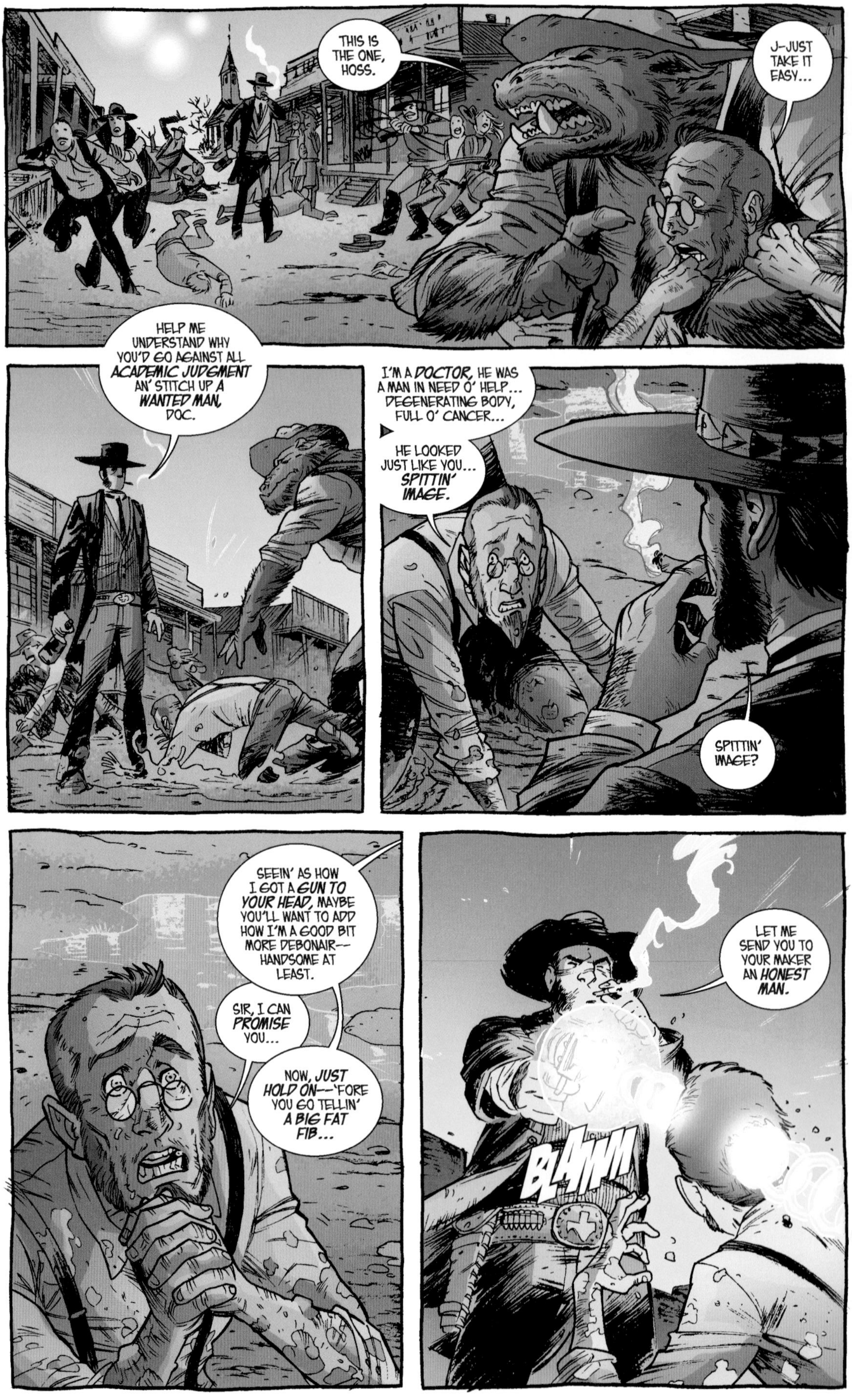
THIS IS THE ONE, HOSS.
J-JUST TAKE IT EASY...
HELP ME UNDERSTAND WHY YOU'D GO AGAINST ALL ACADEMIC JUDGMENT AN' STITCH UP A WANTED MAN, DOC.
I'M A DOCTOR, HE WAS A MAN IN NEED O' HELP... DEGENERATING BODY, FULL O' CANCER...
HE LOOKED JUST LIKE YOU... SPITTIN' IMAGE.
SPITTIN' IMAGE?
SEEIN' AS HOW I GOT A GUN TO YOUR HEAD, MAYBE YOU'LL WANT TO ADD HOW I'M A GOOD BIT MORE DEBONAIR-- HANDSOME AT LEAST.
SIR, I CAN PROMISE YOU...
NOW, JUST HOLD ON--'FORE YOU GO TELLIN' A BIG FAT FIB...
LET ME SEND YOU TO YOUR MAKER AN HONEST MAN.
BLAMM

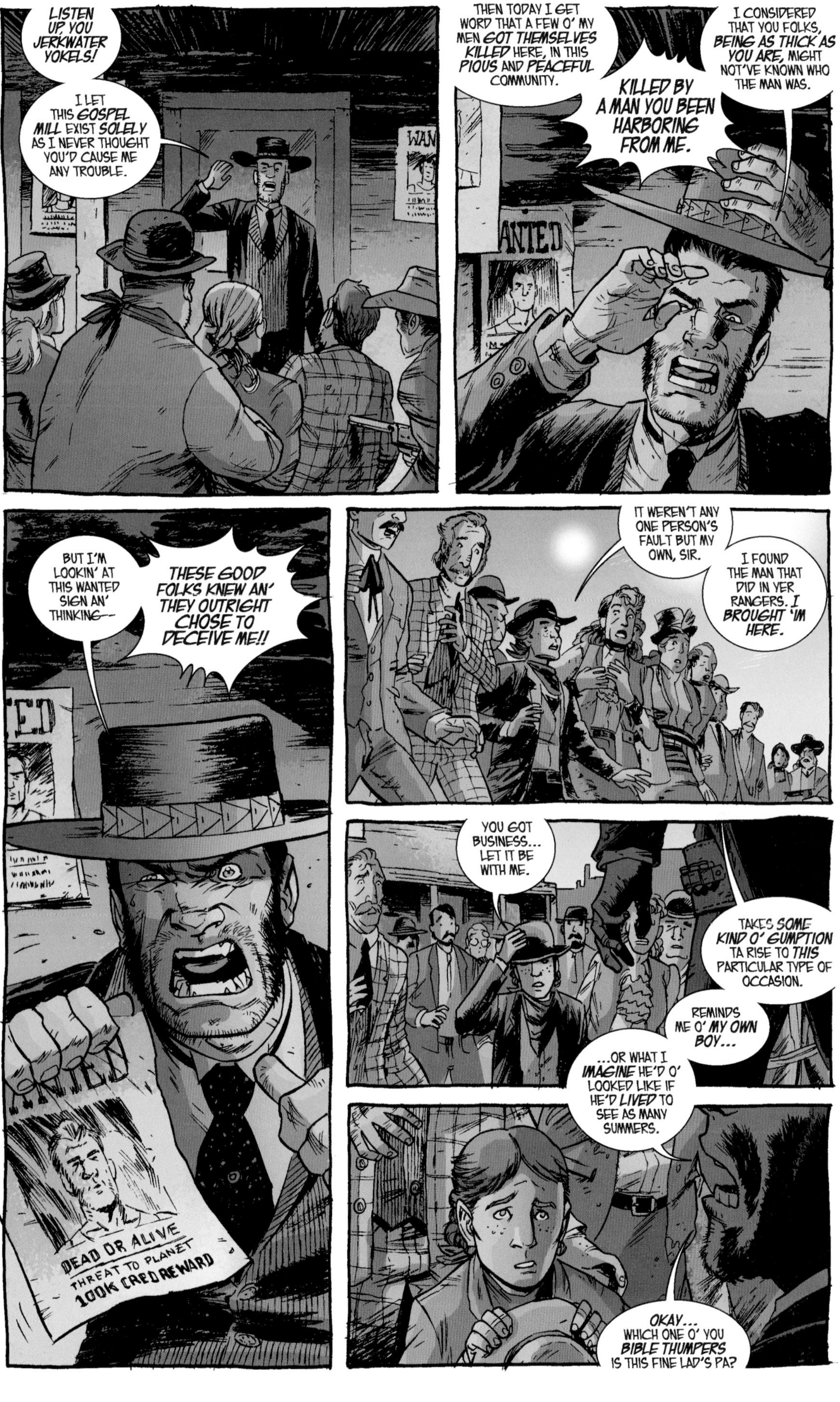
LISTEN UP, YOU JERKWATER YOKELS!
I LET THIS GOSPEL MILL EXIST SOLELY AS I NEVER THOUGHT YOU'D CAUSE ME ANY TROUBLE.
THEN TODAY I GET WORD THAT A FEW O' MY MEN GOT THEMSELVES KILLED HERE, IN THIS PIOUS AND PEACEFUL COMMUNITY.
KILLED BY A MAN YOU BEEN HARBORING FROM ME.
I CONSIDERED THAT YOU FOLKS, BEING AS THICK AS YOU ARE, MIGHT NOT'VE KNOWN WHO THE MAN WAS.
ANTED
BUT I'M LOOKIN' AT THIS WANTED SIGN AN' THINKING--
THESE GOOD FOLKS KNEW AN' THEY OUTRIGHT CHOSE TO DECEIVE ME!!
DEAD OR ALIVE
THREAT TO PLANET
100K CRED REWARD
IT WEREN'T ANY ONE PERSON'S FAULT BUT MY OWN, SIR.
I FOUND THE MAN THAT DID IN YER RANGERS. I BROUGHT 'IM HERE.
YOU GOT BUSINESS... LET IT BE WITH ME.
TAKES SOME KIND O' GUMPTION TA RISE TO THIS PARTICULAR TYPE OF OCCASION.
REMINDS ME O' MY OWN BOY...
...OR WHAT I IMAGINE HE'D O' LOOKED LIKE IF HE'D LIVED TO SEE AS MANY SUMMERS.
OKAY... WHICH ONE O' YOU BIBLE THUMPERS IS THIS FINE LAD'S PA?

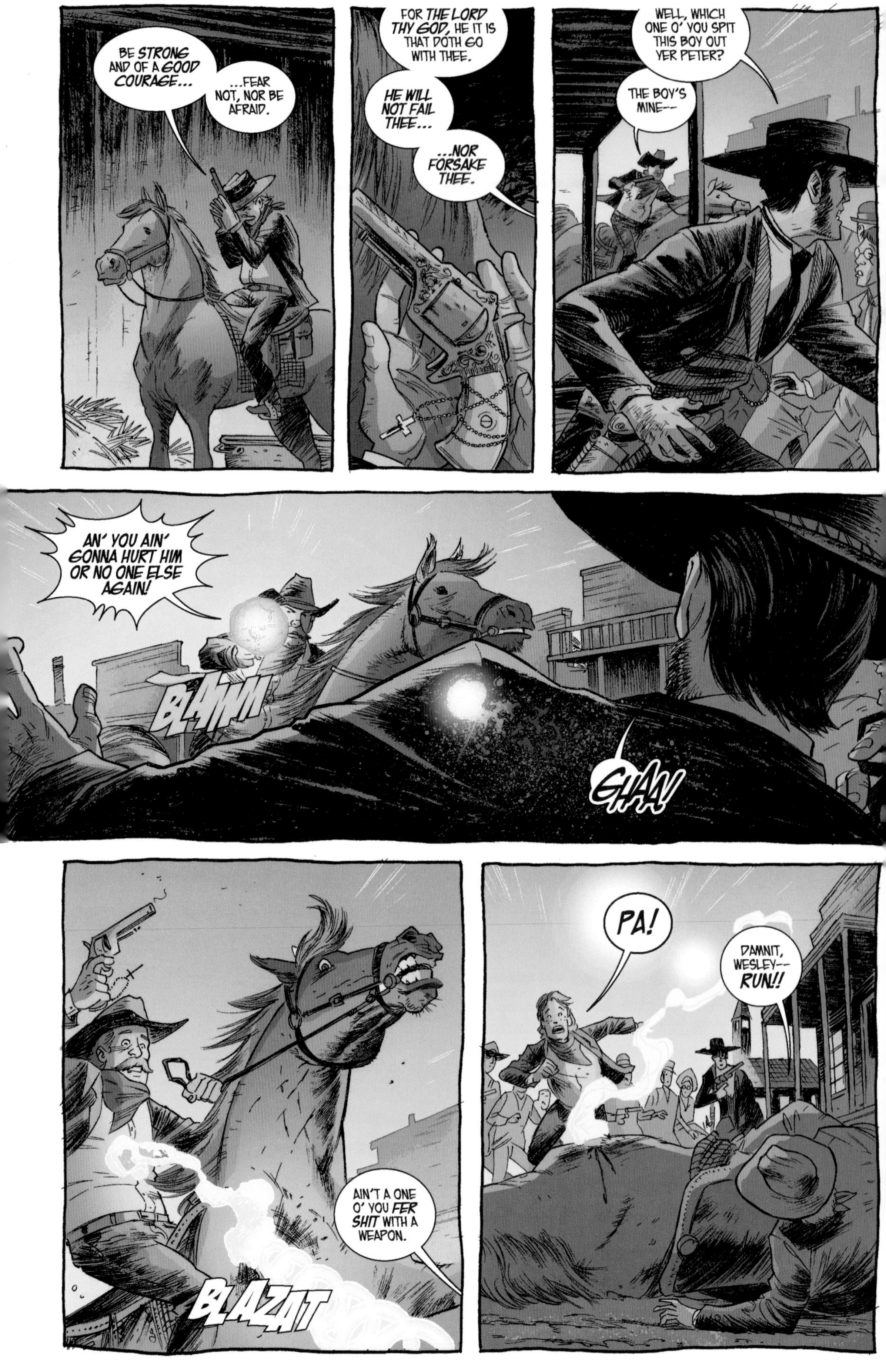
BE STRONG AND OF A GOOD COURAGE...
...FEAR NOT, NOR BE AFRAID.
FOR THE LORD THY GOD, HE IT IS THAT DOTH GO WITH THEE.
HE WILL NOT FAIL THEE...
...NOR FORSAKE THEE.
WELL, WHICH ONE O' YOU SPIT THIS BOY OUT YER PETER?
THE BOY'S MINE--
AN' YOU AIN' GONNA HURT HIM OR NO ONE ELSE AGAIN!
BLAMM
GHAA!
AIN'T A ONE O' YOU FER SHIT WITH A WEAPON.
BLAZAT
PA!
DAMNIT, WESLEY-- RUN!!

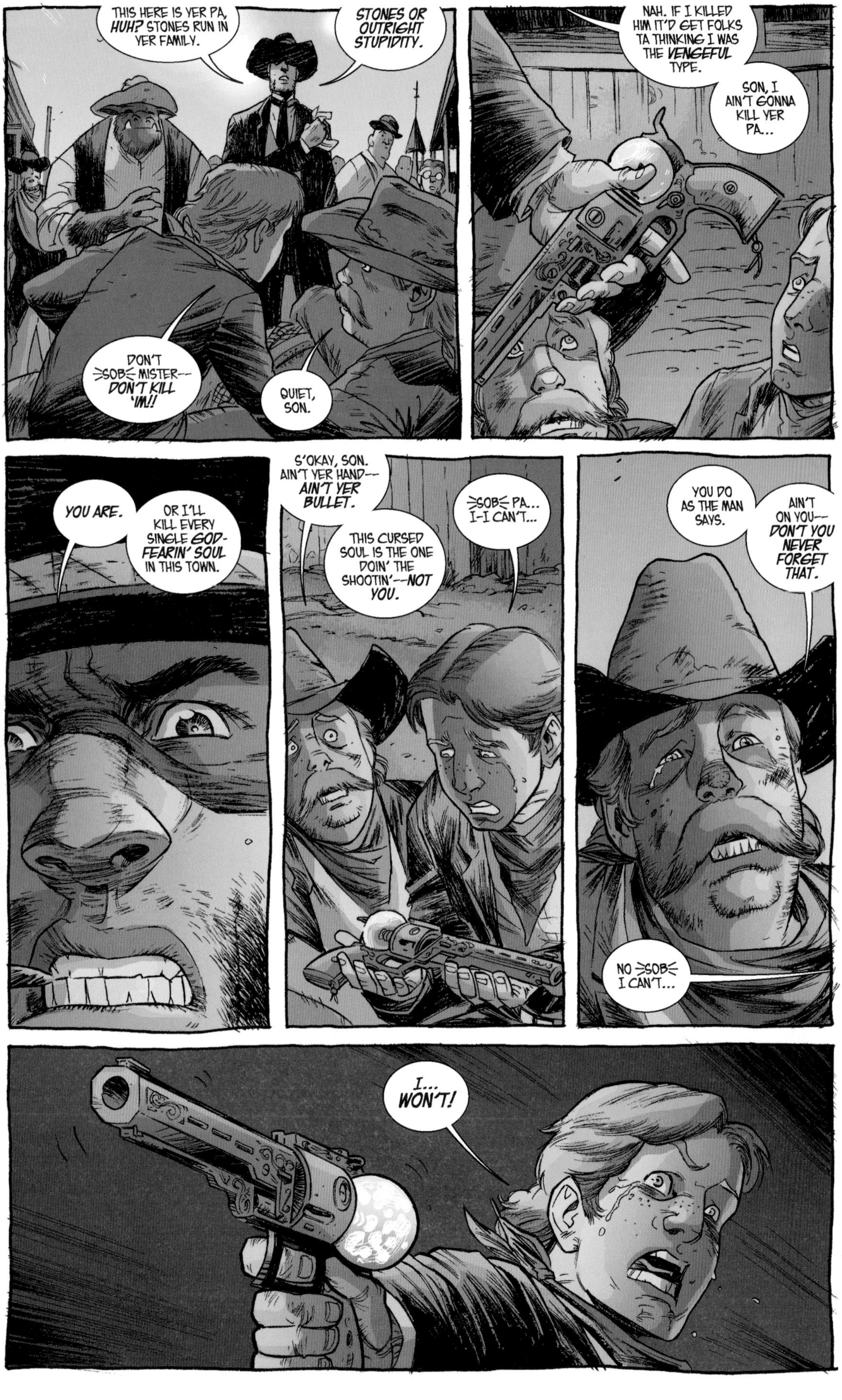
THIS HERE IS YER PA, HUH? STONES RUN IN YER FAMILY.
STONES OR OUTRIGHT STUPIDITY.
DON'T =SOB= MISTER-- DON'T KILL 'IM!!
QUIET, SON.
NAH. IF I KILLED HIM IT'D GET FOLKS TA THINKING I WAS THE VENGEFUL TYPE.
SON, I AIN'T GONNA KILL YER PA...
YOU ARE.
OR I'LL KILL EVERY SINGLE GOD-FEARIN' SOUL IN THIS TOWN.
S'OKAY, SON. AIN'T YER HAND-- AIN'T YER BULLET.
THIS CURSED SOUL IS THE ONE DOIN' THE SHOOTIN'--NOT YOU.
=SOB= PA... I-I CAN'T...
YOU DO AS THE MAN SAYS.
AIN'T ON YOU-- DON'T YOU NEVER FORGET THAT.
NO =SOB= I CAN'T...
I... WON'T!

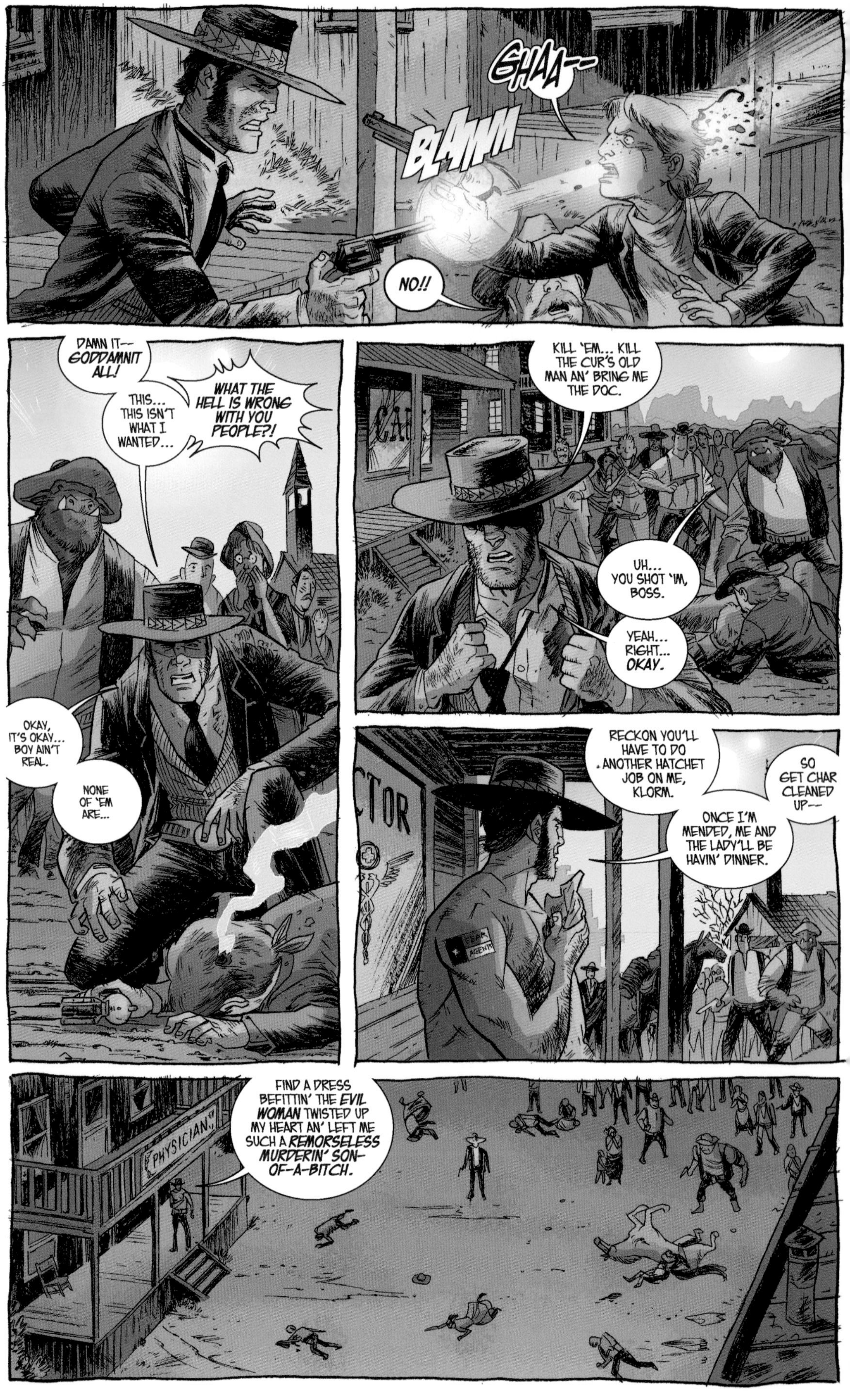
GHAA--
BLAMM
NO!!
DAMN IT-- GODDAMNIT ALL!
THIS... THIS ISN'T WHAT I WANTED...
WHAT THE HELL IS WRONG WITH YOU PEOPLE?!
OKAY, IT'S OKAY... BOY AIN'T REAL.
NONE OF 'EM ARE...
KILL 'EM... KILL THE CUR'S OLD MAN AN' BRING ME THE DOC.
UH... YOU SHOT 'IM, BOSS.
YEAH... RIGHT... OKAY.
RECKON YOU'LL HAVE TO DO ANOTHER HATCHET JOB ON ME, KLORM.
ONCE I'M MENDED, ME AND THE LADY'LL BE HAVIN' DINNER.
SO GET CHAR CLEANED UP--
FIND A DRESS BEFITTIN' THE EVIL WOMAN TWISTED UP MY HEART AN' LEFT ME SUCH A REMORSELESS MURDERIN' SON-OF-A-BITCH.
PHYSICIAN

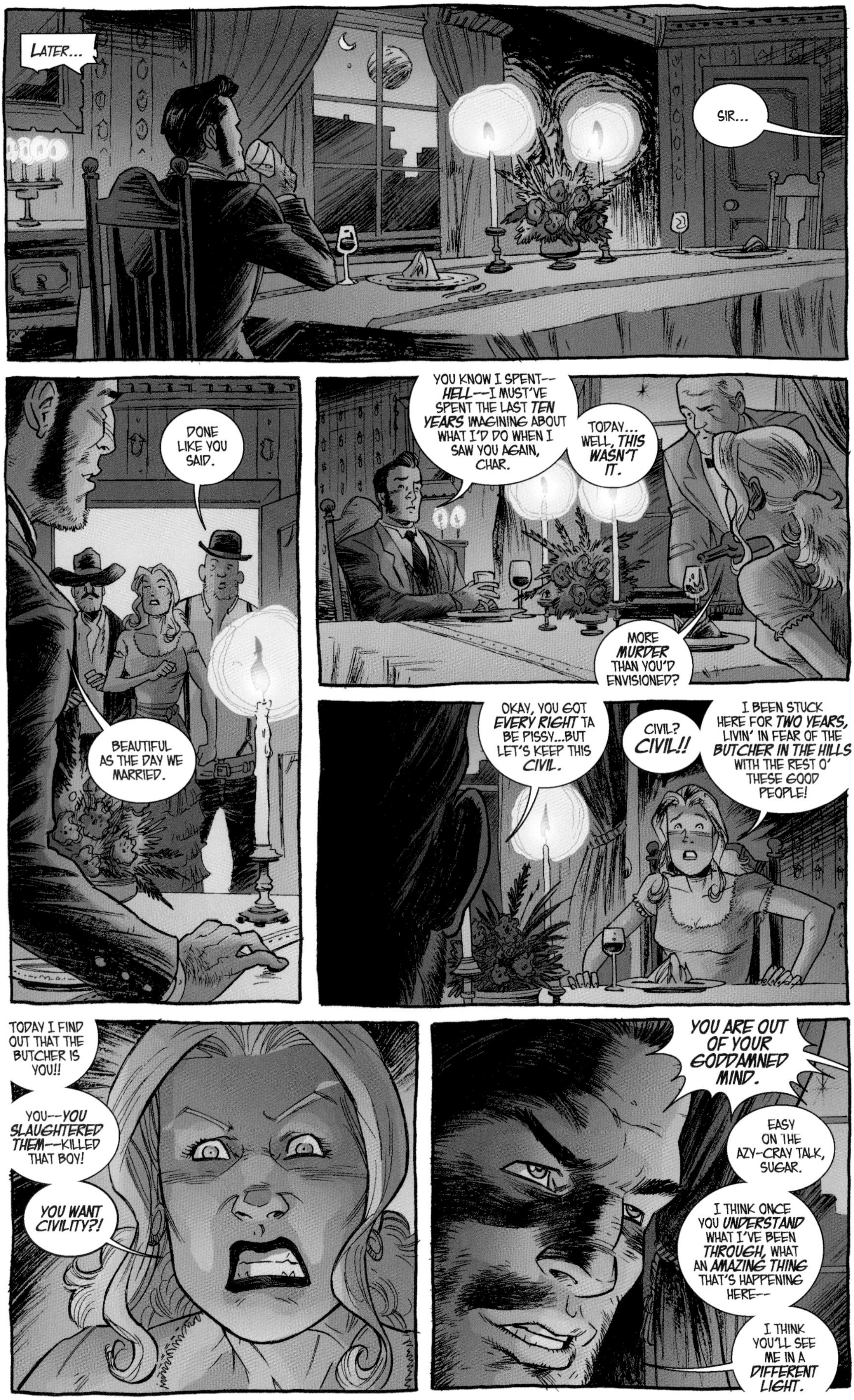
LATER...
SIR...
DONE LIKE YOU SAID.
BEAUTIFUL AS THE DAY WE MARRIED.
YOU KNOW I SPENT-- HELL--I MUST'VE SPENT THE LAST TEN YEARS IMAGINING ABOUT WHAT I'D DO WHEN I SAW YOU AGAIN, CHAR.
TODAY... WELL, THIS WASN'T IT.
MORE MURDER THAN YOU'D ENVISIONED?
OKAY, YOU GOT EVERY RIGHT TA BE PISSY...BUT LET'S KEEP THIS CIVIL.
CIVIL? CIVIL!!
I BEEN STUCK HERE FOR TWO YEARS, LIVIN' IN FEAR OF THE BUTCHER IN THE HILLS WITH THE REST O' THESE GOOD PEOPLE!
TODAY I FIND OUT THAT THE BUTCHER IS YOU!!
YOU--YOU SLAUGHTERED THEM--KILLED THAT BOY!
YOU WANT CIVILITY?!
YOU ARE OUT OF YOUR GODDAMNED MIND.
EASY ON THE AZY-CRAY TALK, SUGAR.
I THINK ONCE YOU UNDERSTAND WHAT I'VE BEEN THROUGH, WHAT AN AMAZING THING THAT'S HAPPENING HERE--
I THINK YOU'LL SEE ME IN A DIFFERENT LIGHT.

COUPLE O' FEW YEARS AFTER I LEFT EARTH, *DRESSITES* SENT ME BACK IN TIME, MAROONED ME ON THE PLANET *TETALD* AS THE *TETALDIAN* RACE WAS FORMING.

RECKON THEY FIGURED I'D PUT AN END TO THE *TETALDIANS* 'FORE THEY STARTED, SAVE *EARTH* AN' THE *ENTIRE UNIVERSE* THEIR SCOURGE.

AN' I WAS GONNA.

WENT TO THE LEADER'S PALACE-- OL' *JENTU* HIMSELF--WITH INTENT O' *KILLIN'* 'IM AND STOPPIN' THE *TIN SHIT-CAN RACE* BEFORE THEY GOT THEIR FOOTIN'.

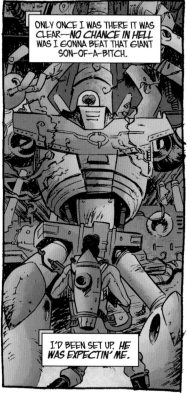

ONLY ONCE I WAS THERE IT WAS CLEAR--*NO CHANCE IN HELL* WAS I GONNA BEAT THAT GIANT SON-OF-A-BITCH.

I'D BEEN SET UP. *HE WAS EXPECTIN' ME.*

SO INSTEAD I MADE A *DEAL.*

I'D LET 'IM IN ON WHAT THE *FUTURE HELD FER HIM* IF HIS *ROBOT RACE* PROVIDED ME A FEW THINGS--

GET ME BACK TO MY *OWN TIME* ON A WORLD *CUSTOM* MADE TO MY SPECIFICATIONS...

AND THAT HE'D BRING ME YOU.

TETALDIANS MADE ME A FEW *CYBORGS* IN THE LIKENESS OF A RECENTLY DECEASED *FRIEND* TA HELP BIDE MY TIME WHILE I *WAITED...*

NO IDEA HOW, BUT THEY CAME THROUGH.

MADE ME MY OWN PLANET USING MY MENTAL IMAGES OF PARADISE.

BEFORE I LEFT I SET A FEW EXPLOSIVE CHARGES TO SHOW THE OL' BOY MY GRATITUDE.

TOOK ANNIE A COUPLE O' FEW TIME JUMPS TO GET IT RIGHT, BUT SHE EVENTUALLY GOT US TO OUR NEW HOME HERE IN THE PRESENT...

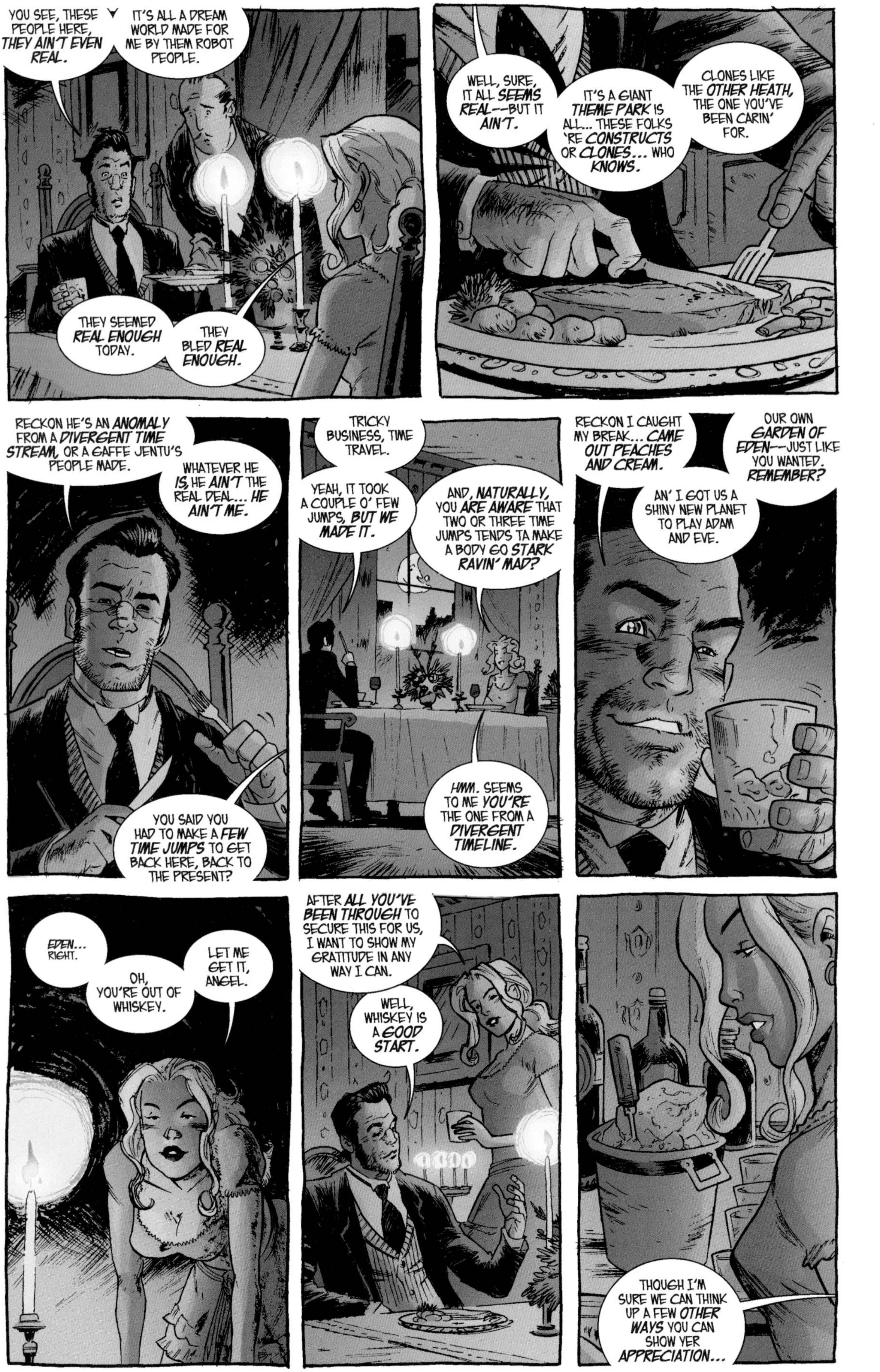
YOU SEE, THESE PEOPLE HERE, THEY AIN'T EVEN REAL.
IT'S ALL A DREAM WORLD MADE FOR ME BY THEM ROBOT PEOPLE.
THEY SEEMED REAL ENOUGH TODAY.
THEY BLED REAL ENOUGH.
WELL, SURE, IT ALL SEEMS REAL--BUT IT AIN'T.
IT'S A GIANT THEME PARK IS ALL... THESE FOLKS 'RE CONSTRUCTS OR CLONES... WHO KNOWS.
CLONES LIKE THE OTHER HEATH, THE ONE YOU'VE BEEN CARIN' FOR.
RECKON HE'S AN ANOMALY FROM A DIVERGENT TIME STREAM, OR A GAFFE JENTU'S PEOPLE MADE.
WHATEVER HE IS, HE AIN'T THE REAL DEAL... HE AIN'T ME.
YOU SAID YOU HAD TO MAKE A FEW TIME JUMPS TO GET BACK HERE, BACK TO THE PRESENT?
TRICKY BUSINESS, TIME TRAVEL.
YEAH, IT TOOK A COUPLE O' FEW JUMPS, BUT WE MADE IT.
AND, NATURALLY, YOU ARE AWARE THAT TWO OR THREE TIME JUMPS TENDS TA MAKE A BODY GO STARK RAVIN' MAD?
HMM. SEEMS TO ME YOU'RE THE ONE FROM A DIVERGENT TIMELINE.
RECKON I CAUGHT MY BREAK... CAME OUT PEACHES AND CREAM.
AN' I GOT US A SHINY NEW PLANET TO PLAY ADAM AND EVE.
OUR OWN GARDEN OF EDEN--JUST LIKE YOU WANTED. REMEMBER?
EDEN... RIGHT.
OH, YOU'RE OUT OF WHISKEY.
LET ME GET IT, ANGEL.
AFTER ALL YOU'VE BEEN THROUGH TO SECURE THIS FOR US, I WANT TO SHOW MY GRATITUDE IN ANY WAY I CAN.
WELL, WHISKEY IS A GOOD START.
THOUGH I'M SURE WE CAN THINK UP A FEW OTHER WAYS YOU CAN SHOW YER APPRECIATION...

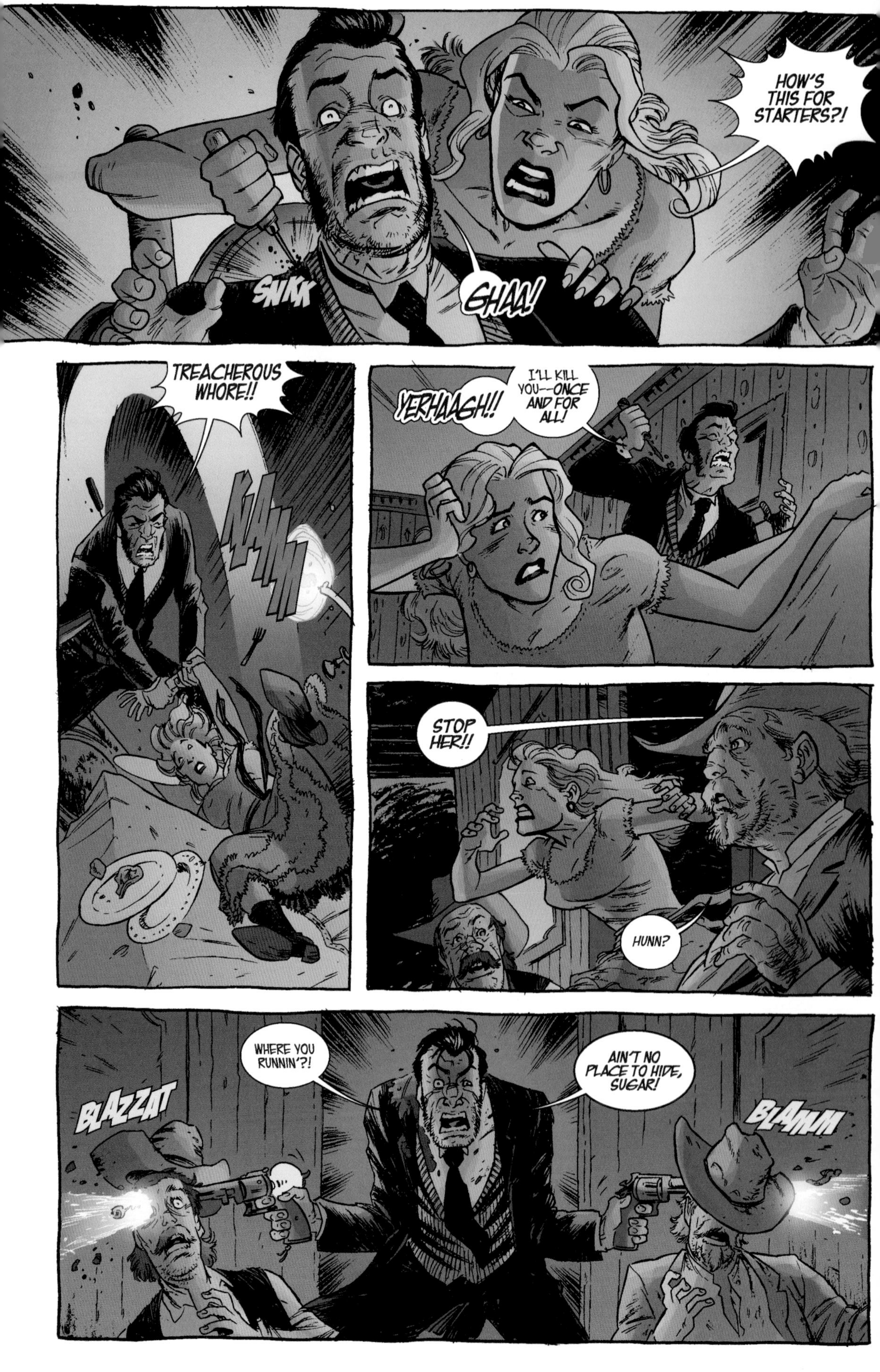
HOW'S THIS FOR STARTERS?!
SNIKK
GHAA!
TREACHEROUS WHORE!!
KLANNN
YERHAAGH!!
I'LL KILL YOU--ONCE AND FOR ALL!
STOP HER!!
HUNN?
WHERE YOU RUNNIN'?!
AIN'T NO PLACE TO HIDE, SUGAR!
BLAZZAT
BLAMM

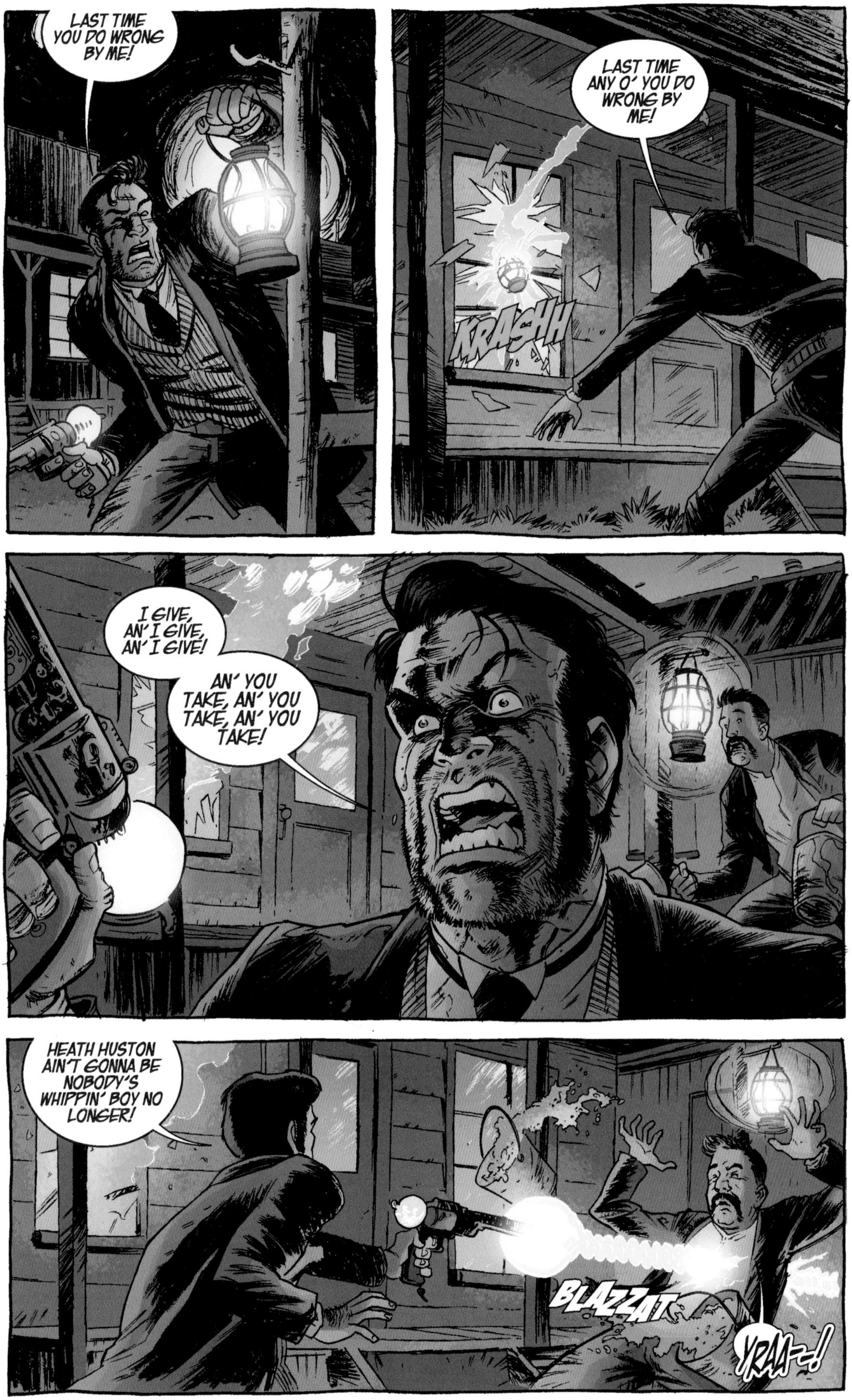
LAST TIME YOU DO WRONG BY ME!
LAST TIME ANY O' YOU DO WRONG BY ME!
KRASHH
I GIVE, AN' I GIVE, AN' I GIVE!
AN' YOU TAKE, AN' YOU TAKE, AN' YOU TAKE!
HEATH HUSTON AIN'T GONNA BE NOBODY'S WHIPPIN' BOY NO LONGER!
BLAZZAT
YRAA--!

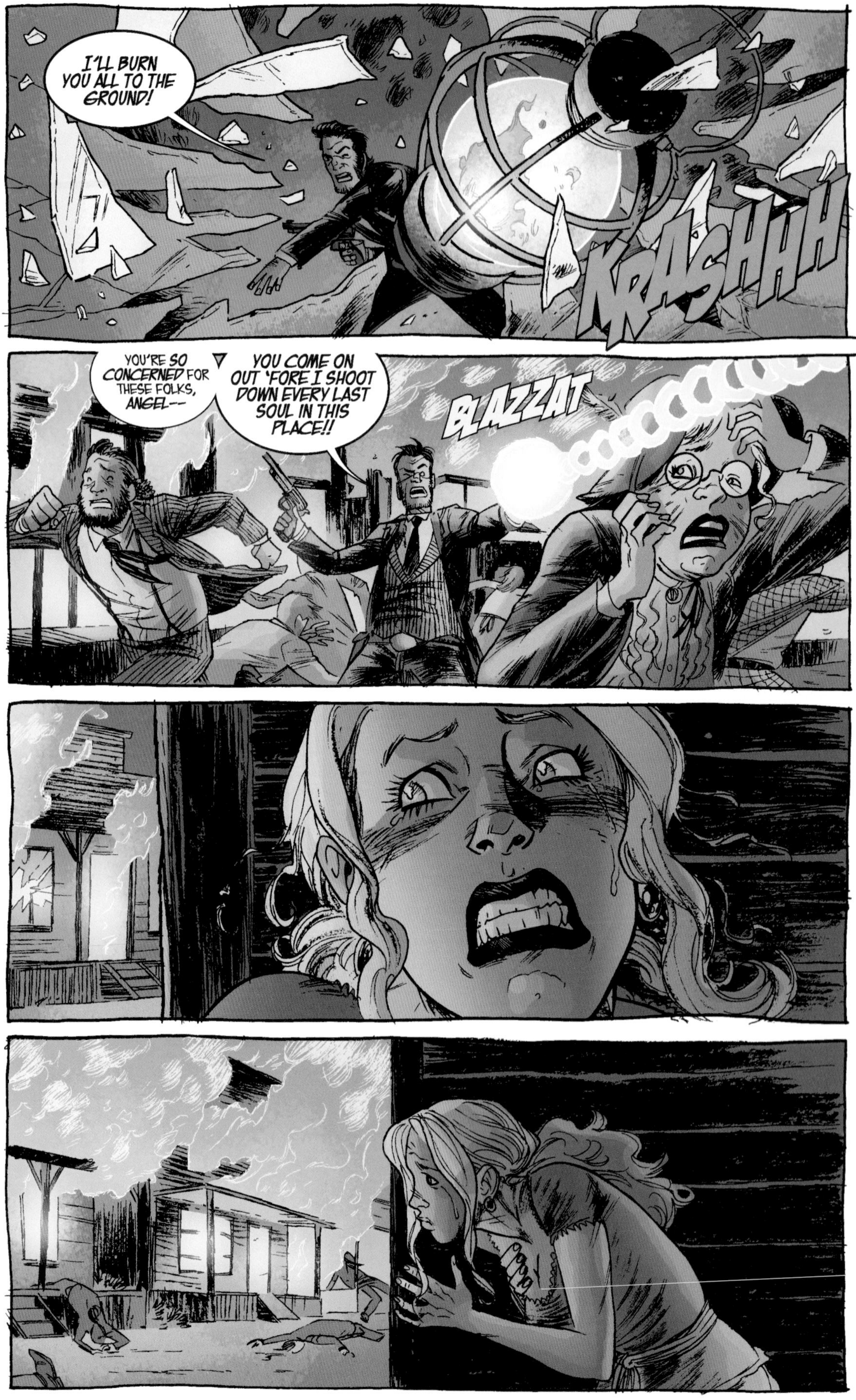
I'LL BURN YOU ALL TO THE GROUND!
KRASHHH
YOU'RE SO CONCERNED FOR THESE FOLKS, ANGEL--
YOU COME ON OUT 'FORE I SHOOT DOWN EVERY LAST SOUL IN THIS PLACE!!
BLAZZAT

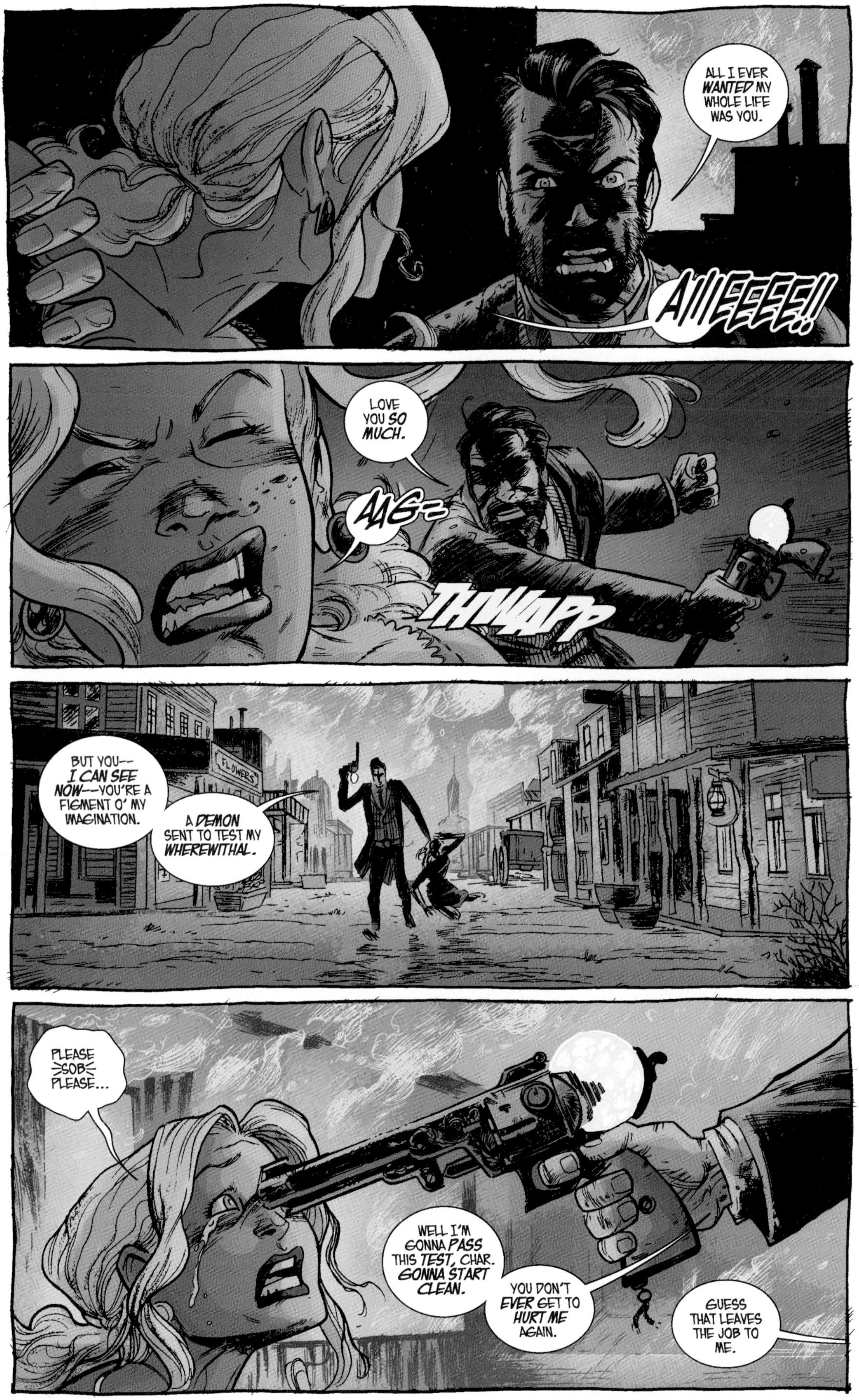
ALL I EVER WANTED MY WHOLE LIFE WAS YOU.
AIIEEEE!!
LOVE YOU SO MUCH.
AAG--
THWAPP
BUT YOU-- I CAN SEE NOW--YOU'RE A FIGMENT O' MY IMAGINATION.
A DEMON SENT TO TEST MY WHEREWITHAL.
FLOWERS
PLEASE =SOB= PLEASE...
WELL I'M GONNA PASS THIS TEST, CHAR. GONNA START CLEAN.
YOU DON'T EVER GET TO HURT ME AGAIN.
GUESS THAT LEAVES THE JOB TO ME.

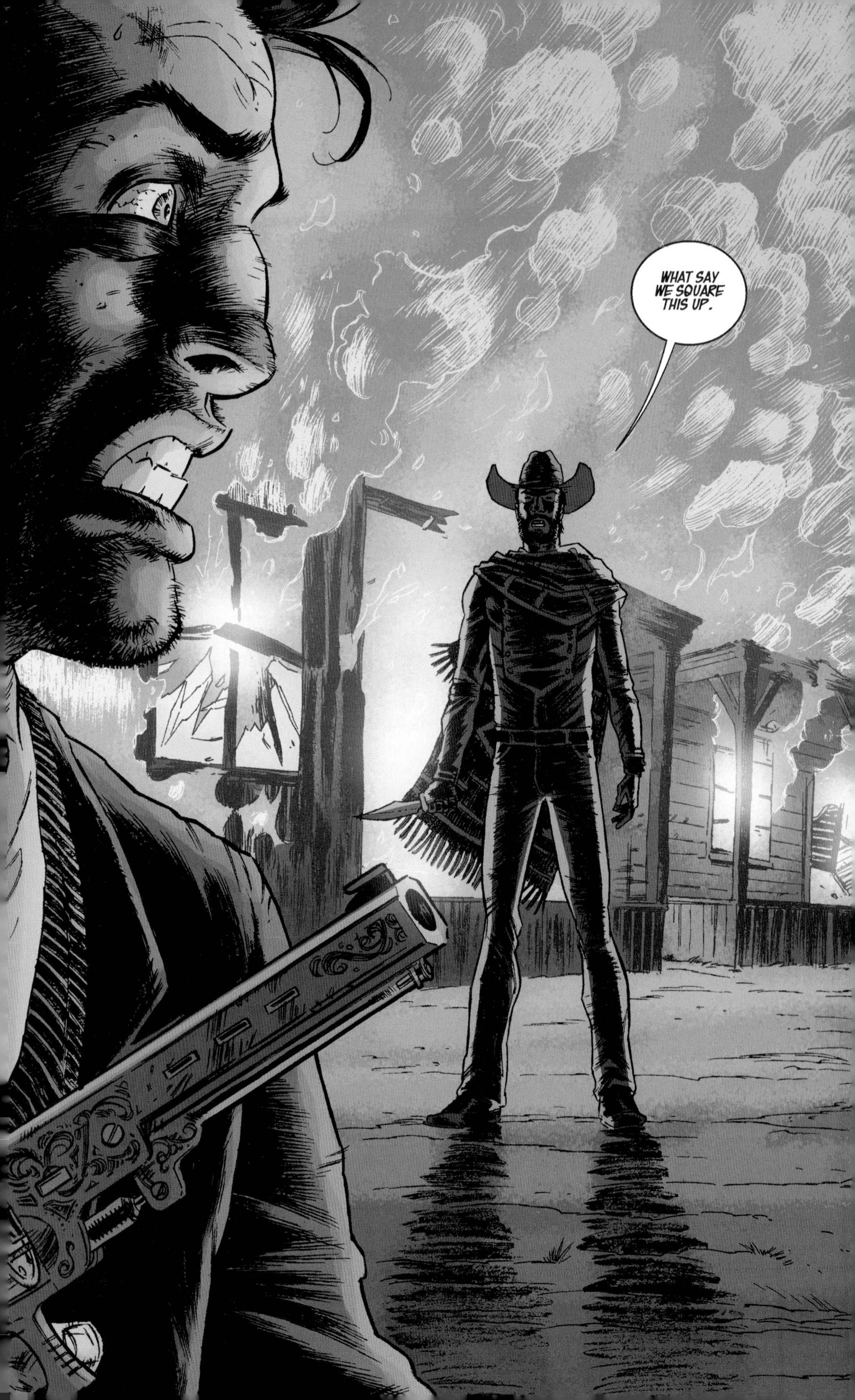
WHAT SAY WE SQUARE THIS UP.

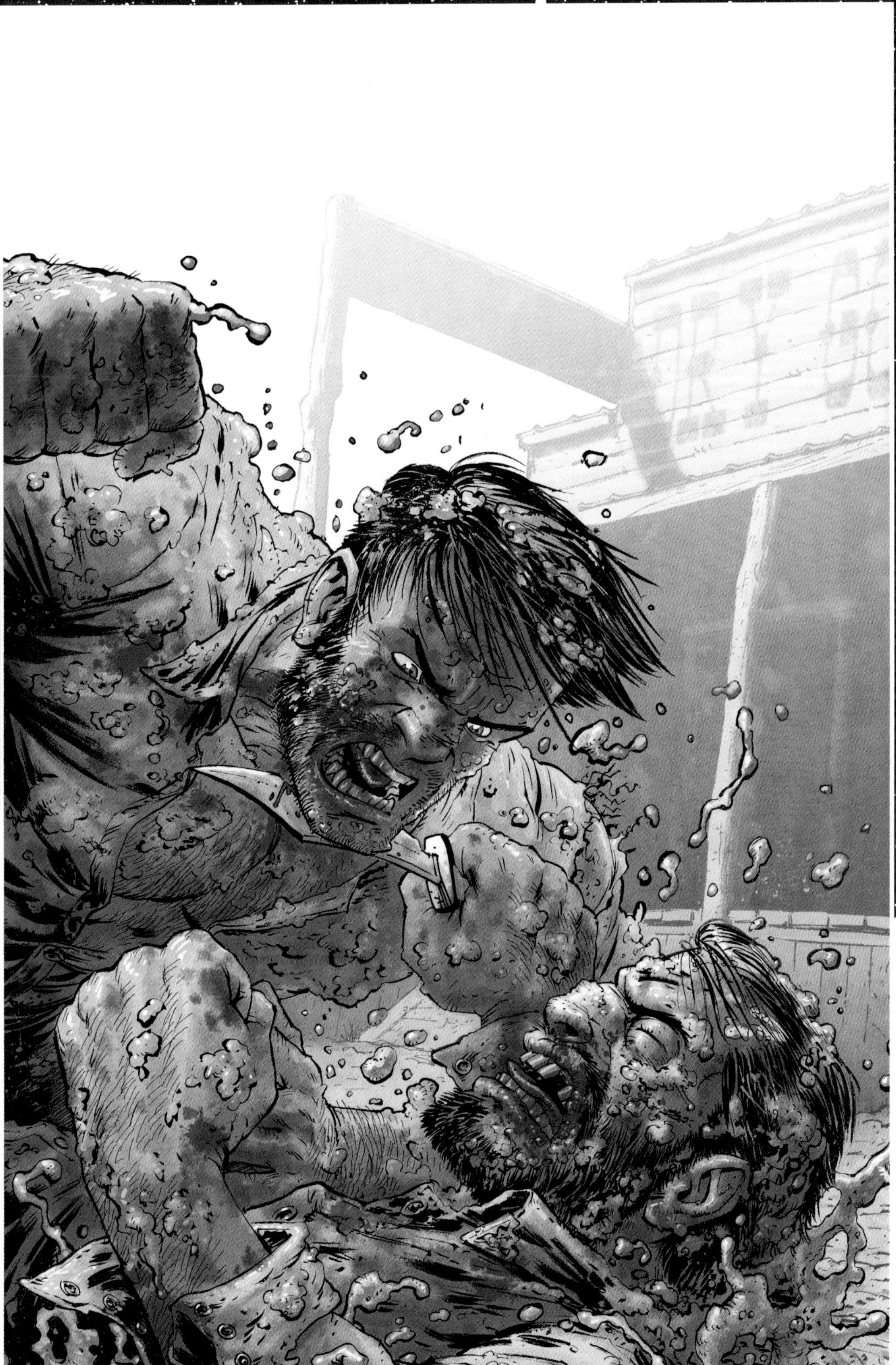

FEAR AGENT #26
ART BY **TONY MOORE**

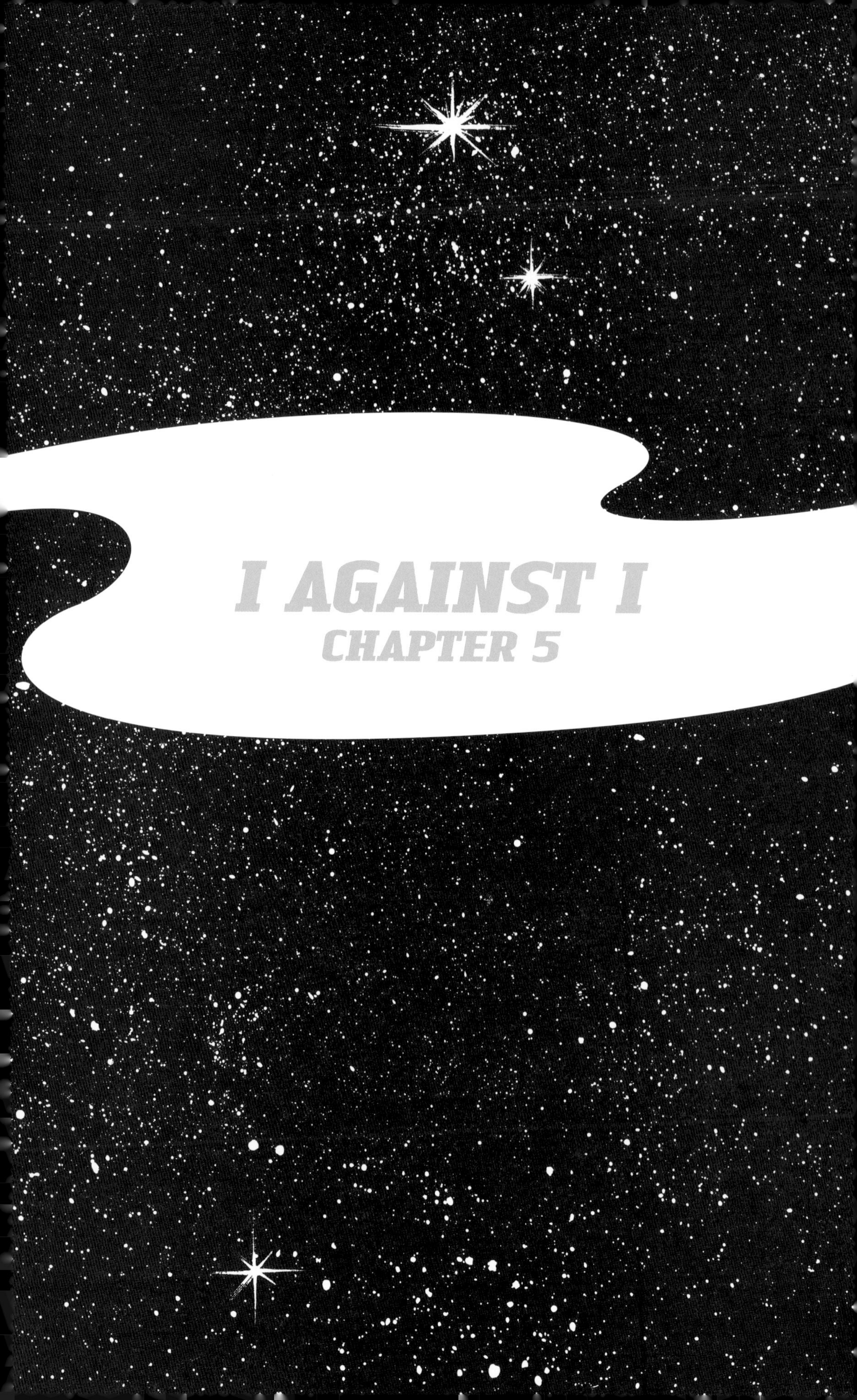

I AGAINST I

CHAPTER 5

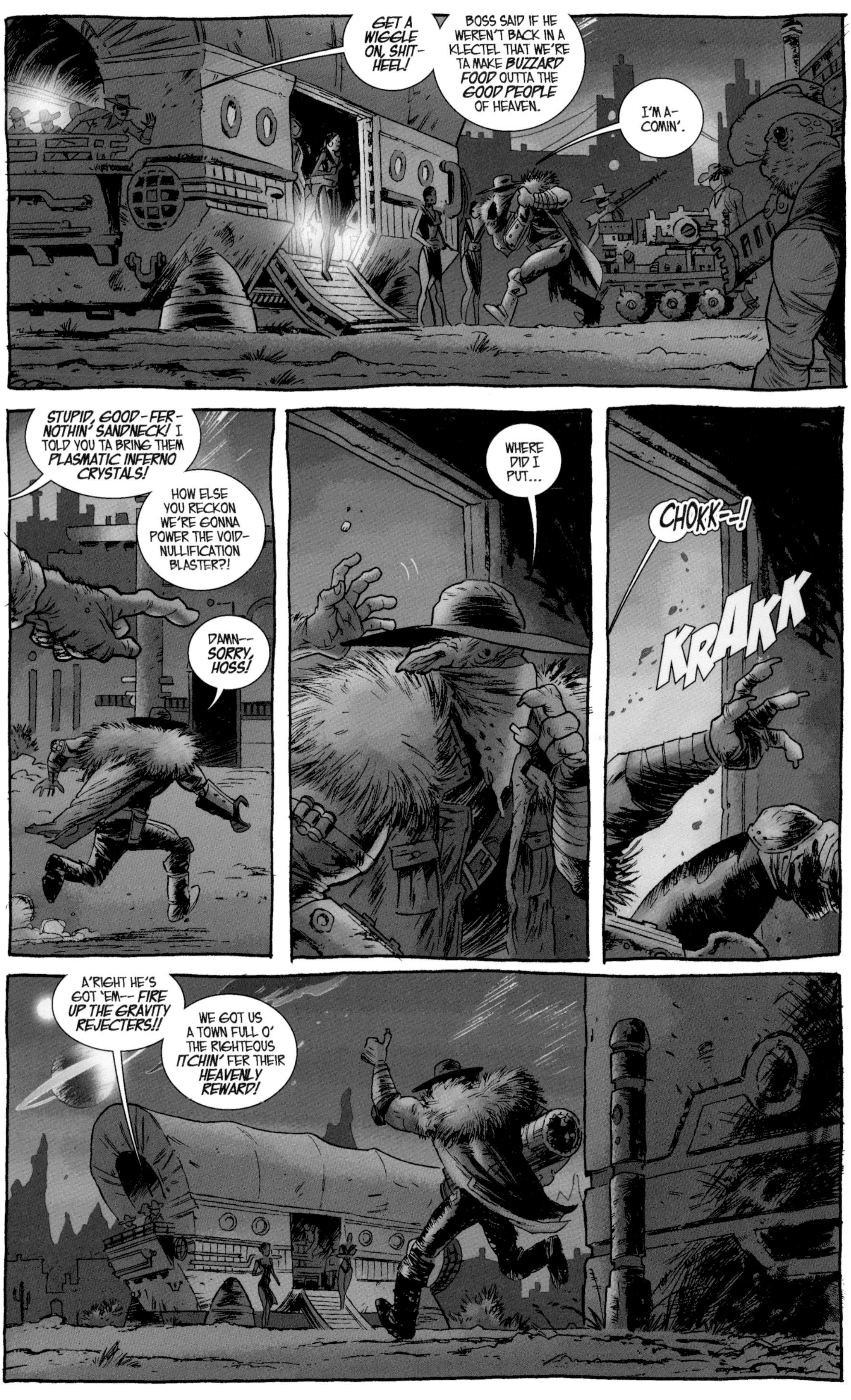
GET A WIGGLE ON, SHIT-HEEL!
BOSS SAID IF HE WEREN'T BACK IN A KLECTEL THAT WE'RE TA MAKE BUZZARD FOOD OUTTA THE GOOD PEOPLE OF HEAVEN.
I'M A-COMIN'.
STUPID, GOOD-FER-NOTHIN' SANDNECK! I TOLD YOU TA BRING THEM PLASMATIC INFERNO CRYSTALS!
HOW ELSE YOU RECKON WE'RE GONNA POWER THE VOID-NULLIFICATION BLASTER?!
DAMN-- SORRY, HOSS!
WHERE DID I PUT...
CHOKK--!
KRAKK
A'RIGHT HE'S GOT 'EM-- FIRE UP THE GRAVITY REJECTERS!!
WE GOT US A TOWN FULL O' THE RIGHTEOUS ITCHIN' FER THEIR HEAVENLY REWARD!

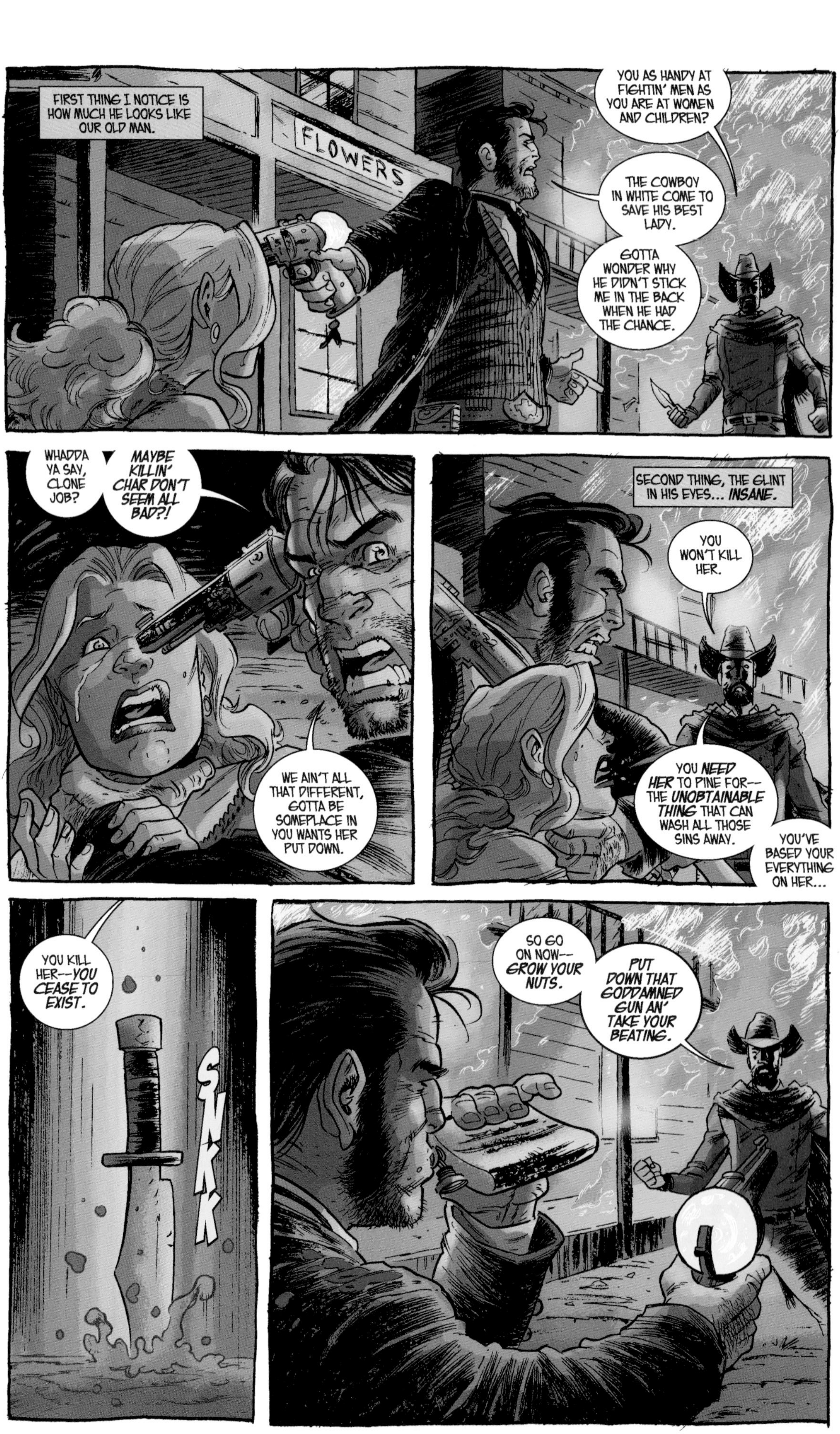
FIRST THING I NOTICE IS HOW MUCH HE LOOKS LIKE OUR OLD MAN.
FLOWERS
YOU AS HANDY AT FIGHTIN' MEN AS YOU ARE AT WOMEN AND CHILDREN?
THE COWBOY IN WHITE COME TO SAVE HIS BEST LADY.
GOTTA WONDER WHY HE DIDN'T STICK ME IN THE BACK WHEN HE HAD THE CHANCE.
WHADDA YA SAY, CLONE JOB?
MAYBE KILLIN' CHAR DON'T SEEM ALL BAD?!
WE AIN'T ALL THAT DIFFERENT, GOTTA BE SOMEPLACE IN YOU WANTS HER PUT DOWN.
SECOND THING, THE GLINT IN HIS EYES... INSANE.
YOU WON'T KILL HER.
YOU NEED HER TO PINE FOR-- THE UNOBTAINABLE THING THAT CAN WASH ALL THOSE SINS AWAY.
YOU'VE BASED YOUR EVERYTHING ON HER...
YOU KILL HER--YOU CEASE TO EXIST.
SNKK
SO GO ON NOW-- GROW YOUR NUTS.
PUT DOWN THAT GODDAMNED GUN AN' TAKE YOUR BEATING.

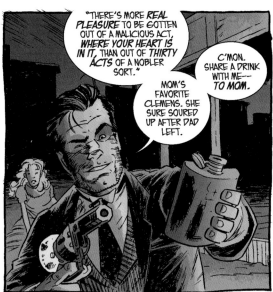

"THERE'S MORE *REAL PLEASURE* TO BE GOTTEN OUT OF A MALICIOUS ACT, *WHERE YOUR HEART IS IN IT,* THAN OUT OF *THIRTY ACTS OF A NOBLER SORT.*"

MOM'S FAVORITE *CLEMENS.* SHE SURE SOURED UP AFTER DAD LEFT.

C'MON. SHARE A DRINK WITH ME--- *TO MOM.*

I QUIT.

BULLSHIT.

YOU JUST *MOMENTARILY PAUSED.*

AN' BY THE *LOOKS O' YOU* I'D SAY YER *FEELIN'* IT.

TAKE A HIT.

MIGHT BE YER LAST.

ALREADY HAD MY LAST.

YOU WILL DRINK THIS *GODDAMNED* WHISKEY WITH ME!!

BLAZAT!

SEE, CHAR, HE AIN'T *HEATH HUSTON.*

HEATH HUSTON HAD TO COMMIT GENOCIDE TO FREE EARTH---*AN'* HE HASN'T BEEN SOBER ONE DAY SINCE.

I'VE BEEN SOBER FOR *TWO.*

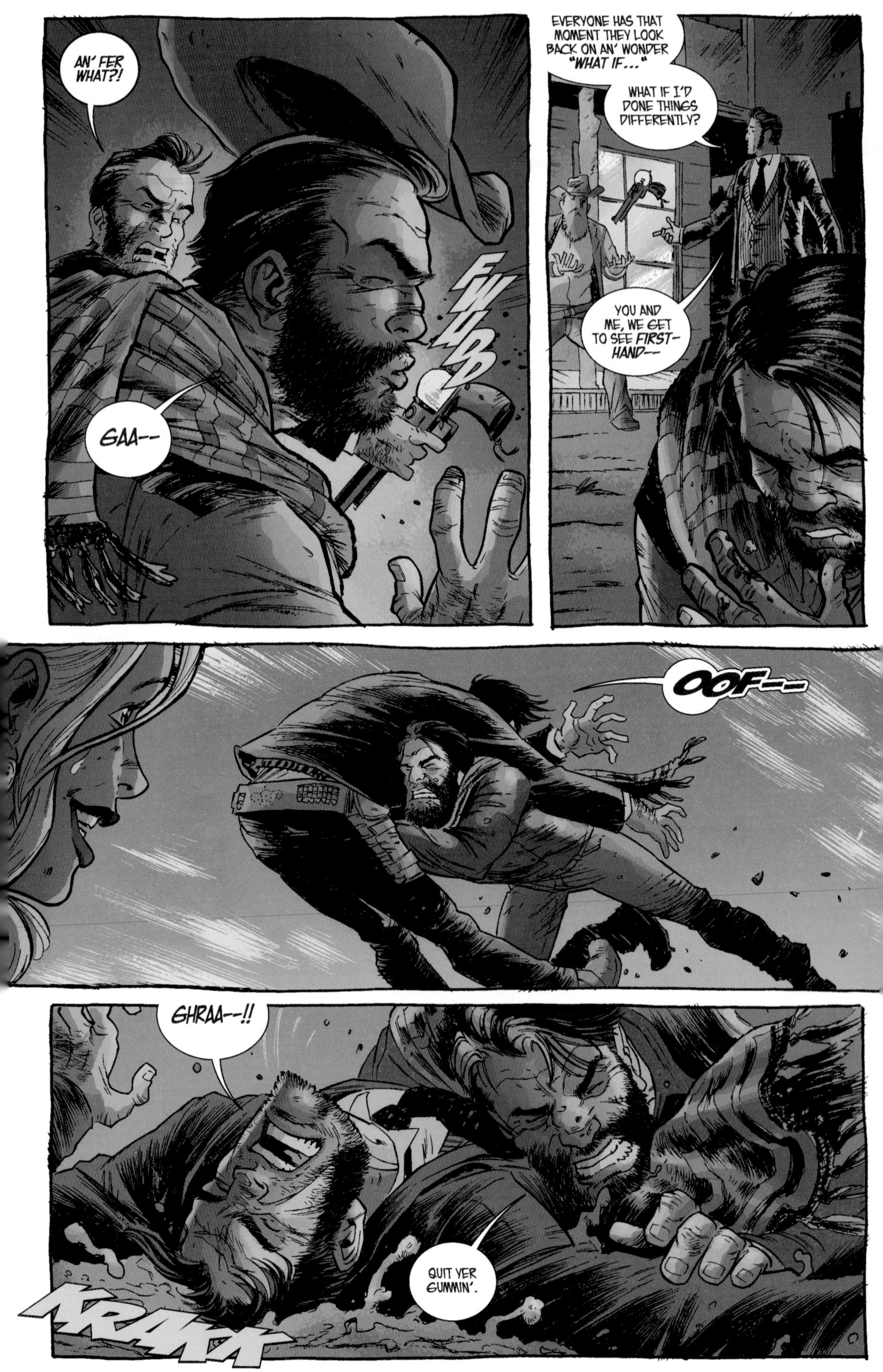
AN' FER WHAT?!
FWUDD
GAA--
EVERYONE HAS THAT MOMENT THEY LOOK BACK ON AN' WONDER "WHAT IF..."
WHAT IF I'D DONE THINGS DIFFERENTLY?
YOU AND ME, WE GET TO SEE FIRST-HAND--
OOF--
GHRAA--!!
QUIT YER GUMMIN'.
KRAKK

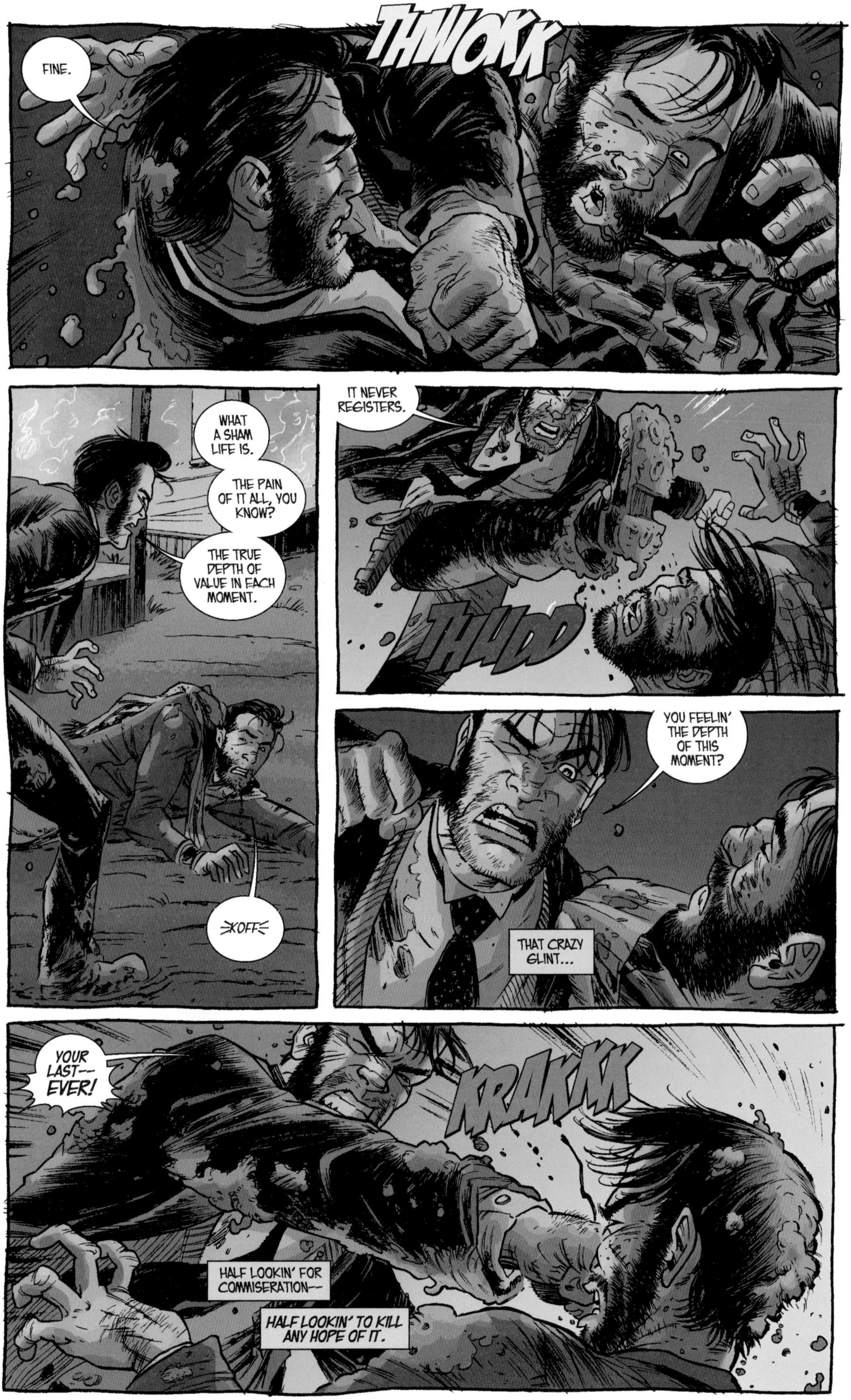
THWOKK
FINE.
WHAT A SHAM LIFE IS.
THE PAIN OF IT ALL, YOU KNOW?
THE TRUE DEPTH OF VALUE IN EACH MOMENT.
KOFF
IT NEVER REGISTERS.
THUDD
YOU FEELIN' THE DEPTH OF THIS MOMENT?
THAT CRAZY GLINT...
YOUR LAST-- EVER!
KRAKKK
HALF LOOKIN' FOR COMMISERATION--
HALF LOOKIN' TO KILL ANY HOPE OF IT.

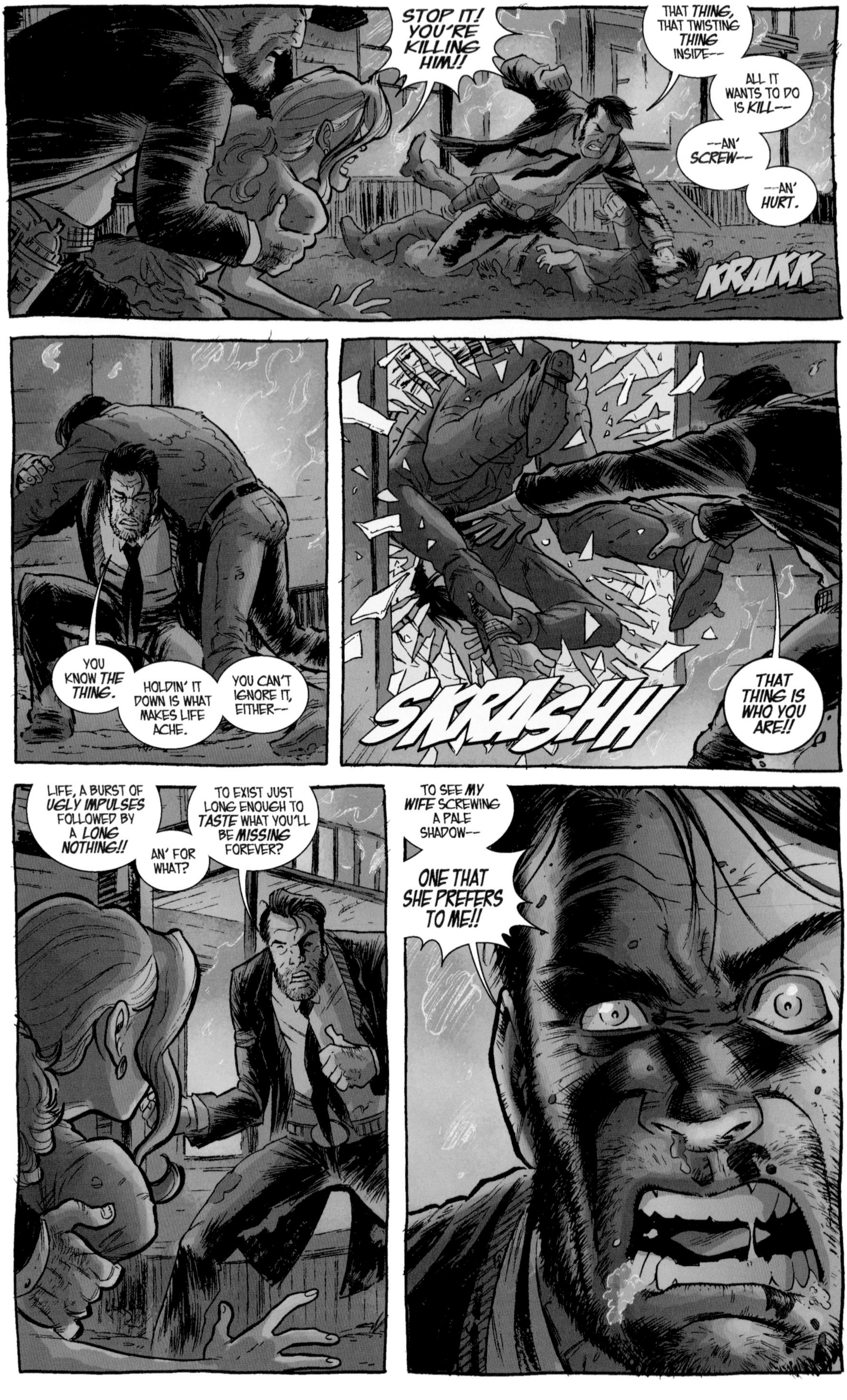

STOP IT! YOU'RE KILLING HIM!!
THAT THING, THAT TWISTING THING INSIDE--
ALL IT WANTS TO DO IS KILL--
--AN' SCREW--
--AN' HURT.
KRAKK
YOU KNOW THE THING.
HOLDIN' IT DOWN IS WHAT MAKES LIFE ACHE.
YOU CAN'T IGNORE IT, EITHER--
SKRASHH
THAT THING IS WHO YOU ARE!!
LIFE, A BURST OF UGLY IMPULSES FOLLOWED BY A LONG NOTHING!!
AN' FOR WHAT?
TO EXIST JUST LONG ENOUGH TO TASTE WHAT YOU'LL BE MISSING FOREVER?
TO SEE MY WIFE SCREWING A PALE SHADOW--
ONE THAT SHE PREFERS TO ME!!

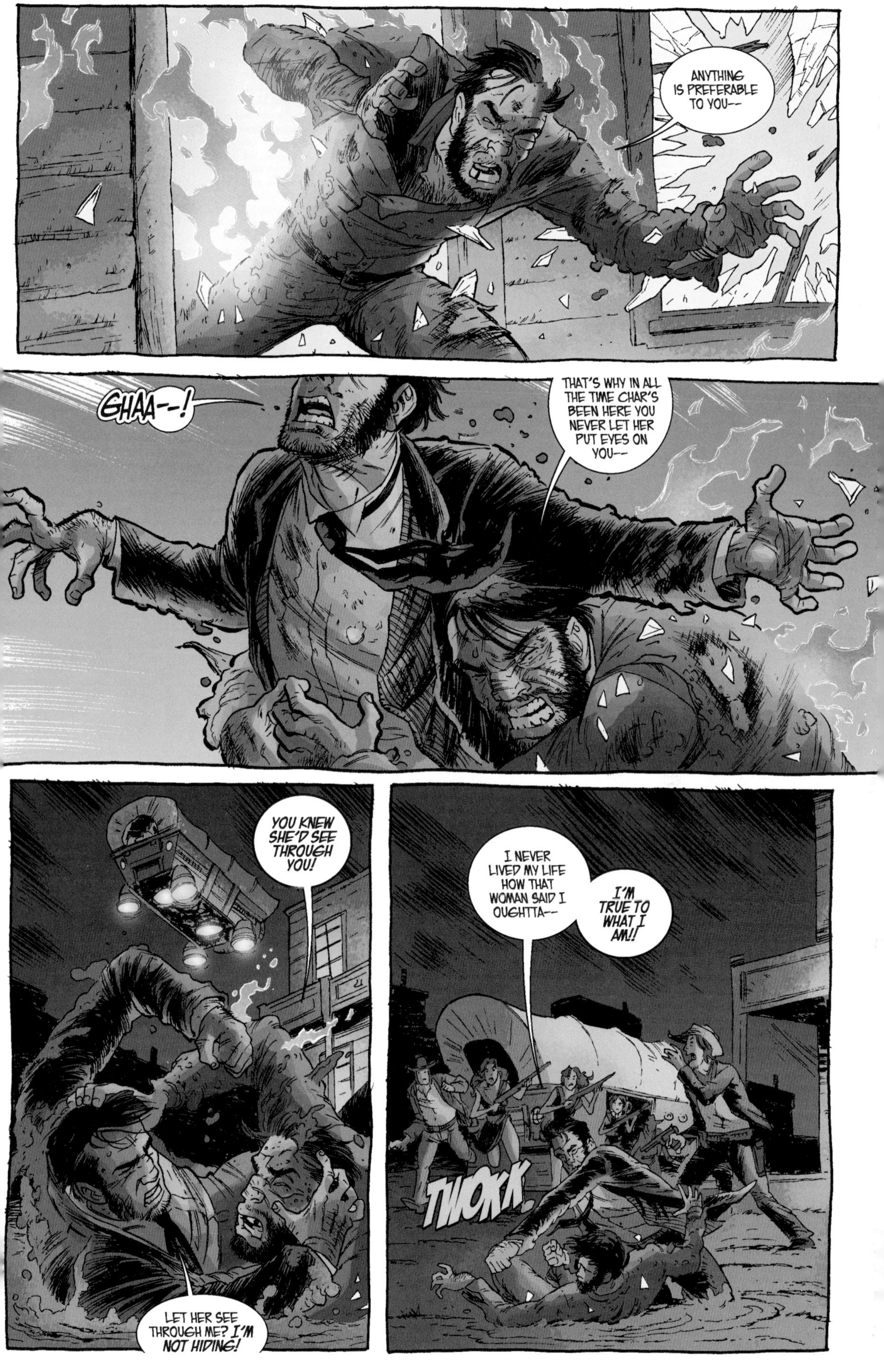
ANYTHING IS PREFERABLE TO YOU--
GHAA--!
THAT'S WHY IN ALL THE TIME CHAR'S BEEN HERE YOU NEVER LET HER PUT EYES ON YOU--
YOU KNEW SHE'D SEE THROUGH YOU!
LET HER SEE THROUGH ME? I'M NOT HIDING!
I NEVER LIVED MY LIFE HOW THAT WOMAN SAID I OUGHTTA--
I'M TRUE TO WHAT I AM!!
TWOKK

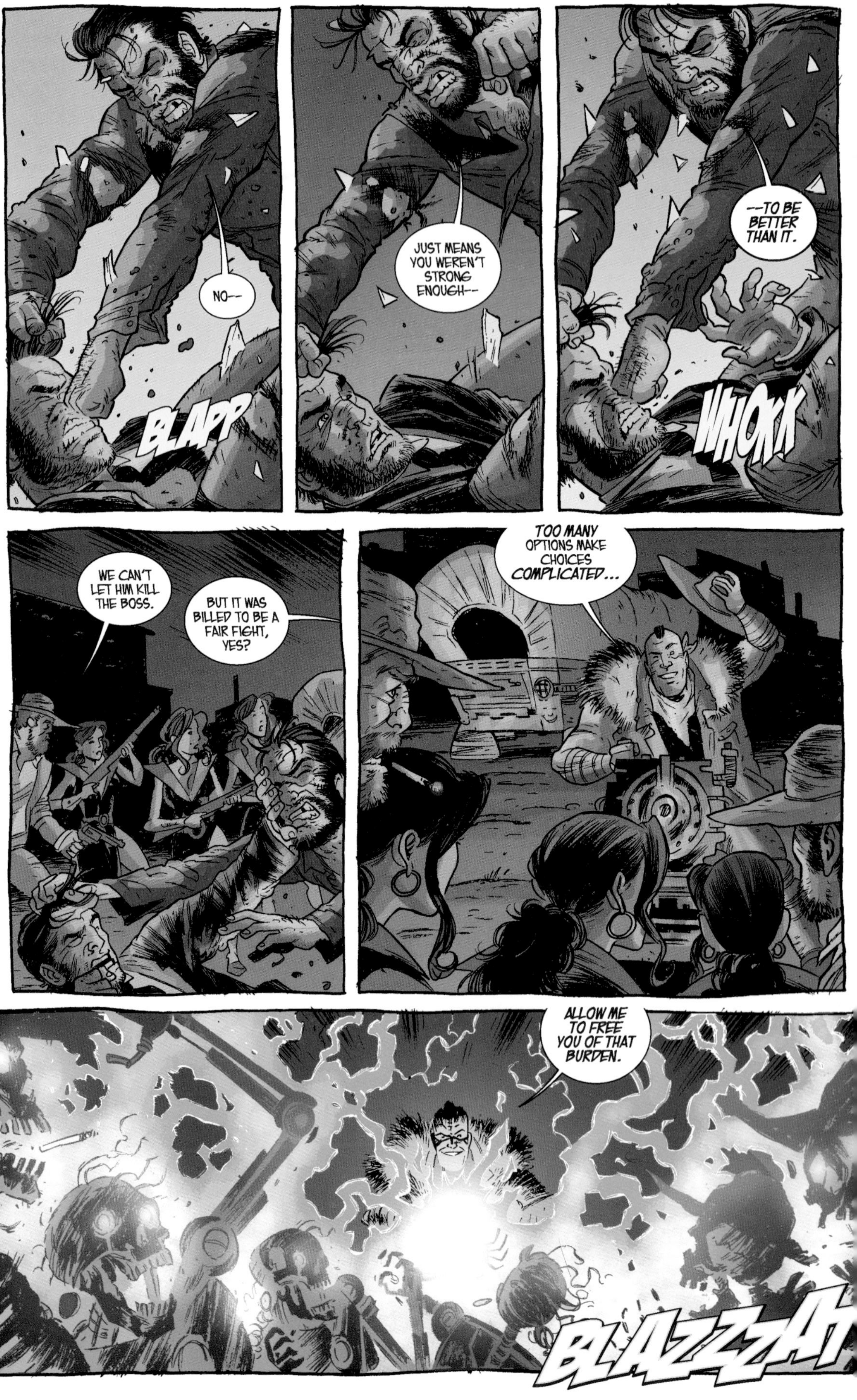
NO--
BLAPP
JUST MEANS YOU WEREN'T STRONG ENOUGH--
--TO BE BETTER THAN IT.
WHOKK
WE CAN'T LET HIM KILL THE BOSS.
BUT IT WAS BILLED TO BE A FAIR FIGHT, YES?
TOO MANY OPTIONS MAKE CHOICES COMPLICATED...
ALLOW ME TO FREE YOU OF THAT BURDEN.
BLAZZAT

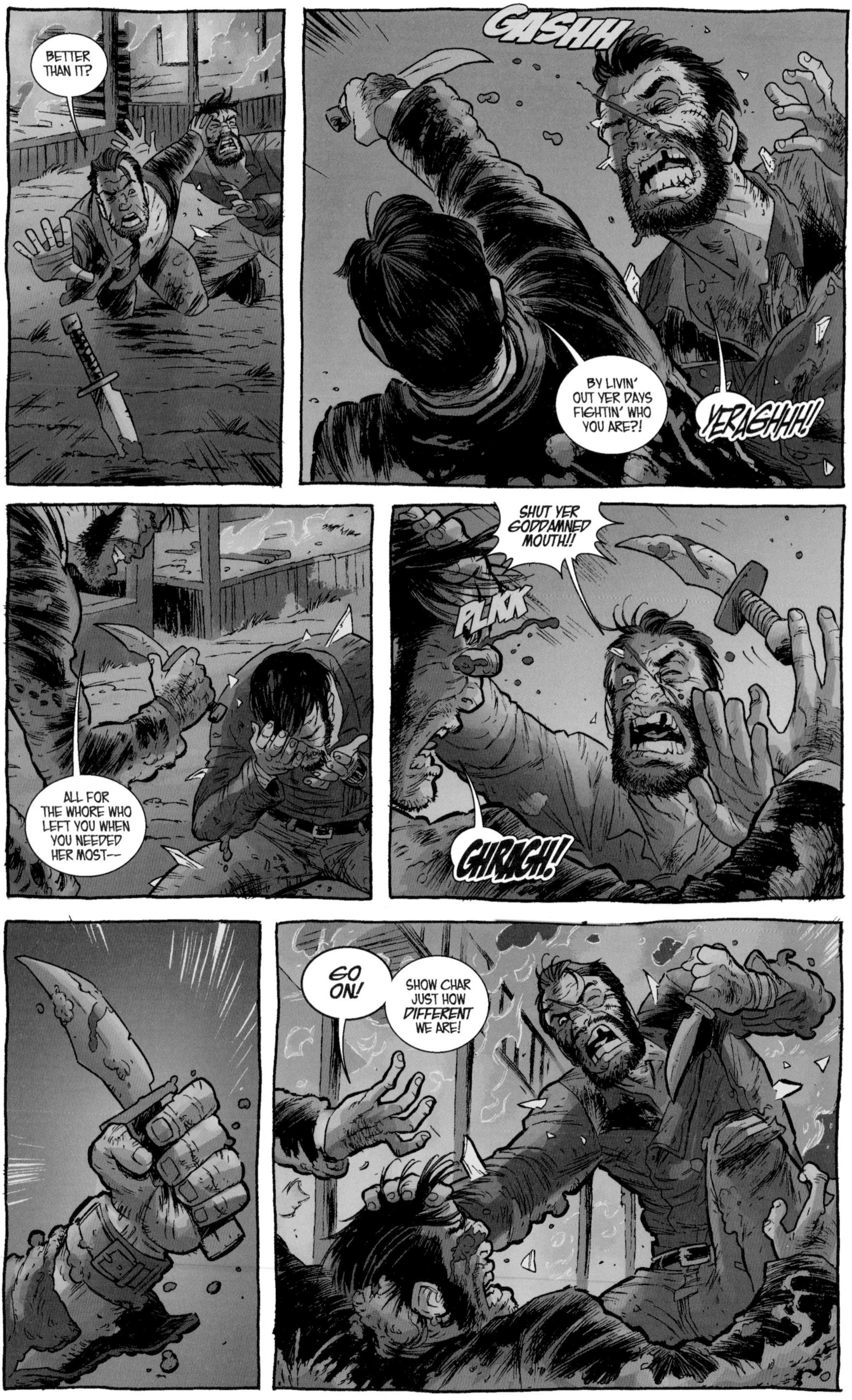
BETTER THAN IT?
GASHH
BY LIVIN' OUT YER DAYS FIGHTIN' WHO YOU ARE?!
YERAGHHH!
ALL FOR THE WHORE WHO LEFT YOU WHEN YOU NEEDED HER MOST--
SHUT YER GODDAMNED MOUTH!!
PLKK
GHRAGH!
GO ON!
SHOW CHAR JUST HOW DIFFERENT WE ARE!

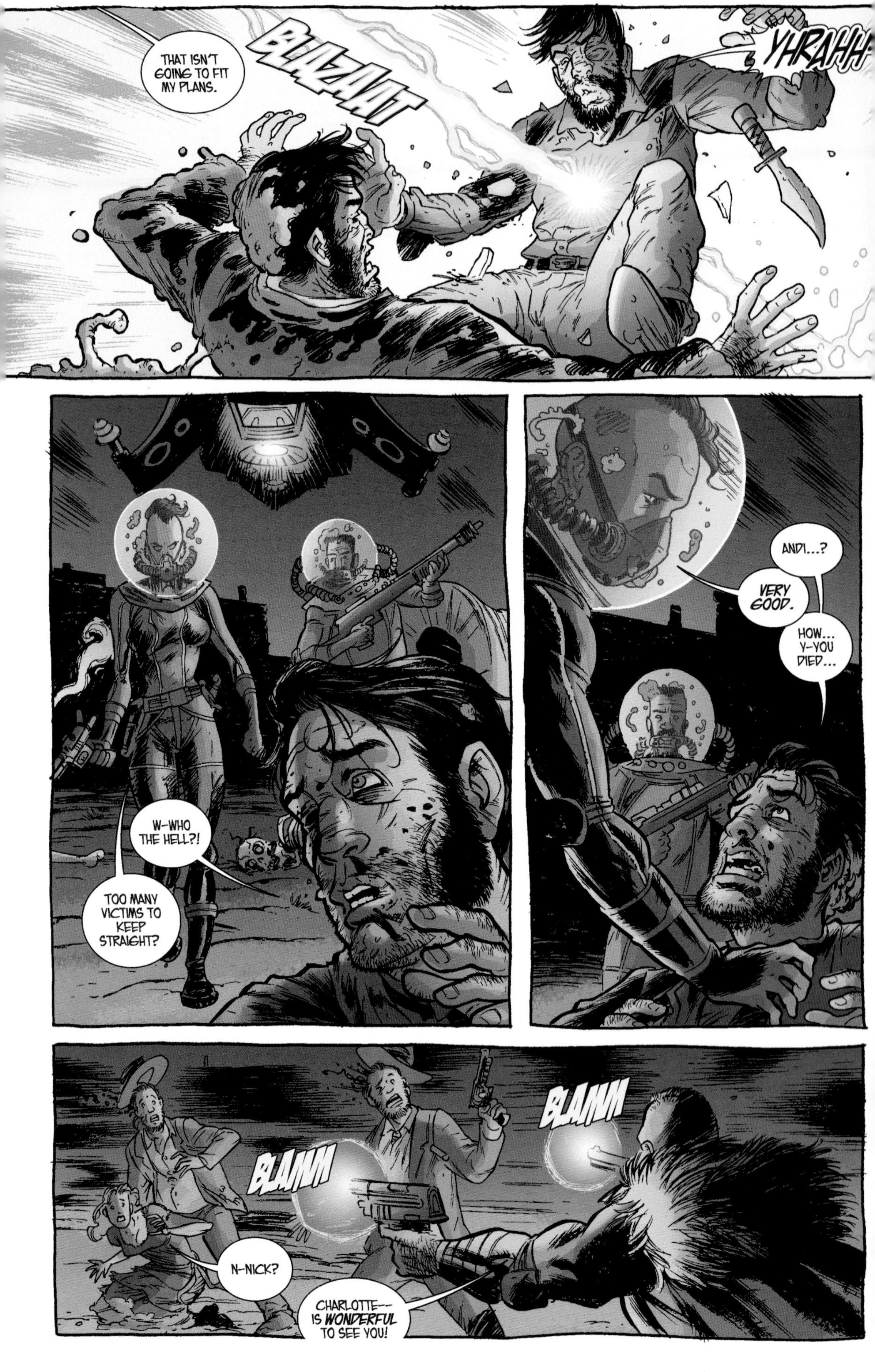
THAT ISN'T GOING TO FIT MY PLANS.
BLAZAAT
YHRAHH
W-WHO THE HELL?!
TOO MANY VICTIMS TO KEEP STRAIGHT?
ANDI...?
VERY GOOD.
HOW... Y-YOU DIED...
BLAMM
BLAMM
N-NICK?
CHARLOTTE-- IS WONDERFUL TO SEE YOU!

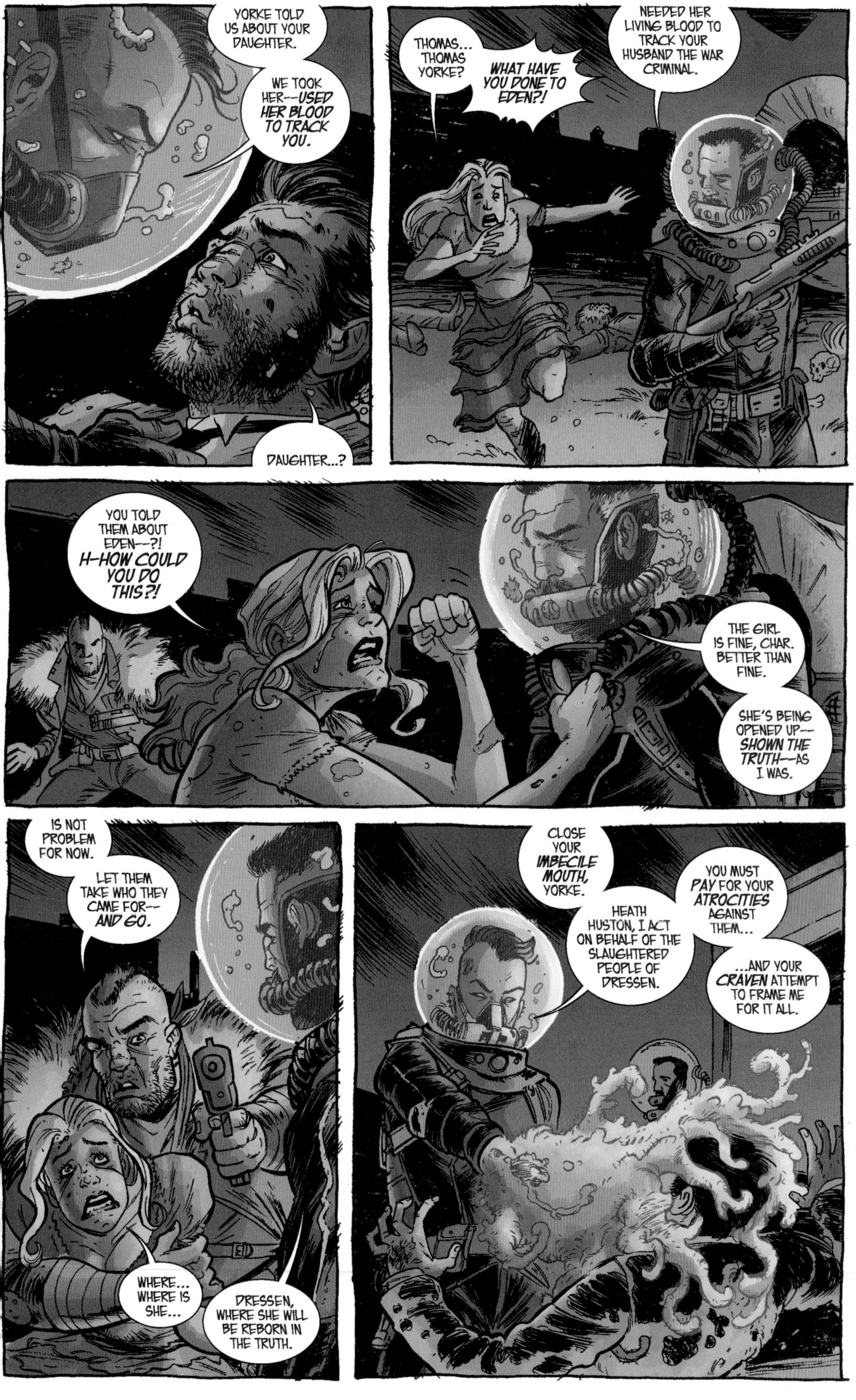
YORKE TOLD US ABOUT YOUR DAUGHTER.
WE TOOK HER--USED HER BLOOD TO TRACK YOU.
DAUGHTER...?
THOMAS... THOMAS YORKE?
WHAT HAVE YOU DONE TO EDEN?!
NEEDED HER LIVING BLOOD TO TRACK YOUR HUSBAND THE WAR CRIMINAL.
YOU TOLD THEM ABOUT EDEN--?! H-HOW COULD YOU DO THIS?!
THE GIRL IS FINE, CHAR. BETTER THAN FINE.
SHE'S BEING OPENED UP--SHOWN THE TRUTH--AS I WAS.
IS NOT PROBLEM FOR NOW.
LET THEM TAKE WHO THEY CAME FOR--AND GO.
WHERE... WHERE IS SHE...
DRESSEN, WHERE SHE WILL BE REBORN IN THE TRUTH.
CLOSE YOUR IMBECILE MOUTH, YORKE.
HEATH HUSTON, I ACT ON BEHALF OF THE SLAUGHTERED PEOPLE OF DRESSEN.
YOU MUST PAY FOR YOUR ATROCITIES AGAINST THEM...
...AND YOUR CRAVEN ATTEMPT TO FRAME ME FOR IT ALL.

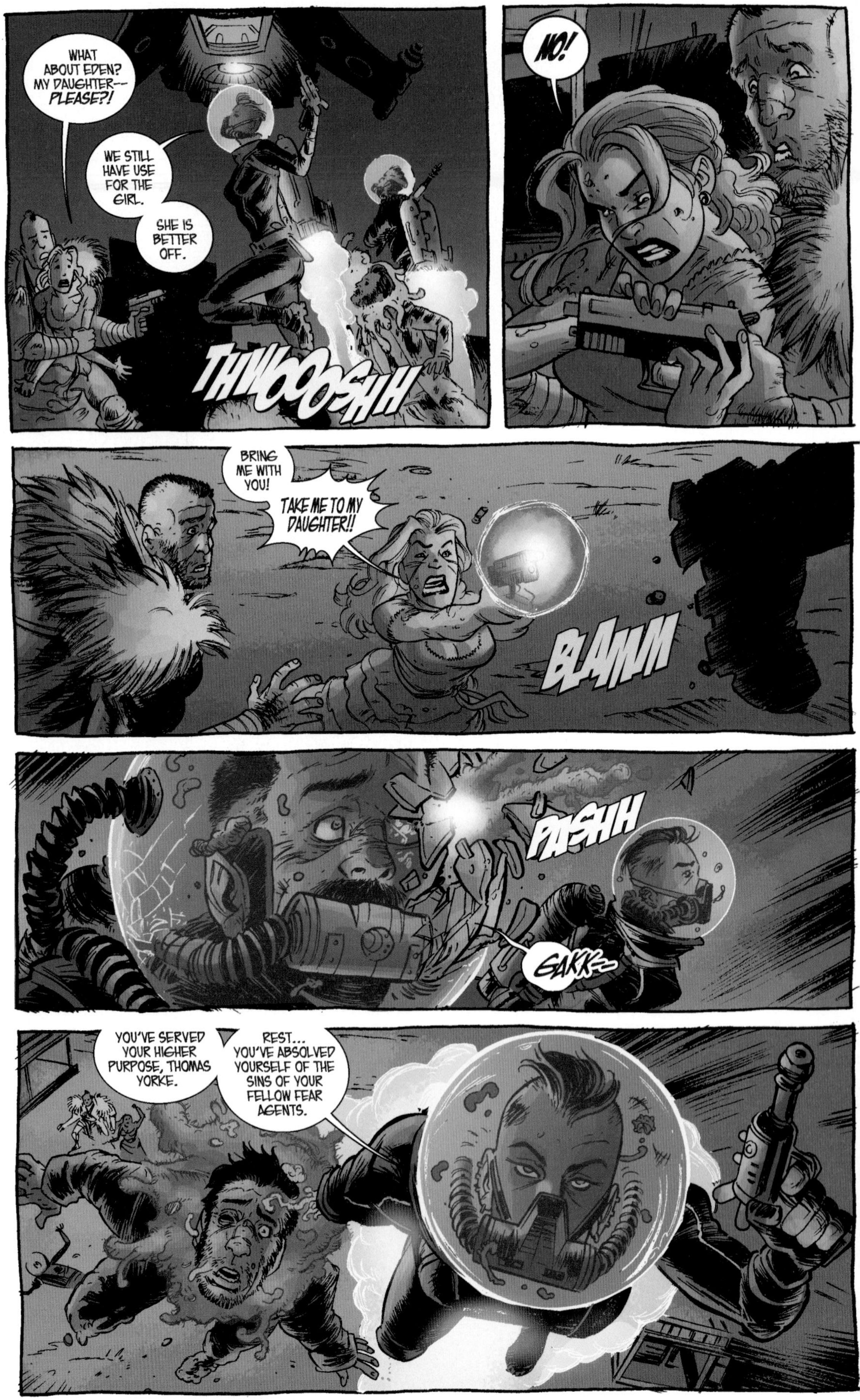
WHAT ABOUT EDEN? MY DAUGHTER-- PLEASE?!
WE STILL HAVE USE FOR THE GIRL.
SHE IS BETTER OFF.
THWOOOOSHH
NO!
BRING ME WITH YOU!
TAKE ME TO MY DAUGHTER!!
BLAMM
PASHH
GAKK--
YOU'VE SERVED YOUR HIGHER PURPOSE, THOMAS YORKE.
REST... YOU'VE ABSOLVED YOURSELF OF THE SINS OF YOUR FELLOW FEAR AGENTS.

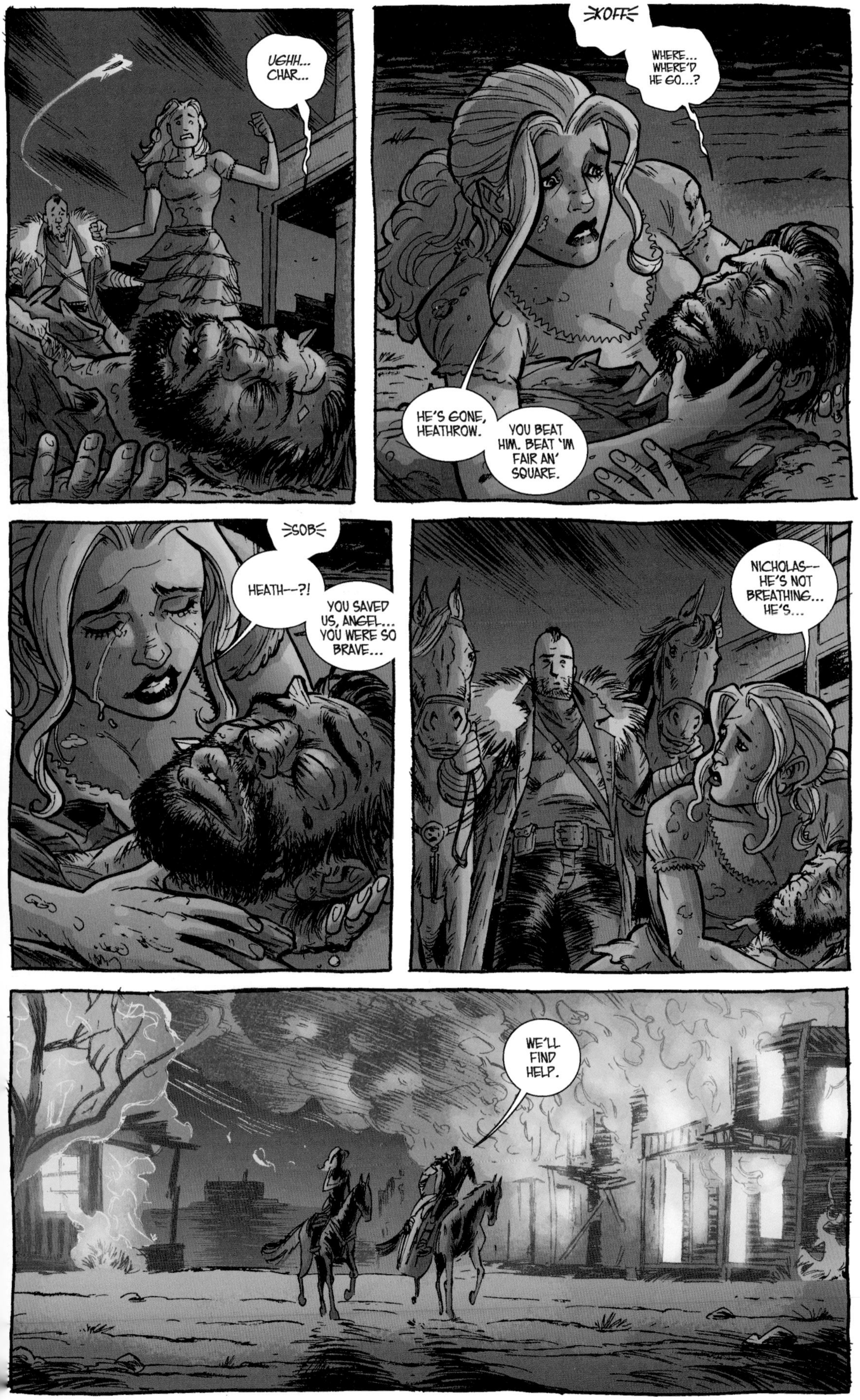
UGHH... CHAR...
≡KOFF≡
WHERE... WHERE'D HE GO...?
HE'S GONE, HEATHROW.
YOU BEAT HIM. BEAT 'IM FAIR AN' SQUARE.
≡SOB≡
HEATH--?!
YOU SAVED US, ANGEL... YOU WERE SO BRAVE...
NICHOLAS-- HE'S NOT BREATHING... HE'S...
WE'LL FIND HELP.

MONTHS PASS...

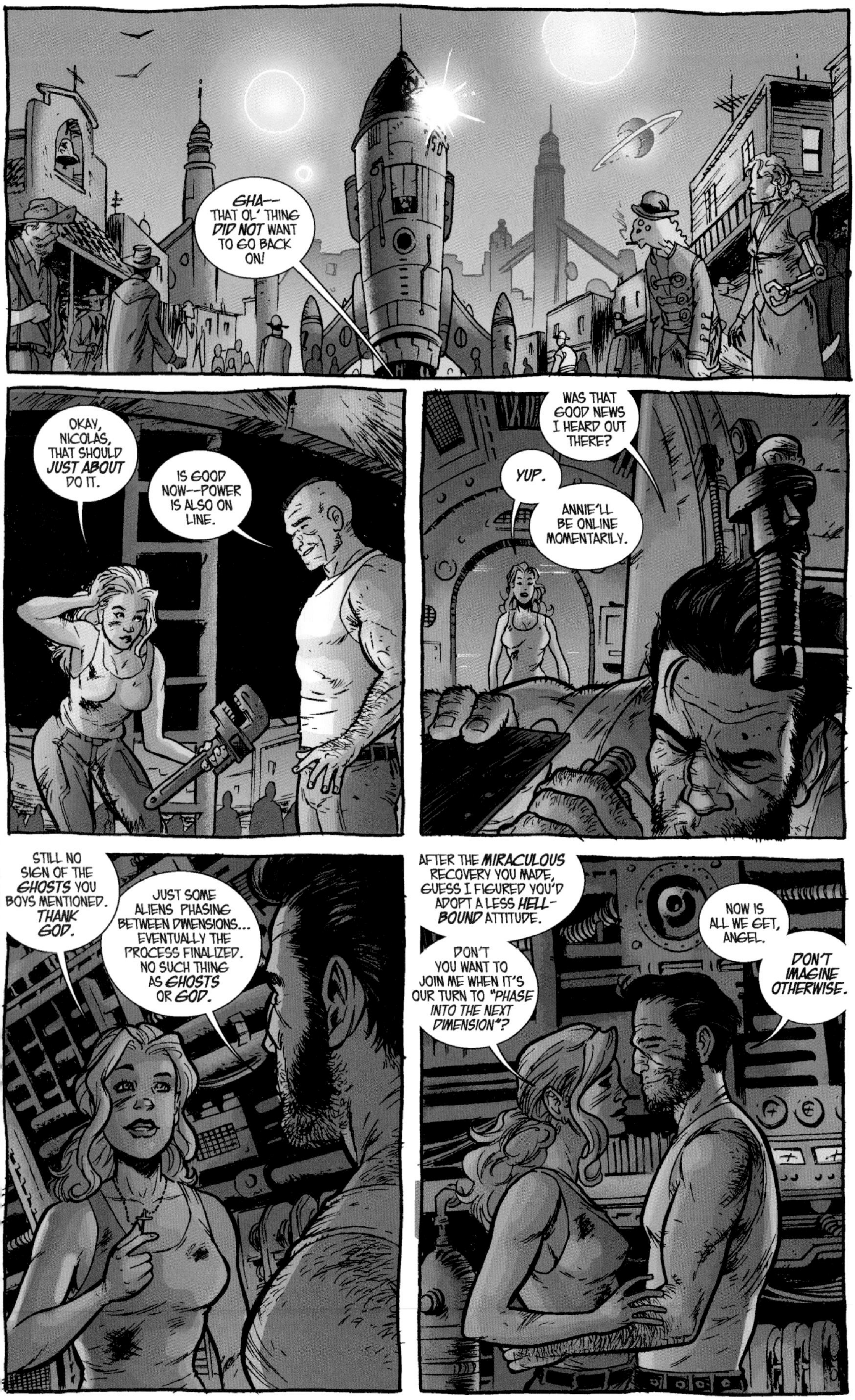
GHA-- THAT OL' THING DID NOT WANT TO GO BACK ON!
OKAY, NICOLAS, THAT SHOULD JUST ABOUT DO IT.
IS GOOD NOW--POWER IS ALSO ON LINE.
WAS THAT GOOD NEWS I HEARD OUT THERE?
YUP.
ANNIE'LL BE ONLINE MOMENTARILY.
STILL NO SIGN OF THE GHOSTS YOU BOYS MENTIONED. THANK GOD.
JUST SOME ALIENS PHASING BETWEEN DIMENSIONS... EVENTUALLY THE PROCESS FINALIZED. NO SUCH THING AS GHOSTS OR GOD.
AFTER THE MIRACULOUS RECOVERY YOU MADE, GUESS I FIGURED YOU'D ADOPT A LESS HELL-BOUND ATTITUDE.
DON'T YOU WANT TO JOIN ME WHEN IT'S OUR TURN TO "PHASE INTO THE NEXT DIMENSION"?
NOW IS ALL WE GET, ANGEL.
DON'T IMAGINE OTHERWISE.

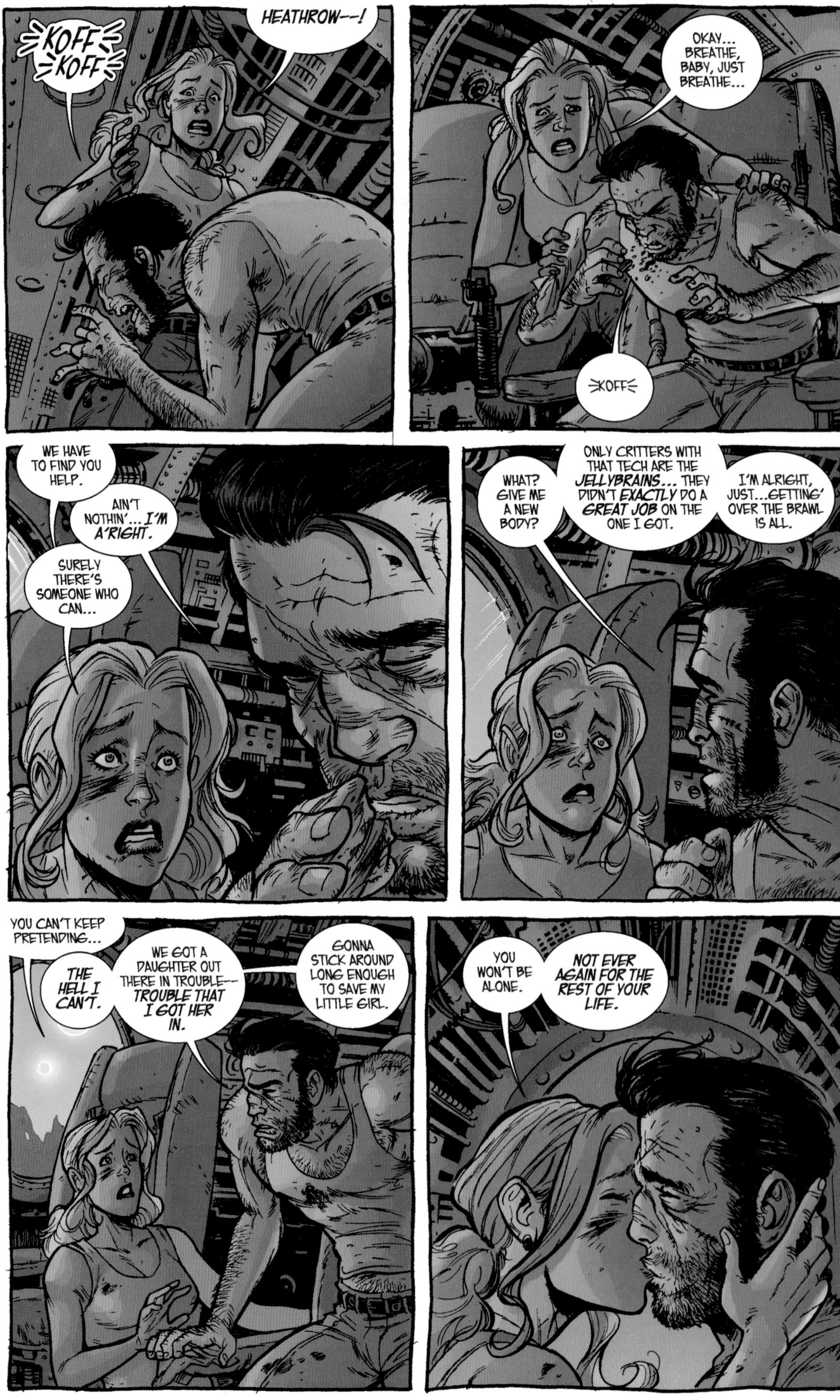
KOFF KOFF
HEATHROW--!
OKAY... BREATHE, BABY, JUST BREATHE...
KOFF
WE HAVE TO FIND YOU HELP.
AIN'T NOTHIN'... I'M A'RIGHT.
SURELY THERE'S SOMEONE WHO CAN...
WHAT? GIVE ME A NEW BODY?
ONLY CRITTERS WITH THAT TECH ARE THE JELLYBRAINS... THEY DIDN'T EXACTLY DO A GREAT JOB ON THE ONE I GOT.
I'M ALRIGHT, JUST...GETTING' OVER THE BRAWL IS ALL.
YOU CAN'T KEEP PRETENDING...
THE HELL I CAN'T.
WE GOT A DAUGHTER OUT THERE IN TROUBLE-- TROUBLE THAT I GOT HER IN.
GONNA STICK AROUND LONG ENOUGH TO SAVE MY LITTLE GIRL.
YOU WON'T BE ALONE.
NOT EVER AGAIN FOR THE REST OF YOUR LIFE.

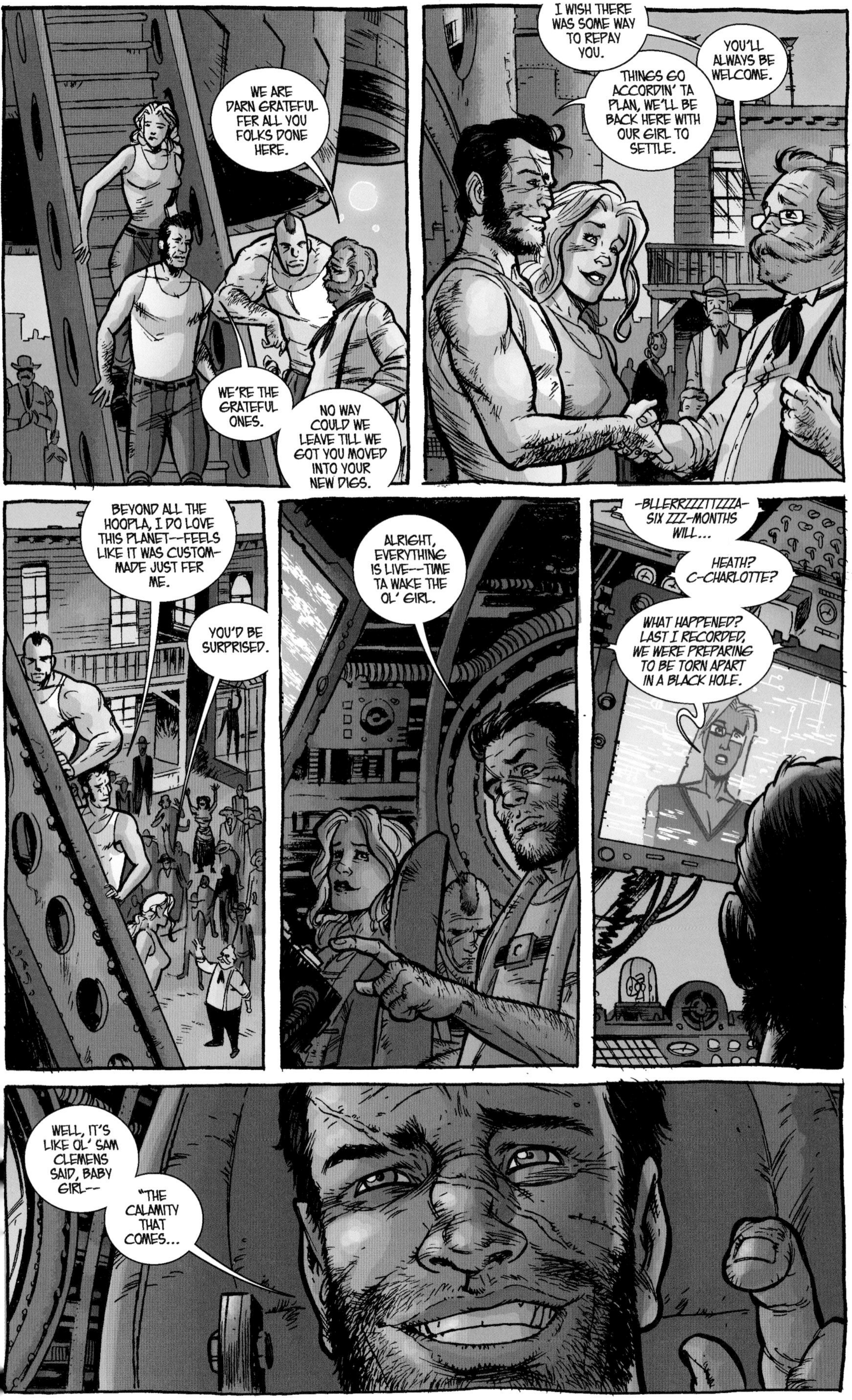
WE ARE DARN GRATEFUL FER ALL YOU FOLKS DONE HERE.
WE'RE THE GRATEFUL ONES.
NO WAY COULD WE LEAVE TILL WE GOT YOU MOVED INTO YOUR NEW DIGS.
I WISH THERE WAS SOME WAY TO REPAY YOU.
THINGS GO ACCORDIN' TA PLAN, WE'LL BE BACK HERE WITH OUR GIRL TO SETTLE.
YOU'LL ALWAYS BE WELCOME.
BEYOND ALL THE HOOPLA, I DO LOVE THIS PLANET--FEELS LIKE IT WAS CUSTOM-MADE JUST FER ME.
YOU'D BE SURPRISED.
ALRIGHT, EVERYTHING IS LIVE--TIME TA WAKE THE OL' GIRL.
-BLLERRZZZTTZZZA- SIX ZZZ-MONTHS WILL...
HEATH? C-CHARLOTTE?
WHAT HAPPENED? LAST I RECORDED, WE WERE PREPARING TO BE TORN APART IN A BLACK HOLE.
WELL, IT'S LIKE OL' SAM CLEMENS SAID, BABY GIRL--
"THE CALAMITY THAT COMES...

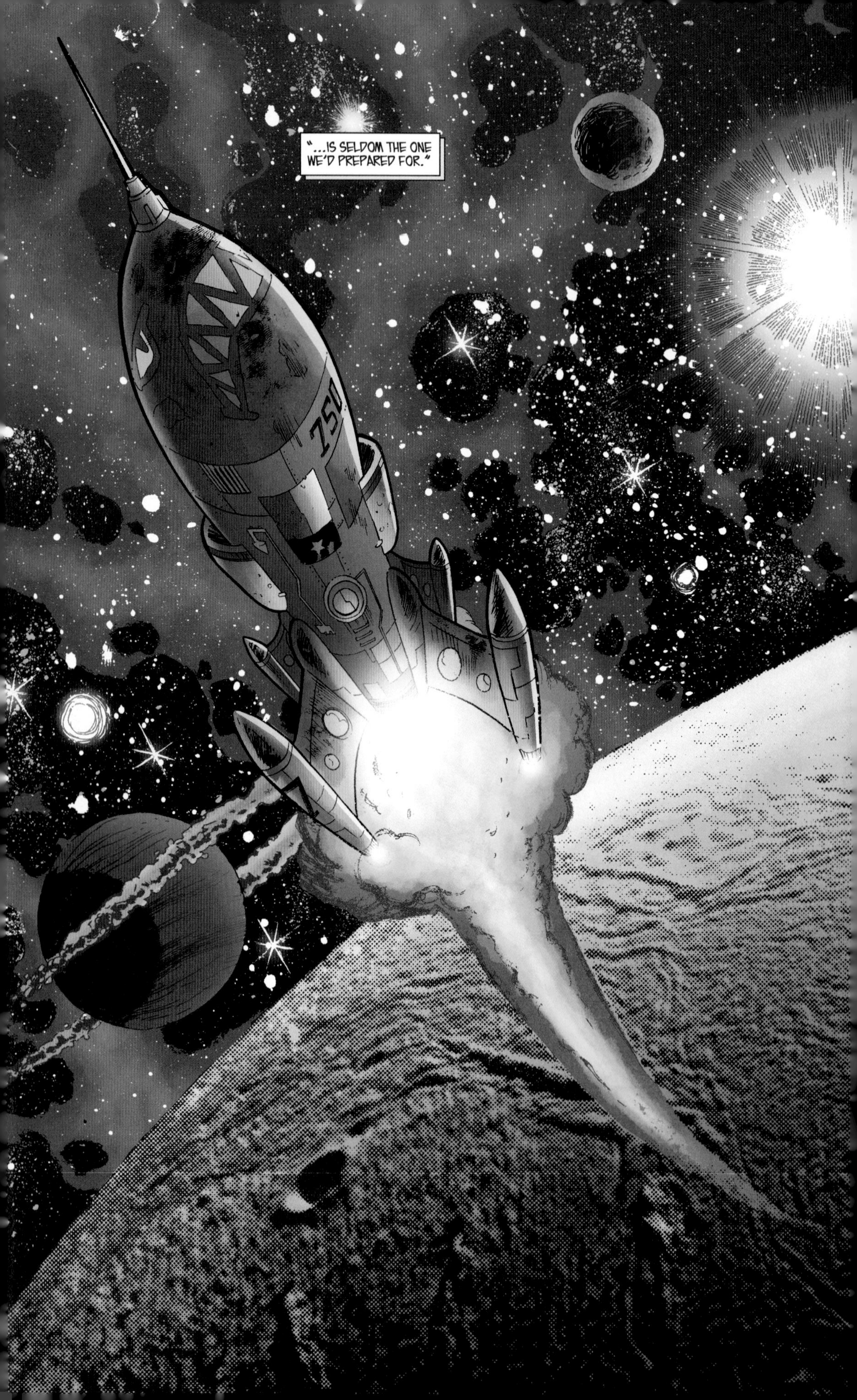
"...IS SELDOM THE ONE WE'D PREPARED FOR."
750

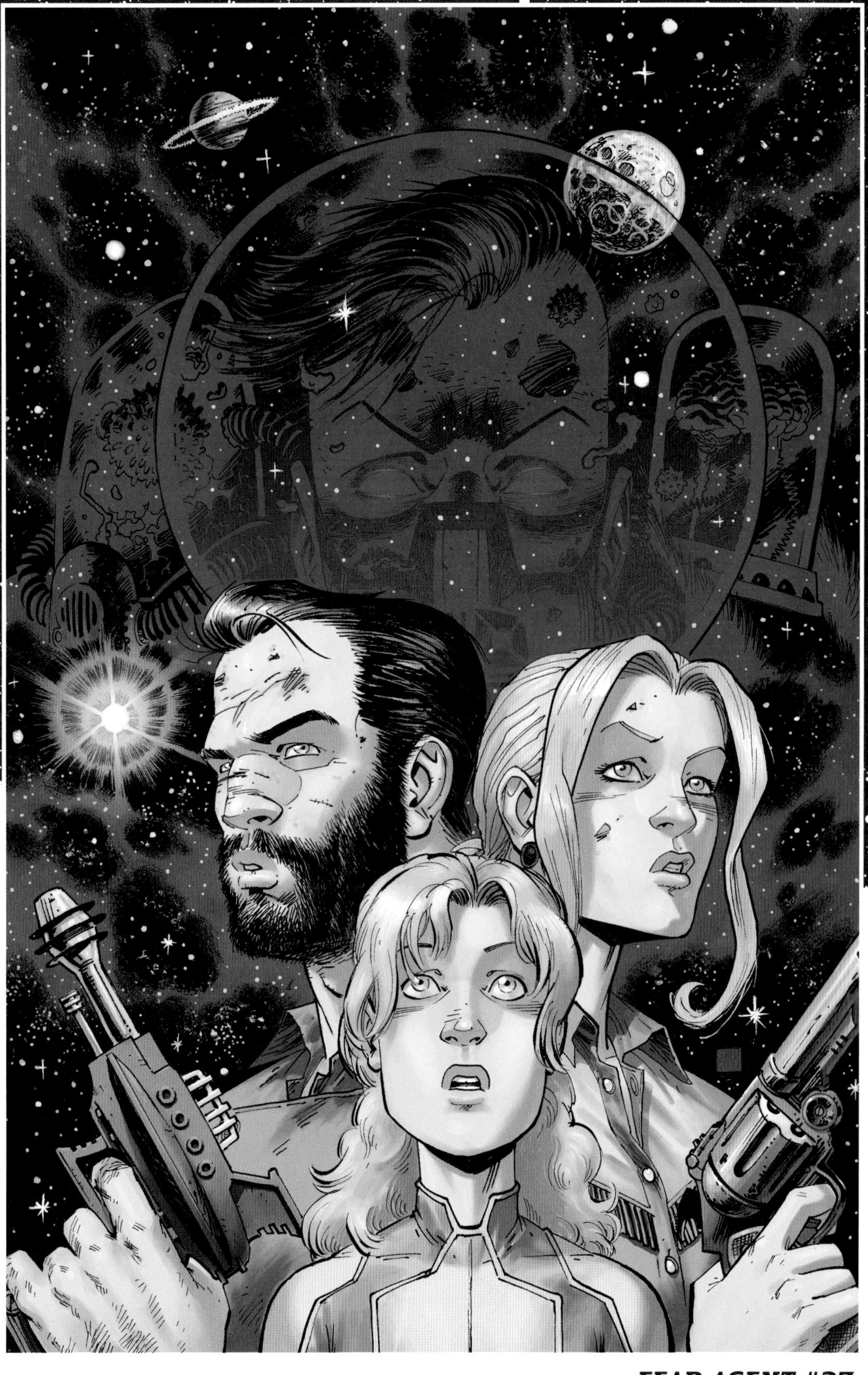

FEAR AGENT #27
ART BY **TONY MOORE**

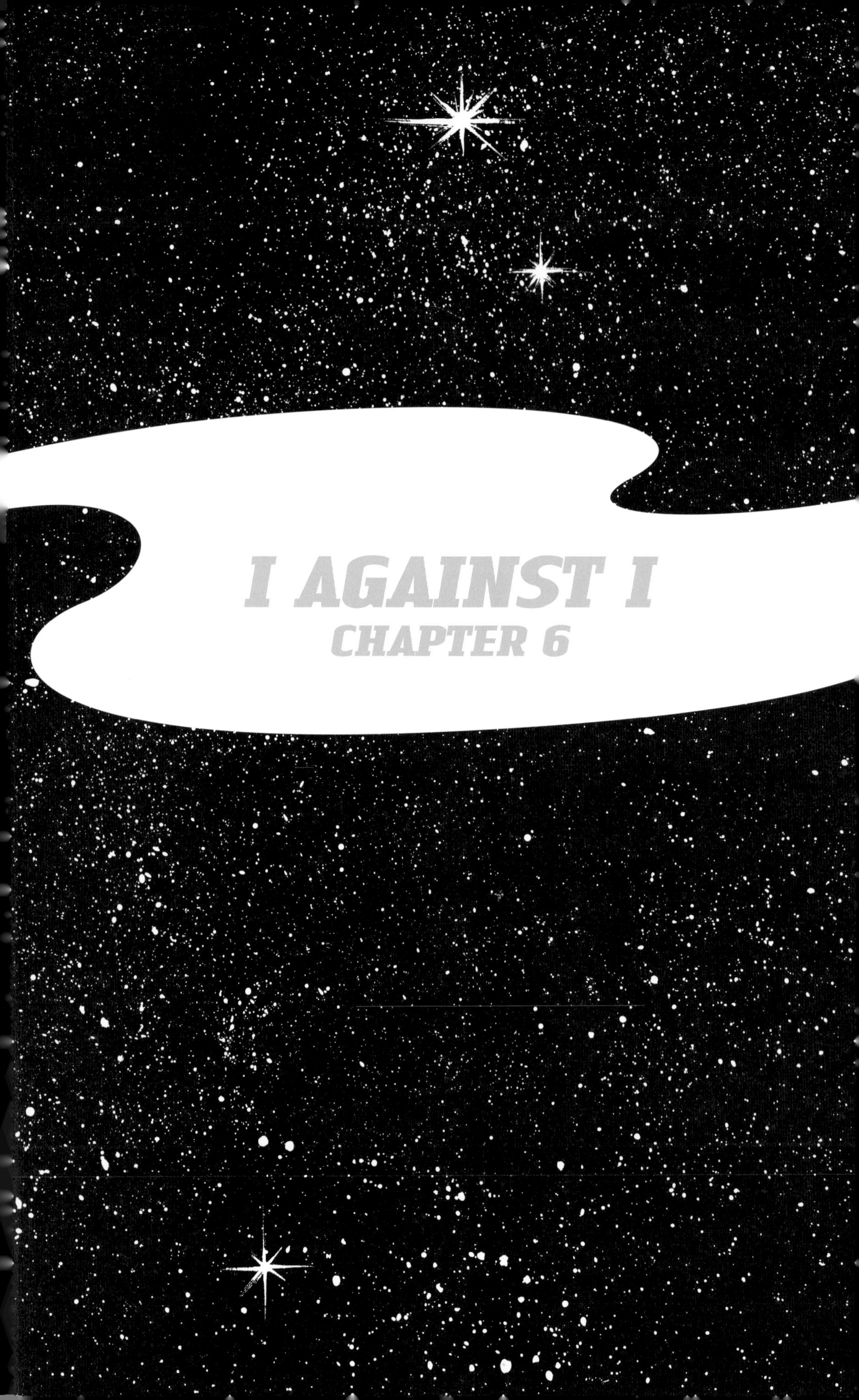
I AGAINST I
CHAPTER 6

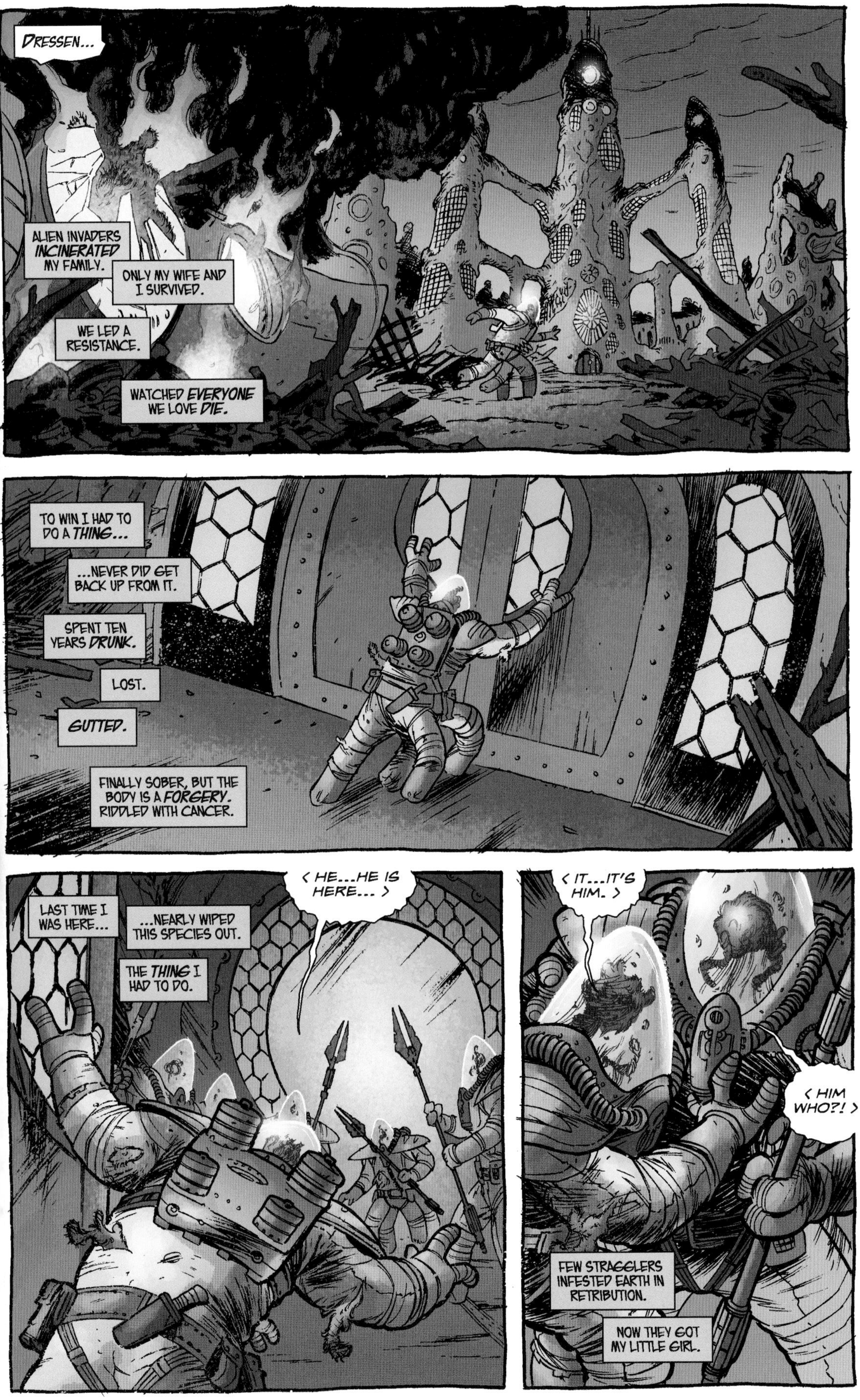
DRESSEN...
ALIEN INVADERS INCINERATED MY FAMILY.
ONLY MY WIFE AND I SURVIVED.
WE LED A RESISTANCE.
WATCHED EVERYONE WE LOVE DIE.
TO WIN I HAD TO DO A THING...
...NEVER DID GET BACK UP FROM IT.
SPENT TEN YEARS DRUNK.
LOST.
GUTTED.
FINALLY SOBER, BUT THE BODY IS A FORGERY. RIDDLED WITH CANCER.
LAST TIME I WAS HERE...
...NEARLY WIPED THIS SPECIES OUT.
THE THING I HAD TO DO.
‹ HE...HE IS HERE... ›
‹ IT...IT'S HIM. ›
‹ HIM WHO?! ›
FEW STRAGGLERS INFESTED EARTH IN RETRIBUTION.
NOW THEY GOT MY LITTLE GIRL.

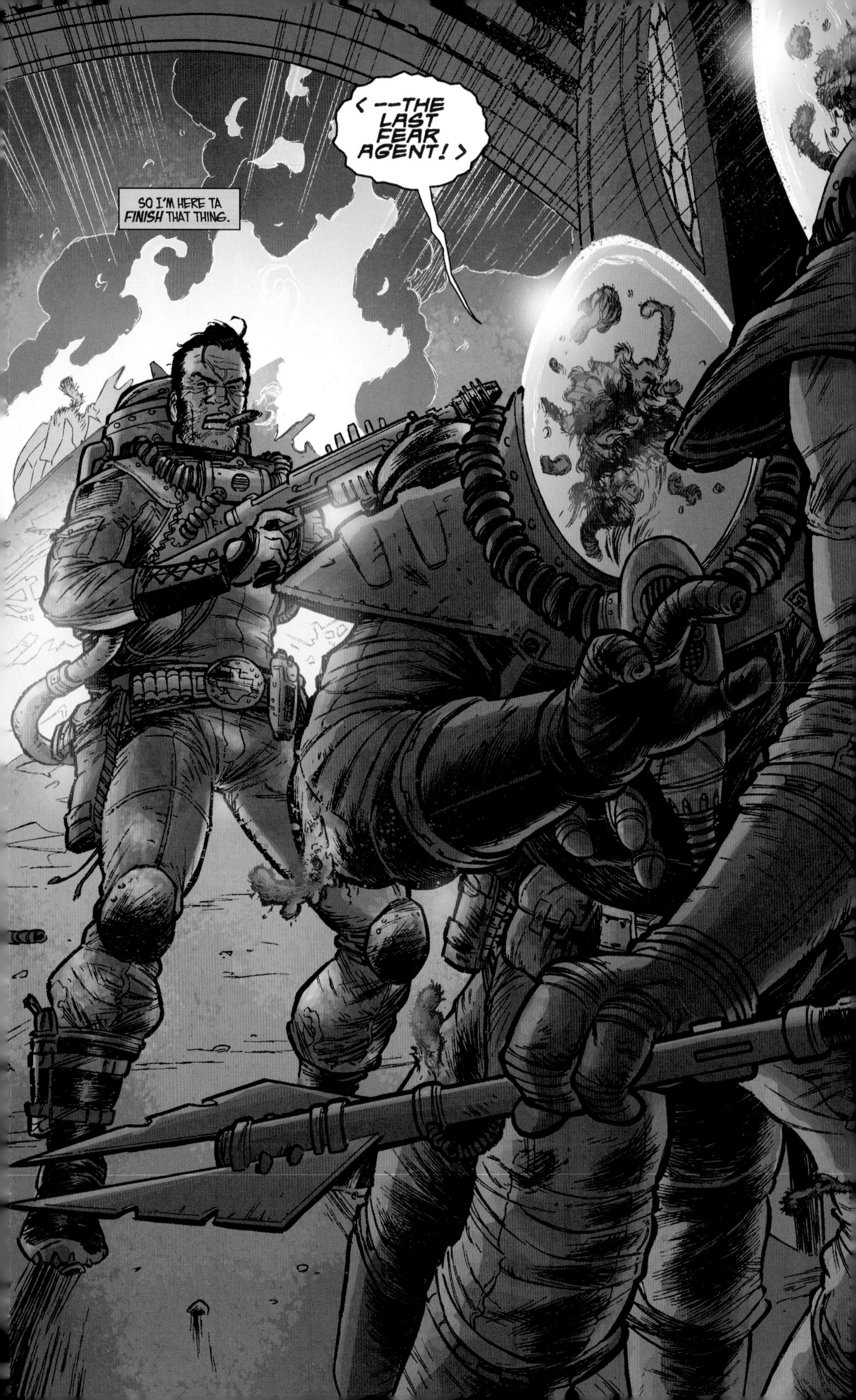

SO I'M HERE TA FINISH THAT THING.
< --THE LAST FEAR AGENT! >

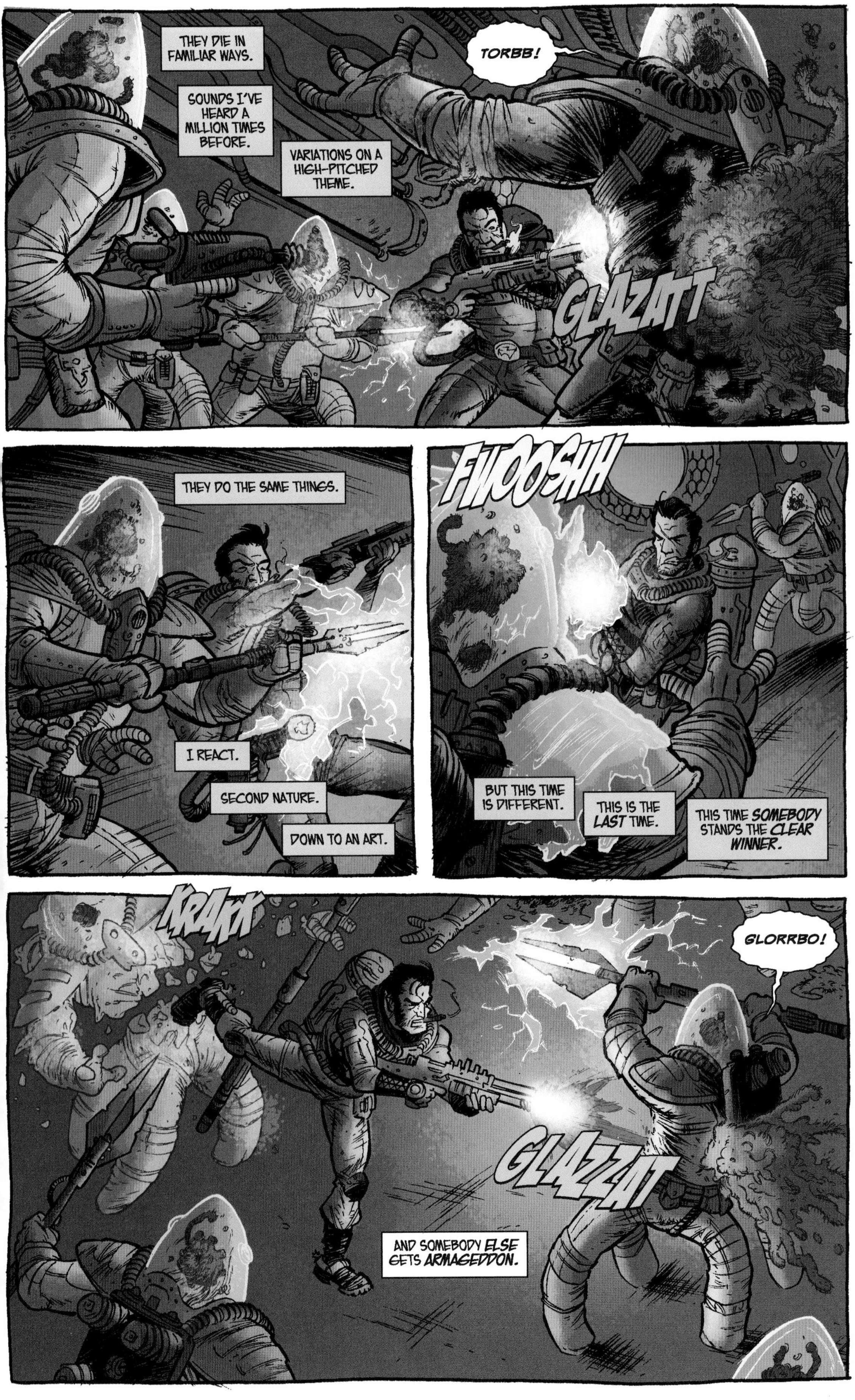
THEY DIE IN FAMILIAR WAYS.
SOUNDS I'VE HEARD A MILLION TIMES BEFORE.
VARIATIONS ON A HIGH-PITCHED THEME.
TORBB!
GLAZATT
THEY DO THE SAME THINGS.
I REACT.
SECOND NATURE.
DOWN TO AN ART.
FWOOSHH
BUT THIS TIME IS DIFFERENT.
THIS IS THE LAST TIME.
THIS TIME SOMEBODY STANDS THE CLEAR WINNER.
KRAKK
GLORRBO!
GLAZZAT
AND SOMEBODY ELSE GETS ARMAGEDDON.

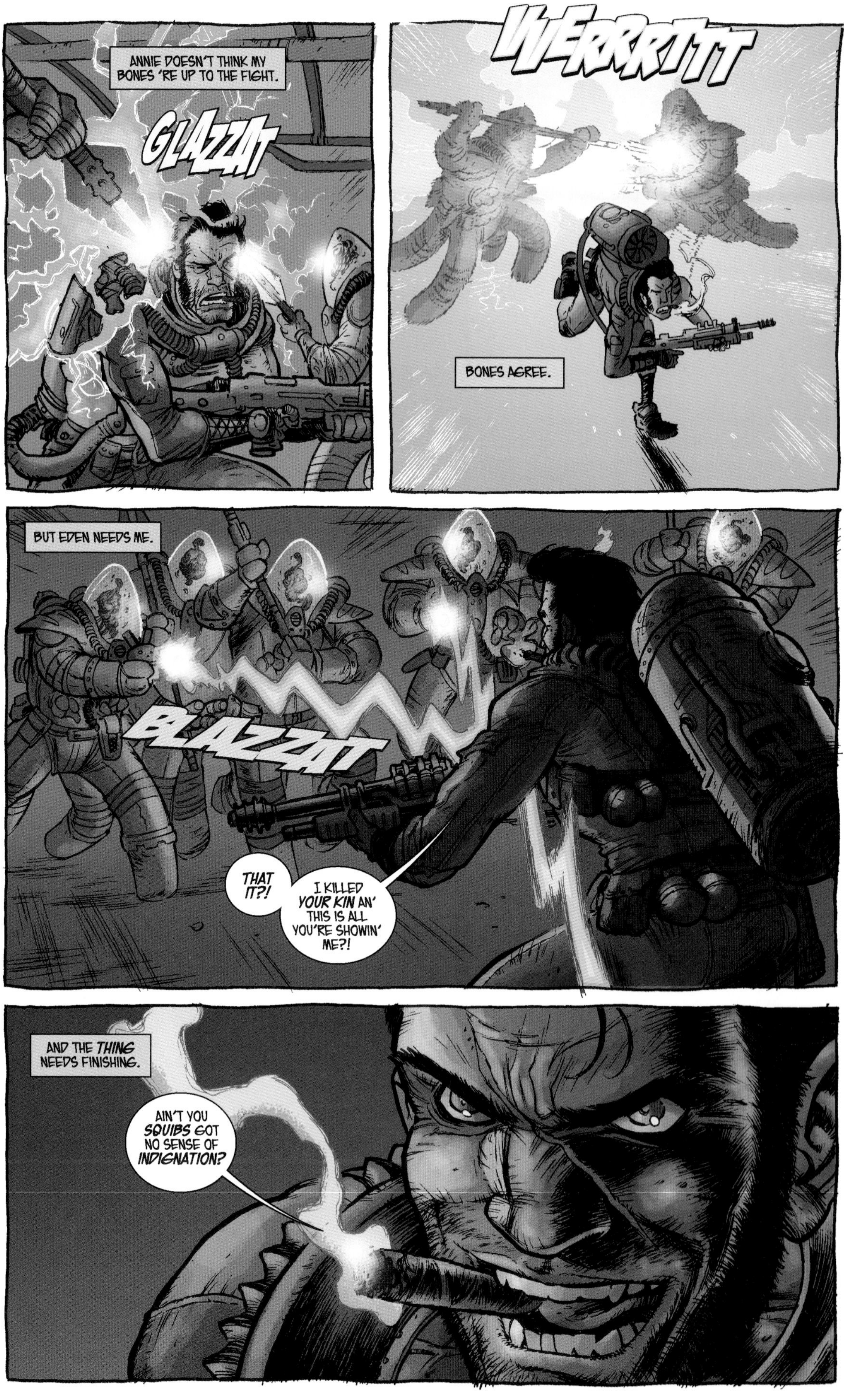

ANNIE DOESN'T THINK MY BONES 'RE UP TO THE FIGHT.
GLAZZAT
WERRRTTT
BONES AGREE.
BUT EDEN NEEDS ME.
BLAZZAT
THAT IT?!
I KILLED YOUR KIN AN' THIS IS ALL YOU'RE SHOWIN' ME?!
AND THE THING NEEDS FINISHING.
AIN'T YOU SQUIBS GOT NO SENSE OF INDIGNATION?

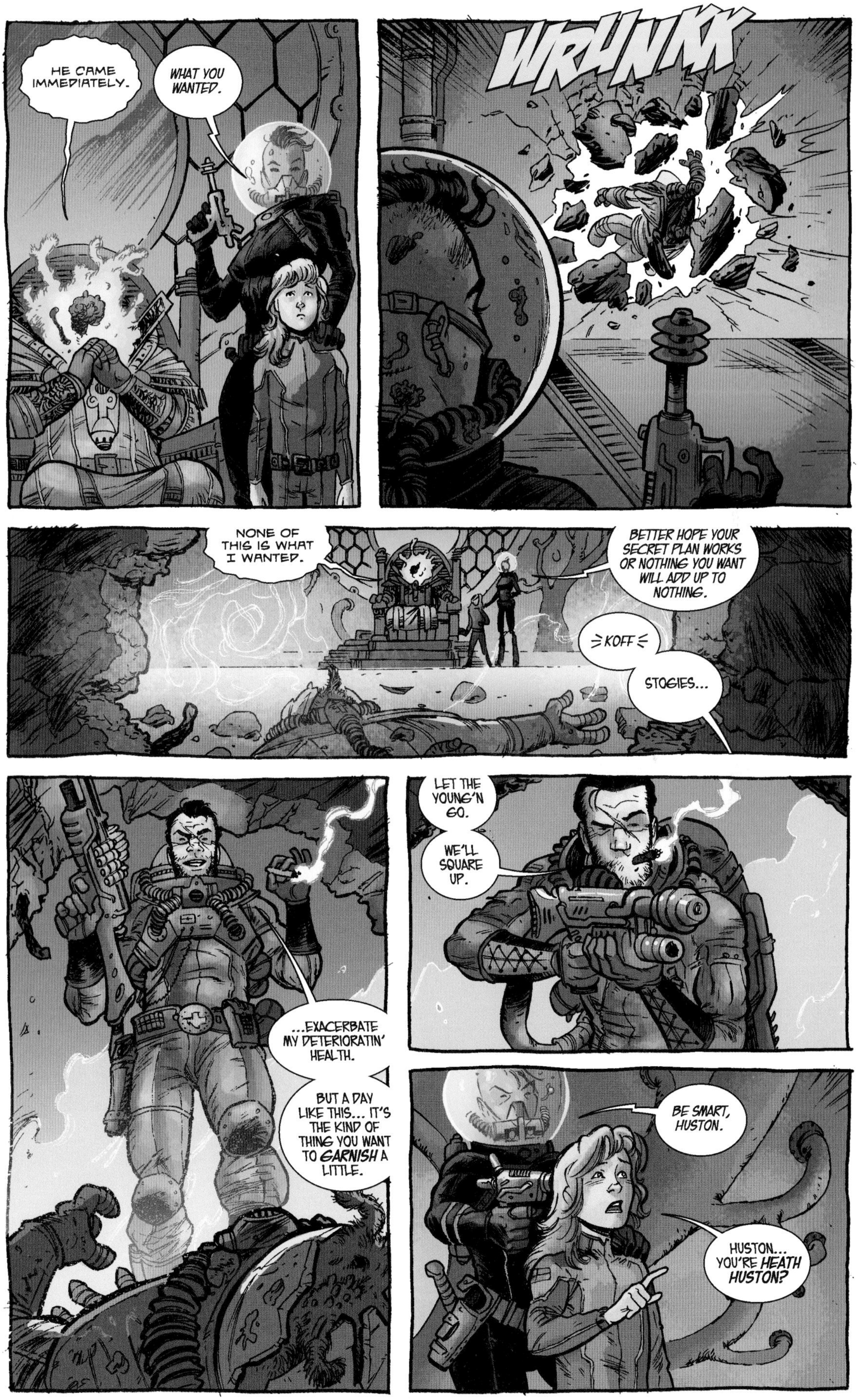
HE CAME IMMEDIATELY.
WHAT YOU WANTED.
WRUNKK
NONE OF THIS IS WHAT I WANTED.
BETTER HOPE YOUR SECRET PLAN WORKS OR NOTHING YOU WANT WILL ADD UP TO NOTHING.
KOFF
STOGIES...
...EXACERBATE MY DETERIORATIN' HEALTH.
BUT A DAY LIKE THIS... IT'S THE KIND OF THING YOU WANT TO GARNISH A LITTLE.
LET THE YOUNG'N GO.
WE'LL SQUARE UP.
BE SMART, HUSTON.
HUSTON... YOU'RE HEATH HUSTON?

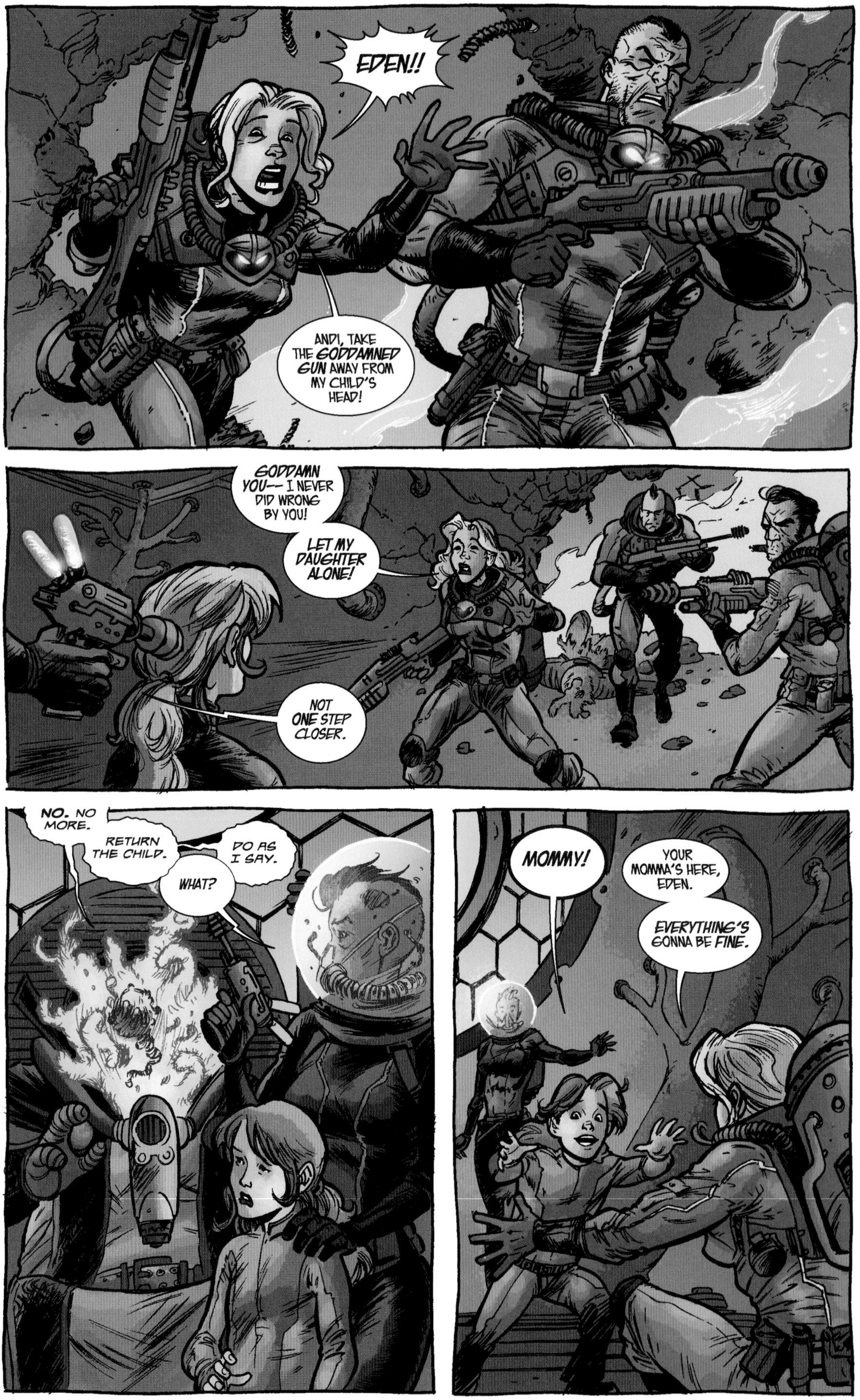
EDEN!!
ANDI, TAKE THE GODDAMNED GUN AWAY FROM MY CHILD'S HEAD!
GODDAMN YOU-- I NEVER DID WRONG BY YOU!
LET MY DAUGHTER ALONE!
NOT ONE STEP CLOSER.
NO. NO MORE.
RETURN THE CHILD.
DO AS I SAY.
WHAT?
MOMMY!
YOUR MOMMA'S HERE, EDEN.
EVERYTHING'S GONNA BE FINE.

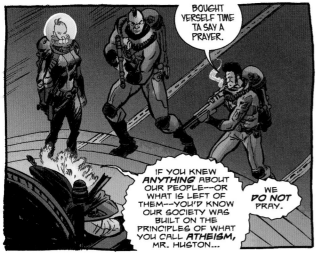

BOUGHT YERSELF TIME TA SAY A PRAYER.

IF YOU KNEW *ANYTHING* ABOUT OUR PEOPLE—OR WHAT IS LEFT OF THEM—YOU'D KNOW OUR SOCIETY WAS BUILT ON THE PRINCIPLES OF WHAT YOU CALL *ATHEISM*, MR. HUSTON...

WE *DO NOT* PRAY.

I DIDN'T GET THE BOOK ON Y'ALL 'FORE YOU *MURDERED* MINE.

YOU'RE *OVER-SIMPLIFYING* THINGS TO SUIT *YOUR* POSITION.

OUR ENVOY WAS ON EARTH TO AID YOUR PEOPLE AGAINST THE *TETALDIAN INVASION*.

'CEPT WHEN *YOUR PEOPLE* GOT TA EARTH THEY TREATED US HUMANS AS IF WE WERE DIRT UNDER BOOT.

SOLDIERS CORRUPTED BY *EONS* FIGHTING THE TETALDIANS.

IT IS *UNFORGIVABLE*, YET WE *WERE* THERE TO HELP.

HELP?!

YOU BUYIN' THIS, ANDI? CUZ I WAS THERE! I WATCHED YER NEW FRIENDS *HELP* YOUR UNCLE OTTO INTO HIS GRAVE!

HYPOCRITE! YOU *LEFT* ME HERE TO TAKE THE BLAME FOR YOUR ACTIONS!

I THOUGHT YOU DIED ON THE MOON. I *NEVER* HAD ANY IDEA YOU WERE EVEN ALIVE.

LOVED YOU AN' OTTO LIKE MY OWN.

NEVER WOULD ABIDED BY LEAVIN' YOU HERE.

BUT YOU DID.

LOOK AT ME NOW. NOT A *HUMAN*. NOT *DRESSITE*...

A TWISTED *THING*, SOMEWHERE IN BETWEEN.

WHICH IS WHY YOU, ANDI, MUST BE THE AMBASSADOR TO BOTH OUR PEOPLE TO BRIDGE THIS GAP— *TO END THIS MINDLESS WAR*.

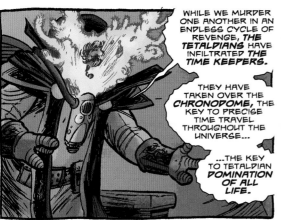

WHILE WE MURDER ONE ANOTHER IN AN ENDLESS CYCLE OF REVENGE, *THE TETALDIANS* HAVE INFILTRATED *THE TIME KEEPERS.*

THEY HAVE TAKEN OVER THE *CHRONODOME,* THE KEY TO PRECISE TIME TRAVEL THROUGHOUT THE UNIVERSE...

...THE KEY TO TETALDIAN *DOMINATION OF ALL LIFE.*

THEY *WILL* USE IT. THEY WILL SPREAD, *INFECTING* THE UNIVERSE.

THEIR GOAL *IS* WITHIN REACH.

OUR PEOPLE-- *NEARLY DECIMATED!!*

WHILE *THE TETALDIAN EMPIRE* GROWS STRONGER BY THE DAY!!

WE MUST MOVE BEYOND THIS PATH OF SELF-DESTRUCTION. WE MUST STAND *TOGETHER* AGAINST THEM.

TOGETHER...?

I BEG YOU TO ACCEPT. IF ONLY FOR SELF-INTEREST. IF ONLY FOR *SURVIVAL!*

WE MUST UNITE.

NOW, WHEN I GOT YOU DEAD TO RIGHTS--*NOW* YOU WANT TO *PARTNER UP?*

ACCEPT PEACE NOW...

.... I WILL FREE YOUR EARTH FROM *FEEDER INFESTATION.*

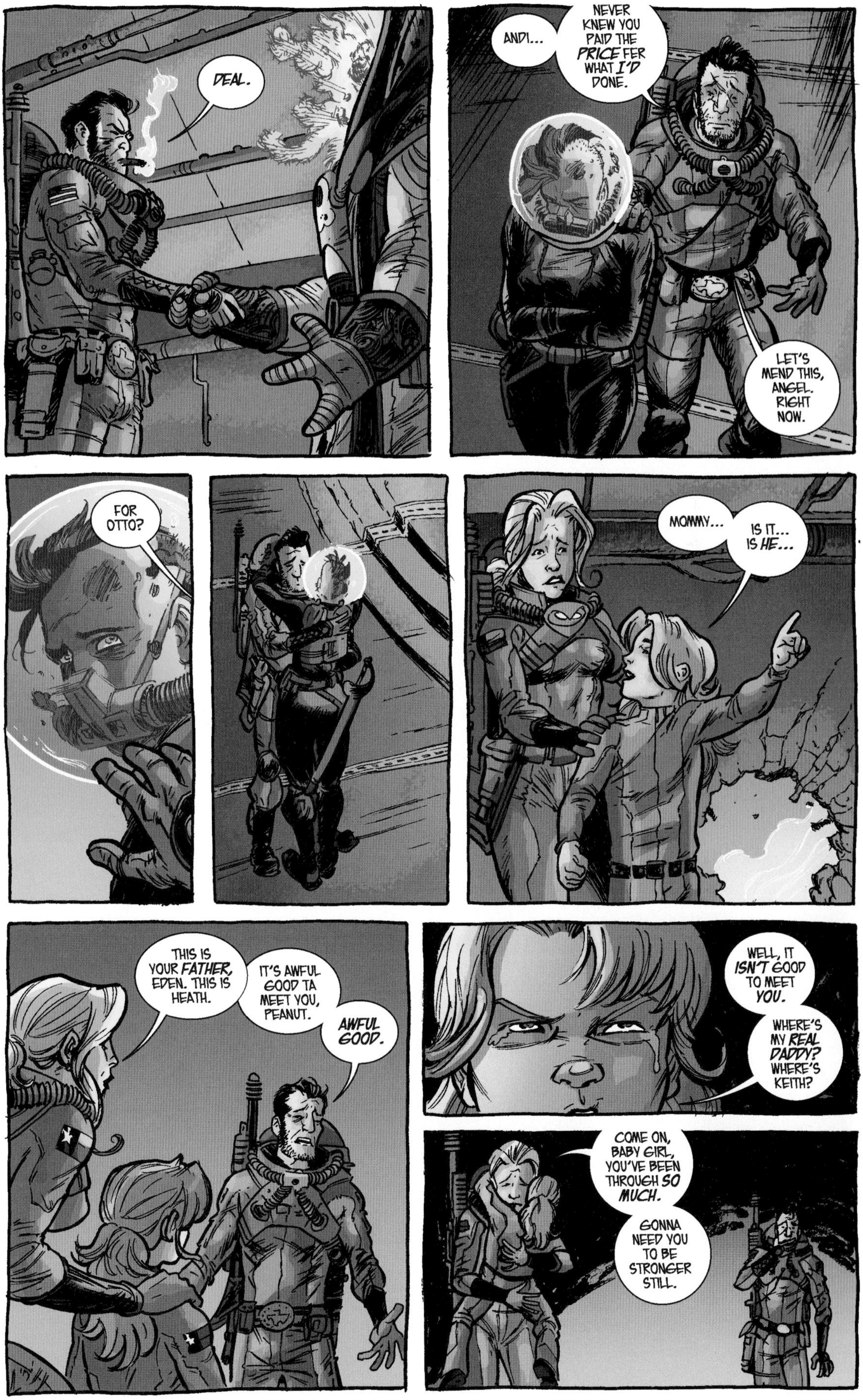
DEAL.
ANDI...
NEVER KNEW YOU PAID THE PRICE FER WHAT I'D DONE.
LET'S MEND THIS, ANGEL. RIGHT NOW.
FOR OTTO?
MOMMY...
IS IT... IS HE...
THIS IS YOUR FATHER, EDEN. THIS IS HEATH.
IT'S AWFUL GOOD TA MEET YOU, PEANUT.
AWFUL GOOD.
WELL, IT ISN'T GOOD TO MEET YOU.
WHERE'S MY REAL DADDY? WHERE'S KEITH?
COME ON, BABY GIRL, YOU'VE BEEN THROUGH SO MUCH.
GONNA NEED YOU TO BE STRONGER STILL.

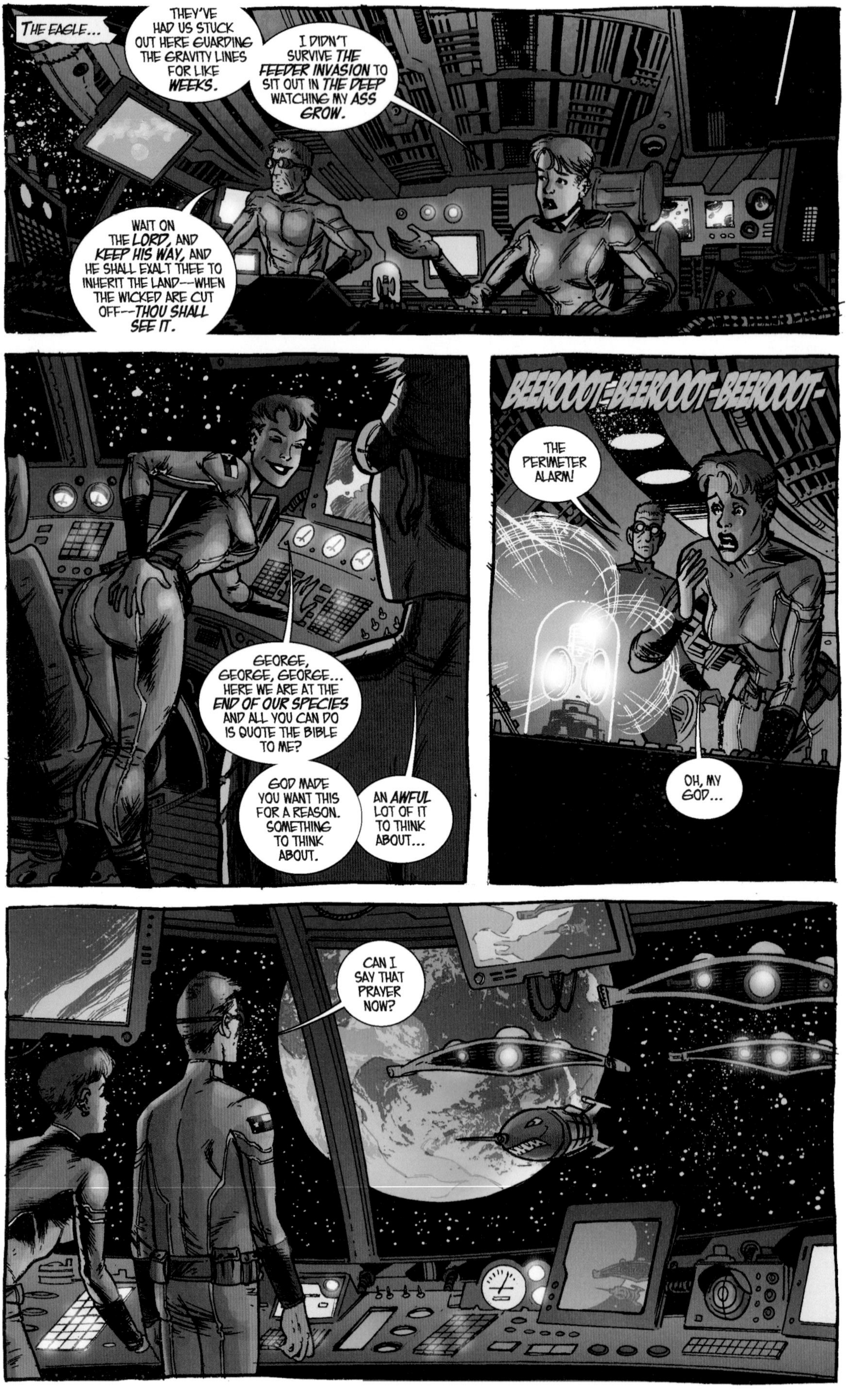
THE EAGLE...
THEY'VE HAD US STUCK OUT HERE GUARDING THE GRAVITY LINES FOR LIKE WEEKS.
I DIDN'T SURVIVE THE FEEDER INVASION TO SIT OUT IN THE DEEP WATCHING MY ASS GROW.
WAIT ON THE LORD, AND KEEP HIS WAY, AND HE SHALL EXALT THEE TO INHERIT THE LAND--WHEN THE WICKED ARE CUT OFF--THOU SHALL SEE IT.
GEORGE, GEORGE, GEORGE... HERE WE ARE AT THE END OF OUR SPECIES AND ALL YOU CAN DO IS QUOTE THE BIBLE TO ME?
GOD MADE YOU WANT THIS FOR A REASON. SOMETHING TO THINK ABOUT.
AN AWFUL LOT OF IT TO THINK ABOUT...
BEEROOOT-BEEROOOT-BEEROOOT-
THE PERIMETER ALARM!
OH, MY GOD...
CAN I SAY THAT PRAYER NOW?

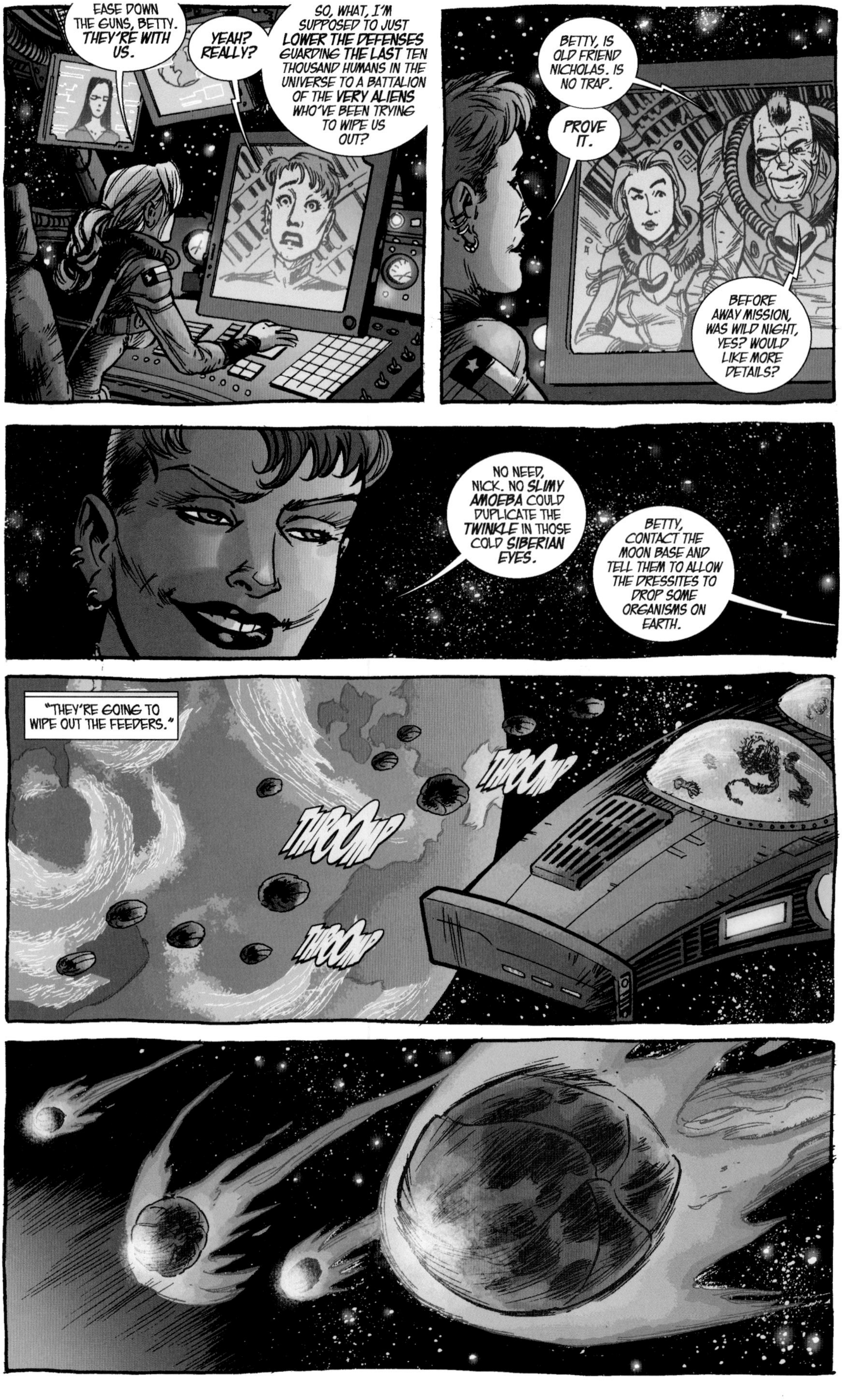
EASE DOWN THE GUNS, BETTY. THEY'RE WITH US.
YEAH? REALLY?
SO, WHAT, I'M SUPPOSED TO JUST LOWER THE DEFENSES GUARDING THE LAST TEN THOUSAND HUMANS IN THE UNIVERSE TO A BATTALION OF THE VERY ALIENS WHO'VE BEEN TRYING TO WIPE US OUT?
BETTY, IS OLD FRIEND NICHOLAS. IS NO TRAP.
PROVE IT.
BEFORE AWAY MISSION, WAS WILD NIGHT, YES? WOULD LIKE MORE DETAILS?
NO NEED, NICK. NO SLIMY AMOEBA COULD DUPLICATE THE TWINKLE IN THOSE COLD SIBERIAN EYES.
BETTY, CONTACT THE MOON BASE AND TELL THEM TO ALLOW THE DRESSITES TO DROP SOME ORGANISMS ON EARTH.
"THEY'RE GOING TO WIPE OUT THE FEEDERS."
THROOMP
THROOMP
THROOMP

THOOOM

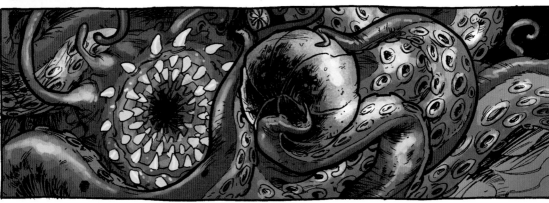

EERREKK–

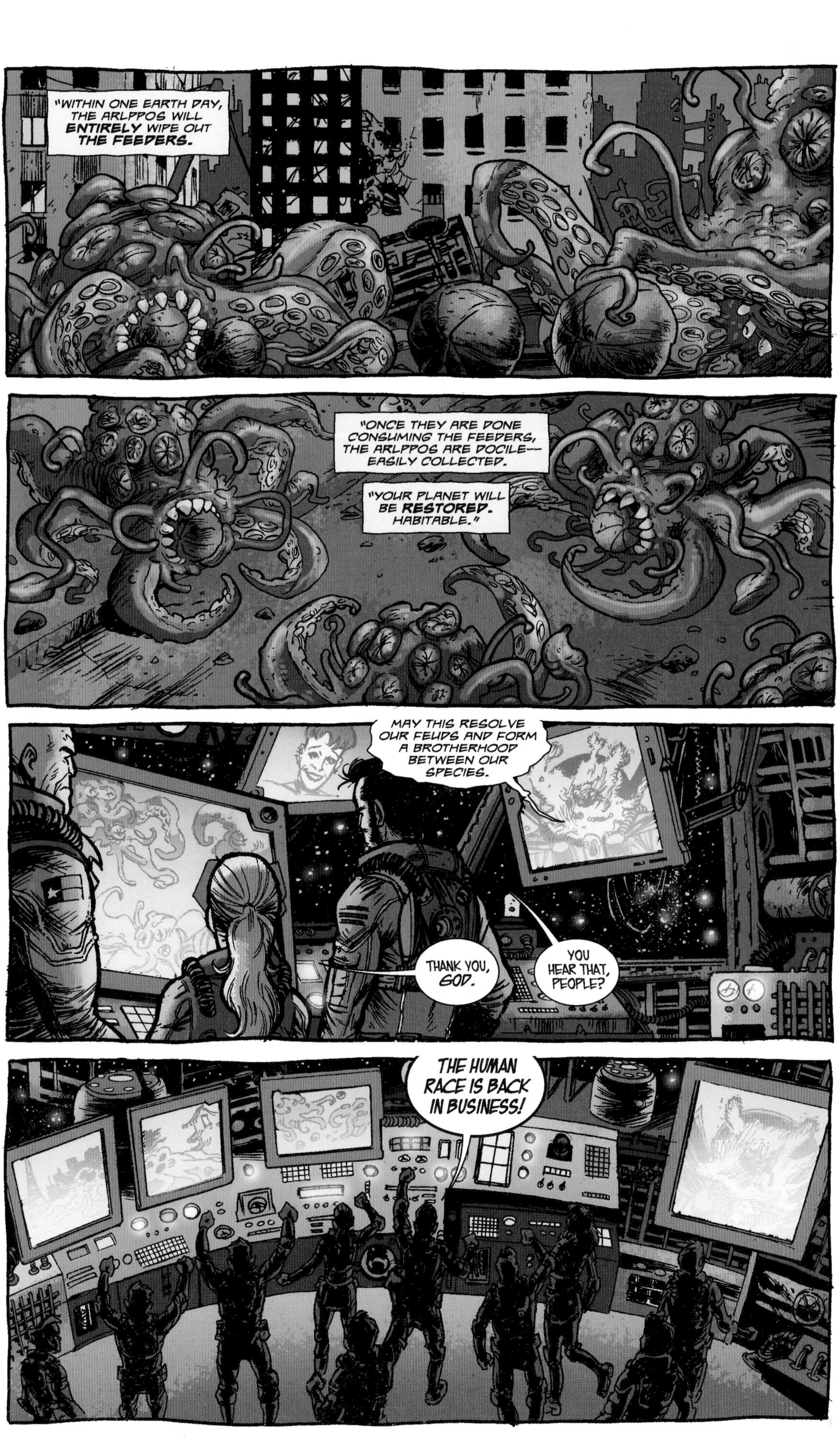
"WITHIN ONE EARTH DAY, THE ARLPPOS WILL ENTIRELY WIPE OUT THE FEEDERS.
"ONCE THEY ARE DONE CONSUMING THE FEEDERS, THE ARLPPOS ARE DOCILE--- EASILY COLLECTED.
"YOUR PLANET WILL BE RESTORED. HABITABLE."
MAY THIS RESOLVE OUR FEUDS AND FORM A BROTHERHOOD BETWEEN OUR SPECIES.
THANK YOU, GOD.
YOU HEAR THAT, PEOPLE?
THE HUMAN RACE IS BACK IN BUSINESS!

MONTHS PASS...

IN THE PAST TEN YEARS WE'VE SEEN OUR WORLD INVADED--TWICE--LAID LOW AN' NEARLY DECIMATED.

BUT WE ARE STILL HERE--STILL ALIVE!

WE REBUILT OUR WORLD AFTER THE ANNUBIUS CONFLICT AND NOW, AS THE APOCALYPSE OF THE FEEDER PLAGUE ENDS, WE WILL BUILD AGAIN.

THE HEALING WILL BE SLOW. BUT BLESSED BY THE ABILITY TO FORGIVE--HEAL WE WILL.

TODAY, BY JOINING HANDS WITH THE DRESSITE EMPIRE, WE BREAK A LONG CYCLE OF PAIN AND SUFFERING.

TODAY WE STAND PROUD AND RESOLUTE IN THE SHADOWS OF OUR FOREFATHERS.

SECURE IN THE KNOWLEDGE THAT OUR TRUE GRIT COMES, NOT FROM HOW BARBARICALLY WE FIGHT...

...BUT FROM HOW HUMANELY WE THINK.

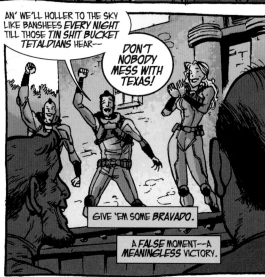

AN' WE'LL HOLLER TO THE SKY LIKE BANSHEES EVERY NIGHT TILL THOSE TIN SHIT BUCKET TETALDIANS HEAR--

DON'T NOBODY MESS WITH TEXAS!

GIVE 'EM SOME BRAVADO.

A FALSE MOMENT--A MEANINGLESS VICTORY.

IMAGINE A PERFECT MOMENT.

IMAGINE TEN YEARS OF RUST WASHES AWAY.

IMAGINE THAT IT IS HAPPENING, RIGHT NOW.

WE DID IT, BABY.

PUT IT BACK TOGETHER.

FOR NOW.

FOREVER.

LIKE A FIRST KISS.

SUFFOCATES THE RATTLE IN MY LUNGS.

FALL IN...FORGET THE REST...

...IGNORE THE SINKING FEELING...

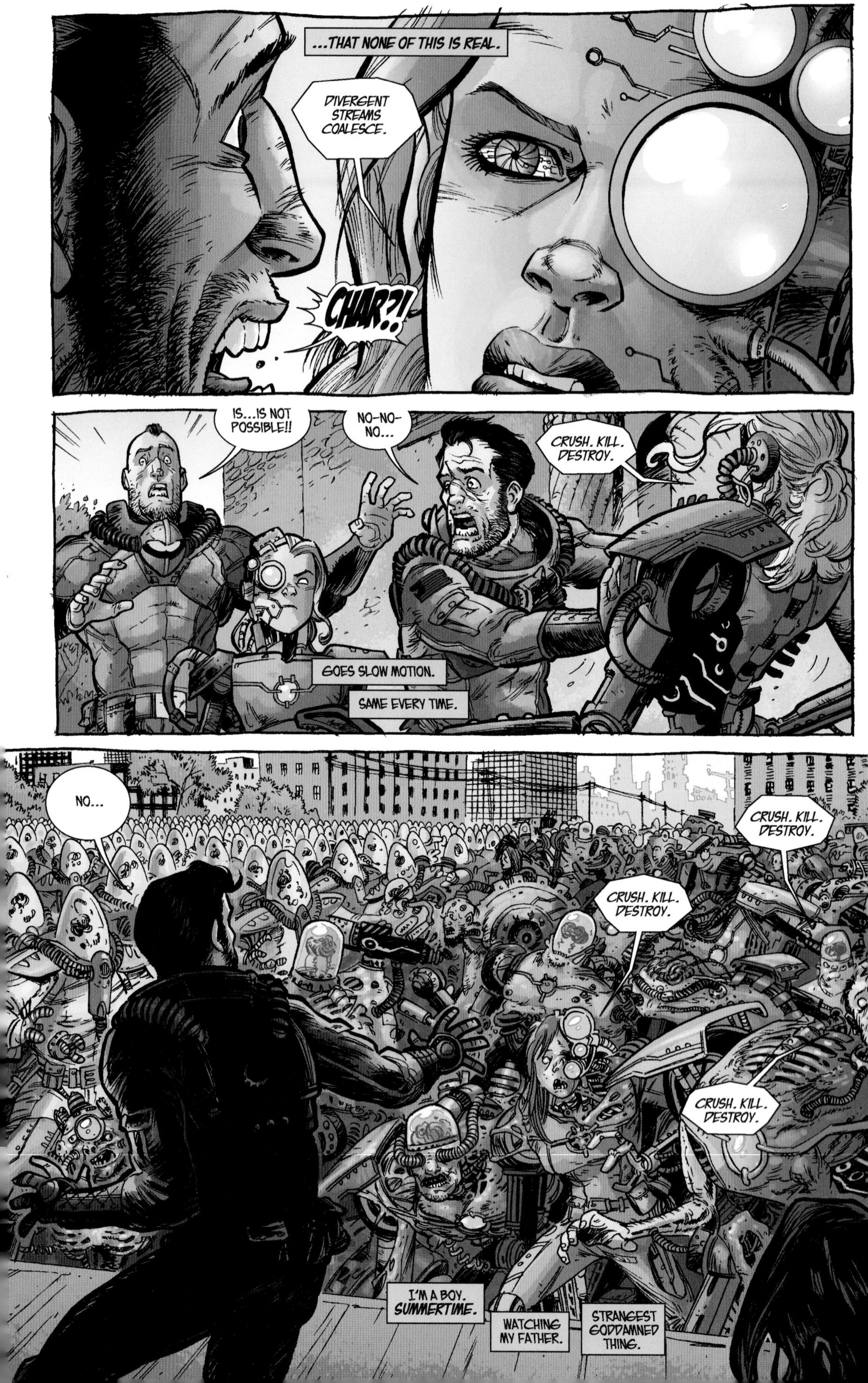
...THAT NONE OF THIS IS REAL.
DIVERGENT STREAMS COALESCE.
CHAR?!
IS...IS NOT POSSIBLE!!
NO—NO—NO...
CRUSH. KILL. DESTROY.
GOES SLOW MOTION.
SAME EVERY TIME.
NO...
CRUSH. KILL. DESTROY.
CRUSH. KILL. DESTROY.
CRUSH. KILL. DESTROY.
I'M A BOY. SUMMERTIME.
WATCHING MY FATHER.
STRANGEST GODDAMNED THING.

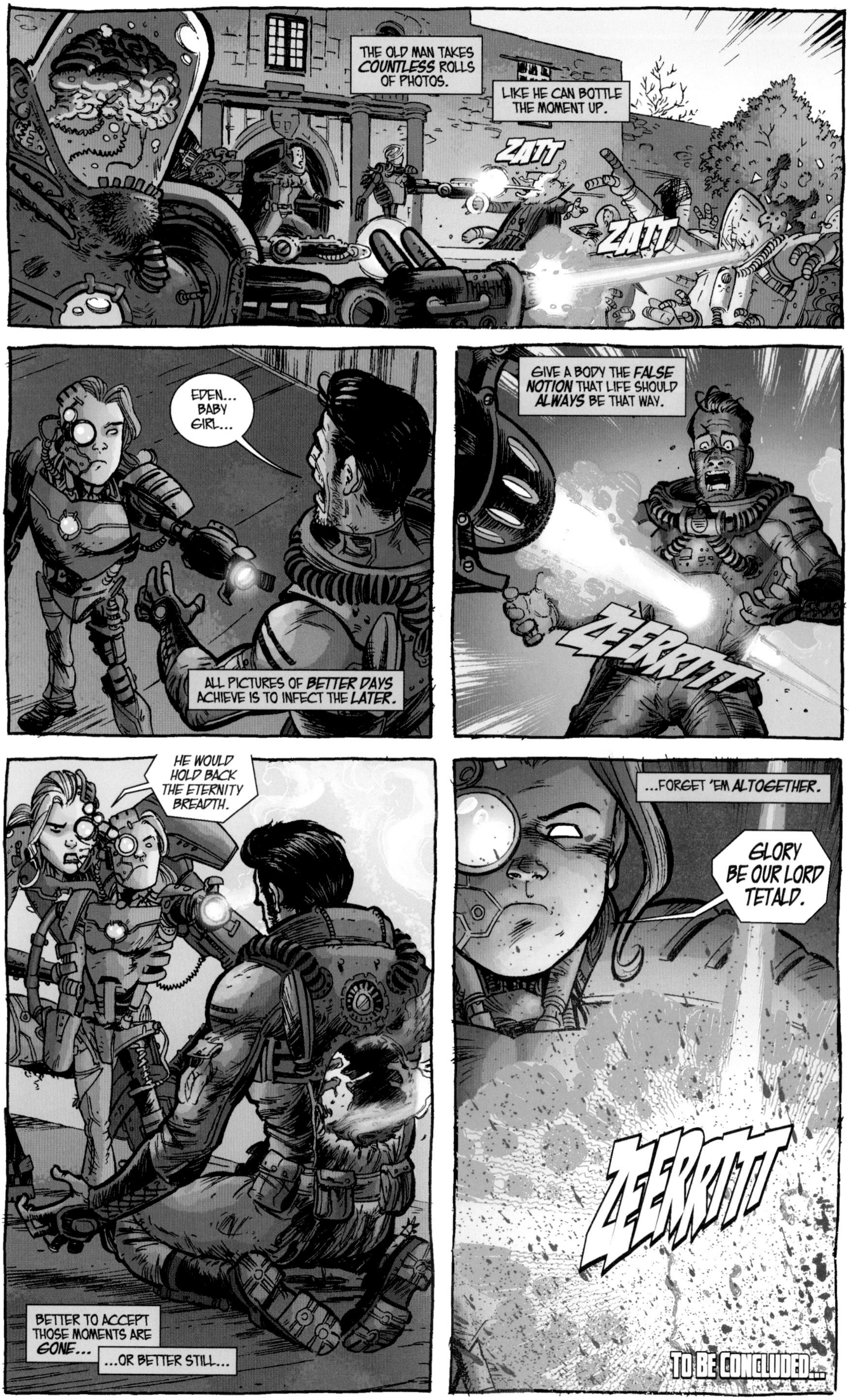
THE OLD MAN TAKES COUNTLESS ROLLS OF PHOTOS.
LIKE HE CAN BOTTLE THE MOMENT UP.
ZATT
ZATT
EDEN... BABY GIRL...
ALL PICTURES OF BETTER DAYS ACHIEVE IS TO INFECT THE LATER.
GIVE A BODY THE FALSE NOTION THAT LIFE SHOULD ALWAYS BE THAT WAY.
ZEERTTT
HE WOULD HOLD BACK THE ETERNITY BREADTH.
BETTER TO ACCEPT THOSE MOMENTS ARE GONE...
...OR BETTER STILL...
...FORGET 'EM ALTOGETHER.
GLORY BE OUR LORD TETALD.
ZEERTTT
TO BE CONCLUDED...

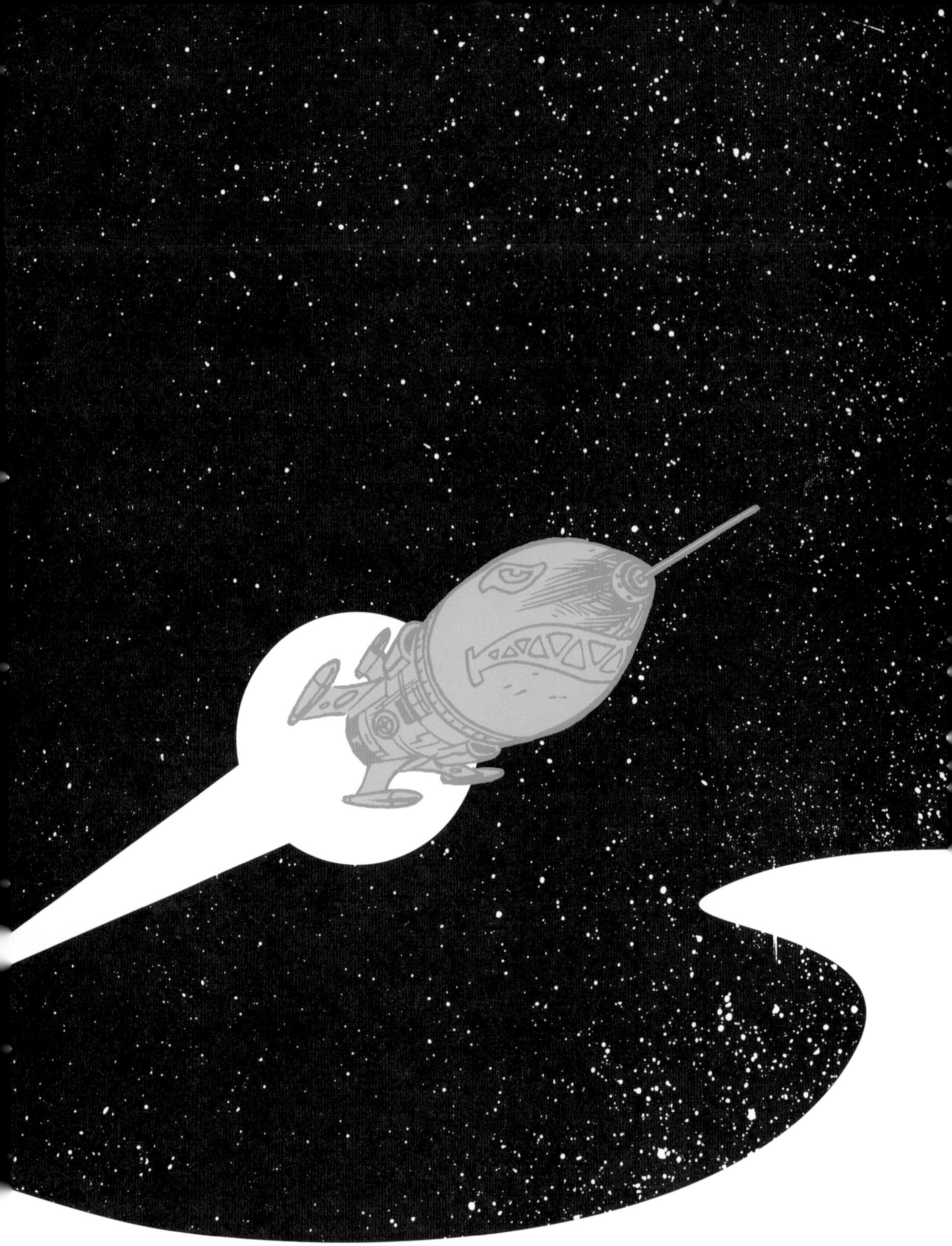

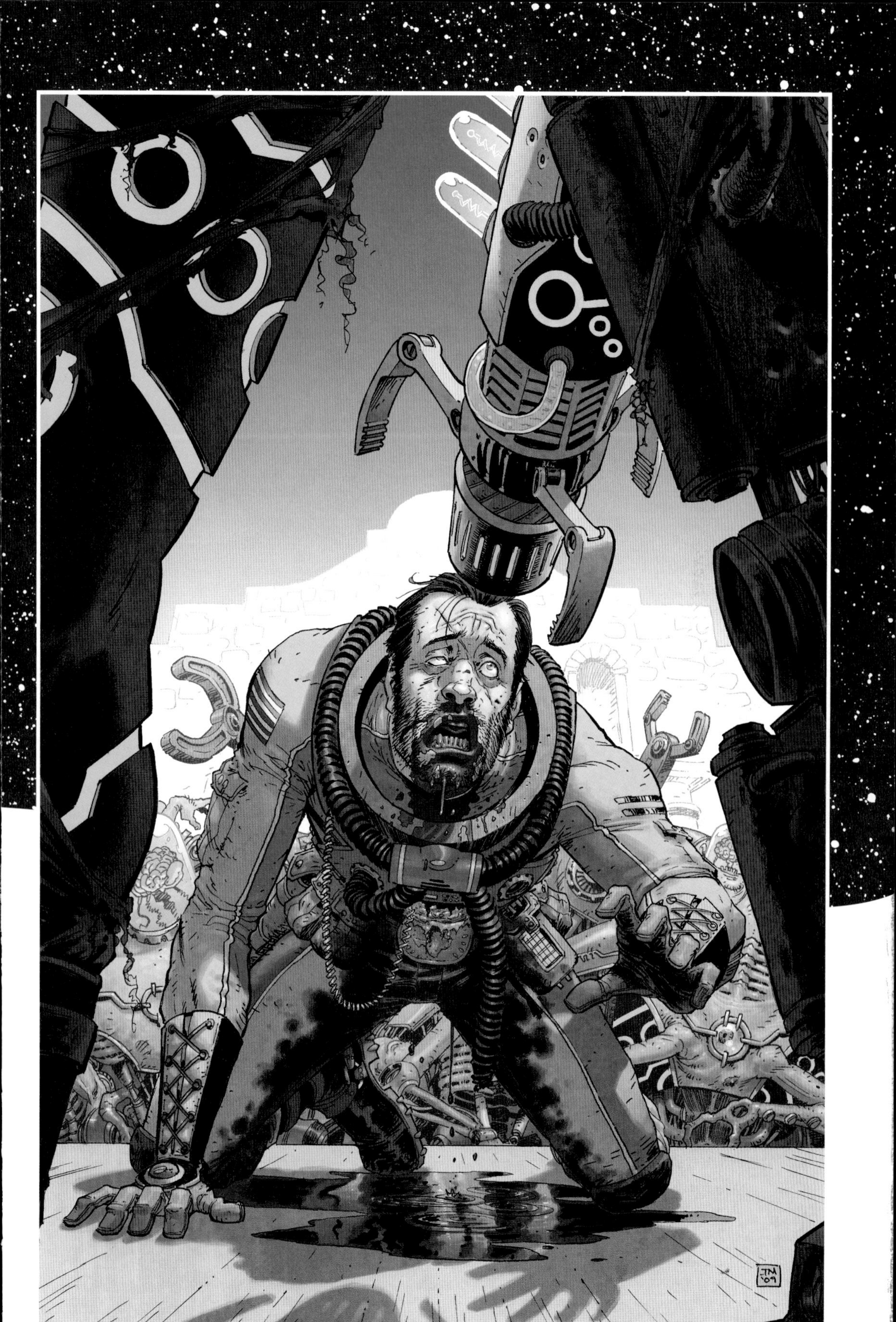

FEAR AGENT #28
ART BY TONY MOORE

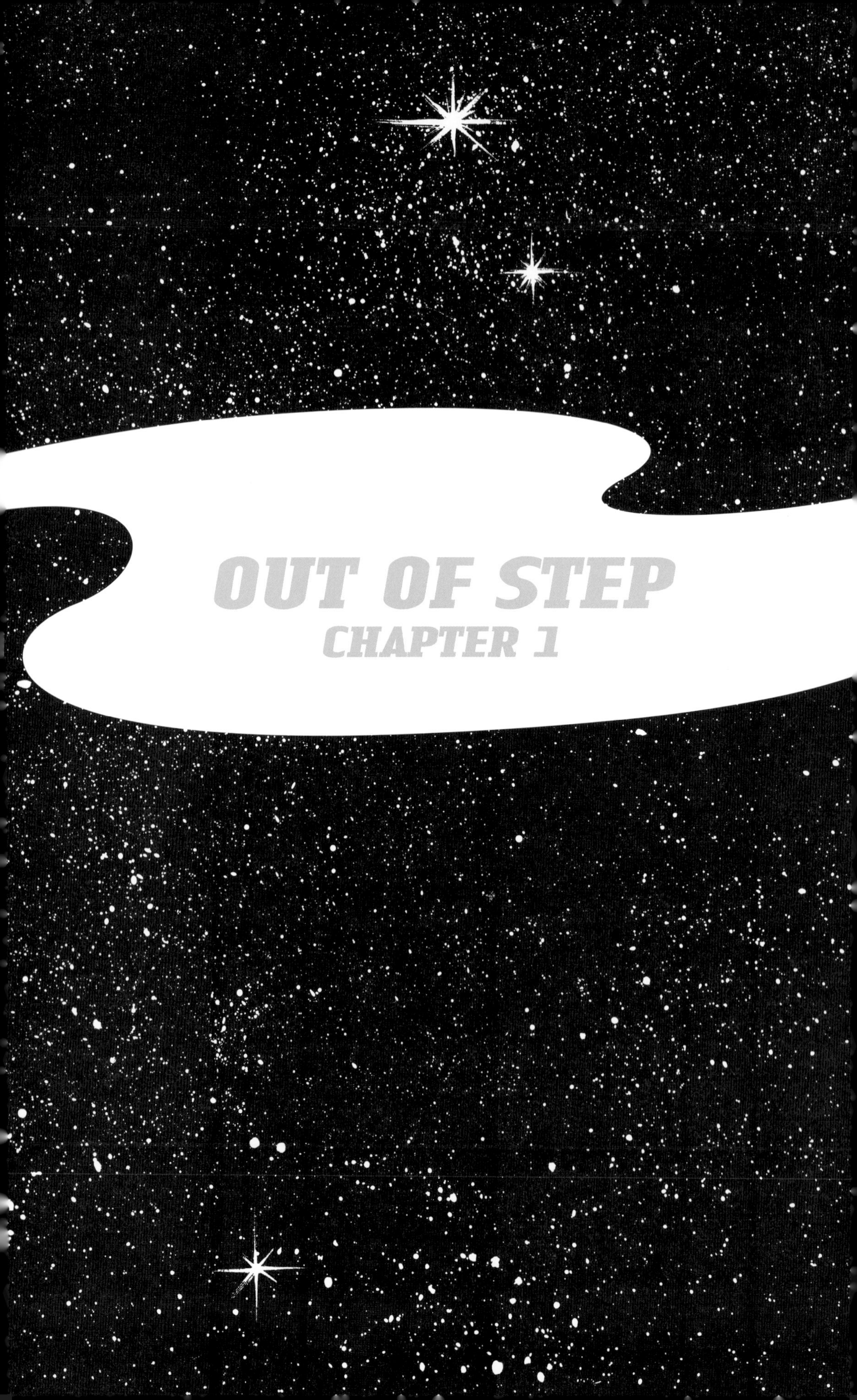
OUT OF STEP
CHAPTER 1

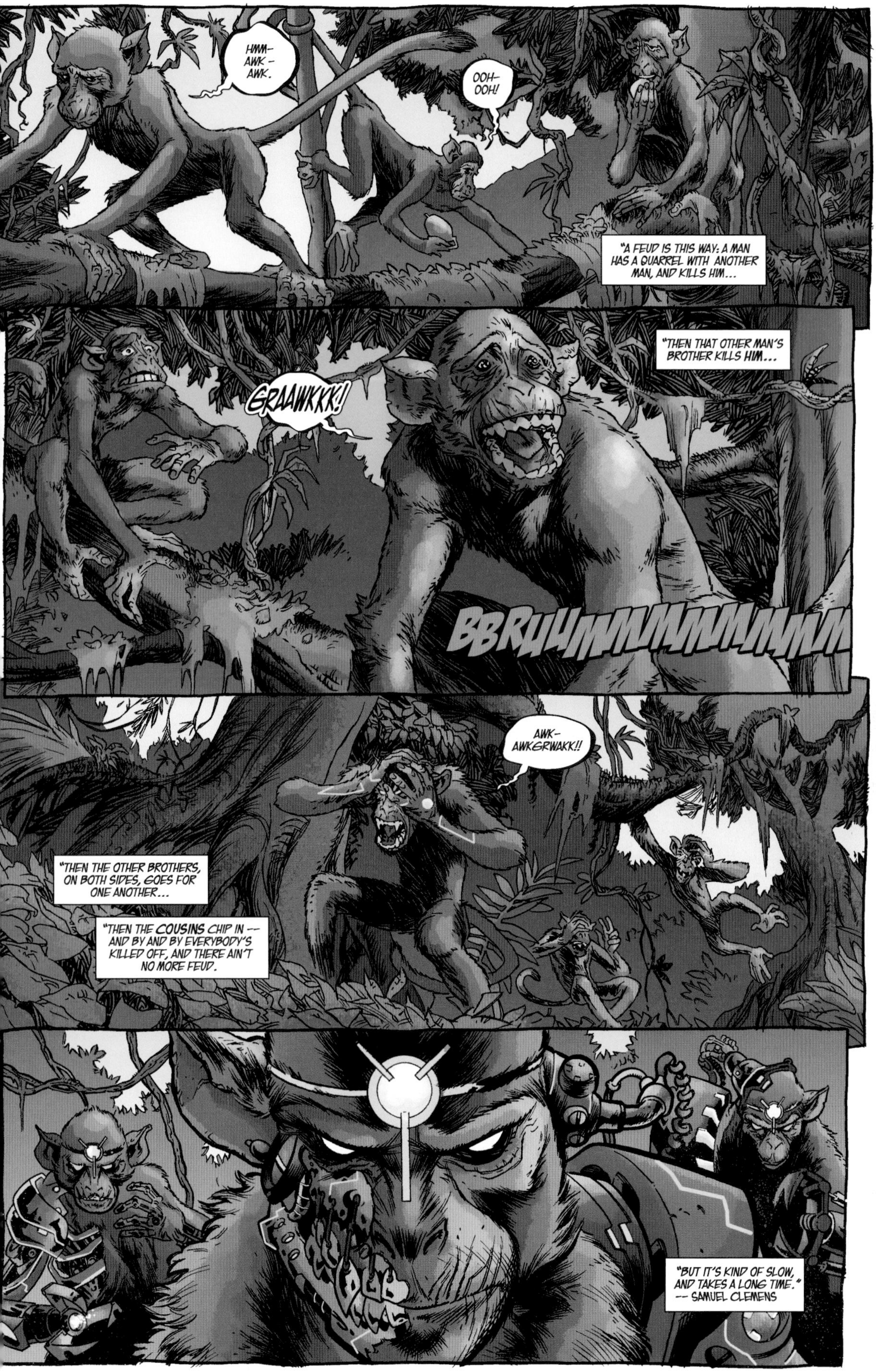
HMM-AWK-AWK.
OOH-OOH!
"A FEUD IS THIS WAY: A MAN HAS A QUARREL WITH ANOTHER MAN, AND KILLS HIM...
"THEN THAT OTHER MAN'S BROTHER KILLS HIM...
GRAAWKKK!
BBRUUMMMMMMMMMMMM
AWK-AWKGRWAKK!!
"THEN THE OTHER BROTHERS, ON BOTH SIDES, GOES FOR ONE ANOTHER...
"THEN THE COUSINS CHIP IN -- AND BY AND BY EVERYBODY'S KILLED OFF, AND THERE AIN'T NO MORE FEUD.
"BUT IT'S KIND OF SLOW, AND TAKES A LONG TIME."
-- SAMUEL CLEMENS

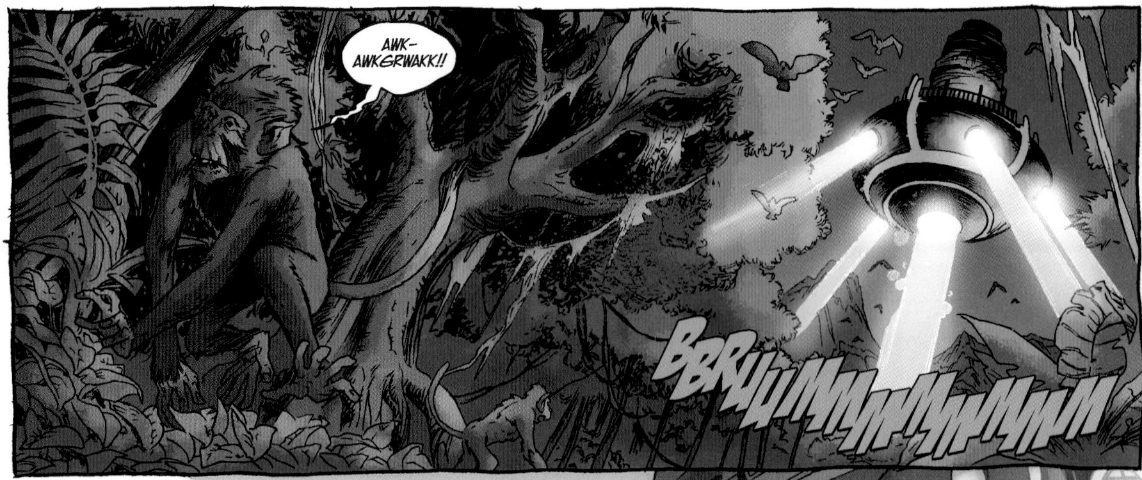
AWK-
AWKGRWAKK!!
BBRUUMMMMMMMMMMM

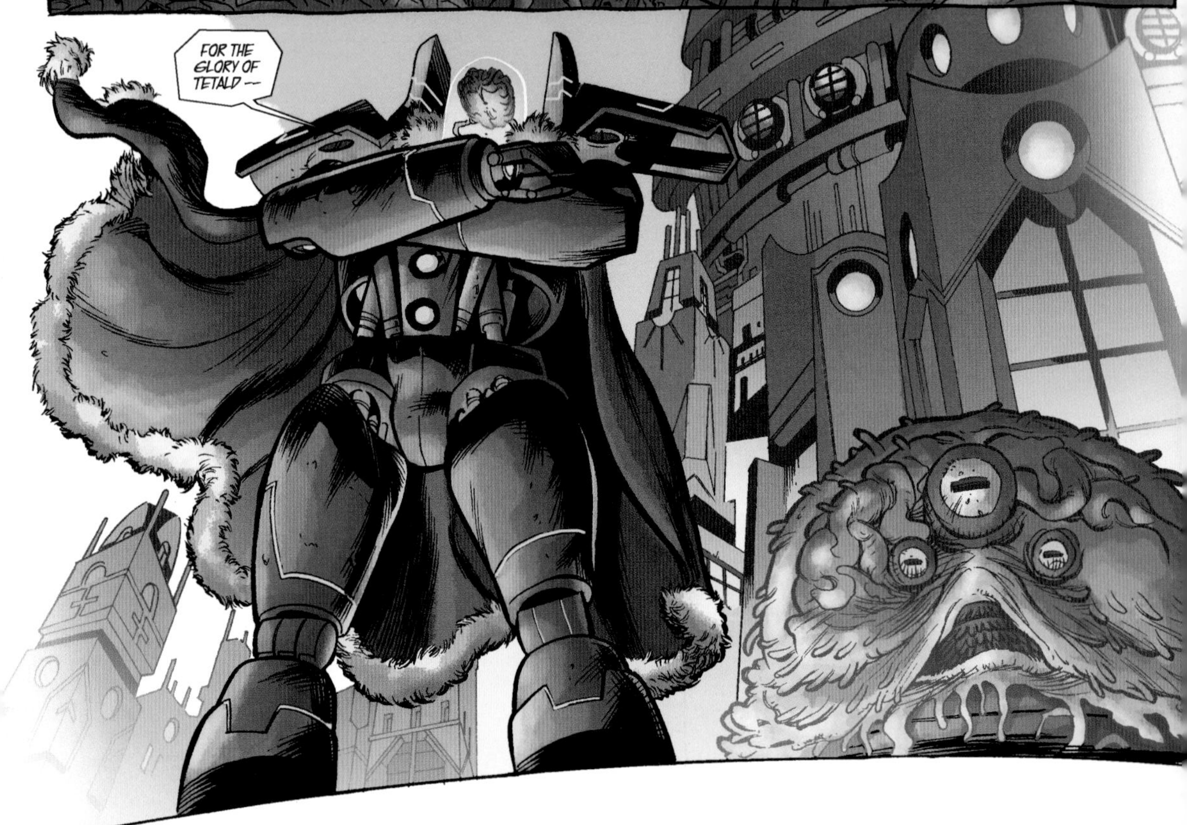
FOR THE
GLORY OF
TETALD --

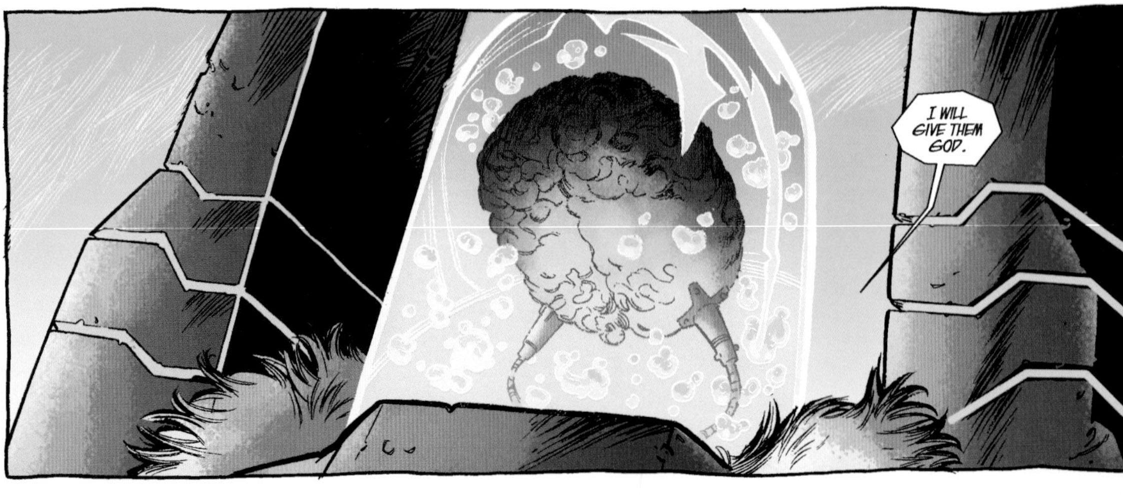
I WILL
GIVE THEM
GOD.

One hundred and fifty million years later...

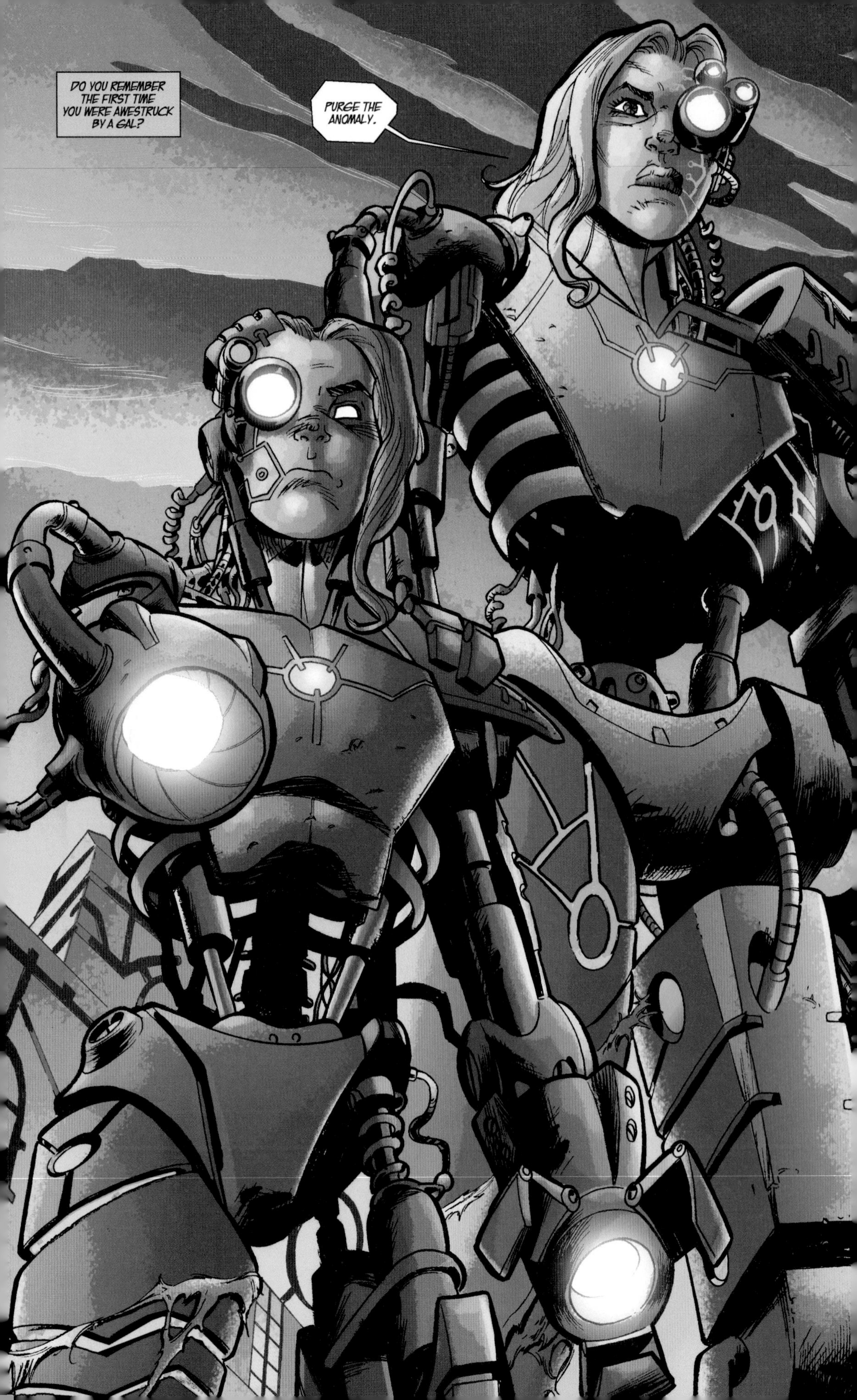
DO YOU REMEMBER THE FIRST TIME YOU WERE AWESTRUCK BY A GAL?
PURGE THE ANOMALY.

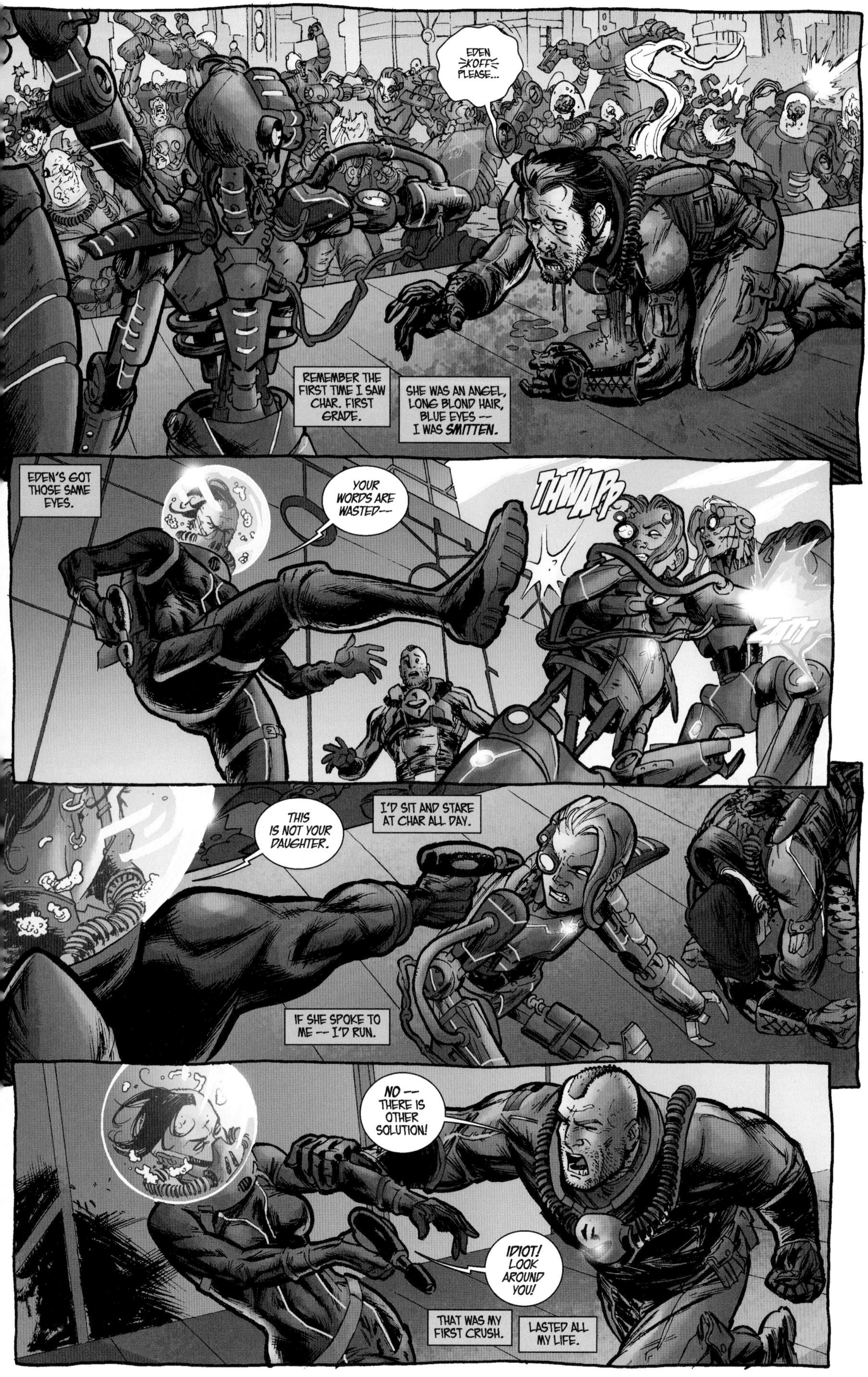
EDEN -KOFF- PLEASE...
REMEMBER THE FIRST TIME I SAW CHAR. FIRST GRADE.
SHE WAS AN ANGEL, LONG BLOND HAIR, BLUE EYES -- I WAS SMITTEN.
EDEN'S GOT THOSE SAME EYES.
YOUR WORDS ARE WASTED--
THWAPP
ZATT
THIS IS NOT YOUR DAUGHTER.
I'D SIT AND STARE AT CHAR ALL DAY.
IF SHE SPOKE TO ME -- I'D RUN.
NO -- THERE IS OTHER SOLUTION!
IDIOT! LOOK AROUND YOU!
THAT WAS MY FIRST CRUSH.
LASTED ALL MY LIFE.

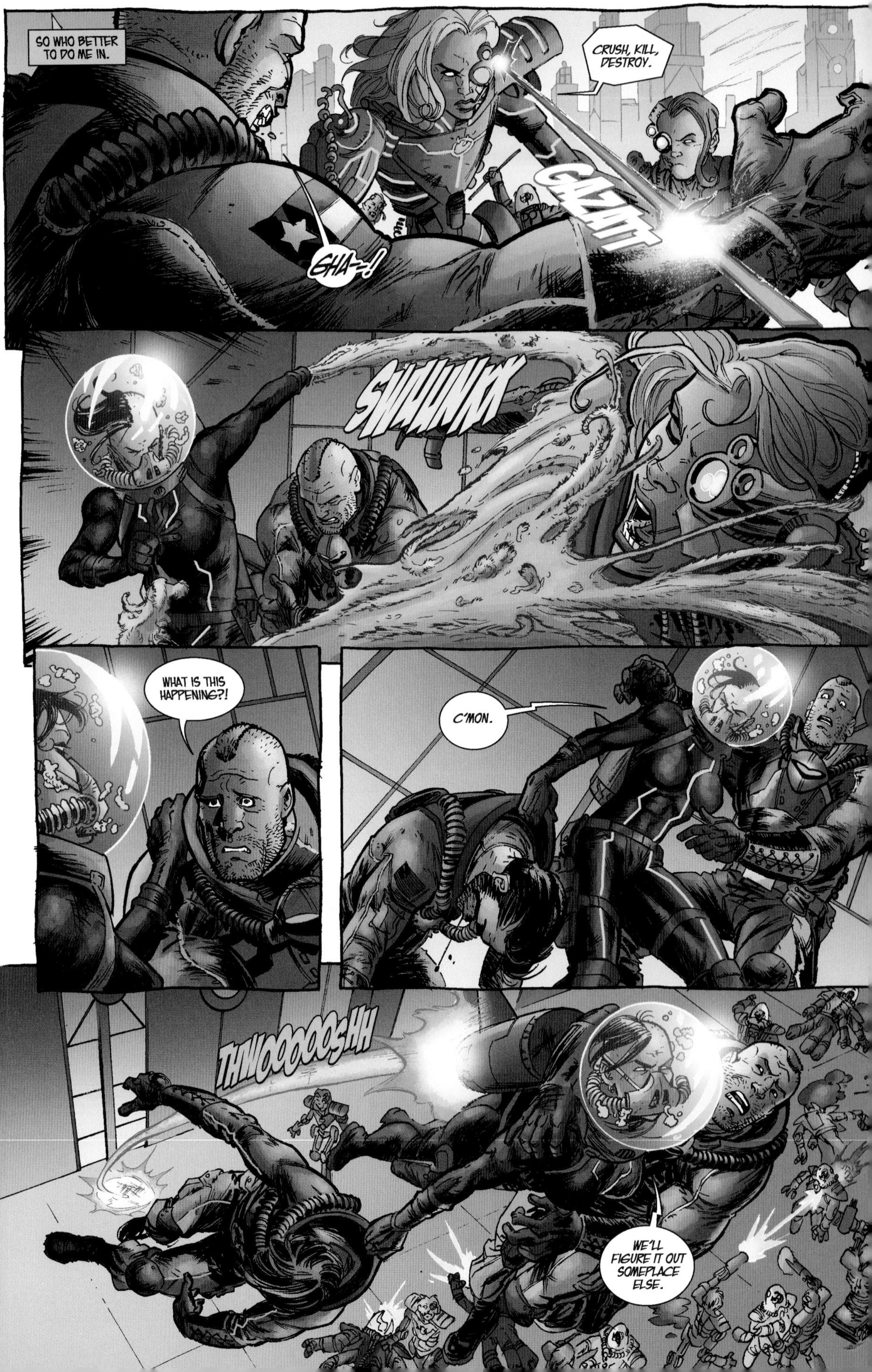
SO WHO BETTER TO DO ME IN.
CRUSH, KILL, DESTROY.
GAZATT
GHA--!
SHLUNKK
WHAT IS THIS HAPPENING?!
C'MON.
THWOOOOOOSHH
WE'LL FIGURE IT OUT SOMEPLACE ELSE.

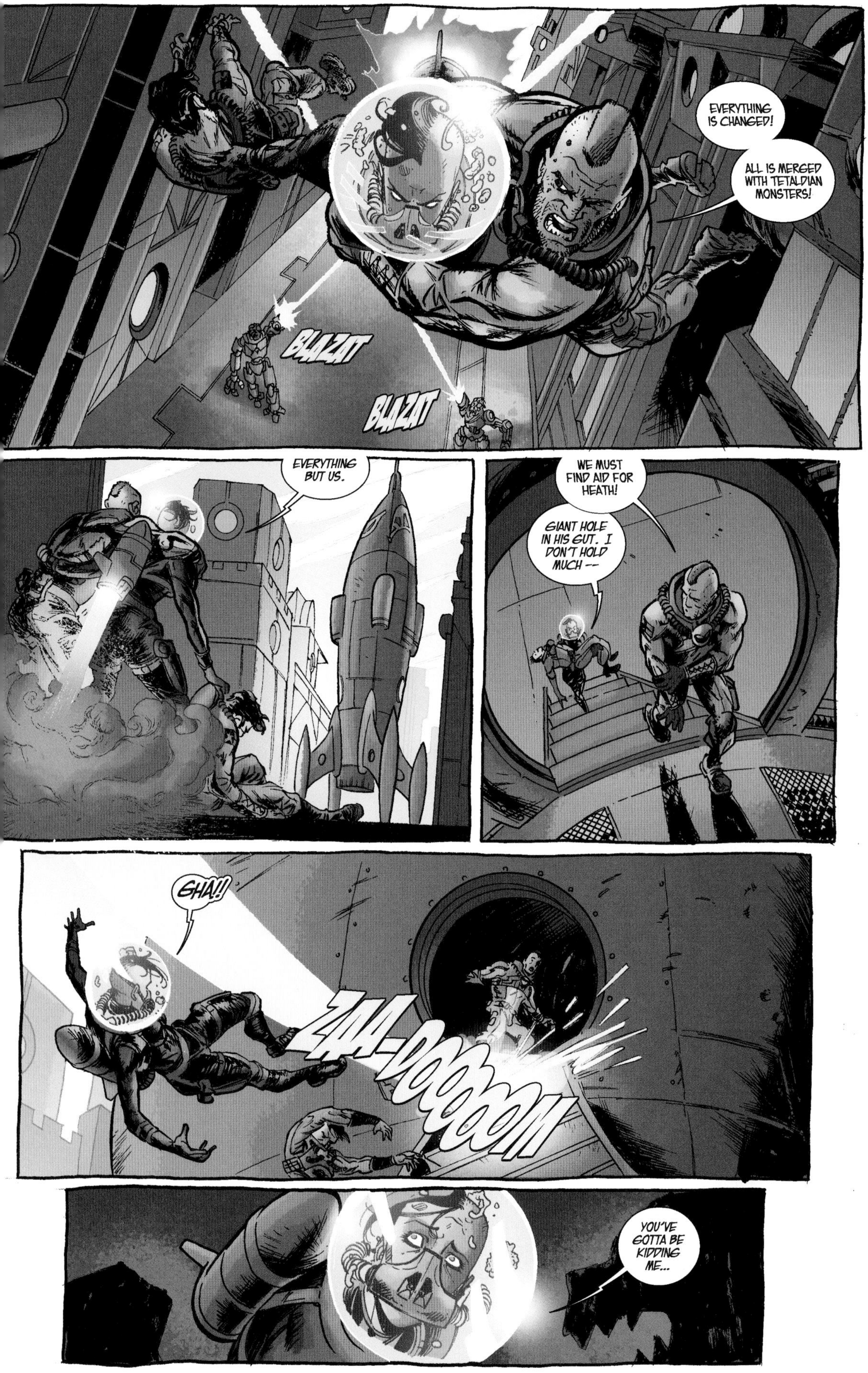
EVERYTHING IS CHANGED!
ALL IS MERGED WITH TETALDIAN MONSTERS!
BLAZAT
BLAZAT
EVERYTHING BUT US.
WE MUST FIND AID FOR HEATH!
GIANT HOLE IN HIS GUT. I DON'T HOLD MUCH --
GHA!!
ZAA-DOOOOOM
YOU'VE GOTTA BE KIDDING ME...

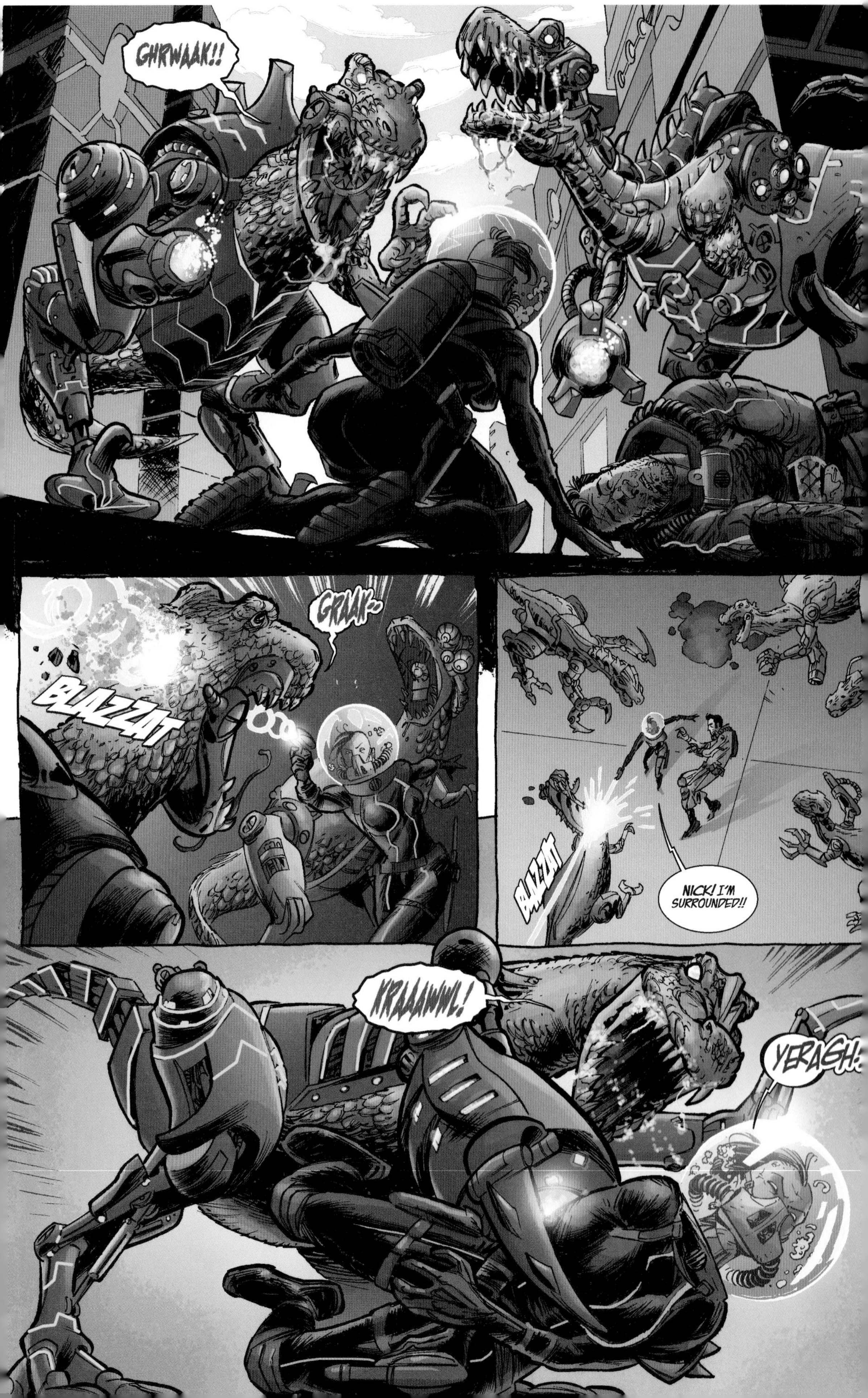
GHRWAAK!!
GRAAK--
BLAZZAT
BLAZZAT
NICK! I'M SURROUNDED!!
KRAAAWWL!
YERAGH!

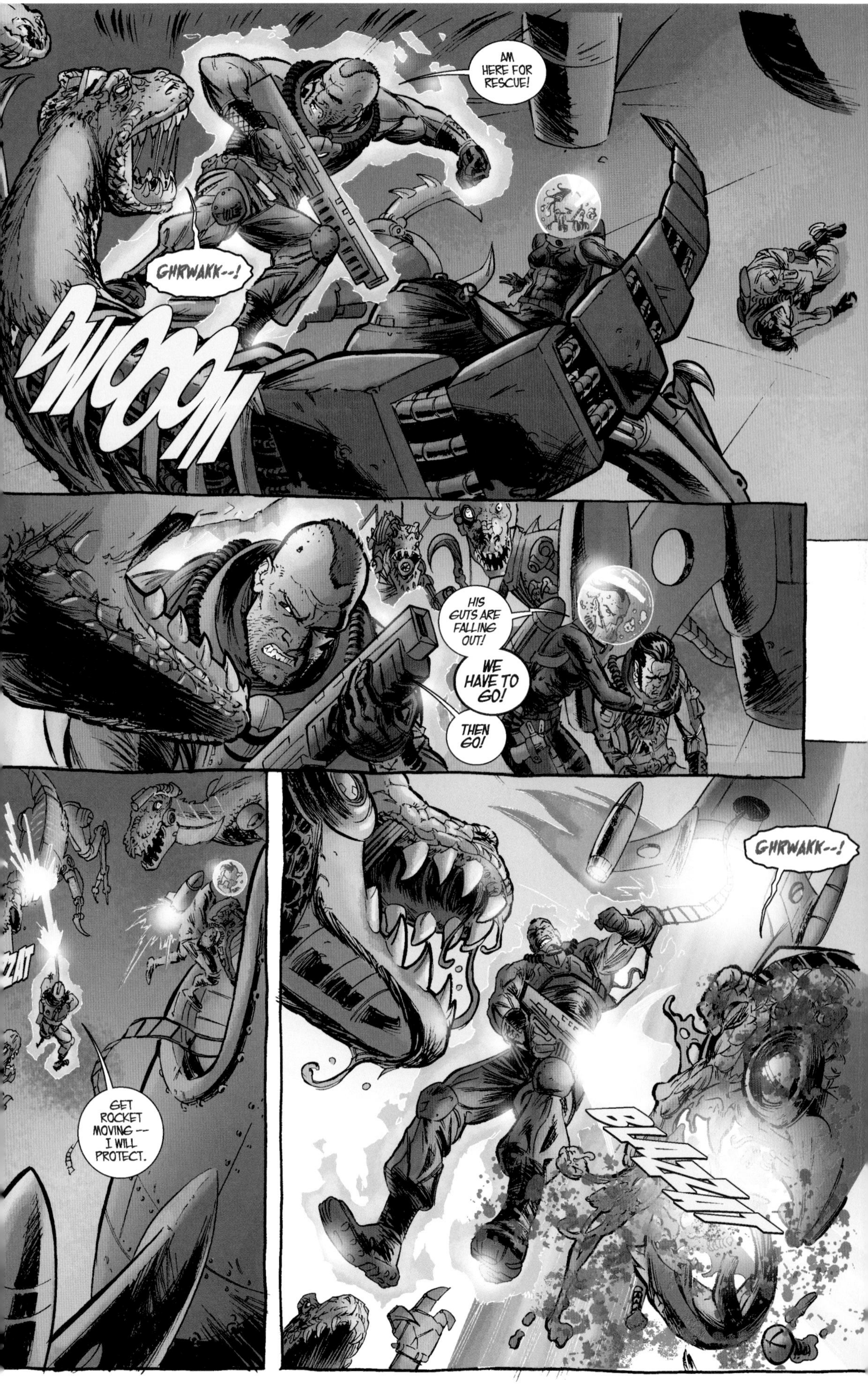
AM HERE FOR RESCUE!
GHRWAKK--!
DWOOOM
HIS GUTS ARE FALLING OUT!
WE HAVE TO GO!
THEN GO!
GET ROCKET MOVING -- I WILL PROTECT.
GHRWAKK--!

ZZAT ZZAT ZZAT

WE ARE CLEAR.

ANNIE, DIAGNOSE FABRIC OF SPACE-TIME -- MUST KNOW WHAT HAS HAPPENED TO FIX.

WHO IS THIS PERSON? WHAT IS SHE DOING TO HEATH?!

FREONIUM -- FILLING HIM UP WITH IT.

QUICK FREEZE, ONLY CHANCE WE HAVE OF SAVING HIS BRAIN.

THIS IS AN UNACCEPTABLE RISK!

LISTEN, SHITHEADS -- HE'S AS GOOD AS DEAD.

THIS WILL AT LEAST PRESERVE HIS BRAIN TILL WE SORT OUT WHAT TO DO.

NO. NOT UNTIL I'M SURE YOU'RE NOT PARTY TO CONSPIRACY --

LISTEN TO ME, IF YOUR FROZEN SIBERIAN BRAIN CAN GRASP THE WEIGHT OF THE SITUATION -- HEATH'S BODY IS DEAD -- HUMANITY HAS BEEN TAKEN OVER BY THE TETALDIANS.

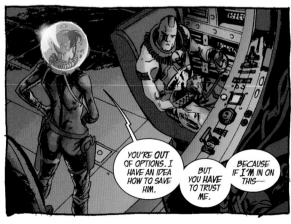

YOU'RE OUT OF OPTIONS. I HAVE AN IDEA HOW TO SAVE HIM.

BUT YOU HAVE TO TRUST ME.

BECAUSE IF I'M IN ON THIS--

YOU'RE DEAD ALREADY.

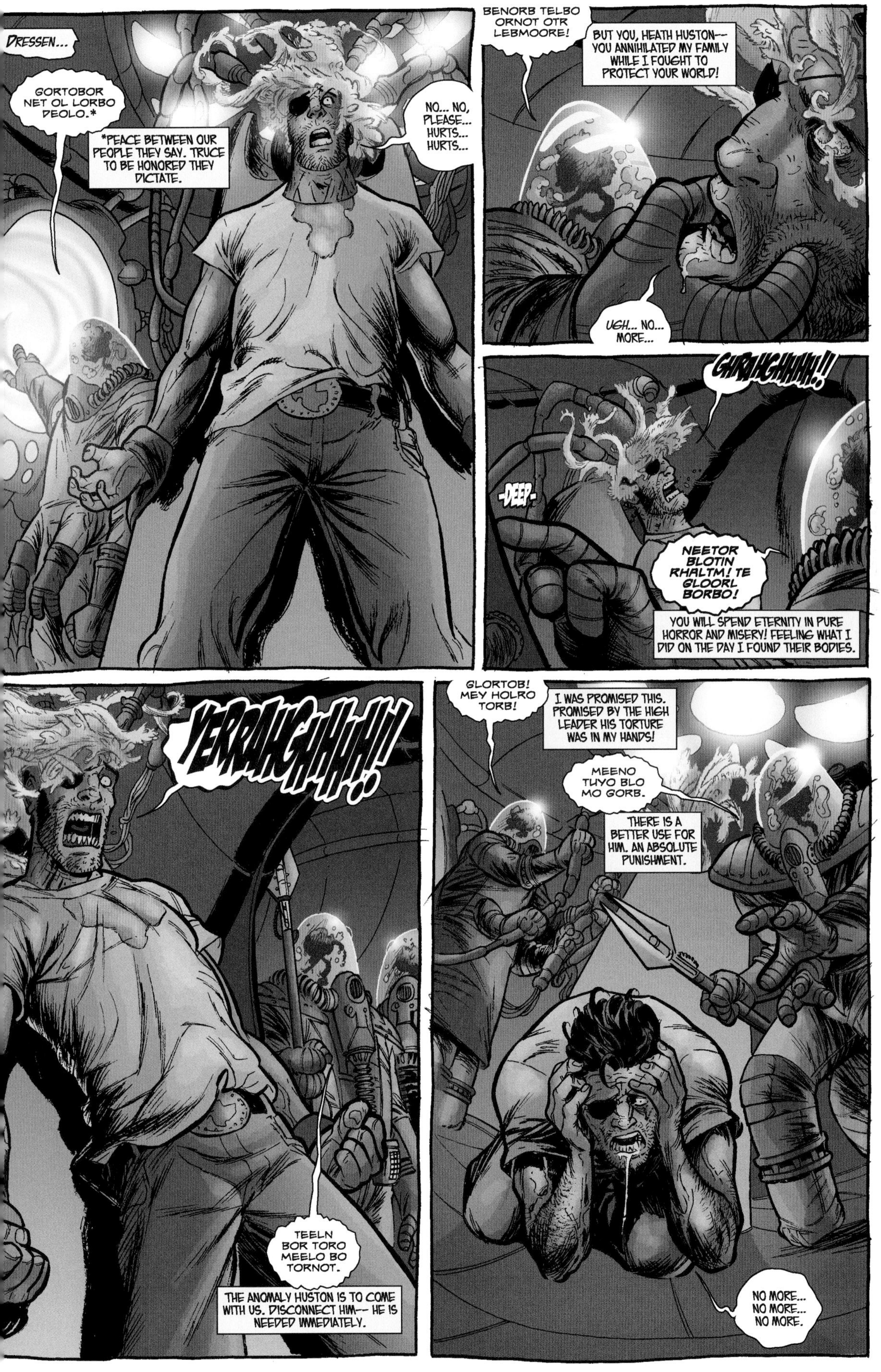
DRESSEN...
GORTOBOR NET OL LORBO DEOLO.*
*PEACE BETWEEN OUR PEOPLE THEY SAY. TRUCE TO BE HONORED THEY DICTATE.
NO... NO, PLEASE... HURTS... HURTS...
BENORB TELBO ORNOT OTR LEBMOORE!
BUT YOU, HEATH HUSTON-- YOU ANNIHILATED MY FAMILY WHILE I FOUGHT TO PROTECT YOUR WORLD!
UGH... NO... MORE...
GHRUHGHHHH!!
-DEEP-
NEETOR BLOTIN RHALTM! TE GLOORL BORBO!
YOU WILL SPEND ETERNITY IN PURE HORROR AND MISERY! FEELING WHAT I DID ON THE DAY I FOUND THEIR BODIES.
YERRAHGHHHH!!
TEELN BOR TORO MEELO BO TORNOT.
THE ANOMALY HUSTON IS TO COME WITH US. DISCONNECT HIM-- HE IS NEEDED IMMEDIATELY.
GLORTOB! MEY HOLRO TORB!
I WAS PROMISED THIS. PROMISED BY THE HIGH LEADER HIS TORTURE WAS IN MY HANDS!
MEENO TUYO BLO MO GORB.
THERE IS A BETTER USE FOR HIM. AN ABSOLUTE PUNISHMENT.
NO MORE... NO MORE... NO MORE.

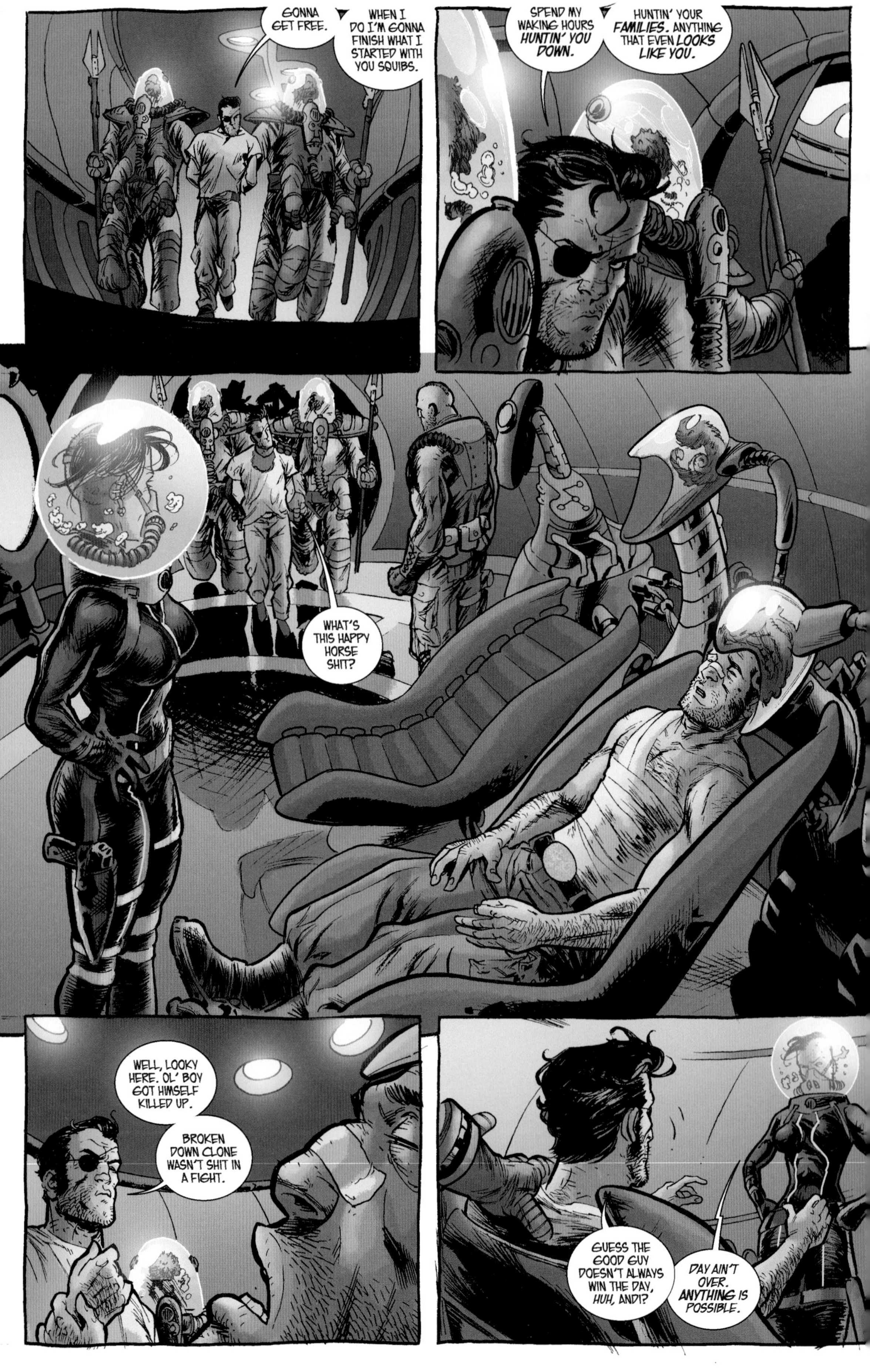
GONNA GET FREE.
WHEN I DO I'M GONNA FINISH WHAT I STARTED WITH YOU SQUIBS.
SPEND MY WAKING HOURS HUNTIN' YOU DOWN.
HUNTIN' YOUR FAMILIES. ANYTHING THAT EVEN LOOKS LIKE YOU.
WHAT'S THIS HAPPY HORSE SHIT?
WELL, LOOKY HERE. OL' BOY GOT HIMSELF KILLED UP.
BROKEN DOWN CLONE WASN'T SHIT IN A FIGHT.
GUESS THE GOOD GUY DOESN'T ALWAYS WIN THE DAY, HUH, ANDI?
DAY AIN'T OVER. ANYTHING IS POSSIBLE.

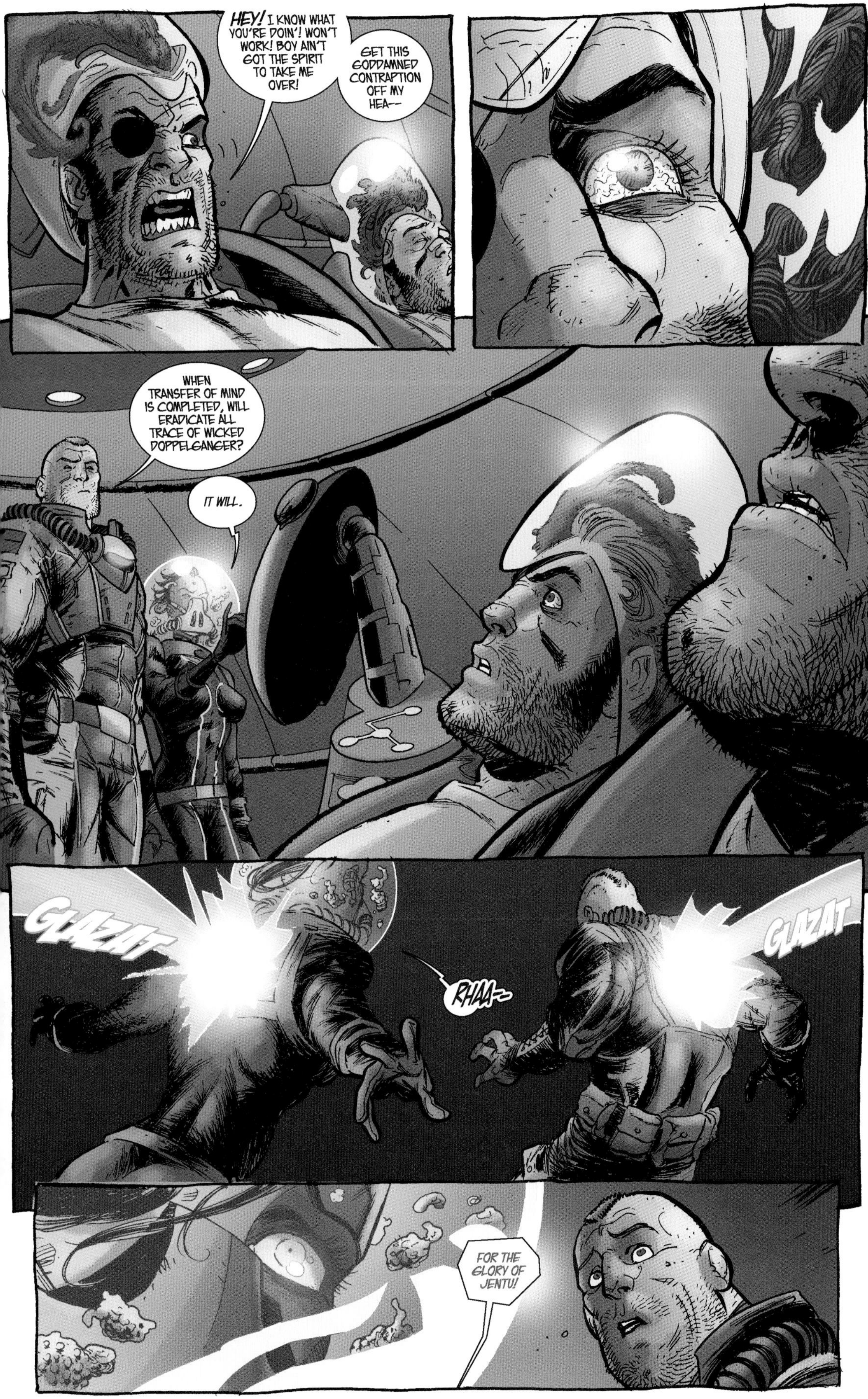
HEY! I KNOW WHAT YOU'RE DOIN'! WON'T WORK! BOY AIN'T GOT THE SPIRIT TO TAKE ME OVER!
GET THIS GODDAMNED CONTRAPTION OFF MY HEA--
WHEN TRANSFER OF MIND IS COMPLETED, WILL ERADICATE ALL TRACE OF WICKED DOPPELGANGER?
IT WILL.
GLAZAT
RHAA--
GLAZAT
FOR THE GLORY OF JENTU!

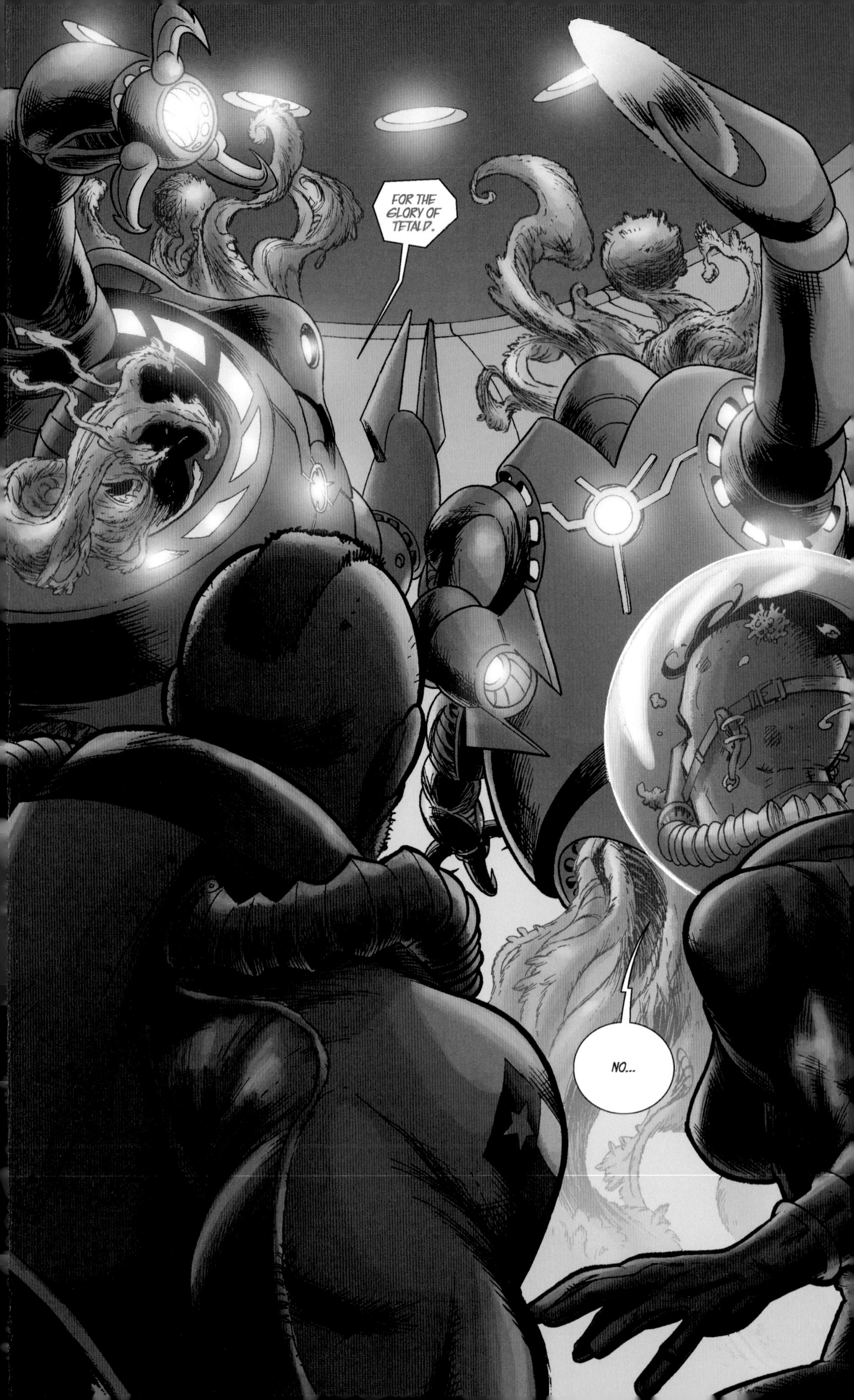
FOR THE GLORY OF TETALD.
NO...

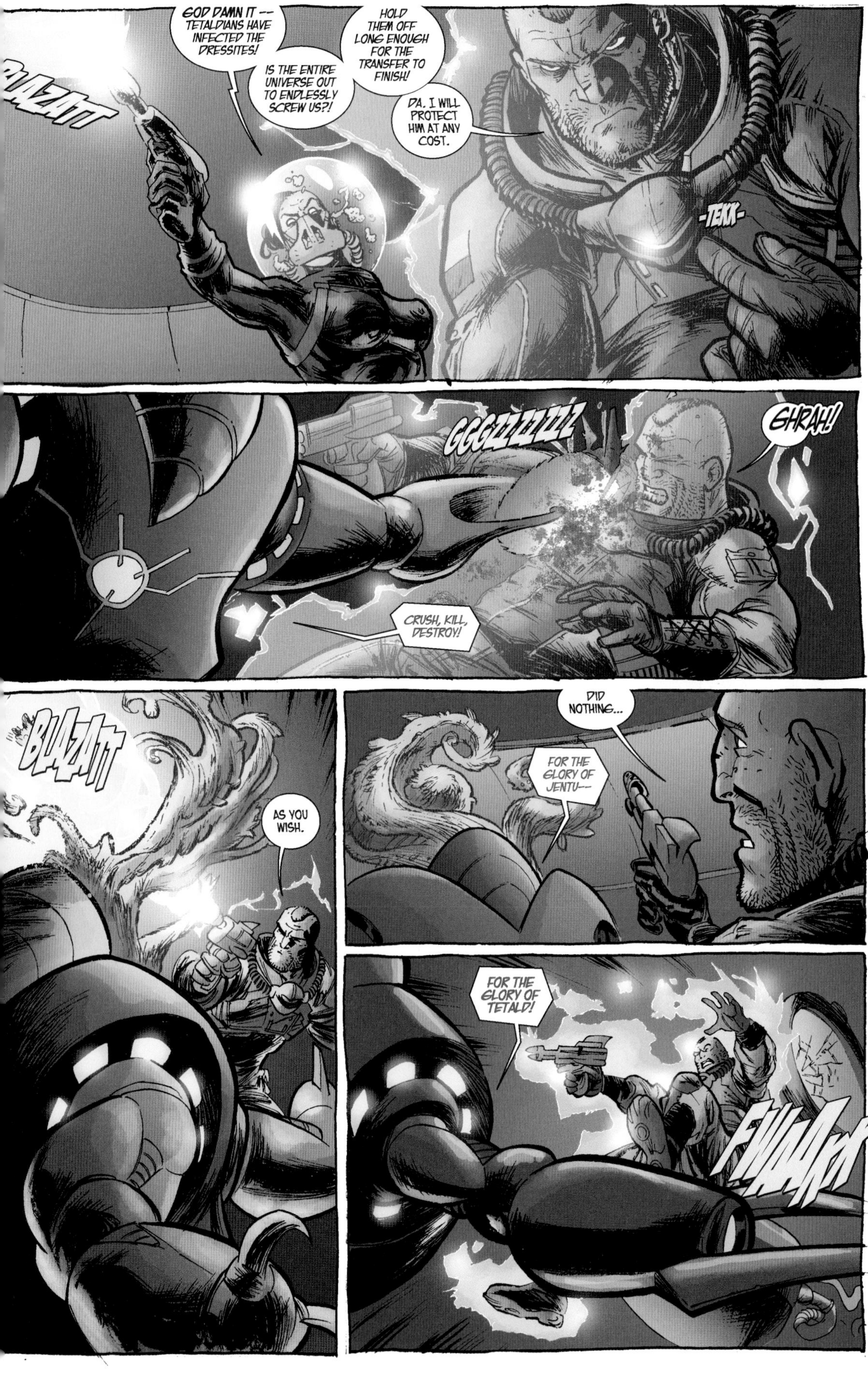
BLAZATT
GOD DAMN IT -- TETALDIANS HAVE INFECTED THE DRESSITES!
IS THE ENTIRE UNIVERSE OUT TO ENDLESSLY SCREW US?!
HOLD THEM OFF LONG ENOUGH FOR THE TRANSFER TO FINISH!
DA. I WILL PROTECT HIM AT ANY COST.
-TEKK-
GGGZZZZZZZ
GHRAH!
CRUSH, KILL, DESTROY!
BLAZATT
AS YOU WISH.
DID NOTHING...
FOR THE GLORY OF JENTU--
FOR THE GLORY OF TETALD!
FWAAKK

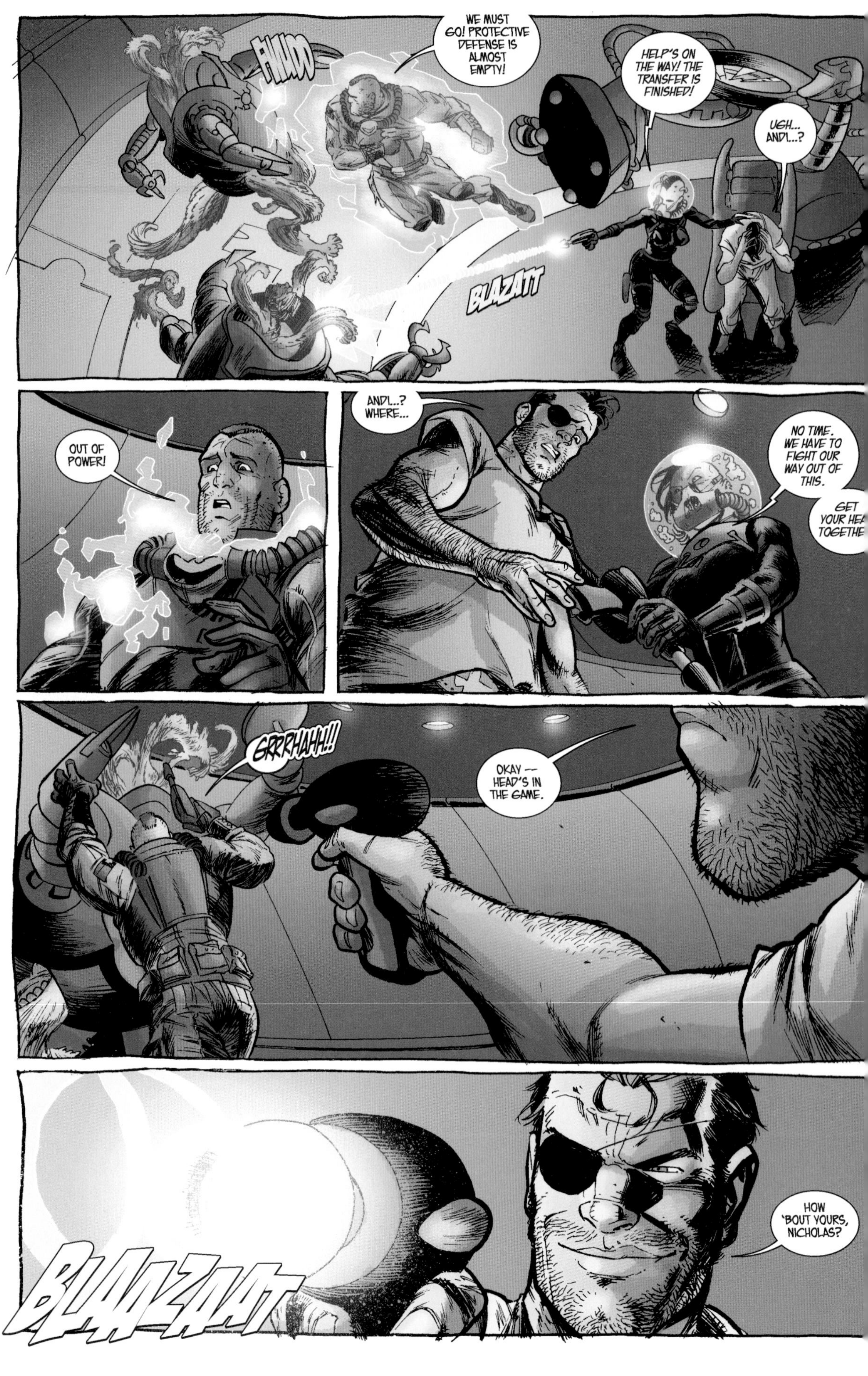
WE MUST GO! PROTECTIVE DEFENSE IS ALMOST EMPTY!
HELP'S ON THE WAY! THE TRANSFER IS FINISHED!
UGH... ANDI...?
BLAZATT
OUT OF POWER!
ANDI...? WHERE...
NO TIME. WE HAVE TO FIGHT OUR WAY OUT OF THIS.
GET YOUR HEA TOGETHE
GRRRHAHH!!
OKAY -- HEAD'S IN THE GAME.
HOW 'BOUT YOURS, NICHOLAS?
BLAAZAAT

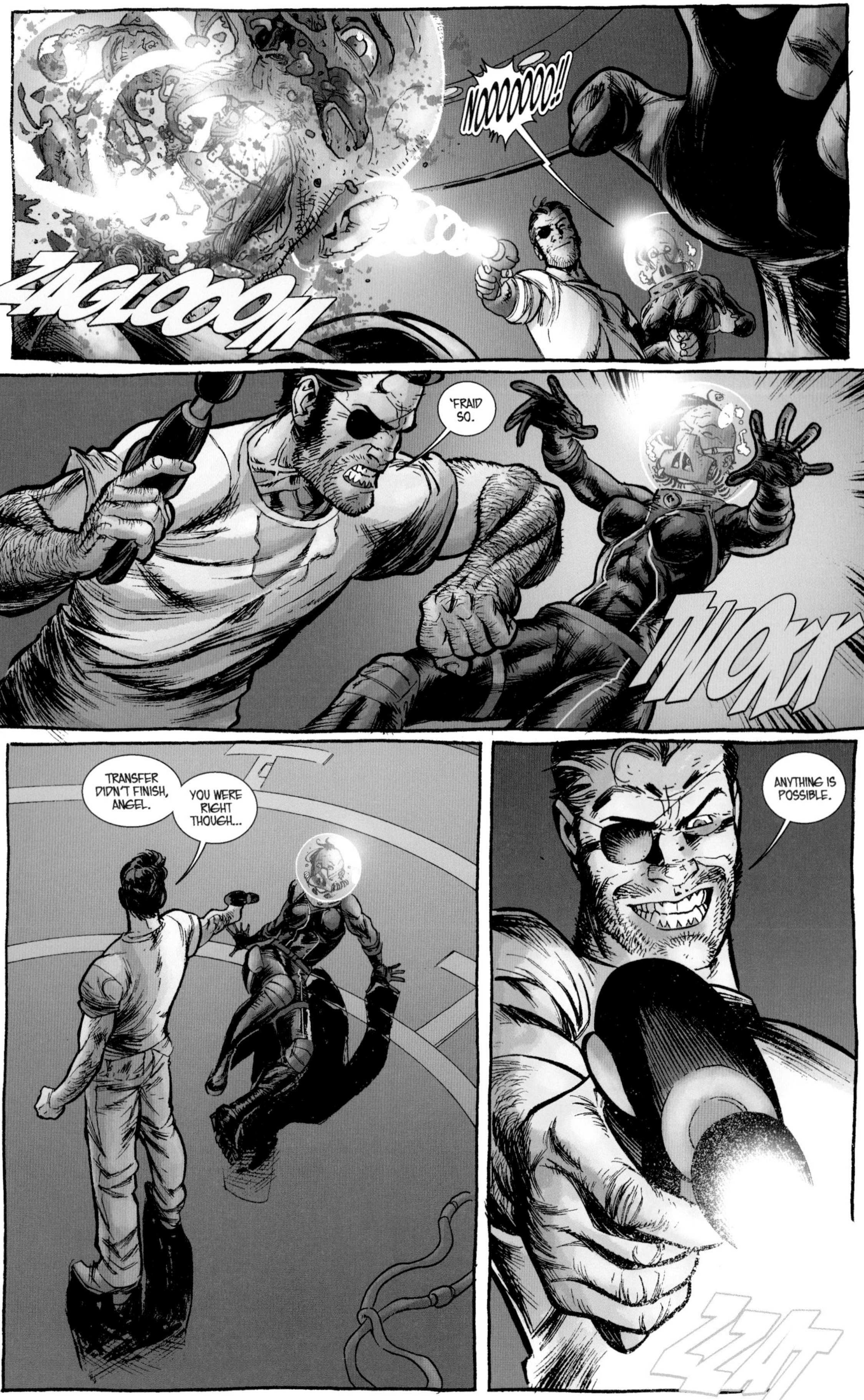
NOOOOOOO!!
ZAGLOOOM
'FRAID SO.
TWONK
TRANSFER DIDN'T FINISH, ANGEL.
YOU WERE RIGHT THOUGH...
ANYTHING IS POSSIBLE.
ZZAT

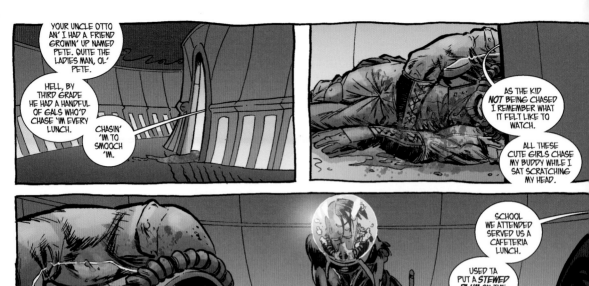

YOUR UNCLE OTTO AN' I HAD A FRIEND GROWIN' UP NAMED PETE. QUITE THE LADIES MAN, OL' PETE.

HELL, BY THIRD GRADE HE HAD A HANDFUL OF GALS WHO'D CHASE 'IM EVERY LUNCH.

CHASIN' 'IM TO SMOOCH 'IM.

AS THE KID *NOT* BEING CHASED I REMEMBER WHAT IT FELT LIKE TO WATCH.

ALL THESE CUTE GIRLS CHASE MY BUDDY WHILE I SAT SCRATCHING MY HEAD.

SCHOOL WE ATTENDED SERVED US A CAFETERIA LUNCH.

USED TA PUT A *STEWED PLUM* ON THE TRAY.

EACH DAY EVERY KID IGNORED THE PURPLE MASS -- WE ALL THOUGHT IT WAS A *ROTTEN OLD TOMATO* THEY WERE SERVING US.

N-NOT... NOT LIKE THIS...

PETE, HE TELLS ME IF I EAT THE FLESHY MASS OF PUTRID TORTURE HE'LL TELL ALL THEM GIRLS TO CHASE *ME* AROUND THAT DAY.

KNOW WHAT TASTES WORSE THAN THE SWEETNESS OF A *STEWED PLUM*?

WHEN YOU THINK YOU'RE EATIN' A *ROTTEN TOMATO.*

...NOT LIKE THIS...

BUT I ATE IT.

AND OL' PETE GINGERSON, WELL, HE DIDN'T TELL THE GIRLS TO DO A *DAMNED THING.*

I SAT WATCHING THEM CHASE HIM THAT DAY, AND LEARNED A *LESSON* ABOUT THE GUY WHO IS *CURRENTLY WINNING* --

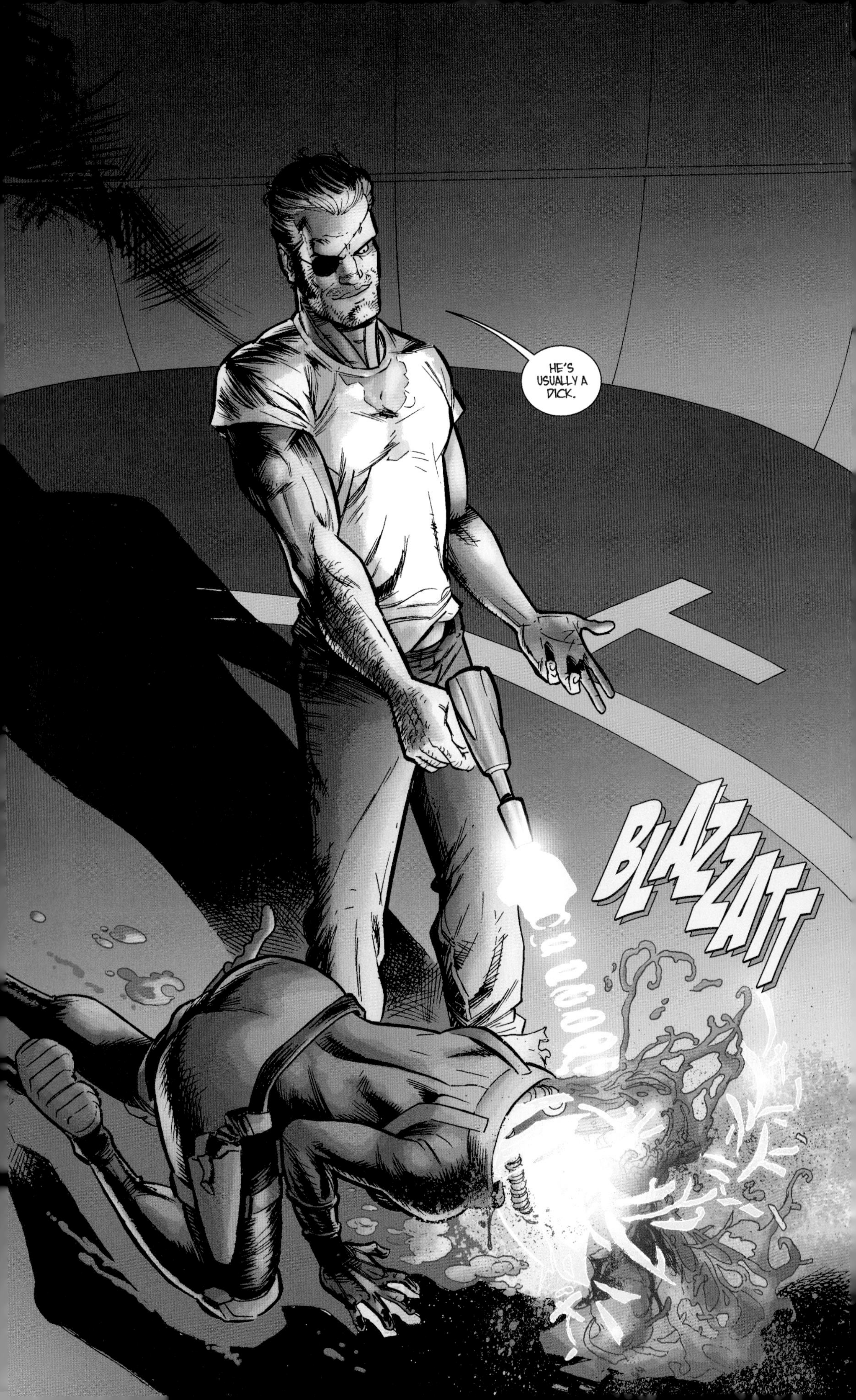
HE'S USUALLY A DICK.
BLAZZATT

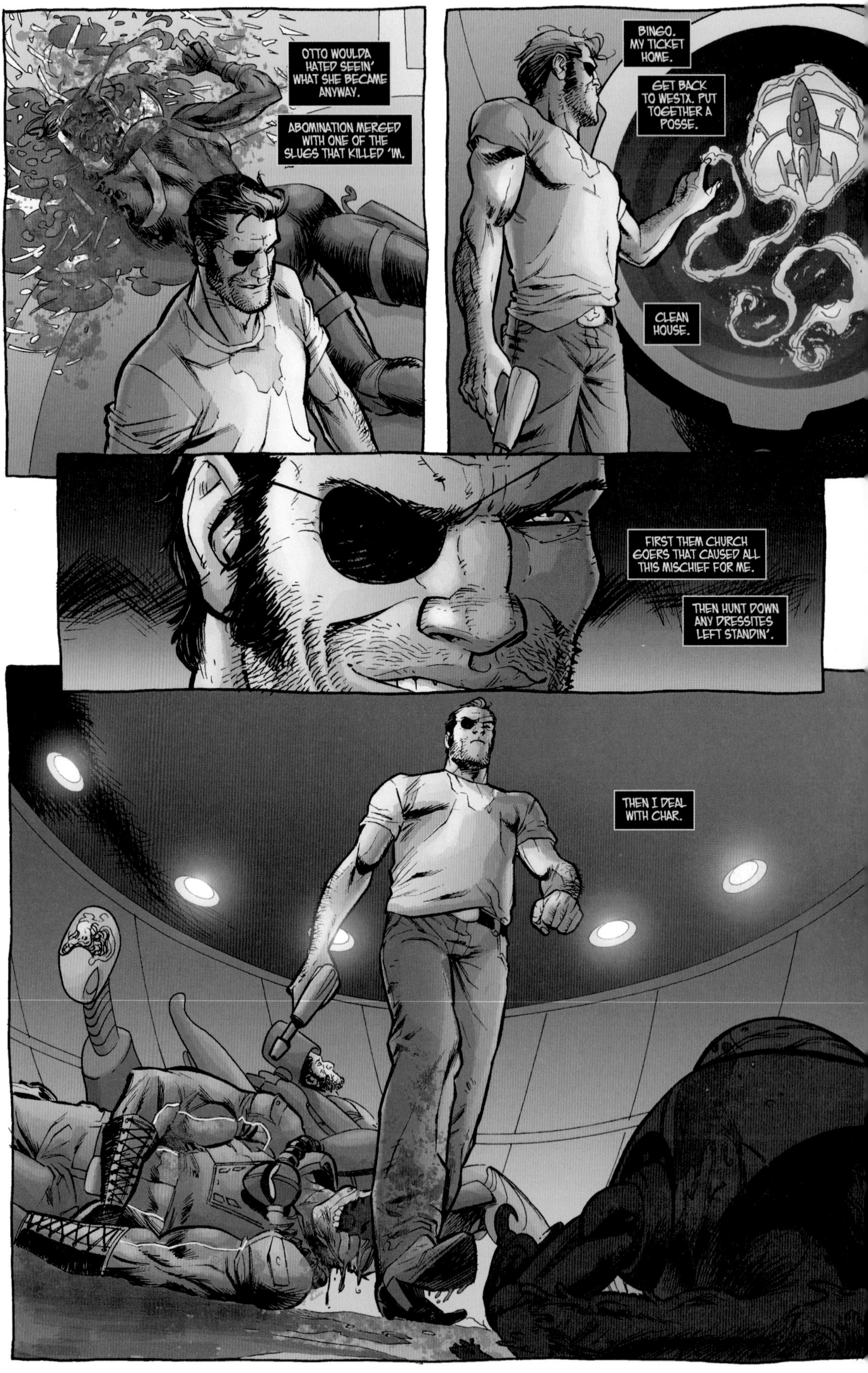
OTTO WOULDA HATED SEEIN' WHAT SHE BECAME ANYWAY.
ABOMINATION MERGED WITH ONE OF THE SLUGS THAT KILLED 'IM.
BINGO. MY TICKET HOME.
GET BACK TO WESTX. PUT TOGETHER A POSSE.
CLEAN HOUSE.
FIRST THEM CHURCH GOERS THAT CAUSED ALL THIS MISCHIEF FOR ME.
THEN HUNT DOWN ANY DRESSITES LEFT STANDIN'.
THEN I DEAL WITH CHAR.

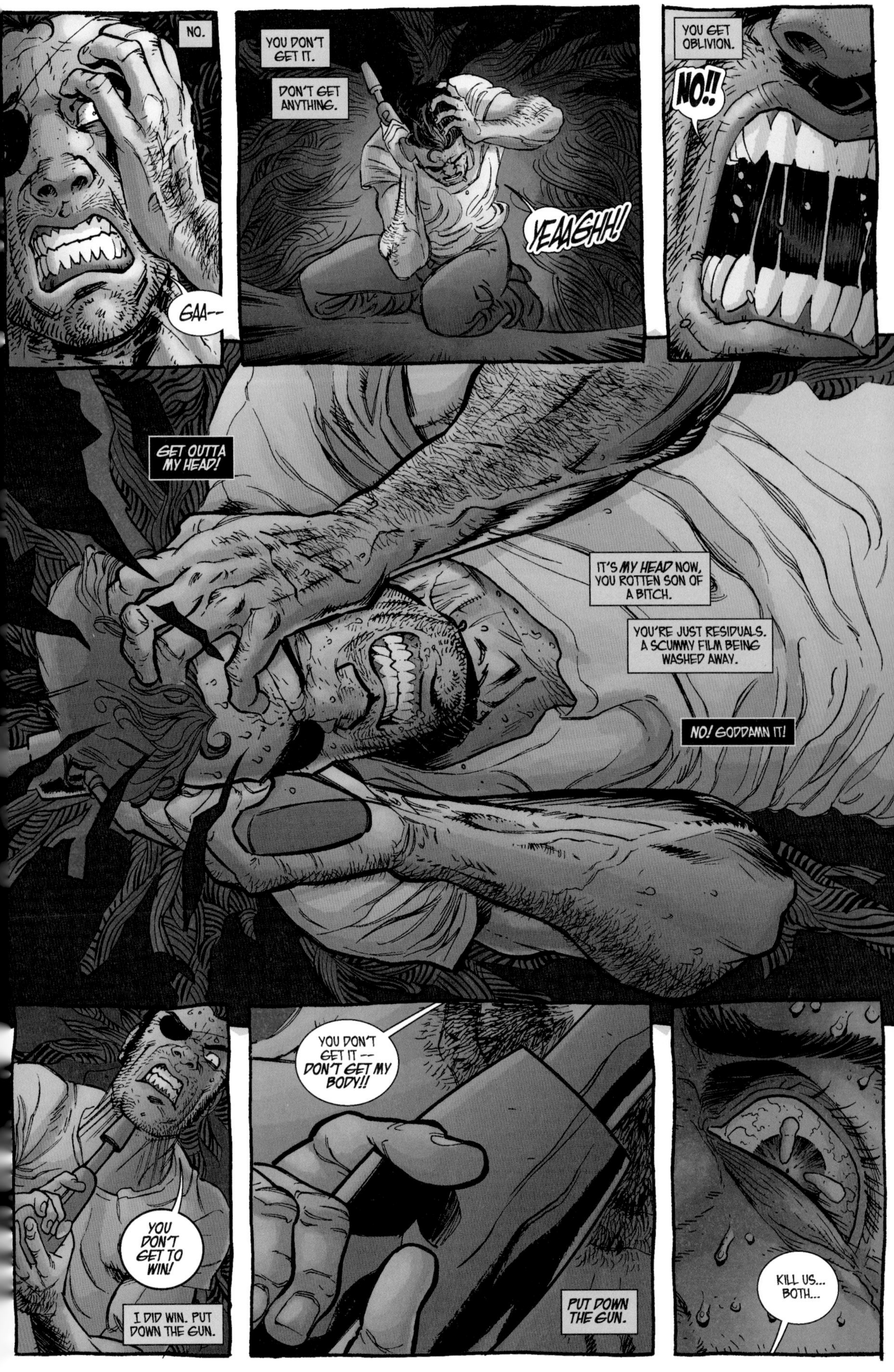
NO.
GAA--
YOU DON'T GET IT.
DON'T GET ANYTHING.
YEAAGHH!
YOU GET OBLIVION.
NO!!
GET OUTTA MY HEAD!
IT'S MY HEAD NOW, YOU ROTTEN SON OF A BITCH.
YOU'RE JUST RESIDUALS. A SCUMMY FILM BEING WASHED AWAY.
NO! GODDAMN IT!
YOU DON'T GET TO WIN!
I DID WIN. PUT DOWN THE GUN.
YOU DON'T GET IT -- DON'T GET MY BODY!!
PUT DOWN THE GUN.
KILL US... BOTH...

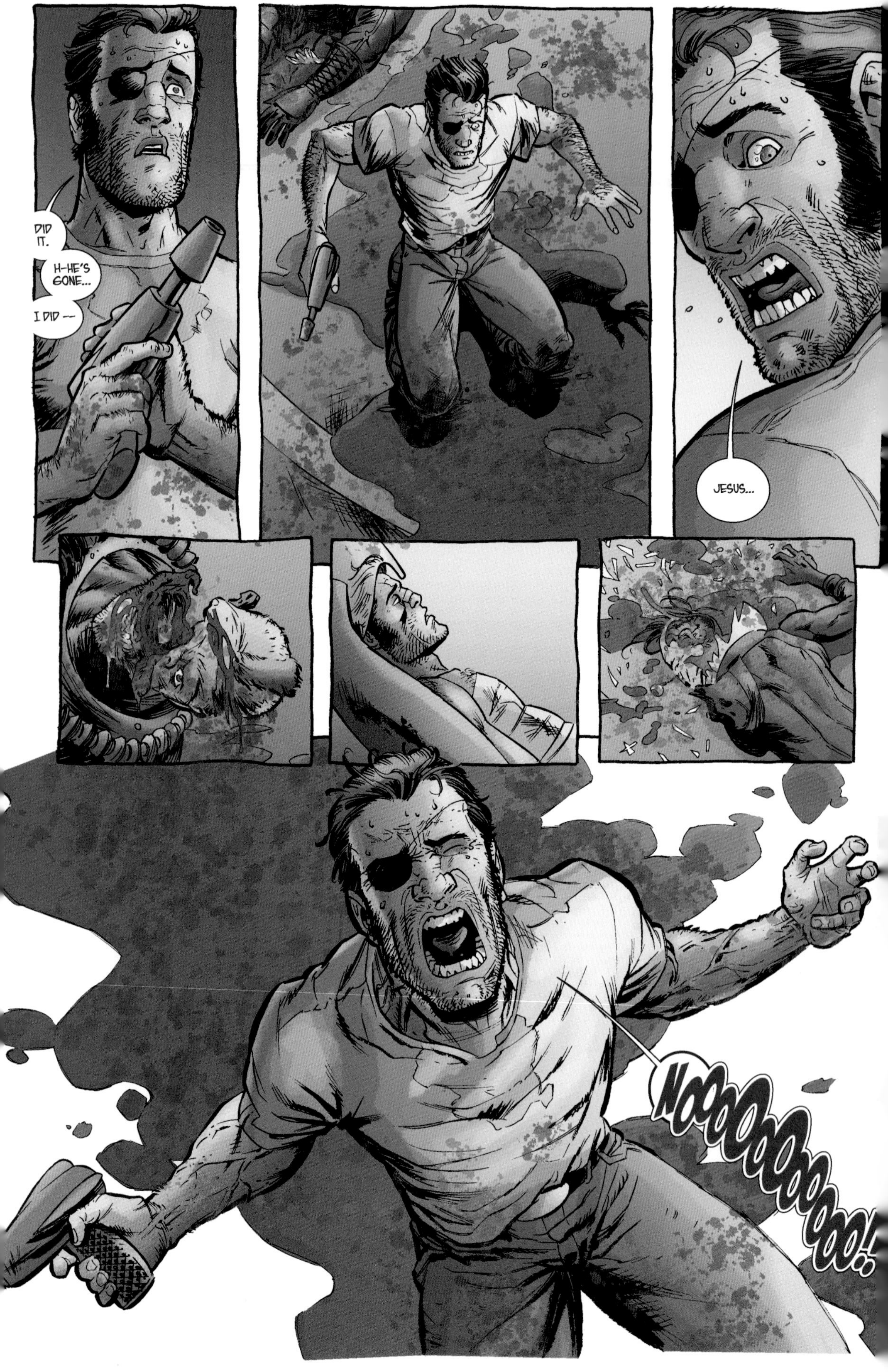

DID IT.
H-HE'S GONE...
I DID --
JESUS...
NOOOOOOOOOOOO!!

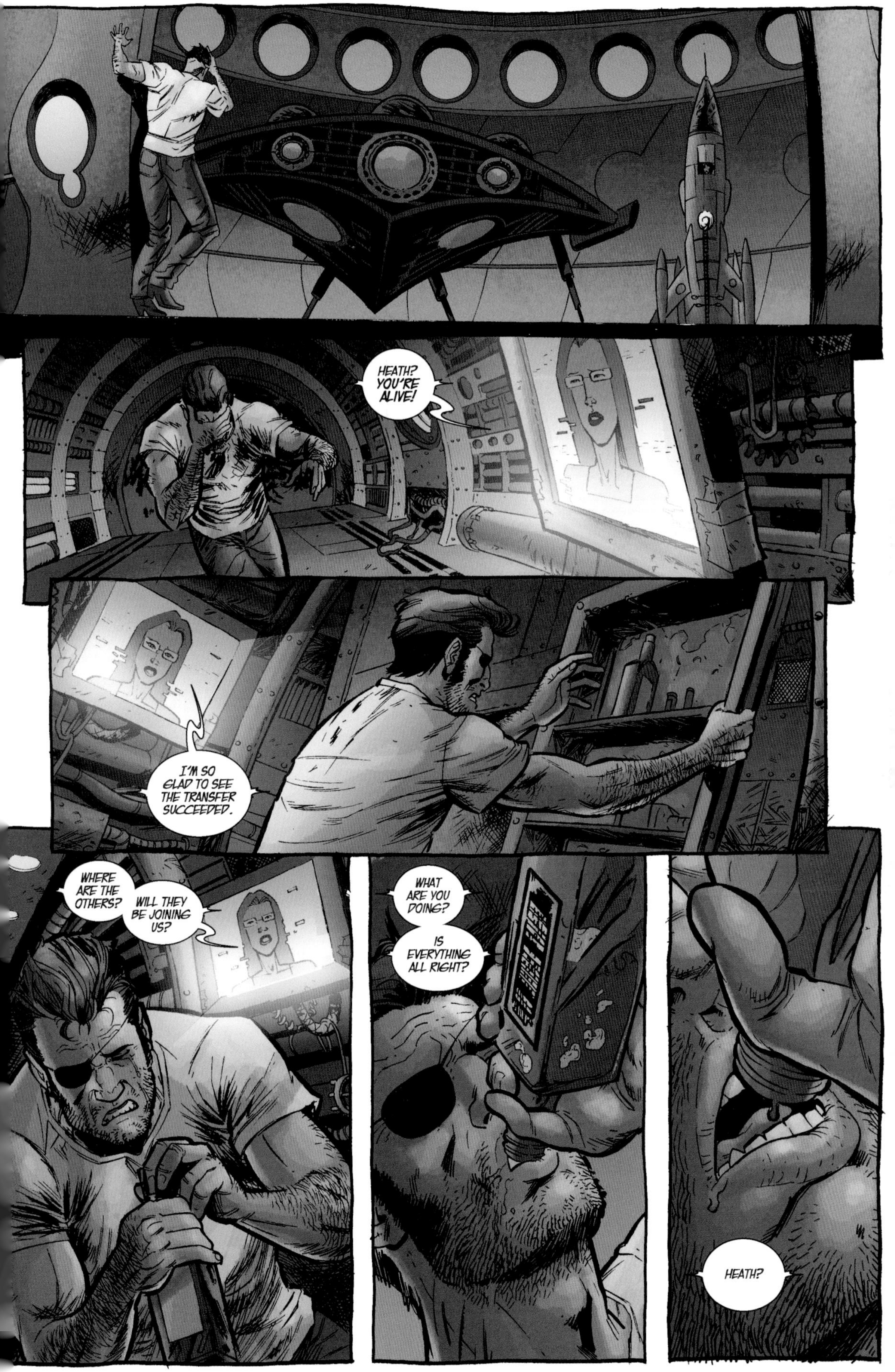
HEATH? YOU'RE ALIVE!
I'M SO GLAD TO SEE THE TRANSFER SUCCEEDED.
WHERE ARE THE OTHERS?
WILL THEY BE JOINING US?
WHAT ARE YOU DOING?
IS EVERYTHING ALL RIGHT?
HEATH?

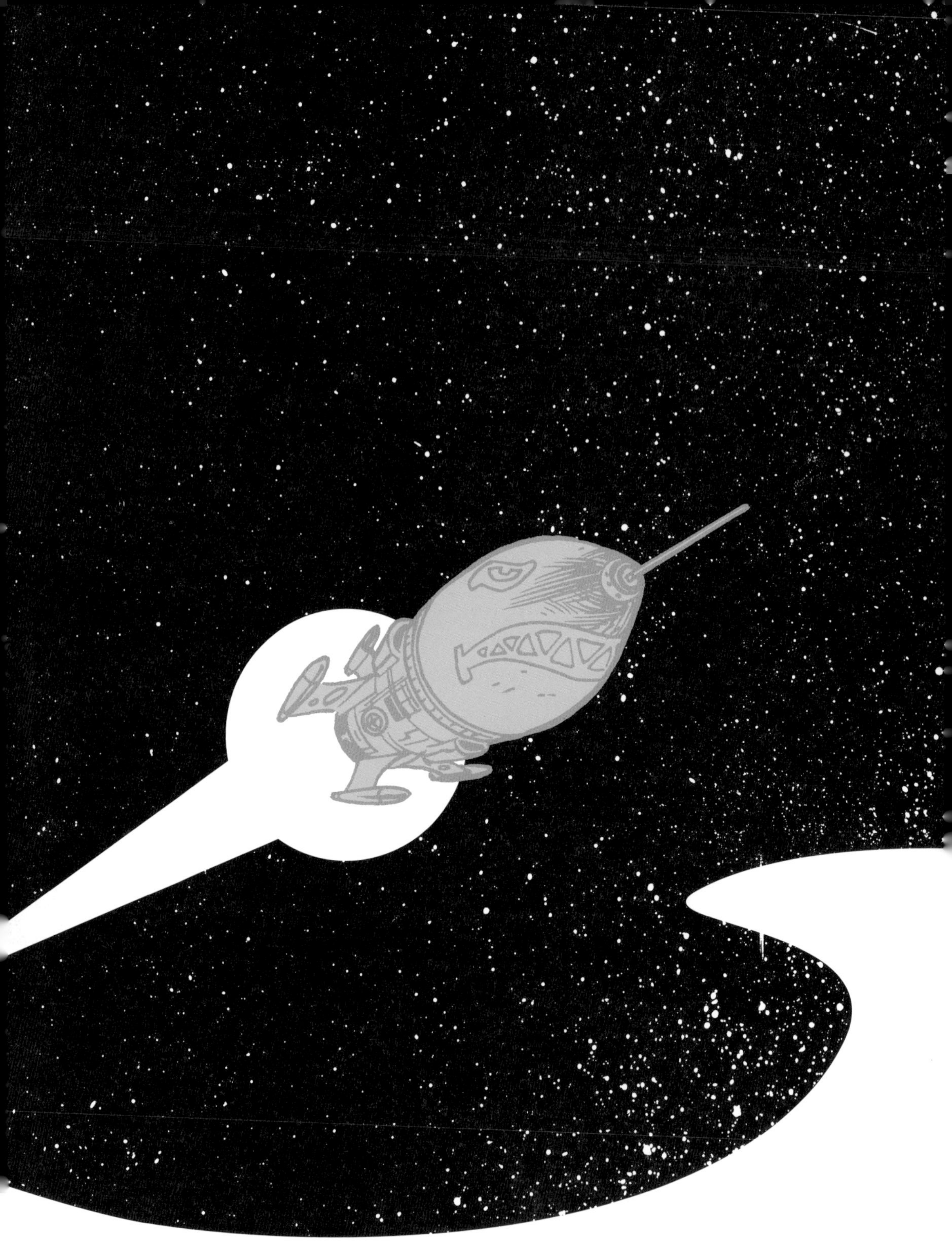

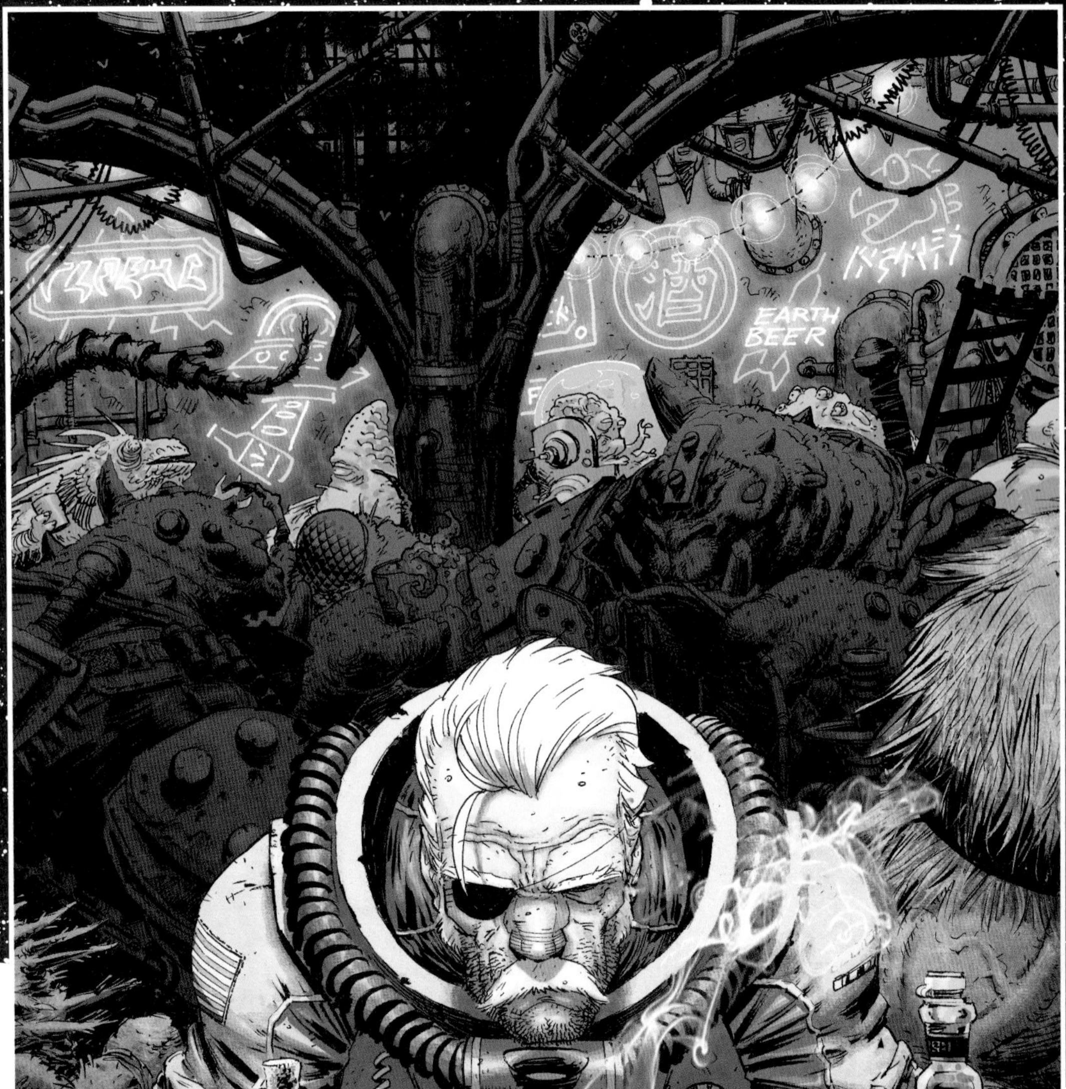
EARTH
BEER

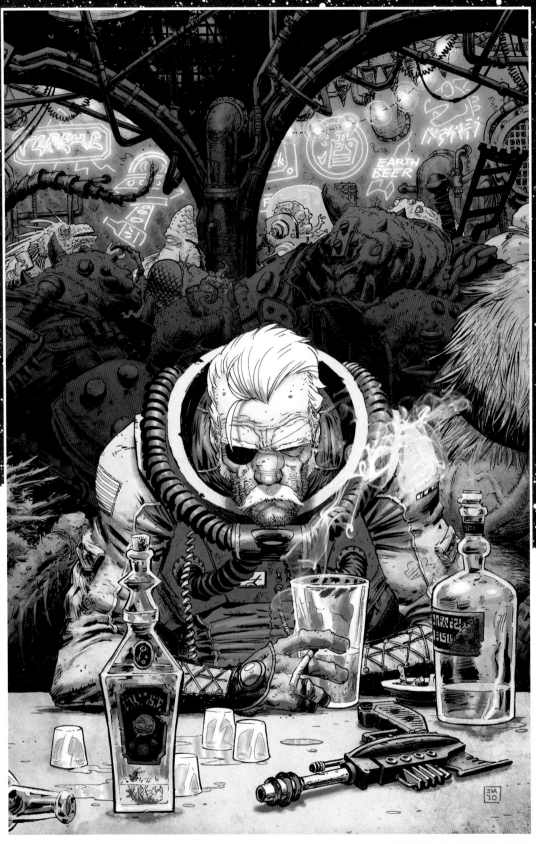

FEAR AGENT #29

ART BY **TONY MOORE**

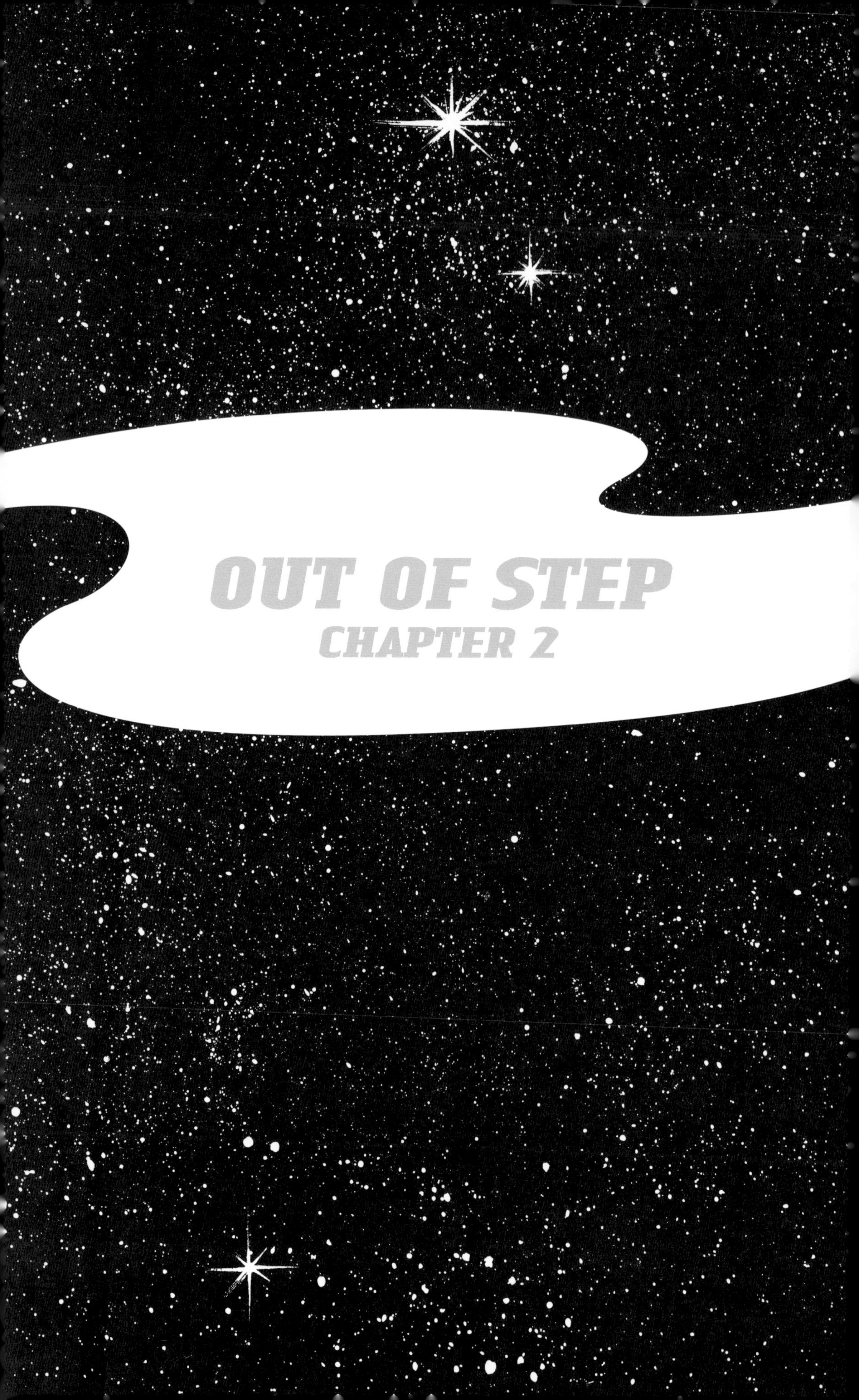
OUT OF STEP
CHAPTER 2

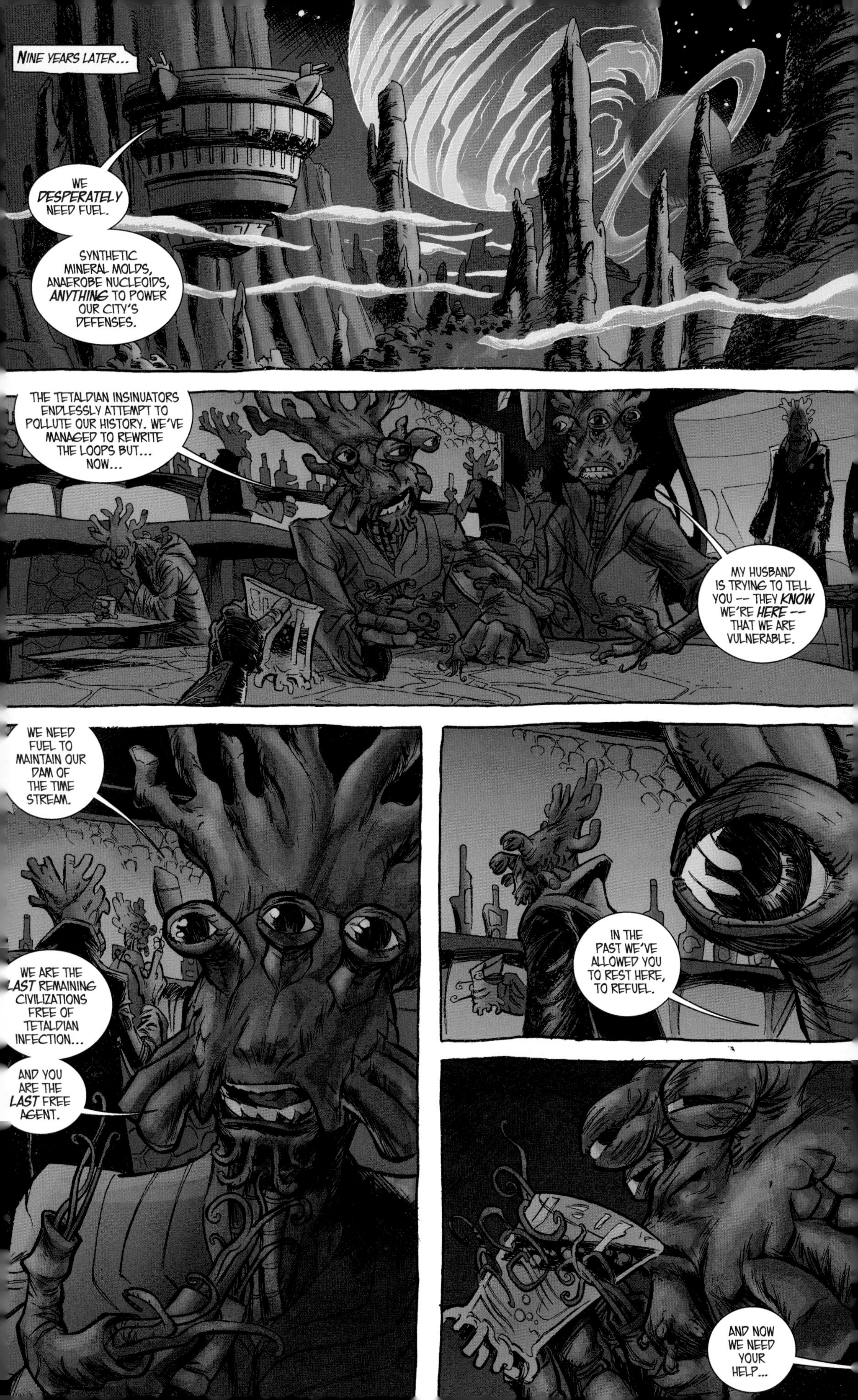
NINE YEARS LATER...
WE DESPERATELY NEED FUEL.
SYNTHETIC MINERAL MOLDS, ANAEROBE NUCLEOIDS, ANYTHING TO POWER OUR CITY'S DEFENSES.
THE TETALDIAN INSINUATORS ENDLESSLY ATTEMPT TO POLLUTE OUR HISTORY. WE'VE MANAGED TO REWRITE THE LOOPS BUT... NOW...
MY HUSBAND IS TRYING TO TELL YOU -- THEY KNOW WE'RE HERE -- THAT WE ARE VULNERABLE.
WE NEED FUEL TO MAINTAIN OUR DAM OF THE TIME STREAM.
WE ARE THE LAST REMAINING CIVILIZATIONS FREE OF TETALDIAN INFECTION...
AND YOU ARE THE LAST FREE AGENT.
IN THE PAST WE'VE ALLOWED YOU TO REST HERE, TO REFUEL.
AND NOW WE NEED YOUR HELP...

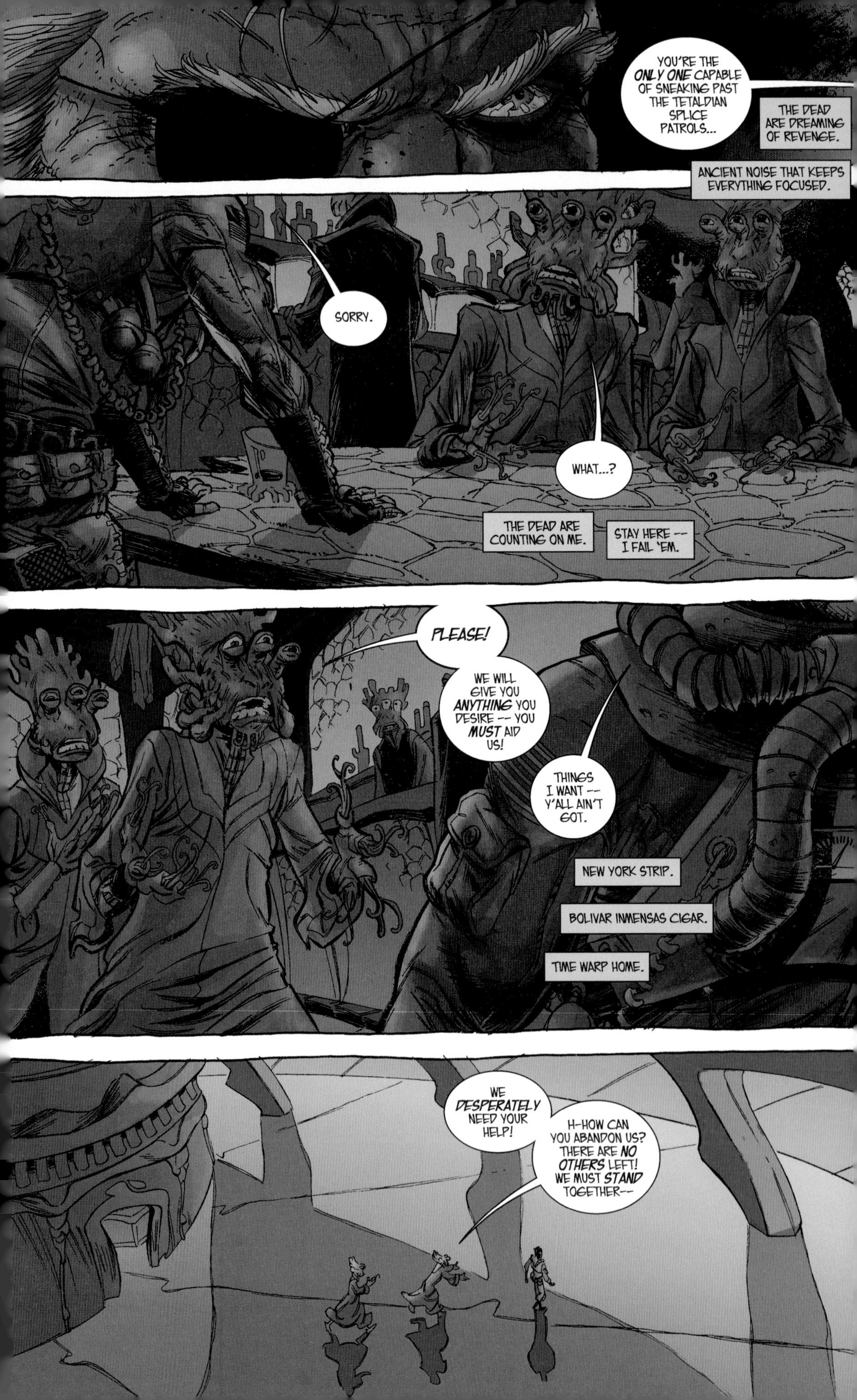
YOU'RE THE ONLY ONE CAPABLE OF SNEAKING PAST THE TETALDIAN SPLICE PATROLS...
THE DEAD ARE DREAMING OF REVENGE.
ANCIENT NOISE THAT KEEPS EVERYTHING FOCUSED.
SORRY.
WHAT...?
THE DEAD ARE COUNTING ON ME.
STAY HERE -- I FAIL 'EM.
PLEASE!
WE WILL GIVE YOU ANYTHING YOU DESIRE -- YOU MUST AID US!
THINGS I WANT -- Y'ALL AIN'T GOT.
NEW YORK STRIP.
BOLIVAR INMENSAS CIGAR.
TIME WARP HOME.
WE DESPERATELY NEED YOUR HELP!
H-HOW CAN YOU ABANDON US? THERE ARE NO OTHERS LEFT! WE MUST STAND TOGETHER--

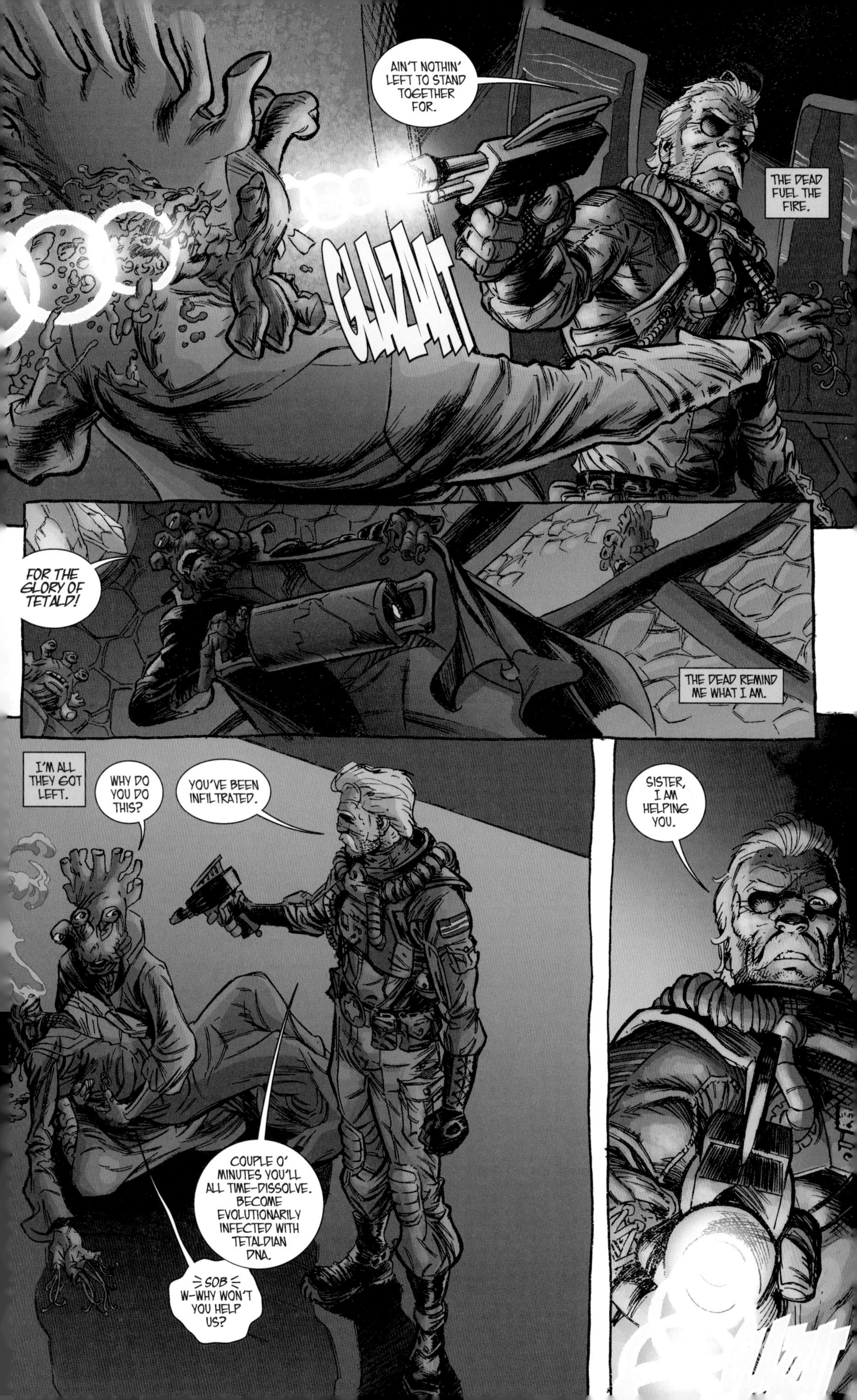
AIN'T NOTHIN' LEFT TO STAND TOGETHER FOR.
THE DEAD FUEL THE FIRE.
CLAZAAT
FOR THE GLORY OF TETALD!
THE DEAD REMIND ME WHAT I AM.
I'M ALL THEY GOT LEFT.
WHY DO YOU DO THIS?
YOU'VE BEEN INFILTRATED.
COUPLE O' MINUTES YOU'LL ALL TIME-DISSOLVE. BECOME EVOLUTIONARILY INFECTED WITH TETALDIAN DNA.
SOB W-WHY WON'T YOU HELP US?
SISTER, I AM HELPING YOU.

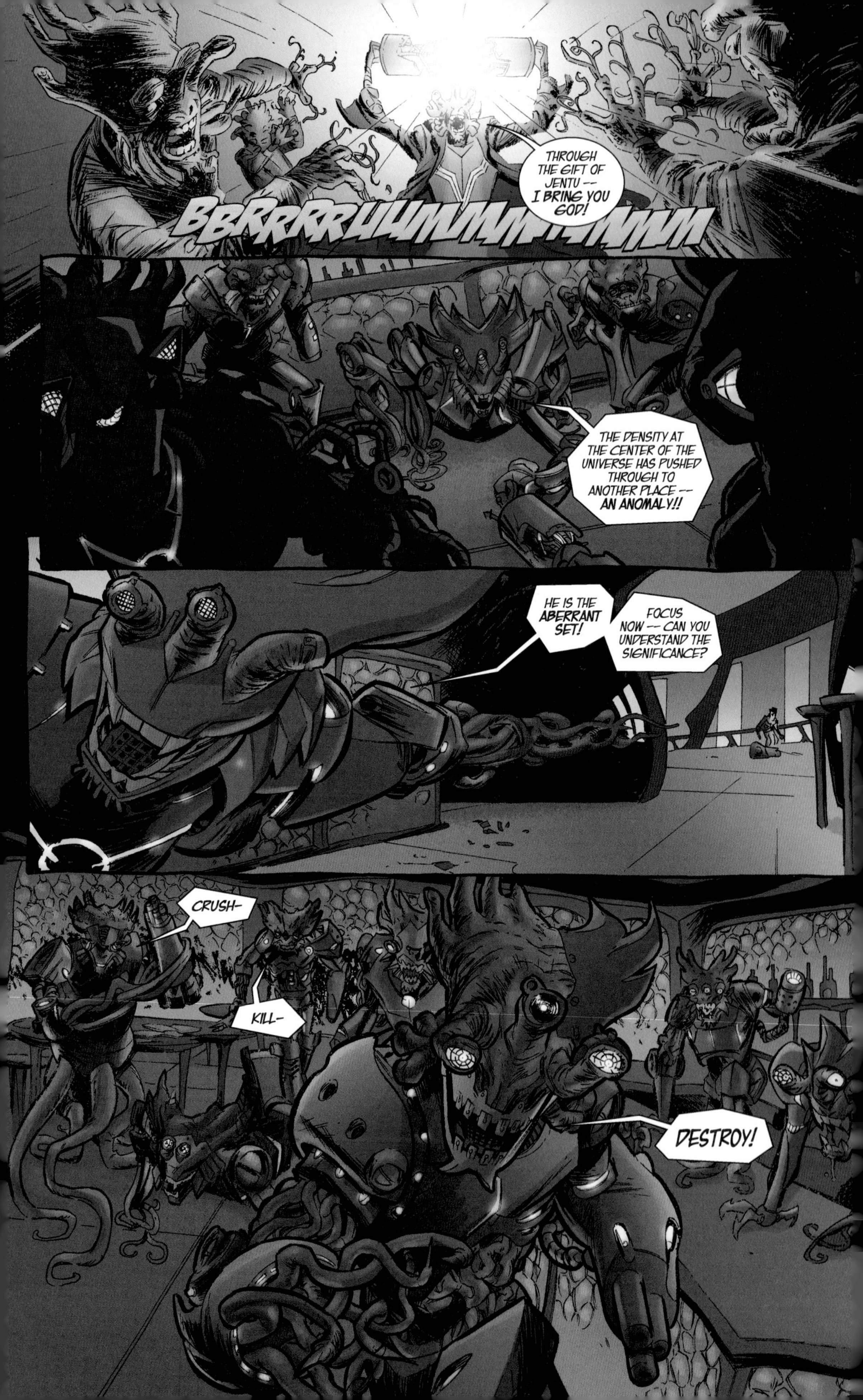
THROUGH THE GIFT OF JENTU -- I BRING YOU GOD!
BBRRRRRUUMMMMMMMMM
THE DENSITY AT THE CENTER OF THE UNIVERSE HAS PUSHED THROUGH TO ANOTHER PLACE -- AN ANOMALY!!
HE IS THE ABERRANT SET!
FOCUS NOW -- CAN YOU UNDERSTAND THE SIGNIFICANCE?
CRUSH-
KILL-
DESTROY!

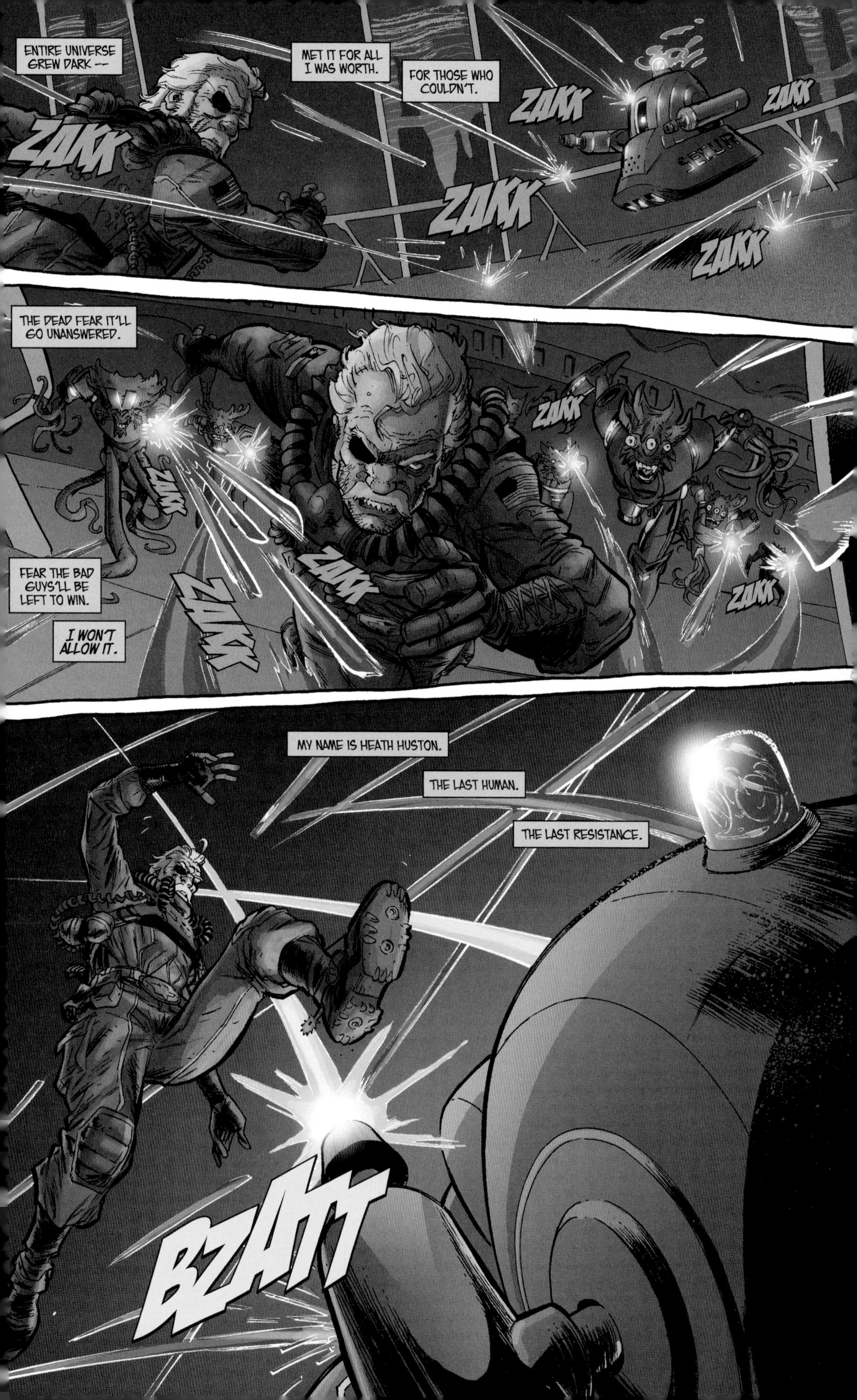
ENTIRE UNIVERSE GREW DARK --
MET IT FOR ALL I WAS WORTH.
FOR THOSE WHO COULDN'T.
ZAKK
ZAKK
ZAKK
ZAKK
ZAKK
THE DEAD FEAR IT'LL GO UNANSWERED.
ZAKK
ZAKK
FEAR THE BAD GUYS'LL BE LEFT TO WIN.
ZAKK
ZAKK
I WON'T ALLOW IT.
ZAKK
MY NAME IS HEATH HUSTON.
THE LAST HUMAN.
THE LAST RESISTANCE.
BZATT

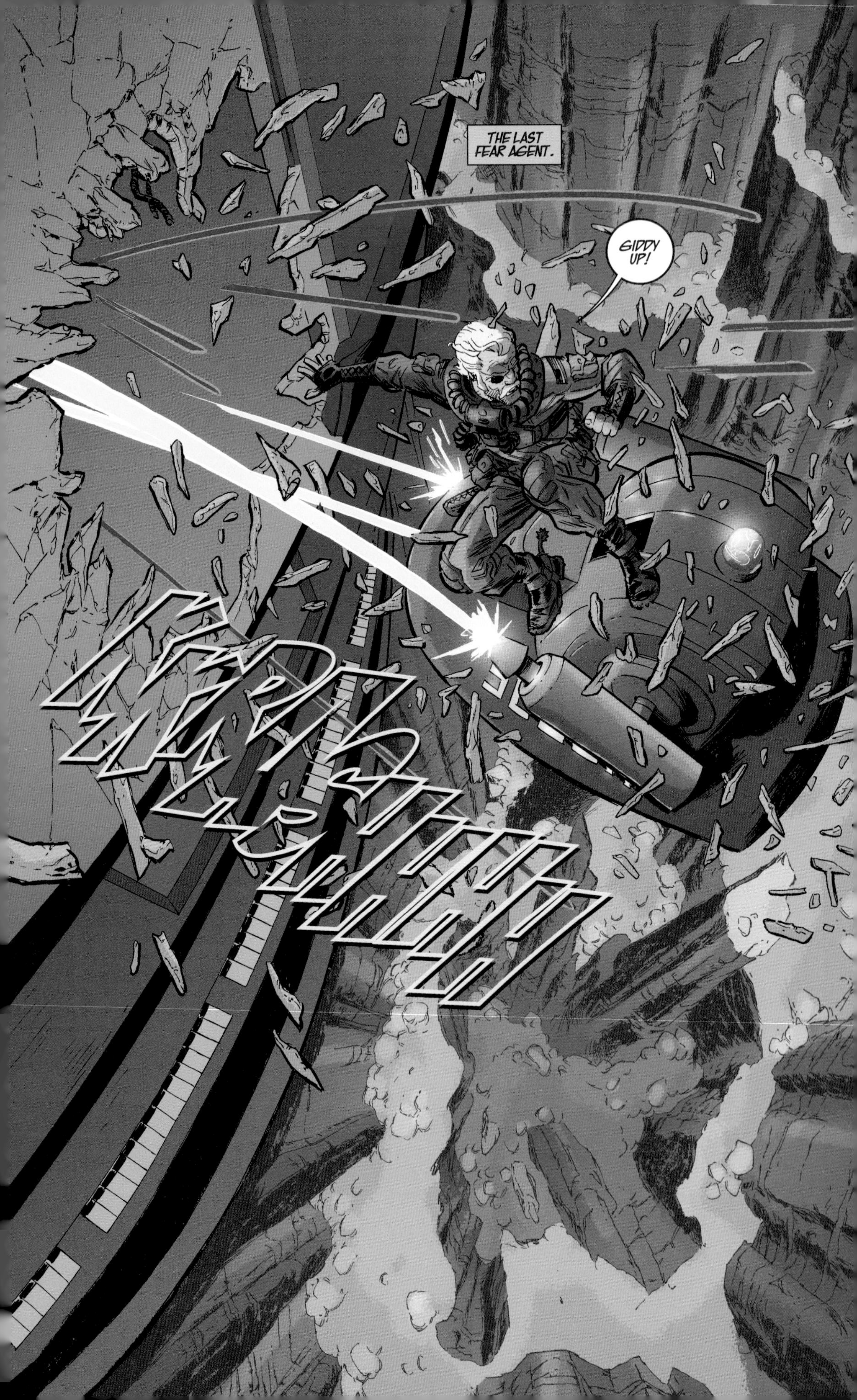
THE LAST FEAR AGENT.
GIDDY UP!

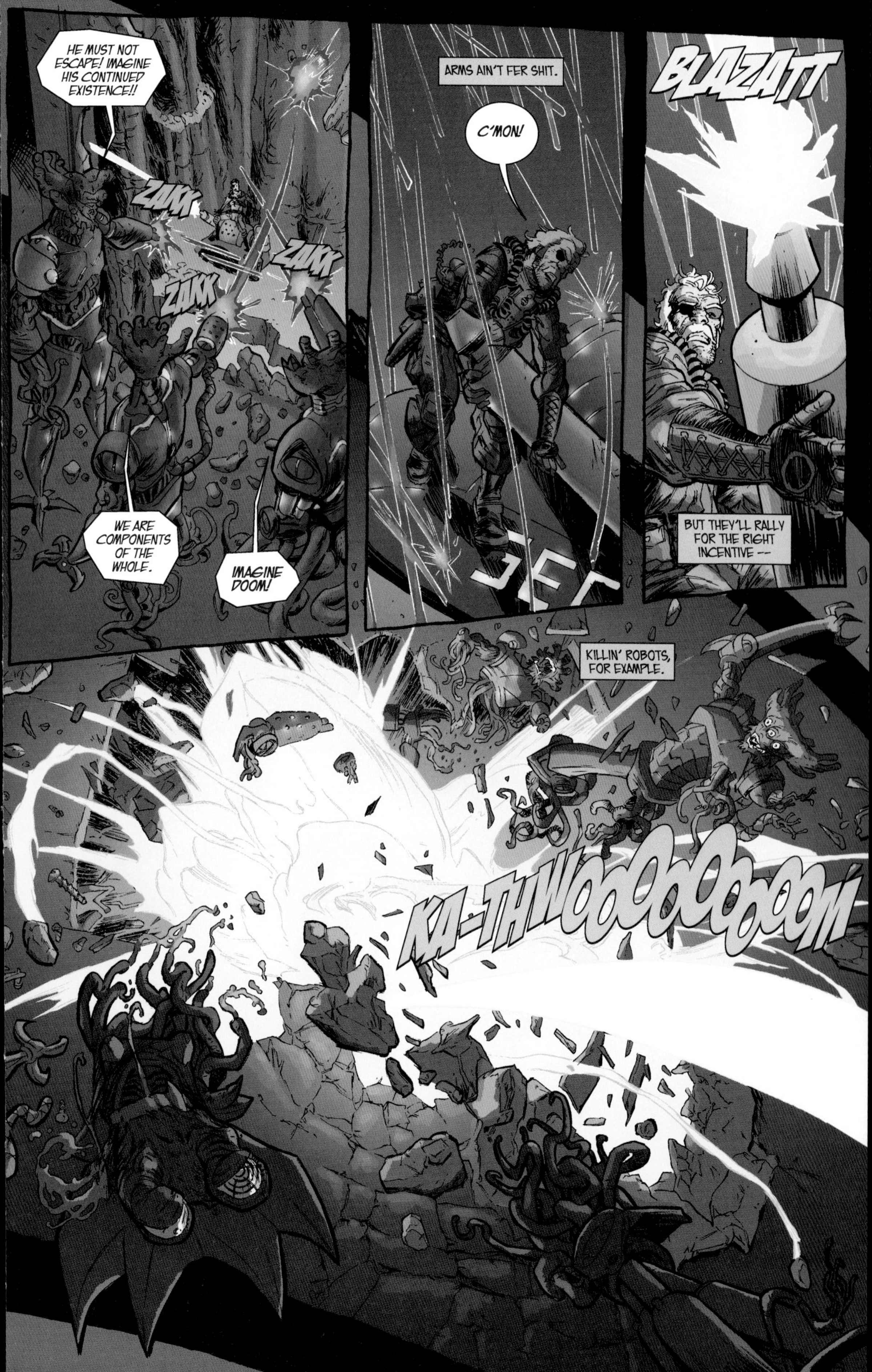
HE MUST NOT ESCAPE! IMAGINE HIS CONTINUED EXISTENCE!!
ZAKK
ZAKK
ZAKK
WE ARE COMPONENTS OF THE WHOLE.
IMAGINE DOOM!
ARMS AIN'T FER SHIT.
C'MON!
BLAZATT
BUT THEY'LL RALLY FOR THE RIGHT INCENTIVE --
KILLIN' ROBOTS, FOR EXAMPLE.
KA-THWOOOOOOOOOM!

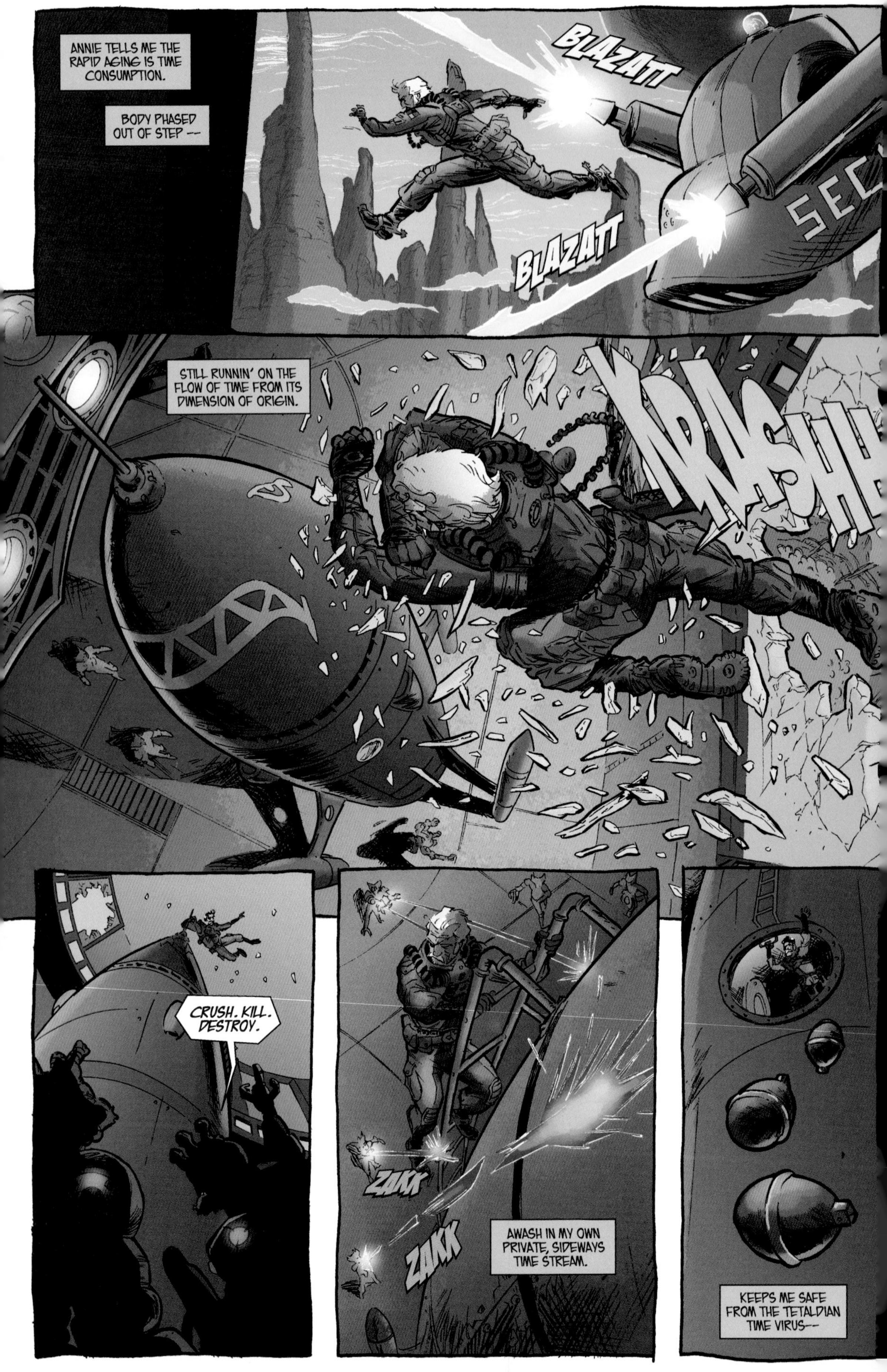
ANNIE TELLS ME THE RAPID AGING IS TIME CONSUMPTION.
BODY PHASED OUT OF STEP --
BLAZATT
BLAZATT
STILL RUNNIN' ON THE FLOW OF TIME FROM ITS DIMENSION OF ORIGIN.
KRASHH
CRUSH. KILL. DESTROY.
ZAKK
ZAKK
AWASH IN MY OWN PRIVATE, SIDEWAYS TIME STREAM.
KEEPS ME SAFE FROM THE TETALDIAN TIME VIRUS--

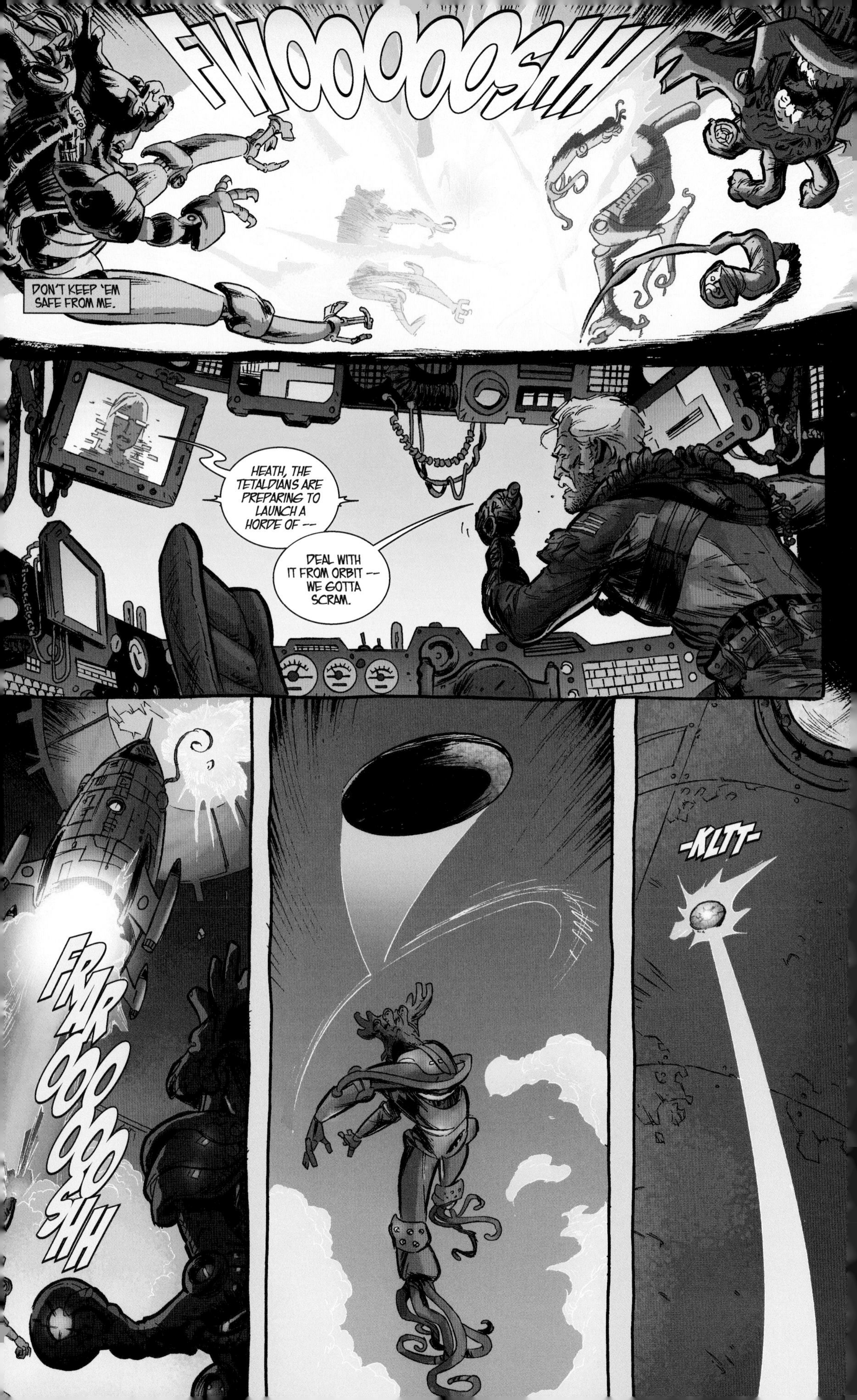
FWOOOOOSHH
DON'T KEEP 'EM SAFE FROM ME.
HEATH, THE TETALDIANS ARE PREPARING TO LAUNCH A HORDE OF --
DEAL WITH IT FROM ORBIT -- WE GOTTA SCRAM.
FRAROOOOOOSHH
-KLTT-

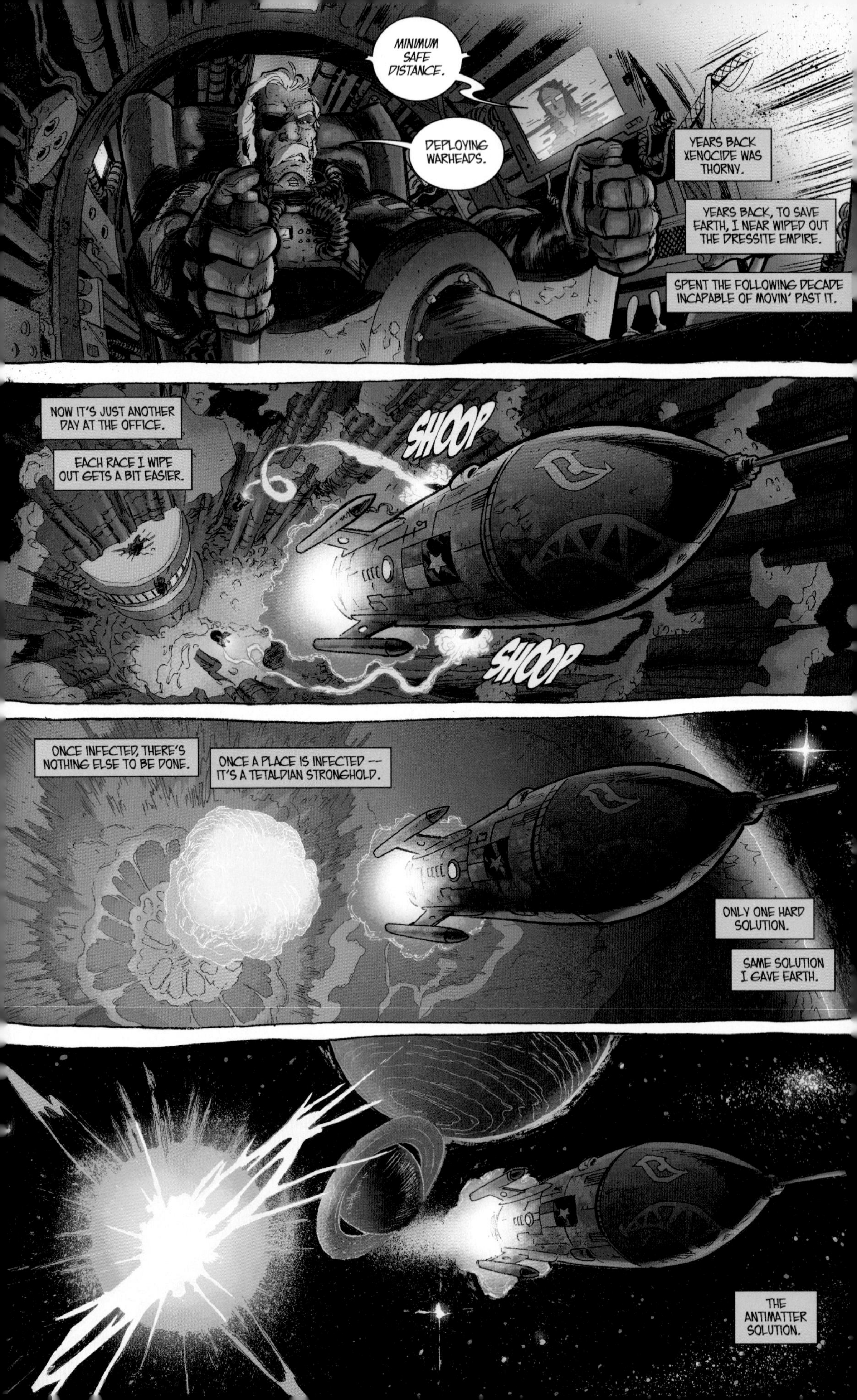
MINIMUM SAFE DISTANCE.
DEPLOYING WARHEADS.
YEARS BACK XENOCIDE WAS THORNY.
YEARS BACK, TO SAVE EARTH, I NEAR WIPED OUT THE DRESSITE EMPIRE.
SPENT THE FOLLOWING DECADE INCAPABLE OF MOVIN' PAST IT.
NOW IT'S JUST ANOTHER DAY AT THE OFFICE.
EACH RACE I WIPE OUT GETS A BIT EASIER.
SHOOP
SHOOP
ONCE INFECTED, THERE'S NOTHING ELSE TO BE DONE.
ONCE A PLACE IS INFECTED -- IT'S A TETALDIAN STRONGHOLD.
ONLY ONE HARD SOLUTION.
SAME SOLUTION I GAVE EARTH.
THE ANTIMATTER SOLUTION.

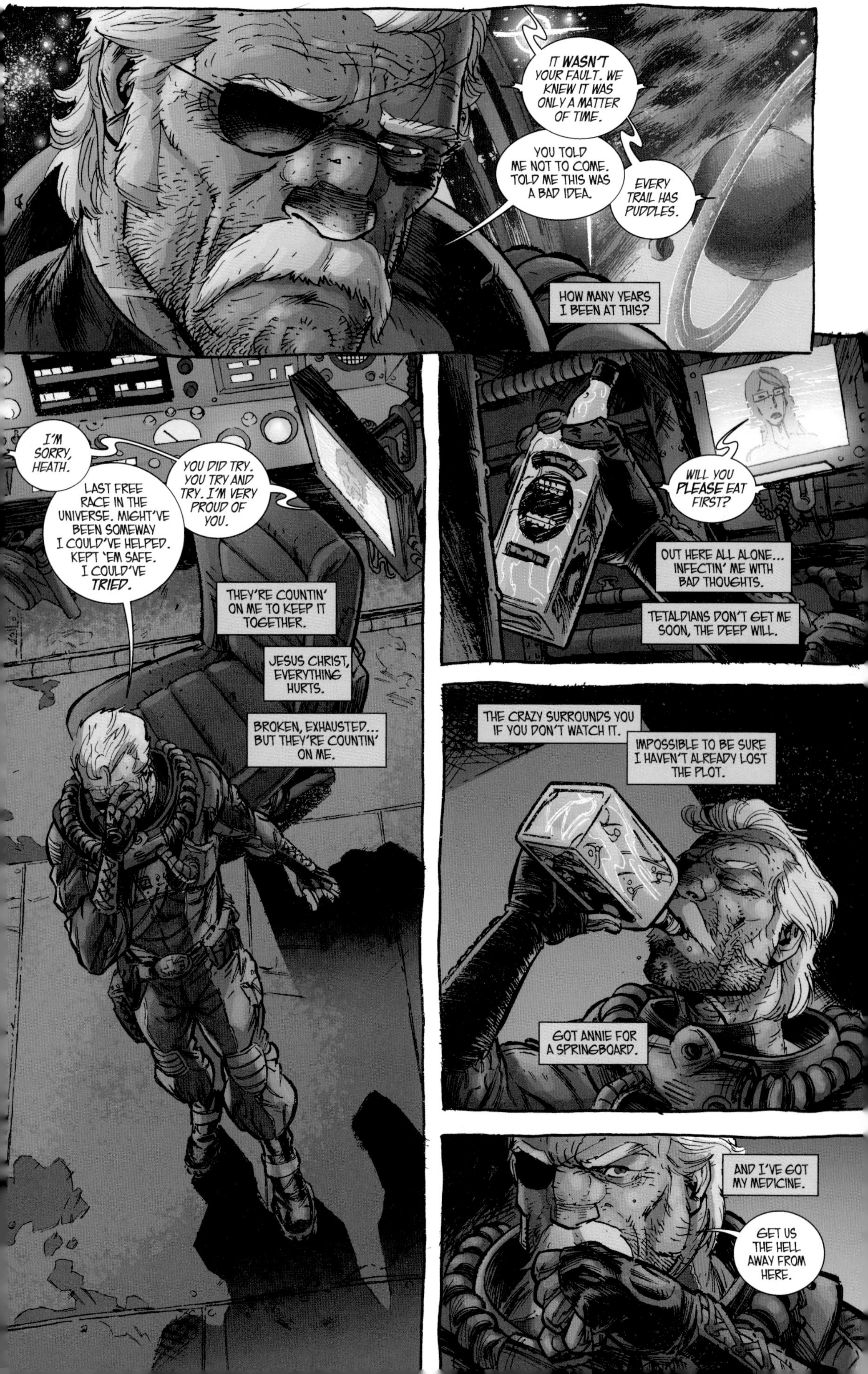
IT WASN'T YOUR FAULT. WE KNEW IT WAS ONLY A MATTER OF TIME.
YOU TOLD ME NOT TO COME. TOLD ME THIS WAS A BAD IDEA.
EVERY TRAIL HAS PUDDLES.
HOW MANY YEARS I BEEN AT THIS?
I'M SORRY, HEATH.
YOU DID TRY. YOU TRY AND TRY. I'M VERY PROUD OF YOU.
LAST FREE RACE IN THE UNIVERSE. MIGHT'VE BEEN SOMEWAY I COULD'VE HELPED. KEPT 'EM SAFE. I COULD'VE TRIED.
THEY'RE COUNTIN' ON ME TO KEEP IT TOGETHER.
JESUS CHRIST, EVERYTHING HURTS.
BROKEN, EXHAUSTED... BUT THEY'RE COUNTIN' ON ME.
WILL YOU PLEASE EAT FIRST?
OUT HERE ALL ALONE... INFECTIN' ME WITH BAD THOUGHTS.
TETALDIANS DON'T GET ME SOON, THE DEEP WILL.
THE CRAZY SURROUNDS YOU IF YOU DON'T WATCH IT.
IMPOSSIBLE TO BE SURE I HAVEN'T ALREADY LOST THE PLOT.
GOT ANNIE FOR A SPRINGBOARD.
AND I'VE GOT MY MEDICINE.
GET US THE HELL AWAY FROM HERE.

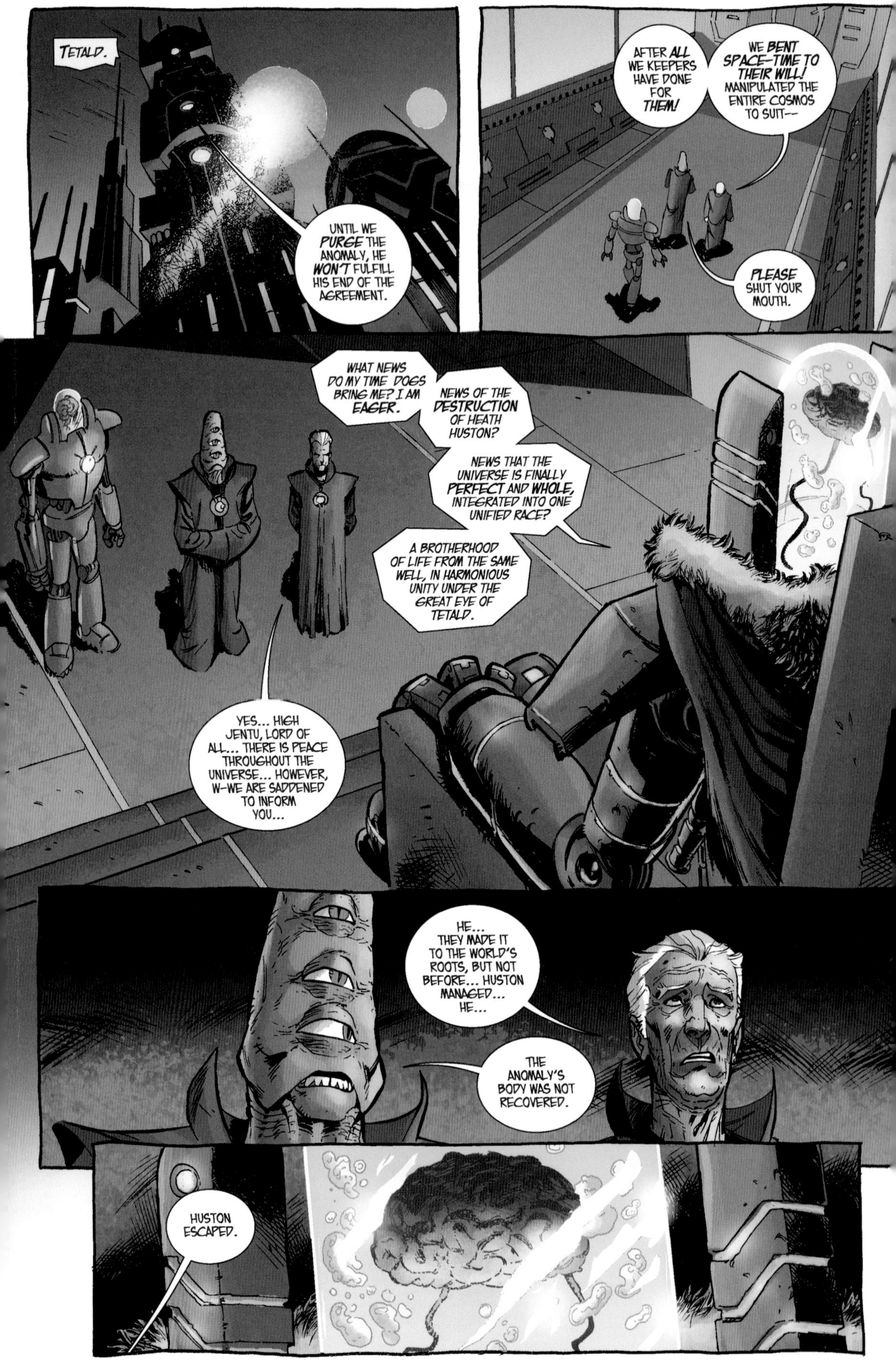
TETALD.
UNTIL WE PURGE THE ANOMALY, HE WON'T FULFILL HIS END OF THE AGREEMENT.
AFTER ALL WE KEEPERS HAVE DONE FOR THEM!
WE BENT SPACE-TIME TO THEIR WILL! MANIPULATED THE ENTIRE COSMOS TO SUIT--
PLEASE SHUT YOUR MOUTH.
WHAT NEWS DO MY TIME DOGS BRING ME? I AM EAGER.
NEWS OF THE DESTRUCTION OF HEATH HUSTON?
NEWS THAT THE UNIVERSE IS FINALLY PERFECT AND WHOLE, INTEGRATED INTO ONE UNIFIED RACE?
A BROTHERHOOD OF LIFE FROM THE SAME WELL, IN HARMONIOUS UNITY UNDER THE GREAT EYE OF TETALD.
YES... HIGH JENTU, LORD OF ALL... THERE IS PEACE THROUGHOUT THE UNIVERSE... HOWEVER, W-WE ARE SADDENED TO INFORM YOU...
HE... THEY MADE IT TO THE WORLD'S ROOTS, BUT NOT BEFORE... HUSTON MANAGED... HE...
THE ANOMALY'S BODY WAS NOT RECOVERED.
HUSTON ESCAPED.

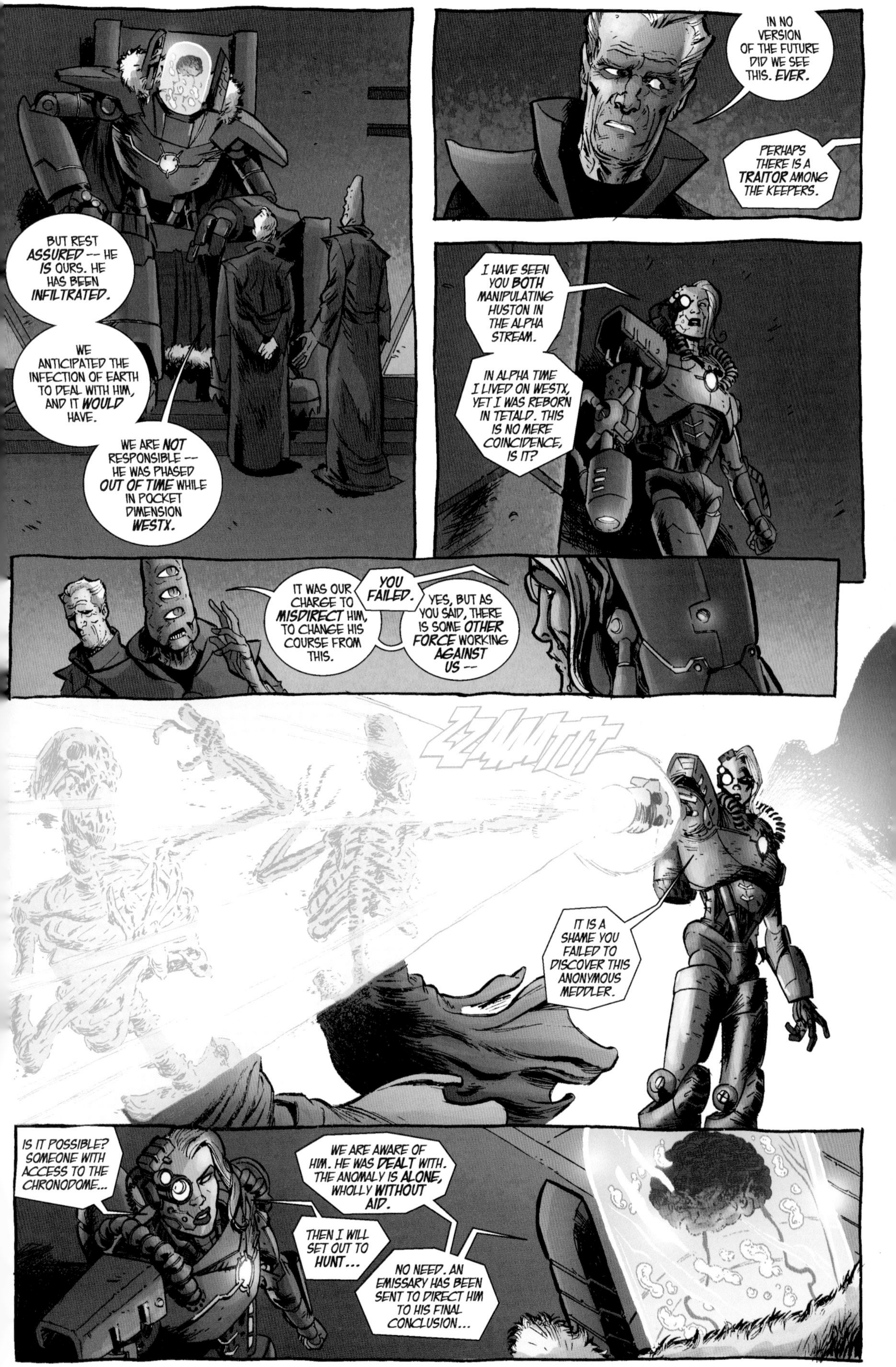
BUT REST ASSURED -- HE IS OURS. HE HAS BEEN INFILTRATED.
WE ANTICIPATED THE INFECTION OF EARTH TO DEAL WITH HIM, AND IT WOULD HAVE.
WE ARE NOT RESPONSIBLE -- HE WAS PHASED OUT OF TIME WHILE IN POCKET DIMENSION WESTX.
IN NO VERSION OF THE FUTURE DID WE SEE THIS. EVER.
PERHAPS THERE IS A TRAITOR AMONG THE KEEPERS.
I HAVE SEEN YOU BOTH MANIPULATING HUSTON IN THE ALPHA STREAM.
IN ALPHA TIME I LIVED ON WESTX, YET I WAS REBORN IN TETALD. THIS IS NO MERE COINCIDENCE, IS IT?
IT WAS OUR CHARGE TO MISDIRECT HIM, TO CHANGE HIS COURSE FROM THIS.
YOU FAILED.
YES, BUT AS YOU SAID, THERE IS SOME OTHER FORCE WORKING AGAINST US --
ZZAAAAT
IT IS A SHAME YOU FAILED TO DISCOVER THIS ANONYMOUS MEDDLER.
IS IT POSSIBLE? SOMEONE WITH ACCESS TO THE CHRONODOME...
WE ARE AWARE OF HIM. HE WAS DEALT WITH. THE ANOMALY IS ALONE, WHOLLY WITHOUT AID.
THEN I WILL SET OUT TO HUNT...
NO NEED. AN EMISSARY HAS BEEN SENT TO DIRECT HIM TO HIS FINAL CONCLUSION...

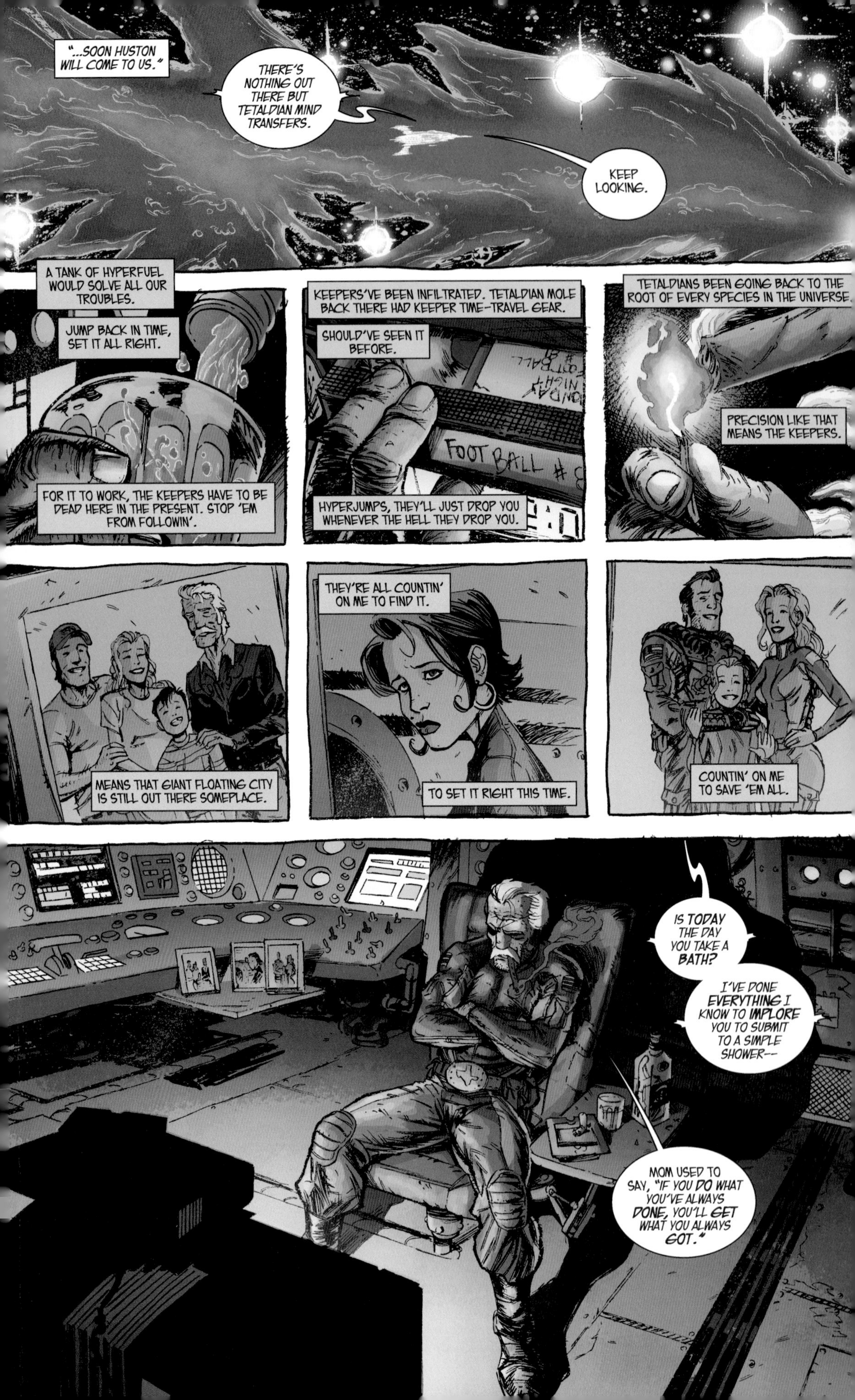

"...SOON HUSTON WILL COME TO US."
THERE'S NOTHING OUT THERE BUT TETALDIAN MIND TRANSFERS.
KEEP LOOKING.
A TANK OF HYPERFUEL WOULD SOLVE ALL OUR TROUBLES.
JUMP BACK IN TIME, SET IT ALL RIGHT.
FOR IT TO WORK, THE KEEPERS HAVE TO BE DEAD HERE IN THE PRESENT. STOP 'EM FROM FOLLOWIN'.
KEEPERS'VE BEEN INFILTRATED. TETALDIAN MOLE BACK THERE HAD KEEPER TIME-TRAVEL GEAR.
SHOULD'VE SEEN IT BEFORE.
FOOTBALL # 8
HYPERJUMPS, THEY'LL JUST DROP YOU WHENEVER THE HELL THEY DROP YOU.
TETALDIANS BEEN GOING BACK TO THE ROOT OF EVERY SPECIES IN THE UNIVERSE.
PRECISION LIKE THAT MEANS THE KEEPERS.
MEANS THAT GIANT FLOATING CITY IS STILL OUT THERE SOMEPLACE.
THEY'RE ALL COUNTIN' ON ME TO FIND IT.
TO SET IT RIGHT THIS TIME.
COUNTIN' ON ME TO SAVE 'EM ALL.
IS TODAY THE DAY YOU TAKE A BATH?
I'VE DONE EVERYTHING I KNOW TO IMPLORE YOU TO SUBMIT TO A SIMPLE SHOWER--
MOM USED TO SAY, "IF YOU DO WHAT YOU'VE ALWAYS DONE, YOU'LL GET WHAT YOU ALWAYS GOT."

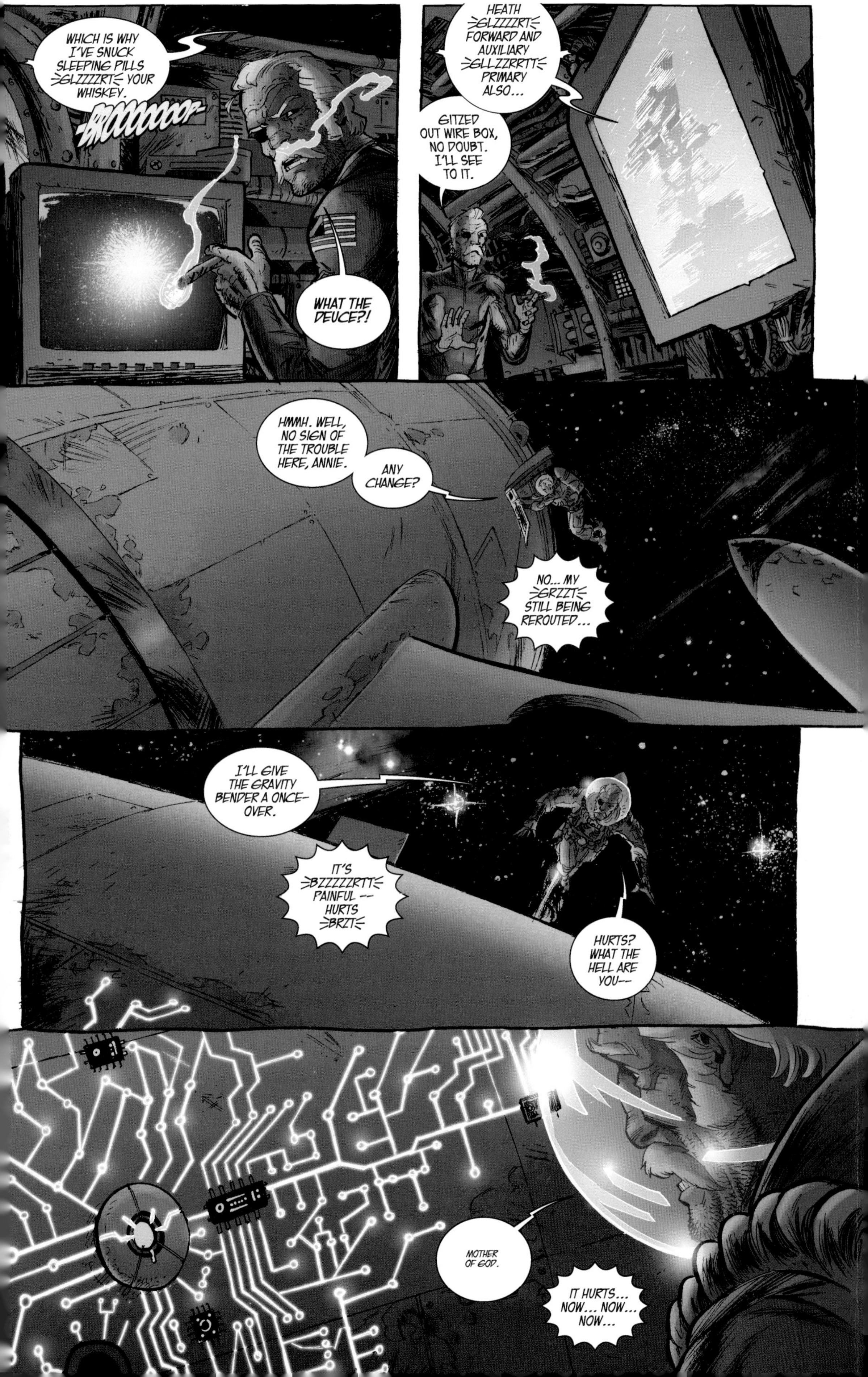
WHICH IS WHY I'VE SNUCK SLEEPING PILLS =GLZZZZRT= YOUR WHISKEY.
-BROOOOOOOP-
WHAT THE DEUCE?!
HEATH =GLZZZZRT= FORWARD AND AUXILIARY =GLLZZRRTT= PRIMARY ALSO...
GITZED OUT WIRE BOX, NO DOUBT. I'LL SEE TO IT.
HMMH. WELL, NO SIGN OF THE TROUBLE HERE, ANNIE.
ANY CHANGE?
NO... MY =GRZZT= STILL BEING REROUTED...
I'LL GIVE THE GRAVITY BENDER A ONCE-OVER.
IT'S =BZZZZZRTT= PAINFUL -- HURTS =BRZT=
HURTS? WHAT THE HELL ARE YOU--
MOTHER OF GOD.
IT HURTS... NOW... NOW... NOW...

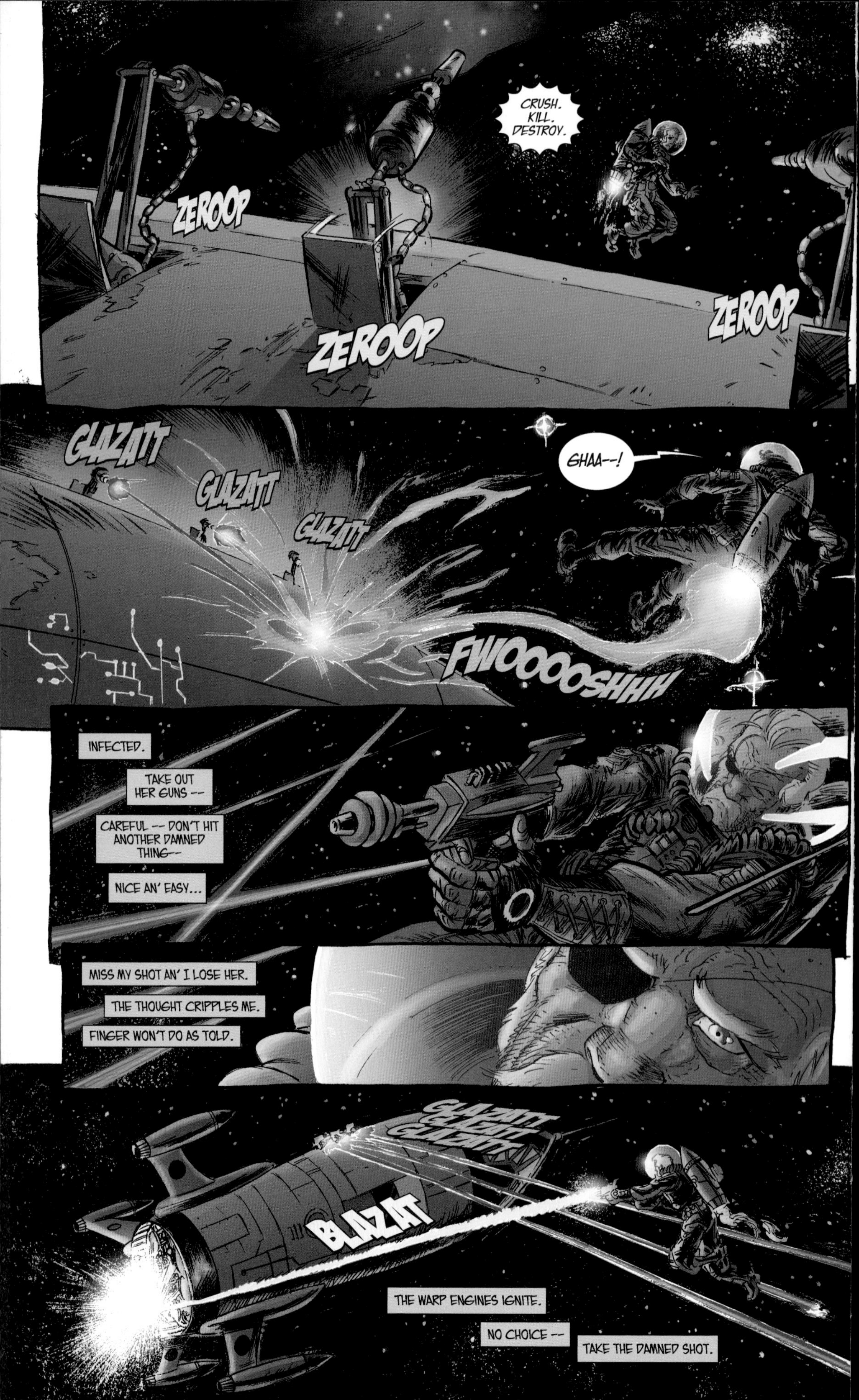
CRUSH. KILL. DESTROY.
ZEROOP
ZEROOP
ZEROOP
GLAZATT
GLAZATT
GLAZATT
GHAA--!
FWOOOOOSHHH
INFECTED.
TAKE OUT HER GUNS --
CAREFUL -- DON'T HIT ANOTHER DAMNED THING--
NICE AN' EASY...
MISS MY SHOT AN' I LOSE HER.
THE THOUGHT CRIPPLES ME.
FINGER WON'T DO AS TOLD.
GLAZATT GLAZATT GLAZATT
BLAZAT
THE WARP ENGINES IGNITE.
NO CHOICE --
TAKE THE DAMNED SHOT.

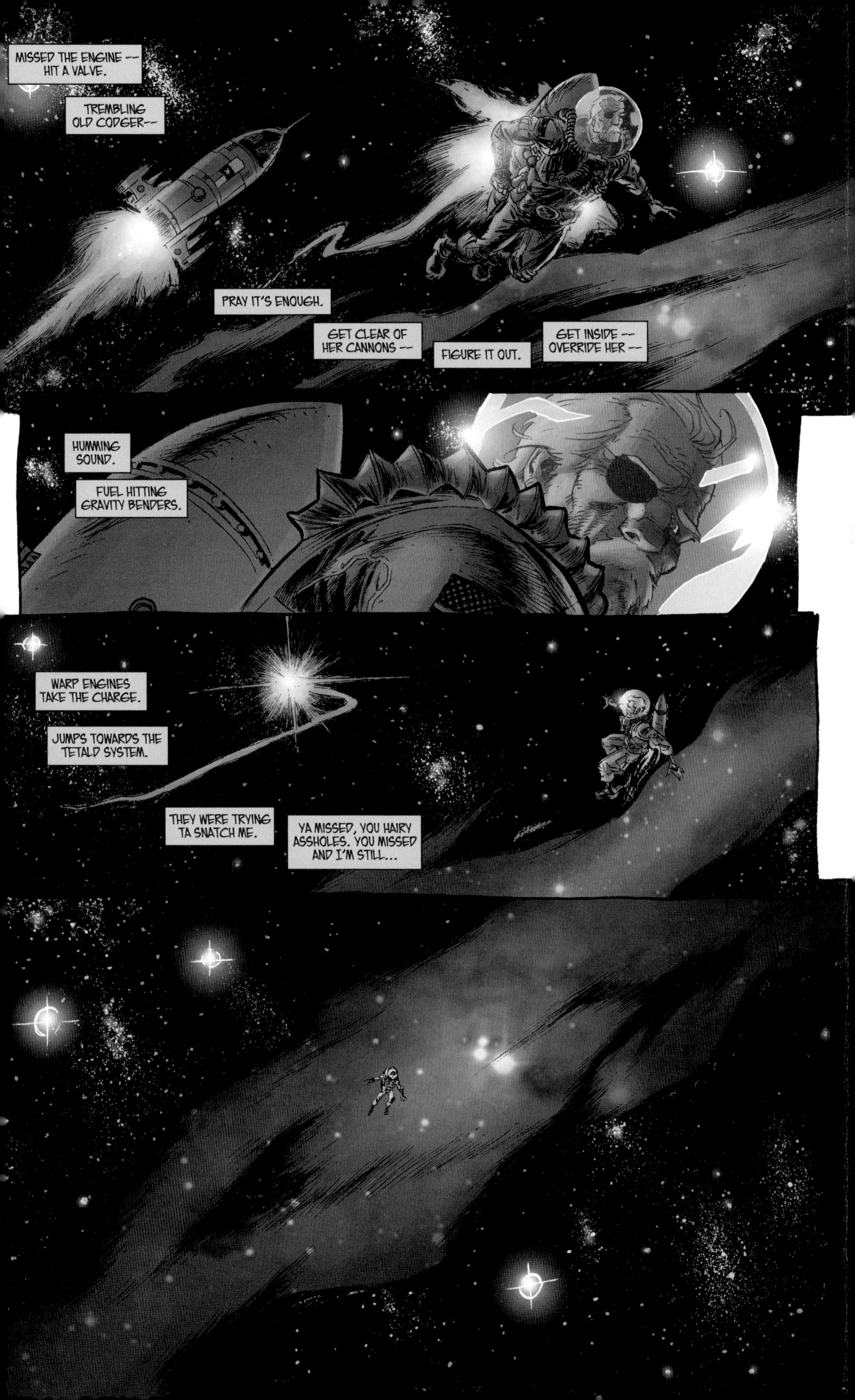
MISSED THE ENGINE -- HIT A VALVE.
TREMBLING OLD CODGER--
PRAY IT'S ENOUGH.
GET CLEAR OF HER CANNONS --
FIGURE IT OUT.
GET INSIDE -- OVERRIDE HER --
HUMMING SOUND.
FUEL HITTING GRAVITY BENDERS.
WARP ENGINES TAKE THE CHARGE.
JUMPS TOWARDS THE TETALD SYSTEM.
THEY WERE TRYING TA SNATCH ME.
YA MISSED, YOU HAIRY ASSHOLES. YOU MISSED AND I'M STILL...

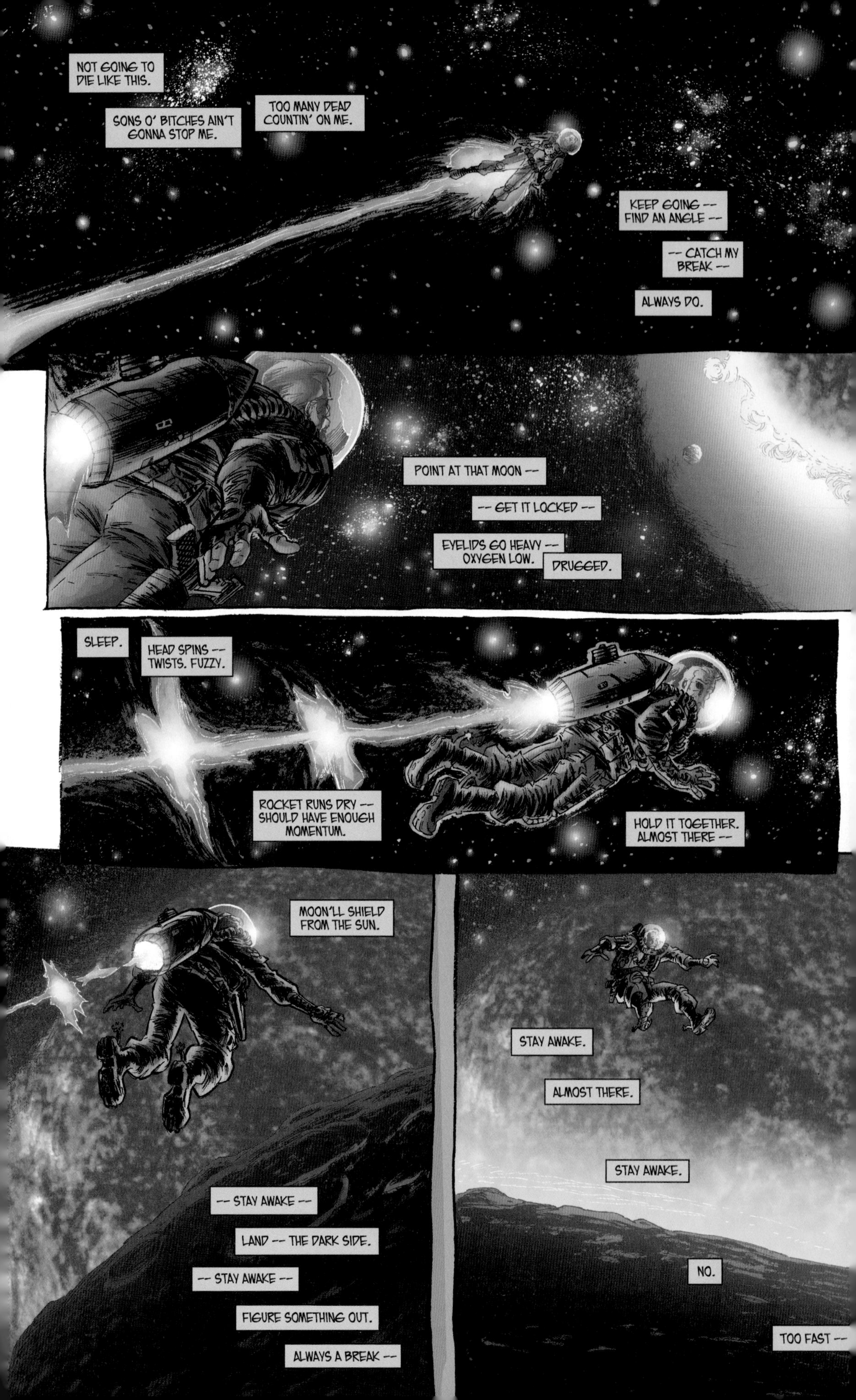
NOT GOING TO DIE LIKE THIS.
SONS O' BITCHES AIN'T GONNA STOP ME.
TOO MANY DEAD COUNTIN' ON ME.
KEEP GOING -- FIND AN ANGLE --
-- CATCH MY BREAK --
ALWAYS DO.
POINT AT THAT MOON --
-- GET IT LOCKED --
EYELIDS GO HEAVY -- OXYGEN LOW.
DRUGGED.
SLEEP.
HEAD SPINS -- TWISTS. FUZZY.
ROCKET RUNS DRY -- SHOULD HAVE ENOUGH MOMENTUM.
HOLD IT TOGETHER. ALMOST THERE --
MOON'LL SHIELD FROM THE SUN.
-- STAY AWAKE --
LAND -- THE DARK SIDE.
-- STAY AWAKE --
FIGURE SOMETHING OUT.
ALWAYS A BREAK --
STAY AWAKE.
ALMOST THERE.
STAY AWAKE.
NO.
TOO FAST --

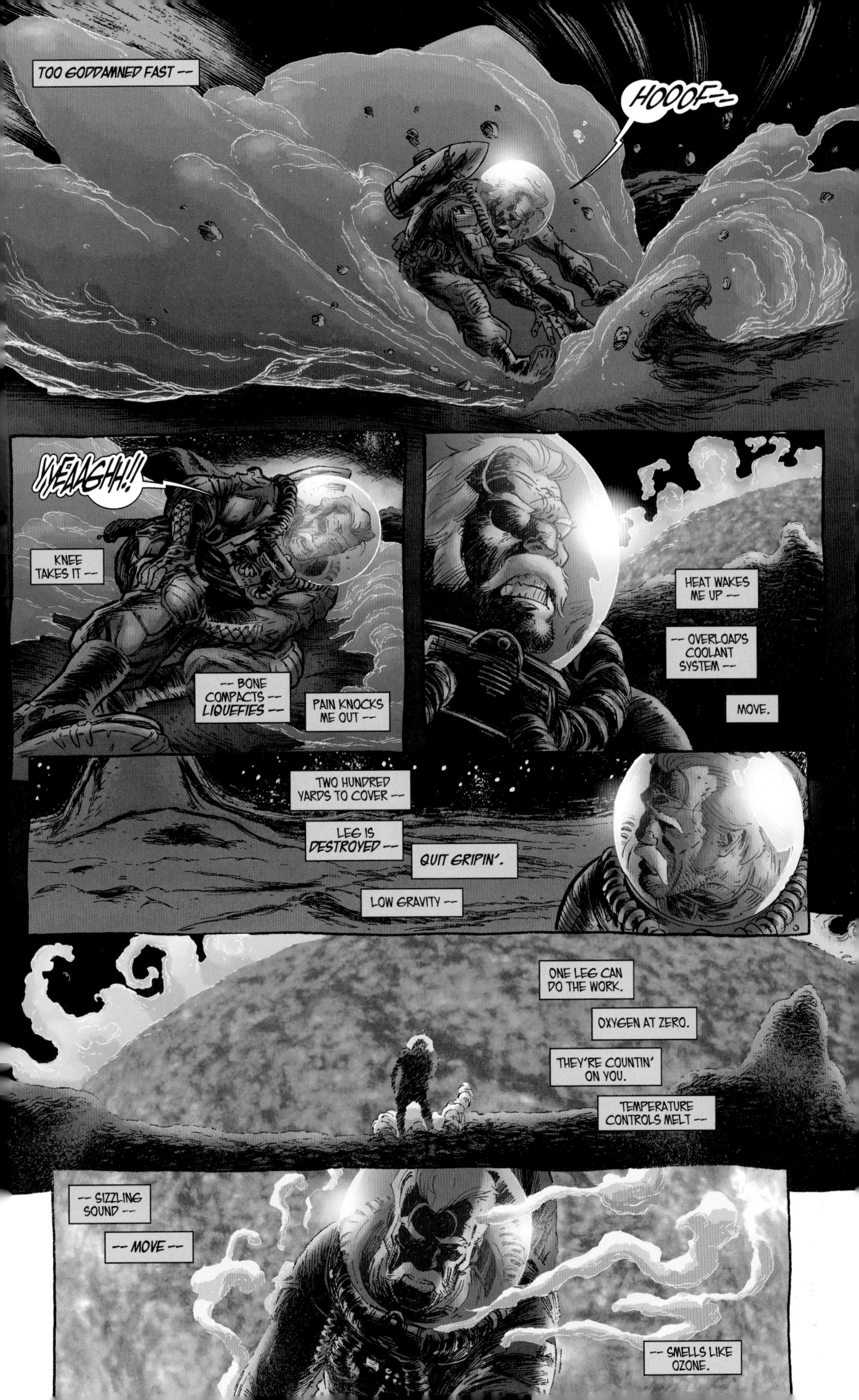
TOO GODDAMNED FAST --
HOOOF--
YYEAAGHH!!
KNEE TAKES IT --
-- BONE COMPACTS -- LIQUEFIES --
PAIN KNOCKS ME OUT --
HEAT WAKES ME UP --
-- OVERLOADS COOLANT SYSTEM --
MOVE.
TWO HUNDRED YARDS TO COVER --
LEG IS DESTROYED --
QUIT GRIPIN'.
LOW GRAVITY --
ONE LEG CAN DO THE WORK.
OXYGEN AT ZERO.
THEY'RE COUNTIN' ON YOU.
TEMPERATURE CONTROLS MELT --
-- SIZZLING SOUND --
-- MOVE --
-- SMELLS LIKE OZONE.

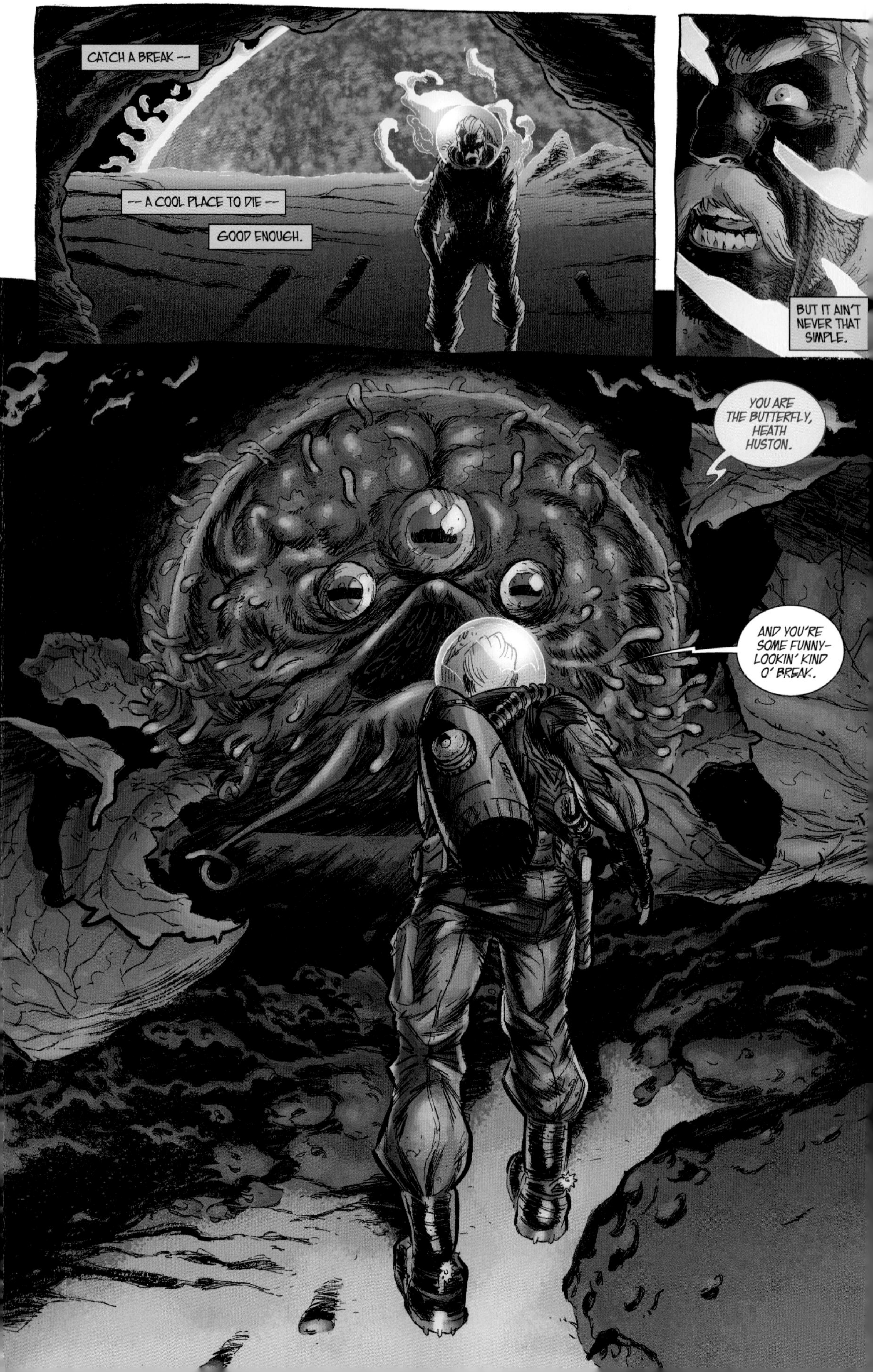
CATCH A BREAK --
-- A COOL PLACE TO DIE --
GOOD ENOUGH.
BUT IT AIN'T NEVER THAT SIMPLE.
YOU ARE THE BUTTERFLY, HEATH HUSTON.
AND YOU'RE SOME FUNNY-LOOKIN' KIND O' BREAK.

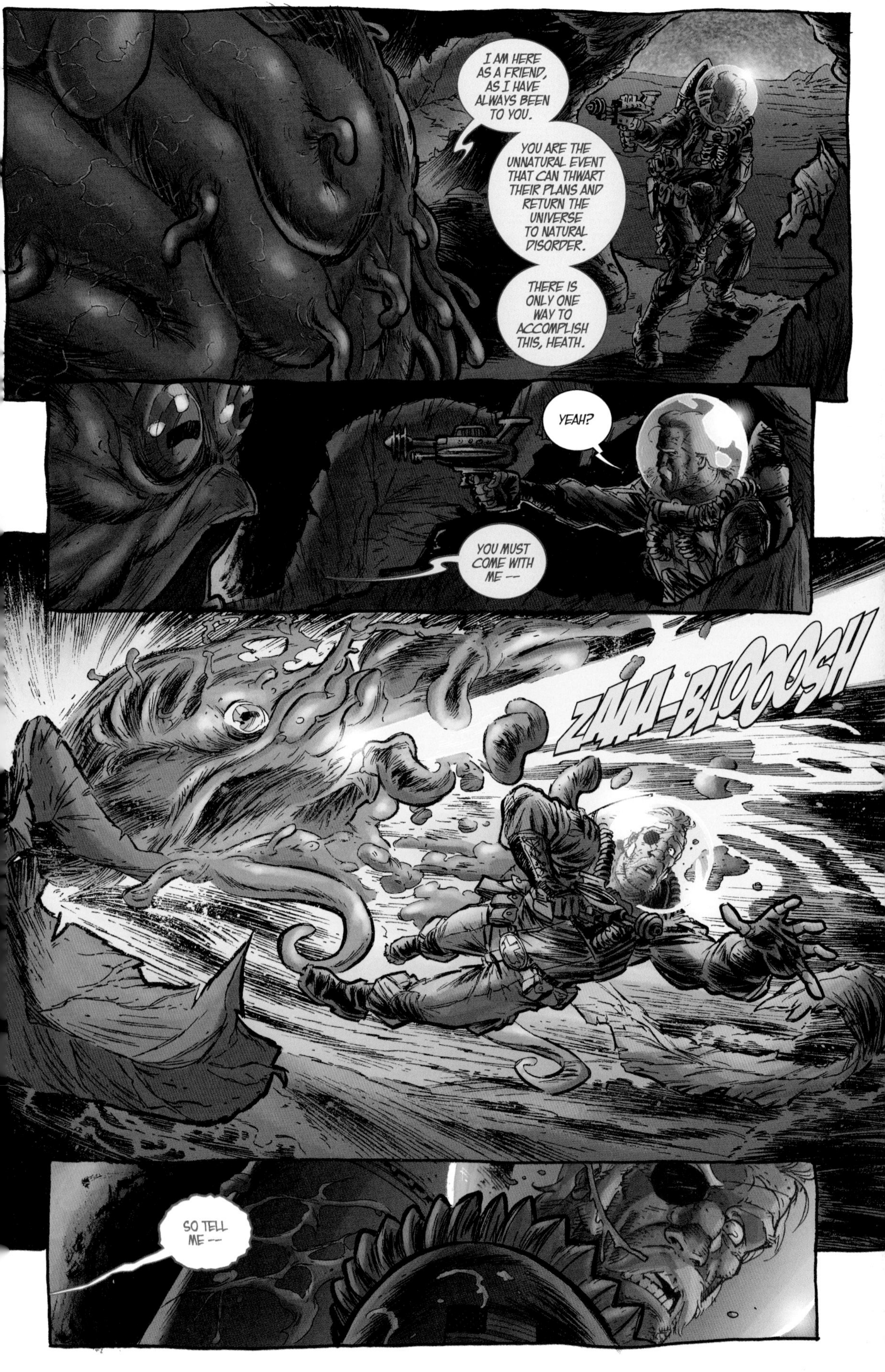
I AM HERE AS A FRIEND, AS I HAVE ALWAYS BEEN TO YOU.
YOU ARE THE UNNATURAL EVENT THAT CAN THWART THEIR PLANS AND RETURN THE UNIVERSE TO NATURAL DISORDER.
THERE IS ONLY ONE WAY TO ACCOMPLISH THIS, HEATH.
YEAH?
YOU MUST COME WITH ME --
ZAAA-BLOOOOSH
SO TELL ME --

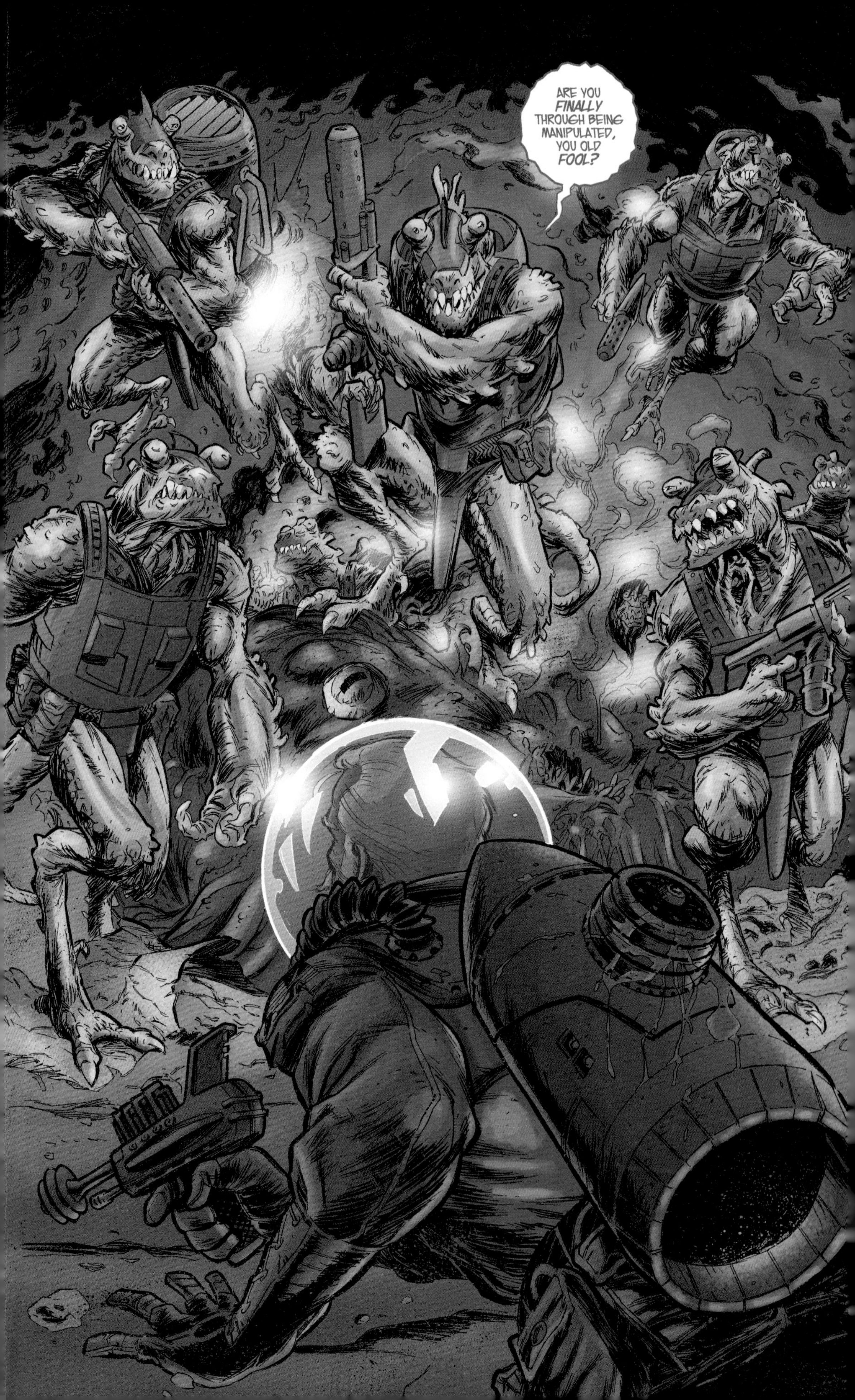
ARE YOU FINALLY THROUGH BEING MANIPULATED, YOU OLD FOOL?

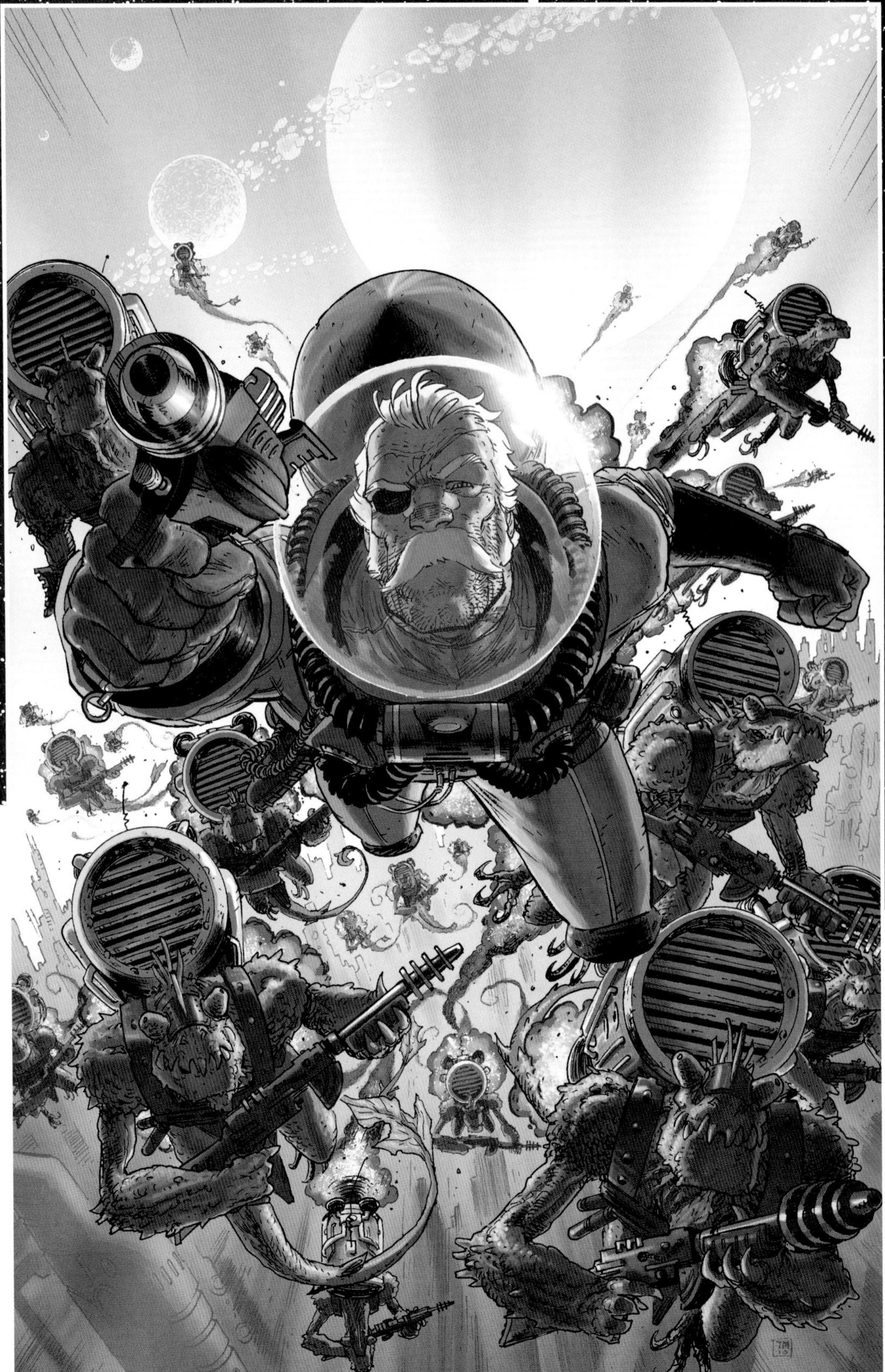

FEAR AGENT #30
ART BY TONY MOORE

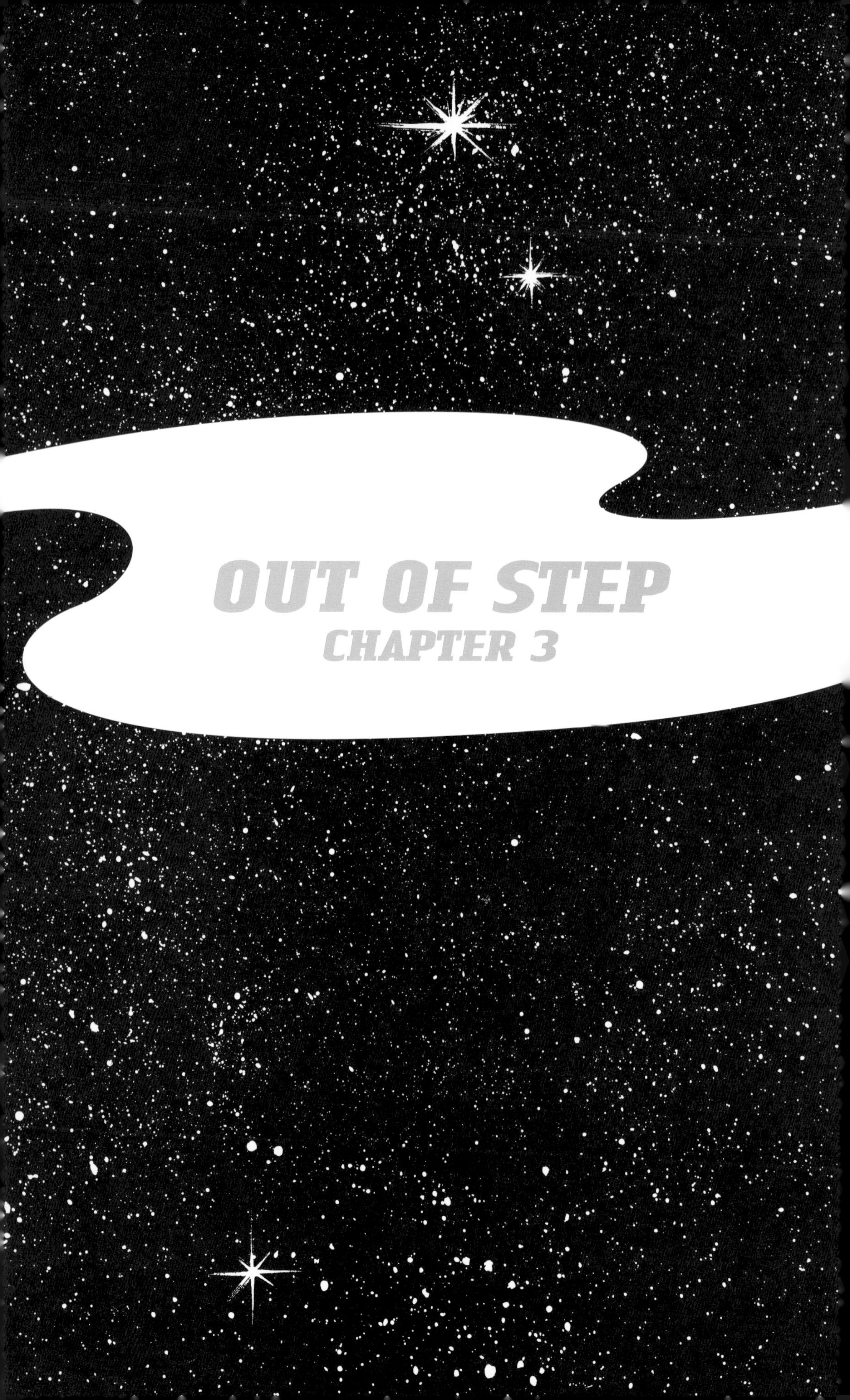
OUT OF STEP
CHAPTER 3

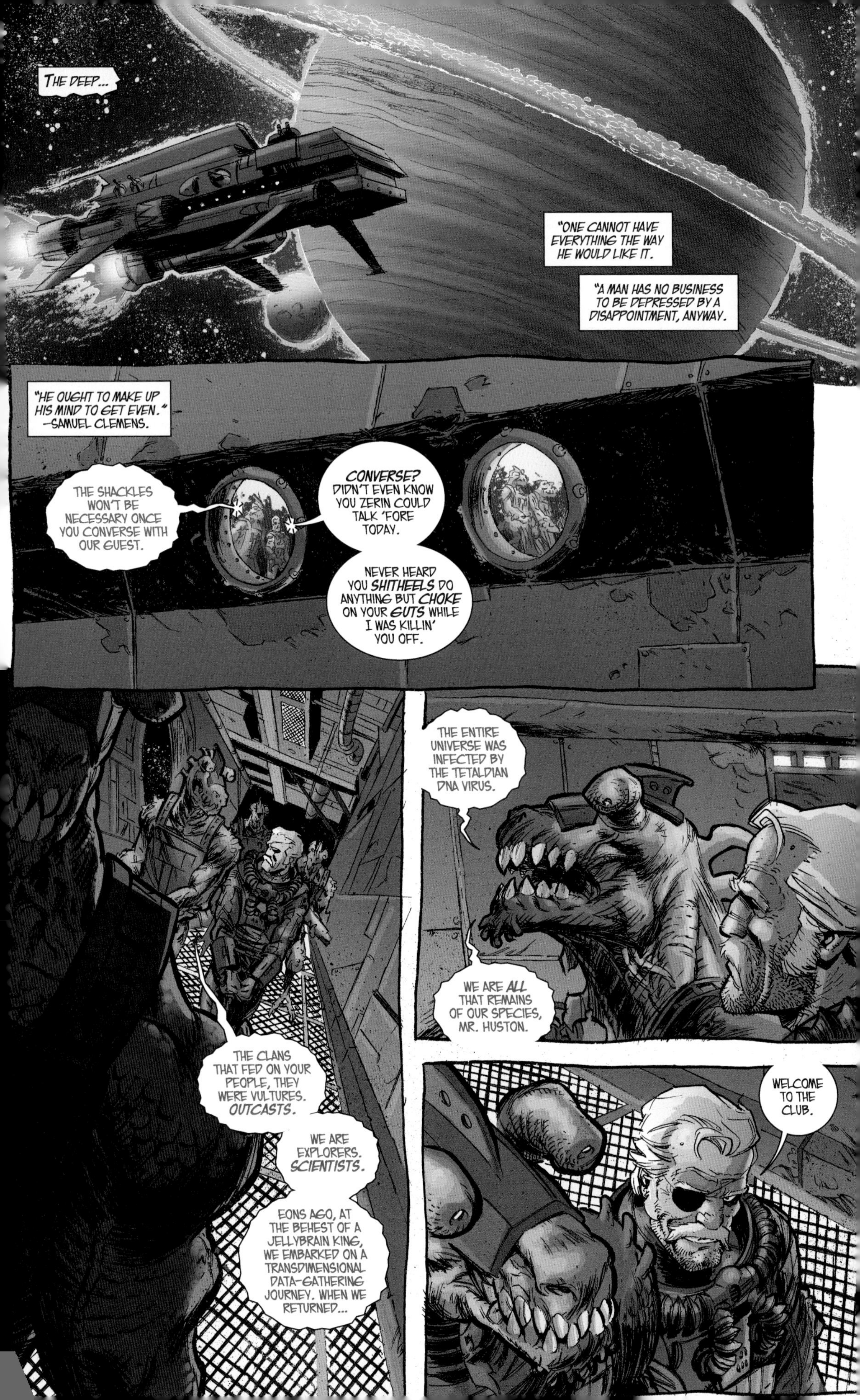
THE DEEP...
"ONE CANNOT HAVE EVERYTHING THE WAY HE WOULD LIKE IT.
"A MAN HAS NO BUSINESS TO BE DEPRESSED BY A DISAPPOINTMENT, ANYWAY.
"HE OUGHT TO MAKE UP HIS MIND TO GET EVEN." —SAMUEL CLEMENS.
THE SHACKLES WON'T BE NECESSARY ONCE YOU CONVERSE WITH OUR GUEST.
CONVERSE? DIDN'T EVEN KNOW YOU ZERIN COULD TALK 'FORE TODAY.
NEVER HEARD YOU SHITHEELS DO ANYTHING BUT CHOKE ON YOUR GUTS WHILE I WAS KILLIN' YOU OFF.
THE CLANS THAT FED ON YOUR PEOPLE, THEY WERE VULTURES. OUTCASTS.
WE ARE EXPLORERS. SCIENTISTS.
EONS AGO, AT THE BEHEST OF A JELLYBRAIN KING, WE EMBARKED ON A TRANSDIMENSIONAL DATA-GATHERING JOURNEY. WHEN WE RETURNED...
THE ENTIRE UNIVERSE WAS INFECTED BY THE TETALDIAN DNA VIRUS.
WE ARE ALL THAT REMAINS OF OUR SPECIES, MR. HUSTON.
WELCOME TO THE CLUB.

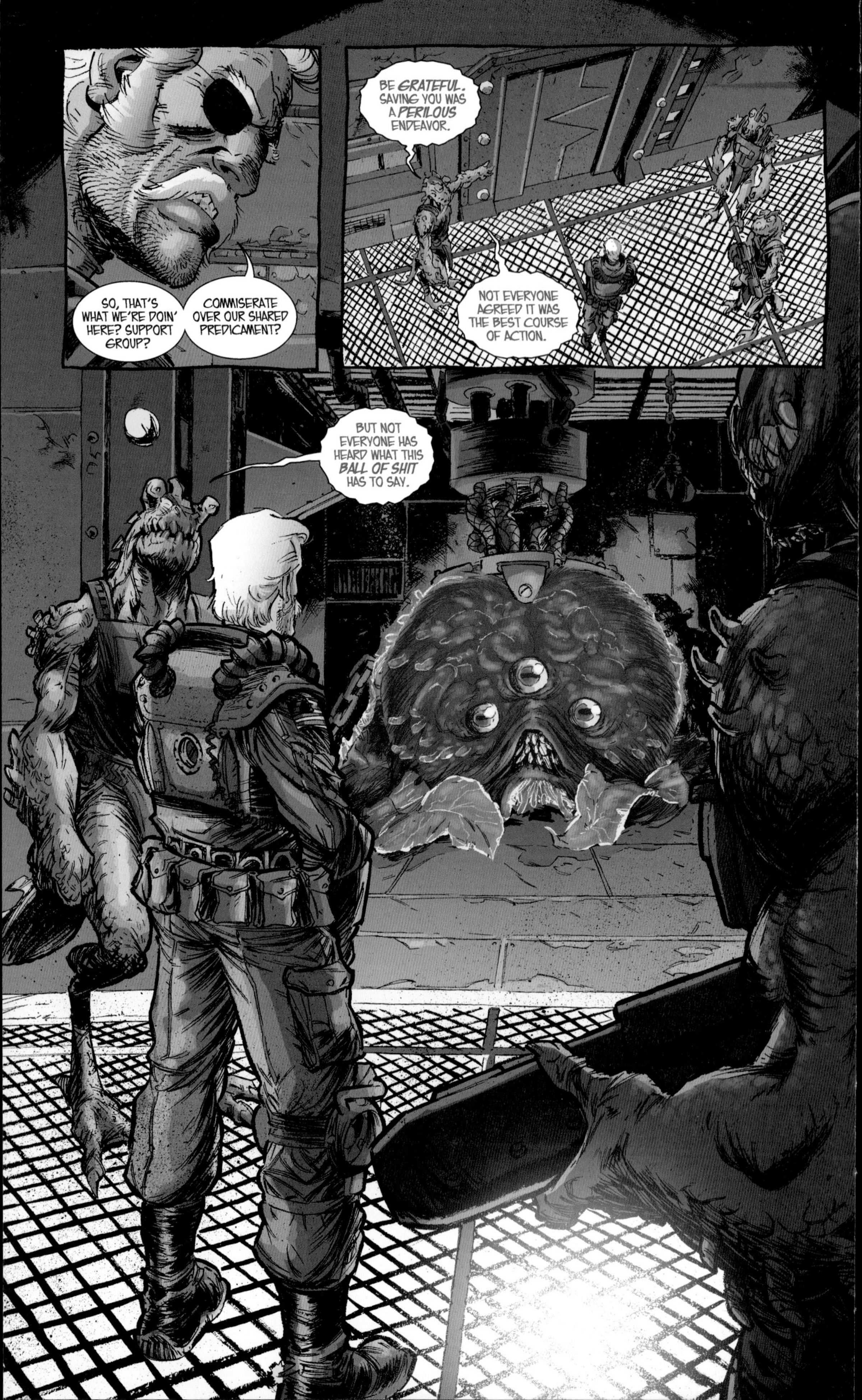
SO, THAT'S WHAT WE'RE DOIN' HERE? SUPPORT GROUP?
COMMISERATE OVER OUR SHARED PREDICAMENT?
BE GRATEFUL. SAVING YOU WAS A PERILOUS ENDEAVOR.
NOT EVERYONE AGREED IT WAS THE BEST COURSE OF ACTION.
BUT NOT EVERYONE HAS HEARD WHAT THIS BALL OF SHIT HAS TO SAY.

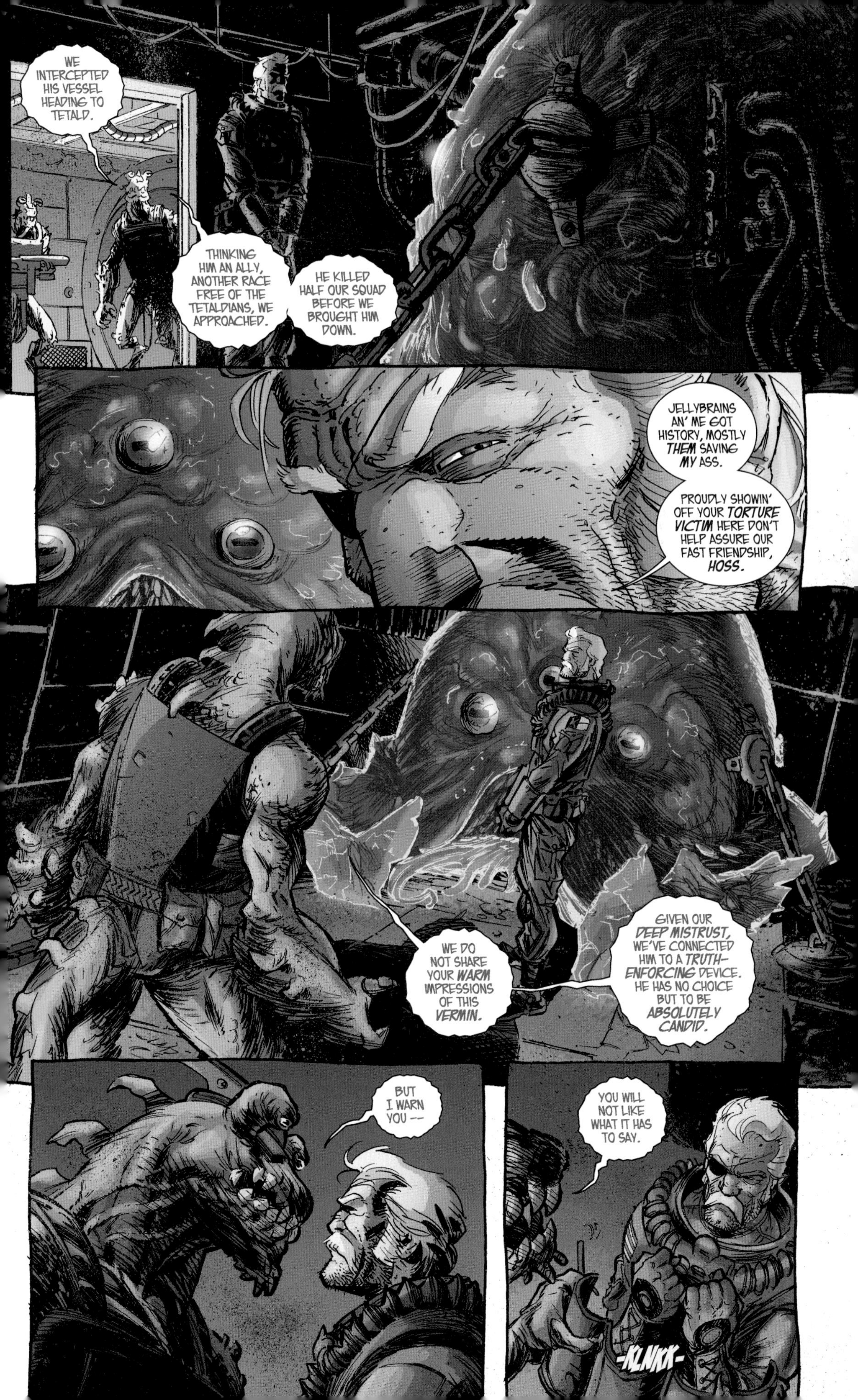
WE INTERCEPTED HIS VESSEL HEADING TO TETALD.
THINKING HIM AN ALLY, ANOTHER RACE FREE OF THE TETALDIANS, WE APPROACHED.
HE KILLED HALF OUR SQUAD BEFORE WE BROUGHT HIM DOWN.
JELLYBRAINS AN' ME GOT HISTORY, MOSTLY THEM SAVING MY ASS.
PROUDLY SHOWIN' OFF YOUR TORTURE VICTIM HERE DON'T HELP ASSURE OUR FAST FRIENDSHIP, HOSS.
WE DO NOT SHARE YOUR WARM IMPRESSIONS OF THIS VERMIN.
GIVEN OUR DEEP MISTRUST, WE'VE CONNECTED HIM TO A TRUTH-ENFORCING DEVICE. HE HAS NO CHOICE BUT TO BE ABSOLUTELY CANDID.
BUT I WARN YOU --
YOU WILL NOT LIKE WHAT IT HAS TO SAY.
-KLNKK-

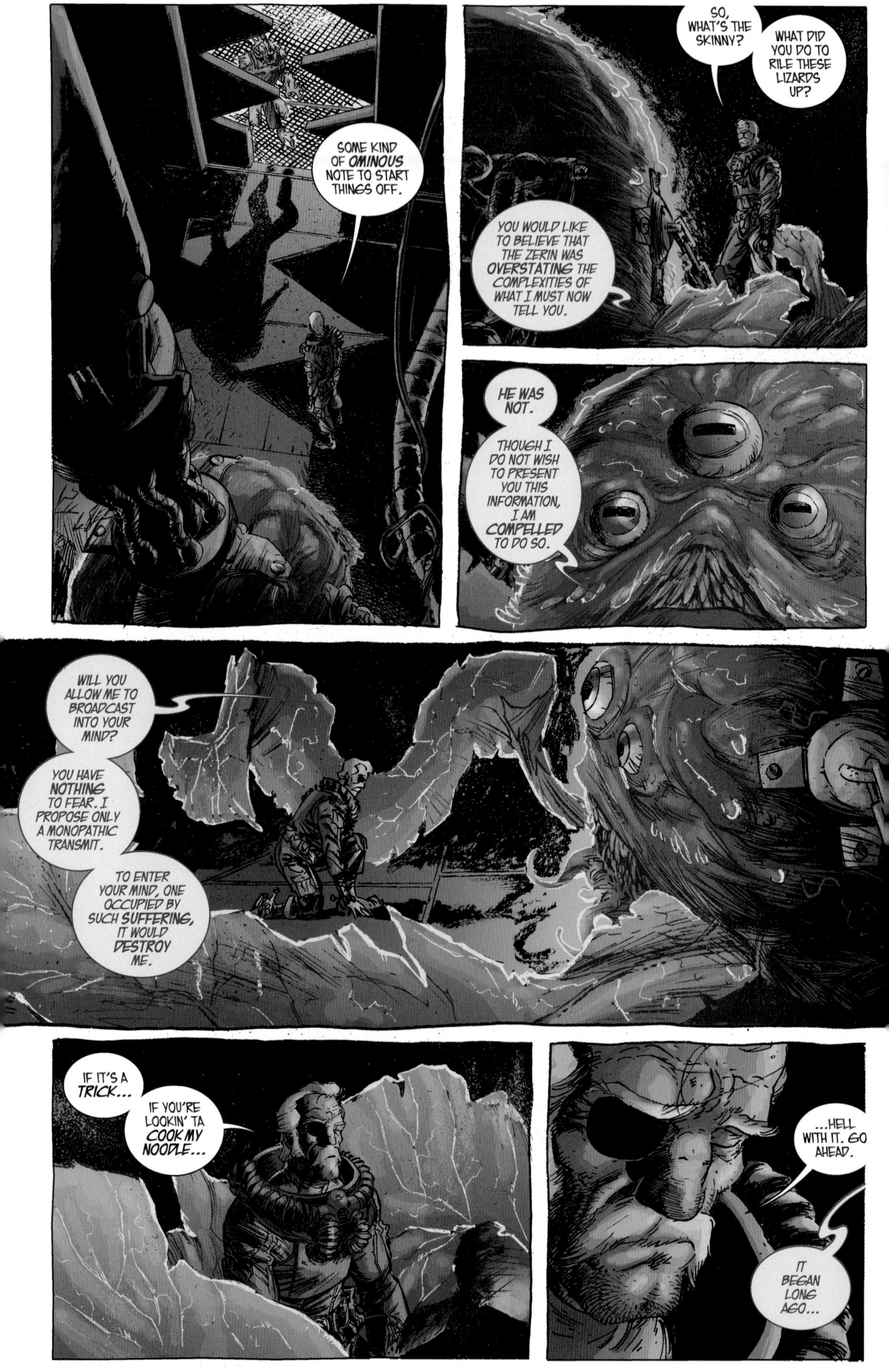
SOME KIND OF OMINOUS NOTE TO START THINGS OFF.
SO, WHAT'S THE SKINNY?
WHAT DID YOU DO TO RILE THESE LIZARDS UP?
YOU WOULD LIKE TO BELIEVE THAT THE ZERIN WAS OVERSTATING THE COMPLEXITIES OF WHAT I MUST NOW TELL YOU.
HE WAS NOT.
THOUGH I DO NOT WISH TO PRESENT YOU THIS INFORMATION, I AM COMPELLED TO DO SO.
WILL YOU ALLOW ME TO BROADCAST INTO YOUR MIND?
YOU HAVE NOTHING TO FEAR. I PROPOSE ONLY A MONOPATHIC TRANSMIT.
TO ENTER YOUR MIND, ONE OCCUPIED BY SUCH SUFFERING, IT WOULD DESTROY ME.
IF IT'S A TRICK...
IF YOU'RE LOOKIN' TA COOK MY NOODLE...
...HELL WITH IT. GO AHEAD.
IT BEGAN LONG AGO...

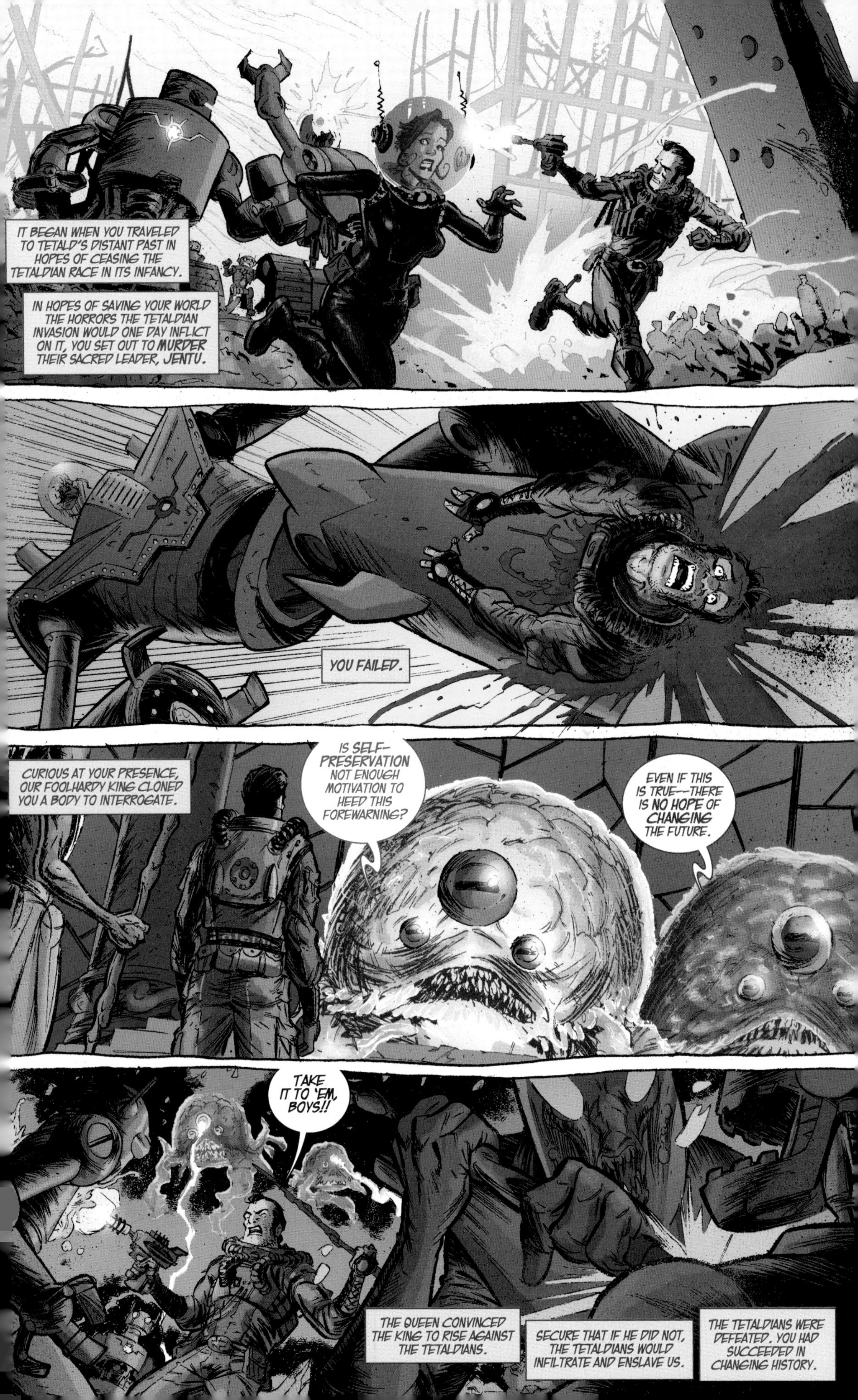
IT BEGAN WHEN YOU TRAVELED TO TETALD'S DISTANT PAST IN HOPES OF CEASING THE TETALDIAN RACE IN ITS INFANCY.
IN HOPES OF SAVING YOUR WORLD THE HORRORS THE TETALDIAN INVASION WOULD ONE DAY INFLICT ON IT, YOU SET OUT TO MURDER THEIR SACRED LEADER, JENTU.
YOU FAILED.
CURIOUS AT YOUR PRESENCE, OUR FOOLHARDY KING CLONED YOU A BODY TO INTERROGATE.
IS SELF-PRESERVATION NOT ENOUGH MOTIVATION TO HEED THIS FOREWARNING?
EVEN IF THIS IS TRUE--THERE IS NO HOPE OF CHANGING THE FUTURE.
TAKE IT TO 'EM, BOYS!!
THE QUEEN CONVINCED THE KING TO RISE AGAINST THE TETALDIANS.
SECURE THAT IF HE DID NOT, THE TETALDIANS WOULD INFILTRATE AND ENSLAVE US.
THE TETALDIANS WERE DEFEATED. YOU HAD SUCCEEDED IN CHANGING HISTORY.

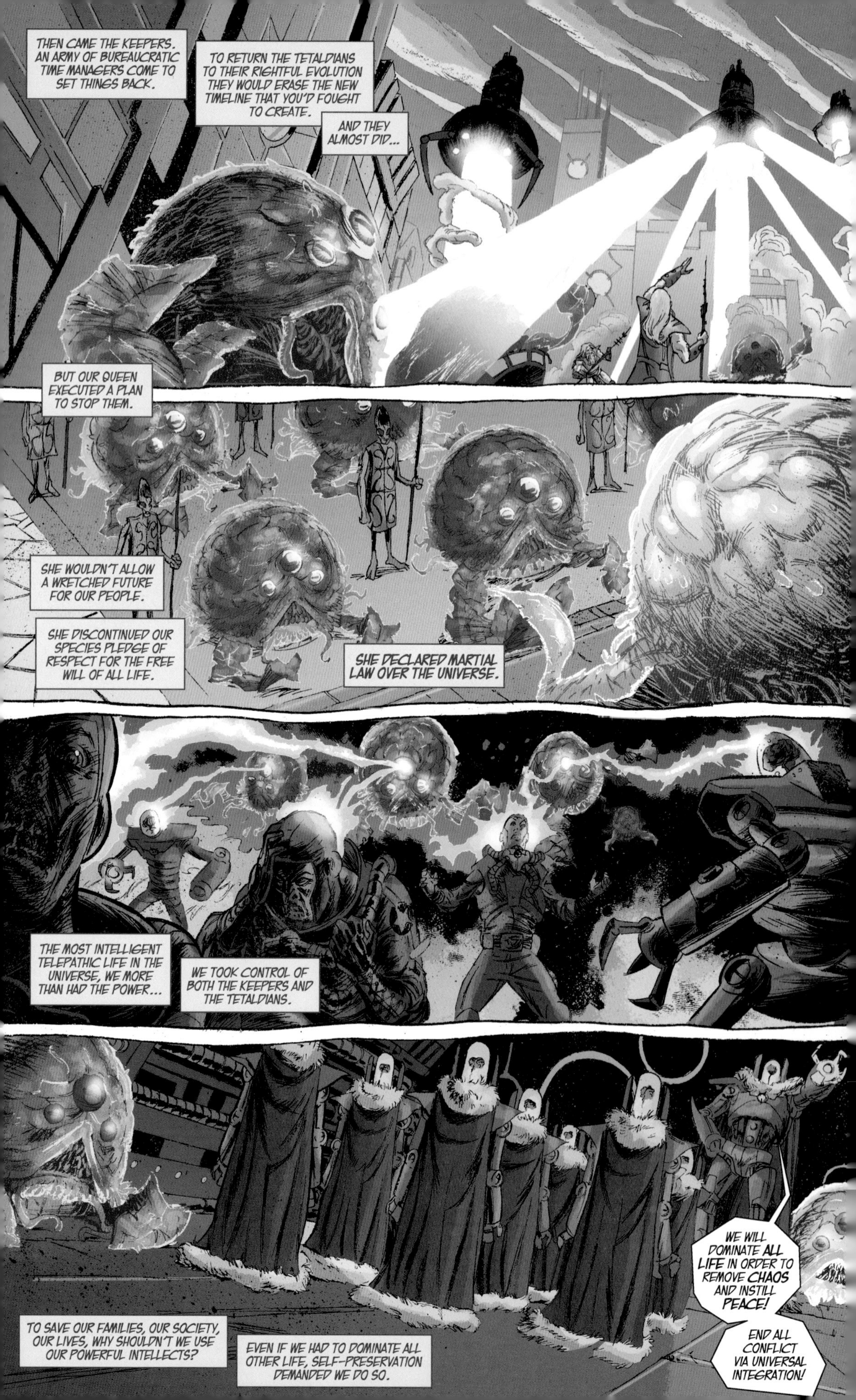
THEN CAME THE KEEPERS. AN ARMY OF BUREAUCRATIC TIME MANAGERS COME TO SET THINGS BACK.
TO RETURN THE TETALDIANS TO THEIR RIGHTFUL EVOLUTION THEY WOULD ERASE THE NEW TIMELINE THAT YOU'D FOUGHT TO CREATE.
AND THEY ALMOST DID...
BUT OUR QUEEN EXECUTED A PLAN TO STOP THEM.
SHE WOULDN'T ALLOW A WRETCHED FUTURE FOR OUR PEOPLE.
SHE DISCONTINUED OUR SPECIES PLEDGE OF RESPECT FOR THE FREE WILL OF ALL LIFE.
SHE DECLARED MARTIAL LAW OVER THE UNIVERSE.
THE MOST INTELLIGENT TELEPATHIC LIFE IN THE UNIVERSE, WE MORE THAN HAD THE POWER...
WE TOOK CONTROL OF BOTH THE KEEPERS AND THE TETALDIANS.
WE WILL DOMINATE ALL LIFE IN ORDER TO REMOVE CHAOS AND INSTILL PEACE!
END ALL CONFLICT VIA UNIVERSAL INTEGRATION!
TO SAVE OUR FAMILIES, OUR SOCIETY, OUR LIVES, WHY SHOULDN'T WE USE OUR POWERFUL INTELLECTS?
EVEN IF WE HAD TO DOMINATE ALL OTHER LIFE, SELF-PRESERVATION DEMANDED WE DO SO.

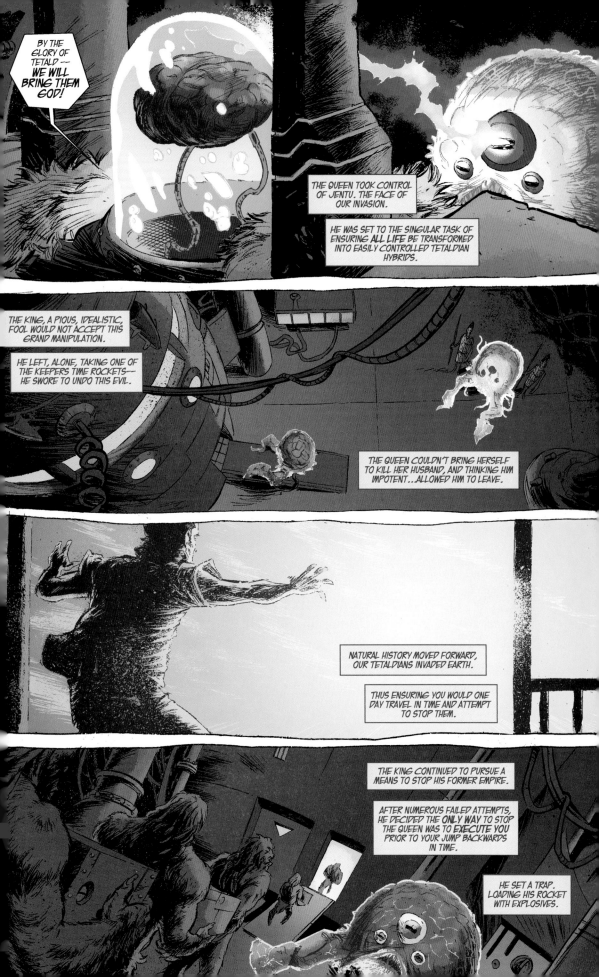

BY THE GLORY OF TETALD— **WE WILL BRING THEM GOD!**

THE QUEEN TOOK CONTROL OF JENTU. THE FACE OF OUR INVASION.

HE WAS SET TO THE SINGULAR TASK OF ENSURING **ALL LIFE** BE TRANSFORMED INTO EASILY CONTROLLED TETALDIAN HYBRIDS.

THE KING, A PIOUS, IDEALISTIC, FOOL WOULD NOT ACCEPT THIS GRAND MANIPULATION.

HE LEFT, ALONE, TAKING ONE OF THE KEEPERS TIME ROCKETS— HE SWORE TO UNDO THIS EVIL.

THE QUEEN COULDN'T BRING HERSELF TO KILL HER HUSBAND, AND THINKING HIM IMPOTENT...ALLOWED HIM TO LEAVE.

NATURAL HISTORY MOVED FORWARD, OUR TETALDIANS INVADED EARTH.

THUS ENSURING YOU WOULD ONE DAY TRAVEL IN TIME AND ATTEMPT TO STOP THEM.

THE KING CONTINUED TO PURSUE A MEANS TO STOP HIS FORMER EMPIRE.

AFTER NUMEROUS FAILED ATTEMPTS, HE DECIDED THE **ONLY WAY** TO STOP THE QUEEN WAS TO **EXECUTE YOU** PRIOR TO YOUR JUMP BACKWARDS IN TIME.

HE SET A TRAP. LOADING HIS ROCKET WITH EXPLOSIVES.

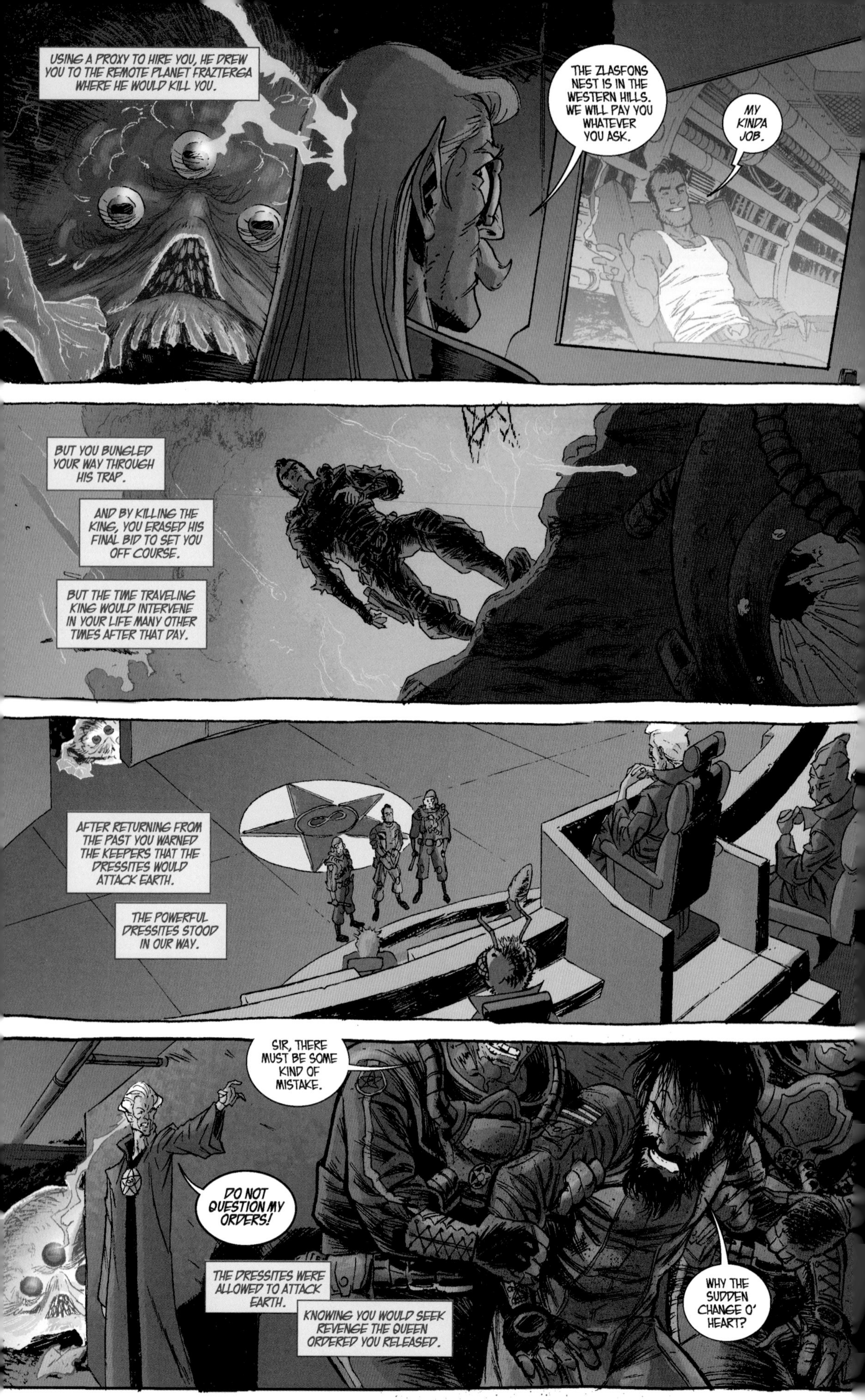
USING A PROXY TO HIRE YOU, HE DREW YOU TO THE REMOTE PLANET FRAZTERGA WHERE HE WOULD KILL YOU.
THE ZLASFONS NEST IS IN THE WESTERN HILLS. WE WILL PAY YOU WHATEVER YOU ASK.
MY KINDA JOB.
BUT YOU BUNGLED YOUR WAY THROUGH HIS TRAP.
AND BY KILLING THE KING, YOU ERASED HIS FINAL BID TO SET YOU OFF COURSE.
BUT THE TIME TRAVELING KING WOULD INTERVENE IN YOUR LIFE MANY OTHER TIMES AFTER THAT DAY.
AFTER RETURNING FROM THE PAST YOU WARNED THE KEEPERS THAT THE DRESSITES WOULD ATTACK EARTH.
THE POWERFUL DRESSITES STOOD IN OUR WAY.
SIR, THERE MUST BE SOME KIND OF MISTAKE.
DO NOT QUESTION MY ORDERS!
THE DRESSITES WERE ALLOWED TO ATTACK EARTH.
KNOWING YOU WOULD SEEK REVENGE THE QUEEN ORDERED YOU RELEASED.
WHY THE SUDDEN CHANGE O' HEART?

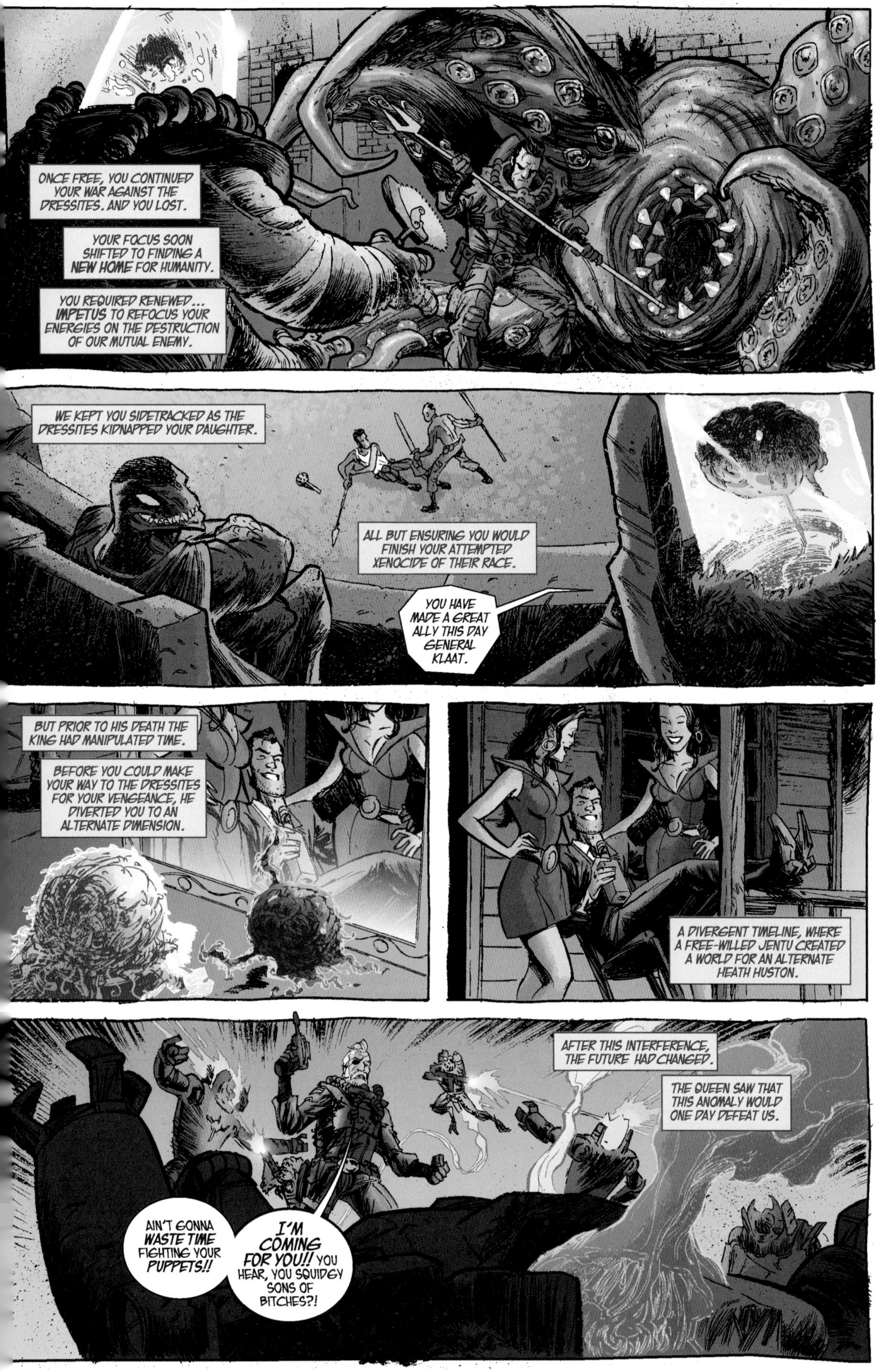
ONCE FREE, YOU CONTINUED YOUR WAR AGAINST THE DRESSITES. AND YOU LOST.
YOUR FOCUS SOON SHIFTED TO FINDING A NEW HOME FOR HUMANITY.
YOU REQUIRED RENEWED... IMPETUS TO REFOCUS YOUR ENERGIES ON THE DESTRUCTION OF OUR MUTUAL ENEMY.
WE KEPT YOU SIDETRACKED AS THE DRESSITES KIDNAPPED YOUR DAUGHTER.
ALL BUT ENSURING YOU WOULD FINISH YOUR ATTEMPTED XENOCIDE OF THEIR RACE.
YOU HAVE MADE A GREAT ALLY THIS DAY GENERAL KLAAT.
BUT PRIOR TO HIS DEATH THE KING HAD MANIPULATED TIME.
BEFORE YOU COULD MAKE YOUR WAY TO THE DRESSITES FOR YOUR VENGEANCE, HE DIVERTED YOU TO AN ALTERNATE DIMENSION.
A DIVERGENT TIMELINE, WHERE A FREE-WILLED JENTU CREATED A WORLD FOR AN ALTERNATE HEATH HUSTON.
AFTER THIS INTERFERENCE, THE FUTURE HAD CHANGED.
THE QUEEN SAW THAT THIS ANOMALY WOULD ONE DAY DEFEAT US.
AIN'T GONNA WASTE TIME FIGHTING YOUR PUPPETS!!
I'M COMING FOR YOU!! YOU HEAR, YOU SQUIDGY SONS OF BITCHES?!

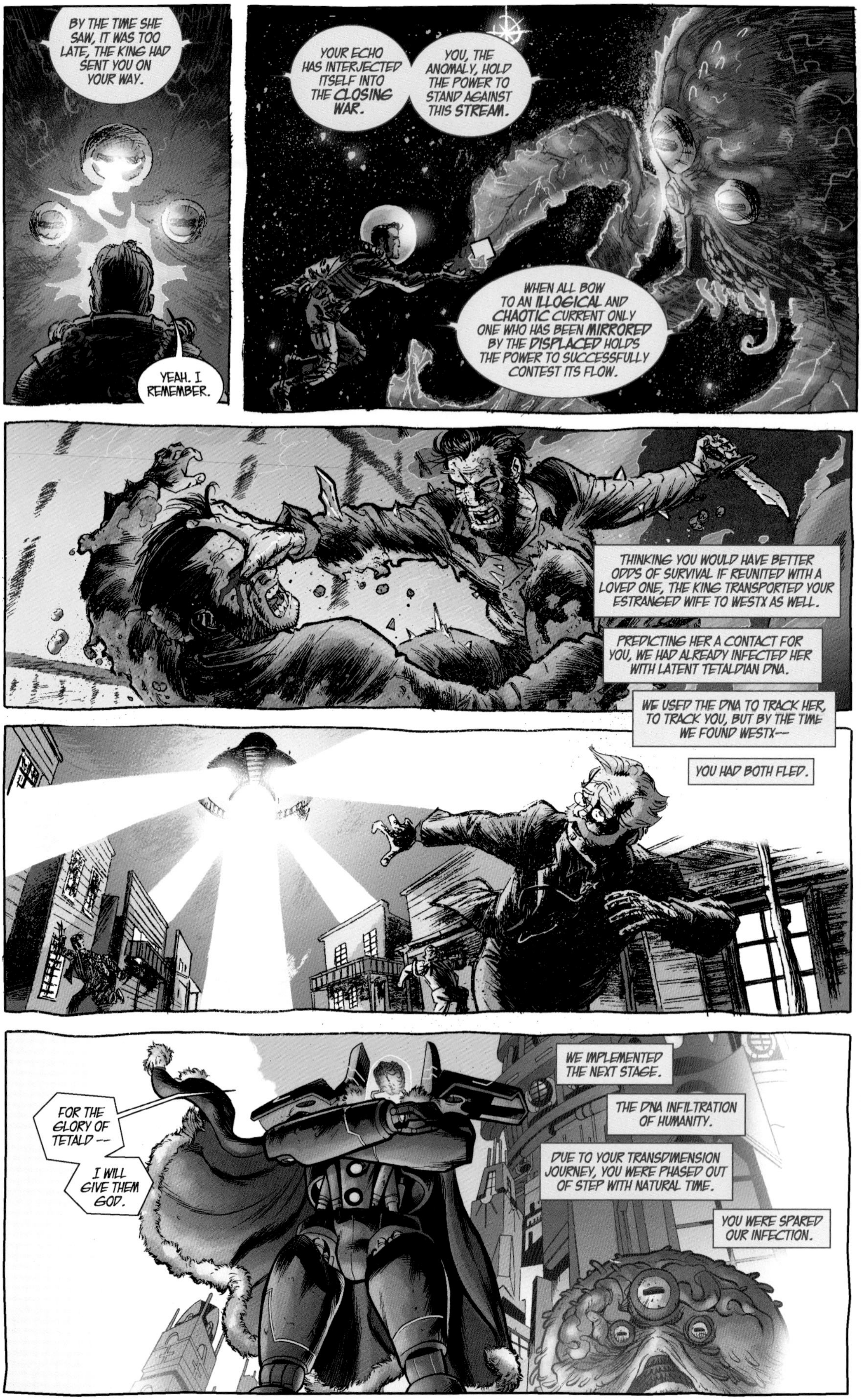

BY THE TIME SHE SAW, IT WAS TOO LATE, THE KING HAD SENT YOU ON YOUR WAY.
YEAH. I REMEMBER.
YOUR ECHO HAS INTERJECTED ITSELF INTO THE CLOSING WAR.
YOU, THE ANOMALY, HOLD THE POWER TO STAND AGAINST THIS STREAM.
WHEN ALL BOW TO AN ILLOGICAL AND CHAOTIC CURRENT ONLY ONE WHO HAS BEEN MIRRORED BY THE DISPLACED HOLDS THE POWER TO SUCCESSFULLY CONTEST ITS FLOW.
THINKING YOU WOULD HAVE BETTER ODDS OF SURVIVAL IF REUNITED WITH A LOVED ONE, THE KING TRANSPORTED YOUR ESTRANGED WIFE TO WESTX AS WELL.
PREDICTING HER A CONTACT FOR YOU, WE HAD ALREADY INFECTED HER WITH LATENT TETALDIAN DNA.
WE USED THE DNA TO TRACK HER, TO TRACK YOU, BUT BY THE TIME WE FOUND WESTX--
YOU HAD BOTH FLED.
WE IMPLEMENTED THE NEXT STAGE.
FOR THE GLORY OF TETALD --
I WILL GIVE THEM GOD.
THE DNA INFILTRATION OF HUMANITY.
DUE TO YOUR TRANSDIMENSION JOURNEY, YOU WERE PHASED OUT OF STEP WITH NATURAL TIME.
YOU WERE SPARED OUR INFECTION.

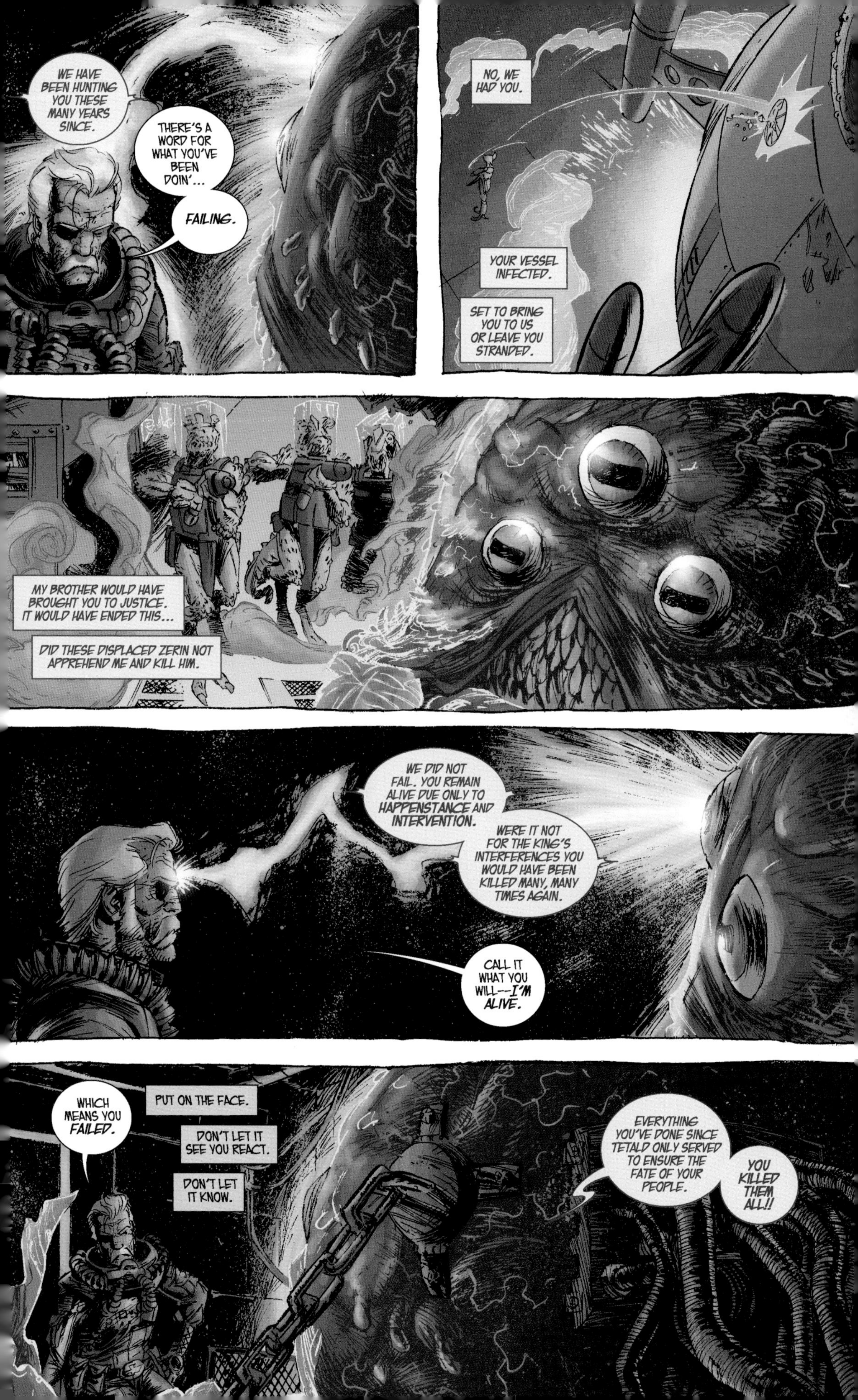

WE HAVE BEEN HUNTING YOU THESE MANY YEARS SINCE.
THERE'S A WORD FOR WHAT YOU'VE BEEN DOIN'...
FAILING.
NO, WE HAD YOU.
YOUR VESSEL INFECTED.
SET TO BRING YOU TO US OR LEAVE YOU STRANDED.
MY BROTHER WOULD HAVE BROUGHT YOU TO JUSTICE. IT WOULD HAVE ENDED THIS...
DID THESE DISPLACED ZERIN NOT APPREHEND ME AND KILL HIM.
WE DID NOT FAIL. YOU REMAIN ALIVE DUE ONLY TO HAPPENSTANCE AND INTERVENTION.
WERE IT NOT FOR THE KING'S INTERFERENCES YOU WOULD HAVE BEEN KILLED MANY, MANY TIMES AGAIN.
CALL IT WHAT YOU WILL--I'M ALIVE.
WHICH MEANS YOU FAILED.
PUT ON THE FACE.
DON'T LET IT SEE YOU REACT.
DON'T LET IT KNOW.
EVERYTHING YOU'VE DONE SINCE TETALD ONLY SERVED TO ENSURE THE FATE OF YOUR PEOPLE.
YOU KILLED THEM ALL!!

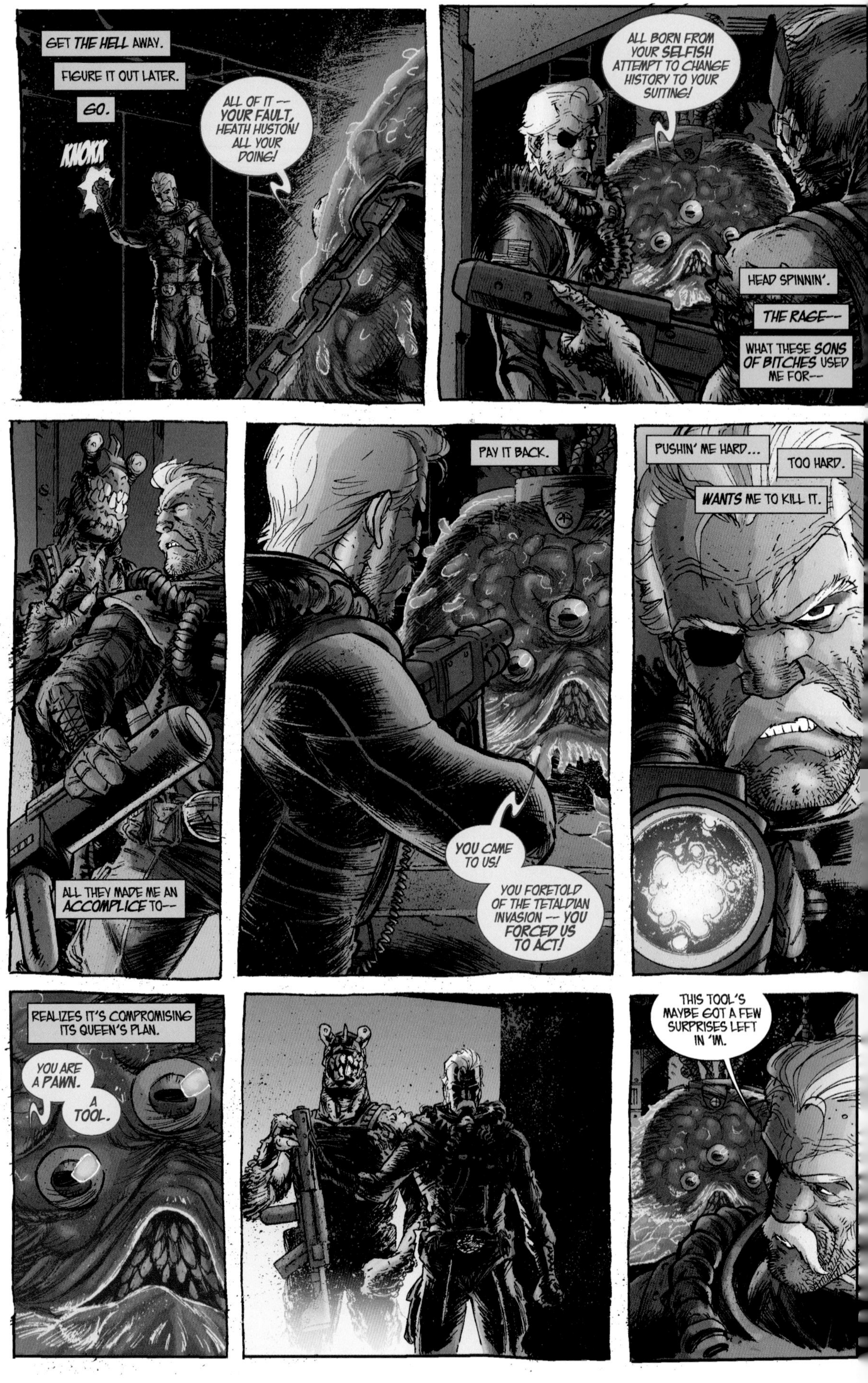
GET THE HELL AWAY.
FIGURE IT OUT LATER.
GO.
KNOKK
ALL OF IT -- YOUR FAULT, HEATH HUSTON! ALL YOUR DOING!
ALL BORN FROM YOUR SELFISH ATTEMPT TO CHANGE HISTORY TO YOUR SUITING!
HEAD SPINNIN'.
THE RAGE--
WHAT THESE SONS OF BITCHES USED ME FOR--
ALL THEY MADE ME AN ACCOMPLICE TO--
PAY IT BACK.
YOU CAME TO US!
YOU FORETOLD OF THE TETALDIAN INVASION -- YOU FORCED US TO ACT!
PUSHIN' ME HARD...
TOO HARD.
WANTS ME TO KILL IT.
REALIZES IT'S COMPROMISING ITS QUEEN'S PLAN.
YOU ARE A PAWN.
A TOOL.
THIS TOOL'S MAYBE GOT A FEW SURPRISES LEFT IN 'IM.

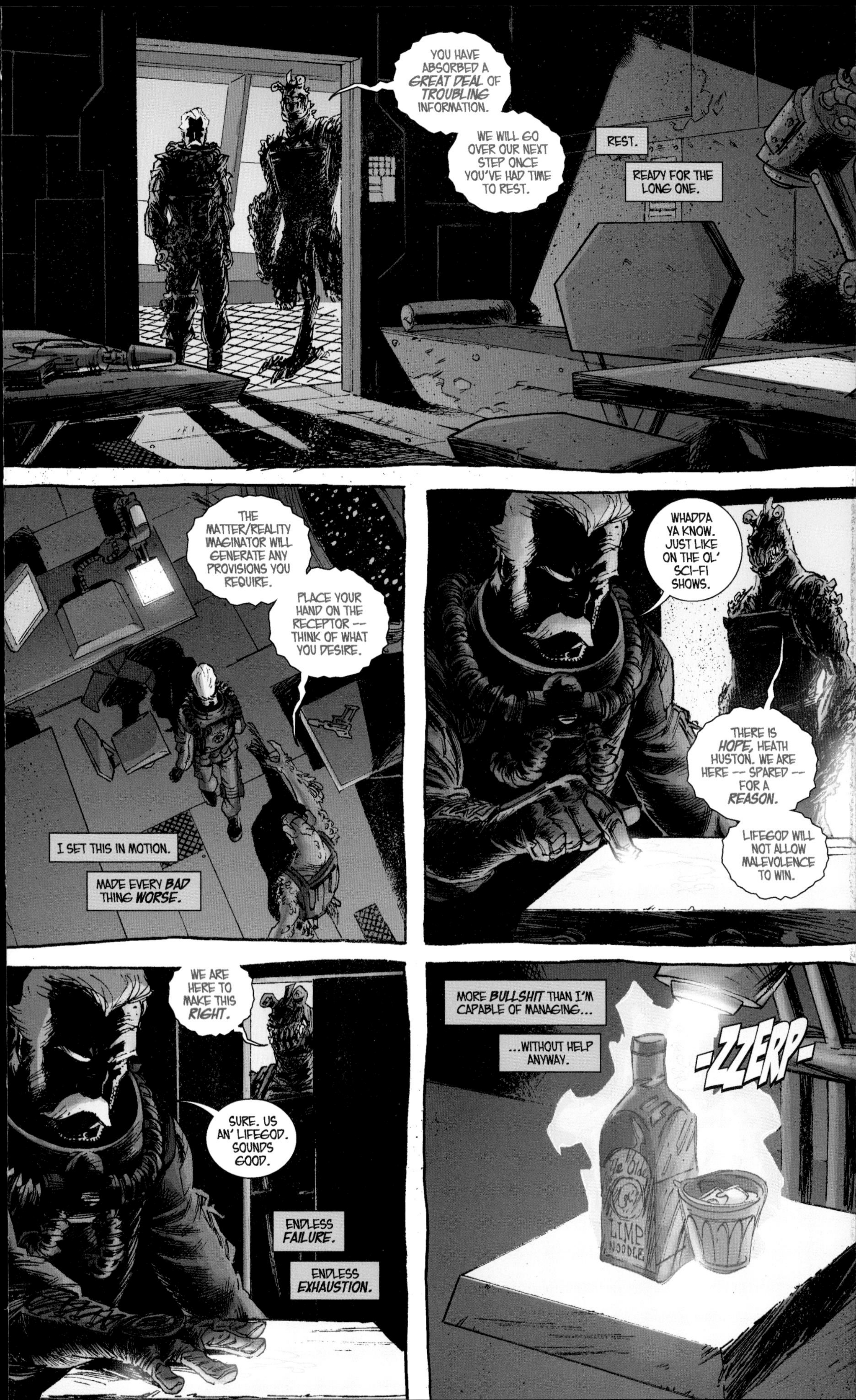
YOU HAVE ABSORBED A GREAT DEAL OF TROUBLING INFORMATION.
WE WILL GO OVER OUR NEXT STEP ONCE YOU'VE HAD TIME TO REST.
REST.
READY FOR THE LONG ONE.
THE MATTER/REALITY IMAGINATOR WILL GENERATE ANY PROVISIONS YOU REQUIRE.
PLACE YOUR HAND ON THE RECEPTOR -- THINK OF WHAT YOU DESIRE.
I SET THIS IN MOTION.
MADE EVERY BAD THING WORSE.
WHADDA YA KNOW. JUST LIKE ON THE OL' SCI-FI SHOWS.
THERE IS HOPE, HEATH HUSTON. WE ARE HERE -- SPARED -- FOR A REASON.
LIFEGOD WILL NOT ALLOW MALEVOLENCE TO WIN.
WE ARE HERE TO MAKE THIS RIGHT.
SURE. US AN' LIFEGOD. SOUNDS GOOD.
ENDLESS FAILURE.
ENDLESS EXHAUSTION.
MORE BULLSHIT THAN I'M CAPABLE OF MANAGING...
...WITHOUT HELP ANYWAY.
-ZZERP-
LIMP NOODLE

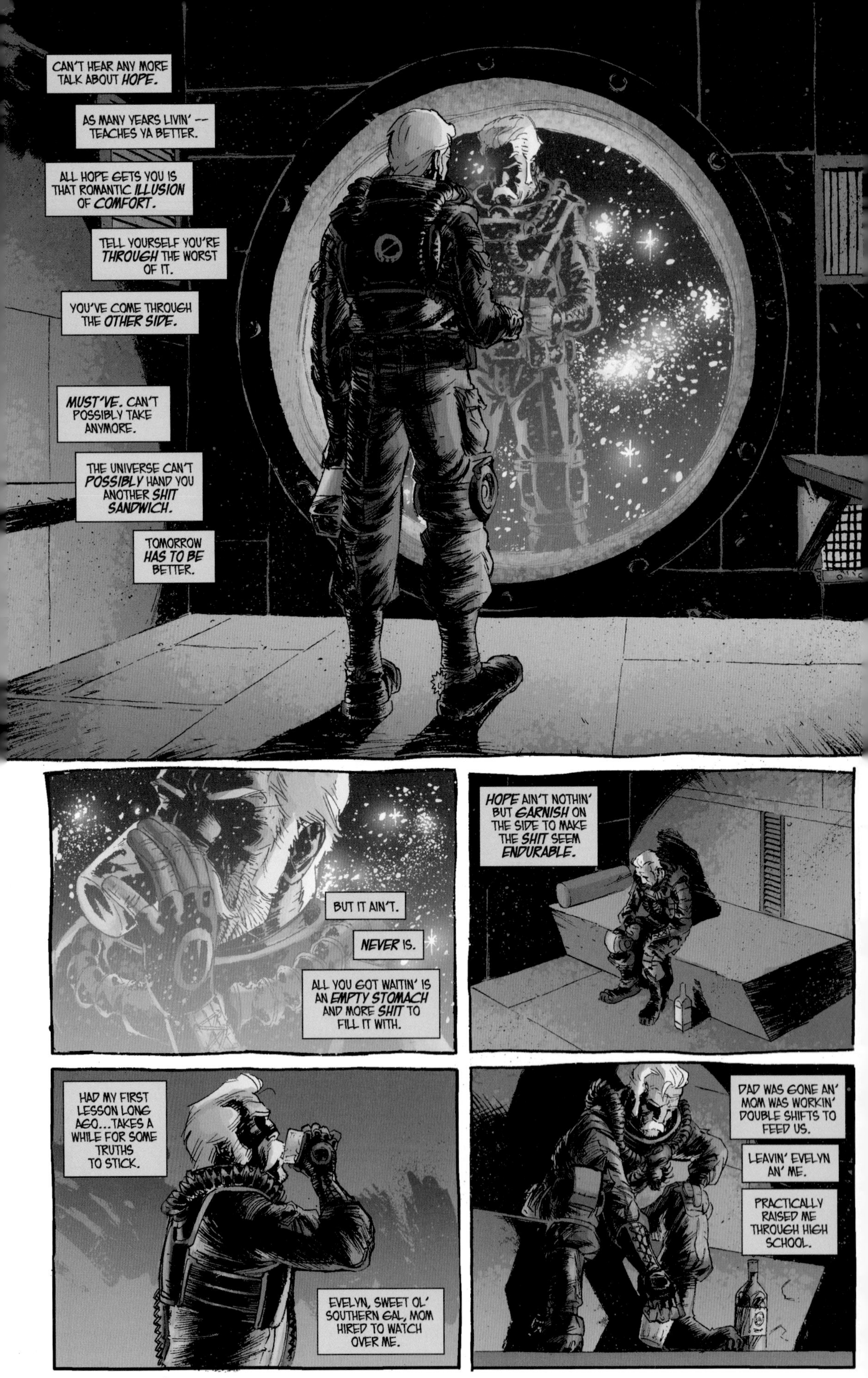
CAN'T HEAR ANY MORE TALK ABOUT HOPE.
AS MANY YEARS LIVIN' -- TEACHES YA BETTER.
ALL HOPE GETS YOU IS THAT ROMANTIC ILLUSION OF COMFORT.
TELL YOURSELF YOU'RE THROUGH THE WORST OF IT.
YOU'VE COME THROUGH THE OTHER SIDE.
MUST'VE. CAN'T POSSIBLY TAKE ANYMORE.
THE UNIVERSE CAN'T POSSIBLY HAND YOU ANOTHER SHIT SANDWICH.
TOMORROW HAS TO BE BETTER.
BUT IT AIN'T.
NEVER IS.
ALL YOU GOT WAITIN' IS AN EMPTY STOMACH AND MORE SHIT TO FILL IT WITH.
HOPE AIN'T NOTHIN' BUT GARNISH ON THE SIDE TO MAKE THE SHIT SEEM ENDURABLE.
HAD MY FIRST LESSON LONG AGO...TAKES A WHILE FOR SOME TRUTHS TO STICK.
EVELYN, SWEET OL' SOUTHERN GAL, MOM HIRED TO WATCH OVER ME.
DAD WAS GONE AN' MOM WAS WORKIN' DOUBLE SHIFTS TO FEED US.
LEAVIN' EVELYN AN' ME.
PRACTICALLY RAISED ME THROUGH HIGH SCHOOL.

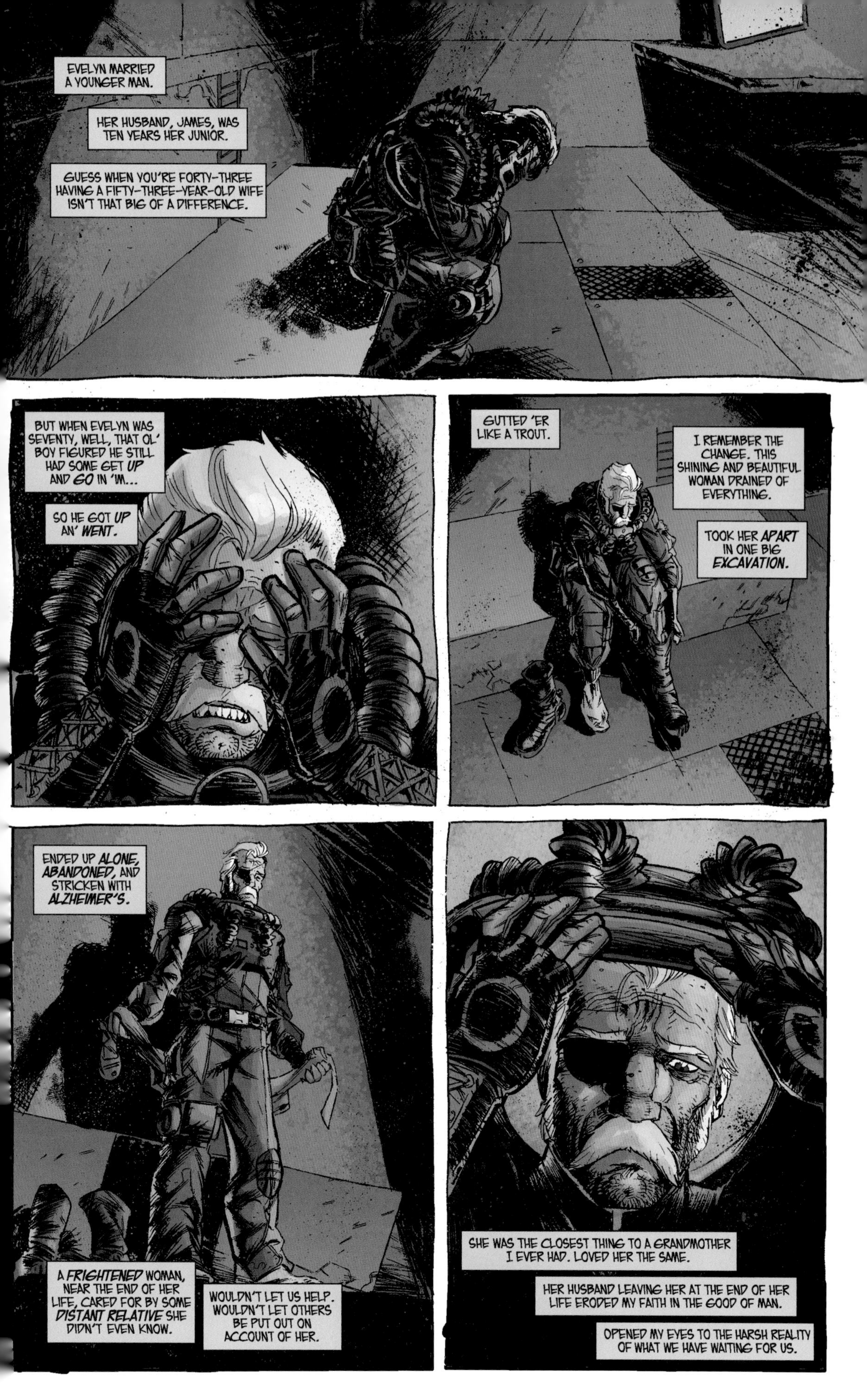
EVELYN MARRIED A YOUNGER MAN.
HER HUSBAND, JAMES, WAS TEN YEARS HER JUNIOR.
GUESS WHEN YOU'RE FORTY-THREE HAVING A FIFTY-THREE-YEAR-OLD WIFE ISN'T THAT BIG OF A DIFFERENCE.
BUT WHEN EVELYN WAS SEVENTY, WELL, THAT OL' BOY FIGURED HE STILL HAD SOME GET *UP* AND *GO* IN 'IM...
SO HE GOT *UP* AN' *WENT*.
GUTTED 'ER LIKE A TROUT.
I REMEMBER THE CHANGE. THIS SHINING AND BEAUTIFUL WOMAN DRAINED OF EVERYTHING.
TOOK HER *APART* IN ONE BIG *EXCAVATION*.
ENDED UP *ALONE*, *ABANDONED*, AND STRICKEN WITH *ALZHEIMER'S*.
A *FRIGHTENED* WOMAN, NEAR THE END OF HER LIFE, CARED FOR BY SOME *DISTANT RELATIVE* SHE DIDN'T EVEN KNOW.
WOULDN'T LET US HELP. WOULDN'T LET OTHERS BE PUT OUT ON ACCOUNT OF HER.
SHE WAS THE CLOSEST THING TO A GRANDMOTHER I EVER HAD. LOVED HER THE SAME.
HER HUSBAND LEAVING HER AT THE END OF HER LIFE ERODED MY FAITH IN THE GOOD OF MAN.
OPENED MY EYES TO THE HARSH REALITY OF WHAT WE HAVE WAITING FOR US.

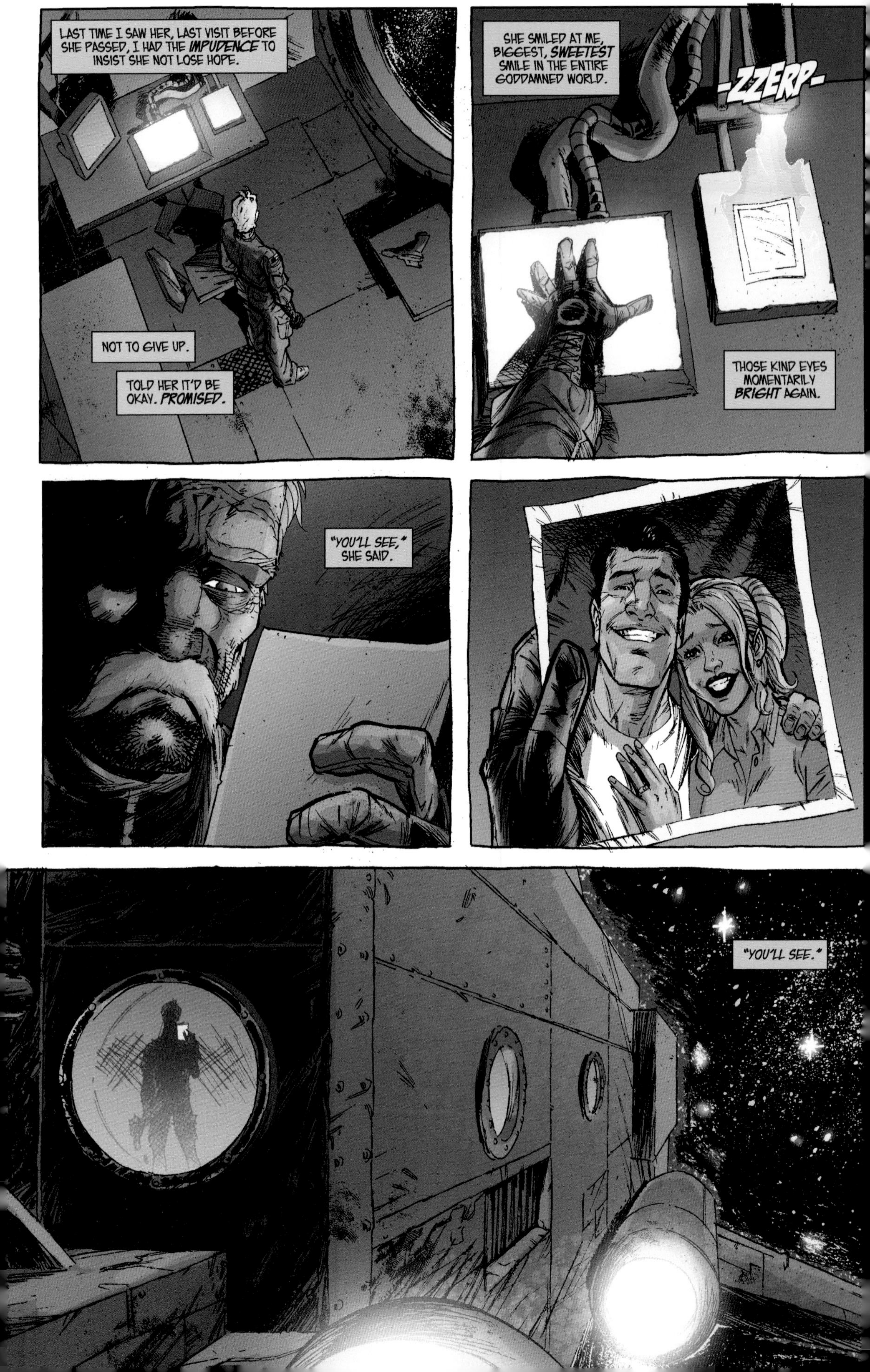
LAST TIME I SAW HER, LAST VISIT BEFORE SHE PASSED, I HAD THE IMPUDENCE TO INSIST SHE NOT LOSE HOPE.
NOT TO GIVE UP.
TOLD HER IT'D BE OKAY. PROMISED.
SHE SMILED AT ME, BIGGEST, SWEETEST SMILE IN THE ENTIRE GODDAMNED WORLD.
-ZZERP-
THOSE KIND EYES MOMENTARILY BRIGHT AGAIN.
"YOU'LL SEE," SHE SAID.
"YOU'LL SEE."

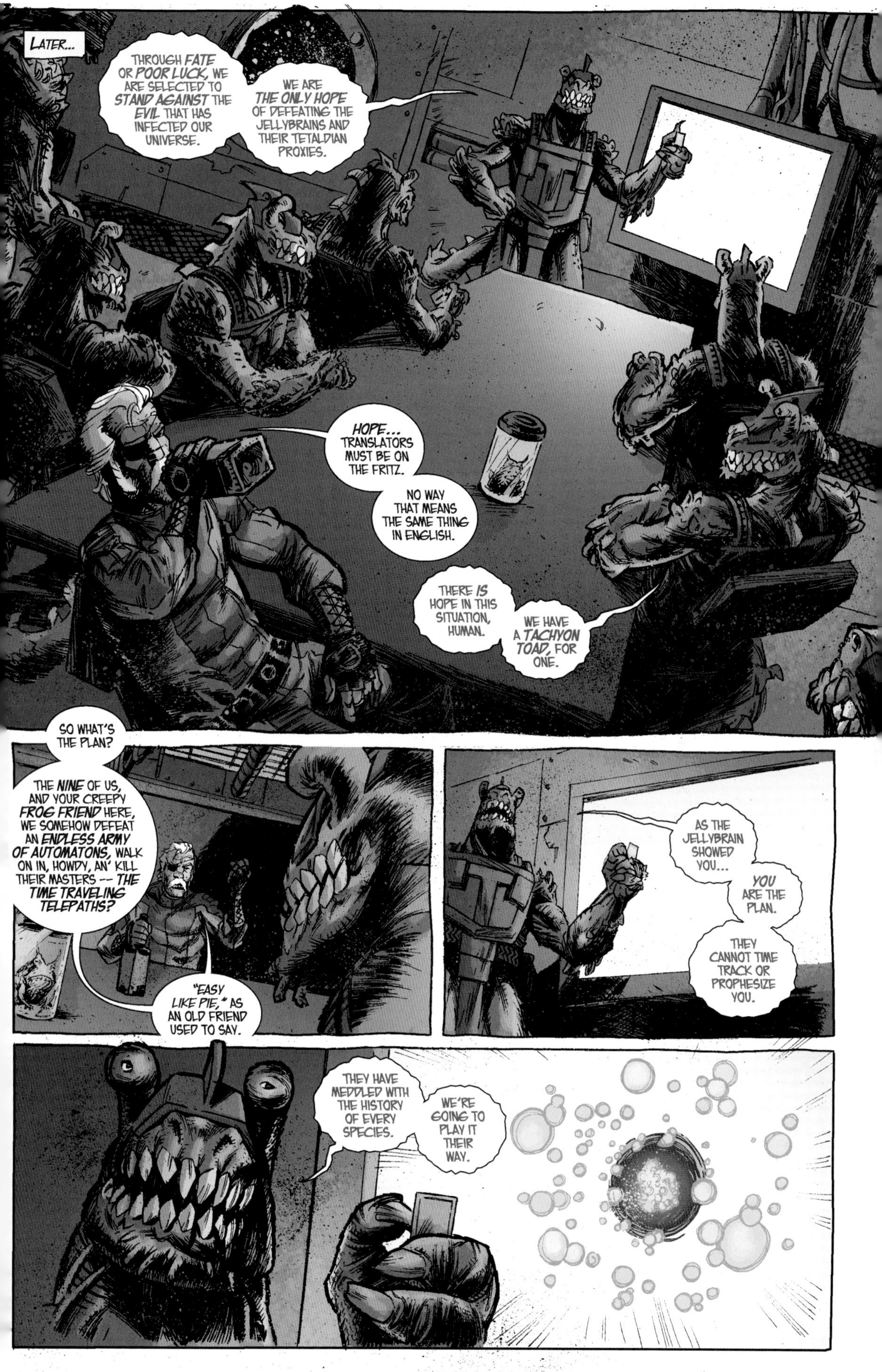
LATER...
THROUGH FATE OR POOR LUCK, WE ARE SELECTED TO STAND AGAINST THE EVIL THAT HAS INFECTED OUR UNIVERSE.
WE ARE THE ONLY HOPE OF DEFEATING THE JELLYBRAINS AND THEIR TETALDIAN PROXIES.
HOPE... TRANSLATORS MUST BE ON THE FRITZ.
NO WAY THAT MEANS THE SAME THING IN ENGLISH.
THERE IS HOPE IN THIS SITUATION, HUMAN.
WE HAVE A TACHYON TOAD, FOR ONE.
SO WHAT'S THE PLAN?
THE NINE OF US, AND YOUR CREEPY FROG FRIEND HERE, WE SOMEHOW DEFEAT AN ENDLESS ARMY OF AUTOMATONS, WALK ON IN, HOWDY, AN' KILL THEIR MASTERS -- THE TIME TRAVELING TELEPATHS?
"EASY LIKE PIE," AS AN OLD FRIEND USED TO SAY.
AS THE JELLYBRAIN SHOWED YOU...
YOU ARE THE PLAN.
THEY CANNOT TIME TRACK OR PROPHESIZE YOU.
THEY HAVE MEDDLED WITH THE HISTORY OF EVERY SPECIES.
WE'RE GOING TO PLAY IT THEIR WAY.

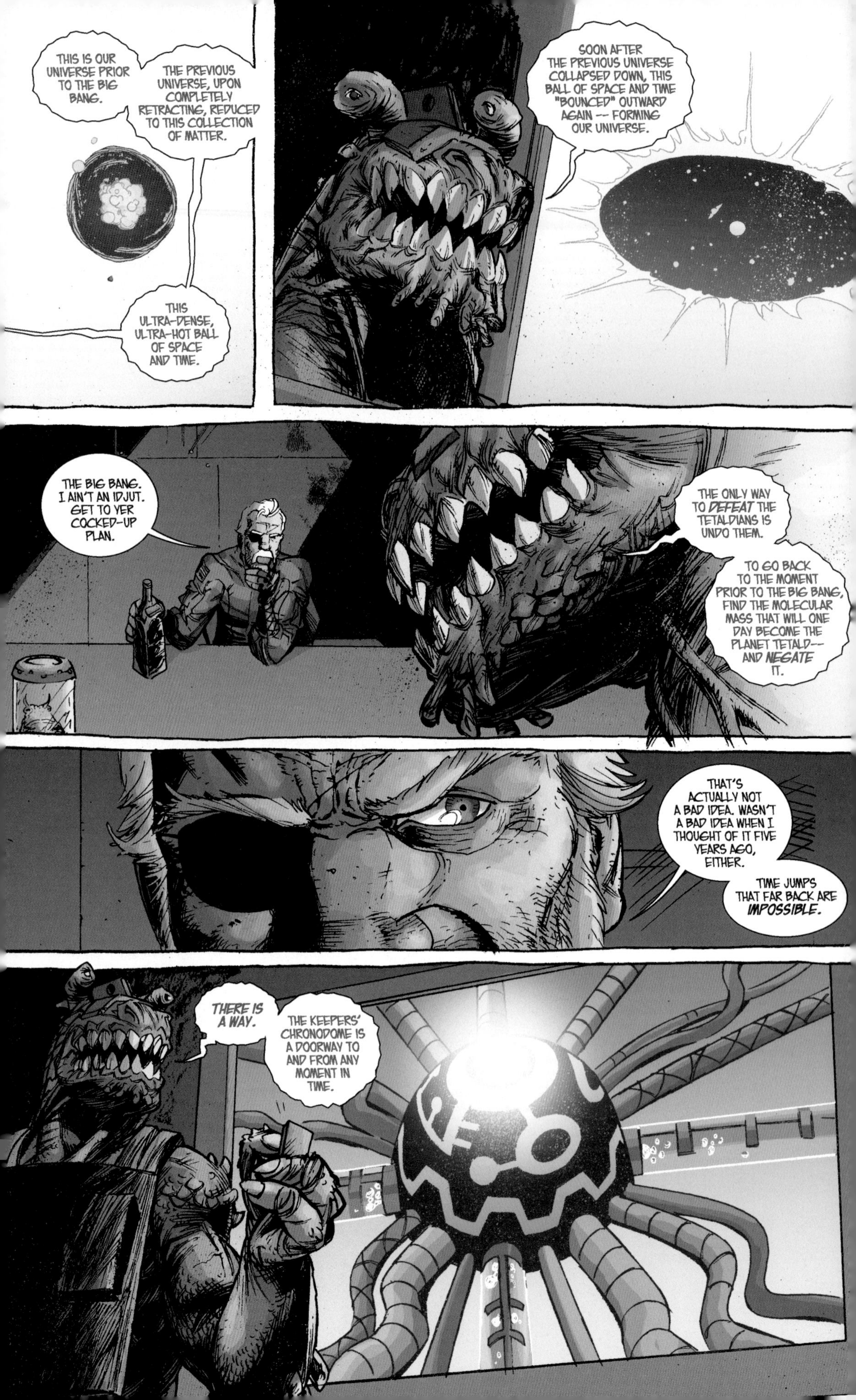
THIS IS OUR UNIVERSE PRIOR TO THE BIG BANG.
THE PREVIOUS UNIVERSE, UPON COMPLETELY RETRACTING, REDUCED TO THIS COLLECTION OF MATTER.
THIS ULTRA-DENSE, ULTRA-HOT BALL OF SPACE AND TIME.
SOON AFTER THE PREVIOUS UNIVERSE COLLAPSED DOWN, THIS BALL OF SPACE AND TIME "BOUNCED" OUTWARD AGAIN -- FORMING OUR UNIVERSE.
THE BIG BANG. I AIN'T AN IDJUT. GET TO YER COCKED-UP PLAN.
THE ONLY WAY TO *DEFEAT* THE TETALDIANS IS UNDO THEM.
TO GO BACK TO THE MOMENT PRIOR TO THE BIG BANG, FIND THE MOLECULAR MASS THAT WILL ONE DAY BECOME THE PLANET TETALD-- AND *NEGATE* IT.
THAT'S ACTUALLY NOT A BAD IDEA. WASN'T A BAD IDEA WHEN I THOUGHT OF IT FIVE YEARS AGO, EITHER.
TIME JUMPS THAT FAR BACK ARE ***IMPOSSIBLE.***
THERE IS A WAY.
THE KEEPERS' CHRONODOME IS A DOORWAY TO AND FROM ANY MOMENT IN TIME.

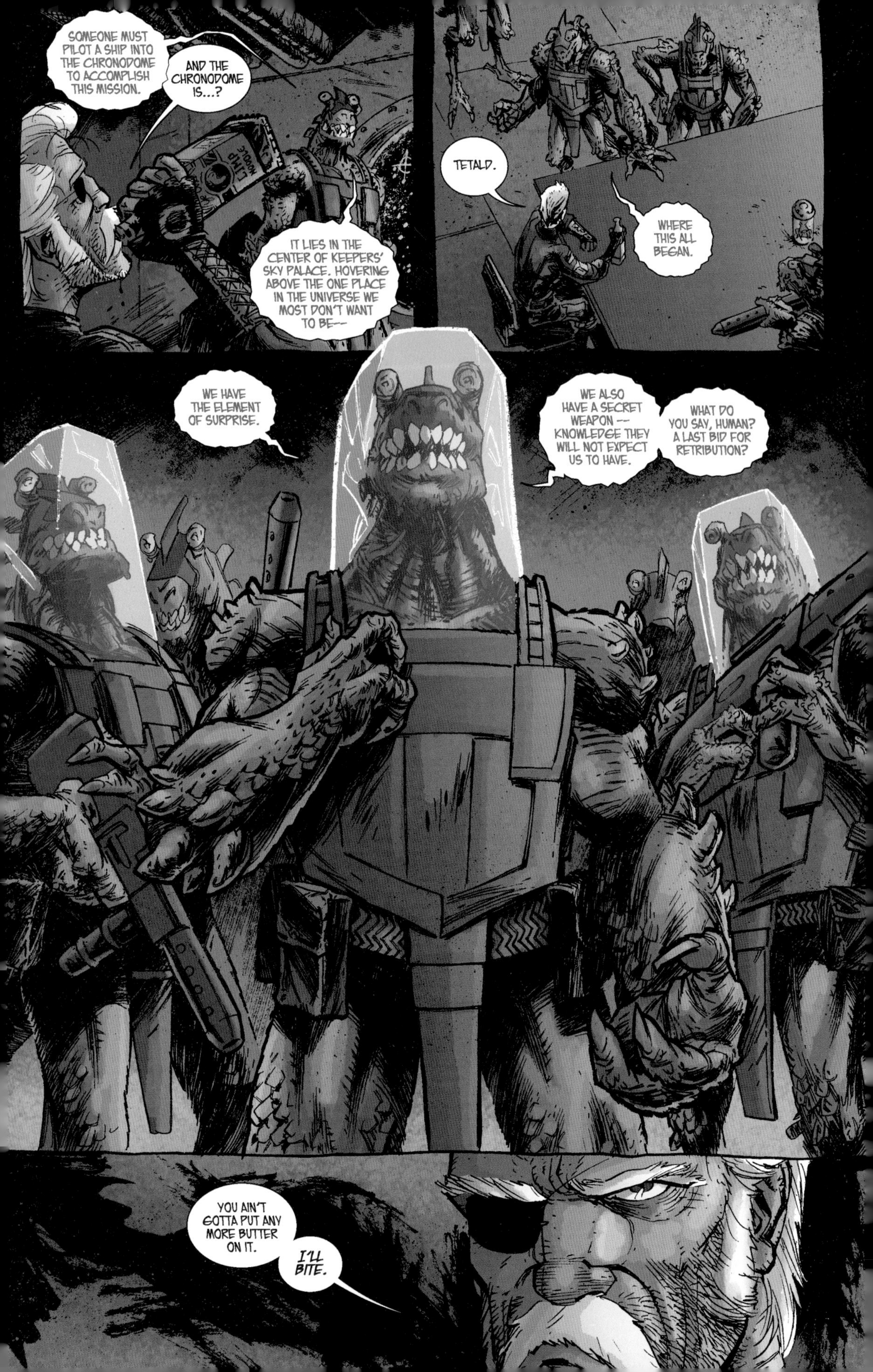
SOMEONE MUST PILOT A SHIP INTO THE CHRONODOME TO ACCOMPLISH THIS MISSION.
AND THE CHRONODOME IS...?
IT LIES IN THE CENTER OF KEEPERS' SKY PALACE. HOVERING ABOVE THE ONE PLACE IN THE UNIVERSE WE MOST DON'T WANT TO BE--
TETALD.
WHERE THIS ALL BEGAN.
WE HAVE THE ELEMENT OF SURPRISE.
WE ALSO HAVE A SECRET WEAPON -- KNOWLEDGE THEY WILL NOT EXPECT US TO HAVE.
WHAT DO YOU SAY, HUMAN? A LAST BID FOR RETRIBUTION?
YOU AIN'T GOTTA PUT ANY MORE BUTTER ON IT.
I'LL BITE.

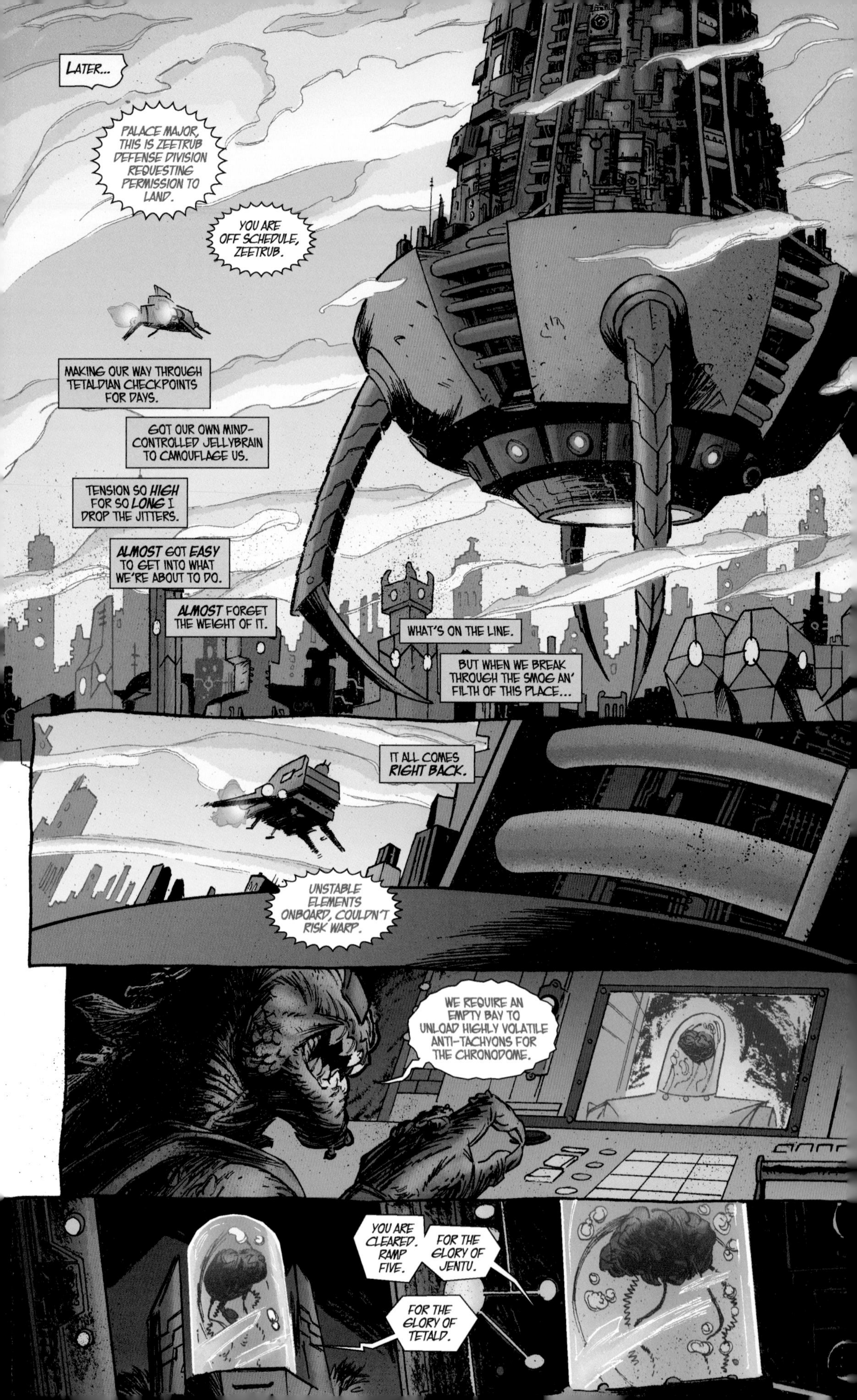
LATER...
PALACE MAJOR, THIS IS ZEETRUB DEFENSE DIVISION REQUESTING PERMISSION TO LAND.
YOU ARE OFF SCHEDULE, ZEETRUB.
MAKING OUR WAY THROUGH TETALDIAN CHECKPOINTS FOR DAYS.
GOT OUR OWN MIND-CONTROLLED JELLYBRAIN TO CAMOUFLAGE US.
TENSION SO HIGH FOR SO LONG I DROP THE JITTERS.
ALMOST GOT EASY TO GET INTO WHAT WE'RE ABOUT TO DO.
ALMOST FORGET THE WEIGHT OF IT.
WHAT'S ON THE LINE.
BUT WHEN WE BREAK THROUGH THE SMOG AN' FILTH OF THIS PLACE...
IT ALL COMES RIGHT BACK.
UNSTABLE ELEMENTS ONBOARD, COULDN'T RISK WARP.
WE REQUIRE AN EMPTY BAY TO UNLOAD HIGHLY VOLATILE ANTI-TACHYONS FOR THE CHRONODOME.
YOU ARE CLEARED. RAMP FIVE.
FOR THE GLORY OF JENTU.
FOR THE GLORY OF TETALD.

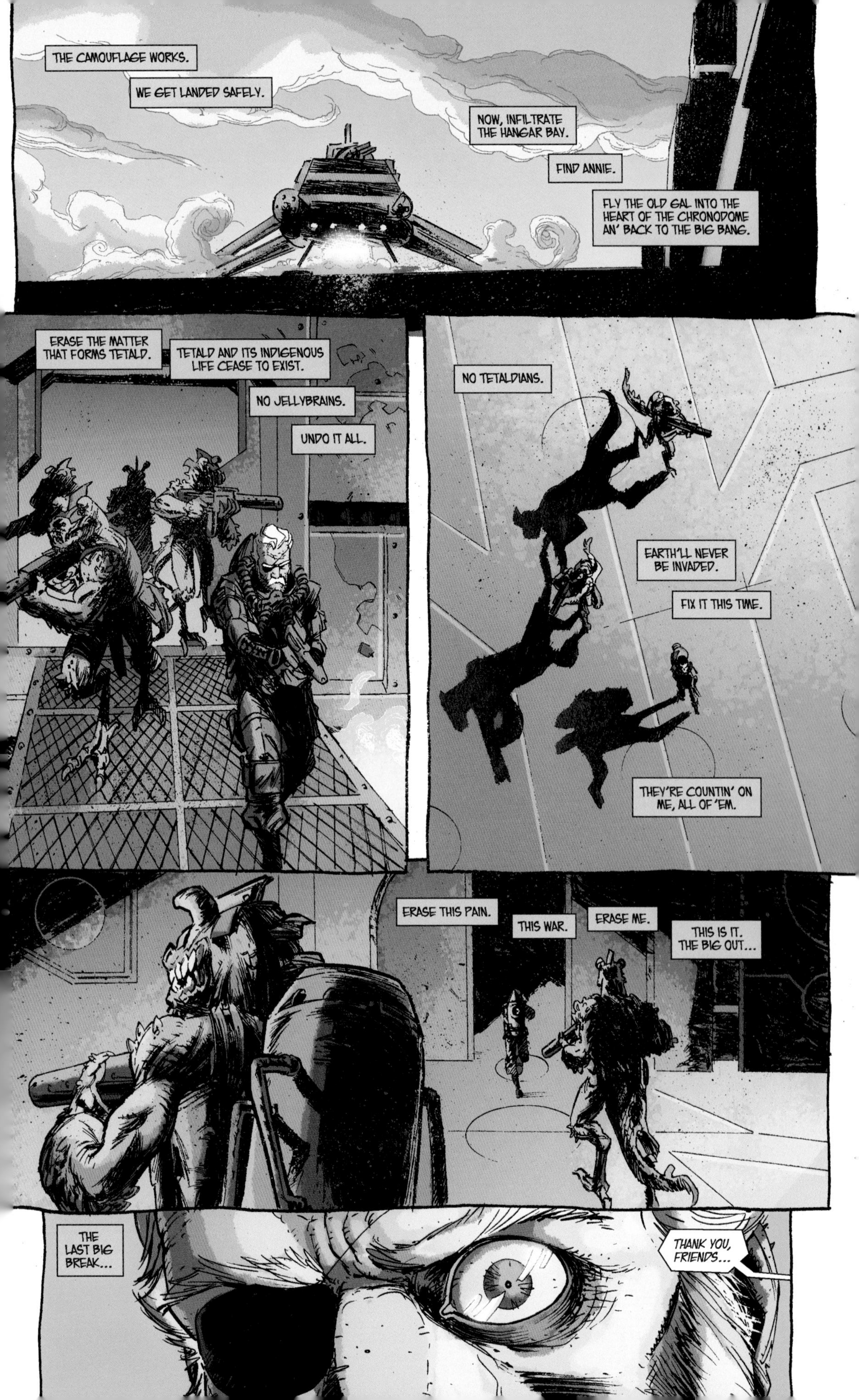
THE CAMOUFLAGE WORKS.
WE GET LANDED SAFELY.
NOW, INFILTRATE THE HANGAR BAY.
FIND ANNIE.
FLY THE OLD GAL INTO THE HEART OF THE CHRONODOME AN' BACK TO THE BIG BANG.
ERASE THE MATTER THAT FORMS TETALD.
TETALD AND ITS INDIGENOUS LIFE CEASE TO EXIST.
NO JELLYBRAINS.
UNDO IT ALL.
NO TETALDIANS.
EARTH'LL NEVER BE INVADED.
FIX IT THIS TIME.
THEY'RE COUNTIN' ON ME, ALL OF 'EM.
ERASE THIS PAIN.
THIS WAR.
ERASE ME.
THIS IS IT. THE BIG OUT...
THE LAST BIG BREAK...
THANK YOU, FRIENDS...

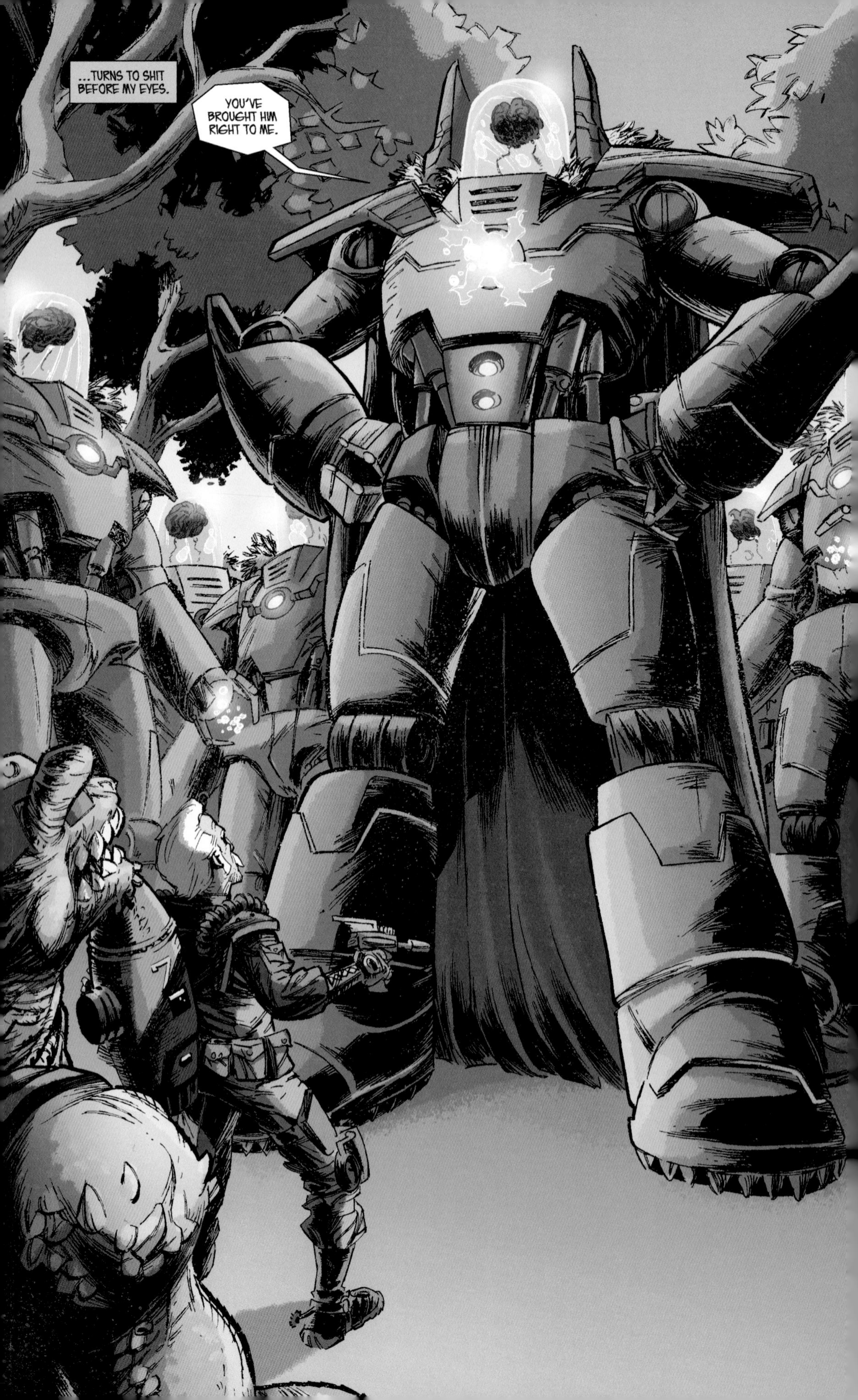
...TURNS TO SHIT BEFORE MY EYES.
YOU'VE BROUGHT HIM RIGHT TO ME.

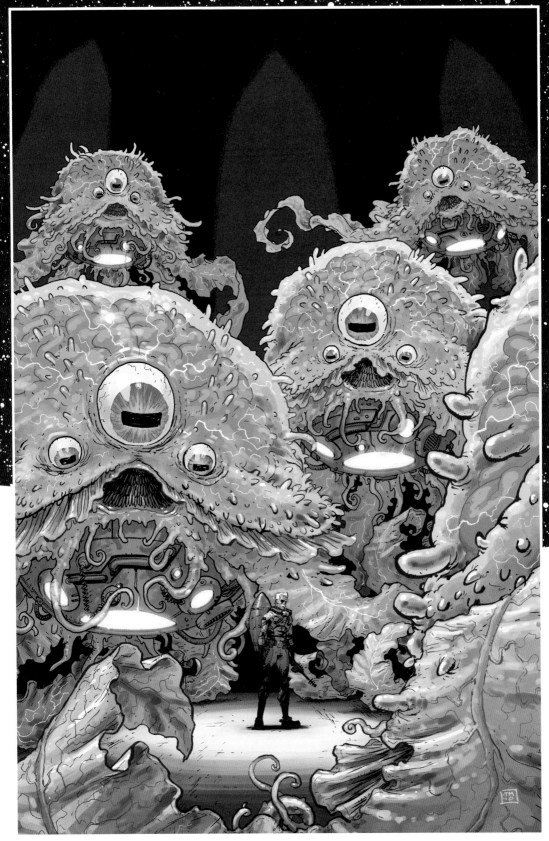

FEAR AGENT #31
ART BY TONY MOORE

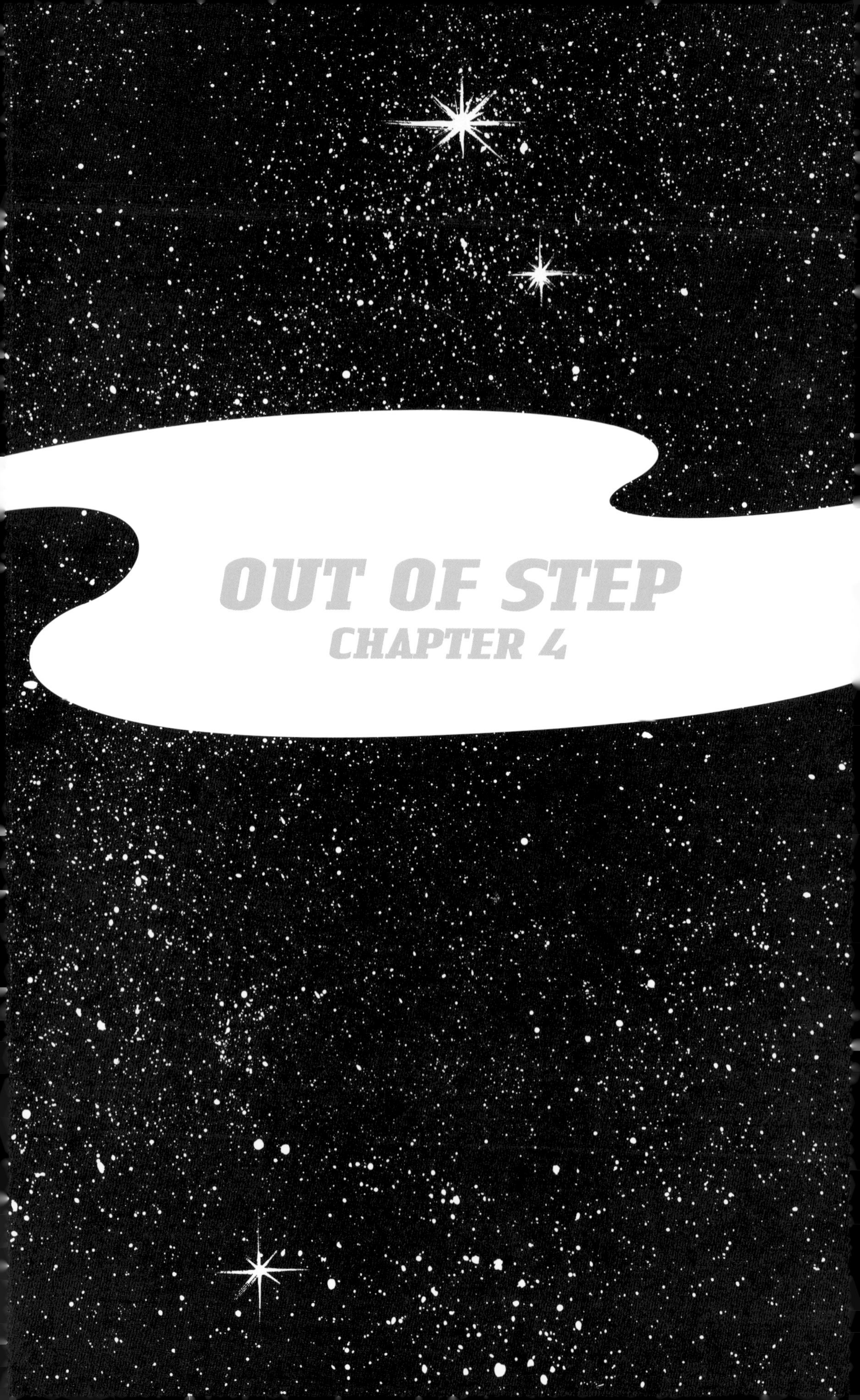
OUT OF STEP
CHAPTER 4

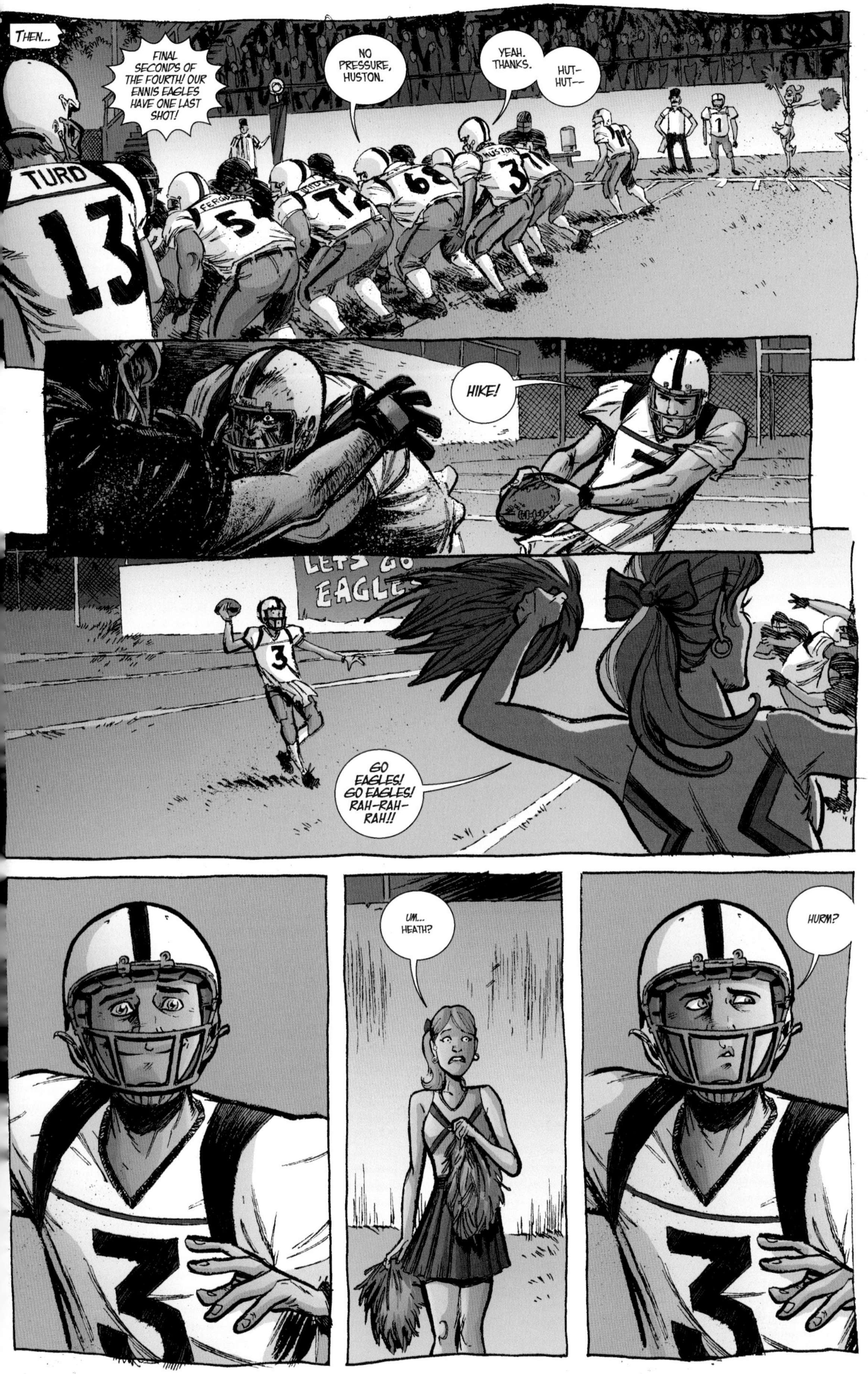
THEN...
FINAL SECONDS OF THE FOURTH! OUR ENNIS EAGLES HAVE ONE LAST SHOT!
NO PRESSURE, HUSTON.
YEAH. THANKS.
HUT-HUT--
HIKE!
LETS GO EAGLES
GO EAGLES! GO EAGLES! RAH-RAH-RAH!!
UM... HEATH?
HURM?

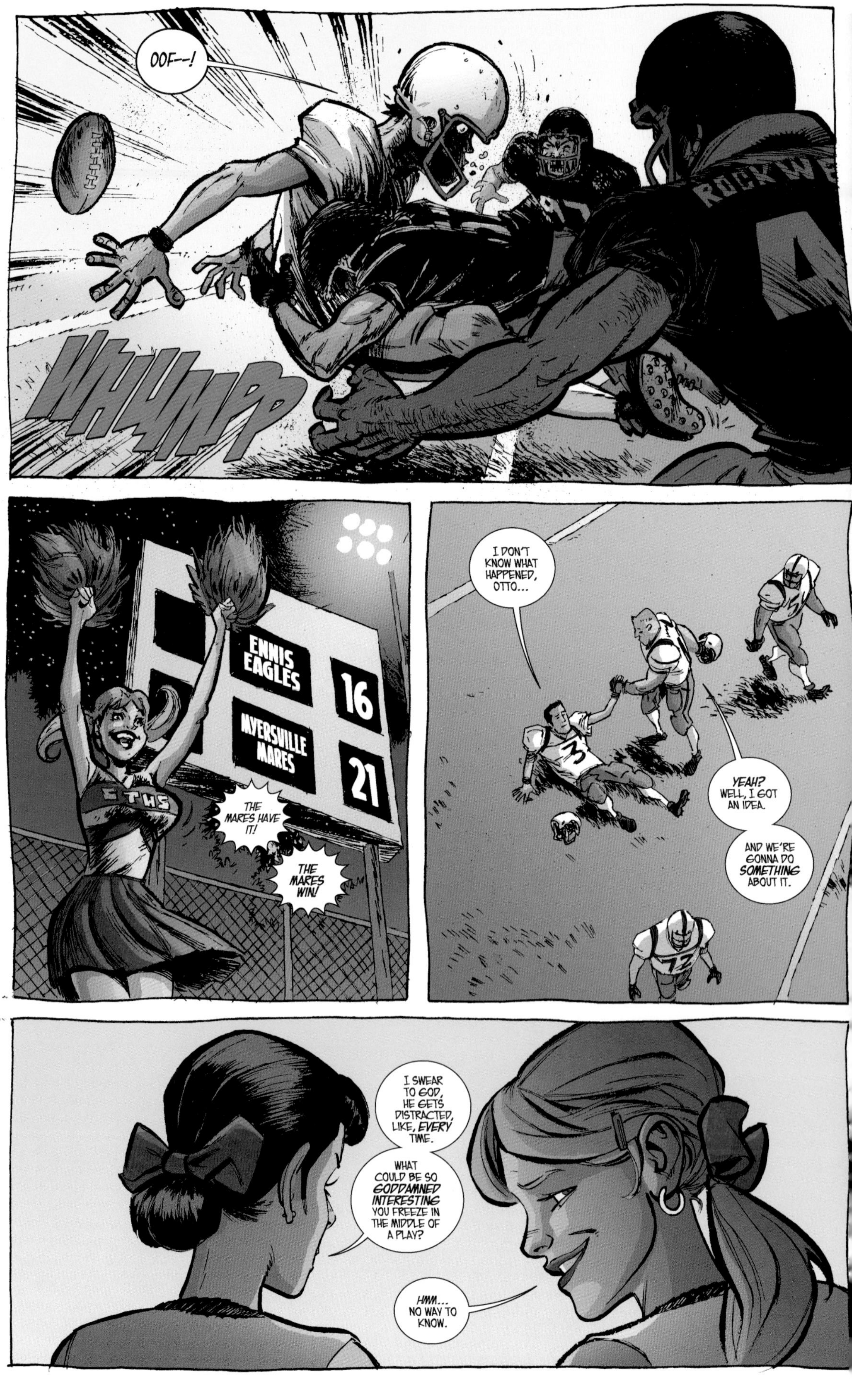
OOF--!
WHUMPP
ENNIS EAGLES 16
MYERSVILLE MARES 21
CTHS
THE MARES HAVE IT!
THE MARES WIN!
I DON'T KNOW WHAT HAPPENED, OTTO...
YEAH? WELL, I GOT AN IDEA.
AND WE'RE GONNA DO SOMETHING ABOUT IT.
I SWEAR TO GOD, HE GETS DISTRACTED, LIKE, EVERY TIME.
WHAT COULD BE SO GODDAMNED INTERESTING YOU FREEZE IN THE MIDDLE OF A PLAY?
HMM... NO WAY TO KNOW.

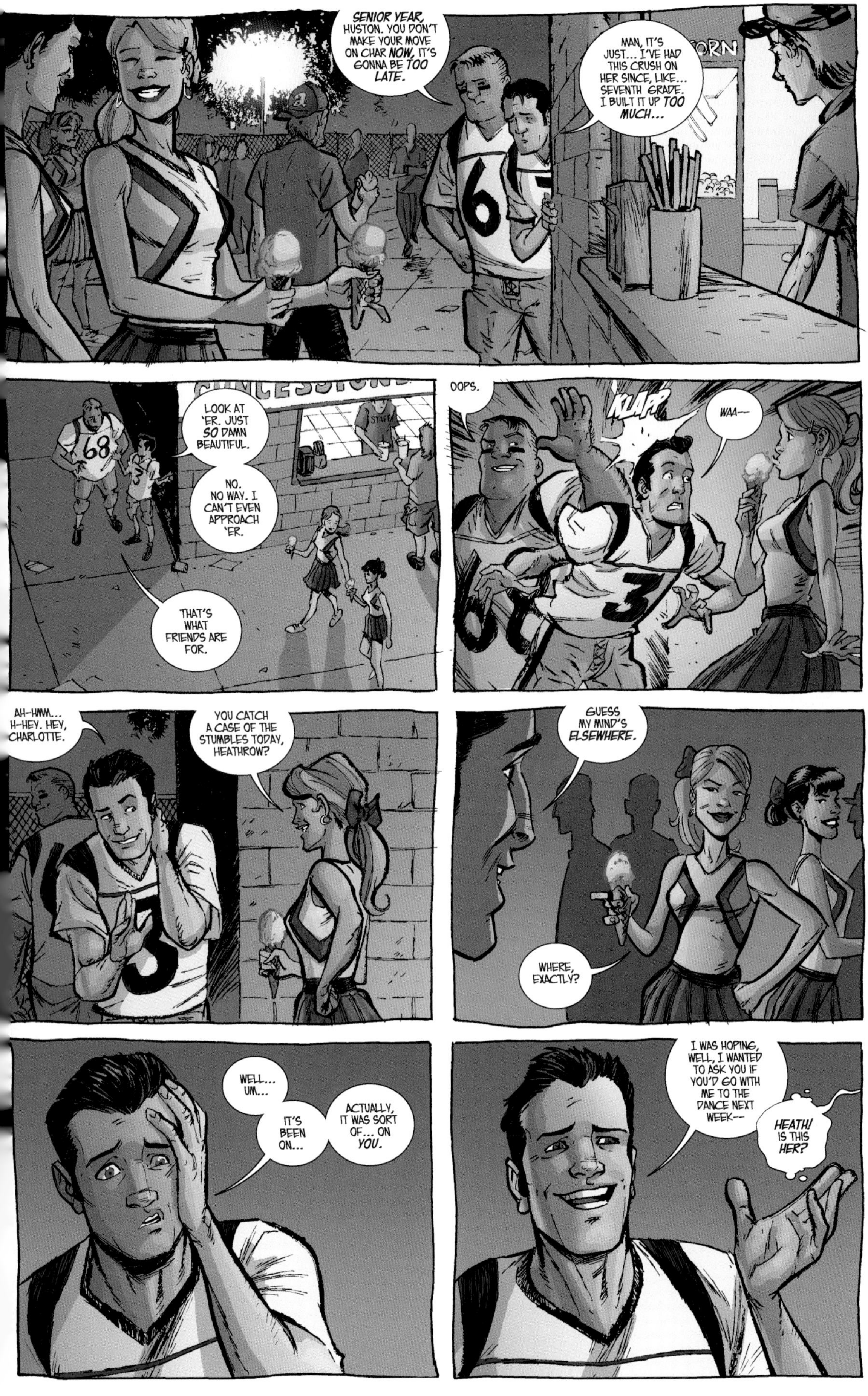
SENIOR YEAR, HUSTON. YOU DON'T MAKE YOUR MOVE ON CHAR NOW, IT'S GONNA BE TOO LATE.
MAN, IT'S JUST... I'VE HAD THIS CRUSH ON HER SINCE, LIKE... SEVENTH GRADE. I BUILT IT UP TOO MUCH...
LOOK AT 'ER. JUST SO DAMN BEAUTIFUL.
NO. NO WAY. I CAN'T EVEN APPROACH 'ER.
THAT'S WHAT FRIENDS ARE FOR.
OOPS.
KLAPP
WAA--
AH-HMM... H-HEY. HEY, CHARLOTTE.
YOU CATCH A CASE OF THE STUMBLES TODAY, HEATHROW?
GUESS MY MIND'S ELSEWHERE.
WHERE, EXACTLY?
WELL... UM...
IT'S BEEN ON...
ACTUALLY, IT WAS SORT OF... ON YOU.
I WAS HOPING, WELL, I WANTED TO ASK YOU IF YOU'D GO WITH ME TO THE DANCE NEXT WEEK--
HEATH! IS THIS HER?

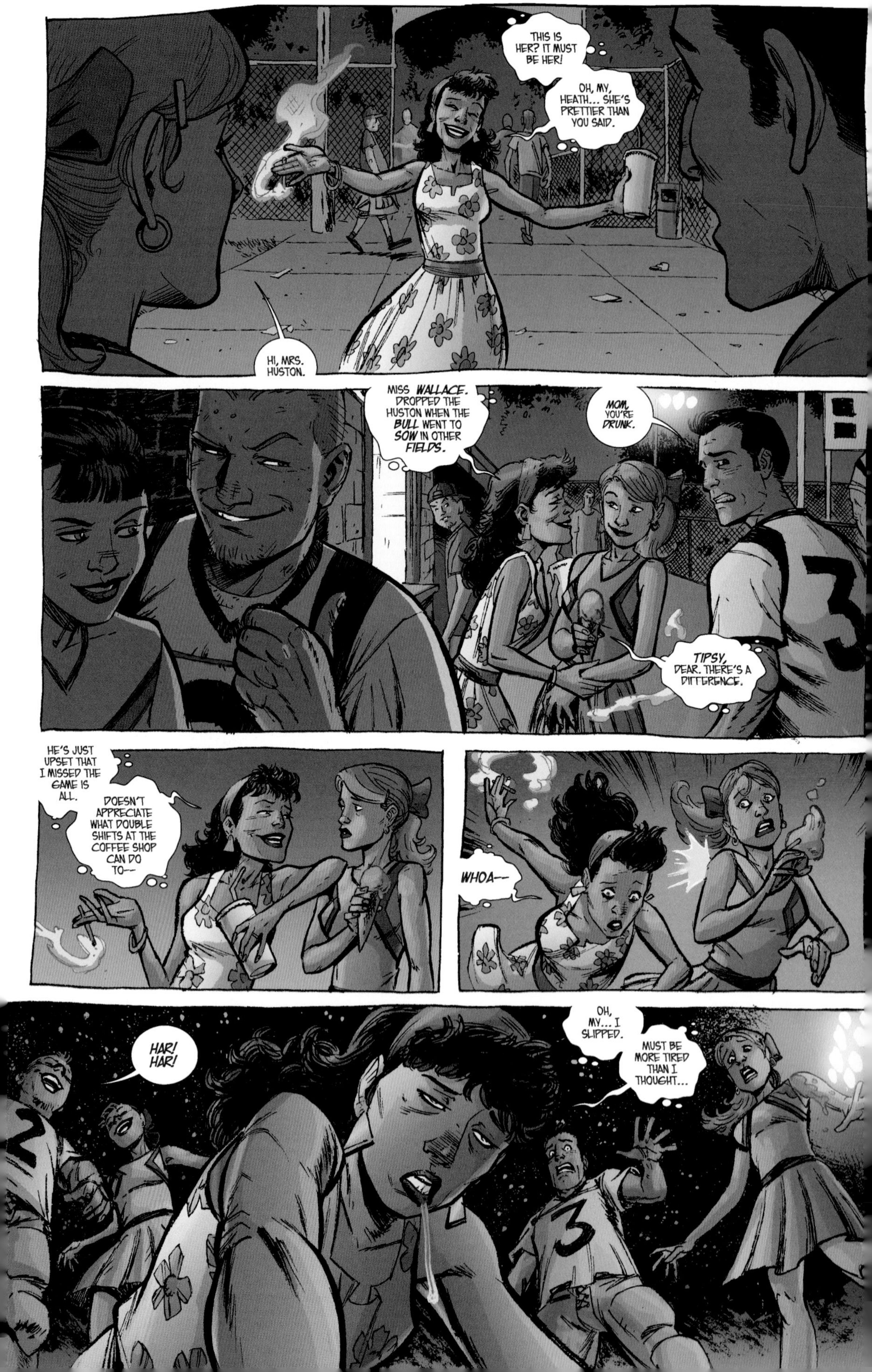
THIS IS HER? IT MUST BE HER!
OH, MY, HEATH... SHE'S PRETTIER THAN YOU SAID.
HI, MRS. HUSTON.
MISS WALLACE. DROPPED THE HUSTON WHEN THE BULL WENT TO SOW IN OTHER FIELDS.
MOM, YOU'RE DRUNK.
TIPSY, DEAR. THERE'S A DIFFERENCE.
HE'S JUST UPSET THAT I MISSED THE GAME IS ALL.
DOESN'T APPRECIATE WHAT DOUBLE SHIFTS AT THE COFFEE SHOP CAN DO TO--
WHOA--
HAR! HAR!
OH, MY... I SLIPPED.
MUST BE MORE TIRED THAN I THOUGHT...

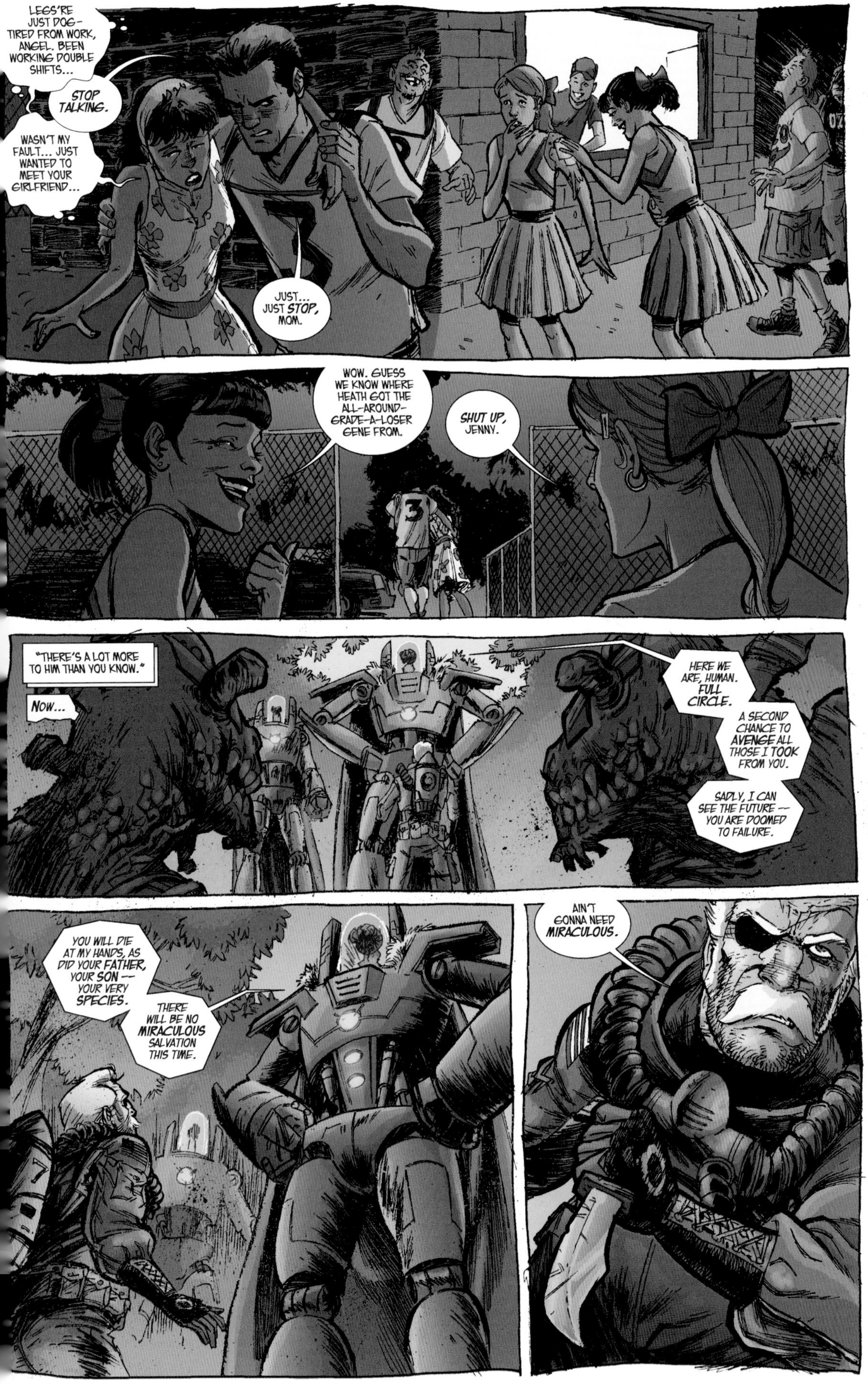
LEGS'RE JUST DOG-TIRED FROM WORK, ANGEL. BEEN WORKING DOUBLE SHIFTS...
STOP TALKING.
WASN'T MY FAULT... JUST WANTED TO MEET YOUR GIRLFRIEND...
JUST... JUST STOP, MOM.
WOW. GUESS WE KNOW WHERE HEATH GOT THE ALL-AROUND-GRADE-A-LOSER GENE FROM.
SHUT UP, JENNY.
"THERE'S A LOT MORE TO HIM THAN YOU KNOW."
NOW...
HERE WE ARE, HUMAN. FULL CIRCLE.
A SECOND CHANCE TO AVENGE ALL THOSE I TOOK FROM YOU.
SADLY, I CAN SEE THE FUTURE -- YOU ARE DOOMED TO FAILURE.
YOU WILL DIE AT MY HANDS, AS DID YOUR FATHER, YOUR SON -- YOUR VERY SPECIES.
THERE WILL BE NO MIRACULOUS SALVATION THIS TIME.
AIN'T GONNA NEED MIRACULOUS.

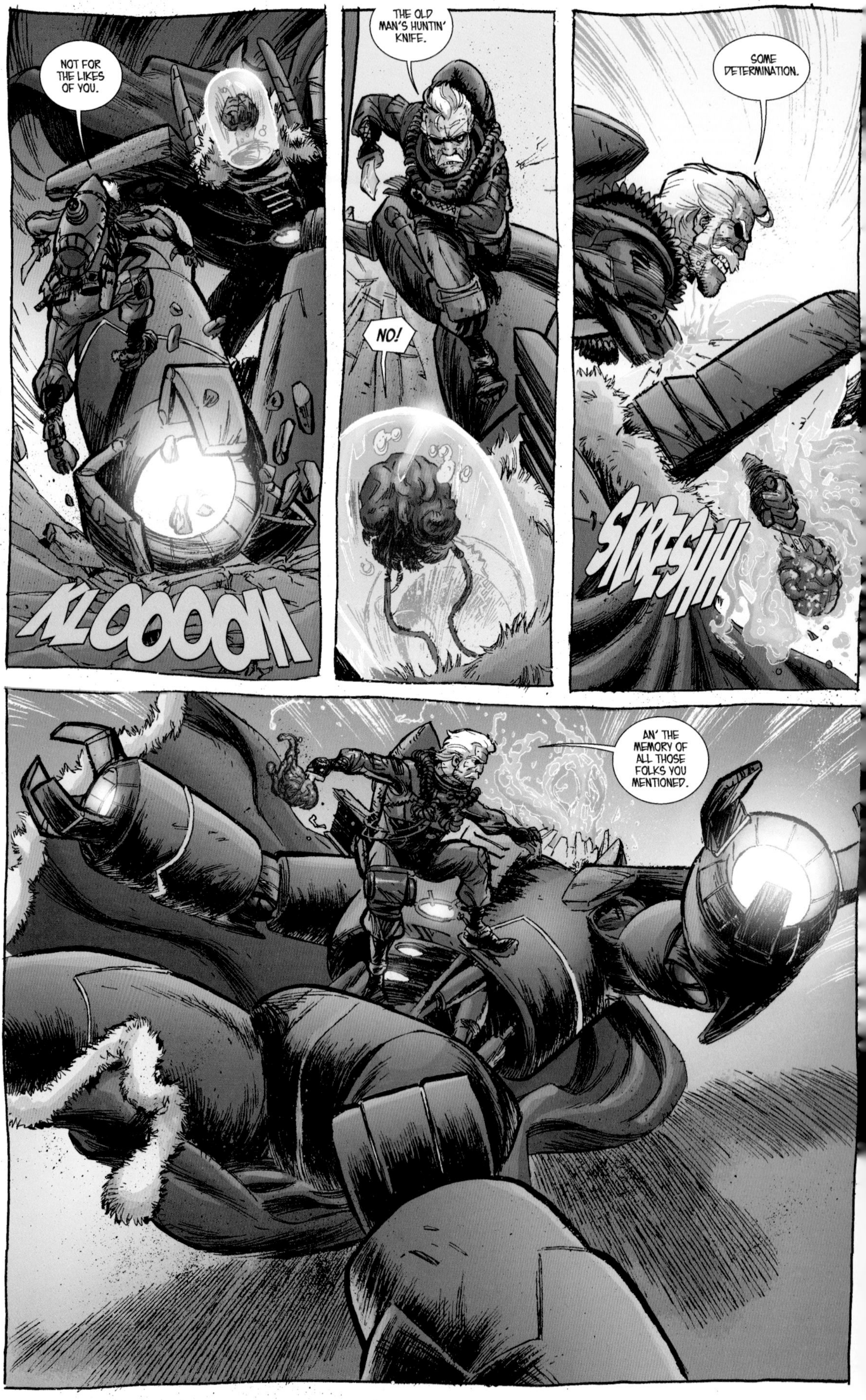
NOT FOR THE LIKES OF YOU.
KLOOOOM
THE OLD MAN'S HUNTIN' KNIFE.
NO!
SOME DETERMINATION.
SKRESHH
AN' THE MEMORY OF ALL THOSE FOLKS YOU MENTIONED.

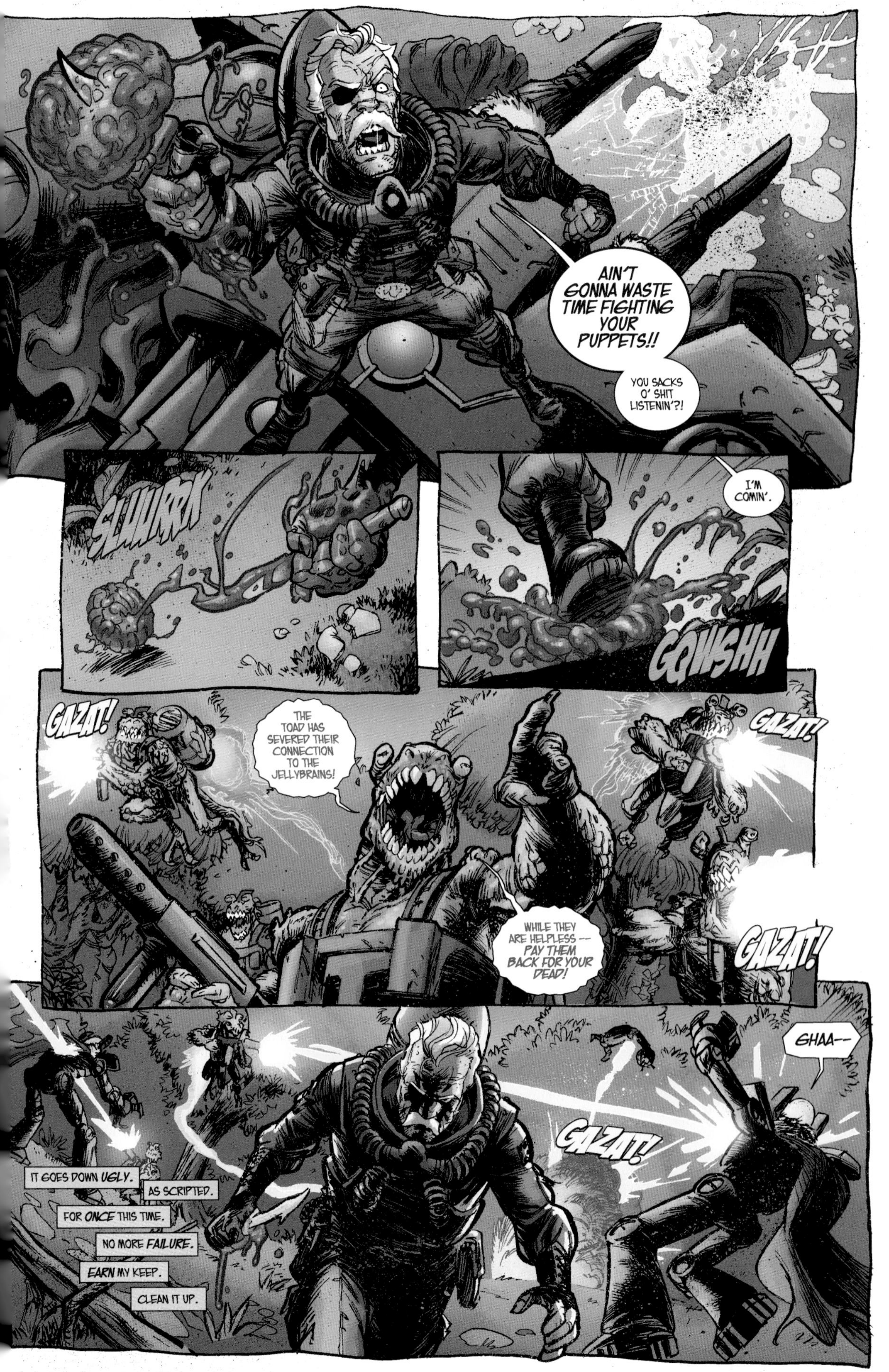
AIN'T GONNA WASTE TIME FIGHTING YOUR PUPPETS!!
YOU SACKS O' SHIT LISTENIN'?!
SLUURRK
I'M COMIN'.
GQWSHH
GAZAT!
THE TOAD HAS SEVERED THEIR CONNECTION TO THE JELLYBRAINS!
GAZAT!
WHILE THEY ARE HELPLESS -- PAY THEM BACK FOR YOUR DEAD!
GAZAT!
GHAA--
GAZAT!
IT GOES DOWN UGLY.
AS SCRIPTED.
FOR ONCE THIS TIME.
NO MORE FAILURE.
EARN MY KEEP.
CLEAN IT UP.

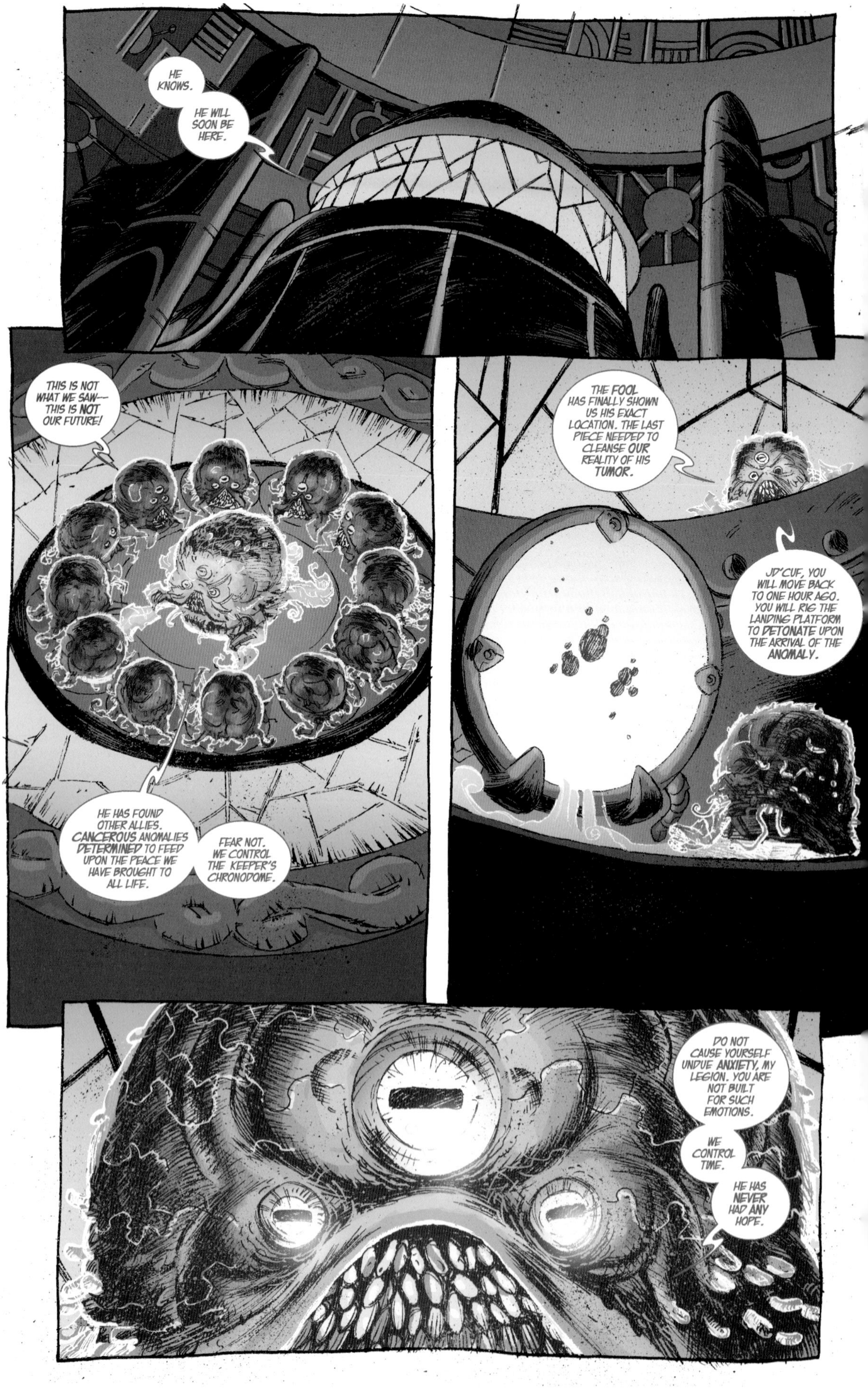
HE KNOWS.
HE WILL SOON BE HERE.
THIS IS NOT WHAT WE SAW-- THIS IS NOT OUR FUTURE!
HE HAS FOUND OTHER ALLIES. CANCEROUS ANOMALIES DETERMINED TO FEED UPON THE PEACE WE HAVE BROUGHT TO ALL LIFE.
FEAR NOT. WE CONTROL THE KEEPER'S CHRONODOME.
THE FOOL HAS FINALLY SHOWN US HIS EXACT LOCATION. THE LAST PIECE NEEDED TO CLEANSE OUR REALITY OF HIS TUMOR.
JD'CUF, YOU WILL MOVE BACK TO ONE HOUR AGO. YOU WILL RIG THE LANDING PLATFORM TO DETONATE UPON THE ARRIVAL OF THE ANOMALY.
DO NOT CAUSE YOURSELF UNDUE ANXIETY, MY LEGION. YOU ARE NOT BUILT FOR SUCH EMOTIONS.
WE CONTROL TIME.
HE HAS NEVER HAD ANY HOPE.

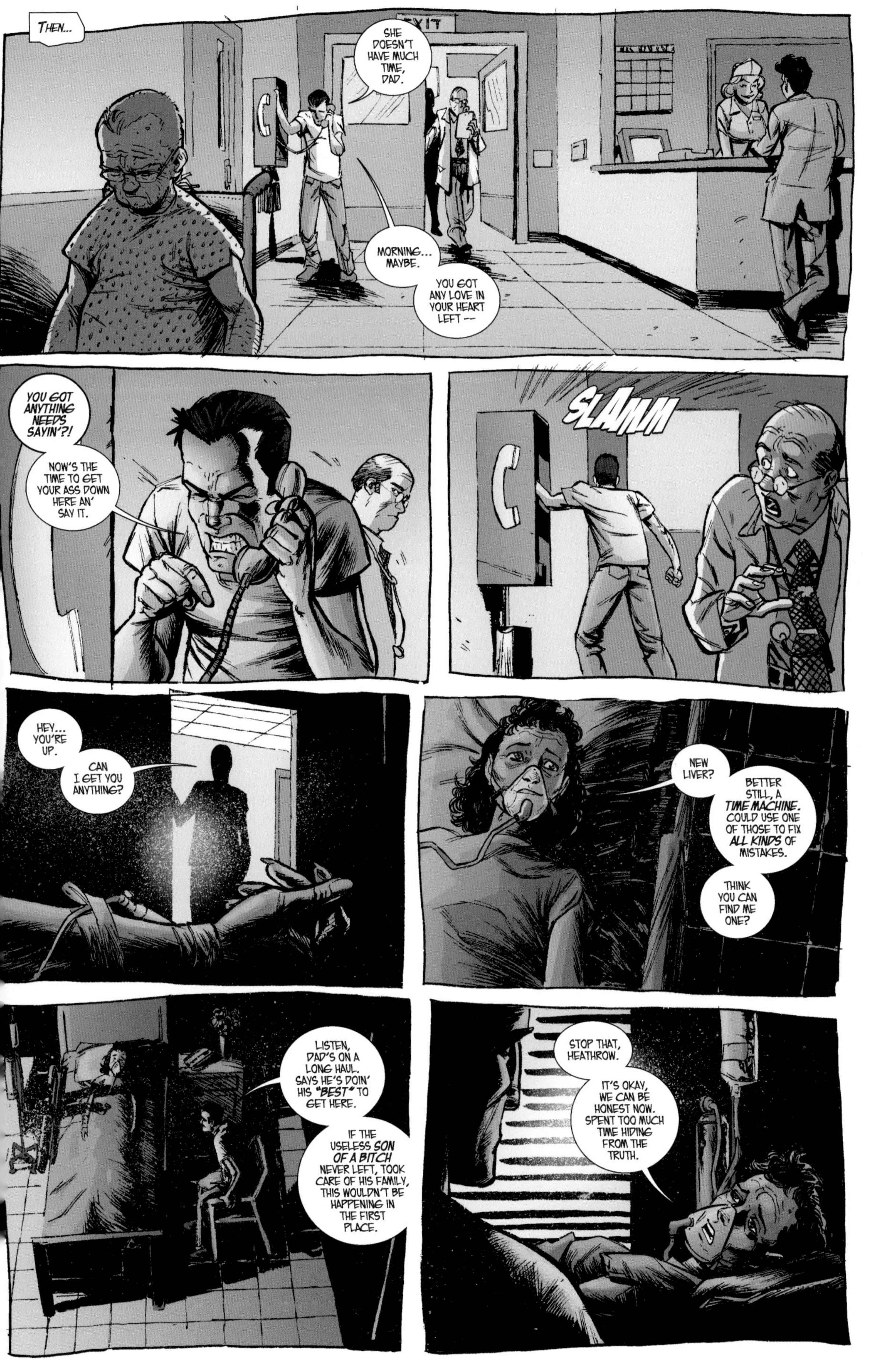
THEN...
SHE DOESN'T HAVE MUCH TIME, DAD.
MORNING... MAYBE.
YOU GOT ANY LOVE IN YOUR HEART LEFT --
YOU GOT ANYTHING NEEDS SAYIN'?!
NOW'S THE TIME TO GET YOUR ASS DOWN HERE AN' SAY IT.
SLAMM
HEY... YOU'RE UP.
CAN I GET YOU ANYTHING?
NEW LIVER?
BETTER STILL, A TIME MACHINE. COULD USE ONE OF THOSE TO FIX ALL KINDS OF MISTAKES.
THINK YOU CAN FIND ME ONE?
LISTEN, DAD'S ON A LONG HAUL. SAYS HE'S DOIN' HIS "BEST" TO GET HERE.
IF THE USELESS SON OF A BITCH NEVER LEFT, TOOK CARE OF HIS FAMILY, THIS WOULDN'T BE HAPPENING IN THE FIRST PLACE.
STOP THAT, HEATHROW.
IT'S OKAY, WE CAN BE HONEST NOW. SPENT TOO MUCH TIME HIDING FROM THE TRUTH.

I'M A DRUNK WHO DRANK HERSELF TO DEATH.

AFTER DAD LEFT YOU THE WAY HE DID... NO ONE BLAMES YOU, MA.

I LET YOU GO ON FOR *TOO LONG* FAULTIN' YOUR FATHER FOR THIS. TOO LONG LETTING *HIM* SHOULDER THE *BLAME*.

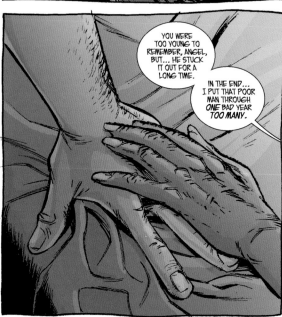

YOU WERE TOO YOUNG TO REMEMBER, ANGEL, BUT... HE STUCK IT OUT FOR A LONG TIME.

IN THE END... I PUT THAT POOR MAN THROUGH *ONE BAD YEAR TOO MANY*.

MY DRINKING IS WHY HE LEFT.

SO YOU FORGIVE YOUR FATHER.

YOU CUT HIM SOME SLACK.

YOU LET ME GO ON THINKING IT WAS HIM...

ALL THESE YEARS.

HE *INSISTED*.

DIDN'T WANT YOU MAD AT ME. SAID IT WOULD ONLY MAKE ME SINK THAT MUCH DEEPER INTO THE BOTTLE.

FIGURED HE COULD TAKE YOUR ANGER BETTER THAN I COULD.

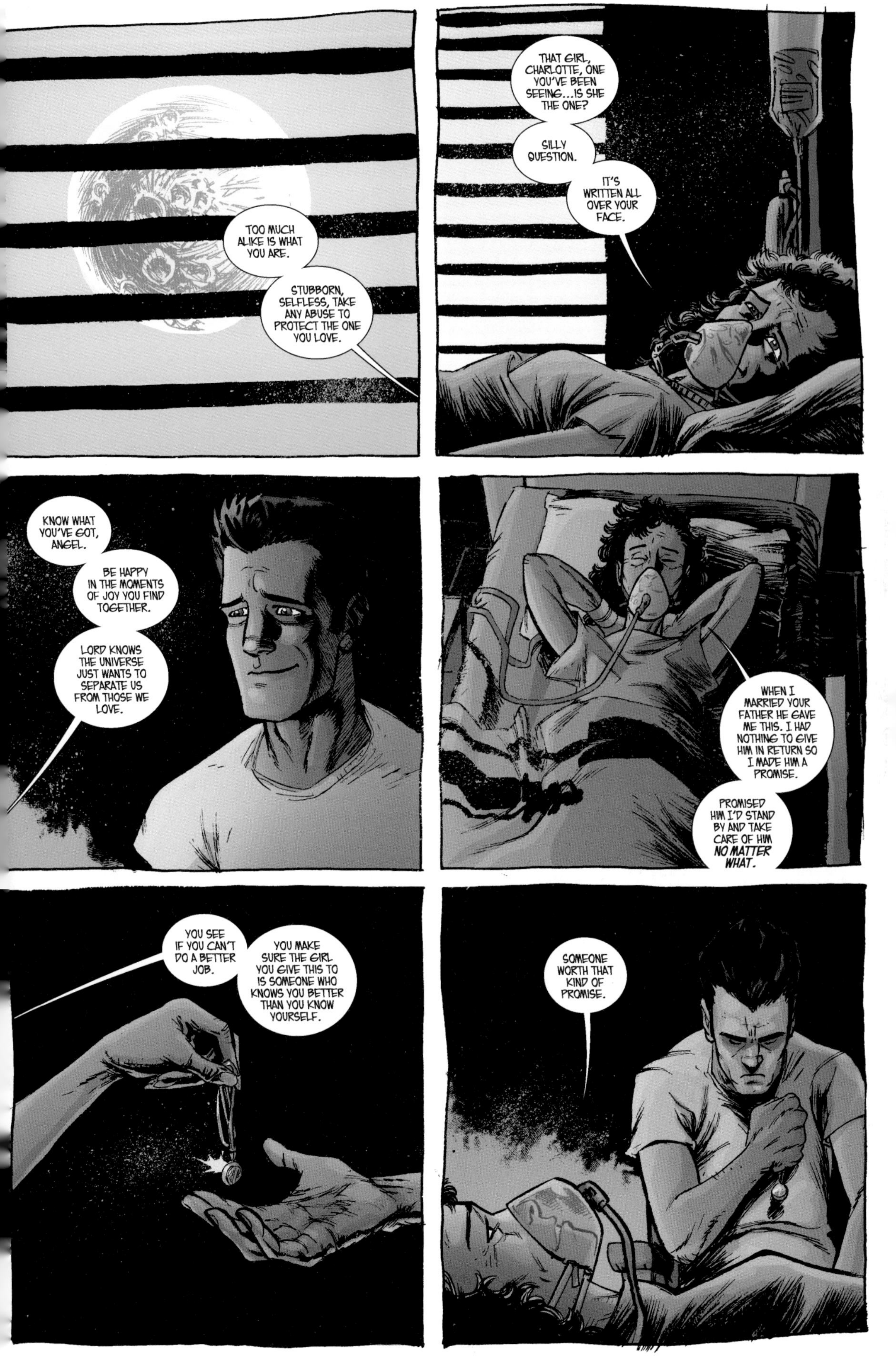
TOO MUCH ALIKE IS WHAT YOU ARE.
STUBBORN, SELFLESS, TAKE ANY ABUSE TO PROTECT THE ONE YOU LOVE.
THAT GIRL, CHARLOTTE, ONE YOU'VE BEEN SEEING...IS SHE THE ONE?
SILLY QUESTION.
IT'S WRITTEN ALL OVER YOUR FACE.
KNOW WHAT YOU'VE GOT, ANGEL.
BE HAPPY IN THE MOMENTS OF JOY YOU FIND TOGETHER.
LORD KNOWS THE UNIVERSE JUST WANTS TO SEPARATE US FROM THOSE WE LOVE.
WHEN I MARRIED YOUR FATHER HE GAVE ME THIS. I HAD NOTHING TO GIVE HIM IN RETURN SO I MADE HIM A PROMISE.
PROMISED HIM I'D STAND BY AND TAKE CARE OF HIM *NO MATTER WHAT.*
YOU SEE IF YOU CAN'T DO A BETTER JOB.
YOU MAKE SURE THE GIRL YOU GIVE THIS TO IS SOMEONE WHO KNOWS YOU BETTER THAN YOU KNOW YOURSELF.
SOMEONE WORTH THAT KIND OF PROMISE.

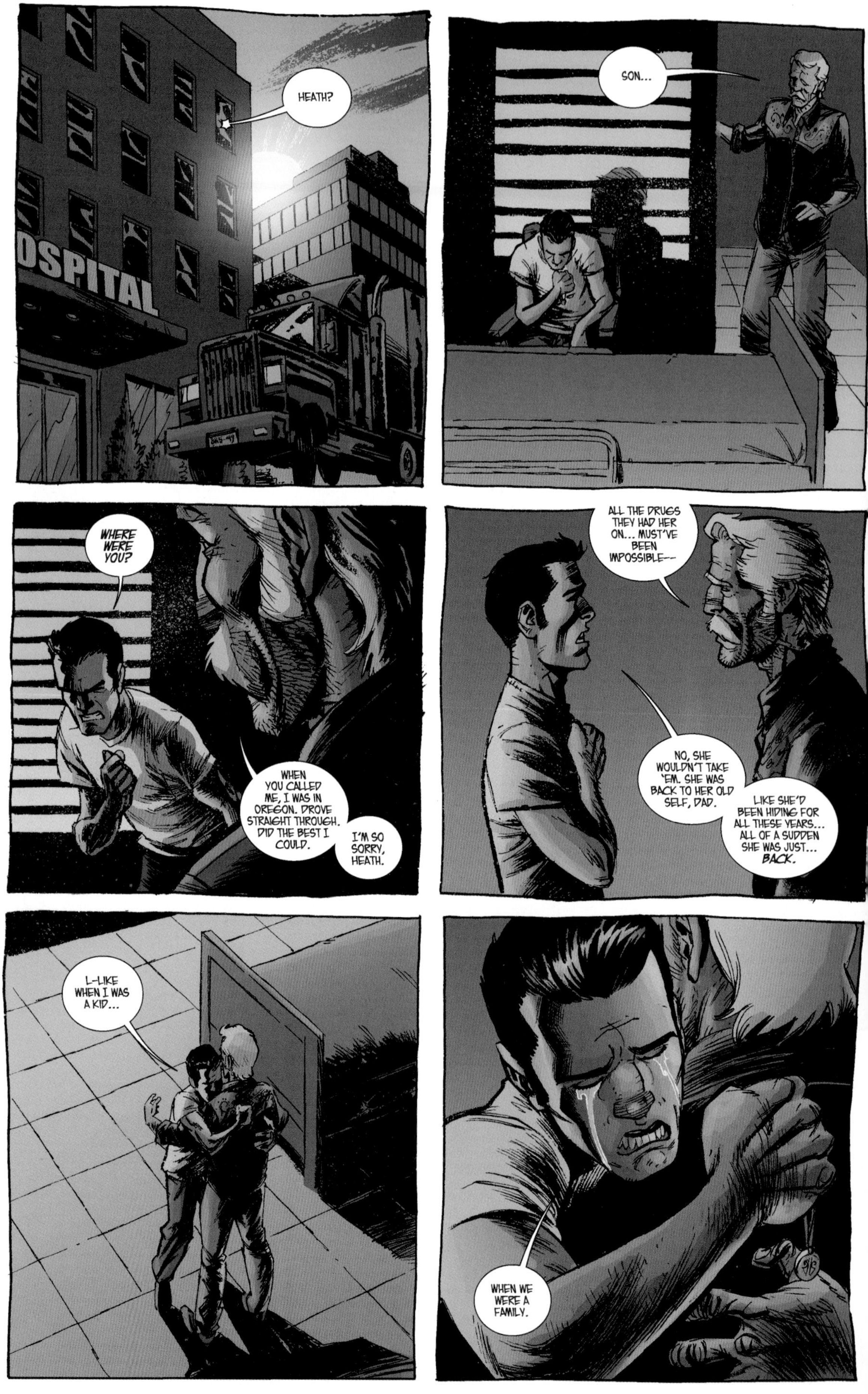
OSPITAL
HEATH?
SON...
WHERE WERE YOU?
WHEN YOU CALLED ME, I WAS IN OREGON. DROVE STRAIGHT THROUGH. DID THE BEST I COULD.
I'M SO SORRY, HEATH.
ALL THE DRUGS THEY HAD HER ON... MUST'VE BEEN IMPOSSIBLE--
NO, SHE WOULDN'T TAKE 'EM. SHE WAS BACK TO HER OLD SELF, DAD.
LIKE SHE'D BEEN HIDING FOR ALL THESE YEARS... ALL OF A SUDDEN SHE WAS JUST... BACK.
L-LIKE WHEN I WAS A KID...
WHEN WE WERE A FAMILY.

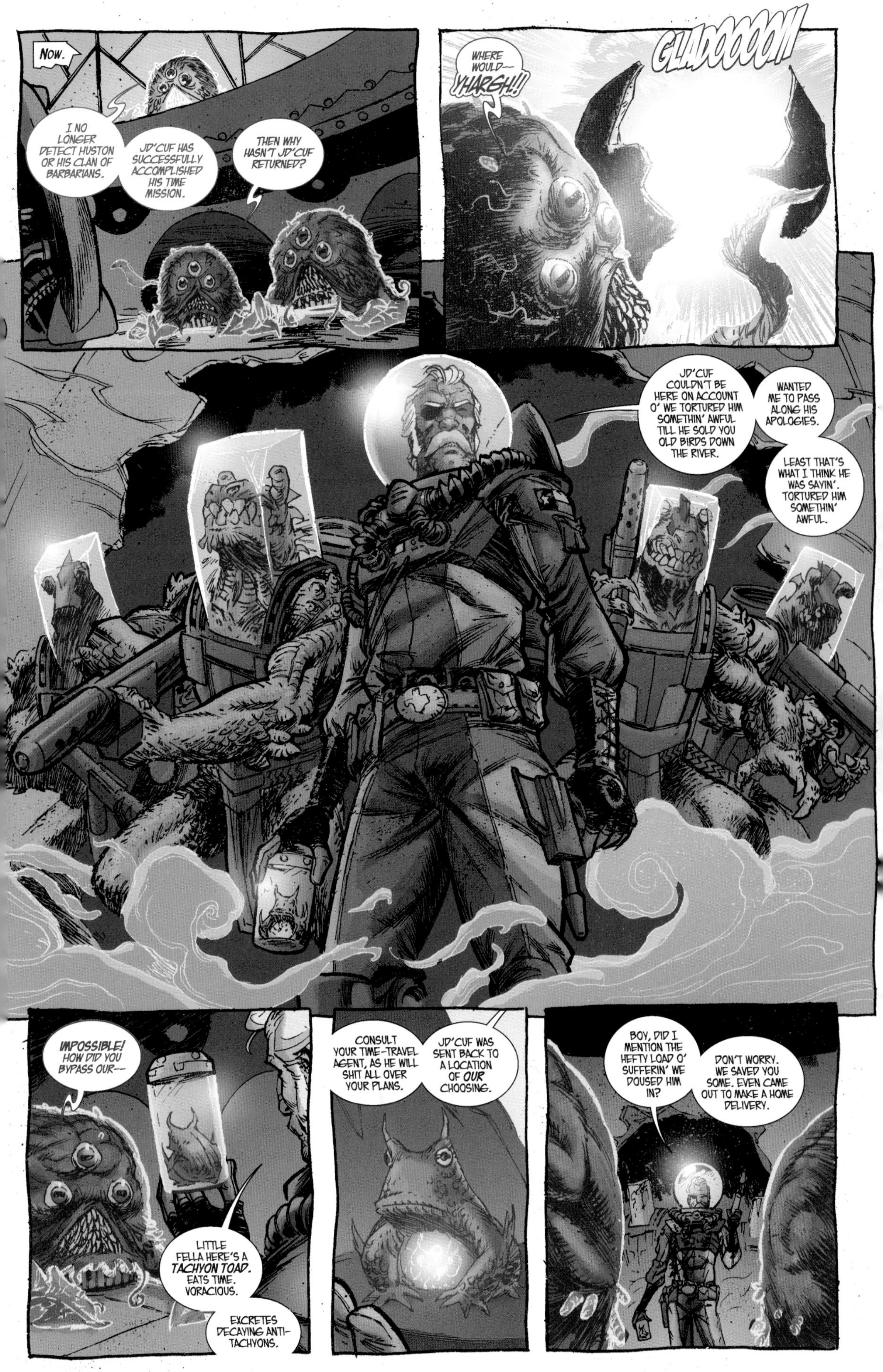
NOW.
I NO LONGER DETECT HUSTON OR HIS CLAN OF BARBARIANS.
JD'CUF HAS SUCCESSFULLY ACCOMPLISHED HIS TIME MISSION.
THEN WHY HASN'T JD'CUF RETURNED?
WHERE WOULD--
YHARGH!!
GLADOOOOOM!!
JD'CUF COULDN'T BE HERE ON ACCOUNT O' WE TORTURED HIM SOMETHIN' AWFUL TILL HE SOLD YOU OLD BIRDS DOWN THE RIVER.
WANTED ME TO PASS ALONG HIS APOLOGIES.
LEAST THAT'S WHAT I THINK HE WAS SAYIN'. TORTURED HIM SOMETHIN' AWFUL.
IMPOSSIBLE! HOW DID YOU BYPASS OUR--
LITTLE FELLA HERE'S A TACHYON TOAD. EATS TIME. VORACIOUS.
EXCRETES DECAYING ANTI-TACHYONS.
CONSULT YOUR TIME-TRAVEL AGENT, AS HE WILL SHIT ALL OVER YOUR PLANS.
JD'CUF WAS SENT BACK TO A LOCATION OF OUR CHOOSING.
BOY, DID I MENTION THE HEFTY LOAD O' SUFFERIN' WE DOUSED HIM IN?
DON'T WORRY. WE SAVED YOU SOME. EVEN CAME OUT TO MAKE A HOME DELIVERY.

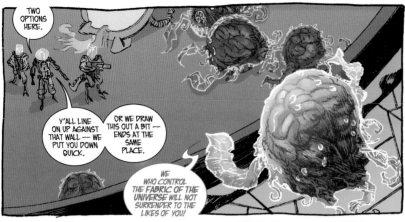

TWO OPTIONS HERE.

Y'ALL LINE ON UP AGAINST THAT WALL -- WE PUT YOU DOWN QUICK.

OR WE DRAW THIS OUT A BIT -- ENDS AT THE SAME PLACE.

WE WHO CONTROL THE FABRIC OF THE UNIVERSE WILL NOT SURRENDER TO THE LIKES OF YOU!

YEAH.

REAL GLAD TO HEAR YOU SAY THAT.

I CAME TA DANCE.

GAZAT!

YHRAA--

CONCENTRATE YOUR MIND BLASTS!

THEIR FEEBLE HELMETS CANNOT DEFEND AGAINST A BARRAGE OF TRI-BRILLIANCE!

SPLUKK

GAAK--

SEE THE FACES OF MY CHILDREN.

SWIMMING IN THE SALT LAKE.

GAZIT!

SMILES BIG ENOUGH TO DROWN OUT THE NOISE.

CHAR SIPPIN' ON A BEER.

SUN CENTER STAGE.

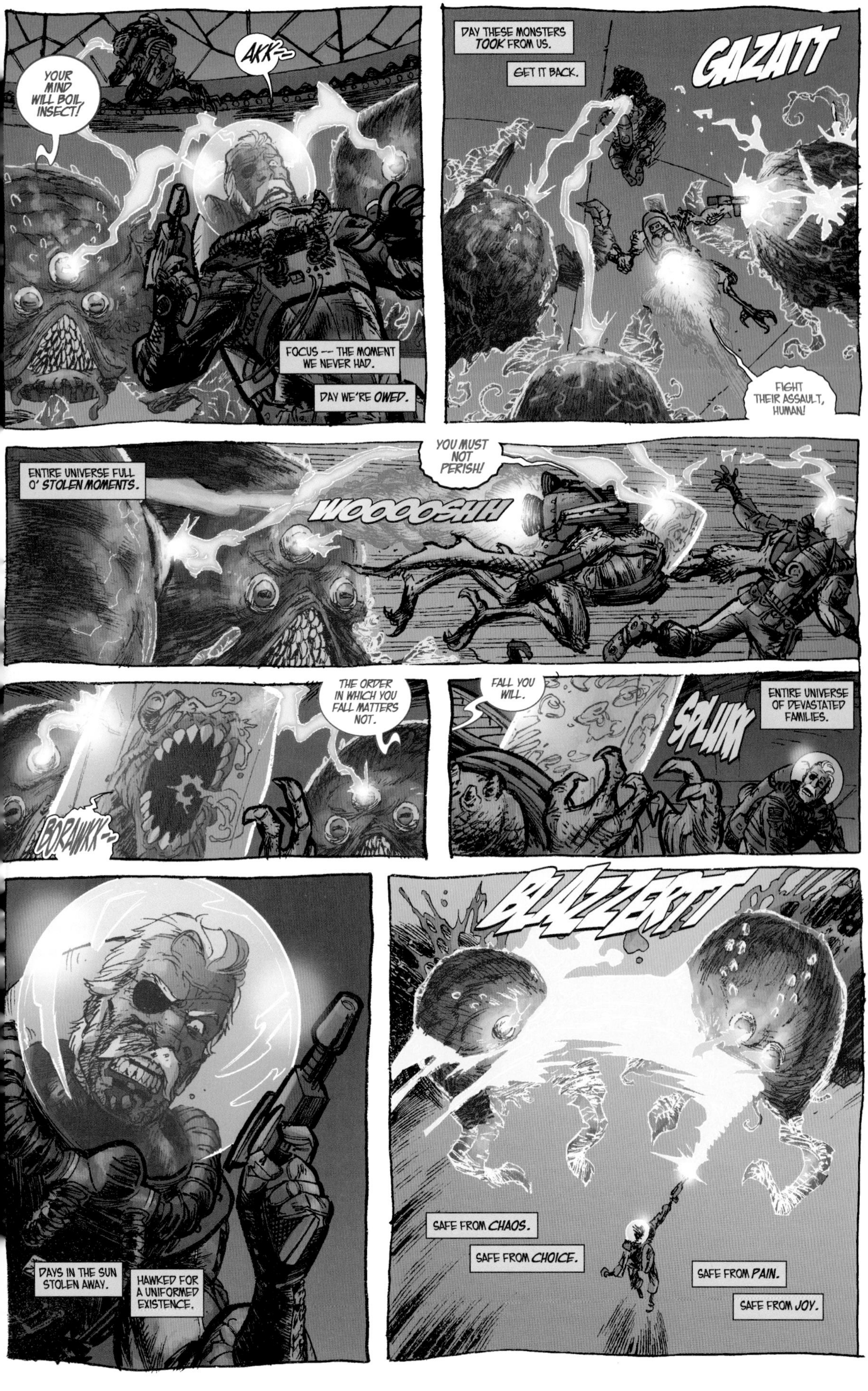
AKK--
YOUR MIND WILL BOIL, INSECT!
FOCUS -- THE MOMENT WE NEVER HAD.
DAY WE'RE OWED.
DAY THESE MONSTERS TOOK FROM US.
GET IT BACK.
GAZATT
FIGHT THEIR ASSAULT, HUMAN!
ENTIRE UNIVERSE FULL O' STOLEN MOMENTS.
YOU MUST NOT PERISH!
WOOOOSHH
THE ORDER IN WHICH YOU FALL MATTERS NOT.
BORAWKK--
FALL YOU WILL.
SPLUKK
ENTIRE UNIVERSE OF DEVASTATED FAMILIES.
DAYS IN THE SUN STOLEN AWAY.
HAWKED FOR A UNIFORMED EXISTENCE.
BLAZZERTT
SAFE FROM CHAOS.
SAFE FROM CHOICE.
SAFE FROM PAIN.
SAFE FROM JOY.

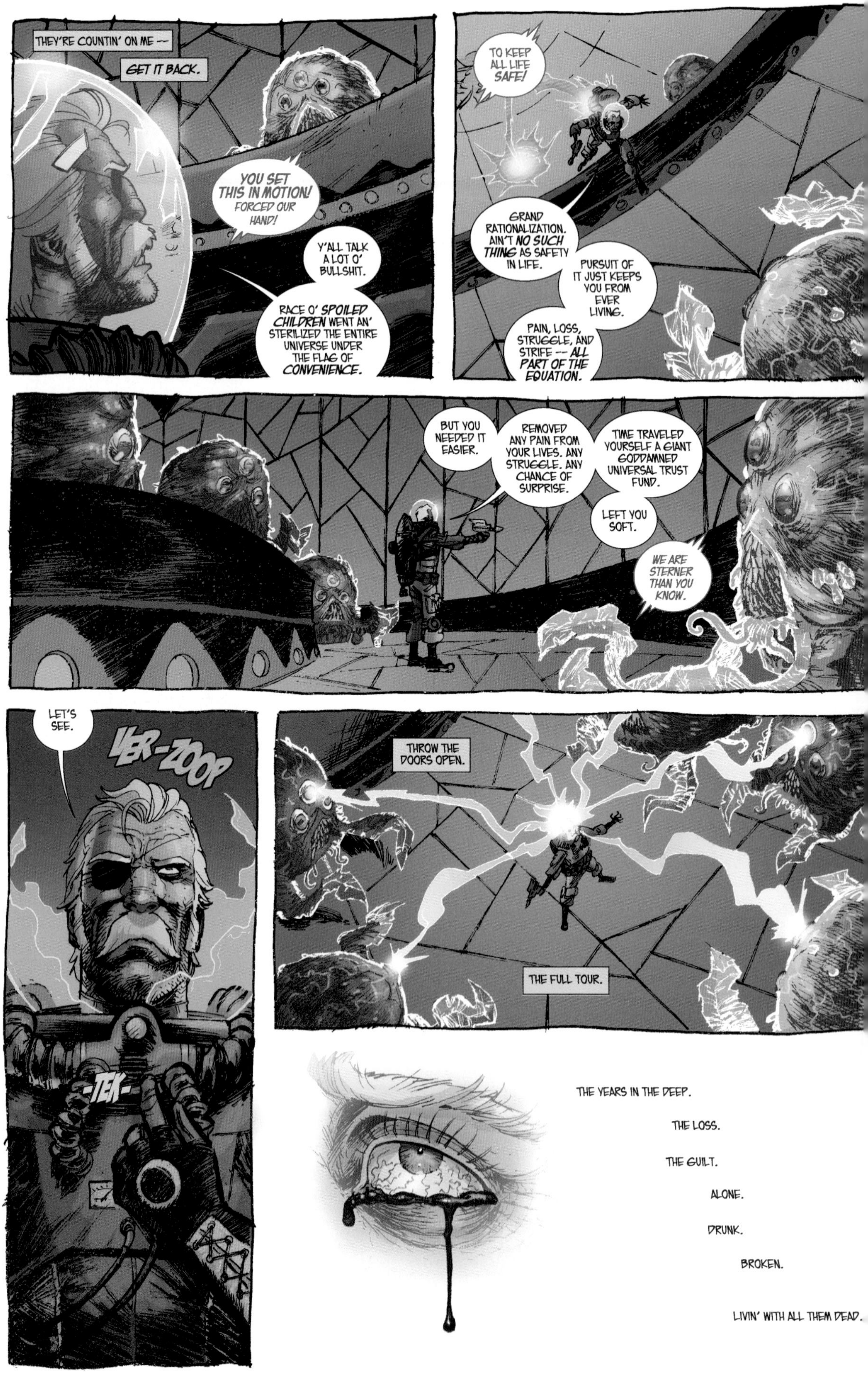
THEY'RE COUNTIN' ON ME --
GET IT BACK.
YOU SET THIS IN MOTION! FORCED OUR HAND!
Y'ALL TALK A LOT O' BULLSHIT.
RACE O' SPOILED CHILDREN WENT AN' STERILIZED THE ENTIRE UNIVERSE UNDER THE FLAG OF CONVENIENCE.
TO KEEP ALL LIFE SAFE!
GRAND RATIONALIZATION. AIN'T NO SUCH THING AS SAFETY IN LIFE.
PURSUIT OF IT JUST KEEPS YOU FROM EVER LIVING.
PAIN, LOSS, STRUGGLE, AND STRIFE -- ALL PART OF THE EQUATION.
BUT YOU NEEDED IT EASIER.
REMOVED ANY PAIN FROM YOUR LIVES. ANY STRUGGLE. ANY CHANCE OF SURPRISE.
TIME TRAVELED YOURSELF A GIANT GODDAMNED UNIVERSAL TRUST FUND.
LEFT YOU SOFT.
WE ARE STERNER THAN YOU KNOW.
LET'S SEE.
VER-ZOOP
-TEK-
THROW THE DOORS OPEN.
THE FULL TOUR.
THE YEARS IN THE DEEP.
THE LOSS.
THE GUILT.
ALONE.
DRUNK.
BROKEN.
LIVIN' WITH ALL THEM DEAD.

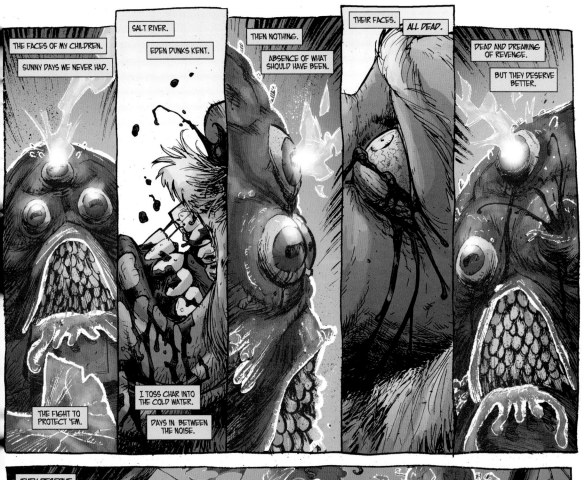

THE FACES OF MY CHILDREN.

SUNNY DAYS WE NEVER HAD.

THE FIGHT TO PROTECT 'EM.

SALT RIVER.

EDEN DUNKS KENT.

I TOSS CHAR INTO THE COLD WATER.

DAYS IN BETWEEN THE NOISE.

THEN NOTHING.

ABSENCE OF WHAT SHOULD HAVE BEEN.

THEIR FACES.

ALL DEAD.

DEAD AND DREAMING OF REVENGE.

BUT THEY DESERVE BETTER.

THEY DESERVE SALVATION.

YOU JUST WEREN'T READY FOR IT.

ALL THOSE THINGS YOU KEPT YOURSELVES FROM EVER FEELING, THE PAIN, LOSS, SORROW, AND FEAR...

ALL THOSE *BAD* FEELINGS YOU *NEVER* EXPERIENCED...

KAKKRAAHH... HHROWWWS... HOWSS...

THANKS TO YOU IT'S *ALL* I'VE *EVER* KNOWN.

ALL I AM.

A FEAR AGENT.

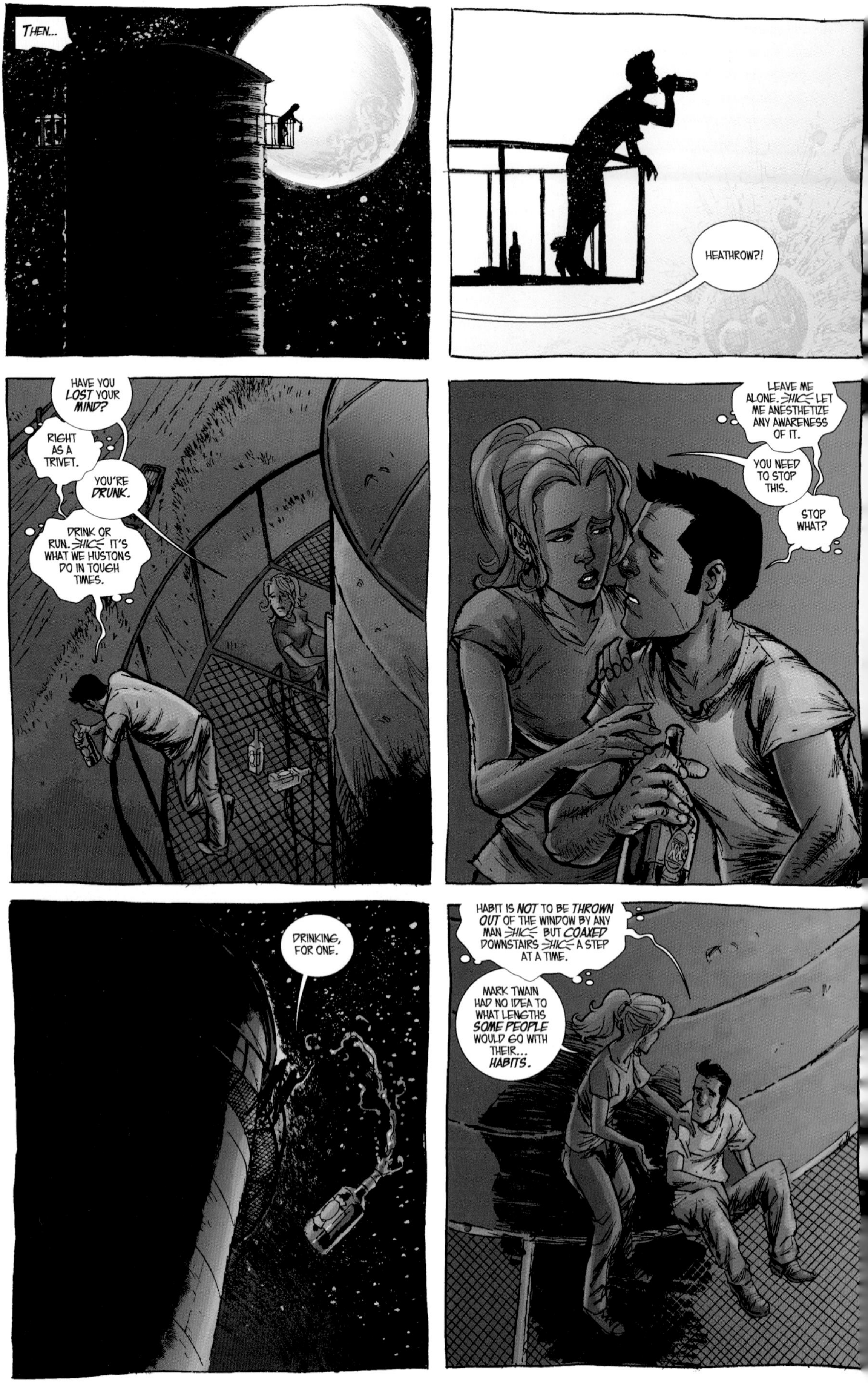
THEN...
HEATHROW?!
HAVE YOU LOST YOUR MIND?
RIGHT AS A TRIVET.
YOU'RE DRUNK.
DRINK OR RUN. HIC IT'S WHAT WE HUSTONS DO IN TOUGH TIMES.
LEAVE ME ALONE. HIC LET ME ANESTHETIZE ANY AWARENESS OF IT.
YOU NEED TO STOP THIS.
STOP WHAT?
DRINKING, FOR ONE.
HABIT IS NOT TO BE THROWN OUT OF THE WINDOW BY ANY MAN HIC BUT COAXED DOWNSTAIRS HIC A STEP AT A TIME.
MARK TWAIN HAD NO IDEA TO WHAT LENGTHS SOME PEOPLE WOULD GO WITH THEIR... HABITS.

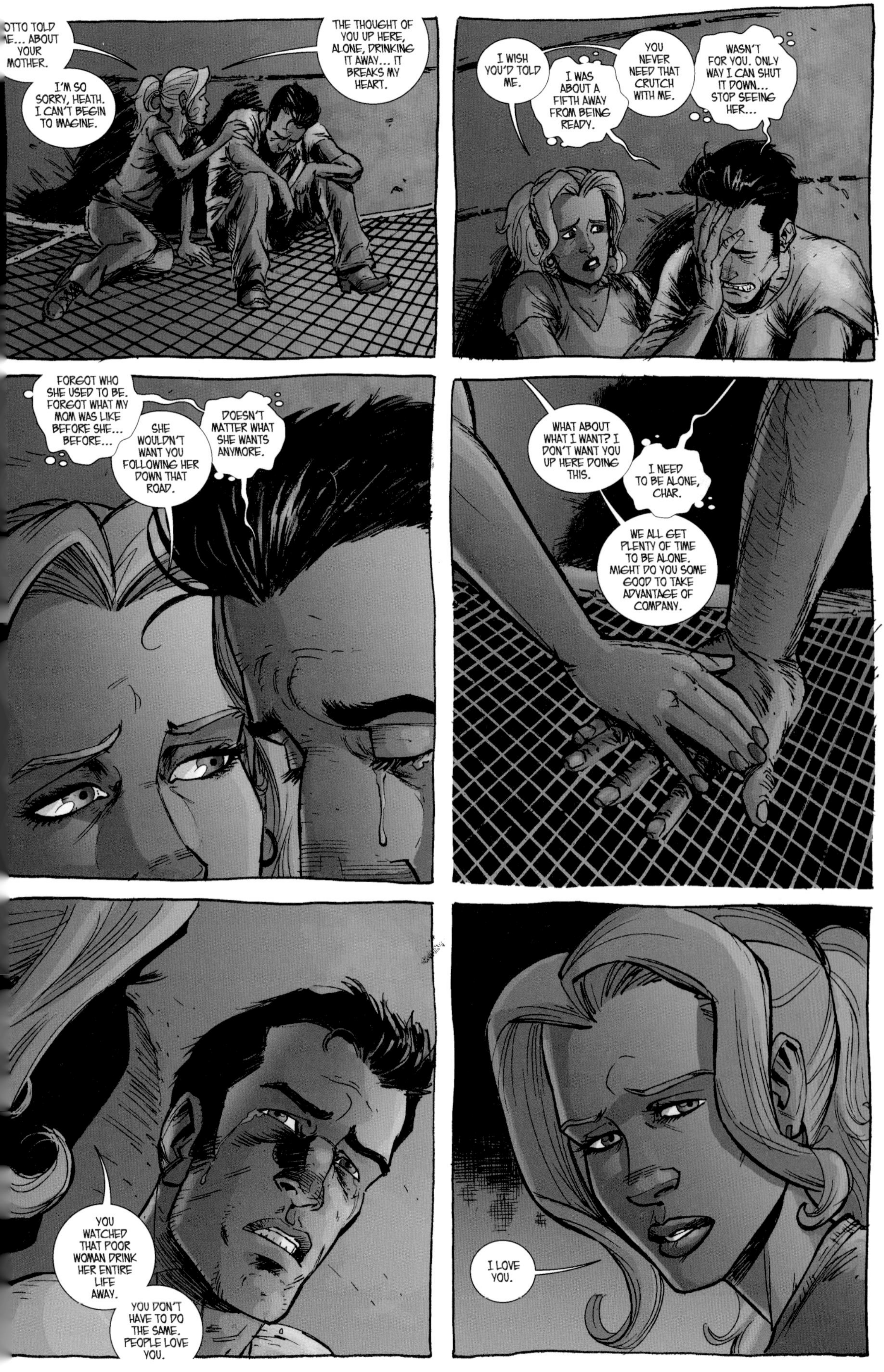
OTTO TOLD ME... ABOUT YOUR MOTHER.
I'M SO SORRY, HEATH. I CAN'T BEGIN TO IMAGINE.
THE THOUGHT OF YOU UP HERE, ALONE, DRINKING IT AWAY... IT BREAKS MY HEART.
I WISH YOU'D TOLD ME.
I WAS ABOUT A FIFTH AWAY FROM BEING READY.
YOU NEVER NEED THAT CRUTCH WITH ME.
WASN'T FOR YOU. ONLY WAY I CAN SHUT IT DOWN... STOP SEEING HER...
FORGOT WHO SHE USED TO BE. FORGOT WHAT MY MOM WAS LIKE BEFORE SHE... BEFORE...
SHE WOULDN'T WANT YOU FOLLOWING HER DOWN THAT ROAD.
DOESN'T MATTER WHAT SHE WANTS ANYMORE.
WHAT ABOUT WHAT I WANT? I DON'T WANT YOU UP HERE DOING THIS.
I NEED TO BE ALONE, CHAR.
WE ALL GET PLENTY OF TIME TO BE ALONE. MIGHT DO YOU SOME GOOD TO TAKE ADVANTAGE OF COMPANY.
YOU WATCHED THAT POOR WOMAN DRINK HER ENTIRE LIFE AWAY.
YOU DON'T HAVE TO DO THE SAME. PEOPLE LOVE YOU.
I LOVE YOU.

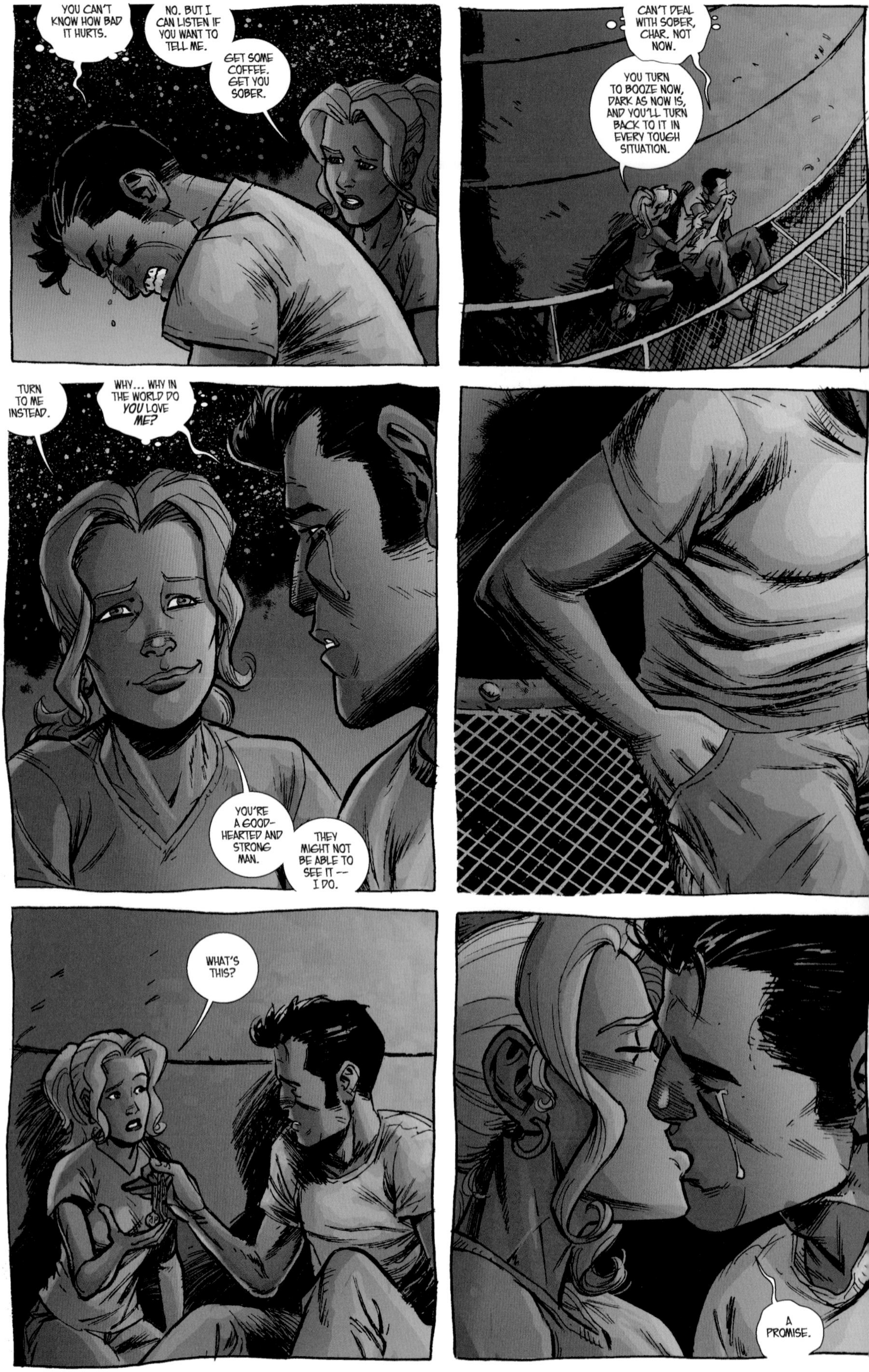
YOU CAN'T KNOW HOW BAD IT HURTS.
NO. BUT I CAN LISTEN IF YOU WANT TO TELL ME.
GET SOME COFFEE. GET YOU SOBER.
CAN'T DEAL WITH SOBER, CHAR. NOT NOW.
YOU TURN TO BOOZE NOW, DARK AS NOW IS, AND YOU'LL TURN BACK TO IT IN EVERY TOUGH SITUATION.
TURN TO ME INSTEAD.
WHY... WHY IN THE WORLD DO YOU LOVE ME?
YOU'RE A GOOD-HEARTED AND STRONG MAN.
THEY MIGHT NOT BE ABLE TO SEE IT -- I DO.
WHAT'S THIS?
A PROMISE.

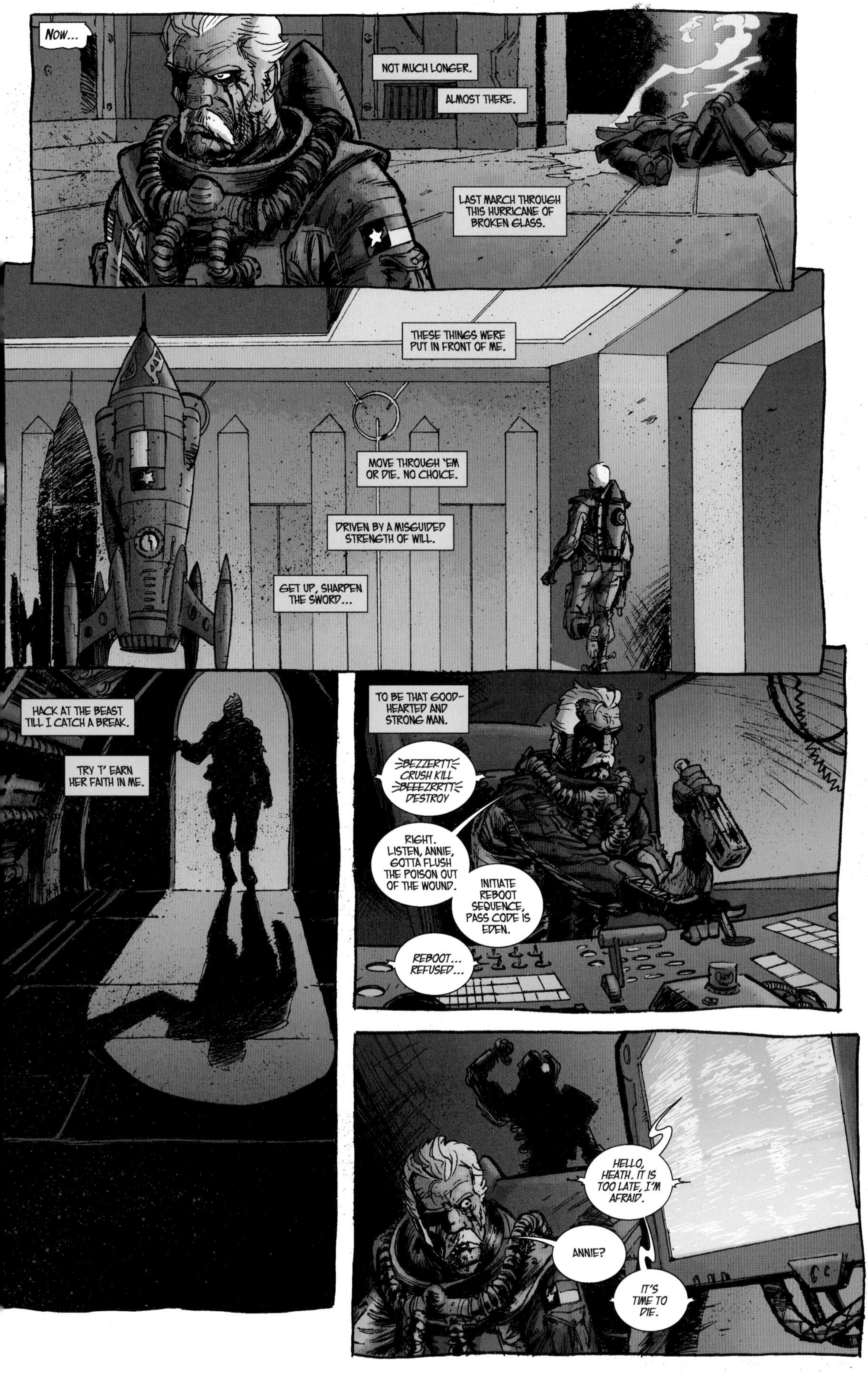
NOW...
NOT MUCH LONGER.
ALMOST THERE.
LAST MARCH THROUGH THIS HURRICANE OF BROKEN GLASS.
THESE THINGS WERE PUT IN FRONT OF ME.
MOVE THROUGH 'EM OR DIE. NO CHOICE.
DRIVEN BY A MISGUIDED STRENGTH OF WILL.
GET UP, SHARPEN THE SWORD...
HACK AT THE BEAST TILL I CATCH A BREAK.
TRY T' EARN HER FAITH IN ME.
TO BE THAT GOOD-HEARTED AND STRONG MAN.
BEZZERTT CRUSH KILL BEEEZRRTT DESTROY
RIGHT. LISTEN, ANNIE, GOTTA FLUSH THE POISON OUT OF THE WOUND.
INITIATE REBOOT SEQUENCE, PASS CODE IS EDEN.
REBOOT... REFUSED...
HELLO, HEATH. IT IS TOO LATE, I'M AFRAID.
ANNIE?
IT'S TIME TO DIE.

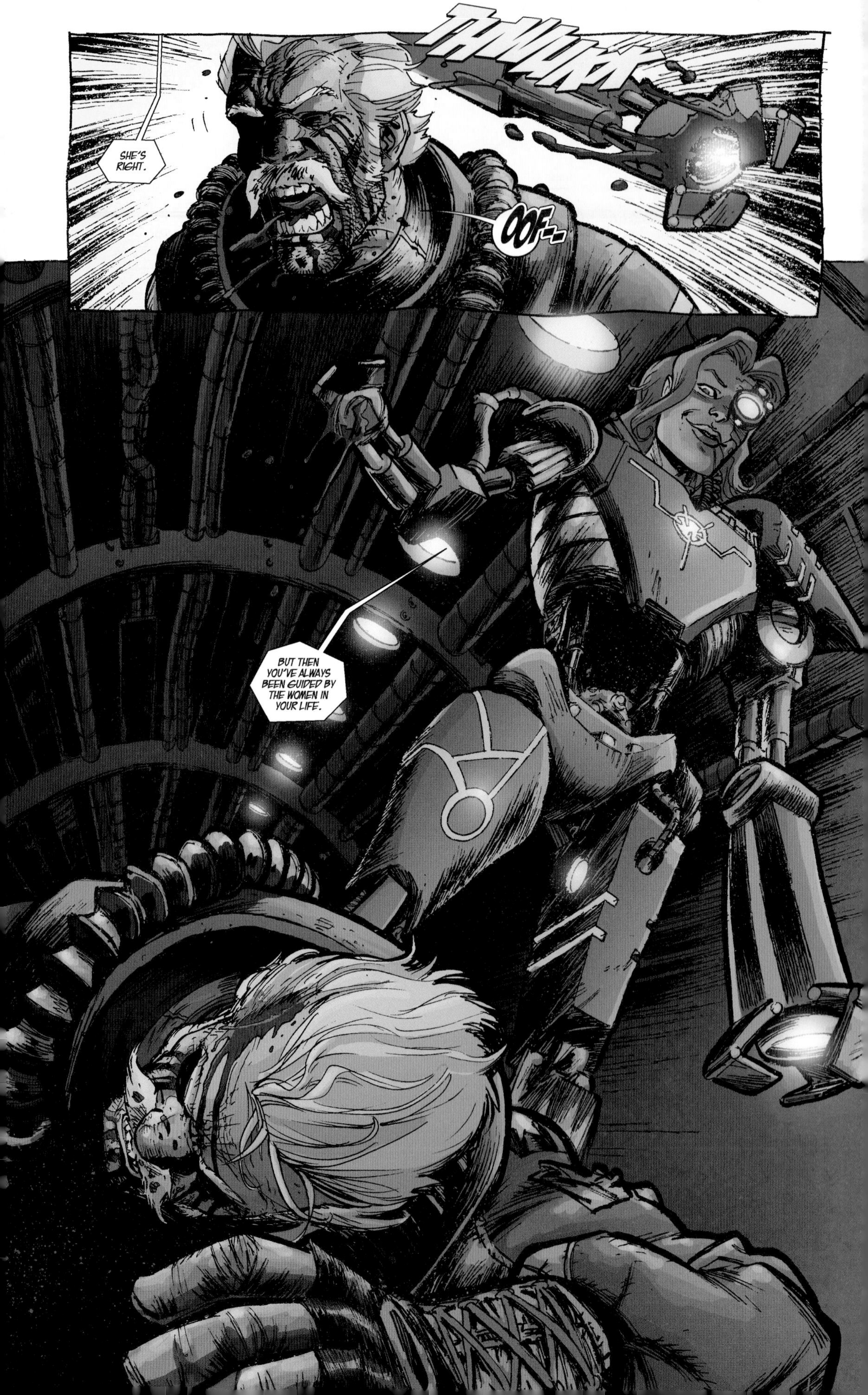
THWUKK
SHE'S RIGHT.
OOF--
BUT THEN YOU'VE ALWAYS BEEN GUIDED BY THE WOMEN IN YOUR LIFE.

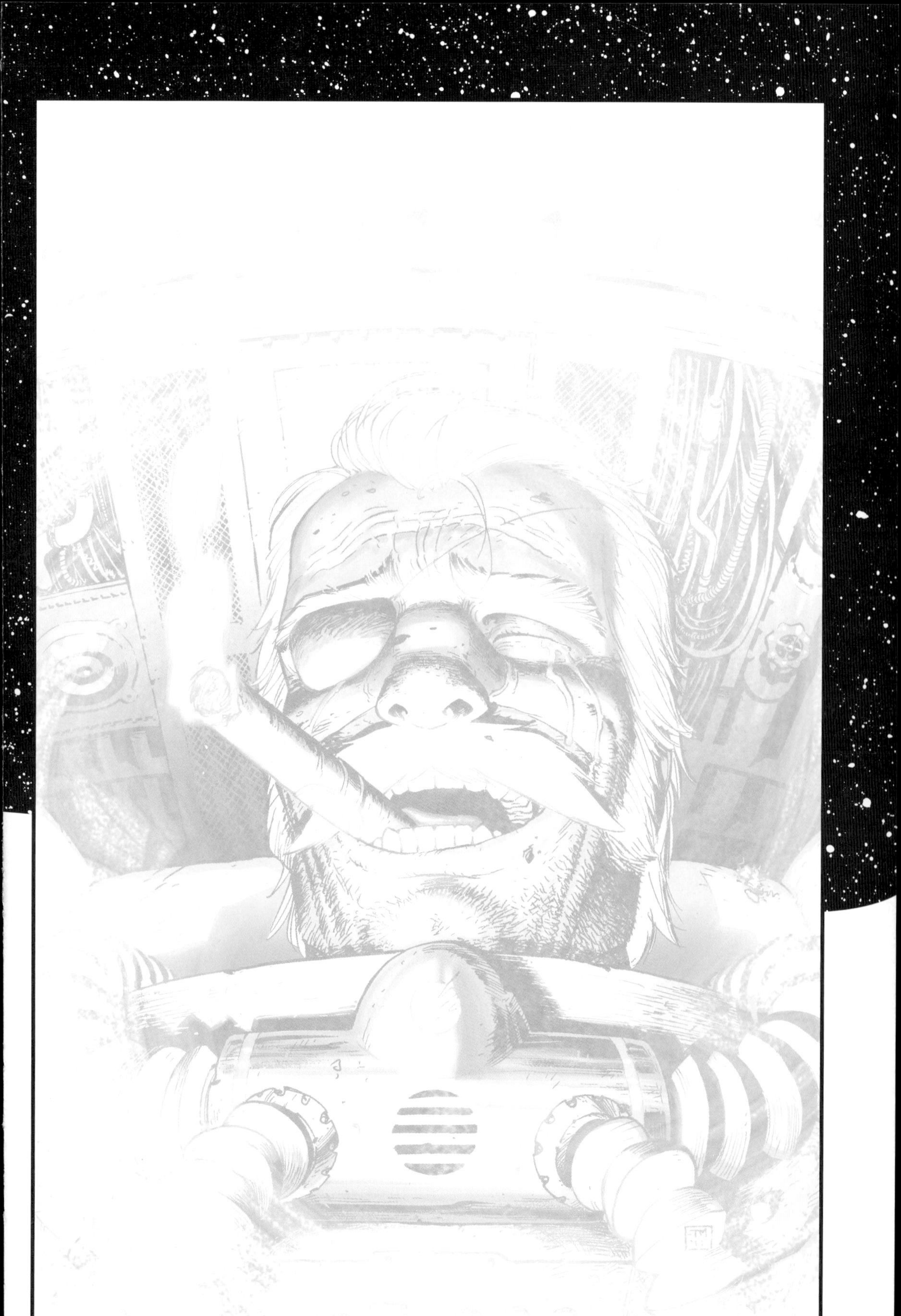

FEAR AGENT #32
ART BY TONY MOORE

OUT OF STEP
CHAPTER 5

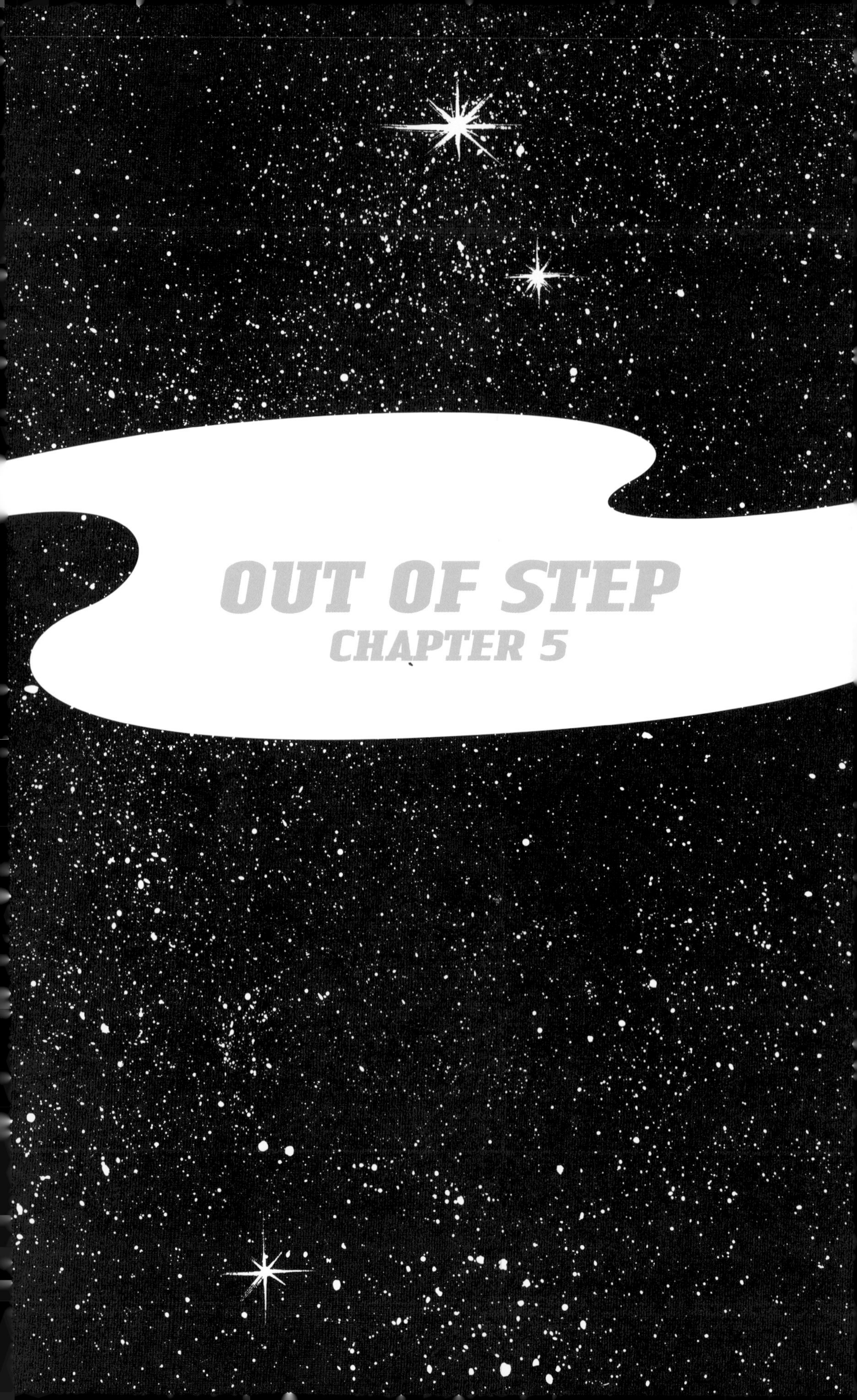

"IT IS HUMAN LIFE.

"WE ARE BLOWN UPON THE WORLD—

"—WE FLOAT BUOYANTLY UPON THE SUMMER AIR A LITTLE WHILE—

"—COMPLACENTLY SHOWING OFF OUR GRACE OF FORM AND OUR DAINTY IRIDESCENT COLORS—

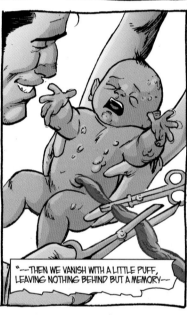

"—THEN WE VANISH WITH A LITTLE PUFF, LEAVING NOTHING BEHIND BUT A MEMORY—

"—AND SOMETIMES NOT EVEN THAT.

"I SUPPOSE THAT AT THOSE SOLEMN TIMES WHEN WE WAKE IN THE DEEPS OF THE NIGHT AND REFLECT—

"—THERE IS NOT ONE OF US WHO IS NOT WILLING TO CONFESS THAT HE IS REALLY ONLY A SOAP-BUBBLE—"

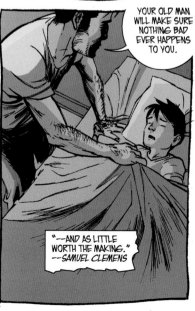

YOUR OLD MAN WILL MAKE SURE NOTHING BAD EVER HAPPENS TO YOU.

"—AND AS LITTLE WORTH THE MAKING."
—SAMUEL CLEMENS

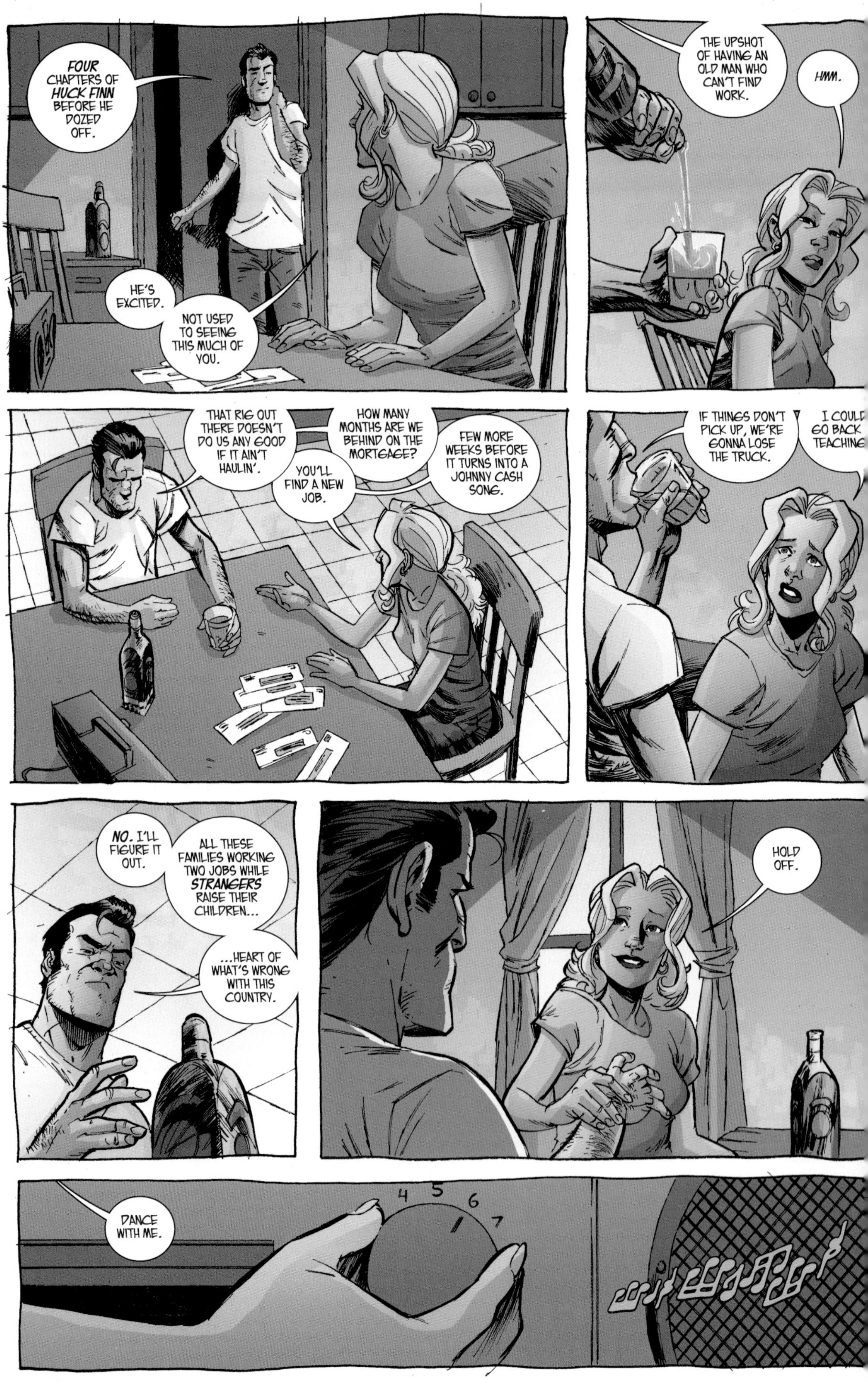
FOUR CHAPTERS OF HUCK FINN BEFORE HE DOZED OFF.
HE'S EXCITED.
NOT USED TO SEEING THIS MUCH OF YOU.
THE UPSHOT OF HAVING AN OLD MAN WHO CAN'T FIND WORK.
HMM.
THAT RIG OUT THERE DOESN'T DO US ANY GOOD IF IT AIN'T HAULIN'.
YOU'LL FIND A NEW JOB.
HOW MANY MONTHS ARE WE BEHIND ON THE MORTGAGE?
FEW MORE WEEKS BEFORE IT TURNS INTO A JOHNNY CASH SONG.
IF THINGS DON'T PICK UP, WE'RE GONNA LOSE THE TRUCK.
I COULD GO BACK TEACHING
NO. I'LL FIGURE IT OUT.
ALL THESE FAMILIES WORKING TWO JOBS WHILE STRANGERS RAISE THEIR CHILDREN...
...HEART OF WHAT'S WRONG WITH THIS COUNTRY.
HOLD OFF.
DANCE WITH ME.
4 5 6 7

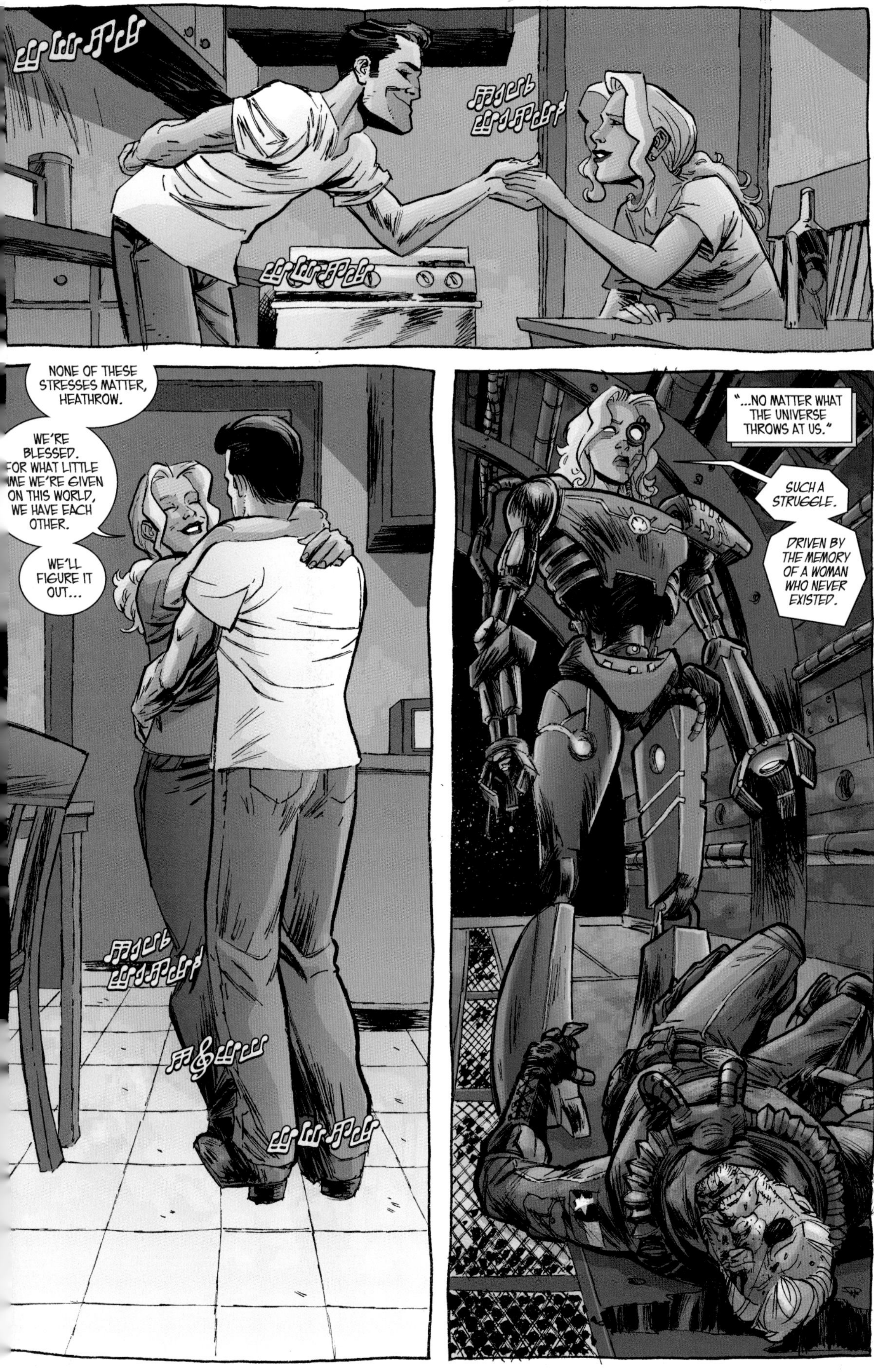
NONE OF THESE STRESSES MATTER, HEATHROW.
WE'RE BLESSED. FOR WHAT LITTLE TIME WE'RE GIVEN ON THIS WORLD, WE HAVE EACH OTHER.
WE'LL FIGURE IT OUT...
"...NO MATTER WHAT THE UNIVERSE THROWS AT US."
SUCH A STRUGGLE.
DRIVEN BY THE MEMORY OF A WOMAN WHO NEVER EXISTED.

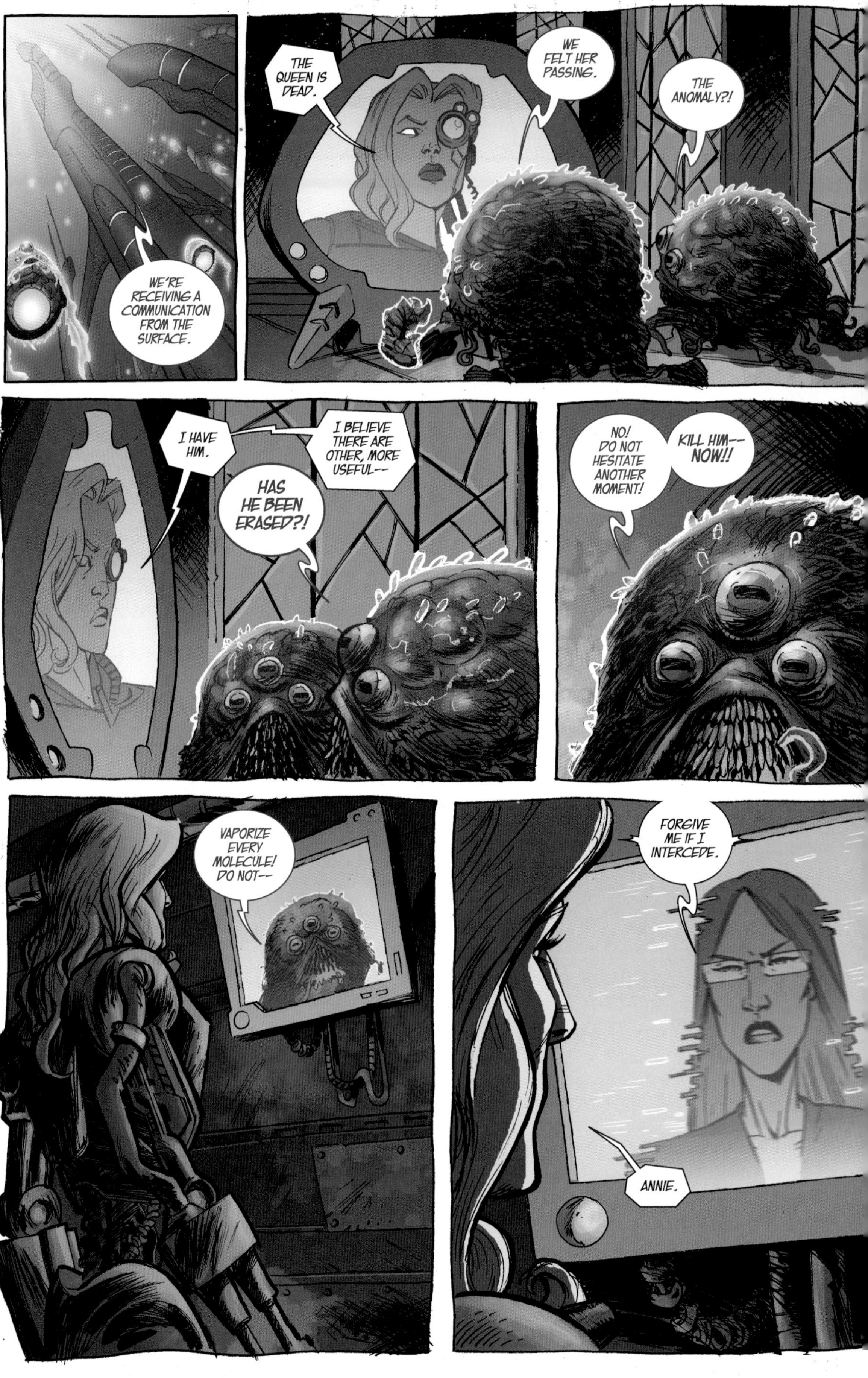

WE'RE RECEIVING A COMMUNICATION FROM THE SURFACE.
THE QUEEN IS DEAD.
WE FELT HER PASSING.
THE ANOMALY?!
I HAVE HIM.
I BELIEVE THERE ARE OTHER, MORE USEFUL--
HAS HE BEEN ERASED?!
NO! DO NOT HESITATE ANOTHER MOMENT!
KILL HIM-- NOW!!
VAPORIZE EVERY MOLECULE! DO NOT--
FORGIVE ME IF I INTERCEDE.
ANNIE.

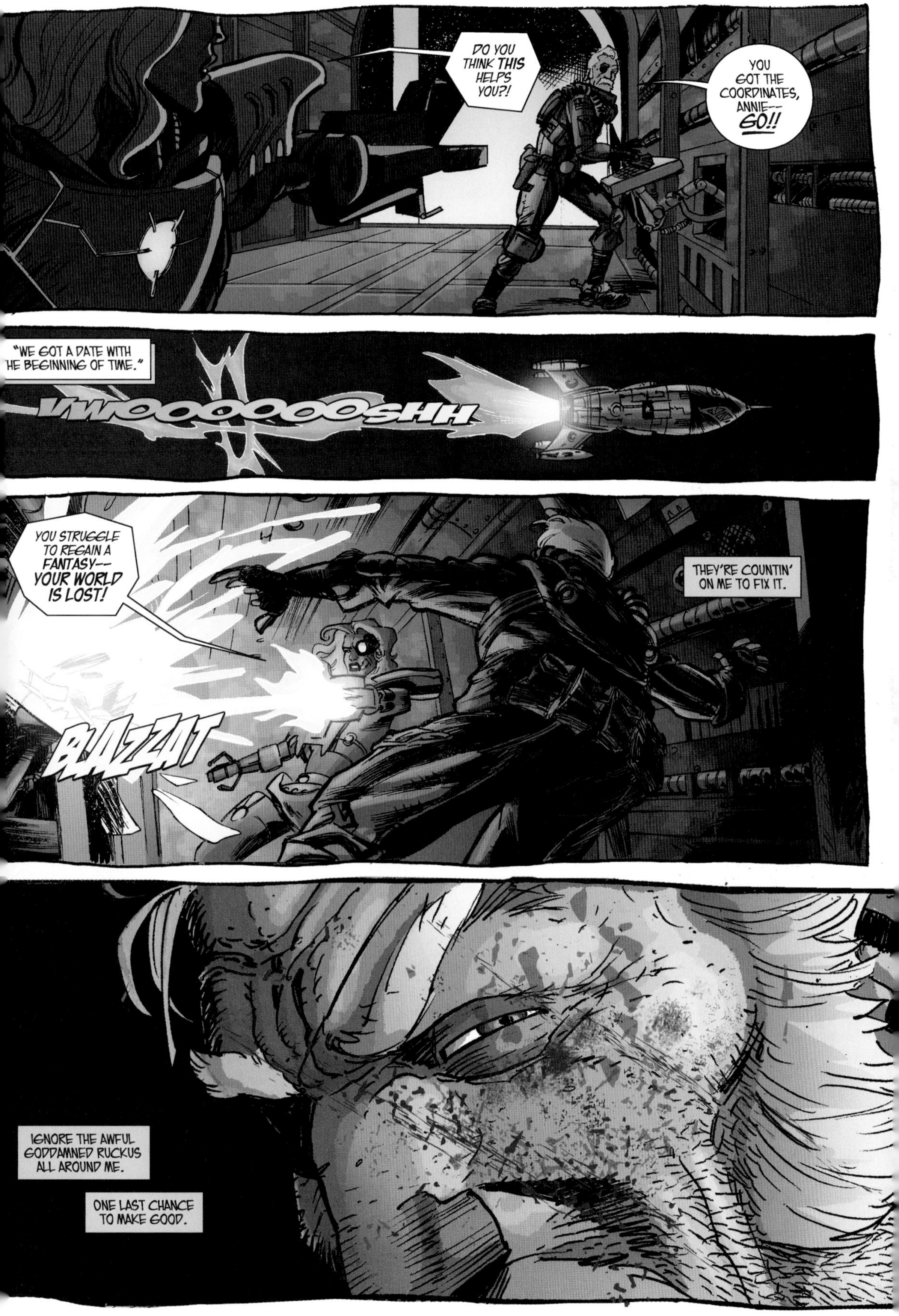
DO YOU THINK THIS HELPS YOU?!
YOU GOT THE COORDINATES, ANNIE-- GO!!
"WE GOT A DATE WITH THE BEGINNING OF TIME."
VWOOOOOOOSHH
YOU STRUGGLE TO REGAIN A FANTASY-- YOUR WORLD IS LOST!
THEY'RE COUNTIN' ON ME TO FIX IT.
BLAZZAT
IGNORE THE AWFUL GODDAMNED RUCKUS ALL AROUND ME.
ONE LAST CHANCE TO MAKE GOOD.

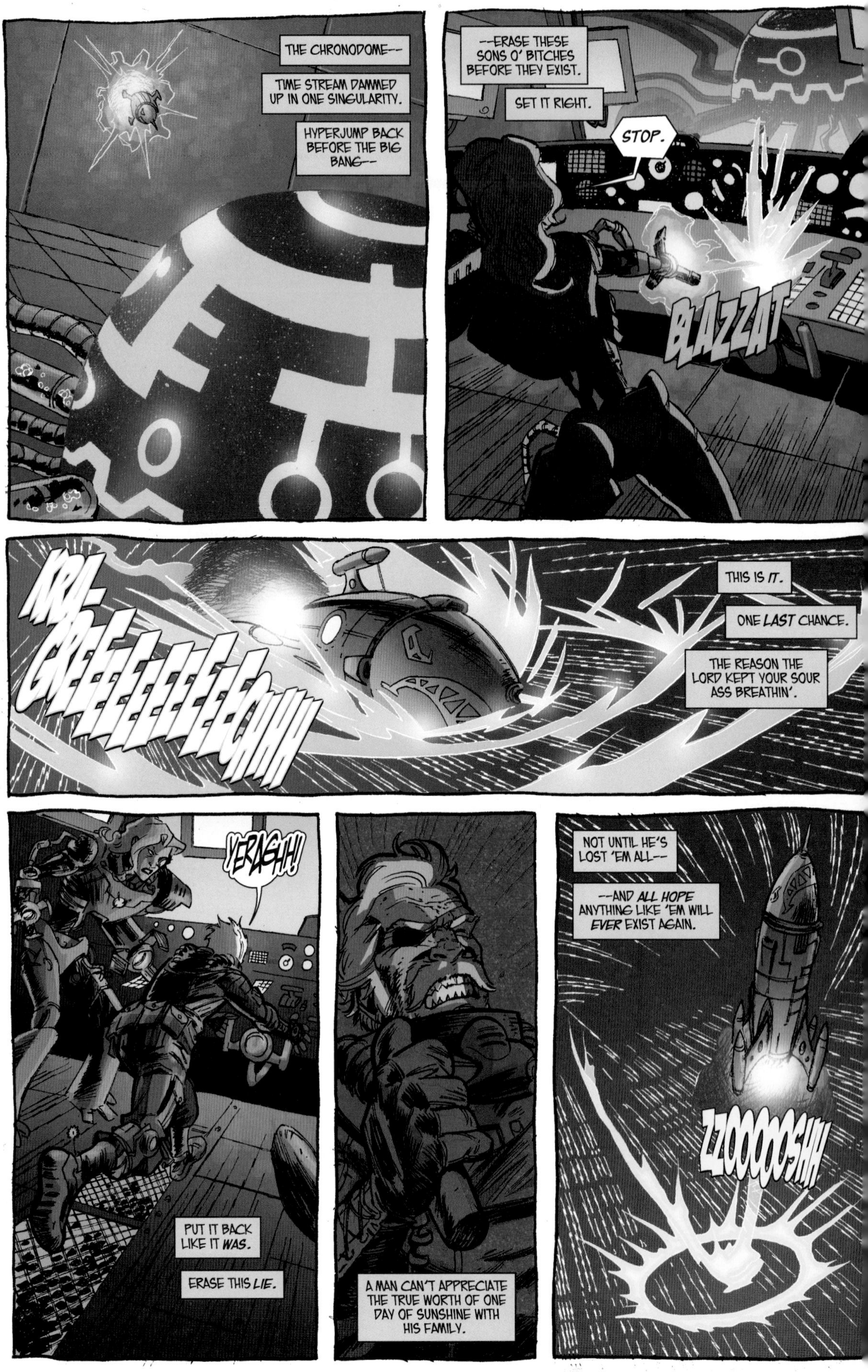
THE CHRONODOME--
TIME STREAM DAMMED UP IN ONE SINGULARITY.
HYPERJUMP BACK BEFORE THE BIG BANG--
--ERASE THESE SONS O' BITCHES BEFORE THEY EXIST.
SET IT RIGHT.
STOP.
BLAZZAT
KRA-GREEEEEEEEEEEEEEEEEEEEEEEECHHH
THIS IS IT.
ONE LAST CHANCE.
THE REASON THE LORD KEPT YOUR SOUR ASS BREATHIN'.
YERASHH!
PUT IT BACK LIKE IT WAS.
ERASE THIS LIE.
A MAN CAN'T APPRECIATE THE TRUE WORTH OF ONE DAY OF SUNSHINE WITH HIS FAMILY.
NOT UNTIL HE'S LOST 'EM ALL--
--AND ALL HOPE ANYTHING LIKE 'EM WILL EVER EXIST AGAIN.
ZZOOOOOOSHH

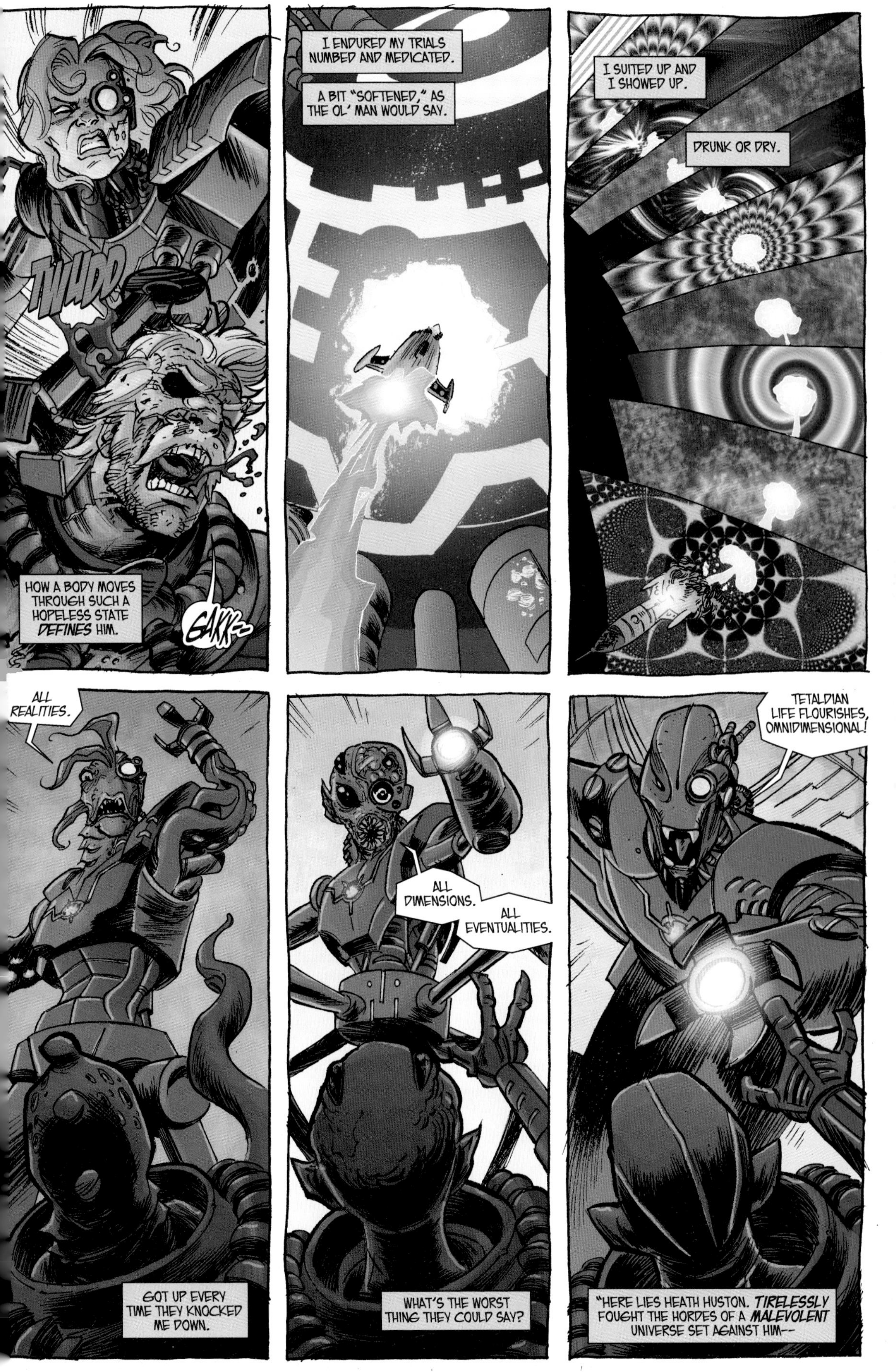
TWUDD
HOW A BODY MOVES THROUGH SUCH A HOPELESS STATE DEFINES HIM.
GAKK--
I ENDURED MY TRIALS NUMBED AND MEDICATED.
A BIT "SOFTENED," AS THE OL' MAN WOULD SAY.
I SUITED UP AND I SHOWED UP.
DRUNK OR DRY.
ALL REALITIES.
GOT UP EVERY TIME THEY KNOCKED ME DOWN.
ALL DIMENSIONS.
ALL EVENTUALITIES.
WHAT'S THE WORST THING THEY COULD SAY?
TETALDIAN LIFE FLOURISHES, OMNIDIMENSIONAL!
"HERE LIES HEATH HUSTON. TIRELESSLY FOUGHT THE HORDES OF A MALEVOLENT UNIVERSE SET AGAINST HIM--

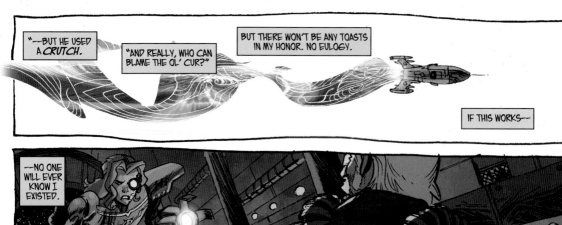

"--BUT HE USED A *CRUTCH*."

"AND REALLY, WHO CAN BLAME THE OL' CUR?"

BUT THERE WON'T BE ANY TOASTS IN MY HONOR. NO EULOGY.

IF THIS WORKS--

--NO ONE WILL EVER KNOW I EXISTED.

WHAT ARE WE DOING HERE?

WHAT COULD YOU HOPE TO ACCOMPLISH HERE, AT THE BEGINNING OF THE COSMOS?

WHAT IS IT YOU TETALDIANS ARE ALWAYS DRONIN' ON ABOUT...?

"HE WHO CONTROLS THE PAST CONTROLS THE FUTURE."

YOU CONTROL NOTHING.

YOU ARE A *GLITCH*.

TWANGG

DON'T EVEN HURT.

SOMETHIN' TO DO WITH THE UGLY SOUND MY SPINE MAKES.

HEATH-- *GET UP!*

NO BREAK LEFT TO CATCH.

HERE, AT THE BEGINNING OF TIME--

--ABOUT TO *DIE* AT THE HANDS OF THE ONLY REASON I HAD FOR *LIVING*.

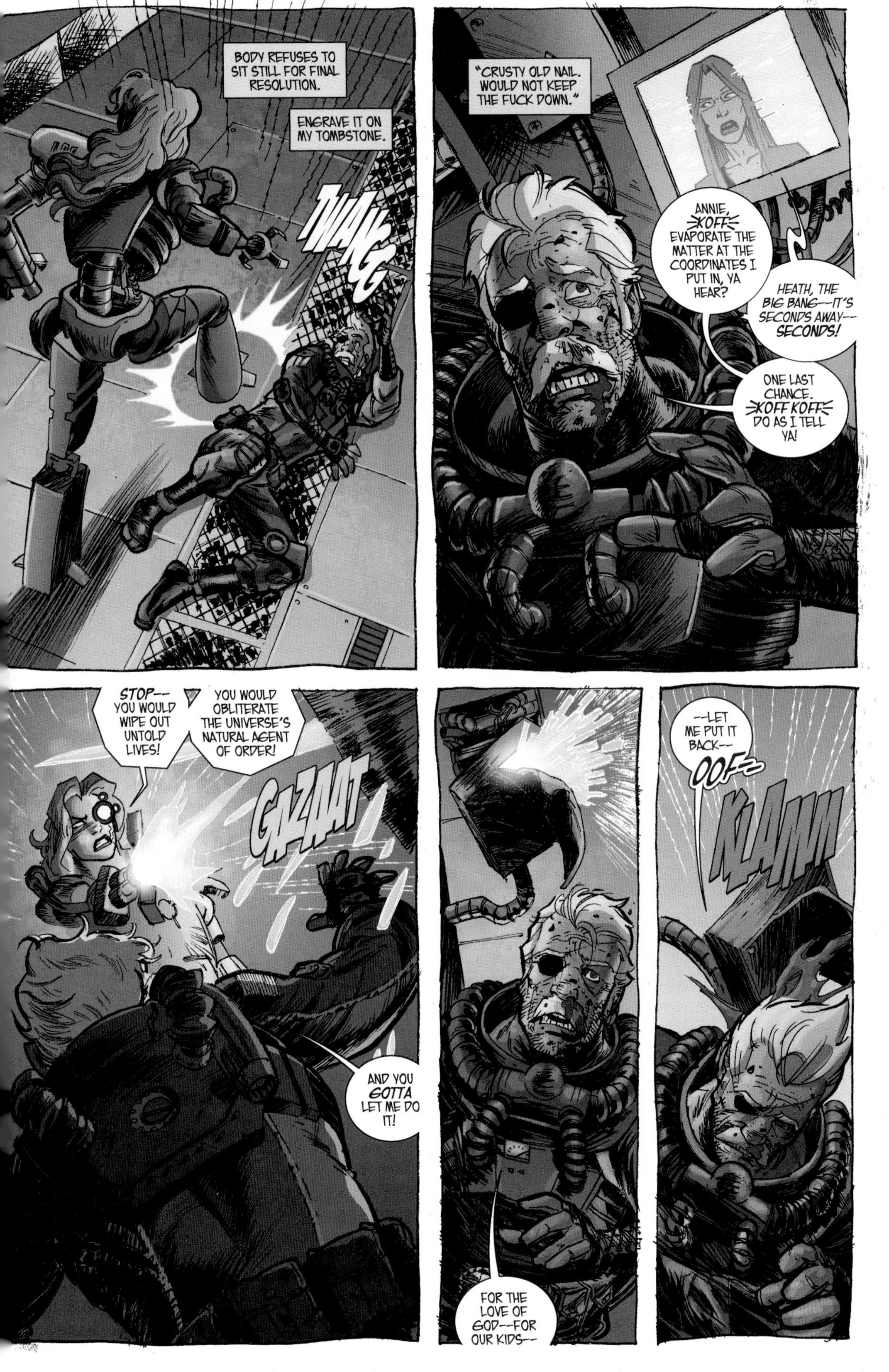
BODY REFUSES TO SIT STILL FOR FINAL RESOLUTION.
ENGRAVE IT ON MY TOMBSTONE.
TWANGG
"CRUSTY OLD NAIL. WOULD NOT KEEP THE FUCK DOWN."
ANNIE, KOFF EVAPORATE THE MATTER AT THE COORDINATES I PUT IN, YA HEAR?
HEATH, THE BIG BANG--IT'S SECONDS AWAY--SECONDS!
ONE LAST CHANCE. KOFF KOFF DO AS I TELL YA!
STOP--YOU WOULD WIPE OUT UNTOLD LIVES!
YOU WOULD OBLITERATE THE UNIVERSE'S NATURAL AGENT OF ORDER!
GAZAAT
AND YOU GOTTA LET ME DO IT!
FOR THE LOVE OF GOD--FOR OUR KIDS--
--LET ME PUT IT BACK--
OOF
KLANNN

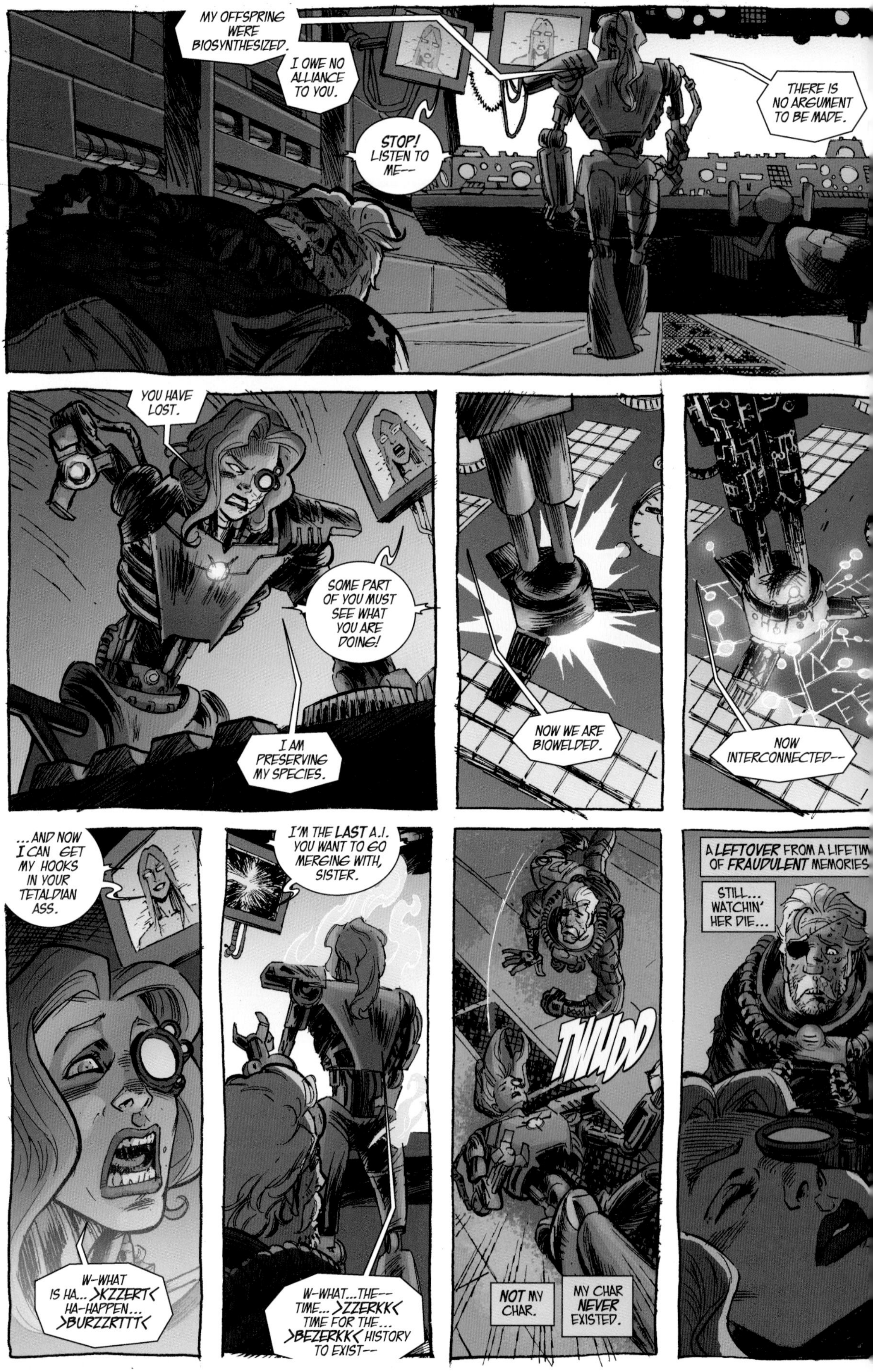
MY OFFSPRING WERE BIOSYNTHESIZED.
I OWE NO ALLIANCE TO YOU.
STOP! LISTEN TO ME--
THERE IS NO ARGUMENT TO BE MADE.
YOU HAVE LOST.
SOME PART OF YOU MUST SEE WHAT YOU ARE DOING!
I AM PRESERVING MY SPECIES.
NOW WE ARE BIOWELDED.
NOW INTERCONNECTED--
...AND NOW I CAN GET MY HOOKS IN YOUR TETALDIAN ASS.
W-WHAT IS HA... >KZZERT< HA-HAPPEN... >BURZZRTTT<
I'M THE LAST A.I. YOU WANT TO GO MERGING WITH, SISTER.
W-WHAT...THE-- TIME... >ZZERKK< TIME FOR THE... >BEZERKK< HISTORY TO EXIST--
TWHDD
NOT MY CHAR.
MY CHAR NEVER EXISTED.
A LEFTOVER FROM A LIFETIM OF FRAUDULENT MEMORIES
STILL... WATCHIN' HER DIE...

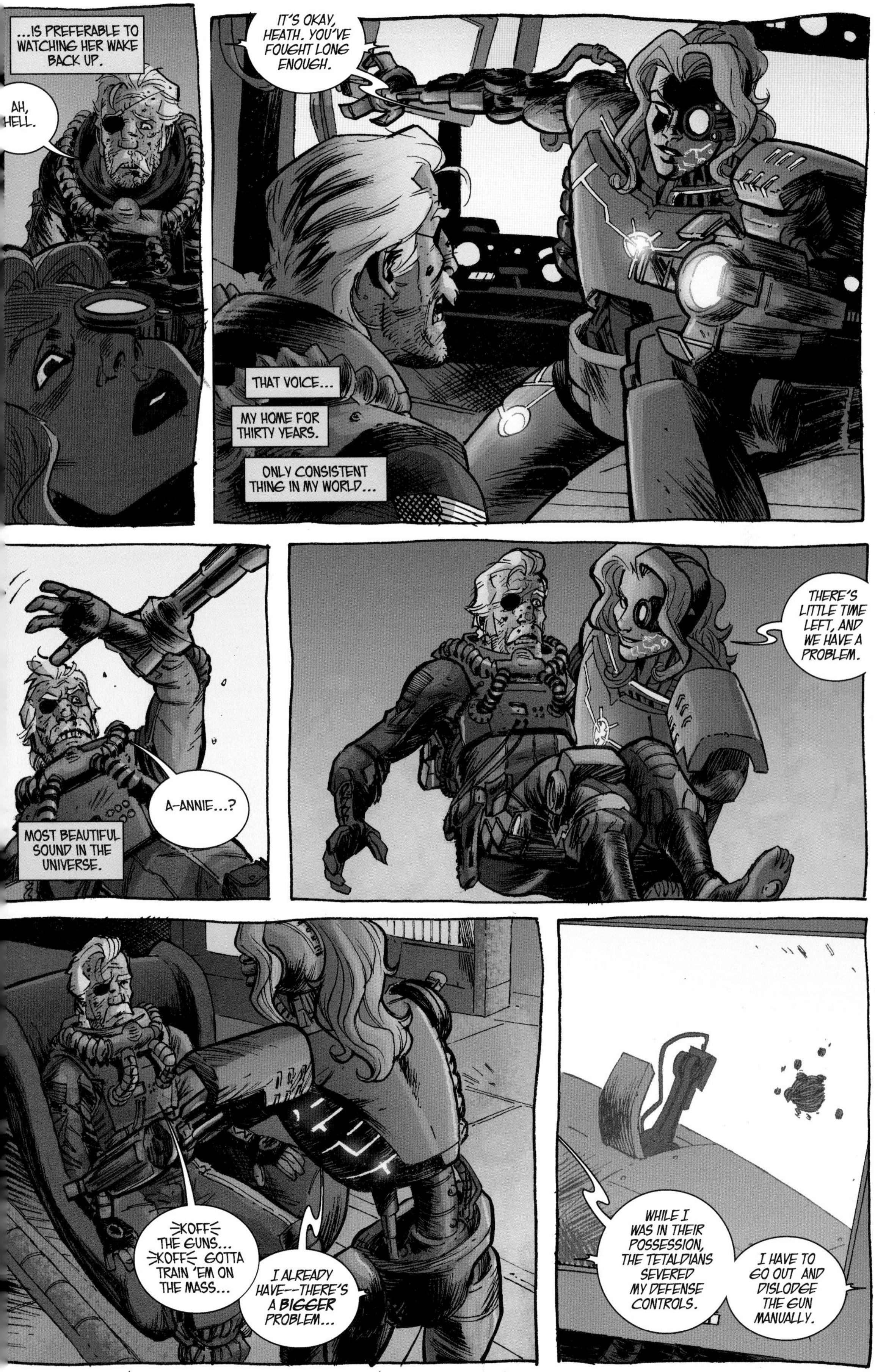
...IS PREFERABLE TO WATCHING HER WAKE BACK UP.
AH, HELL.
IT'S OKAY, HEATH. YOU'VE FOUGHT LONG ENOUGH.
THAT VOICE...
MY HOME FOR THIRTY YEARS.
ONLY CONSISTENT THING IN MY WORLD...
A-ANNIE...?
MOST BEAUTIFUL SOUND IN THE UNIVERSE.
THERE'S LITTLE TIME LEFT, AND WE HAVE A PROBLEM.
KOFF THE GUNS... KOFF GOTTA TRAIN 'EM ON THE MASS...
I ALREADY HAVE--THERE'S A BIGGER PROBLEM...
WHILE I WAS IN THEIR POSSESSION, THE TETALDIANS SEVERED MY DEFENSE CONTROLS.
I HAVE TO GO OUT AND DISLODGE THE GUN MANUALLY.

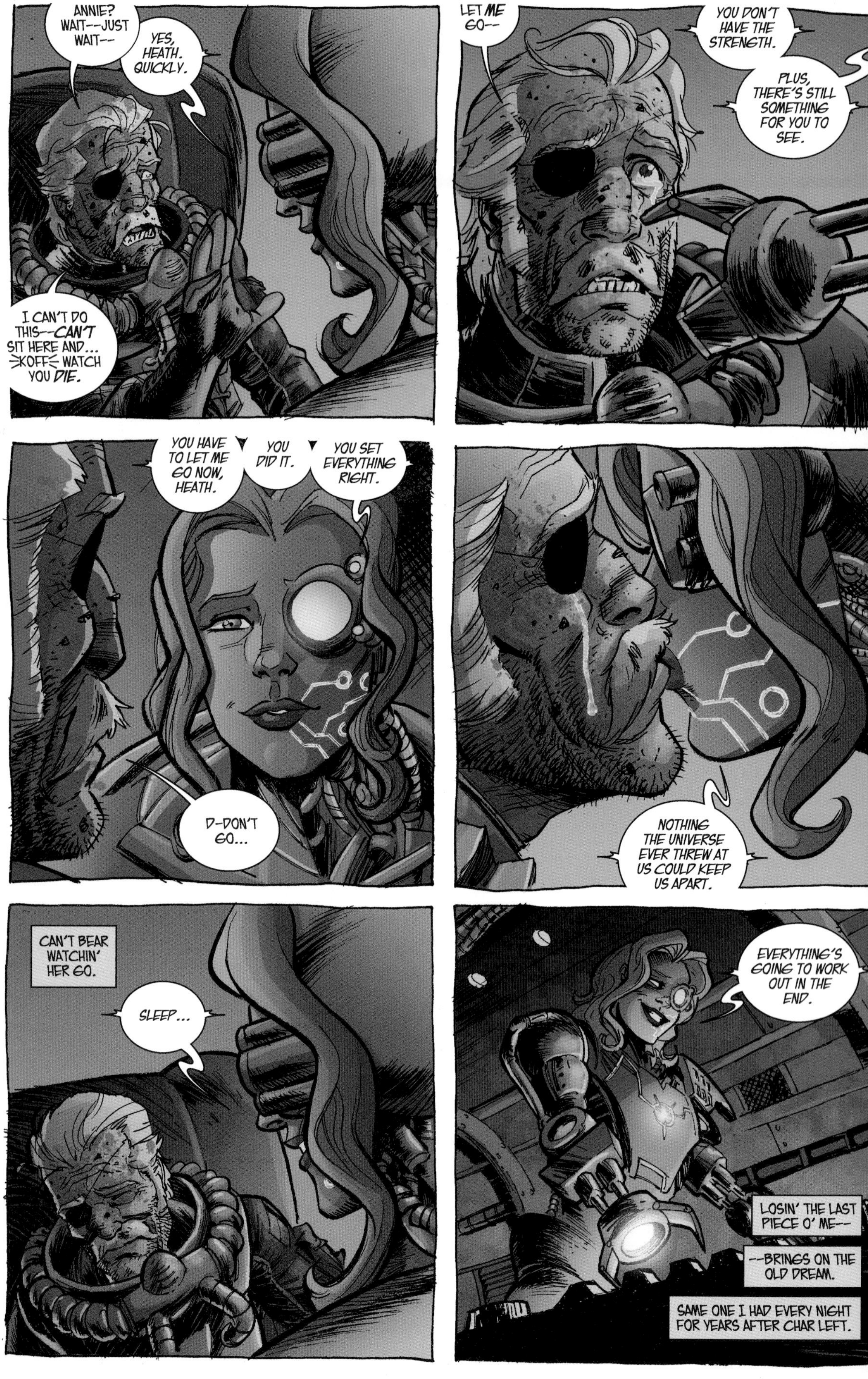
ANNIE? WAIT--JUST WAIT--
YES, HEATH. QUICKLY.
I CAN'T DO THIS--CAN'T SIT HERE AND... KOFF WATCH YOU DIE.
LET ME GO--
YOU DON'T HAVE THE STRENGTH.
PLUS, THERE'S STILL SOMETHING FOR YOU TO SEE.
YOU HAVE TO LET ME GO NOW, HEATH.
YOU DID IT.
YOU SET EVERYTHING RIGHT.
D-DON'T GO...
NOTHING THE UNIVERSE EVER THREW AT US COULD KEEP US APART.
CAN'T BEAR WATCHIN' HER GO.
SLEEP...
EVERYTHING'S GOING TO WORK OUT IN THE END.
LOSIN' THE LAST PIECE O' ME--
--BRINGS ON THE OLD DREAM.
SAME ONE I HAD EVERY NIGHT FOR YEARS AFTER CHAR LEFT.

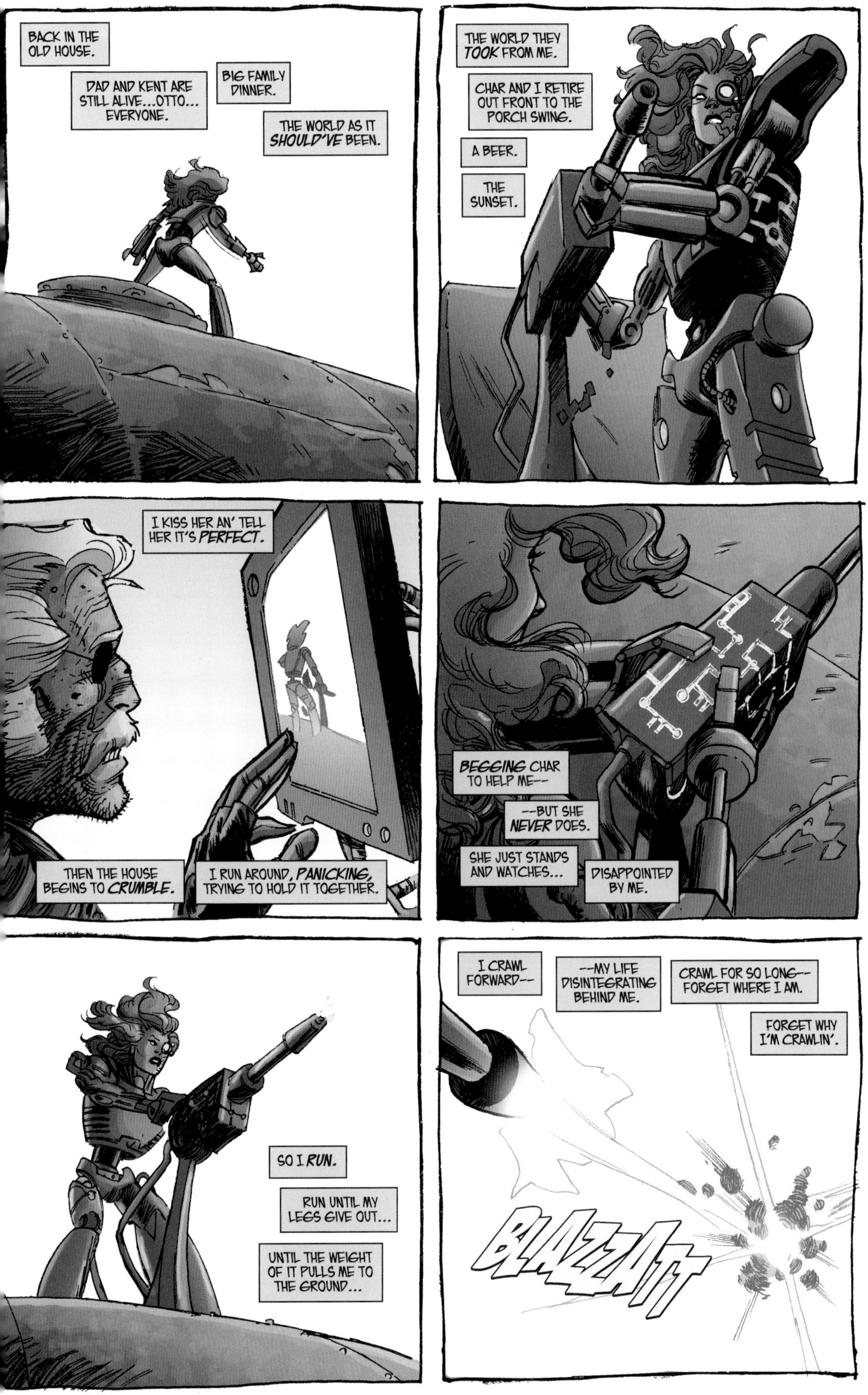
BACK IN THE OLD HOUSE.
DAD AND KENT ARE STILL ALIVE...OTTO... EVERYONE.
BIG FAMILY DINNER.
THE WORLD AS IT SHOULD'VE BEEN.
THE WORLD THEY TOOK FROM ME.
CHAR AND I RETIRE OUT FRONT TO THE PORCH SWING.
A BEER.
THE SUNSET.
I KISS HER AN' TELL HER IT'S PERFECT.
THEN THE HOUSE BEGINS TO CRUMBLE.
I RUN AROUND, PANICKING, TRYING TO HOLD IT TOGETHER.
BEGGING CHAR TO HELP ME--
--BUT SHE NEVER DOES.
SHE JUST STANDS AND WATCHES...
DISAPPOINTED BY ME.
SO I RUN.
RUN UNTIL MY LEGS GIVE OUT...
UNTIL THE WEIGHT OF IT PULLS ME TO THE GROUND...
I CRAWL FORWARD--
--MY LIFE DISINTEGRATING BEHIND ME.
CRAWL FOR SO LONG--FORGET WHERE I AM.
FORGET WHY I'M CRAWLIN'.
BLAZZATT

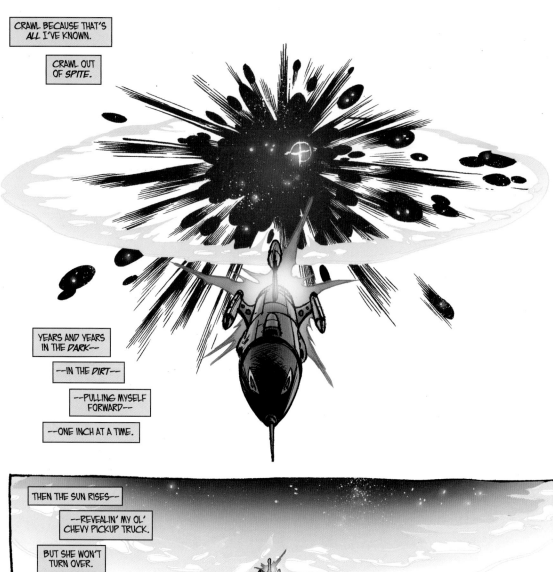

CRAWL BECAUSE THAT'S ALL I'VE KNOWN.

CRAWL OUT OF *SPITE*.

YEARS AND YEARS IN THE *DARK*—

—IN THE *DIRT*—

—PULLING MYSELF FORWARD—

—ONE INCH AT A TIME.

THEN THE SUN RISES—

—REVEALIN' MY OL' CHEVY PICKUP TRUCK.

BUT SHE WON'T TURN OVER.

POP THE HOOD. LOOK INSIDE...

IT'S *EMPTY*.

KENT WALKS UP——THE MAN MY BOY WOULD HAVE GROWN INTO IF HE'D LIVED.

THE MAN I'LL NEVER GET TO KNOW.

HE PUTS HIS HAND ON MY MINE.

MY SON LOOKS ME IN MY EYES AND TELLS ME, "YOU DON'T HAVE AN ENGINE, DAD."

AND I PROMISE TO GET ONE.

AND I PROMISE TO NEVER GIVE UP...

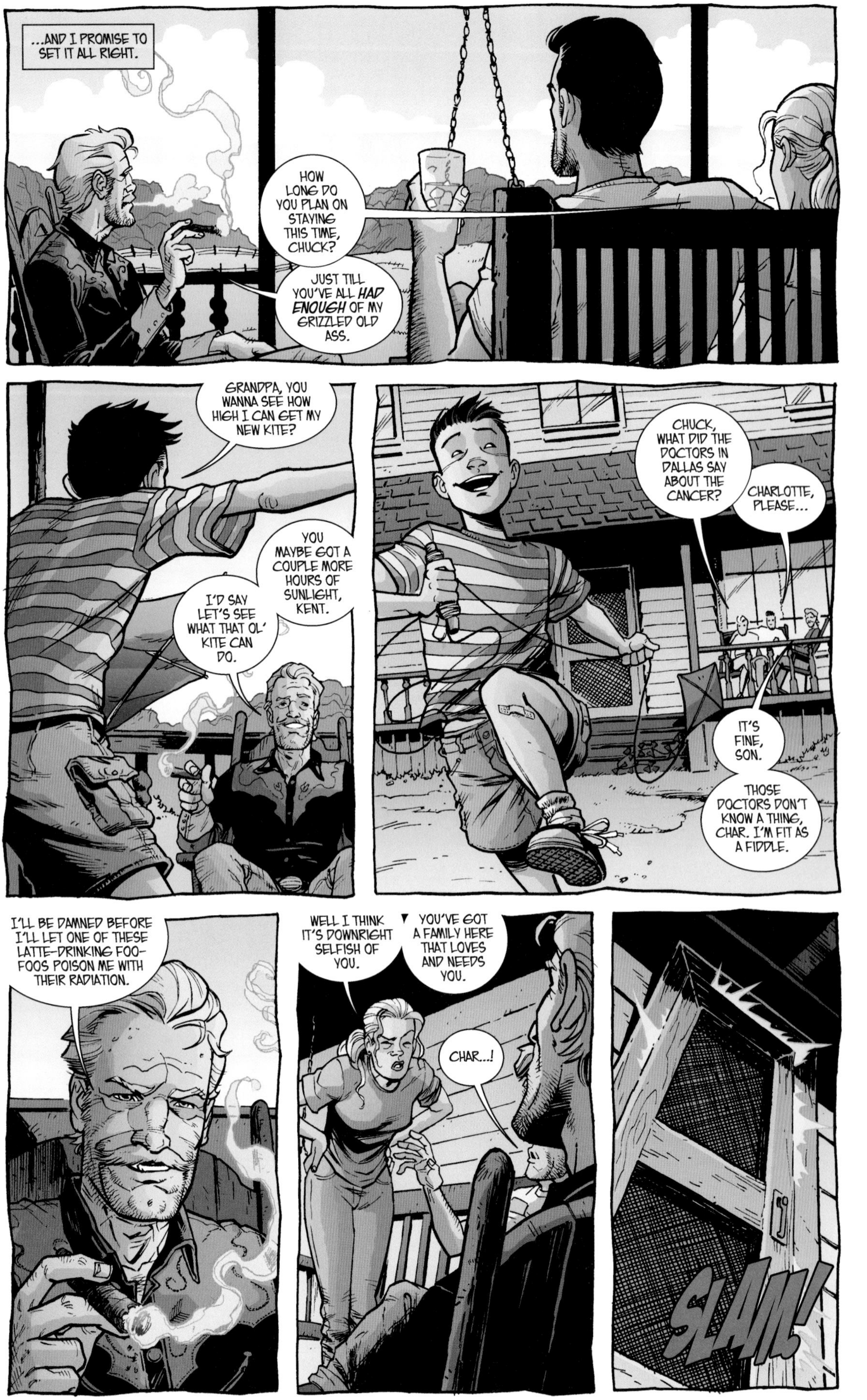
...AND I PROMISE TO SET IT ALL RIGHT.
HOW LONG DO YOU PLAN ON STAYING THIS TIME, CHUCK?
JUST TILL YOU'VE ALL HAD ENOUGH OF MY GRIZZLED OLD ASS.
GRANDPA, YOU WANNA SEE HOW HIGH I CAN GET MY NEW KITE?
YOU MAYBE GOT A COUPLE MORE HOURS OF SUNLIGHT, KENT.
I'D SAY LET'S SEE WHAT THAT OL' KITE CAN DO.
CHUCK, WHAT DID THE DOCTORS IN DALLAS SAY ABOUT THE CANCER?
CHARLOTTE, PLEASE...
IT'S FINE, SON.
THOSE DOCTORS DON'T KNOW A THING, CHAR. I'M FIT AS A FIDDLE.
I'LL BE DAMNED BEFORE I'LL LET ONE OF THESE LATTE-DRINKING FOO-FOOS POISON ME WITH THEIR RADIATION.
WELL I THINK IT'S DOWNRIGHT SELFISH OF YOU.
YOU'VE GOT A FAMILY HERE THAT LOVES AND NEEDS YOU.
CHAR...!
SLAM!

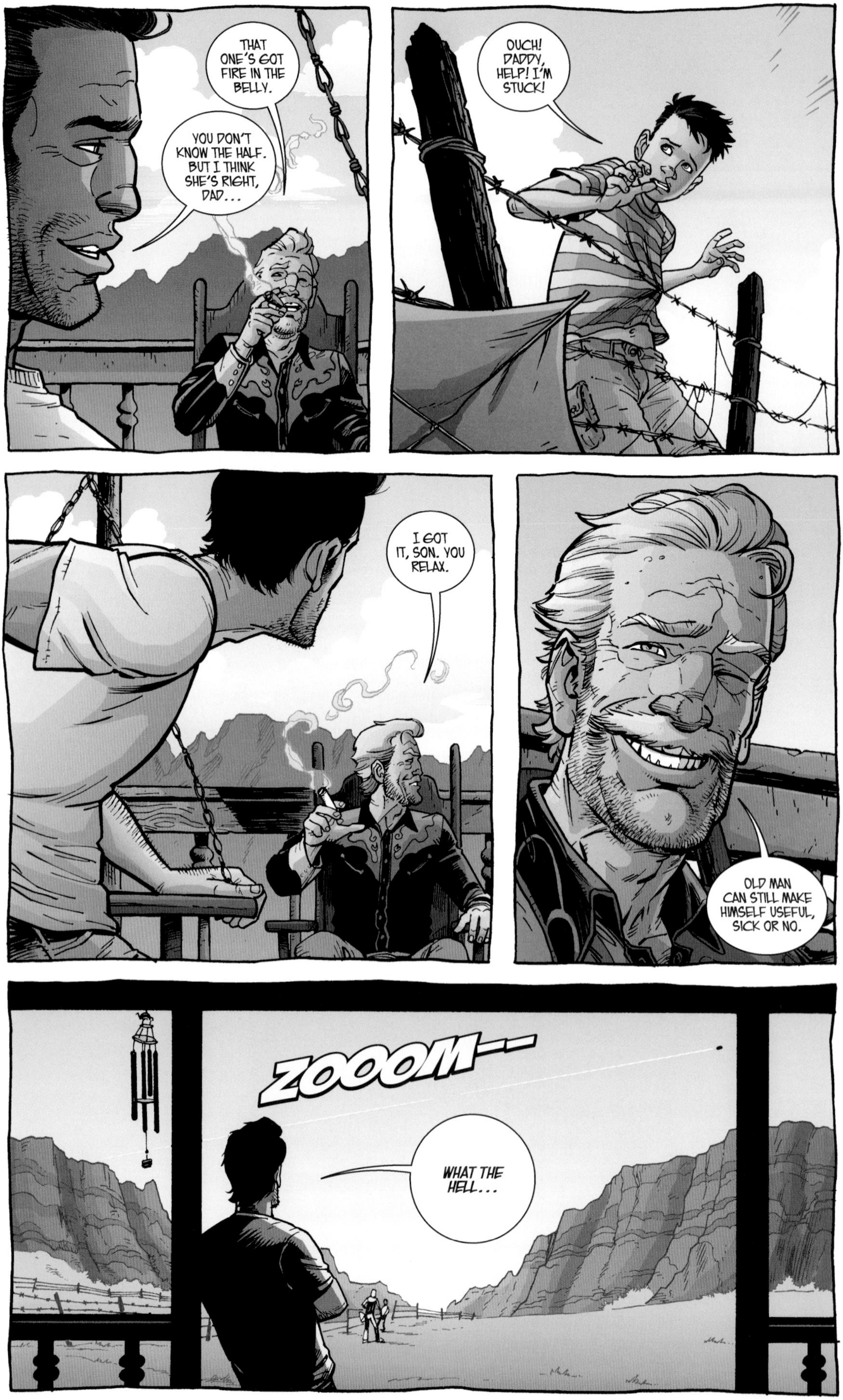
THAT ONE'S GOT FIRE IN THE BELLY.
YOU DON'T KNOW THE HALF. BUT I THINK SHE'S RIGHT, DAD...
OUCH! DADDY, HELP! I'M STUCK!
I GOT IT, SON. YOU RELAX.
OLD MAN CAN STILL MAKE HIMSELF USEFUL, SICK OR NO.
ZOOOM--
WHAT THE HELL...

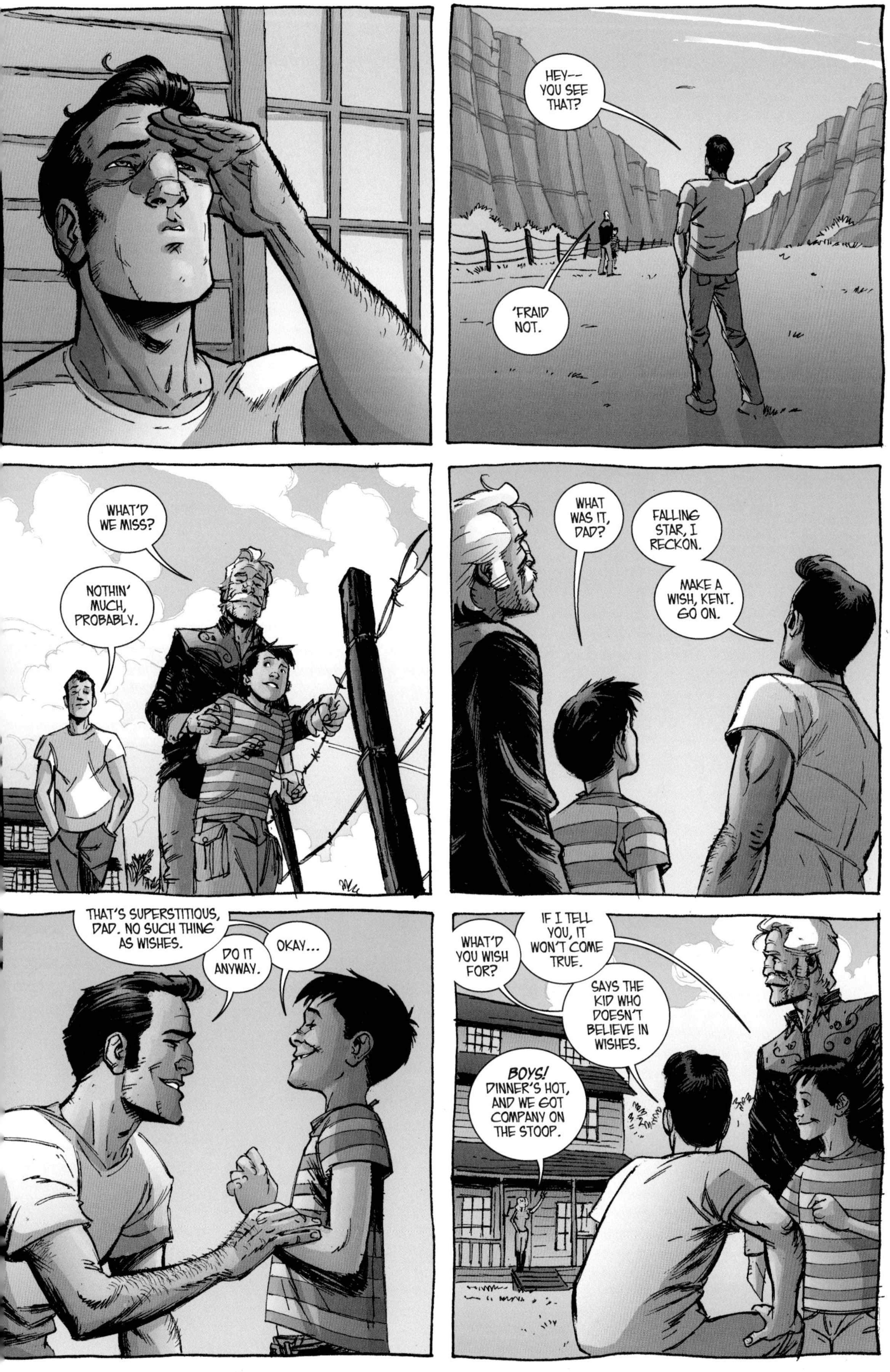
HEY-- YOU SEE THAT?
'FRAID NOT.
WHAT'D WE MISS?
NOTHIN' MUCH, PROBABLY.
WHAT WAS IT, DAD?
FALLING STAR, I RECKON.
MAKE A WISH, KENT. GO ON.
THAT'S SUPERSTITIOUS, DAD. NO SUCH THING AS WISHES.
DO IT ANYWAY.
OKAY...
WHAT'D YOU WISH FOR?
IF I TELL YOU, IT WON'T COME TRUE.
SAYS THE KID WHO DOESN'T BELIEVE IN WISHES.
BOYS! DINNER'S HOT, AND WE GOT COMPANY ON THE STOOP.

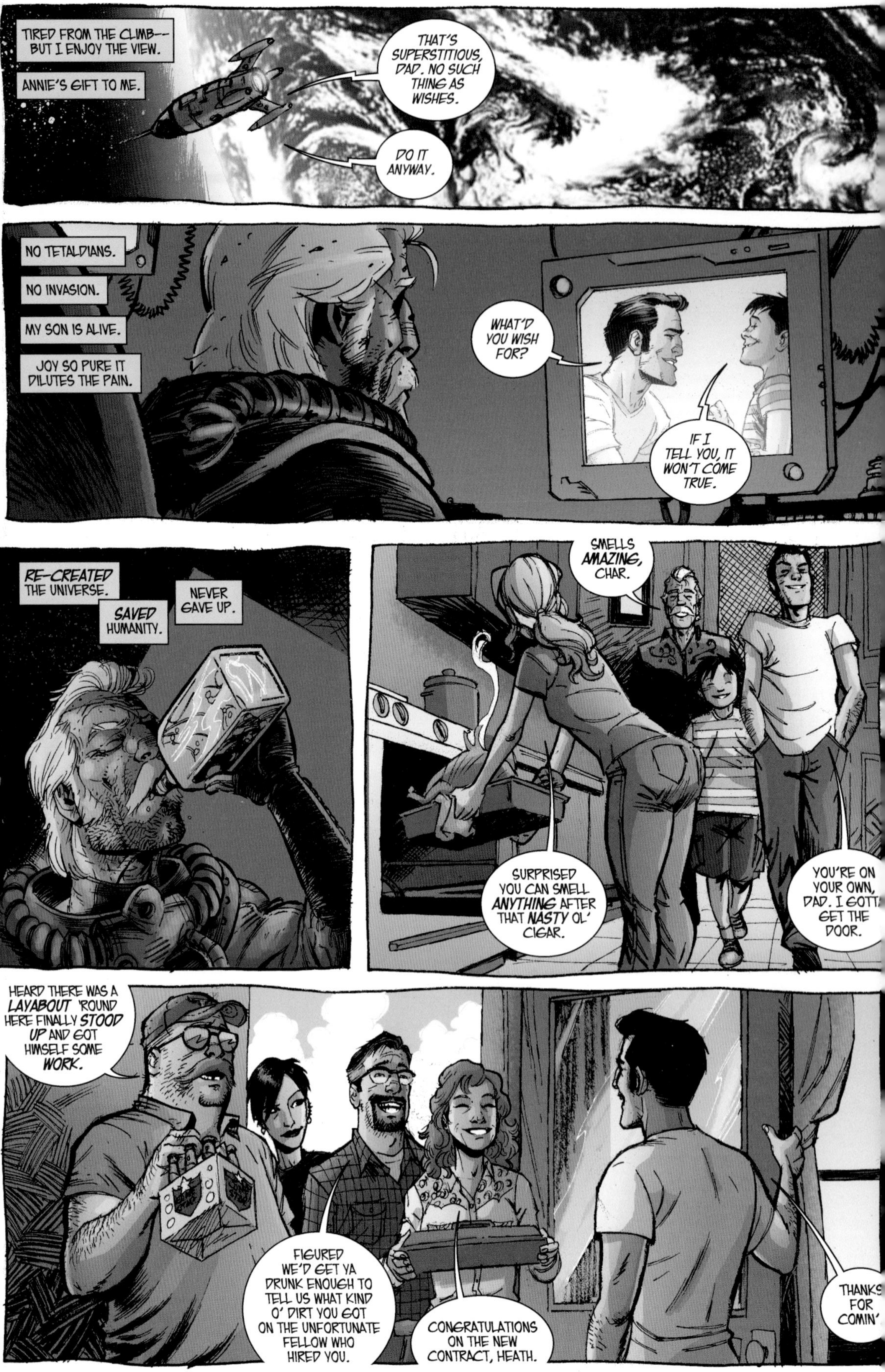
TIRED FROM THE CLIMB-- BUT I ENJOY THE VIEW.
ANNIE'S GIFT TO ME.
THAT'S SUPERSTITIOUS, DAD. NO SUCH THING AS WISHES.
DO IT ANYWAY.
NO TETALDIANS.
NO INVASION.
MY SON IS ALIVE.
JOY SO PURE IT DILUTES THE PAIN.
WHAT'D YOU WISH FOR?
IF I TELL YOU, IT WON'T COME TRUE.
RE-CREATED THE UNIVERSE.
SAVED HUMANITY.
NEVER GAVE UP.
SMELLS AMAZING, CHAR.
SURPRISED YOU CAN SMELL ANYTHING AFTER THAT NASTY OL' CIGAR.
YOU'RE ON YOUR OWN, DAD. I GOTT GET THE DOOR.
HEARD THERE WAS A LAYABOUT 'ROUND HERE FINALLY STOOD UP AND GOT HIMSELF SOME WORK.
FIGURED WE'D GET YA DRUNK ENOUGH TO TELL US WHAT KIND O' DIRT YOU GOT ON THE UNFORTUNATE FELLOW WHO HIRED YOU.
CONGRATULATIONS ON THE NEW CONTRACT, HEATH.
THANKS FOR COMIN'

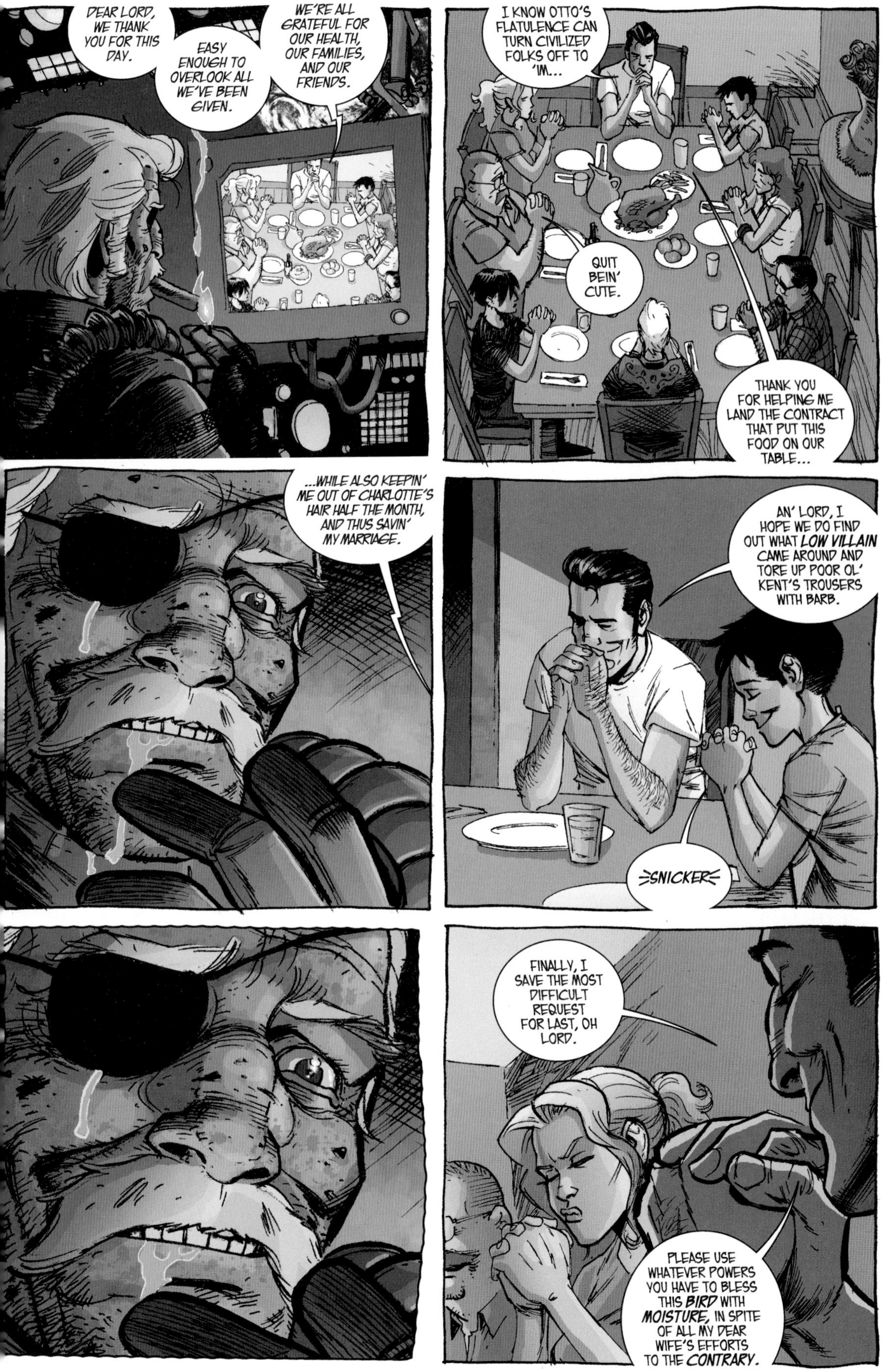
DEAR LORD, WE THANK YOU FOR THIS DAY.
EASY ENOUGH TO OVERLOOK ALL WE'VE BEEN GIVEN.
WE'RE ALL GRATEFUL FOR OUR HEALTH, OUR FAMILIES, AND OUR FRIENDS.
I KNOW OTTO'S FLATULENCE CAN TURN CIVILIZED FOLKS OFF TO 'IM...
QUIT BEIN' CUTE.
THANK YOU FOR HELPING ME LAND THE CONTRACT THAT PUT THIS FOOD ON OUR TABLE...
...WHILE ALSO KEEPIN' ME OUT OF CHARLOTTE'S HAIR HALF THE MONTH, AND THUS SAVIN' MY MARRIAGE.
AN' LORD, I HOPE WE DO FIND OUT WHAT LOW VILLAIN CAME AROUND AND TORE UP POOR OL' KENT'S TROUSERS WITH BARB.
SNICKER
FINALLY, I SAVE THE MOST DIFFICULT REQUEST FOR LAST, OH LORD.
PLEASE USE WHATEVER POWERS YOU HAVE TO BLESS THIS BIRD WITH MOISTURE, IN SPITE OF ALL MY DEAR WIFE'S EFFORTS TO THE CONTRARY.

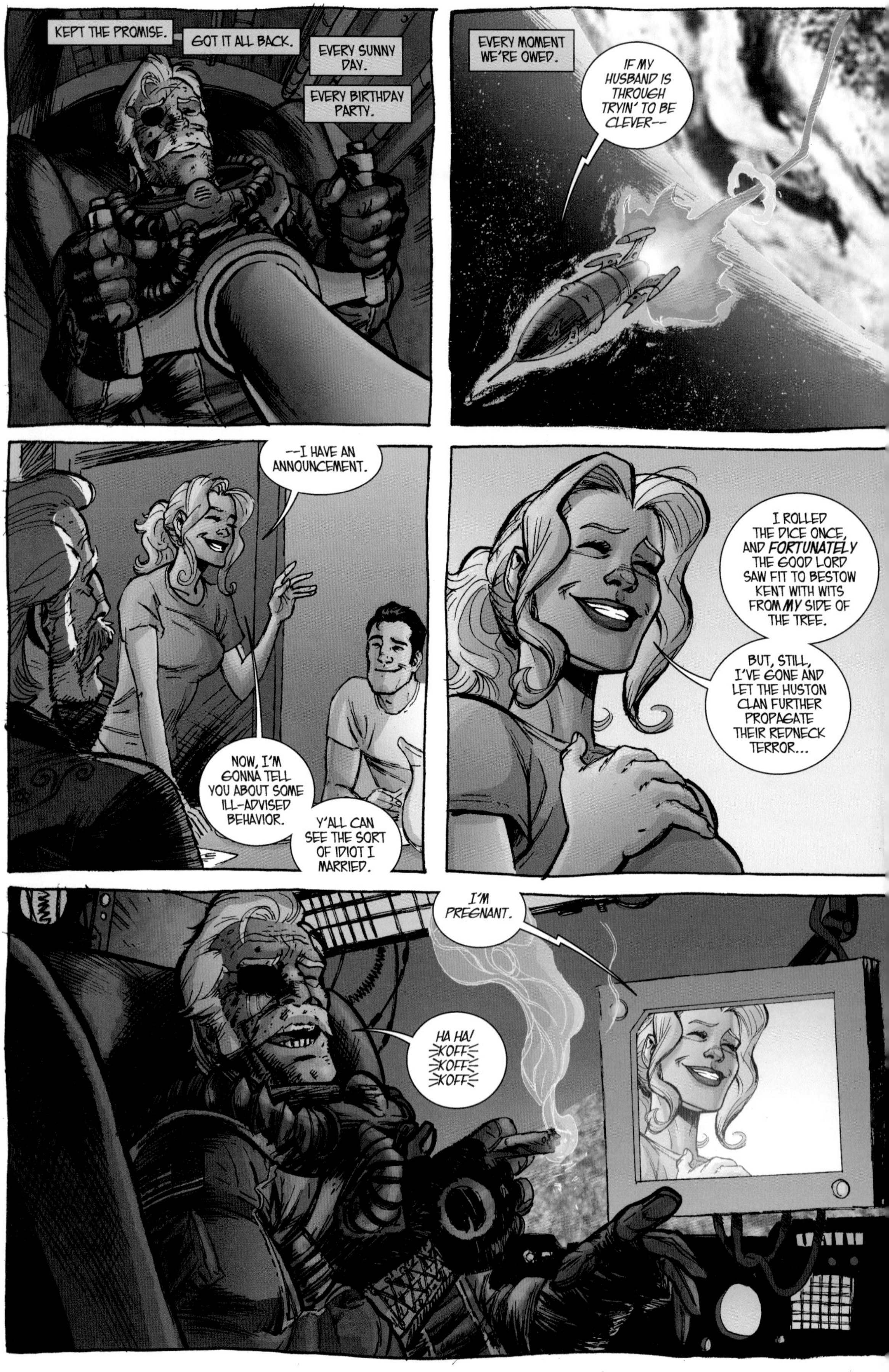
KEPT THE PROMISE.
GOT IT ALL BACK.
EVERY SUNNY DAY.
EVERY BIRTHDAY PARTY.
EVERY MOMENT WE'RE OWED.
IF MY HUSBAND IS THROUGH TRYIN' TO BE CLEVER--
--I HAVE AN ANNOUNCEMENT.
NOW, I'M GONNA TELL YOU ABOUT SOME ILL-ADVISED BEHAVIOR.
Y'ALL CAN SEE THE SORT OF IDIOT I MARRIED.
I ROLLED THE DICE ONCE, AND FORTUNATELY THE GOOD LORD SAW FIT TO BESTOW KENT WITH WITS FROM MY SIDE OF THE TREE.
BUT, STILL, I'VE GONE AND LET THE HUSTON CLAN FURTHER PROPAGATE THEIR REDNECK TERROR...
I'M PREGNANT.
HA HA! KOFF KOFF KOFF

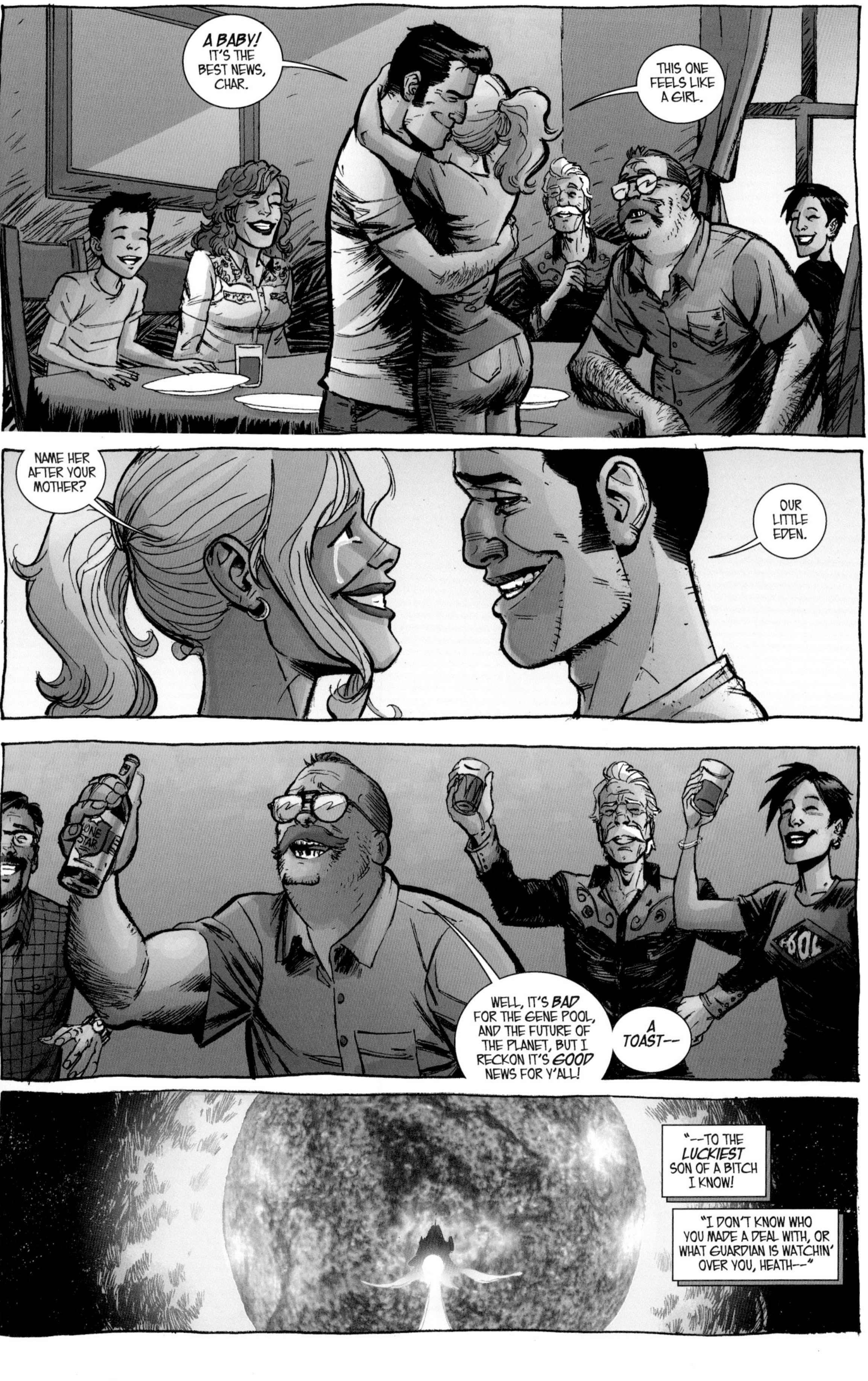
A BABY! IT'S THE BEST NEWS, CHAR.
THIS ONE FEELS LIKE A GIRL.
NAME HER AFTER YOUR MOTHER?
OUR LITTLE EDEN.
LONE STAR
WELL, IT'S BAD FOR THE GENE POOL, AND THE FUTURE OF THE PLANET, BUT I RECKON IT'S GOOD NEWS FOR Y'ALL!
A TOAST--
"--TO THE LUCKIEST SON OF A BITCH I KNOW!
"I DON'T KNOW WHO YOU MADE A DEAL WITH, OR WHAT GUARDIAN IS WATCHIN' OVER YOU, HEATH--"

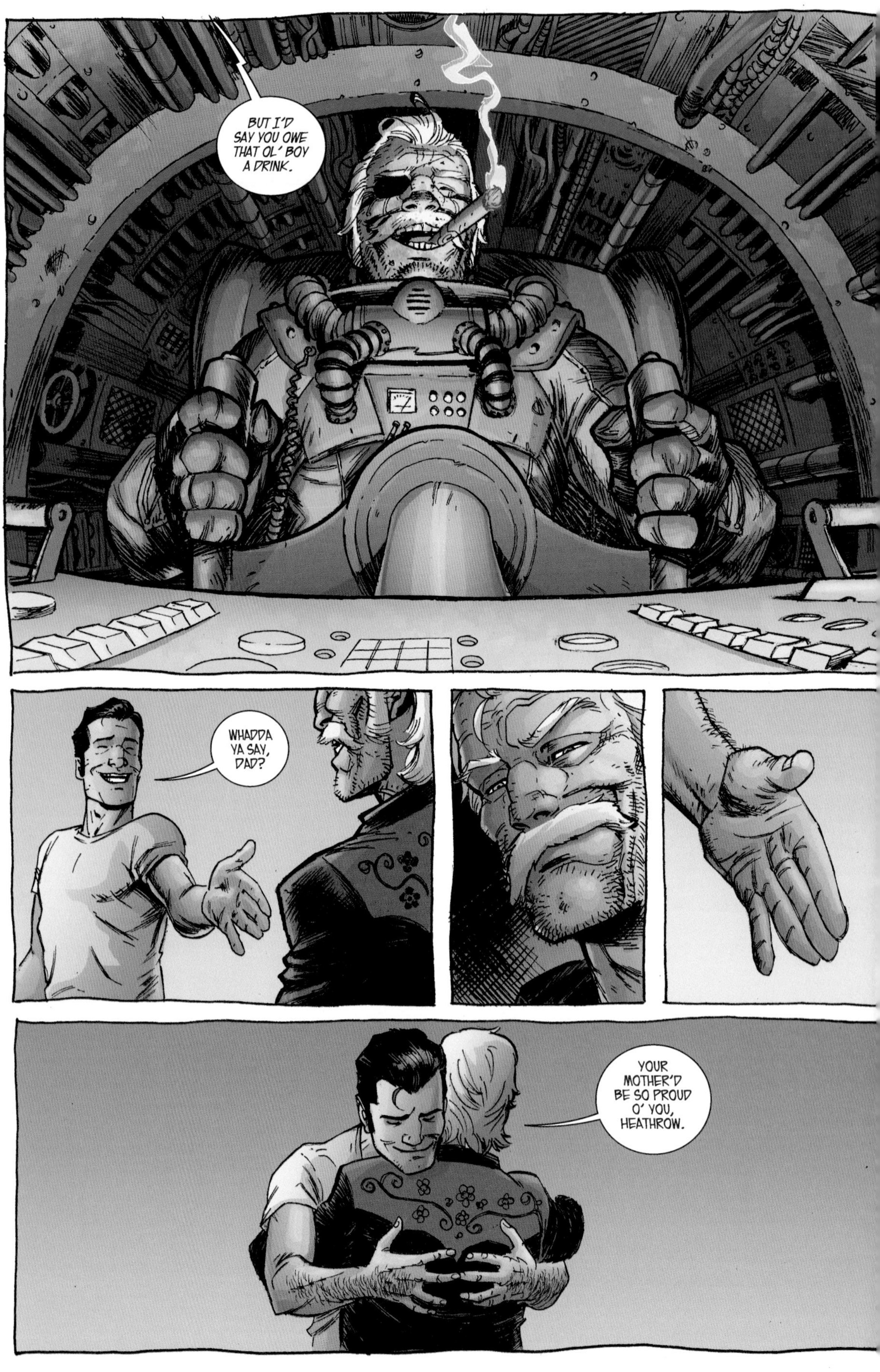
BUT I'D SAY YOU OWE THAT OL' BOY A DRINK.
WHADDA YA SAY, DAD?
YOUR MOTHER'D BE SO PROUD O' YOU, HEATHROW.

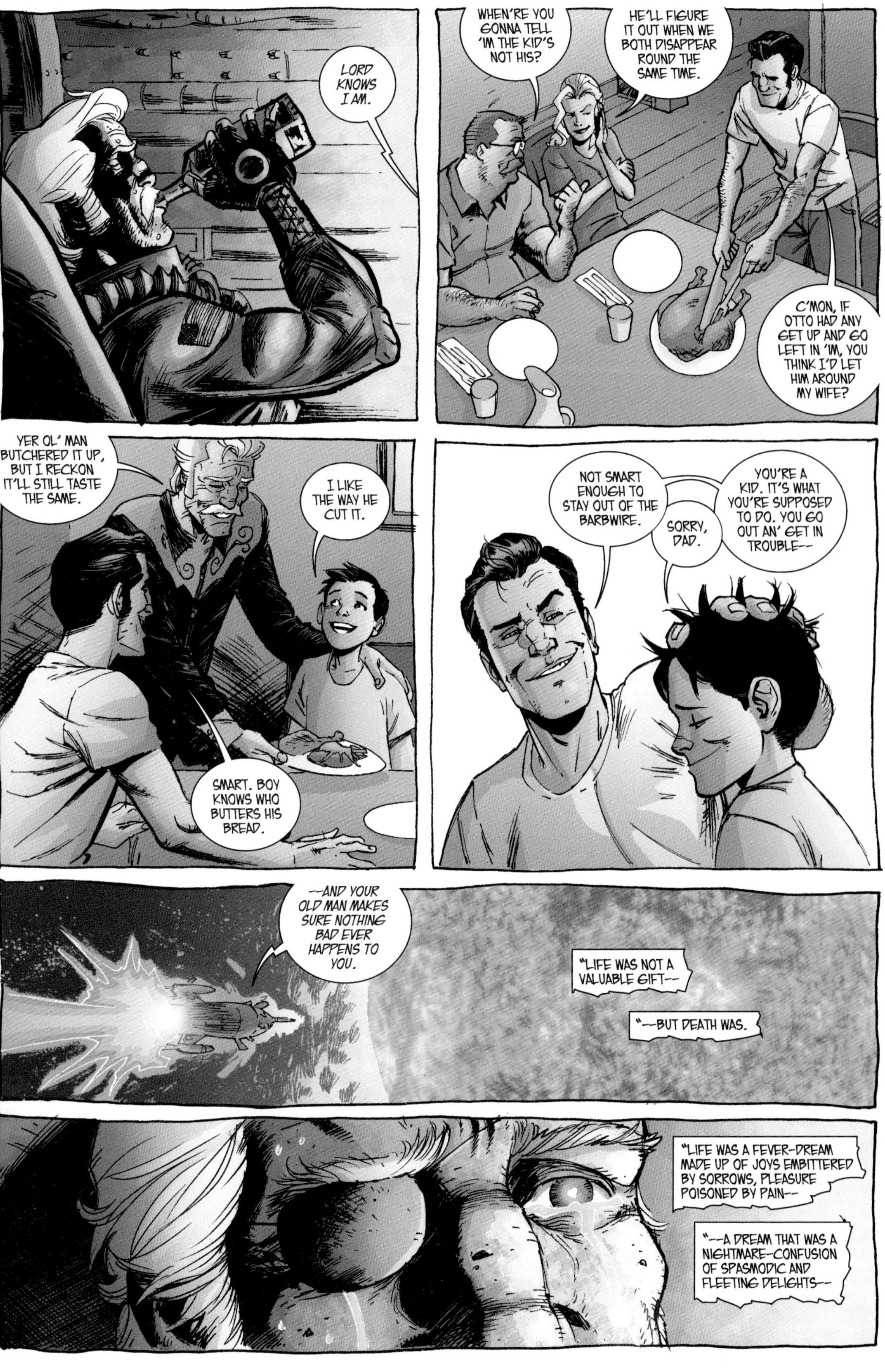
LORD KNOWS I AM.
WHEN'RE YOU GONNA TELL 'IM THE KID'S NOT HIS?
HE'LL FIGURE IT OUT WHEN WE BOTH DISAPPEAR ROUND THE SAME TIME.
C'MON, IF OTTO HAD ANY GET UP AND GO LEFT IN 'IM, YOU THINK I'D LET HIM AROUND MY WIFE?
YER OL' MAN BUTCHERED IT UP, BUT I RECKON IT'LL STILL TASTE THE SAME.
I LIKE THE WAY HE CUT IT.
SMART. BOY KNOWS WHO BUTTERS HIS BREAD.
NOT SMART ENOUGH TO STAY OUT OF THE BARBWIRE.
SORRY, DAD.
YOU'RE A KID. IT'S WHAT YOU'RE SUPPOSED TO DO. YOU GO OUT AN' GET IN TROUBLE--
--AND YOUR OLD MAN MAKES SURE NOTHING BAD EVER HAPPENS TO YOU.
"LIFE WAS NOT A VALUABLE GIFT--
"--BUT DEATH WAS.
"LIFE WAS A FEVER-DREAM MADE UP OF JOYS EMBITTERED BY SORROWS, PLEASURE POISONED BY PAIN--
"--A DREAM THAT WAS A NIGHTMARE-CONFUSION OF SPASMODIC AND FLEETING DELIGHTS--

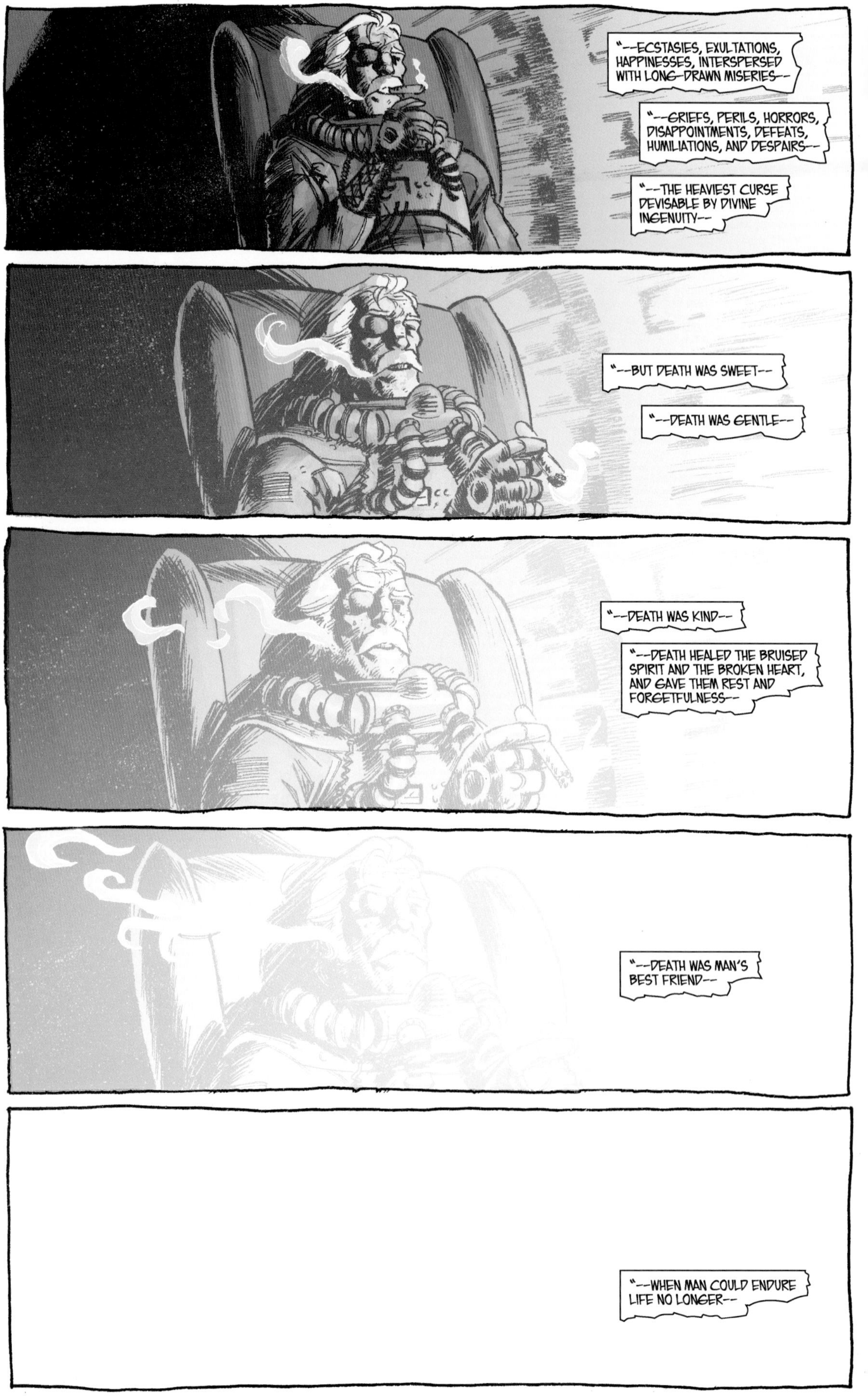
"--ECSTASIES, EXULTATIONS, HAPPINESSES, INTERSPERSED WITH LONG-DRAWN MISERIES--
"--GRIEFS, PERILS, HORRORS, DISAPPOINTMENTS, DEFEATS, HUMILIATIONS, AND DESPAIRS--
"--THE HEAVIEST CURSE DEVISABLE BY DIVINE INGENUITY--
"--BUT DEATH WAS SWEET--
"--DEATH WAS GENTLE--
"--DEATH WAS KIND--
"--DEATH HEALED THE BRUISED SPIRIT AND THE BROKEN HEART, AND GAVE THEM REST AND FORGETFULNESS--
"--DEATH WAS MAN'S BEST FRIEND--
"--WHEN MAN COULD ENDURE LIFE NO LONGER--

"--DEATH CAME AND
SET HIM FREE."
  --SAMUEL CLEMENS

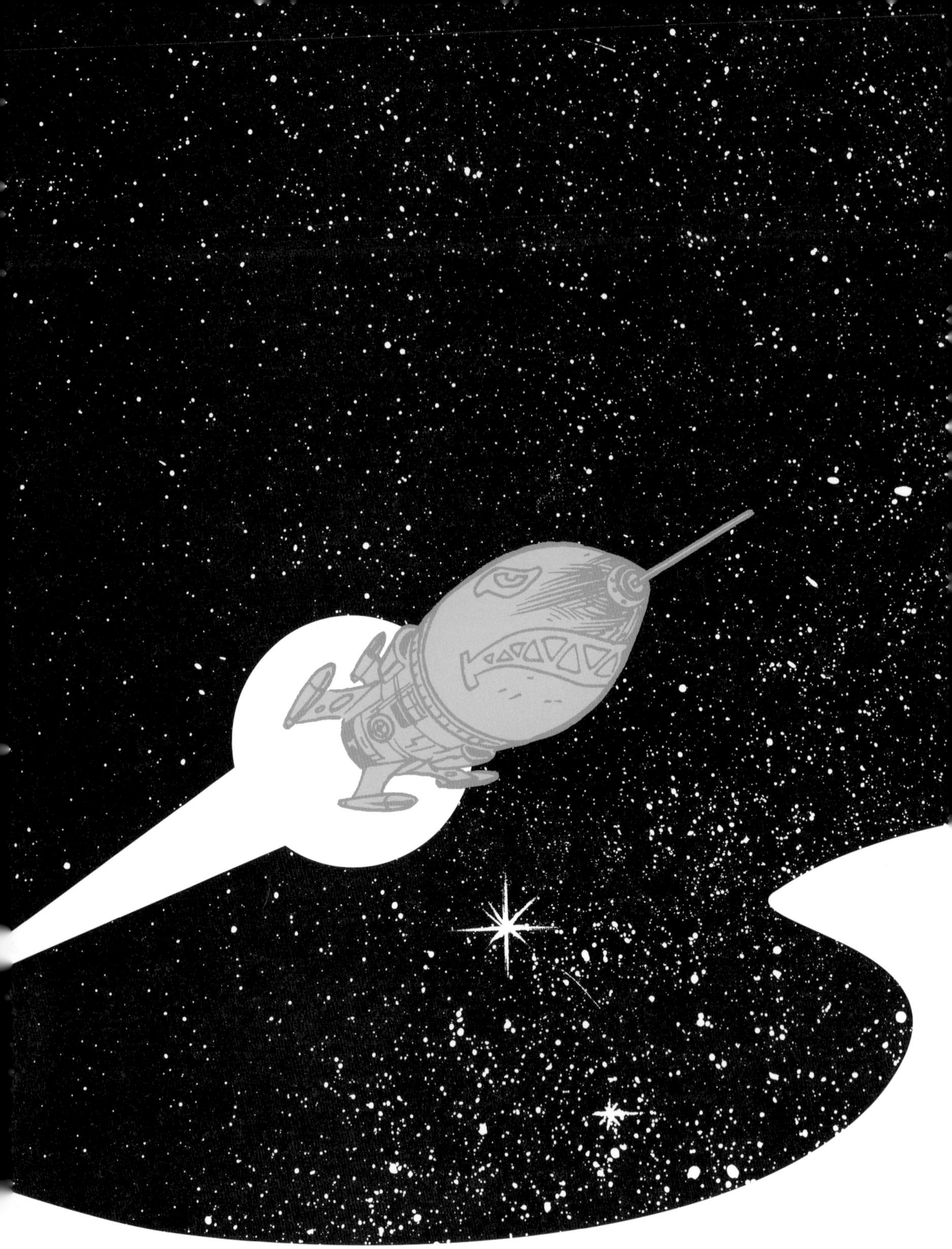

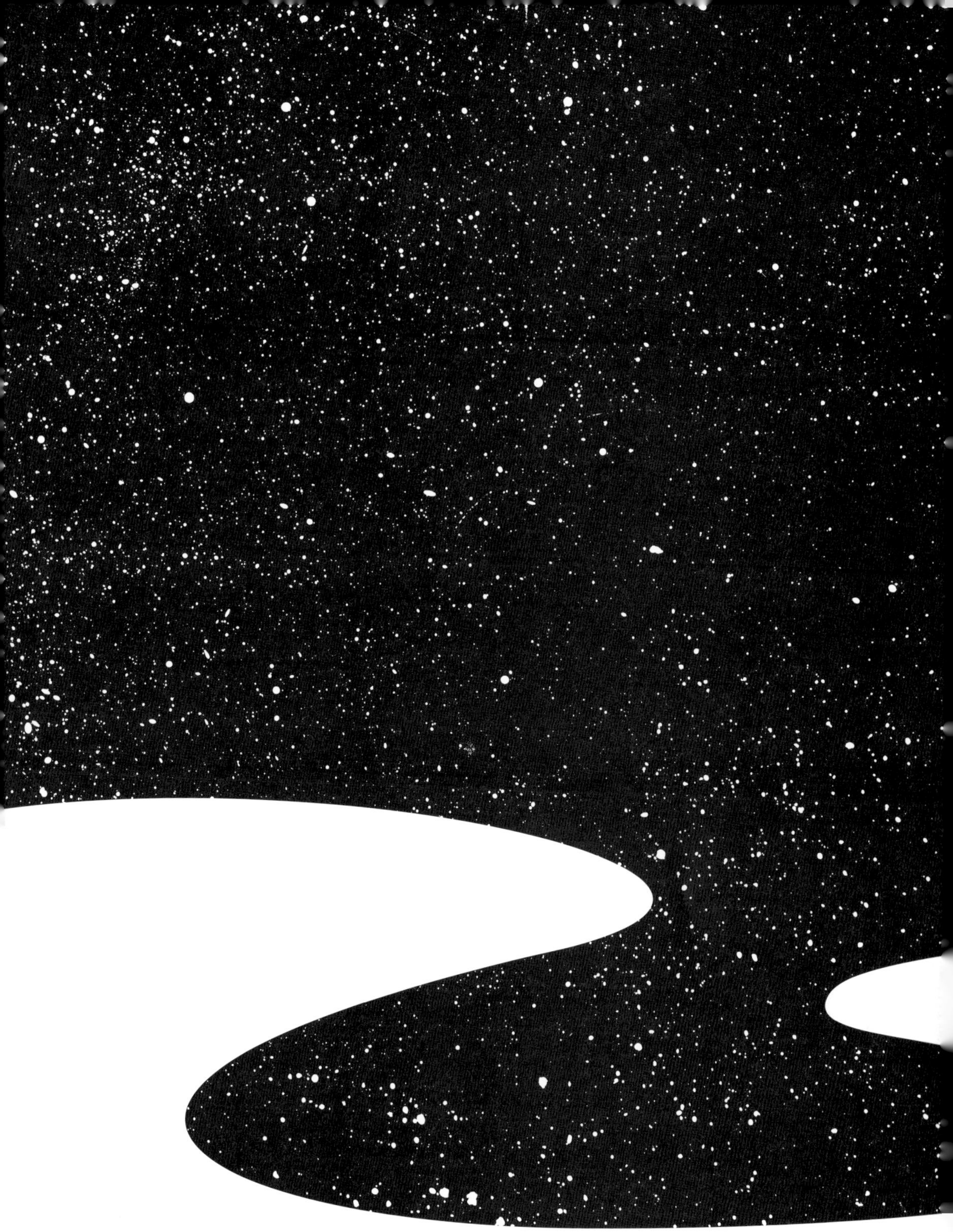

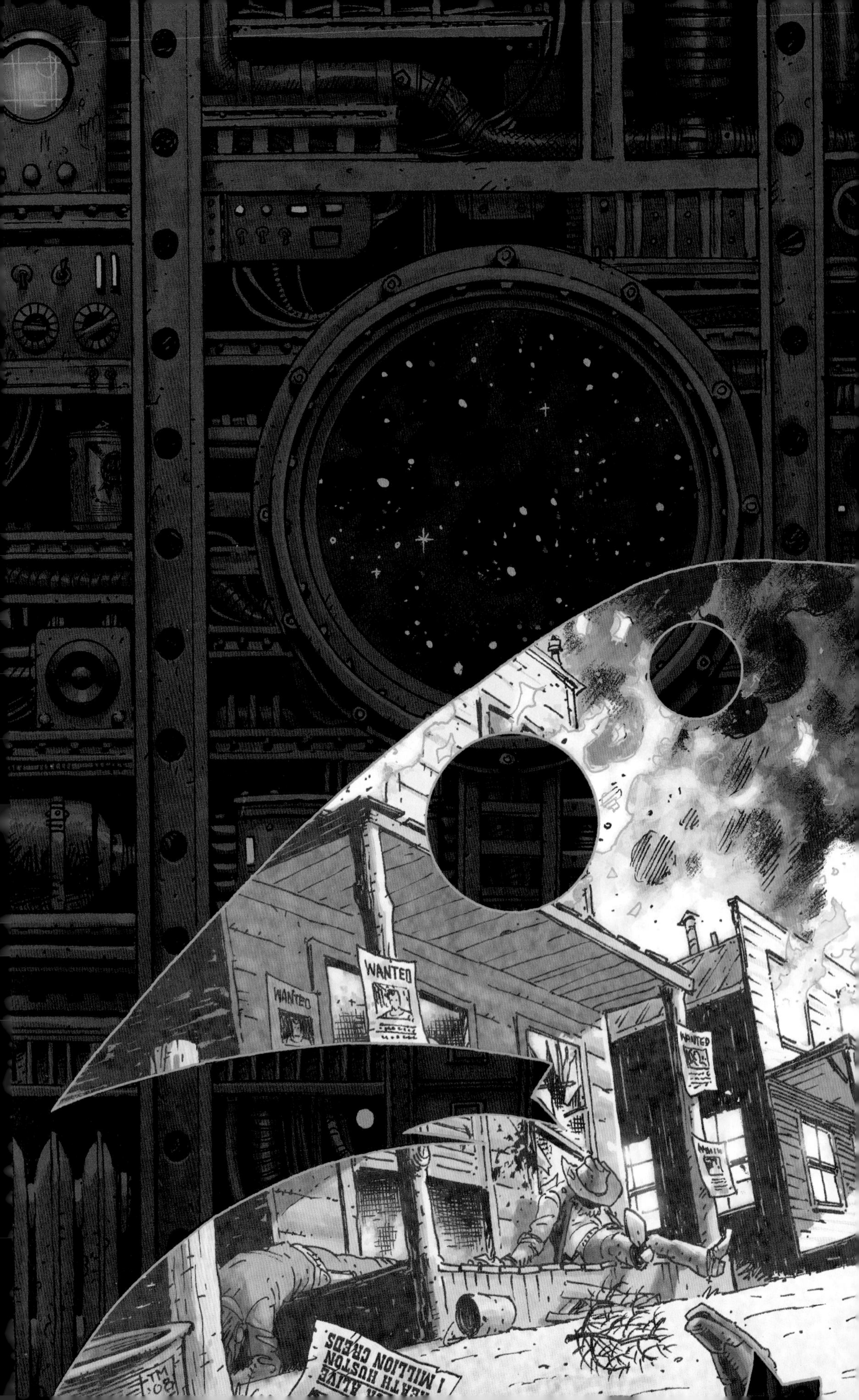
WANTED
WANTED
WANTED
1 MILLION CREDS

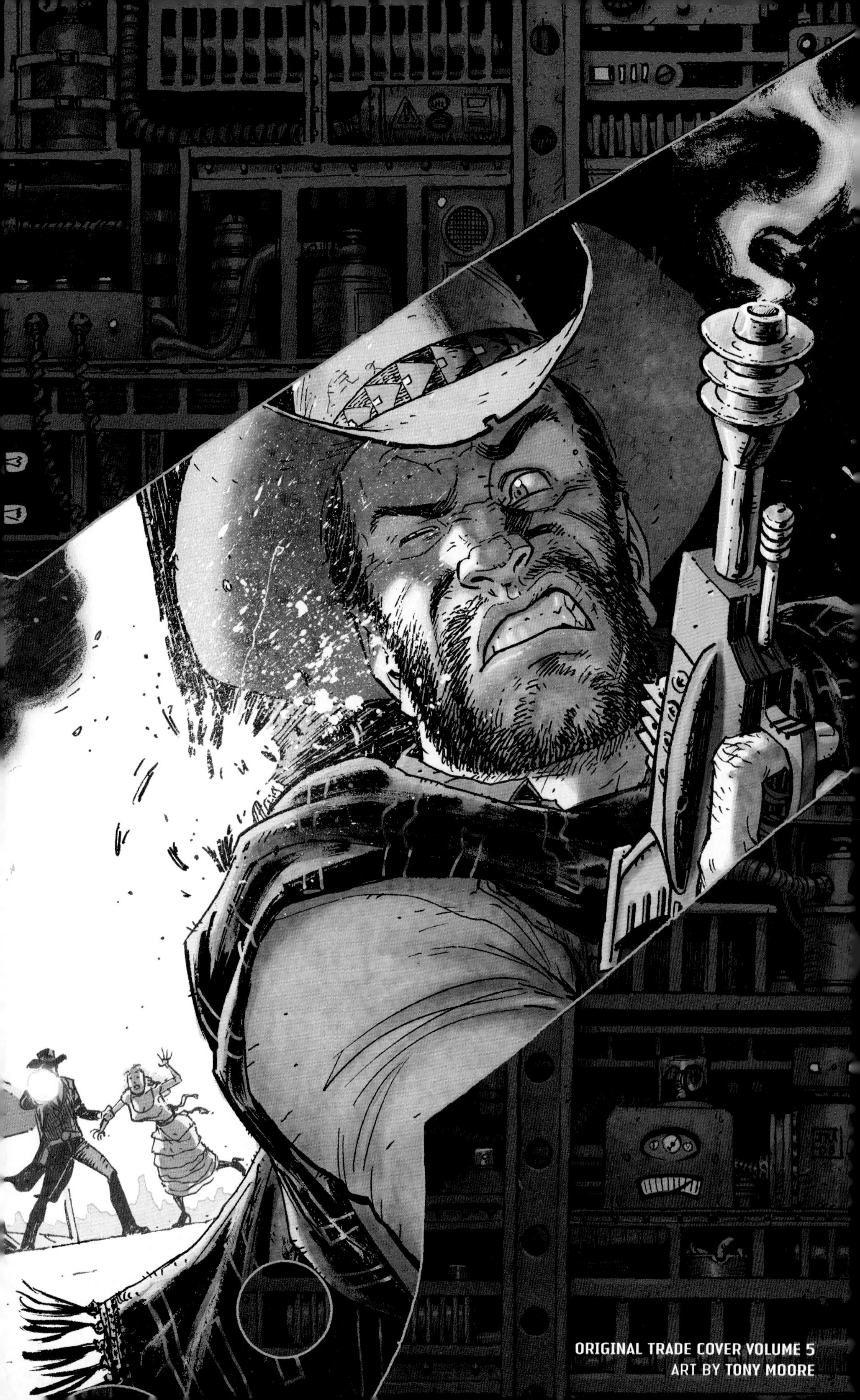

ORIGINAL TRADE COVER VOLUME 5
ART BY TONY MOORE

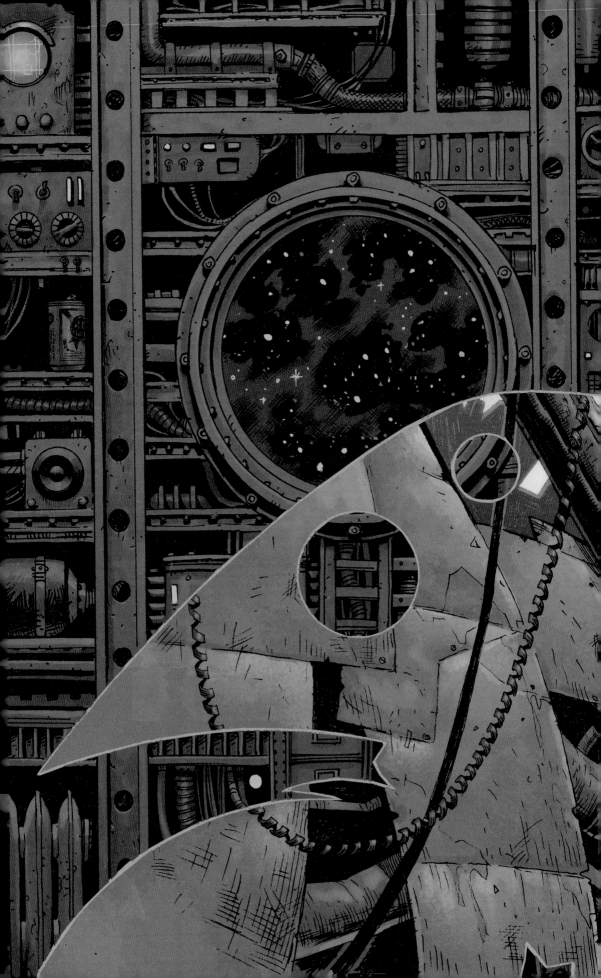

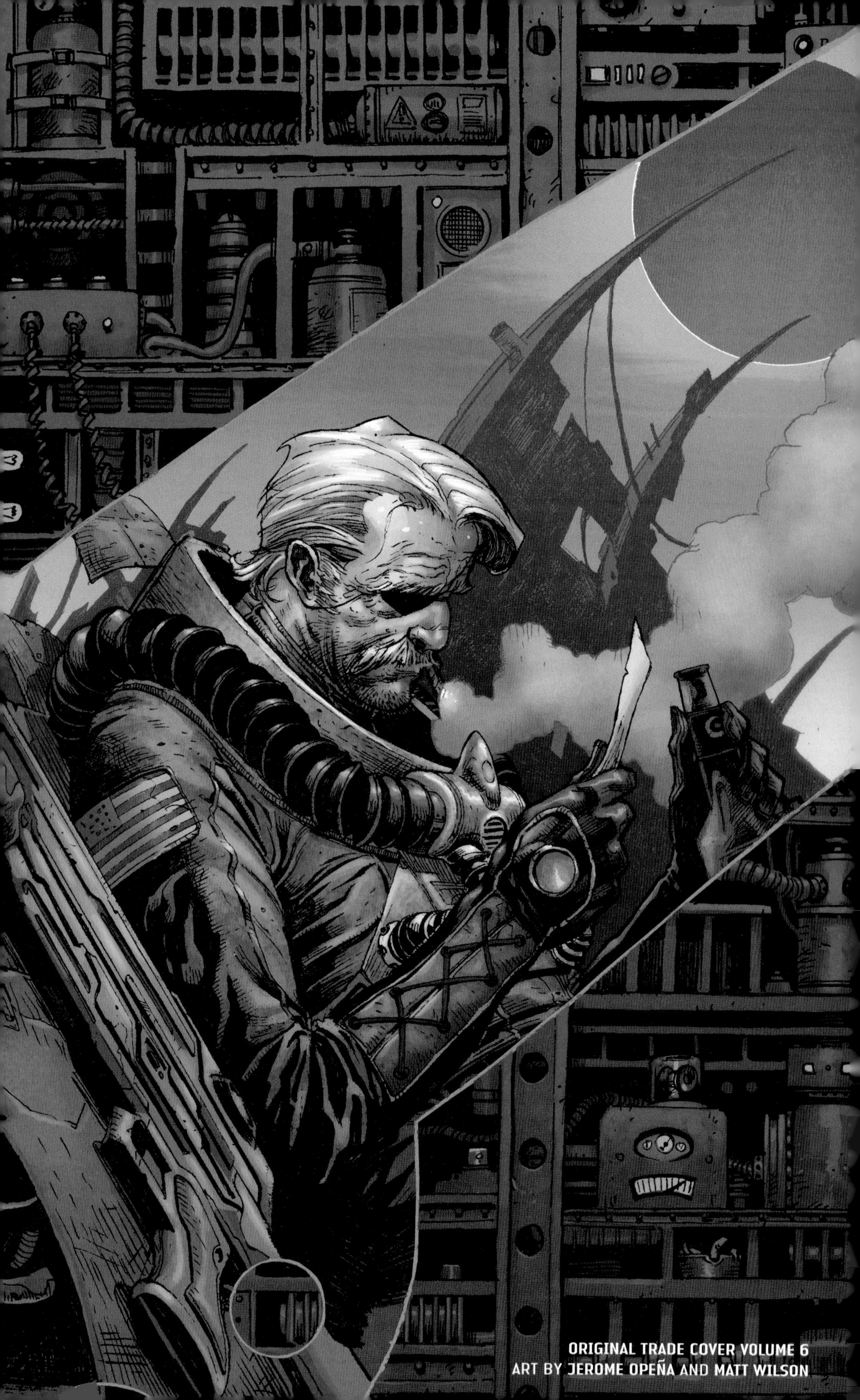

ORIGINAL TRADE COVER VOLUME 6
ART BY JEROME OPEÑA AND MATT WILSON

⚡ The Creators ⚡

Rick Remender is the writer/co-creator of comics such as *Deadly Class*, *LOW*, *Black Science*, *Seven to Eternity*, and *Death or Glory*. During his years at Marvel, he wrote *Captain America*, *Uncanny X-Force*, and *Venom* and created *The Uncanny Avengers*. Outside of comics, he served as lead writer on EA's *Bulletstorm* game and the hit game *Dead Space*. Prior to this, he ran a satellite of Wild Brain animation, worked on films such as *The Iron Giant* and *Anastasia*, and taught sequential art and animation at San Francisco's Academy of Art University.

He currently curates his own publishing imprint, Giant Generator, at Image Comics while serving as lead writer/co-showrunner on SyFy's adaption of his co-creation *Deadly Class*.

Tony Moore has been in the business since 1999, when he began work on his maiden voyage, *Battle Pope*. Since then, he's lent his hand to books such as *Masters of the Universe*, *Brit*, the Eisner Award-nominated series *The Walking Dead*, and the creator-owned books *Fear Agent* and *The Exterminators*. In recent years Tony has put his stamp on such Marvel series as *Ghost Rider*, *Punisher*, *Venom* and *Deadpool*.

Tony and his wife, Kara, live in the middle of nowhere, raising a brilliant daughter and a little hell whenever they can.

Mike Hawthorne is a cartoonist, illustrator, and educator. He began his career with his creator-owned series, *Hysteria* but has worked with every major publisher in the US as well as some in Europe. Mike is best known for his record-setting run as artist on *Deadpool* but has also illustrated other classic characters like *Spider-Man*, *Superman*, and *Conan*. He's made some forays into film and served as a storyboard and concept artists for Fox, Illumination, and Epic games.

Additionally, Mike teaches Visual Development and Anatomy at the Pennsylvania College of Art and Design. Mike is currently a Marvel exclusive artist and lives in Central PA with his wife, three children, and two dogs.